CALIBAN'S WAR

BOOK TWO OF THE EXPANSE

JAMES S. A. COREY

orbit

www.orbitbooks.net

ORBIT

First published in Great Britain in 2012 by Orbit
This paperback edition published in 2013 by Orbit

9 11 12 10

A CIP catalogue record for this book
is available from the British Library.

ISBN 978-1-84149-991-8

Printed and bound by CPI Group (UK) Ltd, Croydon, CR0 4YY

Papers used by Orbit are from well-managed forests
and other responsible sources.

Orbit
An imprint of
Little, Brown Book Group
Carmelite House
50 Victoria Embankment
London EC4Y 0DZ

An Hachette UK Company
www.hachette.co.uk

www.orbitbooks.net

CALIBAN'S WAR

The Earth forces weren't attacking. They were retreating.

Before the UN soldiers could cross the half-kilometer line that would cause the Martians to open fire, the thing caught them.

"Oh, holy shit," Bobbie whispered. "Holy *shit*."

It grabbed one UN Marine in its huge hands and tore him in half like paper. Titanium-and-ceramic armor ripped as easily as the flesh inside, spilling broken bits of technology and wet human viscera indiscriminately onto the ice. The remaining five soldiers ran even harder, but the monster chasing them barely slowed as it killed.

"Shoot it shoot it shoot it," Bobbie yelled, and opened fire. Her training and the technology of her combat suit combined to make her an extremely efficient killing machine. As soon as her finger pulled the trigger on her suit's gun, a stream of two-millimeter armor-piercing rounds streaked out at the creature at more than a thousand meters per second. In just under a second she'd fired fifty rounds at it. The creature was a relatively slow-moving human-sized target, running in a straight line. Her targeting computer could do ballistic corrections that would let her hit a softball-sized object moving at supersonic speeds. Every bullet she fired at the monster hit.

It didn't matter.

BY JAMES S. A. COREY

The Expanse
Leviathan Wakes
Caliban's War
Abaddon's Gate
Cibola Burn
Nemesis Games
Babylon's Ashes

To Bester and Clarke, who got us here

Prologue: Mei

Mei?" Miss Carrie said. "Please put your painting work away now. Your mother is here."

It took her a few seconds to understand what the teacher was saying, not because Mei didn't know the words—she was four now, and not a toddler anymore—but because they didn't fit with the world as she knew it. Her mother couldn't come get her. Mommy had left Ganymede and gone to live on Ceres Station, because, as her daddy put it, she needed some mommy-alone-time. Then, her heart starting to race, Mei thought, *She came back*.

"Mommy?"

From where Mei sat at her scaled-down easel, Miss Carrie's knee blocked her view of the coatroom door. Mei's hands were sticky with finger paints, red and blue and green swirling on her palms. She shifted forward and grabbed for Miss Carrie's leg as much to move it as to help her stand up.

"Mei!" Miss Carrie shouted.

Mei looked at the smear of paint on Miss Carrie's pants and the controlled anger on the woman's broad, dark face.

"I'm sorry, Miss Carrie."

"It's okay," the teacher said in a tight voice that meant it wasn't, really, but Mei wasn't going to be punished. "Please go wash your hands and then come put away your painting work. I'll get this down and you can give it to your mother. It is a doggie?"

"It's a space monster."

"It's a very nice space monster. Now go wash your hands, please, sweetheart."

Mei nodded, turned, and ran for the bathroom, her smock flapping around her like a rag caught in an air duct.

"And don't touch the wall!"

"I'm sorry, Miss Carrie."

"It's okay. Just clean it off after you've washed your hands."

She turned the water on full blast, the colors and swirls rushing off her skin. She went through the motions of drying her hands without caring whether she was dripping water or not. It felt like gravity had shifted, pulling her toward the doorway and the ante-room instead of down toward the ground. The other children watched, excited because she was excited, as Mei scrubbed the finger marks mostly off the wall and slammed the paint pots back into their box and the box onto its shelf. She pulled the smock up over her head rather than wait for Miss Carrie to help her, and stuffed it into the recycling bin.

In the anteroom, Miss Carrie was standing with two other grown-ups, neither of them Mommy. One was a woman Mei didn't know, space monster painting held gently in her hand and a polite smile on her face. The other was Doctor Strickland.

"No, she's been very good about getting to the toilet," Miss Carrie was saying. "There are accidents now and then, of course."

"Of course," the woman said.

"Mei!" Doctor Strickland said, bending down so that he was hardly taller than she was. "How is my favorite girl?"

"Where's—" she began, but before she could say *Mommy*, Doctor Strickland scooped her up into his arms. He was bigger than Daddy, and he smelled like salt. He tipped her backward, tickling her sides, and she laughed hard enough that she couldn't talk anymore.

"Thank you so much," the woman said.

"It's a pleasure to meet you," Miss Carrie said, shaking the woman's hand. "We really love having Mei in the classroom."

Doctor Strickland kept tickling Mei until the door to the Montessori cycled closed behind them. Then Mei caught her breath.

"Where's Mommy?"

"She's waiting for us," Doctor Strickland said. "We're taking you to her right now."

The newer hallways of Ganymede were wide and lush and the air recyclers barely ran. The knife-thin blades of areca palm fronds spilled up and out from dozens of hydroponic planters. The broad yellow-green striated leaves of devil's ivy spilled down the walls. The dark green primitive leaves of Mother-in-Law's Tongue thrust up beneath them both. Full-spectrum LEDs glowed white-gold. Daddy said it was just what sunlight looked like on Earth, and Mei pictured that planet as a huge complicated network of plants and hallways with the sun running in lines above them in a bright blue ceiling-sky, and you could climb over the walls and end up anywhere.

Mei leaned her head on Doctor Strickland's shoulder, looking over his back and naming each plant as they passed. *Sansevieria trifasciata. Epipremnum aureum.* Getting the names right always made Daddy grin. When she did it by herself, it made her body feel calmer.

"More?" the woman asked. She was pretty, but Mei didn't like her voice.

"No," Doctor Strickland said. "Mei here is the last one."

"*Chysalidocarpus lutenscens*," Mei said.

"All right," the woman said, and then again, more softly: "All right."

The closer to the surface they got, the narrower the corridors became. The older hallways seemed dirtier even though there really wasn't any dirt on them. It was just that they were more used up. The quarters and labs near the surface were where Mei's grandparents had lived when they'd come to Ganymede. Back then, there hadn't been anything deeper. The air up there smelled funny, and the recyclers always had to run, humming and thumping.

The grown-ups didn't talk to each other, but every now and then Doctor Strickland would remember Mei was there and ask her questions: What was her favorite cartoon on the station feed? Who was her best friend in school? What kinds of food did she eat for lunch that day? Mei expected him to start asking the other questions, the ones he always asked next, and she had her answers ready.

Does your throat feel scratchy? No.

Did you wake up sweaty? No.

Was there any blood in your poop this week? No.

Did you get your medicine both times every day? Yes.

But this time, Doctor Strickland didn't ask any of that. The corridors they went down got older and thinner until the woman had to walk behind them so that the men coming the other direction could pass. The woman still had Mei's painting in her hand, rolled up in a tube so the paper wouldn't get wrinkles.

Doctor Strickland stopped at an unmarked door, shifted Mei to his other hip, and took his hand terminal out of his pants pocket. He keyed something into a program Mei had never seen before, and the door cycled open, seals making a rough popping sound like something out of an old movie. The hallway they walked into was full of junk and old metal boxes.

"This isn't the hospital," Mei said.

"This is a special hospital," Doctor Strickland said. "I don't think you've ever been here, have you?"

It didn't look like a hospital to Mei. It looked like one of the abandoned tubes that Daddy talked about sometimes. Leftover spaces from when Ganymede had first been built that no one used anymore except as storage. This one had a kind of airlock at the end, though, and when they passed through it, things looked a little more like a hospital. They were cleaner, anyway, and there was the smell of ozone, like in the decontamination cells.

"Mei! Hi, Mei!"

It was one of the big boys. Sandro. He was almost five. Mei waved at him as Doctor Strickland walked past. Mei felt better knowing the big boys were here too. If they were, then it was probably okay, even if the woman walking with Doctor Strickland wasn't her mommy. Which reminded her...

"Where's Mommy?"

"We're going to go see Mommy in just a few minutes," Doctor Strickland said. "We just have a couple more little things we need to do first."

"No," Mei said. "I don't want that."

He carried her into a room that looked a little like an examination room, only there weren't any cartoon lions on the walls, and the tables weren't shaped like grinning hippos. Doctor Strickland put her onto a steel examination table and rubbed her head. Mei crossed her arms and scowled.

"I want Mommy," Mei said, and made the same impatient grunt that Daddy would.

"Well, you just wait right here, and I'll see what I can do about that," Doctor Strickland said with a smile. "Umea?"

"I think we're good to go. Check with ops, load up, and let's release it."

"I'll go let them know. You stay here."

The woman nodded, and Doctor Strickland walked back out the door. The woman looked down at her, the pretty face not smiling at all. Mei didn't like her.

"I want my painting," Mei said. "That's not for you. That's for Mommy."

The woman looked at the painting in her hand as if she'd forgotten it was there. She unrolled it.

"It's Mommy's space monster," Mei said. This time, the woman smiled. She held out the painting, and Mei snatched it away. She made some wrinkles in the paper when she did, but she didn't care. She crossed her arms again and scowled and grunted.

"You like space monsters, kid?" the woman asked.

"I want my mommy."

The woman stepped close. She smelled like fake flowers and her fingers were skinny. She lifted Mei down to the floor.

"C'mon, kid," she said. "I'll show you something."

The woman walked away and for a moment Mei hesitated. She didn't like the woman, but she liked being alone even less. She followed. The woman walked down a short hallway, punched a keycode into a big metal door, like an old-fashioned airlock, and walked through when the door swung open. Mei followed her. The new room was cold. Mei didn't like it. There wasn't an examination table here, just a big glass box like they kept fish in at the aquarium, only it was dry inside, and the thing sitting there wasn't a fish. The woman motioned Mei closer and, when Mei came near, knocked sharply on the glass.

The thing inside looked up at the sound. It was a man, but he was naked and his skin didn't look like skin. His eyes glowed blue like there was a fire in his head. And something was wrong with his hands.

He reached toward the glass, and Mei started screaming.

Chapter One: Bobbie

Snoopy's out again," Private Hillman said. "I think his CO must be pissed at him."

Gunnery Sergeant Roberta Draper of the Martian Marine Corps upped the magnification on her armor's heads-up display and looked in the direction Hillman was pointing. Twenty-five hundred meters away, a squad of four United Nations Marines were tromping around their outpost, backlit by the giant greenhouse dome they were guarding. A greenhouse dome identical in nearly all respects to the dome her own squad was currently guarding.

One of the four UN Marines had black smudges on the sides of his helmet that looked like beagle ears.

"Yep, that's Snoopy," Bobbie said. "Been on every patrol detail so far today. Wonder what he did."

Guard duty around the greenhouses on Ganymede meant

doing what you could to keep your mind occupied. Including speculating on the lives of the Marines on the other side.

The other side. Eighteen months before, there hadn't been sides. The inner planets had all been one big, happy, slightly dysfunctional family. Then Eros, and now the two superpowers were dividing up the solar system between them, and the one moon neither side was willing to give up was Ganymede, breadbasket of the Jovian system.

As the only moon with any magnetosphere, it was the only place where dome-grown crops stood a chance in Jupiter's harsh radiation belt, and even then the domes and habitats still had to be shielded to protect civilians from the eight rems a day burning off Jupiter and onto the moon's surface.

Bobbie's armor had been designed to let a soldier walk through a nuclear bomb crater minutes after the blast. It also worked well at keeping Jupiter from frying Martian Marines.

Behind the Earth soldiers on patrol, their dome glowed in a shaft of weak sunlight captured by enormous orbital mirrors. Even with the mirrors, most terrestrial plants would have died, starved of sunlight. Only the heavily modified versions the Ganymede scientists cranked out could hope to survive in the trickle of light the mirrors fed them.

"Be sunset soon," Bobbie said, still watching the Earth Marines outside their little guard hut, knowing they were watching her too. In addition to Snoopy, she spotted the one they called Stumpy because he or she couldn't be much over a meter and a quarter tall. She wondered what their nickname for her was. Maybe Big Red. Her armor still had the Martian surface camouflage on it. She hadn't been on Ganymede long enough to get it resurfaced with mottled gray and white.

One by one over the course of five minutes, the orbital mirrors winked out as Ganymede passed behind Jupiter for a few hours. The glow from the greenhouse behind her changed to actinic blue as the artificial lights came on. While the overall light level didn't go down much, the shadows shifted in strange and subtle ways.

Above, the sun—not even a disk from here as much as the brightest star—flashed as it passed behind Jupiter's limb, and for a moment the planet's faint ring system was visible.

"They're going back in," Corporal Travis said. "Snoop's bringing up the rear. Poor guy. Can we bail too?"

Bobbie looked around at the featureless dirty ice of Ganymede. Even in her high-tech armor she could feel the moon's chill.

"Nope."

Her squad grumbled but fell in line as she led them on a slow low-gravity shuffle around the dome. In addition to Hillman and Travis, she had a green private named Gourab on this particular patrol. And even though he'd been in the Marines all of about a minute and a half, he grumbled just as loud as the other two in his Mariner Valley drawl.

She couldn't blame them. It was make-work. Something for the Martian soldiers on Ganymede to do to keep them busy. If Earth decided it needed Ganymede all to itself, four grunts walking around the greenhouse dome wouldn't stop them. With dozens of Earth and Mars warships in a tense standoff in orbit, if hostilities broke out the ground pounders would probably find out only when the surface bombardment began.

To her left, the dome rose to almost half a kilometer: triangular glass panels separated by gleaming copper-colored struts that turned the entire structure into a massive Faraday cage. Bobbie had never been inside one of the greenhouse domes. She'd been sent out from Mars as part of a surge in troops to the outer planets and had been walking patrols on the surface almost since day one. Ganymede to her was a spaceport, a small Marine base, and the even smaller guard outpost she currently called home.

As they shuffled around the dome, Bobbie watched the unremarkable landscape. Ganymede didn't change much without a catastrophic event. The surface was mostly silicate rock and water ice a few degrees warmer than space. The atmosphere was oxygen so thin it could pass as an industrial vacuum. Ganymede didn't erode or weather. It changed when rocks fell on it from space, or when warm water from the liquid core forced itself onto the surface and created short-lived lakes. Neither thing happened all that often. At home on Mars, wind and dust changed the landscape hourly. Here, she was walking through the footsteps of the day before and the day before and the day before. And if she never came back, those footprints would outlive her. Privately, she thought it was sort of creepy.

A rhythmic squeaking started to cut through the normally smooth hiss and thump sounds her powered armor made. She usually kept the suit's HUD minimized. It got so crowded with information that a marine knew everything except what was actually in front of her. Now she pulled it up, using blinks and eye movements to page over to the suit diagnostic screen. A yellow telltale warned her that the suit's left knee actuator was low on hydraulic fluid. Must be a leak somewhere, but a slow one, because the suit couldn't find it.

"Hey, guys, hold up a minute," Bobbie said. "Hilly, you have any extra hydraulic fluid in your pack?"

"Yep," said Hillman, already pulling it out.

"Give my left knee a squirt, would you?"

While Hillman crouched in front of her, working on her suit, Gourab and Travis began an argument that seemed to be about sports. Bobbie tuned it out.

"This suit is ancient," Hillman said. "You really oughta upgrade. This sort of thing is just going to happen more and more often, you know."

"Yeah, I should," Bobbie said. But the truth was that was easier said than done. Bobbie was not the right shape to fit into one of the standard suits, and the Marines made her jump through a series of flaming hoops every time she requisitioned a new custom one. At a bit over two meters tall, she was only slightly above average height for a Martian male, but thanks in part to her Polynesian ancestry, she weighed in at over a hundred kilos at one g. None of it was fat, but her muscles seemed to get bigger every time she even walked through a weight room. As a marine, she trained all the time.

The suit she had now was the first one in twelve years of active duty that actually fit well. And even though it was beginning to show its age, it was just easier to try to keep it running than beg and plead for a new one.

Hillman was starting to put his tools away when Bobbie's radio crackled to life.

"Outpost four to stickman. Come in, stickman."

"Roger four," Bobbie replied. "This is stickman one. Go ahead."

"Stickman one, where are you guys? You're half an hour late and some shit is going down over here."

"Sorry, four, equipment trouble," Bobbie said, wondering what sort of shit might be going down, but not enough to ask about it over an open frequency.

"Return to the outpost immediately. We have shots fired at the UN outpost. We're going into lockdown."

It took Bobbie a moment to parse that. She could see her men staring at her, their faces a mix of puzzlement and fear.

"Uh, the Earth guys are shooting at you?" she finally asked.

"Not yet, but they're shooting. Get your asses back here."

Hillman pushed to his feet. Bobbie flexed her knee once and got greens on her diagnostic. She gave Hilly a nod of thanks, then said, "Double-time it back to the outpost. Go."

Bobbie and her squad were still half a kilometer from the outpost when the general alert went out. Her suit's HUD came up on its own, switching to combat mode. The sensor package went to work looking for hostiles and linked up to one of the satellites for a top-down view. She felt the click as the gun built into the suit's right arm switched to free-fire mode.

A thousand alarms would be sounding if an orbital bombardment had begun, but she couldn't help looking up at the sky anyway. No flashes or missile trails. Nothing but Jupiter's bulk.

Bobbie took off for the outpost in a long, loping run. Her squad followed without a word. A person trained in the use of a strength-augmenting suit running in low gravity could cover a lot of ground quickly. The outpost came into view around the curve of the dome in just a few seconds, and a few seconds after that, the cause of the alarm.

UN Marines were charging the Martian outpost. The yearlong cold war was going hot. Somewhere deep behind the cool mental habits of training and discipline, she was surprised. She hadn't really thought this day would come.

The rest of her platoon were out of the outpost and arranged in a firing line facing the UN position. Someone had driven *Yojimbo* out onto the line, and the four-meter-tall combat mech towered over the other marines, looking like a headless giant in power armor, its massive cannon moving slowly as it tracked the incoming Earth troops. The UN soldiers were covering the 2,500 meters between the two outposts at a dead run.

Why isn't anyone talking? she wondered. The silence coming from her platoon was eerie.

And then, just as her squad got to the firing line, her suit squealed a jamming warning at her. The top-down vanished as she lost contact with the satellite. Her team's life signs and equipment status reports went dead as her link to their suits was cut off. The faint static of the open comm channel disappeared, leaving an even more unsettling silence.

She used hand motions to place her team at the right flank, then moved up the line to find Lieutenant Givens, her CO. She spotted his suit right at the center of the line, standing almost directly under *Yojimbo*. She ran up and placed her helmet against his.

"What the fuck is going on, El Tee?" she shouted.

He gave her an irritated look and yelled, "Your guess is as good as mine. We can't tell them to back off because of the jamming, and visual warnings are being ignored. Before the radio cut out, I got authorization to fire if they come within half a klick of our position."

Bobbie had a couple hundred more questions, but the UN troops would cross the five-hundred-meter mark in just a few more seconds, so she ran back to anchor the right flank with her squad. Along the way, she had her suit count the incoming forces and mark them all as hostiles. The suit reported seven targets. Less than a third of the UN troops at their outpost.

This makes no sense.

She had her suit draw a line on the HUD at the five-hundred-meter mark. She didn't tell her boys that was the free-fire zone. She didn't need to. They'd open fire when she did without needing to know why.

The UN soldiers had crossed the one-kilometer mark, still without firing a shot. They were coming in a scattered formation, with six out front in a ragged line and a seventh bringing up the rear about seventy meters behind. Her suit HUD selected the figure on the far left of the enemy line as her target, picking the one closest to her by default. Something itched at the back of her brain, and she overrode the suit and selected the target at the rear and told it to magnify.

The small figure suddenly enlarged in her targeting reticule. She felt a chill move down her back, and magnified again.

The figure chasing the six UN Marines wasn't wearing an environment suit. Nor was it, properly speaking, human. Its skin was covered in chitinous plates, like large black scales. Its head was a massive horror, easily twice as large as it should have been and covered in strange protruding growths.

But most disturbing of all were its hands. Far too large for its body, and too long for their width, they were a childhood nightmare version of hands. The hands of the troll under the bed or the witch sneaking in through the window. They flexed and grasped at nothing with a constant manic energy.

The Earth forces weren't attacking. They were retreating.

"Shoot the thing chasing them," Bobbie yelled to no one.

Before the UN soldiers could cross the half-kilometer line that would cause the Martians to open fire, the thing caught them.

"Oh, holy shit," Bobbie whispered. "Holy *shit*."

It grabbed one UN Marine in its huge hands and tore him in half like paper. Titanium-and-ceramic armor ripped as easily as the flesh inside, spilling broken bits of technology and wet human viscera indiscriminately onto the ice. The remaining five soldiers ran even harder, but the monster chasing them barely slowed as it killed.

"Shoot it shoot it shoot it," Bobbie yelled, and opened fire. Her training and the technology of her combat suit combined to make her an extremely efficient killing machine. As soon as her finger pulled the trigger on her suit's gun, a stream of two-millimeter armor-piercing rounds streaked out at the creature at more than a thousand meters per second. In just under a second she'd fired fifty rounds at it. The creature was a relatively slow-moving human-sized target, running in a straight line. Her targeting computer could do ballistic corrections that would let her hit a softball-sized object moving at supersonic speeds. Every bullet she fired at the monster hit.

It didn't matter.

The rounds went through it, probably not slowing appreciably before they exited. Each exit wound sprouted a spray of black filaments that fell onto the snow instead of blood. It was like shooting water. The wounds closed almost faster than they were created; the only sign the thing had even been hit was the trail of black fibers in its wake.

And then it caught a second UN Marine. Instead of tearing him to pieces like it had the last one, it spun and hurled the fully armored Earther—probably massing more than five hundred kilos total—toward Bobbie. Her HUD tracked the UN soldier on his upward arc and helpfully informed her that the monster had thrown him not *toward* her but *at* her. In a very flat trajectory. Which meant fast.

She dove to the side as quickly as her bulky suit would let her.

The hapless UN Marine swiped Hillman, who'd been standing next to her, and then both of them were gone, bouncing down the ice at lethal speeds.

By the time she'd turned back to the monster, it had killed two more UN soldiers.

The entire Martian line opened fire on it, including *Yojimbo*'s big cannon. The two remaining Earth soldiers diverged and ran at angles away from the thing, trying to give their Martian counterparts an open firing lane. The creature was hit hundreds, thousands of times. It stitched itself back together while remaining at a full run, never more than slowing when one of *Yojimbo*'s cannon shots detonated nearby.

Bobbie, back on her feet, joined in the barrage of fire but it didn't make any difference. The creature slammed into the Martian line, killing two marines faster than the eye could follow. *Yojimbo* slid to one side, far more nimble than a machine of its size should be. Bobbie thought Sa'id must be driving it. He bragged he could make the big mech dance the tango when he wanted to. That didn't matter either. Even before Sa'id could bring the mech's cannon around for a point-blank shot, the creature ran right up its side, gripped the pilot hatch, and tore the door off its hinges. Sa'id was snatched from his cockpit harness and hurled sixty meters straight up.

The other marines had begun to fall back, firing as they went. Without radio, there was no way to coordinate the retreat. Bobbie found herself running toward the dome with the rest. The small and distant part of her mind that wasn't panicking knew that the dome's glass and metal would offer no protection against something that could tear an armored man in half or rip a nine-ton mech to pieces. That part of her mind recognized the futility in attempting to override her terror.

By the time she found the external door into the dome, there was only one other marine left with her. Gourab. Up close, she could see his face through the armored glass of his helmet. He screamed something at her she couldn't hear. She started to lean forward to touch helmets with him when he shoved her backward onto the ice. He was hammering on the door controls with one metal fist, trying to smash his way in, when the creature caught him and peeled the helmet off his suit with one casual swipe. Gourab stood for a moment, face in vacuum, eyes blinking and mouth open in a soundless scream; then the creature tore off his head as easily as it had his helmet.

It turned and looked at Bobbie, still flat on her back.

Up close, she could see that it had bright blue eyes. A glowing, electric blue. They were beautiful. She raised her gun and held down the trigger for half a second before she realized she'd run out of ammo long before. The creature looked at her gun with what she would have sworn was curiosity, then looked into her eyes and cocked its head to one side.

This is it, she thought. *This is how I go out, and I'm not going to know what did it, or why.* Dying she could handle. Dying without any answers seemed terribly cruel.

The creature took one step toward her, then stopped and shuddered. A new pair of limbs burst out of its midsection and writhed in the air like tentacles. Its head, already grotesque, seemed to swell up. The blue eyes flashed as bright as the lights in the domes.

And then it exploded in a ball of fire that hurled her away across the ice and slammed her into a low ridge hard enough for the impact-absorbing gel in her suit to go rigid, freezing her in place.

She lay on her back, fading toward unconsciousness. The night sky above her began to flash with light. The ships in orbit, shooting each other.

Cease fire, she thought, pressing it out into the blackness. *They were retreating. Cease fire.* Her radio was still out, her suit dead. She couldn't tell anyone that the UN Marines hadn't been attacking.

Or that something else had.

Chapter Two: Holden

The coffeemaker was broken again.

Again.

Jim Holden clicked the red brew button in and out several more times, knowing it wouldn't matter, but helpless to stop himself. The massive and gleaming coffeemaker, designed to brew enough to keep a Martian naval crew happy, refused to make a single cup. Or even a noise. It wasn't just refusing to brew; it was refusing to *try.* Holden closed his eyes against the caffeine headache that threatened in his temples and hit the button on the nearest wall panel to open the shipwide comm.

"Amos," he said.

The comm wasn't working.

Feeling increasingly ridiculous, he pushed the button for the 1MC channel several more times. Nothing. He opened his eyes and saw that all the lights on the panel were out. Then he turned around and saw that the lights on the refrigerator and the ovens were out. It wasn't just the coffeemaker; the entire galley was in open revolt. Holden looked at the ship name, *Rocinante*, newly stenciled onto the galley wall, and said, "Baby, why do you hurt me when I love you so much?"

He pulled out his hand terminal and called Naomi.

After several moments, she finally answered, "Uh, hello?"

"The galley doesn't work, where's Amos?"

A pause. "You called me from the galley? While we are on the same ship? The wall panel just one step too far away?"

"The wall panel in the galley doesn't work either. When I said, 'The galley doesn't work,' it wasn't clever hyperbole. It literally means that not one thing in the galley works. I called you because you carry your terminal and Amos almost never does. And also because he never tells me what he's working on, but he always tells you. So, where is Amos?"

Naomi laughed. It was a lovely sound, and it never failed to put a smile on Holden's face. "He told me he was going to be doing some rewiring."

"Do you have power up there? Are we hurtling out of control and you guys were trying to figure out how to break the news to me?"

Holden could hear tapping from Naomi's end. She hummed to herself as she worked.

"Nope," she said. "Only area without power seems to be the galley. Also, Alex says we're less than an hour from fighting with space pirates. Want to come up to ops and fight pirates?"

"I can't fight pirates without coffee. I'm going to find Amos," Holden said, then hung up and put his terminal back in his pocket.

Holden moved to the ladder that ran down the keel of the ship, and called up the lift. The fleeing pirate ship could only sustain about 1 g for extended flight, so Holden's pilot, Alex Kamal, had them flying at 1.3 g to intercept. Anything over 1 g made the ladder dangerous to use.

A few seconds later, the deck hatch clanged open, and the lift whined to a stop at his feet. He stepped on and tapped the button for the engineering deck. The lift began its slow crawl down the shaft, deck hatches opening at its approach, then slamming shut once he had passed.

Amos Burton was in the machine shop, one deck above engineering. He had a complex-looking device half disassembled on the workbench in front of him and was working on it with a solder gun. He wore a gray jumpsuit several sizes too small for him, which strained to contain his broad shoulders when he moved, the old ship name *Tachi* still embroidered on the back.

Holden stopped the lift and said, "Amos, the galley doesn't work."

Amos waved one thick arm in an impatient gesture without stopping his work. Holden waited. After another couple seconds of soldering, Amos finally put down the tool and turned around.

"Yep, it doesn't work because I got this little fucker yanked out of it," he said, pointing at the device he'd been soldering.

"Can you put it back?"

"Nope, at least not yet. Not done working on it."

Holden sighed. "Is it important that we disable the galley to fix this thing just before confronting a bloodthirsty band of space pirates? Because my head is really starting to ache, and I'd love to get a cup of coffee before, you know, doing battle."

"Yep, it was important," Amos said. "Should I explain why? Or you want to take my word for it?"

Holden nodded. While he didn't miss much about his days in the Earth Navy, he did find that he occasionally got nostalgic for the absolute respect for the chain of command. On the *Rocinante* the title "captain" was much more nebulously defined. Rewiring things was Amos' job, and he would resist the idea that he had to inform Holden anytime he was doing it.

Holden let it drop.

"Okay," he said. "But I wish you'd warned me ahead of time. I'm going to be cranky without my coffee."

Amos grinned at him and pushed his cap back on his mostly bald head.

"Shit, Cap, I can cover you on that," he said, then reached back and grabbed a massive metal thermos off the bench. "I made some emergency supplies before I shut the galley down."

"Amos, I apologize for all the mean things I was thinking about you just now."

Amos waved it off and turned back to his work. "Take it. I already had a cup."

Holden climbed back onto the lift and rode it up to the operations deck, the thermos clutched in both hands like a life preserver.

Naomi was seated at the sensor and communications panel, tracking their progress in pursuit of the fleeing pirates. Holden could see at a glance that they were much closer than the last estimate he'd received. He strapped himself into the combat operations couch. He opened a nearby cabinet and, guessing they might be at low g or in free fall in the near future, pulled out a drinking bulb for his coffee.

As he filled it from the thermos's nipple, he said, "We're closing awful fast. What's up?"

"Pirate ship has slowed down quite a bit from its initial one g acceleration. They dropped to half a g for a couple minutes, then stopped accelerating altogether a minute ago. The computer tracked some fluctuations in drive output just before they slowed, so I think we chased them too hard."

"They broke their ship?"

"They broke their ship."

Holden took a long drink out of the bulb, scalding his tongue in the process and not caring.

"How long to intercept now?"

"Five minutes, tops. Alex was waiting to do the final decel burn until you were up here and belted in."

Holden tapped the comm panel's 1MC button and said, "Amos, buckle up. Five minutes to badguys." Then he switched to the cockpit channel and said, "Alex, what's the word?"

"I do believe they broke their ship," Alex replied in his Martian Mariner Valley drawl.

"That seems to be the consensus," Holden said.

"Makes runnin' away a bit harder."

The Mariner Valley had originally been settled by Chinese, East Indians, and Texans. Alex had the dark complexion and jet-black hair of an East Indian. Coming as he did from Earth, Holden always found it strangely disconcerting when an exaggerated Texas drawl came from someone his brain said should be speaking with Punjabi accents.

"And it makes our day easier," Holden replied, warming up the combat ops panel. "Bring us to relative stop at ten thousand klicks. I'm going to paint them with the targeting laser and turn on the point defense cannons. Open the outer doors to the tubes, too. No reason not to look as threatening as possible."

"Roger that, boss," Alex replied.

Naomi swiveled in her chair and gave Holden a grin. "Fighting space pirates. Very romantic."

Holden couldn't help smiling back. Even wearing a Martian naval officer's jumpsuit that was three sizes too short and five sizes too big around for her long and thin Belter frame, she looked beautiful to him. Her long and curly black hair was pulled into an unruly tail behind her head. Her features were a striking mix of Asian, South American, and African that was unusual even in the melting pot of the Belt. He glanced at his brown-haired Montana farm boy reflection in a darkened panel and felt very generic by comparison.

"You know how much I like anything that gets you to say the word 'romantic,' " he said. "But I'm afraid I lack your enthusiasm. We started out saving the solar system from a horrific alien menace. Now this?"

Holden had only known one cop well, and him briefly. During the massive and unpleasant series of clusterfucks that now went under the shorthand "the Eros incident," Holden had teamed up for a time with a thin, gray, broken man called Miller. By the time they'd met, Miller had already walked away from his official job to obsessively follow a missing persons case.

They'd never precisely been friends, but they'd managed to stop the human race from being wiped out by a corporation's self-induced sociopathy and a recovered alien weapon that everyone in human history had mistaken for a moon of Saturn. By that standard, at least, the partnership had been a success.

Holden had been a naval officer for six years. He'd seen people die, but only from the vantage of a radar screen. On Eros, he'd seen thousands of people die, up close and in horrific ways. He'd killed a couple of them himself. The radiation dose he'd received there meant he had to take constant medications to stop the cancers that kept blooming in his tissues. He'd still gotten off lighter than Miller.

Because of Miller, the alien infection had landed on Venus instead of Earth. But that hadn't killed it. Whatever the alien's hijacked, confused programming was, it was still going on under that planet's thick cloud cover, and no one had so far been able to offer any scientific conclusions more compelling than *Hmm. Weird.*

Saving humanity had cost the old, tired Belter detective his life.

Saving humanity had turned Holden into an employee of the Outer Planets Alliance tracking down pirates. Even on the bad days, he had to think he'd gotten the better end of that deal.

"Thirty seconds to intercept," Alex said.

Holden pulled his mind back to the present and called down to engineering. "You all strapped in down there, Amos?"

"Roger, Cap. Ready to go. Try not to get my girl all shot up."

"No one's shooting anyone today," Holden said after he shut the comm link off. Naomi heard him and raised an eyebrow in question. "Naomi, give me comms. I want to call our friends out there."

A second later, the comm controls appeared on his panel. He aimed a tightbeam at the pirate ship and waited for the link light to go green. When it did, he said, "Undesignated light freighter, this is Captain James Holden of the Outer Planets Alliance missile frigate *Rocinante*. Please respond."

His headset was silent except for the faint static of background radiation.

"Look, guys, let's not play games. I know you know who I am. I also know that five days ago, you attacked the food freighter *Somnambulist*, disabled its engines, and stole six thousand kilos of protein and all of their air. Which is pretty much all I need to know about you."

More staticky silence.

"So here's the deal. I'm tired of following you, and I'm not going to let you stall me while you fix your broken ship and then lead me on another merry chase. If you don't signal your full and complete surrender in the next sixty seconds, I am going to fire a pair of torpedoes with high-yield plasma warheads and melt your ship into glowing slag. Then I'm going to fly back home and sleep really well tonight."

The static was finally broken by a boy who sounded way too young to have already decided on a life of piracy.

"You can't do that. The OPA isn't a real government. You can't legally do shit to me, so back the fuck off," the voice said, sounding like it was on the verge of a pubescent squeak the entire time.

"Seriously? That's the best you've got?" Holden replied. "Look, forget the debate about legality and what constitutes actual governmental authority for a minute. Look at the ladar returns you're getting from my ship. While you are in a cobbled-together light freighter that someone welded a homemade gauss cannon onto, I'm in a state-of-the-art Martian torpedo bomber with enough firepower to slag a small moon."

The voice on the other end didn't reply.

"Guys, even if you don't recognize me as the appropriate legal authority, can we at least agree that I can blow you up anytime I want to?"

The comm remained silent.

Holden sighed and rubbed the bridge of his nose. In spite of the caffeine, his headache was refusing to go away. Leaving the channel open to the pirate ship, he opened another channel to the cockpit.

"Alex, put a short burst from the forward point defense cannons through that freighter. Aim for midships."

"Wait!" yelled the kid on the other ship. "We surrender! Jesus *Christ*!"

Holden stretched out in the zero g, enjoying it after the days of acceleration, and grinned to himself. *No one gets shot today* indeed.

"Naomi, tell our new friends how to give remote control of their ship to you, and let's take them back to Tycho Station for the OPA tribunals to figure out. Alex, once they have their engines back up, plot us a return trip at a nice comfortable half g. I'll be down in sick bay trying to find aspirin."

Holden unbuckled his crash couch harness and pushed off to the deck ladder. Along the way, his hand terminal started beeping. It was Fred Johnson, the nominal leader of the OPA and their personal patron on the Tycho corporation's manufacturing station, which was also now doubling as the de facto OPA headquarters.

"Yo, Fred, caught our naughty pirates. Bringing them back for trial."

Fred's large dark face crinkled into a grin. "That's a switch. Got tired of blowing them up?"

"Nope, just finally found some who believed me when I said I would."

Fred's grin turned into a frown. "Listen, Jim, that's not why I called. I need you back at Tycho on the double. Something's happening on Ganymede..."

Chapter Three: Prax

Praxidike Meng stood in the doorway of the staging barn, look-ing out at the fields of softly waving leaves so utterly green they were almost black, and panicked. The dome arched above him, darker than it should have been. Power to the grow lights had been cut, and the mirrors…He couldn't think about the mirrors.

The flickers of fighting ships looked like glitches on a cheap screen, colors and movements that shouldn't have been there. The sign that something was very wrong. He licked his lips. There had to be a way. There had to be some way to save them.

"Prax," Doris said. "We have to go. Now."

The cutting edge of low-resource agricultural botany, the *Glycine kenon*, a type of soybean so heavily modified it was an entirely new species, represented the last eight years of his life. They were the reason his parents still hadn't seen their only granddaughter in the flesh. They, and a few other things, had ended his marriage. He could see the eight subtly different strains of engineered chloroplasts in the fields, each one trying to spin out the most protein per photon. His hands were trembling. He was going to vomit.

"We have maybe five more minutes to impact," Doris said. "We have to evacuate."

"I don't see it," Prax said.

"It's coming fast enough, by the time you see it, you won't see it. Everyone else has already gone. We're the last ones. Now get in the lift."

The great orbital mirrors had always been his allies, shining down on his fields like a hundred pale suns. He couldn't believe that they'd betray him. It was an insane thought. The mirror plummeting toward the surface of Ganymede—toward his greenhouse, his soybeans, his life's work—hadn't chosen anything. It was a victim of cause and effect, the same as everything else.

"I'm about to leave," Doris said. "If you're here in four minutes, you'll die."

"Wait," Prax said. He ran out into the dome. At the edge of the nearest field, he fell to his knees and dug into the rich black soil. The smell of it was like a good patchouli. He pushed his fingers in as deep as he could, cupping a root ball. The small, fragile plant came up in his hands.

Doris was in the industrial lift, ready to descend into the caves and tunnels of the station. Prax sprinted for her. With the plant to save, the dome suddenly felt horribly dangerous. He threw himself through the door and Doris pressed the control display. The wide metal room of the lift lurched, shifted, and began its descent. Normally, it would have carried heavy equipment: the tiller, the tractor, the tons of humus taken from the station recycling processors. Now it was only the three of them: Prax sitting cross-legged on the floor, the soybean seedling nodding in his lap, Doris chewing her lower lip and watching her hand terminal. The lift felt too big.

"The mirror could miss," Prax said.

"It could. But it's thirteen hundred tons of glass and metal. The shock wave will be fairly large."

"The dome might hold."

"No," she said, and Prax stopped talking to her.

The cart hummed and clanked, falling deeper under the surface ice, sliding into the network of tunnels that made up the bulk of the station. The air smelled like heating elements and industrial lubricant. Even now, he couldn't believe they'd done it. He couldn't believe the military bastards had actually started shooting each other. No one, anywhere, could really be that shortsighted. Except that it seemed they could.

In the months since the Earth-Mars alliance had shattered, he'd gone from constant and gnawing fear to cautious hope to complacency. Every day that the United Nations and the Martians hadn't started something had been another bit of evidence that they wouldn't. He'd let himself think that everything was more stable than it looked. Even if things got bad and there was a shooting war, it wouldn't be here. Ganymede was where the food came from. With its magnetosphere, it was the safest place for pregnant women to gestate, claiming the lowest incidence of birth defects and stillbirth in the outer planets. It was the center of everything that made human expansion into the solar system possible. Their work was as precious as it was fragile, and the people in charge would never let the war come here.

Doris said something obscene. Prax looked up at her. She ran a hand through her thin white hair, turned, and spat.

"Lost connectivity," she said, holding up the hand terminal. "Whole network's locked down."

"By who?"

"Station security. United Nations. Mars. How would I know?"

"But if they—"

The concussion was like a giant fist coming down on the cart's roof. The emergency brakes kicked in with a bone-shaking clang. The lights went out, darkness swallowing them for two

hummingbird-fast heartbeats. Four battery-powered emergency
LEDs popped on, then off again as the cart's power came back.
The critical failure diagnostics started to run: motors humming,
lifts clicking, the tracking interface spooling through checksums
like an athlete stretching before a run. Prax stood up and walked
to the control panel. The shaft sensors reported minimal atmospheric pressure and falling. He felt a shudder as containment
doors closed somewhere above them and the exterior pressure
started to rise. The air in the shaft had been blown out into space
before the emergency systems could lock down. His dome was
compromised.

His dome was gone.

He put his hand to his mouth, not realizing he was smearing
soil across his chin until he'd already done it. Part of his mind was
skittering over the things that needed to be done to save the
project—contact his project manager at RMD-Southern, refile
the supplemental grant applications, get the data backups to
rebuild the viral insertion samples—while another part had gone
still and eerily calm. The sense of being two men—one bent on
desperate measures, the other already in the numb of mourning—
felt like the last weeks of his marriage.

Doris turned to him, a weary amusement plucking at her wide
lips. She put out her hand.

"It was a pleasure working with you, Dr. Meng."

The cart shuddered as the emergency brakes retracted. Another
impact came from much farther off. A mirror or a ship falling.
Soldiers shelling each other on the surface. Maybe even fighting
deeper in the station. There was no way to know. He shook her
hand.

"Dr. Bourne," he said. "It has been an honor."

They took a long, silent moment at the graveside of their previous lives. Doris sighed.

"All right," she said. "Let's get the hell out of here."

Mei's day care was deep in the body of the moon, but the tube station was only a few hundred yards from the cart's loading dock, and the express trip down to her was no more than ten minutes. Or would have been if they were running. In three decades of living on Ganymede, Prax had never even noticed that the tube stations had security doors.

The four soldiers standing in front of the closed station wore thick plated armor painted in shifting camouflage lines the same shades of beige and steel as the corridor. They carried intimidatingly large assault rifles and scowled at the crowd of a dozen or more pressing in around them.

"I am on the transportation board," a tall, thin, dark-skinned woman was saying, punctuating each word by tapping her finger on one soldier's chest plate. "If you don't let us past, then you're in trouble. Serious trouble."

"How long is it going to be down?" a man asked. "I need to get home. How long is it going to be down?"

"Ladies and gentlemen," the soldier on the left shouted. She had a powerful voice. It cut through the rumble and murmur of the crowd like a teacher speaking to restless schoolchildren. "This settlement is in security lockdown. Until the military action is resolved, there is no movement between levels except by official personnel."

"Whose side are you on?" someone shouted. "Are you Martians? Whose side are you *on*?"

"In the meantime," the soldier went on, ignoring the question, "we are going to ask you all to be patient. As soon as it's safe to travel, the tube system will be opened. Until that time, we're going to ask you to remain calm for your own safety."

Prax didn't know he was going to speak until he heard his own voice. He sounded whiny.

"My daughter's in the eighth level. Her school's down there."

"Every level is in lockdown, sir," the soldier said. "She'll be just fine. You just have to be patient."

The dark-skinned woman from the transportation board crossed her arms. Prax saw two men abandon the press, walking back down the narrow, dirty hall, talking to each other. In the old tunnels this far up, the air smelled of recyclers—plastic and heat and artificial scents. And now also of fear.

"Ladies and gentlemen," the soldier shouted. "For your own safety, you need to remain calm and stay where you are until the military situation has been resolved."

"What exactly is the military situation?" a woman at Prax's elbow said, her voice making the words a demand.

"It's rapidly evolving," the soldier said. Prax thought there was a dangerous buzz in her voice. She was as scared as anyone. Only she had a gun. So this wasn't going to work. He had to find something else. His one remaining *Glycine kenon* still in his hand, Prax walked away from the tube station.

He'd been eight years old when his father had transferred from the high-population centers of Europa to help build a research lab on Ganymede. The construction had taken ten years, during which Prax had gone through a rocky adolescence. When his parents had packed up to move the family to a new contract on an asteroid in eccentric orbit near Neptune, Prax had stayed behind. He'd gotten a botany internship thinking that he could use it to grow illicit, untaxed marijuana only to discover that every third botany intern had come in with the same plan. The four years he'd spent trying to find a forgotten closet or an abandoned tunnel that wasn't already occupied by an illegal hydroponics experiment left him with a good sense of the tunnel architecture.

He walked through the old, narrow hallways of the first-generation construction. Men and women sat along the walls or in the bars and restaurants, their faces blank or angry or frightened. The display screens were set on old entertainment loops of music or theater or abstract art instead of the usual newsfeeds. No hand terminals chimed with incoming messages.

By the central-air ducts, he found what he'd been looking for. The maintenance transport always had a few old electric scooters lying around. No one used them anymore. Because Prax was a senior researcher, his hand terminal would let him through the rusting chain-link fencing. He found one scooter with a sidecar and half a charge still in the batteries. It had been seven years since he'd been on a scooter. He put the *Glycine kenon* in the sidecar, ran through the diagnostic sequence, and wheeled himself out to the hall.

The first three ramps had soldiers just like the ones he'd seen at the tube station. Prax didn't bother stopping. At the fourth, a supply tunnel that led from the surface warehouses down toward the reactors, there was nobody. He paused, the scooter silent beneath him. There was a bright acid smell in the air that he couldn't quite place. Slowly, other details registered. The scorch marks at the wall panel, a smear of something dark along the floor. He heard a distant popping sound that it took three or four long breaths to recognize as gunfire.

Rapidly evolving apparently meant fighting in the tunnels. The image of Mei's classroom stippled with bullet holes and soaked in children's blood popped into his mind, as vivid as something he was remembering instead of imagining. The panic he'd felt in the dome came down on him again, but a hundred times worse.

"She's fine," he told the plant beside him. "They wouldn't have a firefight in a day care. There're kids there."

The green-black leaves were already starting to wilt. They wouldn't have a war around children. Or food supplies. Or fragile agricultural domes. His hands were trembling again, but not so badly he couldn't steer.

The first explosion came just as he was heading down the ramp from seven to level eight along the side of one of the cathedral-huge unfinished caverns where the raw ice of the moon had been left to weep and refreeze, something between a massive green space and a work of art. There was a flash, then a concussion, and the scooter was fishtailing. The wall loomed up fast, and Prax wrenched his leg out of the way before the impact. Above him, he heard voices shouting. Combat troops would be in armor, talking through their radios. At least, he thought they would. The people screaming up there had to be just people. A second explosion gouged the cavern wall, a section of blue-white ice the size of a tractor calving off the roof and falling slowly and inexorably down to the floor, grinding into it. Prax scrambled to keep the scooter upright. His heart felt like it was trying to break out of his rib cage.

On the upper edge of the curving ramp, he saw figures in armor. He didn't know if they were UN or Mars. One of them turned toward him, lifting a rifle. Prax gunned the scooter, sliding fast down the ramp. The chatter of automatic weapons and the smell of smoke and steam melt followed him.

The school's doors were closed. He didn't know if that was ominous or hopeful. He brought the wobbling scooter to a halt, jumped off. His legs felt weak and unsteady. He meant to knock gently on the steel drop door, but his first try split the skin over his knuckle.

"Open up! My daughter's in there!" He sounded like a madman, but someone inside heard him or saw him on the security monitor. The articulated steel plates of the door shuddered and began to rise. Prax dropped to the ground and scrambled through.

He hadn't met the new teacher, Miss Carrie, more than a few times, when dropping Mei off or picking her up. She couldn't have been more than twenty years old and was Belter-tall and thin. He didn't remember her face being so gray.

The schoolroom was intact, though. The children were in a circle, singing a song about an ant traveling through the solar system, with rhymes for all the major asteroid bodies. There was no blood, no bullet holes, but the smell of burning plastic was seeping through the vents. He had to get Mei someplace safe. He wasn't sure where that would be. He looked at the circle of children, trying to pick out her face, her hair.

"Mei's not here, sir," Miss Carrie said, her voice tight and breathy at the same time. "Her mother got her this morning."

"This morning?" Prax said, but his mind fastened on *her mother*. What was Nicola doing on Ganymede? He'd had a message from her two days earlier about the child support judgment; she *couldn't* have gotten from Ceres to Ganymede in two days…

"Just after snack," the teacher said.

"You mean she was evacuated. Someone came and evacuated Mei."

Another explosion came, shaking the ice. One of the children made a high, frightened sound. The teacher looked from him to the children, then back. When she spoke again, her voice was lower.

"Her mother came just after snack. She took Mei with her. She hasn't been here all day."

Prax pulled up his hand terminal. The connection was still dead, but his wallpaper was a picture from Mei's first birthday, back when things were still good. Lifetimes ago. He held up the picture and pointed at Nicola, laughing and dangling the doughy, delighted bundle that had been Mei.

"Her?" Prax said. "*She* was here?"

The confusion in the teacher's face answered him. There'd been a mistake. Someone—a new nanny or a social worker or something—had come to pick up a kid and gotten the wrong one.

"She was on the computer," the teacher said. "She was in the system. It *showed* her."

The lights flickered. The smell of smoke was getting stronger, and the air recyclers were humming loudly, popping and crackling as they struggled to suck out the volatile particulates. A boy whose name Prax should have known whimpered, and the teacher reflexively tried to turn toward him. Prax took her elbow and wrenched her back.

"No, you made a mistake," he said. "Who did you give Mei to?"

"The system said it was her mother! She had identification. It cleared her."

A stutter of muted gunfire came from the hallway. Someone was screaming outside, and then the kids started to shriek. The teacher pulled her arm away. Something banged against the drop door.

"She was about thirty. Dark hair, dark eyes. She had a doctor with her, she was in the system, and Mei didn't make any kind of fuss about it."

"Did they take her medicine?" he asked. "Did they take her *medicine*?"

"No. I don't know. I don't think so."

Without meaning to, Prax shook the woman. Only once, but hard. If Mei didn't have her medicine, she'd already missed her midday dose. She might make it as long as morning before her immune system started shutting down.

"Show me," Prax said. "Show me the picture. The woman who took her."

"I can't! The system's down!" the teacher shouted. "They're killing people in the hallway!"

The circle of children dissolved, screams riding on the backs of screams. The teacher was crying, her hands pressed to her face. Her skin had an almost blue cast to it. He could feel the raw animal panic leaping through his brain. The calm that fell on him didn't take away from it.

"Is there an evacuation tunnel?" he asked.

"They told us to stay here," the teacher said.

"I'm telling you to evacuate," Prax said, but what he thought was *I have to find Mei.*

Chapter Four: Bobbie

Consciousness returned as an angry buzzing noise and pain. Bobbie blinked once, trying to clear her head, trying to see where she was. Her vision was maddeningly blurry. The buzzing sound resolved into an alarm from her suit. Colored lights flashed in her face as the suit's HUD sent her data she couldn't read. It was in the middle of rebooting and alarms were coming on one by one. She tried to move her arms and found that although weak, she wasn't paralyzed or frozen in place. The impact gel in her suit had returned to a liquid state.

Something moved across the window of faint light that was her helmet's face shield. A head, bobbing in and out of view. Then a click as someone plugged a hardline into her suit's external port. A corpsman, then, downloading her injury data.

A voice, male and young, in her suit's internal speakers said,

"Gotcha, Gunny. We gotcha. Gonna be okay. Gonna be all right. Just hang in there."

He hadn't quite finished saying *there* when she blacked out again.

She woke bouncing down a long white tunnel on a stretcher. She wasn't wearing her suit anymore. Bobbie was afraid that the battlefield med-techs hadn't wasted time taking her out of it the normal way, that they'd just hit the override that blew all the seams and joints apart. It was a fast way to get a wounded soldier out of four hundred kilos of armored exoskeleton, but the suit was destroyed in the process. Bobbie felt a pang of remorse for the loss of her faithful old suit.

A moment later, she remembered that her entire platoon had been ripped to pieces before her eyes, and her sadness about the lost suit seemed trivial and demeaning.

A hard bump on the stretcher sent a jolt of lightning up her spine and hurled her back into darkness.

"Sergeant Draper," a voice said.

Bobbie tried to open her eyes and found it impossible to do. Each eyelid weighed a thousand kilos, and even the attempt left her exhausted. So she tried to answer the voice and was surprised and a little ashamed of the drunken mumble that came out instead.

"She's conscious, but just barely," the voice said. It was a deep, mellow male voice. It seemed filled with warmth and concern. Bobbie hoped that the voice would keep talking until she fell back asleep.

A second voice, female and sharp, replied, "Let her rest. Trying to bring her fully awake right now is dangerous."

The kind voice said, "I don't care if it kills her, Doctor. I need to speak to this soldier, and I need to do it now. So you give her whatever you need to give her to make that happen."

Bobbie smiled to herself, not parsing the words the nice voice said, just the kindly, warm tone. It was good to have someone like that to take care of you. She started to fall back asleep, the coming blackness a welcome friend.

White fire shot up Bobbie's spine, and she sat bolt upright in bed, as awake as she'd ever been. It felt like going on the juice, the chemical cocktail they gave sailors to keep them conscious and alert during high-g maneuvers. Bobbie opened her eyes and then slammed them shut again when the room's bright white light nearly burned them out of her sockets.

"Turn off the lights," she mumbled, the words coming out of her dry throat in a whisper.

The red light seeping in through her closed eyelids dimmed, but when she tried to open them again, it was still too bright. Someone took her hand and held it while a cup was put into it.

"Can you hold that?" the nice voice said.

Bobbie didn't answer; she just brought the cup to her mouth and drank the water in two greedy swallows.

"More," she said, this time in something resembling her old voice.

She heard the sounds of someone scooting a chair and then footsteps away from her on a tile floor. Her brief look at the room had told her she was in a hospital. She could hear the electric hum of medical machines nearby, and the smells of antiseptic and urine competed for dominance. Disheartened, she realized she was the source of the urine smell. A faucet ran for a moment, and then the footsteps came toward her. The cup was put back into her hand. She sipped at it this time, letting the water stay in her mouth awhile before swallowing. It was cool and delicious.

When she was finished, the voice asked, "More?"

She shook her head.

"Maybe later," she said. Then, after a moment: "Am I blind?"

"No. You've been given a combination of focus drugs and

powerful amphetamines. Which means your eyes are fully dilated. Sorry, I didn't think to lower the lights before you woke up."

The voice was still filled with kindness and warmth. Bobbie wanted to see the face behind that voice, so she risked squinting through one eye. The light didn't burn into her like it had before, but it was still uncomfortable. The owner of the nice voice turned out to be a very tall, thin man in a naval intelligence uniform. His face was narrow and tight, the skull beneath it pressing to get out. He gave her a frightening smile that didn't extend past a slight upturn at the corners of his mouth.

"Gunnery Sergeant Roberta W. Draper, 2nd Marine Expeditionary Force," he said, his voice so at odds with his appearance that Bobbie felt like she was watching a movie dubbed from a foreign language.

After several seconds, he still hadn't continued, so Bobbie said, "Yes, sir," then glanced at his bars and added, "Captain."

She could open both eyes now without pain, but a strange tingling sensation was moving up her limbs, making them feel numb and shaky at the same time. She resisted an urge to fidget.

"Sergeant Draper, my name is Captain Thorsson, and I am here to debrief you. We've lost your entire platoon. There's been a two-day pitched battle between the United Nations and Martian Congressional Republic forces on Ganymede. Which, at most recent tally, has resulted in over five billion MCR dollars of infrastructure damage, and the deaths of nearly three thousand military and civilian personnel."

He paused again, staring at her through narrowed eyes that glittered like a snake's. Not sure what response he was looking for, Bobbie just said, "Yes, sir."

"Sergeant Draper, why did your platoon fire on and destroy the UN military outpost at dome fourteen?"

This question was so nonsensical that Bobbie's mind spent several seconds trying to figure out what it really meant.

"Who ordered you to commence firing, and why?"

Of course he couldn't be asking why her people had started the fight. Didn't he know about the monster?

"Don't you know about the monster?"

Captain Thorsson didn't move, but the corners of his mouth dropped into a frown, and his forehead bunched up over his nose.

"Monster," he said, none of the warmth gone from his voice.

"Sir, some kind of monster...mutant...something attacked the UN outpost. The UN troops were running to us to escape it. We didn't fire on them. This...this whatever it was killed them, and then it killed us," she said, nauseated and pausing to swallow at the lemony taste in her mouth. "I mean, everyone but me."

Thorsson frowned for a moment, then reached into one pocket and took out a small digital recorder. He turned it off, then set it on a tray next to Bobbie's bed.

"Sergeant, I'm going to give you a second chance. Up to now, your record has been exemplary. You are a fine marine. One of our best. Would you like to start over?"

He picked up the recorder and placed a finger on the delete button while giving her a knowing look.

"You think I'm lying?" she said. The itchy feeling in her limbs resolved itself into a very real urge to reach out and snap the smug bastard's arm off at the elbow. "We all shot at it. There will be gun camera footage from the entire platoon of this thing killing UN soldiers and then attacking us. Sir."

Thorsson shook his hatchet-shaped head at her, narrowing his eyes until they almost disappeared.

"We have no transmissions from the platoon for the entire fight, and no uploaded data—"

"They were jamming," Bobbie interrupted. "I lost my radio link when I got close to the monster too."

Thorsson continued as though she had not spoken. "And all of the local hardware was lost when an orbital mirror array fell onto the dome. You were outside of the impact area, but the shock wave threw you nearly another quarter of a kilometer. It took us some time to find you."

All of the local hardware was lost. Such a sterile way of putting it. Everyone in Bobbie's platoon blown into shrapnel and vapor when a couple thousand tons of mirror fell out of orbit onto them. A monitor started sounding a low, chiming alert, but no one else paid it any attention, so she didn't either.

"My suit, sir. I shot at it too. My video will still be there."

"Yes," Thorsson said. "We've examined your suit's video log. It's nothing but static."

This is like a bad horror movie, she thought. The heroine who sees the monster, but no one will believe her. She imagined the second act, in which she was court-martialed in disgrace, and only got her redemption in the third act, when the monster showed up again and killed everyone who didn't believe—

"Wait!" she said. "What decompression did you use? My suit is an older model. It uses the version 5.1 video compression. Tell the tech that, and have them try it again."

Thorsson stared at her for a few moments, then pulled out his hand terminal and called someone.

"Have Sergeant Draper's combat suit brought up to her room. Send a tech with video gear with it."

He put the terminal away and then gave Bobbie another of those frightening smiles.

"Sergeant, I admit that I am extremely curious about what you want me to see. If this is still a ruse of some kind, you've only bought yourself a few more moments."

Bobbie didn't reply, but her reaction to Thorsson's attitude had finally shifted from frightened through angry to annoyed. She pushed herself up in the narrow hospital bed and turned sideways, sitting on the edge and tossing the blanket to the side. With her size, her physical presence up close usually either frightened men or turned them on. Either way it made them uncomfortable. She leaned toward Thorsson a bit and was rewarded when he pushed his chair back an equal amount.

She could tell from his disgusted expression that he immediately knew what she'd done, and he looked away from her smile.

The door to the room opened and a pair of Navy techs wheeled in her suit on a rack. It was intact. They hadn't wrecked it taking her out. She felt a lump come up in her throat, and swallowed it back down. She wasn't going to show even a moment's weakness in front of this Thorsson clown.

The clown pointed at the senior of the two techs and said, "You. What's your name?"

The young tech snapped off a salute and said, "Petty Officer Electrician's Mate Singh, sir."

"Mr. Singh, Sergeant Draper here is claiming that her suit has a different video compression than the new suits, and that's why you were unable to read her video data. Is this correct?"

Singh slapped himself on the forehead with his palm.

"Shit. Yeah," he said. "I didn't think— This is the old Mark III Goliath suit. When they started making the Mark IV, they completely rewrote the firmware. Totally different video storage system. Wow, I feel pretty stupid—"

"Yes," interrupted Thorsson. "Do whatever you need to do to display the video stored on that suit. The sooner you do, the less time I will have to dwell on the delays caused by incompetence."

Singh, to his credit, did not reply. He immediately plugged the suit into a monitor and began working. Bobbie examined her suit. It had a lot of scratches and dings but appeared otherwise undamaged. She felt a strong urge to go put it on and then tell Thorsson where he could stick his attitude.

A new set of shakes moved up her arms and legs. Something fluttered in her neck like the heartbeat of a small animal. She reached up and touched it. It was her pulse. She started to say something, but the tech was pumping his fist and high-fiving his assistant.

"Got it, sir," Singh said, then began the playback.

Bobbie tried to watch, but the picture kept getting fuzzy. She reached for Thorsson's arm to get his attention, but missed somehow and just kept tipping forward.

Here we go again, she thought, and there was a brief moment of free fall before the blackness.

"God dammit," the sharp voice said. "I goddamn well told you this would happen. This soldier has suffered internal injuries and a nasty concussion. You can't just pump her full of speed and then interrogate her. It's irresponsible. It's fucking criminal!"

Bobbie opened her eyes. She was back in bed. Thorsson sat in the chair by her side. A stocky blond woman in hospital scrubs stood at the foot of her bed, her face flushed and furious. When she saw Bobbie was awake, she moved to her side and took her hand.

"Sergeant Draper, don't try to move. You took a fall and aggravated some of your injuries. We've got you stabilized, but you need to rest now."

The doctor looked up at Thorsson as she said it, her face placing exclamation marks after every sentence. Bobbie nodded at her, which made her head feel like a bowl of water being carried in shifting gravity. That it didn't hurt probably meant they'd shot her full of every pain medication they had.

"Sergeant Draper's assistance was crucial," Thorsson said, not a hint of apology in his lovely voice. "Because of it, she may have just saved us from an all-out shooting war with Earth. Risking one's own life so others don't have to is pretty much the definition of Roberta's job."

"Don't call me Roberta," Bobbie mumbled.

"Gunny," Thorsson said. "I'm sorry about what happened to your team. But mostly I'm sorry for not believing you. Thank you for responding with professionalism. We avoided a serious mistake because of it."

"Just thought you were an asshole," Bobbie said.

"That's my job, soldier."

Thorsson stood up. "Get some rest. We're shipping you out as soon as you're well enough for the trip."

"Shipping me out? Back to Mars?"

Thorsson didn't answer. He nodded to the doctor, then left. The doctor pushed a button on one of the machines near Bobbie's bed, and something cool shot into her arm. The lights went out.

Gelatin. Why do hospitals always serve gelatin?

Bobbie desultorily poked her spork at the quivering mound of green on her plate. She was finally feeling good enough to really eat, and the soft and see-through foods they kept bringing her were growing more unsatisfying. Even the high-protein, high-carbohydrate slop they cranked out on most Navy ships sounded good right then. Or a thick mushroom steak covered in gravy with a side of couscous…

The door to her room slid open and her doctor, who she now knew was named Trisha Pichon but who insisted that everyone call her Dr. Trish, came in along with Captain Thorsson and a new man she didn't know. Thorsson gave her his creepy smile, but Bobbie had learned that it was just the way the man's face worked. He seemed to lack the muscles necessary for normal smiling. The new man wore a Marine chaplain's uniform of indeterminate religious affiliation.

Dr. Trish spoke first.

"Good news, Bobbie. We're turning you loose tomorrow. How do you feel?"

"Fine. Hungry," Bobbie said, then gave her gelatin another stab.

"We'll see about getting you some real food, then," Dr. Trish said, then smiled and left the room.

Thorsson pointed at the chaplain. "This is Captain Martens. He'll be coming with us on our trip. I'll leave you two to get acquainted."

Thorsson left before Bobbie could respond, and Martens plopped himself down in the chair next to her bed. He stuck out his hand, and she shook it.

"Hello, Sergeant," he said. "I—"

"When I marked my 2790 form as 'none' for religious faith, I was serious about that," Bobbie said, cutting him off.

Martens smiled, apparently not offended by her interruption or her agnosticism.

"I'm not here in a religious capacity, Sergeant. I'm also a trained grief counselor, and since you witnessed the death of every person in your unit, and were almost killed yourself, Captain Thorsson and your doctor agree that you might need me."

Bobbie started to make a dismissive reply, which was cut off by the lump in her chest. She hid her discomfort by taking a long drink of water, then said, "I'm fine. Thanks for coming by."

Martens leaned back in the chair, his smile never wavering.

"If you were really all right after what you've been through, it would be a sign that something was wrong. And you're about to be thrown into a situation with a lot of emotional and intellectual pressure. Once we get to Earth, you won't have the luxury of having an emotional breakdown or post-traumatic stress responses. We have a lot of work to—"

"Earth?" Bobbie pounced on the word. "Waitaminute. Why am I going to *Earth*?"

Chapter Five: Avasarala

Chrisjen Avasarala, assistant to the undersecretary of executive administration, sat near the end of the table. Her sari was orange, the only splash of color in the otherwise military blue-and-gray of the meeting. The seven others with seats at the table were the heads of their respective branches of the United Nations military forces, all of them men. She knew their names, their career paths and psychological profiles, pay rates and political alliances and who they were sleeping with. Against the back wall, personal assistants and staff pages stood in uncomfortable still-ness, like the shy teenagers at a dance. Avasarala snuck a pistachio out of her purse, cracked the shell discreetly, and popped the salted nut into her mouth.

"Any meeting with Martian command is going to have to wait until after the situation on Ganymede is stabilized. Official diplomatic talks before then are only going to make it seem like we've accepted the new status quo." That was Admiral Nguyen, youngest of the men present. Hawkish. Impressed with himself in the way that successful young men tended to be.

General Adiki-Sandoval nodded his bull-wide head.

"Agreed. It's not just Mars we need to think about here. If we start looking weak to the Outer Planets Alliance, you can count on a spike in terrorist activity."

Mikel Agee, from the diplomatic corps, leaned back on his chair and licked his lips anxiously. His slicked-back hair and pinched face made him look like an anthropomorphic rat.

"Gentlemen, I have to disagree—"

"Of course you do," General Nettleford said dryly. Agee ignored him.

"Meeting with Mars at this point is a necessary first step. If we start throwing around preconditions and obstacles, not only is this process going to take longer, but the chances for renewed hostilities go up. If we can take the pressure off, blow off some steam—"

Admiral Nguyen nodded, his face expressionless. When he spoke, his tone was conversational.

"You guys over at Dip have any metaphors more recent than the steam engine?"

Avasarala chuckled with the others. She didn't think much of Agee either.

"Mars has already escalated," General Nettleford said. "Seems to me our best move at this point is to pull the Seventh back from Ceres Station. Get them burning. Put a ticking clock on the wall, then see if the Martians want to stand back on Ganymede."

"Are you talking about moving them to the Jovian system?" Nguyen asked. "Or are you taking them in toward Mars?"

"Taking something in toward Earth looks a lot like taking it in toward Mars," Nettleford said.

Avasarala cleared her throat.

"Do you have anything new on the initial attacker?" she asked.

"The tech guys are working on it," Nettleford said. "But that makes my point. If Mars is testing out new technologies on Ganymede, we can't afford to let them control the tempo. We have to get a threat of our own on the board."

"It was the protomolecule, though?" Agee asked. "I mean, it was whatever was on Eros when it went down?"

"Working on that," Nettleford said again, biting at the words a little. "There are some gross similarities, but there's some basic differences too. It didn't spread the way it did on Eros. Ganymede isn't changing the way the population of Eros did. From the satellite imagery we've got, it looks like it went to Martian territory and either self-destructed or was disposed of by their side. If it's related to Eros at all, it's been refined."

"So Mars got a sample and weaponized it," Admiral Souther said. He didn't talk much. Avasarala always forgot how high his voice was.

"One possibility," Nettleford said. "One very strong possibility."

"Look," Nguyen said with a self-satisfied little smile, like a child who knew he was going to get his way. "I know we've taken first strike off the table here, but we need to talk about what the limits are on immediate response. If this was a dry run for something bigger, waiting may be as good as walking out an airlock."

"We should take the meeting with Mars," Avasarala said.

The room went quiet. Nguyen's face darkened.

"Is that…" he said, but never finished the sentence. Avasarala watched the men look at each other. She took another pistachio from her purse, ate the meat, and tucked the shells away. Agee tried not to look pleased. She really did need to find out who had pulled strings to have him represent the diplomatic corps. He was a terrible choice.

"Security's going to be a problem," Nettleford said. "We're not letting any of their ships inside our effective defense perimeter."

"Well, we can't have it on their terms. If we're going to do this, we want them here, where we control the ground."

"Park them a safe distance away, and have our transports pick them up?"

"They'll never agree to that."

"So let's find out what they will agree to."

Avasarala quietly stood up and headed for the door. Her personal assistant—a European boy named Soren Cottwald—detached himself from the back wall and followed her. The generals pretended not to notice her exit, or maybe they were so wrapped up in the new set of problems she'd handed them, they really didn't. Either way, she was sure they were as pleased to have her out as she was to leave.

The hallways of the United Nations complex in the Hague were clean and wide, the décor a soft style that made everything look like a museum diorama of Portuguese colonies in the 1940s. She paused at an organics recycling unit and started digging the shells out of her bag.

"What's next?" she asked.

"Debriefing with Mr. Errinwright."

"After that?"

"Meeston Gravis about the Afghanistan problem."

"Cancel it."

"What should I tell him?"

Avasarala dusted her hands over the waste container, then turned, walking briskly toward the central commons and the elevators.

"Fuck him," she said. "Tell him the Afghanis have been resisting external rule since before my ancestors were kicking out the British. As soon as I figure out how to change that, I'll let him know."

"Yes, ma'am."

"I also need an updated summary paper on Venus. The latest. And I don't have time to get another PhD to read it, so if it's not in clear, concise language, fire the sonofabitch and get someone who knows how to write."

"Yes, ma'am."

The elevator that rose from the common lobby and meeting rooms up to the offices glittered like spun diamond set in steel and was big enough to seat dinner for four. It recognized them as they stepped in, and began its careful rise through the levels. Outside the windows of the common areas, the Binnenhof seemed to sink and the huge anthill of buildings that was the Hague spread out under a perfect blue sky. It was springtime, and the snow that had touched the city since December was finally gone. The pigeons swirled up from the streets far below. There were thirty billion people on the planet, but they would never crowd out the pigeons.

"They're all fucking men," she said.

"Excuse me?" Soren said.

"The generals. They're all fucking men."

"I thought Souther was the only—"

"I don't mean that they all fuck men. I mean they're all men, the fuckers. How long has it been since a woman was in charge of the armed forces? Not since I came here. So instead, we wind up with another example of what happens to policy when there's too much testosterone in the room. That reminds me: Get in touch with Annette Rabbir in infrastructure. I don't trust Nguyen. If traffic starts going up between him and anyone in the general assembly, I want to know it."

Soren cleared his throat.

"Excuse me, ma'am. Did you just instruct me to spy on Admiral Nguyen?"

"No, I just asked for a comprehensive audit of all network traffic, and I don't give a fuck about any results besides Nguyen's office."

"Of course. My mistake."

The elevator rose past the windows, past the view of the city, and into the dark shaft of the private-office levels. Avasarala cracked her knuckles.

"Just in case, though," she said, "do it on your own initiative."

"Yes, ma'am. That was my thought too."

To those who knew Avasarala only by reputation, her office was deceptively unassuming. It was on the east side of the building, where the lower-ranked officials usually started out. She had a window looking out over the city, but not a corner. The video screen that took up most of the southern wall was left off when it wasn't in active use, leaving it matte black. The other walls were scuffed bamboo paneling. The carpet was industrially short and patterned to hide stains. The only decorations were a small shrine with a clay sculpture of the Gautama Buddha beside the desk, and a cut crystal vase with the flowers that her husband, Arjun, sent every Thursday. The place smelled like fresh blooms and old pipe smoke, though Avasarala had never smoked there and didn't know anyone who had. She walked to the window. Beneath her, the city spread out in vast concrete and ancient stone.

In the darkening sky, Venus burned.

In the twelve years she had been at this desk, in this room, everything had changed. The alliance between Earth and its upstart brother had been an eternal, unshakable thing once. The Belt had been an annoyance and a haven for tiny cells of renegades and troublemakers as likely to die of a ship malfunction as to be called to justice. Humanity had been alone in the universe.

And then the secret discovery that Phoebe, idiosyncratic moon of Saturn, had been an alien weapon, launched at earth when life here was hardly more than an interesting idea wrapped in a lipid bilayer. How could anything be the same after that?

And yet it was. Yes, Earth and Mars were still unsure whether they were permanent allies or deadly enemies. Yes, the OPA, Hezbollah of the vacuum, was on its way to being a real political force in the outer planets. Yes, the thing that had been meant to reshape the primitive biosphere of Earth had instead ridden a rogue asteroid down into the clouds of Venus and started doing no one knew what.

But the spring still came. The election cycle still rose and fell. The evening star still lit the indigo heavens, outshining even the greatest cities of Earth.

Other days, she found that reassuring.

"Mr. Errinwright," Soren said.

Avasarala turned to the dead screen on her wall as it came to life. Sadavir Errinwright was darker skinned than she was, his face round and soft. It would have been in place anywhere in the Punjab, but his voice affected the cool, analytic amusement of Britain. He wore a dark suit and a smart, narrow tie. Wherever he was, it was bright daylight behind him. The link kept fluttering, trying to balance the bright with the dark, leaving him a shadow in a government office or else a man haloed by light.

"Your meeting went well, I hope?"

"It was fine," she said. "We're moving ahead with the Martian summit. They're working out the security arrangements now."

"That was the consensus?"

"Once I told them it was, yes. The Martians are sending their top men to a meeting with officials of the United Nations to personally deliver their apology and discuss how to normalize relations and return Ganymede to blah blah blah. Yes?"

Errinwright scratched his chin.

"I'm not sure that's how our opposites on Mars see it," he said.

"Then they can protest. We'll send out dueling press releases and threaten to cancel the meeting right up to the last minute. High drama is wonderful. It's better than wonderful; it's distracting. Just don't let the bobble-head talk about Venus or Eros."

His flinch was almost subliminal.

"Please, can we not refer to the secretary-general as 'the bobble-head'?"

"Why not? He knows I do. I say it to his face, and he doesn't mind."

"He thinks you're joking."

"That's because he's a fucking bobble-head. Don't let him talk about Venus."

"And the footage?"

It was a fair question. Whatever had made its attack on Ganymede, it had started in the area held by the United Nations. If the back-channel chatter was to be trusted—and it wasn't—Mars had a lone marine's suit camera. Avasarala had seven minutes of high-definition video from forty different cameras of the thing slaughtering the best people Earth had standing for it. Even if the Martians could be convinced to keep it quiet, this was going to be hard to bury.

"Give me until the meeting," Avasarala said. "Let me see what they say and how they say it. Then I'll know what to do. If it's a Martian weapon, they'll show it by what they bring to the table."

"I see," Errinwright said slowly. Meaning he didn't.

"Sir, with all respect," she said, "for the time being, this needs to be something between Earth and Mars."

"High drama between the two major military forces in the system is what we want? How exactly do you see that?"

"I got an alert from Michael-Jon de Uturbé about increased activity on Venus at the *same time* the shooting started on Ganymede. It wasn't a big spike, but it was there. And Venus getting restless just when something happens that looks a damn lot like the protomolecule showed up on Ganymede? That's a problem."

She let that sink in for a moment before she went on. Errinwright's eyes shifted, like he was reading in the air. It was something he did when he was thinking hard.

"Saber rattling we've done before," she said. "We've survived it. It's a known quantity. I have a binder with nine hundred pages of analysis and contingency plans for conflict with Mars, including fourteen different scenarios about what we do if they develop an unexpected new technology. The binder for what we do if something comes up from Venus? It's three pages long, and it begins *Step One: Find God*."

Errinwright looked sober. She could hear Soren behind her, a different and more anxious silence than he usually carried. She'd laid her fear out on the table.

"Three options," she said softly. "One: Mars made it. That's just war. We can handle that. Two: Someone else made it. Unpleasant and dangerous, but solvable. Three: It made itself. And we don't have anything."

"You're going to put more pages in your thin binder?" Errinwright said. He sounded flippant. He wasn't.

"No, sir. I'm going to find out which of the three we're looking at. If it's one of the first two, I'll solve the problem."

"And if the third?"

"Retire," she said. "Let you put some other idiot in charge."

Errinwright had known her long enough to hear the joke in her voice. He smiled and tugged absently at his tie. It was a tell of his. He was as anxious as she was. No one who didn't know him would have seen it.

"That's a tightrope. We can't let the conflict on Ganymede become too heated."

"I'll keep it a sideshow," Avasarala said. "No one starts a war unless I say they can."

"You mean unless the secretary-general issues the executive decision and the general assembly casts an affirming vote."

"And I'll tell him when he can do that," she said. "But you can give him the news. Hearing it from an old grandma like me makes his dick shrink."

"Well, we can't have that, certainly. Let me know what you find. I'll speak with the speech-writing staff and make certain that the text of his announcement doesn't color outside the lines."

"And anyone who leaks the video of the attack answers to me," she said.

"Anyone who leaks it is guilty of treason and will be tried before a legitimate tribunal and sent to the Lunar Penal Colony for life."

"Close enough."

"Don't be a stranger, Chrisjen. We're in difficult times. The fewer surprises, the better."

"Yes, sir," she said. The link died. The screen went dark. She could see herself in it as a smudge of orange topped by the gray of her hair. Soren was a blur of khaki and white.

"You need more work?"

"No, ma'am."

"So get the fuck out."

"Yes, ma'am."

She heard his footsteps retreating behind her.

"Soren!"

"Ma'am?"

"Get me a list of everyone who testified at the Eros incident hearings. And run what they said in testimony past the neuro-psych analysts if it hasn't already been."

"Would you like the transcripts?"

"Yes, that too."

"I'll have them to you as soon as possible."

The door closed behind him, and Avasarala sank into her chair. Her feet hurt, and the presentiment of a headache that had haunted her since morning was stepping forward, clearing its throat. The Buddha smiled serenely, and she chuckled at him, as if sharing a private joke. She wanted to go home, to sit on her porch and listen to Arjun practice his piano.

And instead…

She used her hand terminal rather than the office system to call Arjun. It was a superstitious urge that made her want to keep them separate, even in ways as small as this. He picked up the connection at once. His face was angular, the close-cut beard almost entirely white now. The merriness in his eyes was always there, even when he wept. Just looking at him, she felt something in her breast relax.

"I'm going to be late coming home," she said, immediately regretting the matter-of-fact tone. Arjun nodded.

"I am shocked beyond words," he said. Even the man's sarcasm was gentle. "The mask is heavy today?"

The mask, he called it. As if the person she was when she faced the world was the false one, and the one who spoke to him or played painting games with her granddaughters was authentic. She thought he was wrong, but the fiction was so comforting she had always played along.

"Today, very heavy. What are you doing now, love?"

"Reading Kukurri's thesis draft. It needs work."

"Are you in your office?"

"Yes."

"You should go to the garden," she said.

"Because that's where you want to be? We can go together when you're home."

She sighed.

"I may be very late," she said.

"Wake me, and we can go then."

She touched the screen, and he grinned as if he'd felt the caress. She cut the connection. By long habit, they didn't tell each other goodbye. It was one of a thousand small personal idioms that grew from decades of marriage.

Avasarala turned to her desk system, pulling up the tactical analysis of the battle on Ganymede, the intelligence profiles of the major military figures within Mars, and the master schedule for the meeting, already half filled in by the generals in the time since her conference. She took a pistachio from her purse, cracked its shell, and let the raw information wash over her, her mind dancing through it. In the window behind her, other stars struggled through the light pollution of the Hague, but Venus was still the brightest.

Chapter Six: Holden

Holden was dreaming of long twisting corridors filled with half-human horrors when a loud buzzing woke him to a pitch-black cabin. He struggled for a moment with the unfamiliar straps on the bunk before he unbuckled and floated free in the microgravity. The wall panel buzzed again. Holden pushed off the bed to it and hit the button to bring the cabin lights up. The cabin was tiny. A seventy-year-old crash couch above a personal storage locker crammed up against one bulkhead, a toilet and sink built into a corner, and across from the bunk, a wall panel with the name *Somnambulist* etched above it.

The panel buzzed a third time. This time Holden hit the reply button and said, "Where are we, Naomi?"

"Final braking for high orbit. You're not going to believe this, but they're making us queue up."

"Queue up, as in get in line?"

"Yep," Naomi said. "I think they're boarding all the ships that are landing on Ganymede."

Shit.

"Shit. Which side is it?"

"Does it matter?"

"Well," Holden said. "Earth wants me for stealing a couple thousand of their nuclear missiles and handing them over to the OPA. Mars just wants me for stealing one of their ships. I assume those carry different penalties."

Naomi laughed. "They'd lock you up for eternity either way."

"Call me pedantic, then."

"The group we're in line for look like UN ships, but a Martian frigate is parked right next to them, watching the proceedings."

Holden gave a private prayer of thanks for letting Fred Johnson back on Tycho talk him into taking the recently repaired *Somnambulist* to Ganymede rather than try to land in the *Rocinante*. The freighter was the least suspicious ship in the OPA fleet right now. Far less likely to draw unwanted attention than their stolen Martian warship. They'd left the *Roci* parked a million kilometers away from Jupiter in a spot no one was likely to look. Alex had the ship shut down except for air recycling and passive sensors and was probably huddled in his cabin with a space heater and a lot of blankets, waiting for their call.

"Okay, I'm on my way up. Send a tightbeam to Alex and let him know the situation. If we get arrested, he's to take the *Roci* back to Tycho."

Holden opened the locker under the bunk and pulled out a badly fitting green jumpsuit with *Somnambulist* stenciled on the back and the name Philips on the front pocket. According to the ship's records, provided by the tech wizards back at Tycho, he was crewman first class Walter Philips, engineer and general tool pusher on the food freighter *Somnambulist*. He was also third-in-command out of a crew of three. Given his reputation in the solar system, it was thought best that Holden not have a job on the ship that would require him to speak to anyone in authority.

He washed up in his tiny sink—no actual free-flowing water, but a system of moist towels and soaped pads—scratching unhappily at the scraggly beard he'd been growing as part of his disguise. He'd never tried to grow one before, and was disappointed to discover that his facial hair grew in patches of varying length and curl. Amos had grown a beard as well in an act of solidarity and now had a lush lion's mane, which he was considering keeping because it looked so good.

Holden slid the used towel into its cycling chamber and pushed off toward the compartment hatch and up the crew ladder to the operations deck.

Not that it was much of an ops deck. The *Somnambulist* was nearly a hundred years old and definitely at the end of her life cycle. If they hadn't needed a throwaway ship for this mission, Fred's people would probably have just scrapped the old girl out. Her recent run-in with pirates had left her half dead to begin with. But she'd spent the last twenty years of her life flying the Ganymede-to-Ceres food run, and she'd show up in the registry as a regular visitor to the Jovian moon, a ship that might plausibly arrive with relief supplies. Fred thought that with her regular arrivals at Ganymede, she might just get waved past any customs or blockades without a look.

That, it seemed, had been optimistic.

Naomi was belted into one of the operations stations when Holden arrived. She wore a green jumpsuit similar to his, though the name on her pocket read *Estancia*. She gave him a smile, then waved him over to look at her screen.

"That's the group of ships that are checking everyone out before they land."

"Damn," Holden said, zooming the telescopic image in to get a better look at the hulls and identifying marks. "Definitely UN ships." Something small moved across the image from one of the UN ships to the heavy freighter that was currently at the front of the line. "And that looks like a boarding skiff."

"Well, good thing you haven't groomed in a month," Naomi

said, tugging at a lock of his hair. "With that bush on your head and that awful beard, your own mothers wouldn't recognize you."

"I'm hoping they haven't recruited my mothers," Holden said, trying to match her lightness of tone. "I'll warn Amos that they're coming."

Holden, Naomi, and Amos waited in the short locker-filled hallway just outside the inner airlock door for the boarding party to finish cycling the 'lock. Naomi looked tall and stern in her freshly washed captain's uniform and magnetic boots. Captain Estancia had skippered the *Somnambulist* for ten years before the pirate attack that took her life. Holden thought Naomi made a suitably regal replacement.

Behind her, Amos wore a jumpsuit with a chief engineer's patch and a bored scowl. Even in the microgravity of their current orbit around Ganymede, he seemed to be slouching. Holden did his best to emulate his stance and his half-angry expression.

The airlock finished cycling, and the inner doors slid open. Six marines in combat armor and a junior lieutenant in an environment suit clanked out on mag boots. The lieutenant quickly looked over the crew and checked them against something on his hand terminal. He looked as bored as Amos did. Holden guessed that this poor junior officer had been stuck with the shit duty of boarding ships all day and was probably in as big a hurry to be done as they were to leave.

"Rowena Estancia, captain and majority owner of the Ceres-registered freighter *Weeping Somnambulist*."

He didn't make it a question, but Naomi replied, "Yes, sir."

"I like the name," the lieutenant said without looking up from his terminal.

"Sir?"

"The ship name. It's unusual. I swear, if I board one more ship named after someone's kid or the girl they left behind after that magical weekend on Titan, I'm going to start fining people for general lack of creativity."

Holden felt a tension begin at the base of his spine and creep up toward his scalp. This lieutenant might be bored with his job, but he was smart and perceptive, and he was letting them know it up front.

"Well, this one is named after the tearful three months I spent on Titan after he left me," Naomi said with a grin. "Probably a good thing in the long term. I was going to name her after my goldfish."

The lieutenant's head snapped up in surprise; then he began laughing. "Thanks, Captain. That's the first laugh today. Everyone else is scared shitless of us, and these six slabs of meat"—he gestured at the marines behind him—"have had their senses of humor chemically removed."

Holden shot a look to Amos. *Is he flirting with her? I think he's flirting with her.* Amos' scowl could have meant anything.

The lieutenant tapped something on his terminal and said, "Protein, supplements, water purifiers, and antibiotics. Can I take a quick look?"

"Yes, sir," Naomi said, gesturing toward the hatch. "Right this way."

She left, the UN officer and two of the marines in tow. The other four settled into alert-guard poses next to the airlock. Amos elbowed Holden to get his attention, then said, "How you boys doing today?"

The marines ignored him.

"I was saying to my buddy here, I was saying, 'I bet those fancy tin suits those boys wear bind up something awful in the crotch.' "

Holden closed his eyes and started sending psychic messages to Amos to shut up. It didn't work.

"I mean, all that fancy high-tech gear strapped on everywhere, and the one thing they don't allow for is scratching your balls. Or, God forbid, you get outta alignment and gotta give the works a shift to create some space."

Holden opened his eyes. The marines were all looking at Amos now, but they hadn't moved or spoken. Holden shifted to the back corner of the room and tried to press himself into it. No one even glanced in his direction.

"So," Amos continued, his voice full of companionable good cheer. "I got this theory, and I was hoping you boys could help me out."

The closest marine took a half step forward, but that was all.

"My theory is," Amos said, "that to avoid that whole problem, they just go ahead and cut off all those parts that might get caught up in your suit. And it has the added benefit of reducing your temptation to diddle each other during those long cold nights on the ship."

The marine took another step, and Amos immediately took one of his own to close the distance. With his nose so close to the marine's armored faceplate that his breath fogged the glass, Amos said, "So be straight with me, Joe. The outside of those suits, that's anatomically correct, ain't it?"

There was a long, tense silence that was finally broken when someone cleared his throat at the hatch, and the lieutenant came into the corridor. "There a problem here?"

Amos smiled and stepped back.

"Nope. Just getting to know the fine men and women my tax dollars help pay for."

"Sergeant?" the lieutenant said.

The marine stepped back.

"No, sir. No problem."

The lieutenant turned around and shook Naomi's hand.

"Captain Estancia, it has been a pleasure. Our people will be radioing you with landing clearance shortly. I'm sure the people of Ganymede will be grateful for the supplies you're bringing."

"Happy to help," Naomi said, and gave the young officer a brilliant smile.

When the UN troops had cycled back through the airlock and flown away in their skiff, Naomi let out a long breath and began massaging her cheeks.

"If I had to smile one second longer, my face was going to crack apart."

Holden grabbed Amos by the sleeve.

"What. The. Fuck," he said through gritted teeth, "was *that* all about?"

"What?" Naomi said.

"Amos here did just about everything he could to piss the marines off while you were gone. I'm surprised they didn't shoot him, and then me half a second later."

Amos glanced down at Holden's hand, still gripping his arm, but made no move to pull free.

"Cap, you're a good guy, but you'd be a shitty smuggler."

"What?" Naomi said again.

"The captain here was so nervous even I started to think he was up to something. So I kept the marines' attention until you got back," Amos said. "Oh, and they can't shoot you unless you actually touch them or draw a weapon. You were a UN Navy boy. You should remember the rules."

"So…" Holden started.

"So," Amos interrupted. "If the lieutenant asks them about us, they'll have a story to tell about the asshole engineer who got in their faces, and not the nervous guy with the patchy beard who kept trying to hide in the corner."

"Shit," Holden said.

"You're a good captain, and you can have my back in a fight anytime. But you're a crap criminal. You just don't know how to act like anyone but yourself."

"Wanna be captain again?" Naomi said. "That job sucks."

"Ganymede tower, this is *Somnambulist* repeating our request for a pad assignment," Naomi said. "We've been cleared by the UN patrols, and you've had us holding in low orbit for three hours now."

Naomi flicked off her mic and added, "Asshole."

The voice that replied was different from the one they'd been requesting landing clearance from for the last few hours. This one was older and less annoyed.

"Sorry, *Somnambulist*, we'll get you into the pattern as soon as possible. But we've had launches nonstop for the last ten hours, and we still have a dozen ships to get off of the ground before we start letting people land."

Holden turned on his mic and said, "We talking to the supervisor now?"

"Yep. Senior supervisor Sam Snelling if you're making notes for a complaint. That's Snelling with two *L*s."

"No, no," Holden replied. "Not a complaint. We've been watching the outgoing ships flying by. Are these refugee ships? With the tonnage we've seen lifting off, it looks like half the moon is leaving."

"Nope. We do have a few charters and commercial liners taking people off, but most of the ships leaving right now are food freighters."

"Food freighters?"

"We ship almost a hundred thousand kilos of food a *day*, and the fighting trapped a lot of those shipments on the surface. Now that the blockade is letting people through, they're on their way out to make their deliveries."

"Wait," Holden said. "I'm waiting to land with relief food supplies for people starving on Ganymede, and you're launching a hundred thousand kilos of food *off* the moon?"

"Closer to half a million, what with the backup," Sam said. "But we don't own this food. Most of the food production on Ganymede is owned by corporations that aren't headquartered here. Lot of money tied up in these shipments. Every day it sat on the ground here, people were losing a fortune."

"I..." Holden started, then after a pause said, "*Somnambulist* out."

Holden turned his chair around to face Naomi. Her expression was closed in a way that meant she was as angry as he was.

Amos, lounging near the engineering console and eating an

apple he'd stolen from their relief supplies, said, "This surprises you why, Captain?"

An hour later, they got permission to land.

Seen from low orbit and their descent path, the surface of Ganymede didn't look much different than it ever had. Even at its best, the Jovian moon was a wasteland of gray silicate rock and slightly less gray water ice, the entire thing pocked with craters and flash-frozen lakes. It had looked like a battlefield long before humanity's ancestors crawled up onto dry land for the first time.

But humans, with their great creativity and industriousness in the domain of destruction, had found ways to make their mark. Holden spotted the almost skeletal remains of a destroyer stretched across the landscape at the end of a long black scar. The shock wave of its impact had flattened smaller domes as far as ten kilometers away. Tiny rescue ships flitted about its corpse, looking less for survivors than for bits of information or technology that had survived the crash and couldn't be allowed to fall into enemy hands.

The worst damage visible was the complete loss of one of the enormous greenhouse domes. The agricultural domes were gigantic structures of steel and glass with hectares of carefully cultivated soil and meticulously bred and tended crops beneath them. To see one crushed beneath the twisted metal of what looked like a fallen mirror array was shocking and demoralizing. The domes fed the outer planets with their specially bred crops. The most advanced agricultural science in history happened inside them. And the orbiting mirrors were marvels of engineering that helped make it possible. Slamming one into the other, and leaving both lying in ruins, struck Holden as being as stupidly shortsighted as shitting in your water supply to deny your enemy a drink.

By the time the *Somnambulist* had set her creaking bones to rest on their assigned landing pad, Holden had lost all patience with human stupidity.

So, of course, it came out to meet him.

The customs inspector was waiting for them when they stepped out of the airlock. He was a stick-thin man with a handsome face and an egg-shaped bald head. He was accompanied by two men in nondescript security guard uniforms with Tasers in holsters at their belts.

"Hello, my name is Mr. Vedas. I am the customs inspector for port eleven, pads A14 through A22. Your manifest, please."

Naomi, once again playing captain, stepped forward and said, "The manifest was transmitted to your office prior to landing. I don't—"

Holden saw that Vedas wasn't holding an official cargo-inspection terminal, nor were the guards with him wearing Ganymede Port Authority uniforms. He got the tingling premonition of a bad con job about to be played out. He moved up and waved Naomi off.

"Captain, I'll take care of this."

Customs inspector Vedas looked him up and down and said, "And you are?"

"You can call me Mr. Not-putting-up-with-your-bullshit."

Vedas scowled, and the two security guards shuffled closer. Holden smiled at them, then reached behind his back and under his coat and pulled out a large pistol. He held it at the side of his leg, pointed at the ground, but they stepped back anyway. Vedas blanched.

"I know this shakedown," Holden said. "You ask to look at our manifest; then you tell us which items we have *mistakenly* included on it. And while we are retransmitting to your office with our newly amended manifest, you and your goons take the plum items and sell them on what I'm guessing is a thriving black market for food and medicine."

"I am a legally vested administrator of Ganymede Station," Vedas squeaked. "You think you can bully me with your gun? I'll have port security arrest you and impound your entire ship if you think—"

"No, I'm not going to bully you," Holden said. "But I have had it right up to here with idiots profiting from misery, and I'm going to make myself feel better by having my big friend Amos here beat you senseless for trying to steal food and medicine from refugees."

"Ain't bullying so much as stress relief," Amos said amiably.

Holden nodded at Amos.

"How angry does it make you that this guy wants to steal from refugees, Amos?"

"Pretty fucking angry, Captain."

Holden patted his pistol against his thigh.

"The gun is just to make sure 'port security' there doesn't interfere until Amos has fully worked out his anger issues."

Mr. Vedas, customs inspector for port eleven, pads A14 through A22, turned and ran as though his life depended on it, with his rent-a-cops in hot pursuit.

"You enjoyed that," Naomi said. Her expression was odd and evaluating, her voice in the no-man's-land between accusing and not.

Holden holstered his gun.

"Let's go find out what the hell happened here."

Chapter Seven: Prax

The security center was on the third layer down from the surface. The finished walls and independent power supply seemed like luxury items compared with the raw ice of other places on the station, but really they were important signals. The way some plants advertised their poisons by bright foliage, the security center advertised its impregnability. It wasn't enough that it was impossible to tunnel through the ice and sneak a friend or a lover out of the holding cells. Everyone had to *know* that it was impossible—know just by looking—or else someone would try it.

In all his years on Ganymede, Prax had been there only once before, and then as a witness. As a man there to help the law, not to ask help from it. He'd been back twelve times in the last week, waiting in the long, desperate line, fidgeting and struggling with the almost overpowering sense that he needed to be somewhere else doing something, even if he didn't know what exactly it was.

"I'm sorry, Dr. Meng," the woman at the public information counter said from behind her inch-thick wire-laced window. She looked tired. More than tired, more than exhausted even. Shell-shocked. Dead. "Nothing today either."

"Is there anyone I can talk to? There has to be a way to—"

"I'm sorry," she said, and her eyes looked past him to the next desperate, frightened, unbathed person that she wouldn't be able to help. Prax walked out, teeth grinding in impotent rage. The line was two hours long; men and women and children stood or leaned or sat. Some were weeping. A young woman with red-rimmed eyes smoked a marijuana cigarette, the smell of burning leaves over the stink of close-packed bodies, the smoke curling up past the NO SMOKING sign on the wall. No one protested. All of them had the haunted look of refugees, even the ones who'd been born here.

In the days since the official fighting had stopped, the Martian and Earth militaries had retreated back behind their lines. The breadbasket of the outer planets found itself reduced to a waste-land between them, and the collected intelligence of the station was bent to a single task: getting away.

The ports had started out under lockdown by two military forces in conflict, but they'd soon left the surface for the safety of their ships, and the depth of panic and fear in the station could no longer be contained. The few passenger ships that were permitted out were packed with people trying to get anywhere else. The fares for passage were bankrupting people who'd worked for years in some of the highest-paying material science positions outside Earth. The poorer people were left sneaking out in freight drones or tiny yachts or even space suits strapped onto modified frames and fired off toward Europa in hopes of rescue. Panic drove them from risk to risk until they wound up somewhere else or in the grave. Near the security stations, near the ports, even near the abandoned military cordons set up by Mars and the UN, the corridors were thick with people scrambling for anything they could tell themselves was safety.

Prax wished he was with them.

Instead, his world had fallen into a kind of rhythm. He woke at his rooms, because he always went home at night so that he would be there if Mei came back. He ate whatever he could find. The last two days, there hadn't been anything left in his personal storage, but a few of the ornamental plants in the parkways were edible. He wasn't really hungry anyway.

Then he checked the body drops.

The hospital had maintained a scrolling video feed of the recovered dead to help in identification for the first week. Since then, he'd had to go look at the actual bodies. He was looking for a child, so he didn't have to go through the vast majority of the dead, but the ones he did see haunted him. Twice he'd found a corpse sufficiently mutilated that it might have been Mei, but the first had a stork-bite birthmark at the back of her neck and the other's toenails were the wrong shape. Those dead girls were someone else's tragedies.

Once he'd assured himself that Mei wasn't among the lists of the dead, he went hunting. The first night she'd been gone, he'd taken out his hand terminal and made a list. People to contact who had official power: security, her doctors, the warring armies. People to contact who might have information: the other parents at her school, the other parents in his medical support group, her mother. Favorite places to check: her best friend's home, the common-space parks she liked best, the sweet shop with the lime sherbet she always asked for. Places someone might go to buy a stolen child for sex: a list of bars and brothels off a cached copy of the station directory. The updated directory would be on the system, but it was still locked down. Every day, he crossed as many off the list as he could, and when they were all gone, he started over.

From a list, they'd become a schedule. Security every other day, alternating with whoever would talk to him from the Martian forces or the UN on the other days. The parks in the morning after the body checks. Mei's best friend and her family had made it out, so there was nothing to check there. The sweet shop had been burned out in a riot. Finding her doctors was the hardest. Dr. Astrigan, her pediatrician, had made all the right concerned noises and promised him that she would call him if she heard anything and then, when he checked again three days later, didn't remember having spoken to him. The surgeon who'd helped drain the abscesses along her spine when she'd first been diagnosed hadn't seen her. Dr. Strickland from the support and maintenance group was missing. Nurse Abuakár was dead.

The other families from the group had their own tragedies to work through. Mei wasn't the only child missing. Katoa Merton. Gabby Solyuz. Sandro Ventisiete. He'd seen the fear and desperation that shrieked in the back of his head mirrored in the faces of the other parents. It made those visits harder than looking at bodies. It made the fear hard to forget.

He did it anyway.

Basia Merton—KatoaDaddy, Mei called him—was a thick-necked man who always smelled of peppermint. His wife was pencil thin with a nervous twitch of a smile. Their home was six chambers near the water-management complex five levels down from the surface, decorated in spun silk and bamboo. When Basia opened the door, he didn't smile or say hello; he only turned and walked in, leaving the way open. Prax followed him.

At the table, Basia poured Prax a glass of miraculously unspoiled milk. It was the fifth time Prax had come since Mei had gone missing.

"No sign, then?" Basia said. It wasn't really a question.

"No news," Prax said. "So there's that, at least."

From the back of the house, a young girl's voice rose in outrage, matched by a younger boy's. Basia didn't even turn to look.

"Nothing here either. I'm sorry."

The milk tasted wonderful, smooth and rich and soft. Prax could almost feel the calories and nutrients being sucked in through the membranes in his mouth. It occurred to him that he might technically be starving.

"There's still hope," Prax said.

Basia blew out his breath like the words had been a punch in the gut. His lips were pressed thin and he was staring at the table. The shouting voices in the back resolved into a low boyish wail.

"We're leaving," Basia said. "My cousin works on Luna for Magellan Biotech. They're sending relief ships, and when they put off the medical supplies, there's going to be room for us. It's all arranged."

Prax put down the glass of milk. The chambers around them seemed to go quiet, but he knew that was an illusion. A strange pressure bloomed in his throat, down into his chest. His face felt waxy. He had the sudden physical memory of his wife announcing that she'd filed for divorce. Betrayed. He felt betrayed.

"...after that, another few days," Basia was saying. He'd been talking, but Prax hadn't heard him.

"But what about Katoa?" Prax managed to say around the thickness in his throat. "He's here somewhere."

Basia's gaze flickered up and then away, fast as a bird's wing.

"He's not. He's gone, brother. Boy had a swamp where his immune system should've been. You know that. Without his medicine, he used to start feeling really sick in three, maybe four days. I have to take care of the two kids I still got."

Prax nodded, his body responding without him. He felt like a flywheel had come loose somewhere in the back of his head. The grain of the bamboo table seemed unnaturally sharp. The smell of ice melt. The taste of milk going sour on his tongue.

"You can't know that," he said, trying to keep his voice soft. He didn't do a great job.

"I pretty much can."

"Whoever...whoever took Mei and Katoa, they aren't useful to them dead. They knew. They had to know that they'd need medicine. And so it only makes sense that they'd take them somewhere they could get it."

"No one took them, brother. They got lost. Something happened."

"Mei's teacher said—"

"Mei's teacher was scared crazy. Her whole world was making sure toddlers don't spit in each other's mouths too much, and there's a shooting war outside her room. Who the hell knows what she saw?"

"She said Mei's mother and a *doctor*. She said a doctor—"

"And come on, man. Not useful if they're dead? This station is ass deep in dead people, and I don't see anyone getting *useful*. It's a war. Fuckers started a war." There were tears in his wide, dark eyes now, and sorrow in his voice. But there was no fight. "People die in a war. Kids die. You gotta…ah shit. You got to keep moving."

"You don't know," Prax said. "You don't know that they're dead, and until you know, you're abandoning them."

Basia looked down at the floor. There was a flush rising under the man's skin. He shook his head, the corners of his mouth twitching down.

"You can't go," Prax said. "You have to stay and look for him."

"Don't," Basia said. "And I mean *do not* shout at me in my own home."

"These are our kids, and you don't *get* to walk away from them! What kind of father are you? I mean, *Jesus*…"

Basia was leaning forward now, hunched over the table. Behind him, a girl on the edge of womanhood looked in from the hallway, her eyes wide. Prax felt a deep certainty rising in him.

"You're going to stay," he said.

The silence lasted three heartbeats. Four. Five.

"It's arranged," Basia said.

Prax hit him. He didn't plan it, didn't intend it. His arm rolled through the shoulder, balled fist shooting out of its own accord. His knuckles sank into the flesh of Basia's cheek, snapping his head to the side and rocking him back. The big man boiled across the room at him. The first blow hit just below Prax's collarbone, pushing him back, the next one was to his ribs, and the one after that. Prax felt his chair slide out from under him, and he was falling slowly in the low g but unable to get his feet beneath him. Prax swung wild, kicked out. He felt his foot connect with something, but he couldn't tell if it was the table or Basia.

He hit the floor, and Basia's foot came down on his solar plexus. The world went bright, shimmering, and painful. Somewhere a long way away, a woman was shouting. He couldn't make out the words. And then, slowly, he could.

He's not right. He lost a baby too. He's not right.

Prax rolled over, forced himself up to his knees. There was blood on his chin he was pretty sure came from him. No one else there was bleeding. Basia stood by the table, hands in fists, nostrils flared, breath fast. The daughter stood in front of him, interposed between her enraged father and Prax. All he could really see of her was her ass and her ponytail and her hands, flat out at her father in the universal gesture for *stop*. She was saving his life.

"You'd be better off gone, brother," Basia said.

"Okay," Prax said.

He got to his feet slowly and stumbled to the door, still not quite breathing right. He let himself out.

The secret of closed-system botanical collapse was this: *It's not the thing that breaks you need to watch out for. It's the cascade.* The first time he'd lost a whole crop of *G. kenon*, it had been from a fungus that didn't hurt soybeans at all. The spores had probably come in with a shipment of ladybugs. The fungus took hold in the hydroponic system, merrily taking up nutrients that weren't meant for it and altering the pH. That weakened the bacteria Prax had been using to fix nitrogen to the point that they were vulnerable to a phage that wouldn't have been able to take them out otherwise. The nitrogen balance of the system got out of whack. By the time the bacteria recovered to their initial population, the soybeans were yellow, limp, and past repair.

That was the metaphor he used when he thought about Mei and her immune system. The problem was tiny, really. A mutant allele produced a protein that folded left instead of right. A few base pairs' difference. But that protein catalyzed a critical step in signal trans-duction to the T cells. She could have all the parts of an immune system standing ready to fight off a pathogen, but without twice-daily doses of an artificial catalyzing agent, the alarm would never sound. Myers-Skelton Premature Immunosenescence they called it, and the preliminary studies still hadn't even been able to tell if it was more common outside the well of Earth because of an unknown low-g effect or just the high radiation levels increasing mutations rates generally. It didn't matter. However she'd gotten there, Mei had developed a massive spinal infection when she was four months old. If they'd been anywhere else in the outer planets, she'd have died of it. But everyone came to Ganymede to gestate, so the child health research all happened there. When Dr. Strickland saw her, he knew what he was looking at, and he held back the cascade.

Prax walked down the corridors toward home. His jaw was swelling. He didn't remember being hit in the jaw, but it was swell-ing, and it hurt. His ribs had a sharp pain on the left that hurt if he breathed in too deep, so he kept his breath shallow. He stopped at one of the parks, scrounging a few leaves for dinner. He paused at a large stand of *Epipremnum aureum*. The wide spade-shaped leaves looked wrong. They were still green, but thicker, and with a golden undertone. Someone had put distilled water in the hydroponic sup-ply instead of the mineral-rich solution long-stability hydroponics needed. They could get away with it for another week. Maybe two. Then the air-recycling plants would start to die, and by the time that happened, the cascade would be too far gone to stop. And if they couldn't get the right water to the plants, he couldn't imag-ine they'd be able to set all the mechanical air recyclers going. Someone was going to have to do something about that.

Someone else.

In his rooms, his one small *G. kenon* held its fronds up to the light. Without any particular conscious thought, he put his finger in the soil, testing it. The rich scent of well-balanced soil was like incense. It was doing pretty well, all things considered. He glanced at the time stamp on his hand terminal. Three hours had passed since he'd come home. His jaw had gone past aching into a kind of constantly rediscovered pain.

Without her medicine, the normal flora of her digestive system would start overgrowing. The bacteria that normally lived benignly in her mouth and throat would rise against her. After two weeks, maybe she wouldn't be dead. But even in the best case, she'd be so sick that bringing her back would be problematic.

It was a war. Kids died in wars. It was a cascade. He coughed, and the pain was immense and it was still better than thinking. He needed to go. To get out. Ganymede was dying around him. He wasn't going to do Mei any good. She was gone. His baby girl was gone.

Crying hurt worse than coughing.

He didn't sleep so much as lose consciousness. When he woke, his jaw was swollen badly enough that it clicked when he opened his mouth too wide. His ribs felt a degree better. He sat on the edge of his bed, head in his hands.

He'd go to the port. He'd go to Basia and apologize and ask to go along. Get out of the Jovian system entirely. Go someplace and start over without his past. Without his failed marriage and shattered work. Without Mei.

He switched to a slightly less dirty shirt. Swabbed his armpits with a damp cloth. Combed his hair back. He'd failed. It was pointless. He had to come to terms with the loss and move on. And maybe someday he would.

He checked his hand terminal. That day was checking the Martian body drop, walking the parks, checking with Dr. Astrigan, and then a list of five brothels he hadn't been to, where he could ask after the illicit pleasures of pedophilia, hopefully without being gutted by some right-thinking, civic-minded thug. Thugs had children too. Some probably loved them. With a sigh, he keyed in a new entry: MINERALIZE PARK WATER. He'd need to find someone with physical plant access codes. Maybe security could help with that at least.

And maybe, somewhere along the way, he'd find Mei.

There was still hope.

Chapter Eight: Bobbie

The *Harman Dae-Jung* was a *Donnager*-class dreadnought, half a kilometer in length, and a quarter million tons dry weight. Her interior docking bay was large enough to hold four frigate-class escort ships and a variety of lighter shuttles and repair craft. Currently, it held only two ships: the large and almost opulent shuttle that had ferried the Martian ambassadors and state officials up for the flight to Earth, and the smaller and more functional Navy shuttle Bobbie had ridden up from Ganymede.

Bobbie was using the empty space to jog.

The *Dae-Jung*'s captain was being pressured by the diplomats to get them to Earth as quickly as possible, so the ship was running at a near-constant one g acceleration. While this made most of the Martian civilians uncomfortable, it suited Bobbie just fine. The corps trained at high g all the time and did lengthy endurance drills at one g at least once a month. No one ever said it was to prepare for the possibility of having to fight a ground war on Earth. No one had to.

Her recent tour on Ganymede hadn't allowed her to get in any high-g exercise, and the long trip to Earth seemed like an excellent opportunity to get back into shape. The last thing she wanted was to appear weak to the natives.

"Anything you can do I can do better," she sang to herself in a breathless falsetto as she ran. "I can do anything better than you."

She gave her wristwatch a quick glance. Two hours. At her current leisurely pace, that meant twelve miles. Push for twenty? How many people on Earth regularly ran for twenty miles? Martian propaganda would have her believe that half of the people on Earth didn't even have jobs. They just lived off the government dole and spent their meager allowances on drugs and stim parlors. But probably *some* of them could run for twenty miles. She'd bet Snoopy and his gang of Earther marines could have run twenty miles, the way they were running from—

"Anything you can do I can do better," she sang, then concentrated on nothing but the sound of her shoes slapping on the metal deck.

She didn't see the yeoman enter the docking bay, so when he called out to her, she twisted in surprise and tripped over her own feet, catching herself with her left hand just before she would have dashed her brains out on the deck. She felt something pop in her wrist, and her right knee bounced painfully off the floor as she rolled to absorb the impact.

She lay on her back for a few moments, moving her wrist and knee to see if there was any serious damage. Both hurt, but neither had any grating sensation in it. Nothing broken, then. Barely out of the hospital and already looking for ways to bang herself up again. The yeoman ran up to her and dropped into a crouch at her side.

"Jesus, Gunny, you took a hell of a spill!" the Navy boy said. "A *hell* of a spill!"

He touched her right knee where the bruise was already starting to darken the bare skin below her jogging shorts, then seemed to realize what he was doing and yanked his hand back.

"Sergeant Draper, your presence is requested at a meeting in conference room G at fourteen fifty hours," he said, squeaking a little as he rattled off his message. "How come you don't carry your terminal with you? They've had trouble tracking you down."

Bobbie pushed herself back up to her feet, gingerly testing her knee to see if it would hold her weight.

"You just answered your own question, kid."

Bobbie arrived at the conference room five minutes early, her red-and-khaki service uniform sharply pressed and marred only by the white wrist brace the company medic had given her for what turned out to be a minor sprain. A marine in full battle dress and armed with an assault rifle opened the door for her and gave her a smile as she went by. It was a nice smile, full of even white teeth, below almond-shaped eyes so dark they were almost black.

Bobbie smiled back and glanced at the name on his suit. Corporal Matsuke. Never knew who you'd run into in the galley or the weight room. It didn't hurt to make a friend or two.

She was pulled the rest of the way into the room by someone calling her name.

"Sergeant Draper," Captain Thorsson repeated, gesturing impatiently toward a chair at the long conference table.

"Sir," Bobbie said, and snapped off a salute before taking the seat. She was surprised by how few people were in the room. Just Thorsson from the intelligence corps and two civilians she hadn't met.

"Gunny, we're going over some of the details in your report; we'd appreciate your input."

Bobbie waited a moment to be introduced to the two civilians in the room, but when it became clear Thorsson wasn't going to do it, she just said, "Yes, sir. Whatever I can do to help."

The first civilian, a severe-looking redheaded woman in a very expensive suit, said, "We're trying to create a better timeline of the events leading up to the attack. Can you show us on this map where you and your fire team were when you received the radio message to return to the outpost?"

Bobbie showed them, then went step by step through the events of that day. Looking at the map they'd brought, she saw for the first time how far she'd been flung across the ice by the impact of the orbital mirror. It looked like it had been a matter of centimeters between that and being smashed into dust like the rest of her platoon...

"Sergeant," Thorsson said, his tone of voice letting her know he'd said it a couple of times before.

"Sir, sorry, looking at these photos sent me woolgathering. It won't happen again."

Thorsson nodded, but with a strange expression Bobbie couldn't read.

"What we're trying to pinpoint is precisely where the Anomaly was inserted prior to the attack," the other civilian, a chubby man with thinning brown hair, said.

The Anomaly they called it now. You could hear them capitalize the word when they said it. *Anomaly*, like something that just happens. A strange random event. It was because everyone was still afraid to call it what it really was. The Weapon.

"So," the chubby guy said, "based on how long you had radio contact, and information regarding loss of radio signal from other installations around that area, we are able to pinpoint the source of the jamming signal as the Anomaly itself."

"Wait," Bobbie said, shaking her head. "What? The monster *can't* have jammed our radios. It had no tech. It wasn't even wearing a damned *space suit* to breathe! How could it be carrying jamming equipment?"

Thorsson patted her hand paternally, a move that irritated Bobbie more than it calmed her.

"The data doesn't lie, Sergeant. The zone of radio blackout moved. And always at its center was the...thing. The Anomaly,"

Thorsson said, then turned away from her to speak to the chubby guy and the redhead.

Bobbie sat back, feeling the energy move away from her in the room, like she was the one person at the dance without a date. But since Thorsson hadn't dismissed her, she couldn't just leave.

Redhead said, "Based on our radio loss data, that puts insertion here"—she pointed at something on the map—"and the path to the UN outpost is along this ridge."

"What's in that location?" Thorsson said with a frown.

Chubby pulled up a different map and pored over it for a few seconds.

"Looks like some old service tunnels for the dome's hydro plant. This says they haven't been used in decades."

"So," Thorsson said. "The kind of tunnels one might use to transport something dangerous that needs to be kept secret."

"Yes," Redhead said, "maybe they were delivering it to that Marine outpost and it got loose. The marines cut and ran when they saw it was out of control."

Bobbie gave a dismissive laugh before she could stop herself.

"You have something to add, Sergeant Draper?" Thorsson said.

Thorsson was looking at her with his enigmatic smile, but Bobbie had worked with him long enough now to know that what he hated most was bullshit. If you spoke up, he wanted to make sure you actually had something useful to say. The two civilians were looking at her with surprise, as though she were a cockroach that had suddenly stood up on two legs and started speaking.

She shook her head.

"When I was a boot, you know what my drill sergeant said was the second most dangerous thing in the solar system, after a Martian Marine?"

The civvies continued to stare at her, but Thorsson nodded and mouthed the words along with her as she next spoke.

"A UN Marine."

Chubby and Redhead shared a look and Redhead rolled her

eyes for him. But Thorsson said, "So you don't think the UN soldiers were running from something that got out of their control."

"Not a fucking chance, sir."

"Then give us your take on it."

"That UN outpost was staffed by a full platoon of Marines. Same strength as our outpost. When they finally started running, there were six left. Six. They fought almost to the last man. When they ran to us, they weren't trying to disengage. They were coming so we could help them *continue* the fight."

Chubby picked a leather satchel up off the floor and started rummaging in it. Redhead watched, as though what he was doing was far more interesting than anything Bobbie had to say.

"If this were some secret UN thing that those Marines were tasked to deliver or protect, they wouldn't have come. They'd have died doing it rather than abandon their mission. That's what we would have done."

"Thank you," Thorsson said.

"I mean, it wasn't even our fight, and *we* fought to the last marine to stop that thing. You think the UN Marines would do less?"

"Thank you, Sergeant," Thorsson said again, louder. "I tend to agree, but we have to explore all possibilities. Your comments are noted."

Chubby finally found what he was looking for. A small plastic box of mints. He took one out, then held the box out to Redhead to take one. The sickly sweet smell of spearmint filled the air. Around a mouthful of mint, Chubby said, "Yes, thank you, Sergeant. I think we can proceed here without taking up more of your time."

Bobbie stood up, snapped another salute at Thorsson, and left the room. Her heart was going fast. Her jaw ached where she was grinding her teeth.

Civvies didn't get it. No one did.

When Captain Martens came into the cargo bay, Bobbie had just finished disassembling the gun housing on her combat suit's right arm. She removed the three-barrel Gatling gun from its mount and placed it on the floor next to the two dozen other parts she'd already stripped off. Next to them sat a can of gun cleaner and a bottle of lubricant, along with the various rods and brushes she'd use to clean the parts.

Martens waited until she had the gun on the cleaning mat, then sat down on the floor next to her. She attached a wire brush to the end of one of the cleaning rods, dipped it in the cleaner, and began running the brush through the gun, one barrel at a time. Martens watched.

After a few minutes, she replaced the brush with a small cloth and swabbed the remaining cleanser out of the barrels. Then a fresh cloth soaked in gun lubricant to oil them. When she was applying lube to the complex mesh of gears that composed the Gatling mechanism and ammo feed system, Martens finally spoke.

"You know," he said, "Thorsson is naval intelligence right from the start. Straight into officer training, top of his class at the academy, and first posting at fleet command. He's never done anything but *be* an intelligence wonk. The last time he fired a gun was his six weeks as a boot, twenty years ago. He's never led a fire team. Or served in a combat platoon."

"That," Bobbie said, putting down her lubricant then standing up to put the gun back together, "is a fascinating story. I really appreciate you sharing it."

"So," Martens continued, not missing a beat. "How fucked up do you have to be before Thorsson starts asking me if maybe you aren't a little shell-shocked?"

Bobbie dropped the wrench she was holding, but caught it with her other hand before it could hit the deck.

"Is this an official visit? Because if not, you can f—"

"Me now? I'm not a wonk," Martens said. "I'm a marine. Ten years as an enlisted man before I was offered OCS. Got dual degrees in psychology and theology."

The end of Bobbie's nose itched, and she scratched it without thinking. The sudden smell of gun oil let her know that she'd just rubbed lubricant all over her face. Martens glanced at it but didn't stop talking. She tried to drown him out by putting the gun together as noisily as possible.

"I've done combat drills, CQB training, war games," he said, speaking a little louder. "Did you know I was a boot at the same camp where your father was first sergeant? Sergeant Major Draper is a great man. He was like a god to us boots."

Bobbie's head snapped up and her eyes narrowed. Something about this headshrinker acting like he knew her father felt dirty.

"It's true. And if he were here right now, he'd be telling you to listen to me."

"Fuck you," Bobbie said. She imagined her father wincing at the use of obscenity to hide her fear. "You don't know shit."

"I know that when a gunnery sergeant with your level of training and combat readiness almost gets taken out by a yeoman still at the tail end of puberty, something is goddamned wrong."

Bobbie threw the wrench at the ground, knocking over the gun oil, which began to spread across her mat like a bloodstain.

"I fucking fell down! We were at a full g, and I just…I fell down."

"And in the meeting today? Yelling at two civilian intelligence analysts about how Marines would rather die than fail?"

"I didn't yell," Bobbie said, not sure if that was the truth. Her memories of the meeting had become confused once she was out of the room.

"How many times have you fired that gun since you cleaned it yesterday?"

"What?" Bobbie said, feeling nauseated and not sure why.

"For that matter, how many times had you fired it since you cleaned it the day before that? Or the one before that?"

"Stop it," Bobbie said, waving one hand limply at Martens and looking for a place to sit back down.

"Have you fired that gun even once since you've come on board the *Dae-Jung*? Because I can tell you that you've cleaned it every single day you've been on board, and several times you've cleaned it twice in one day."

"No, I—" Bobbie said, finally sitting down with a thump on an ammo canister. She had no memory of having cleaned the gun before that day. "I didn't know that."

"This is post-traumatic stress disorder, Bobbie. It's not a weakness or some kind of moral failure. It's what happens when you live through something terrible. Right now you're not able to process what happened to you and your men on Ganymede, and you're acting irrationally because of it," Martens said, then moved over to crouch in front of her. She was afraid for a moment that he'd try to take her hand, because if he did, she'd hit him.

He didn't.

"You're ashamed," he said, "but there's nothing to be ashamed of. You're trained to be tough, competent, ready for anything. They taught you that if you just do your job and remember your training, you can deal with any threat. Most of all, they taught you that the most important people in the world are the ones standing next to you on the firing line."

Something twitched in her cheek just under her eye, and Bobbie rubbed at the spot hard enough to make stars explode in her vision.

"Then you ran into something that your training couldn't prepare you for, and against which you had no defense. And you lost your teammates and friends."

Bobbie started to reply and realized she'd been holding her breath, so instead of speaking, she exhaled explosively. Martens didn't stop talking.

"We need you, Roberta. We need you back. I haven't been where you are, but I know a lot of people who have, and I know how to help you. If you let me. If you talk to me. I can't take it away. I can't cure you. But I can make it better."

"Don't call me Roberta," Bobbie said so quietly that she could barely hear herself.

She took a few short breaths, trying to clear her head, trying not to hyperventilate. The scents of the cargo bay washed over her. The smell of rubber and metal from her suit. The acrid, competing scents of gun oil and hydraulic fluid, old and aged right into the metal no matter how many times the Navy boys swabbed the decks. The thought of thousands of sailors and marines passing through this same space, working on their equipment and cleaning these same bulkheads, brought her back to herself.

She moved over to her reassembled gun and picked it up off the mat before the spreading pool of gun oil could touch it.

"No, Captain, talking to you is not what's going to get me better."

"Then what, Sergeant?"

"That thing that killed my friends, and started this war? Somebody put that thing on Ganymede," she said, and seated the gun in its housing with a sharp metallic click. She gave the triple barrels a spin with her hand, and they turned with the fast oily hiss of high-quality bearings. "I'm going to find out who. And I'm going to kill them."

Chapter Nine: Avasarala

The report was more than three pages long, but Soren had managed to find someone with the balls to admit it when he didn't know everything. Strange things were happening on Venus, stranger than Avasarala had known or guessed. A network of filaments had nearly encased the planet in a pattern of fifty-kilometer-wide hexagons, and apart from the fact that they seemed to carry superheated water and electrical currents, no one knew what they were. The gravity of the planet had increased by 3 percent. Paired whirlwinds of benzene and complex hydrocarbons were sweeping the impact craters like synchronized swimmers where the remains of Eros Station had smashed into the planetary surface. The best scientific minds of the system were staring at the data with their jaws slack, and the reason no one was panicking yet was that no one could agree on what they should panic about.

On one hand, the Venusian metamorphosis was the most

powerful scientific tool ever. Whatever happened did so in plain sight of everyone. There were no nondisclosure agreements or anti-competition treaties to be concerned with. Anyone with a scanner sensitive enough could look down through the clouds of sulfuric acid and see what was going on today. Analyses were confidential, follow-up studies were proprietary, but the raw data was orbiting the sun for anyone to see.

Only, so far, it was like a bunch of lizards watching the World Cup. Politely put, they weren't sure what they were looking at.

But the data was clear. The attack on Ganymede and the spike in the energy expended on Venus had come at exactly the same time. And no one knew why.

"Well, that's worth shit," she said.

Avasarala closed down her hand terminal and looked out the window. Around them the commissary murmured softly, like the best kind of restaurant, only without the ugly necessity of paying for anything. The tables were real wood and arranged carefully so that everyone had a view and no one could be overheard unless they wanted to be. It was raining that day. Even if the raindrops hadn't been pelting the windows, blurring city and sky, she'd have known by the smell. Her lunch—cold sag aloo and something that was supposed to be tandoori chicken—sat on the table, untouched. Soren was still sitting across from her, his expression polite and alert as a Labrador retriever's.

"There's no data showing a launch," Soren said. "Whatever's on Venus would have to have gotten out to Ganymede, and there's no sign of that at all."

"Whatever's on Venus thinks inertia's optional and gravity isn't a constant. We don't know what a launch would look like. As far as we know, they could walk to Jupiter."

The boy's nod conceded the point.

"Where do we stand on Mars?"

"They've agreed to meet here. They've got ships on the way with the diplomatic delegation, including their witness."

"The marine? Draper?"

"Yes, ma'am. Admiral Nguyen is in charge of the escort."

"He's playing nice?"

"So far."

"All right, where do we go from here?" Avasarala asked.

"Jules-Pierre Mao's waiting in your office, ma'am."

"Run him down for me. Anything you think's important."

Soren blinked. Lightning lit the clouds from within.

"I sent the briefing…"

She felt a stab of annoyance that was half embarrassment. She'd forgotten that the background on the man was in her queue. There were thirty other documents there too, and she'd slept poorly the night before, troubled by dreams in which Arjun had died unexpectedly. She'd had widowhood nightmares since her son had died in a skiing accident, her mind conflating the only two men she'd ever loved.

She'd meant to review the information before breakfast. She'd forgotten. But she wasn't going to admit it to some European brat just because he was smart, competent, and did everything she said.

"I know what's in the briefing. I know *everything*," she said, standing up. "This is a fucking test. I'm asking what *you* think is important about him."

She walked away, moving toward the carved oak doors with a deliberate speed that made Soren scramble a little to keep up.

"He's the corporate controlling interest of Mao-Kwikowski Mercantile," Soren said, his voice low enough to carry to her and then die. "Before the incident, they were one of Protogen's major suppliers. The medical equipment, the radiation rooms, the surveillance and encryption infrastructure. Almost everything Protogen put on Eros or used to construct their shadow station came from a Mao-Kwik warehouse and on a Mao-Kwik freighter."

"And he's still breathing free air because…?" she said, pushing through the doors and into the hallway beyond.

"No evidence that Mao-Kwik knew what the equipment was for," Soren said. "After Protogen was exposed, Mao-Kwik was one of the first to turn over information to the investigation committee. If they—and by 'they,' I mean 'he'—hadn't turned over a terabyte of confidential correspondence, Gutmansdottir and Kolp might never have been implicated."

A silver-haired man with a broad Andean nose walking the other way in the hall looked up from his hand terminal and nodded to her as they drew near.

"Victor," she said. "I'm sorry about Annette."

"The doctors say she'll be fine," the Andean said. "I'll tell her you asked."

"Tell her I said to get the hell out of bed before her husband starts getting dirty ideas," she said, and the Andean laughed as they passed. Then, to Soren: "Was he cutting a deal? Cooperation for clemency?"

"That was one interpretation, but most people assumed it was personal vengeance for what happened to his daughter."

"She was on Eros," Avasarala said.

"She *was* Eros," Soren said as they stepped into the elevator. "She was the initial infection. The scientists think the protomolecule was building itself using her brain and body as a template."

The elevator doors closed, the car already aware of who she was and where she was going. It dropped smoothly as her eyebrows rose.

"So when they started negotiating with that thing—"

"They were talking to what was left of Jules-Pierre Mao's daughter," Soren said. "I mean, they think they were."

Avasarala whistled low.

"Did I pass the test, ma'am?" Soren asked, keeping his face empty and impassive except for a small twinkle in the corners of his eyes that said he knew she'd been bullshitting him. Despite herself, she grinned.

"No one likes a smart-ass," she said. The elevator stopped; the doors slid open.

Jules-Pierre Mao sat at her desk, radiating a sense of calm with the faintest hint of amusement. Avasarala's eyes flickered over him, taking in the details: well-tailored silk suit that straddled the line between beige and gray, receding hairline unmodified by medical therapies, startling blue eyes that he had probably been born with. He wore his age like a statement that fighting the ravages of time and mortality was beneath his notice. Twenty years earlier, he'd just have been devastatingly handsome. Now he was that and dignified too, and her first, animal impulse was that she wanted to like him.

"Mr. Mao," she said, nodding to him. "Sorry to make you wait."

"I've worked with government before," he said. He had a European accent that would have melted butter. "I understand the constraints. What can I do for you, Assistant Undersecretary?"

Avasarala lowered herself into her chair. The Buddha smiled beatifically from his place by the wall. The rain sheeted down the window, shadows giving the near-subliminal impression that Mao was weeping. She steepled her fingers.

"You want some tea?"

"No, thank you," Mao said.

"Soren! Go get me some tea."

"Yes, ma'am," the boy said.

"Soren."

"Ma'am?"

"Don't hurry."

"Of course not, ma'am."

The door closed behind him. Mao's smile looked weary.

"Should I have brought my attorneys?"

"Those rat fuckers? No," she said, "the trials are all done with. I'm not here to reopen any of the legal wrangling. I've got real work to do."

"I can respect that," Mao said.

"I have a problem," Avasarala said. "And I don't know what it is."

"And you think I do?"

"It's possible. I've been through a lot of hearings about one damn thing and another. Most of the time they're exercises in ass covering. If the unvarnished truth ever came out at one, it would be because someone screwed up."

The bright blue eyes narrowed. The smile grew less warm.

"You think my executives and I were less than forthcoming? I put powerful men in prison for you, Assistant Undersecretary. I burned bridges."

Distant thunder mumbled and complained. The rain redoubled its angry tapping at the pane. Avasarala crossed her arms.

"You did. But that doesn't make you an idiot. There are still things you say under oath and things you dance around. This room isn't monitored. This is off the record. I need to know anything you can tell me about the protomolecule that didn't come out in the hearings."

The silence between them stretched. She watched his face, his body, looking for signs, but the man was unreadable. He'd been doing this too long, and he was too good at it. A professional.

"Things get lost," Avasarala said. "There was one time during the finance crisis that we found a whole auditing division that no one remembered. Because that's how you do it. You take part of a problem and you put it somewhere, get some people working on it, and then you get another part of the problem and get other people working on that. And pretty soon you have seven, eight, a hundred different little boxes with work going on, and no one talking to anyone because it would break security protocol."

"And you think...?"

"We killed Protogen, and you helped. I'm asking whether you know of any little boxes lying around somewhere. And I'm very much hoping you say yes."

"Is this from the secretary-general or Errinwright?"

"No. Just me."

"I've already said everything I know," he said.

"I don't believe that."

The mask of his persona slipped. It lasted less than a second, nothing more than a shift in the angle of his spine and a hardness in his jaw, here and gone again. It was anger. That was interesting.

"They killed my daughter," he said softly. "Even if I'd had something to hide, I wouldn't have."

"How did it come to be your girl?" Avasarala asked. "Did they target her? Was somebody using her against you?"

"It was bad luck. She was out in the deep orbits, trying to prove something. She was young and rebellious and stupid. We were trying to get her to come home but...she was in the wrong place at the wrong time."

Something tickled at the back of Avasarala's mind. A hunch. An impulse. She went with it.

"Have you heard from her since it happened?"

"I don't understand."

"Since Eros Station crashed into Venus, have you heard from her?"

It was interesting watching him pretend to be angry now. It was almost like the real thing. She couldn't have said what about it was inauthentic. The intelligence in his eyes, maybe. The sense that he was more present than he had been before. Real rage swept people away. This was rage as a gambit.

"My Julie is dead," he said, his voice shaking theatrically. "She died when that bastard alien thing went down to Venus. She died saving the Earth."

Avasarala countered soft. She lowered her voice, let her face take on a concerned, grandmotherly expression. If he was going to play the injured man, she could play the mother.

"Something lived," she said. "Something survived that impact, and everybody knows that it did. I have reason to think that it didn't stay there. If some part of your daughter made it through that change, she might have reached out to you. Tried to contact you. Or her mother."

"There is nothing I want more than to have my little girl back," Mao said. "But she's gone."

Avasarala nodded.

"All right," she said.

"Is there anything else?"

Again, the false anger. She ran her tongue against the back of her teeth, thinking. There was something here, something beneath the surface. She didn't know what she was looking at with Mao.

"You know about Ganymede?" she said.

"Fighting broke out," he said.

"Maybe more than that," she said. "The thing that killed your daughter is still out there. It was on Ganymede. I'm going to find out how and why."

He rocked back. Was the shock real?

"I'll help if I can," he said, his voice small.

"Start with this. Is there anything you didn't say during the hearings? A business partner you chose not to mention. A backup program or auxiliary staff you outfitted. If it wasn't legal, I don't care. I can get you amnesty for just about anything, but I need to hear it now. Right now."

"Amnesty?" he said as if she'd been joking.

"If you tell me now, yes."

"If I had it, I would give it to you," he said. "I've said everything I know."

"All right, then. I'm sorry to have taken your time. And ... I'm sorry to open old wounds. I lost a son. Charanpal was fifteen. Skiing accident."

"I'm sorry," Mao said.

"If you find out something more, bring it to me," she said.

"I will," he said, rising from his seat. She let him get almost to the doorway before she spoke again.

"Jules?"

Turning to glance over his shoulder, he looked like a still frame from a film.

"If I find out that you knew something and you didn't tell me, I won't take it well," she said. "I'm not someone you want to fuck with."

"If I didn't know that when I came in, I do now," Mao said. It was as good a parting line as any. The door closed behind him. Avasarala sighed, leaning back in her chair. She shifted to look at the Buddha.

"Fat lot of help you were, you smug bastard," she said. The statue, being only a statue, didn't reply. She thumbed down the lights and let the gray of the storm fill the room. Something about Mao didn't sit well with her.

It might only have been the practiced control of a high-level corporate negotiator, but she had the sense of being cut out of the loop. Excluded. That was interesting too. She wondered if he would try to counter her, maybe go over her head. It would be worth telling Errinwright to expect an angry call.

She wondered. It was a stretch to believe there was anything human down on Venus. The protomolecule, as well as anyone understood it, had been designed to hijack primitive life and remake it into something else. But if... *If* the complexity of a human mind had been too much for it to totally control, and the girl had in some sense survived the descent, *if* she'd reached out to her daddy...

Avasarala reached for her hand terminal and opened a connection to Soren.

"Ma'am?"

"When I said don't hurry, I didn't mean you should take the whole fucking day off. My tea?"

"Coming, ma'am. I got sidetracked. I have a report for you that might be interesting."

"Less interesting if the tea's cold," she said, and dropped the channel.

Putting any kind of real surveillance on Mao would probably be impossible. Mao-Kwikowski Mercantile would have its own communications arrays, its own encryption schemes, and several rival companies at least as well funded as the United Nations already bent on ferreting out corporate secrets. But there might be other ways to track communications coming off Venus and going to Mao-Kwik installations. Or messages going down that well.

Soren came in carrying a tray with a cast-iron teapot and an earthenware cup with no handle. He didn't comment on the darkness, but walked carefully to her desk, set down the tray, poured out a smoky, dark cupful of still-steaming tea, and put his hand terminal on the desk beside it.

"You could just send me a fucking copy," Avasarala said.

"More dramatic this way, ma'am," Soren said. "Presentation is everything."

She snorted and pointedly picked up the cup, blowing across the dark surface before she looked at the terminal. The date stamp at the lower right showed it as coming from outside Ganymede seven hours earlier and the identification code of the associated report. The man in the picture had the stocky bones of an Earther, unkempt dark hair, and a peculiar brand of boyish good looks. Avasarala frowned at the image as she sipped her tea.

"What happened to his face?" she asked.

"The reporting officer suggested the beard was intended as a disguise."

She snorted.

"Well, thank God he didn't put on a pair of glasses, we might never have figured it out. What the fuck is James Holden doing on Ganymede?"

"It's a relief ship. Not the *Rocinante*."

"We have confirmation on that? You know those OPA bastards can fake registration codes."

"The reporting officer did a visual inspection of the interior layout and checked the record when he got back. Also, the crew didn't include Holden's usual pilot, so we assume they've got it parked-and-dark somewhere in tightbeam range," Soren said. He paused. "There is a standing detain-on-sight for Holden."

Avasarala turned the lights back on. The windows became dark mirrors again; the storm was pressed back outside.

"Tell me we didn't enforce it," Avasarala said.

"We didn't enforce it," Soren said. "We have a surveillance detail on him and his team, but the situation on the station isn't conducive to a close watch. Plus which, it doesn't look like Mars knows he's there yet, so we're trying to keep that to ourselves."

"Good that someone out there knows how to run an intelligence operation. Any idea what he's doing?"

"So far, it looks a lot like a relief effort," Soren said with a shrug. "We haven't seen him meeting with anybody of special interest. He's asking questions. Almost got into a fight with some opportunists who've been shaking down relief ships, but the other guys backed down. It's early, though."

Avasarala took another sip of tea. She had to give it to the boy; he could brew a fine pot of tea. Or he knew someone who could, which was just as good. If Holden was there, that meant the OPA was interested in the situation on Ganymede. And that they didn't have someone already on the ground to report to them.

Wanting the intelligence didn't in itself mean much. Even if it had been just a bunch of idiot ground-pounders getting trigger-happy, Ganymede was a critical station for the Jovian system and the Belt. The OPA would want their own eyes on the scene. But to send Holden, the only survivor of Eros Station, seemed more than coincidental.

"They don't know what it is," she said aloud.

"Ma'am?"

"They smuggled in someone with experience in the protomolecule for a reason. They're trying to figure out what the hell's going on. Which means they don't know. Which means..." She sighed. "Which means it wasn't them. Which is a fucking pity, since they've got the only live sample we know about."

"What would you like the surveillance team to do?"

"Surveillance," she snapped. "Watch him, see who he talks to and what he does. Daily reports back if it's boring, real-time updates if it runs hot."

"Yes, ma'am. Do you want him brought in?"

"Pull him and his people in when they try to leave Ganymede. Otherwise stay out of their way and try not to get noticed. Holden's an idiot, but he's not stupid. If he realizes he's being watched, he'll start broadcasting pictures of all our Ganymede sources or something. Do not underestimate his capacity to fuck things up."

"Anything else?"

Another flash of lightning. Another roll of thunder. Another storm among trillions of storms that had assaulted the Earth since back in the beginning, when something had first tried to end all life on the planet. Something that was on Venus right now. And spreading.

"Find a way for me to get a message to Fred Johnson without Nguyen or the Martians finding out," she said. "We may need to do some back-channel negotiation."

Chapter Ten: Prax

"Pas kirrup es I'm to this," the boy sitting on the cot said. "Pinche *salad*, sa-sa? Ten thousand, once was."

He couldn't have been more than twenty. Young enough, technically, to be his son, just as Mei could have been the boy's daughter. Colt-thin from adolescent growth and a life in low g, his thinness was improbable to begin with. And he'd been starving besides.

"I can write you a promissory note if you want," Prax said.

The boy grinned and made a rude gesture.

From his professional work, Prax knew that the inner planets thought of Belter slang as a statement about location. He knew from living as a food botanist on Ganymede that it was also about class. He had grown up with tutors in accent-free Chinese and English. He'd spoken with men and women from everywhere in the system. From the way someone said *allopolyploidy*, he could tell if they came from the universities around Beijing or Brazil, if they'd grown up in the shadow of the Rocky Mountains or Olympus Mons or in the corridors of Ceres. He'd grown up in microgravity himself, but Belt patois was as foreign to him as to anyone fresh up the well. If the boy had wanted to speak past him, it would have been effortless. But Prax was a paying customer, and he knew the boy was making an effort to dial it back.

The programming keyboard was twice as large as a standard hand terminal, the plastic worn by use and time. A progress bar was slowly filling along the side, notations in simplified Chinese cycling with each movement.

The hole was a cheap one near the surface of the moon. No more than ten feet wide, four rough rooms inched into the ice from a public corridor hardly wider or better lit. The old plastic walls glittered and wept with condensation. They were in the room farthest from the corridor, the boy on his cot and Prax standing hunched in the doorway.

"No promise for the full record," the boy said. "What is, is, sabé?"

"Anything you can get would be great."

The boy nodded once. Prax didn't know his name. It wasn't the sort of thing to ask. The days it had taken to track down someone willing to break through the security system had been a long dance between his own ignorance of Ganymede Station's gray economy and the increasing desperation and hunger in even the most corrupt quarters. A month before, the boy might have been skimming commercial data to resell or hold hostage for easily laundered private credit. Today he was looking for Mei in exchange for enough leafy greens to make a small meal. Agricultural barter, the oldest economy in humanity's record, had come to Ganymede.

"Authcopy's gone," the boy said. "Sucked into servers, buried ass deep."

"So if you can't break the security servers—"

"Don't have to. Camera got memory, memory got cache. Since the lockdown, it's just filling and filling. No one watching."

"You're kidding," Prax said. "The two biggest armies in the system are staring each other down, and they're not watching the security cameras?"

"Watching each other. No one half-humps for us."

The progress bar filled completely and chimed. The boy pulled open a list of identifying codes and started paging through them, muttering to himself. From the front room, a baby complained weakly. It sounded hungry. Of course it did.

"Your kid?"

The boy shook his head.

"Collateral," he said, and tapped twice on a code. A new window opened. A wide hall. A door half melted and forced open. Scorch marks on the walls and, worse, a puddle of water. There shouldn't be free water. The environmental controls were getting further and further away from their safe levels. The boy looked up at Prax. "C'est la?"

"Yes," Prax said. "That's it."

The boy nodded and hunched back over his console.

"I need it before the attack. Before the mirror came down," Prax said.

"Hokay, boss. Waybacking. Tod á frames con null delta. Only see when something happens, que si?"

"Fine. That's fine."

Prax moved forward, leaning to look over the boy's shoulder. The image jittered without anything on the screen changing except the puddle, slowly getting smaller. They were going backward through time, through the days and weeks. Toward the moment when it had all fallen apart.

Medics appeared in the screen, appearing to walk backward in the inverted world as they brought a dead body to lay beside the door. Then another draped over it. The two corpses lay motionless; then one moved, pawing gently at the wall, then more strongly until, in an eyeblink, he staggered to his feet and was gone.

"There should be a girl. I'm looking for who brought out a four-year-old girl."

"Sa day care, no? Should be a thousand of them."

"I only care about the one."

The second corpse sat up and then stood, clutching her belly. A man stepped into the frame, a gun in his hand, healing her by sucking the bullet from her guts. They argued, grew calm, parted peaceably. Prax knew he was seeing it all in reverse, but his sleep- and calorie-starved brain kept trying to make the images into a narrative. A group of soldiers crawled backward out of the ruined door, like a breech birth, then huddled, backed away in a rush. A flash of light, and the door had made itself whole, thermite charges clinging to it like fruit until a soldier in a Martian uniform rushed forward to collect them safely. Their technological harvest complete, the soldiers all backed rapidly away, leaving a scooter behind them, leaning against the wall.

And then the door slid open, and Prax saw himself back out. He looked younger. He beat on the door, hands popping off the surface in staccato bursts, then leapt awkwardly onto the scooter and vanished backward.

The door went quiet. Motionless. He held his breath. Walking backward, a woman carrying a five-year-old boy on her hip went to the door, vanished within, and then reappeared. Prax had to remind himself that the woman hadn't been dropping her son off, but retrieving him. Two figures backed down the corridor.

No. Three.

"Stop. That's it," Prax said, his heart banging against his ribs. "That's her."

The boy waited until all three figures were caught in the camera's eye, stepping out into the corridor. Mei's face was petulant; even in the low resolution of the security camera, he knew the expression. And the man holding her...

Relief warred with outrage in his chest, and relief won. It was Dr. Strickland. She'd gone with Dr. Strickland, who knew about her condition, about the medicine, about all the things that needed to be done to keep Mei alive. He sank to his knees, his eyes closed and weeping. If he'd taken her, she wasn't dead. His daughter wasn't dead.

Unless, a thin demonic thought whispered in his brain, Strickland was too.

The woman was a stranger. Dark-haired with features that reminded Prax of the Russian botanists he'd worked with. She was holding a roll of paper in her hand. Her smile might have been one of amusement or impatience. He didn't know.

"Can you follow them?" he asked. "See where they went?"

The boy looked at him, lips curled.

"For salad? No. Box of chicken and atche sauce."

"I don't have any chicken."

"Then you got what you got," the boy said with a shrug. His eyes had gone dead as marbles. Prax wanted to hit him, wanted to choke him until he dug the images out of the dying computers. But it was a fair bet the boy had a gun or something worse, and unlike Prax, he likely knew how to use it.

"Please," Prax said.

"Got your favor, you. No epressa mé, si?"

Humiliation rose in the back of his throat, and he swallowed it down.

"Chicken," he said.

"Si."

Prax opened his satchel and put a double handful of leaves, orange peppers, and snow onions on the cot. The boy snatched up a half of it and stuffed it into his mouth, eyes narrowing in animal pleasure.

"I'll do what I can," Prax said.

He couldn't do anything.

The only edible protein still on the station was either coming in a slow trickle from the relief supplies or walking around on two feet. People had started trying Prax's strategy, grazing off the plants in the parks and hydroponics. They hadn't bothered with the homework, though. Inedibles were eaten all the same, degrading the air-scrubbing functions and throwing the balance of the station's ecosystem further off. One thing was leading to another, and chicken couldn't be had, or anything that might substitute for it. And even if there was, he didn't have time to solve that problem.

In his own home, the lights were dim and wouldn't go bright. The soybean plant had stopped growing but didn't fade, which was an interesting datapoint, or would have been.

Sometime during the day, an automated system had clicked into a conservation routine, limiting energy use. In the big picture, it might be a good sign. Or it might be the fever break just before the catastrophe. It didn't change what he had to do.

As a boy, he'd entered the schools young, shipping up with his family to the sunless reaches of space, chasing a dream of work and prosperity. He hadn't taken the change well. Headaches and anxiety attacks and constant, bone-deep fatigue had haunted those first years when he needed to impress his tutors, be tracked as bright and promising. His father hadn't let him rest. *The window is open until the window is closed*, he'd say, and then push Prax to do a little more, to find a way to think when he was too tired or sick or in pain to think. He'd learned to make lists, notes, outlines.

By capturing his fleeting thoughts, he could drag himself to clarity like a mountain climber inching toward a summit. Now, in the artificial twilight, he made lists. The names of all the children he could remember from Mei's therapy group. He knew there were twenty, but he could only remember sixteen. His mind wandered. He put the image of Strickland and the mystery woman on his hand terminal, staring at it. The confusion of hope and anger swirled in him until it faded. He felt like he was falling asleep, but his pulse was racing. He tried to remember if tachycardia was a symptom of starvation.

For a moment, he came to himself, clear and lucid in a way he only then realized he hadn't been in days. He was starting to crash. His own personal cascade was getting ahead of him, and he wouldn't be able to keep up his investigation much longer without rest. Without protein. He was already half zombie.

He had to get help. His gaze drifted to the list of children's names. He had to get help, but first he'd check, just check. He'd go to...go to...

He closed his eyes, frowned. He knew the answer. He knew that he knew. The security station. He'd go there and ask about each of them. He opened his eyes, writing *security station* down under the list, capturing the thought. Then *UN outreach station. Mars outreach.* All the places he'd been before, day after day, only now with new questions. It would be easy. And then, when he knew, there was something else he was supposed to do. It took a minute to figure out what it was, and then he wrote it at the bottom of the page.

Get help.

"They're all gone," Prax said, his breath ghosting white in the cold. "They're all his patients, and they're all gone. Sixteen out of sixteen. Do you know the probability of that? It's not random."

The security man hadn't shaved in days. A long, angry ice burn reddened his cheek and neck, the wound fresh and untreated. His face must have touched an uninsulated piece of Ganymede. He was lucky to still have skin. He wore a thick coat and gloves. There was frost on the desk.

"I appreciate the information, sir, and I'll see it gets out to the relief stations—"

"No, you don't understand, he took them. They're sick, and he took them."

"Maybe he was trying to keep them safe," the security man said. His voice was a gray rag, limp and weary. There was a problem with that. Prax knew there was a problem with that, but he couldn't remember what it was. The security man reached out, gently moving him aside, and nodded to the woman behind him. Prax found himself staring at her like he was drunk.

"I want to report a murder," she said, her voice shaking.

The security man nodded, neither surprise nor disbelief in his eyes. Prax remembered.

"He took them first," he said. "He took them before the attack happened."

"Three men broke into my apartment," the woman said. "They... My brother was with me and he tried to stop them."

"When did this happen, ma'am?"

"Before the attack," Prax said.

"A couple hours ago," the woman said. "Fourth level. Blue sector. Apartment 1453."

"Okay, ma'am. I'm going to take you over to a desk here. I need you to fill out a report."

"My brother's dead. They shot him."

"And I'm very sorry about that, ma'am. I need you to fill out a report so we can catch the men who did this."

Prax watched them walk away. He turned back to the line of the traumatized and desperate waiting their turns to beg for help, for justice, for law. A flash of anger lit him, then flickered. He needed help, but there wasn't any to be had here. He and Mei were a pebble in space. They didn't signify.

The security man was back, talking to a tall pretty woman about something horrible. Prax hadn't noticed the man returning, hadn't heard the beginning of the woman's tale. He was starting to lose time. That wasn't good.

The small sane part of his brain whispered that if he died, no one would look for Mei. She'd be lost. It whispered that he needed food, that he'd needed it for days. That he didn't have very much time left.

"I have to go to the relief center," he said aloud. The woman and the security man didn't seem to hear. "Thanks anyway."

Now that he had started to notice his own condition, Prax was astonished and alarmed. His gait was a shuffle; his arms were weak and ached badly, though he couldn't remember having done anything to earn the pain. He hadn't lifted anything heavy or gone climbing. He hadn't done his daily exercise routine any time that he could remember. He didn't remember the last time he'd eaten. He remembered the shudder of the falling mirror, the death of his dome, like it was something that had happened in a previous lifetime. No wonder he was falling apart.

The corridors by the relief center were packed like a slaughterhouse. Men and women, many of them who looked stronger and healthier than he was, pushed against each other, making even the widest spaces feel narrow. The closer he got to the port, the more light-headed he felt. The air was almost warm here, the barn-hot of bodies. It stank of keytone-acrid breath. Saint's breath, his mother called it. The smell of protein breakdown, of bodies eating their own muscles to survive. He wondered how many people in the crowd knew what that scent was.

People were yelling. Shoving. The crowd around him surged back and forth the way he imagined waves might press against a beach.

"Then open the doors and let us look!" a woman shouted, far ahead of him.

Oh, Prax thought. *This is a food riot.*

He pushed for the edges, trying to get out. Trying to get away. Ahead of him, people were shouting. Behind him, they pushed. Banks of LEDs in the ceiling glowed white and gold. The walls were industrial gray. He put a hand out. He'd gotten to a wall. Somewhere, the dam burst, and the crowd flowed suddenly forward, the collective movement threatening to pull him swirling away into the flow. He kept a hand on the wall. The crowd thinned, and Prax staggered forward. The loading bay doors stood open. Beside them Prax saw a familiar face but couldn't place it. Someone from the lab, maybe? The man was thick-boned and muscular. An Earther. Maybe someone he'd seen in his travels through the failing station. Had he seen the man grubbing for food? But no, he looked too well fed. There was no gauntness to his cheeks. He was like a friend and also a stranger. Someone Prax knew and also didn't. Like the secretary-general or a famous actor.

Prax knew he was staring, but he couldn't stop. He knew that face. He *knew* it. It had to do with the war.

Prax had a sudden flashbulb memory. He was in his apartment, holding Mei in his arms, trying to calm her. She was barely a year old, not walking, the doctors still tinkering to find the right pharmaceutical cocktail to keep her alive. Over her colic wail, the news streams were a constant alarmed chatter. A man's face played over and over.

My name is James Holden and my ship, the Canterbury, *was just destroyed by a warship with stealth technology and what appear to be parts stamped with Martian Navy serial numbers.*

That was him. That was why he recognized the face and felt that he'd never seen it before. Prax felt a tug from somewhere near the center of his chest and found himself stepping forward. He paused. Beyond the loading doors, someone whooped. Prax took out his hand terminal, looked at his list. Sixteen names, sixteen children gone. And at the bottom of the page, in simple block characters: *Get help.*

Prax turned toward the man who'd started wars and saved planets, suddenly shy and uncertain.

"Get help," he said, and walked forward.

Chapter Eleven: Holden

Santichai and Melissa Supitayaporn were a pair of eighty-year-old earthborn missionaries from the Church of Humanity Ascendant, a religion that eschewed supernaturalism in all forms, and whose theology boiled down to *Humans can be better than they are, so let's do that.* They also ran the relief depot headquarters with the ruthless efficiency of natural-born dictators. Minutes after arriving, Holden had been thoroughly dressed down by Santichai, a frail wisp of a man with thinning white hair, about his altercation with customs officials at the port. After several minutes of trying to explain himself, only to be shouted down by the tiny missionary, he finally just gave up and apologized.

"Don't make our situation here any more precarious," Santichai repeated, apparently mollified by the apology but needing to drive this point home. He shook a sticklike brown finger in Holden's face.

"Got it," Holden said, holding up his hands in surrender. The rest of his crew had vanished at Santichai's first angry outburst, leaving Holden to deal with the man alone. He spotted Naomi across the large open warehouse space of the relief depot, talking calmly to Melissa, Santichai's hopefully less volatile wife. Holden couldn't hear any shouting, though with the voices of several dozen people and the grinding gears and engine whine and reverse alerts of three lift trucks, Melissa could have been flinging grenades at Naomi and he probably wouldn't have heard it.

Looking for an opportunity to escape, Holden pointed at Naomi across the room and said, "Excuse me, I—"

Santichai cut him off with a curt wave of one hand that sent his loose orange robes swirling. Holden found himself unable to disobey the tiny man.

"This," Santichai said, pointing in the direction of the crates being brought in from the *Somnambulist*, "is not enough."

"I—"

"The OPA promised us twenty-two thousand kilos of protein and supplements by last week. This is less than twelve thousand kilos," Santichai said, punctuating his statement with a sharp poke at Holden's bicep.

"I'm not in charge of—"

"Why would they promise us things they have no intention of delivering? Promise twelve thousand if that is what you have. Do *not* promise twenty-two thousand and then deliver twelve," he said, accompanied by more poking.

"I agree," Holden said, backing out of poke range with his hands up. "I totally agree. I'll call my contact on Tycho Station immediately to find out where the rest of the promised supplies are. I'm sure they're on the way."

Santichai shrugged in another swirl of orange.

"See that you do," he said, then steamed off toward one of the lift trucks. "You! *You!* Do you see the sign that says 'medicine'? Why are you putting things that are not medicine in that place?"

Holden used this distraction to make good his escape, and

jogged over to Naomi and Melissa. Naomi had a form open on her terminal and was completing some paperwork while Melissa watched.

Holden glanced around the warehouse space while Naomi worked. The *Somnambulist* was just one of almost twenty relief ships that had landed in the last twenty-four hours, and the massive room was quickly filling up with crates of supplies. The chill air smelled of dust and ozone and hot oil from the lift trucks, but under it there was a vaguely unpleasant smell of decay, like rotting vegetation. As he watched, Santichai darted across the warehouse floor, shouting instructions to a pair of workers carrying a heavy crate.

"Your husband is something else, ma'am," Holden said to Melissa.

Melissa was both taller and heavier than her tiny husband, but she had the same shapeless cloud of thinning white hair he had. She also had bright blue eyes that nearly disappeared in her face when she smiled. As she was doing now.

"I've never met anyone else in my life who cared more about other people's welfare, and less about their feelings," she said. "But at least he'll make sure everyone is well fed before he tells them all the many things they did wrong."

"I think that does it," Naomi said, hitting the key to send the filled-out form to Melissa's terminal, a charmingly outdated model she pulled out of a pocket in her robe when it chimed receipt.

"Mrs. Supitayaporn," Holden said.

"Melissa."

"Melissa, how long have you and your husband been on Ganymede?"

"Almost," she said, tapping her finger against her chin and staring off into the distance, "ten years? Can it be that long? It must be, because Dru had just had her baby, and he—"

"I'm wondering because the one thing no one outside of Ganymede seems to know is how this"—Holden gestured around him—"all got started."

"The station?"

"The crisis."

"Well, the UN and Martian soldiers started shooting at each other; then we started seeing system failures—"

"Yes," Holden said, cutting in again. "I understand that. But *why*? Not one shot during the entire year that Earth and Mars have jointly held this moon. We had a war before the whole Eros thing, and they didn't bring it here. Then all at once everyone everywhere is shooting? What kicked that off?"

Melissa looked puzzled, another expression that made her eyes almost disappear in a mass of wrinkles.

"I don't know," she said. "I'd assumed they were shooting each other everywhere in the system. We don't get much news right now."

"No," Holden said. "It's just here, and it was just for a couple of days. And then it stopped, with no explanation."

"That is odd," Melissa said, "but I don't know that it matters. Whatever happened, it doesn't change what we need to do now."

"I suppose not," Holden agreed.

Melissa smiled, embraced him warmly, then went off to check someone else's paperwork.

Naomi hooked her arm through Holden's, and they started toward the warehouse exit into the rest of the station, dodging crates of supplies and aid workers as they went.

"How can they have had a whole battle here," she said, "and no one knows why?"

"They know," Holden said. "*Someone* knows."

The station looked worse on the ground than from space. The vital, oxygen-producing plants that lined the corridor walls were turning an unhealthy shade of yellow. Many corridors didn't have lights, and the automatic pressure doors had been hand cranked and then wedged open; if one area of the station suddenly lost pressure, many adjoining sections would as well. The few people they ran into either avoided their eyes or stared at them with open hostility. Holden found himself wishing he were wearing his gun openly, rather than in a concealed holster at the small of his back.

"Who's our contact?" Naomi asked quietly.

"Hmmmm?"

"I assume Fred has people here," she replied under her breath as she smiled and nodded at a passing group of men. All of them openly carried weapons, though most were of the stabbing and clubbing variety. They stared back at her with speculative looks on their faces. Holden moved his hand under his coat and toward his gun, but the men moved on, only giving them a few backward glances before they turned a corner and disappeared from view.

"He didn't arrange for us to meet someone?" Naomi finished in a normal voice.

"He gave me some names. But communication with this moon has been so spotty he wasn't able to—"

Holden was cut off by a loud bang from another part of the port. The explosion was followed by a roar that gradually resolved into people shouting. The few people in the corridor with them began to run, some toward the noise, but most away from it.

"Should we…" Naomi said, looking at the people running toward the commotion.

"We're here to see what's going on," Holden replied. "So let's go see."

They quickly became lost in the twisting corridors of Ganymede's port, but it didn't matter as long as they kept moving toward the noise and along with the growing wave of people running in the same direction. A tall, stocky man with spiked red hair ran alongside them for a while. He was carrying a length of black metal pipe in each hand. He grinned at Naomi and tried to hand her one. She waved it off.

" 'Bout fookin' time," he yelled in an accent Holden couldn't place. He held his extra club out to Holden when Naomi didn't take it.

"What is?" Holden asked, taking the club.

"Fookin' bastahds flingin' the victuals up, and the prols jus gotta shove, wut? Well, fook that, ya mudder-humpin' spunk guzzlas!"

Spiky Redhead howled and waved his club in the air, then took off at a faster run and disappeared into the crowd. Naomi laughed and howled at his back as he ran. When Holden shot her a look, she just smiled and said, "It's infectious."

A final bend in the corridor brought them to another large warehouse space, looking almost identical to the one ruled over by the Supitayaporns, except that this room was filled with a mob of angry people pushing toward the loading dock. The doors to the dock were closed, and a small group of port security officers were trying to hold the mob back. When Holden arrived, the crowd was still cowed by the security officers' Tasers and shock prods, but from the rising tension and anger in the air, he could tell that wouldn't last long.

Just behind the front line of rent-a-cops, with their nonlethal deterrents, stood a small clump of men in dark suits and sensible shoes. They carried shotguns with the air of men who were just waiting for someone to give them permission.

That would be the corporate security, then.

Looking over the room, Holden felt the scene snap into place. Beyond that closed loading bay door was one of the few remaining corporate freighters loaded down with the last food being stripped from Ganymede.

And this crowd was hungry.

Holden remembered trying to escape a casino on Eros when it went into security lockdown. Remembered angry crowds facing down men with guns. Remembered the screams and the smells of blood and cordite. Before he knew he'd made a decision, he found himself pushing his way to the front of the crowd. Naomi followed, murmuring apologies in his wake. She grabbed his arm and stopped him for a moment.

"Are you about to do something really stupid?" she asked.

"I'm about to keep these people from being shot for the crime of being hungry," he said, wincing at the self-righteous tone even as he said it.

"Don't," Naomi said, letting him go, "pull your gun on anyone."

"They have guns."

"Guns plural. You have gun singular, which is why you will keep yours in your holster, or you'll do this by yourself."

That's the only way you ever do anything. By yourself. It was the kind of thing Detective Miller would have said. For him, it had been true. That was a strong enough argument against doing it that way.

"Okay." Holden nodded, then resumed pushing his way to the front. By the time he reached it, two people had become the focus of the conflict. A gray-haired port security man wearing a white patch with the word *supervisor* printed on it and a tall, thin dark-skinned woman who could pass for Naomi's mother were yelling at each other while their respective groups looked on, shouting agreements and insults.

"Just open the damn door and let us look!" yelled the woman in a tone that let Holden know this was something she was repeating again and again.

"You won't get anything by yelling at me," the gray-haired supervisor yelled back. Beside him, his fellow security guards held their shock sticks in white-knuckled grips and the corporate boys held their shotguns in a loose cradle that Holden found far more threatening.

The woman stopped shouting when Holden pushed his way up to the supervisor, and stared at him instead.

"Who...?" she said.

Holden climbed up onto the loading dock next to the supervisor. The other guards waved their shock prods around a little, but no one jabbed him. The corporate thugs just narrowed their eyes and shifted their stances a bit. Holden knew that their confusion about who he was would only last so long, and when they finally got past it, he was probably going to get uncomfortably intimate with one of those cattle prods, if not just blasted in the face with a shotgun. Before that could happen, he thrust his hand out to the supervisor and said in a loud voice that would carry to the crowd, "Hi there, I'm Walter Philips, an OPA rep out of Tycho Station, and here as personal representative of Colonel Frederick Johnson."

The supervisor shook his hand like a man in a daze. The corporate gorillas shifted again and held their guns more firmly.

"Mr. Philips," the supervisor said. "The OPA has no authority…"

Holden ignored him and turned to the woman he'd been shouting at.

"Ma'am, what's all the fuss?"

"That ship," she said, pointing at the door, "has almost ten thousand kilos of beans and rice on it, enough to feed the whole station for a week!"

The crowd murmured agreement at her back and shuffled forward a step or two.

"Is that true?" Holden asked the supervisor.

"As I said," the man replied, holding up his hands and making pushing motions at the crowd as though he could drive them back through sheer force of will, "we are not allowed to discuss the cargo manifests of privately owned—"

"Then open the doors and let us look!" the woman shouted again. While she yelled and the crowd picked up her chant—*let us look, let us look*—Holden took the security supervisor by the elbow and pulled his head close.

"In about thirty seconds, that mob is going to tear you and your men to pieces trying to get into that ship," he said. "I think you should let them have it before this turns violent."

"Violent!" The man gave a humorless laugh. "It's already violent. The only reason the ship isn't long gone is because one of them set off a bomb and blew up the docking-clamp release mechanism. If they try to take the ship, we'll—"

"They will not take the ship," said a gravelly voice, and a heavy hand came down on Holden's shoulder. When he turned around, one of the corporate goons was standing behind him. "This ship is Mao-Kwikowski Mercantile property."

Holden pushed the man's hand off his shoulder.

"A dozen guys with Tasers and shotguns isn't going to stop them," he said, pointing out at the chanting mob.

"Mr."—the goon looked him up and down once—"*Philips*. I don't give a drippy shit what you or the OPA thinks about anything, and especially not my chances of doing my job. So why don't you fuck off before the shooting starts?"

Well, he'd tried. Holden smiled at the man and began to reach for the holster at the small of his back. He wished that Amos were here, but he hadn't seen him since they had gotten off the ship. Before he reached the pistol, his hand was enveloped by long slender fingers and squeezed tightly.

"How about this," Naomi said, suddenly at Holden's side. "How about we skip past the posturing and I just tell you how this is actually going to work?"

Both Holden and the goon turned to look at Naomi in surprise. She held up one finger in a *wait a minute* gesture and pulled out her hand terminal. She called someone and turned on the external speaker.

"Amos," she said, still holding her finger up.

"Yep," came the reply.

"A ship is trying to leave from port 11, pad B9. It's full of food we could really use here. If it makes it off the ground, do we have an OPA gunship close enough to intercept?"

There was a long pause; then, with a chuckle, Amos said, "You know we do, boss. Who'm I actually saying this to?"

"Call that ship and have them disable the freighter. Then have an OPA team secure it, strip it of everything, and scuttle it."

Amos just said, "You got it."

Naomi closed up the terminal and put it back into her pocket.

"Don't test us, boy," she said to the goon, a hint of steel in her voice. "Not one word of that was empty threat. Either you give these people the cargo, or we'll take the whole damned ship. Your choice."

The goon stared at her for a moment, then motioned to his team and walked away. Port security followed, and Holden and Naomi had to dodge out of the way of the crowd rushing up the dock and to the loading bay doors.

When they were out of danger of being trampled, Holden said, "That was pretty cool."

"Getting shot standing up for justice probably seemed very heroic to you," she said, the steel not quite gone from her voice. "But I want to keep you around, so stop being an idiot."

"Smart play, threatening the ship," Holden said.

"You were acting like that asshole Detective Miller, so I just acted like you used to. What I said was the kind of thing you say when you're not in a hurry to wave your gun around."

"I wasn't acting like Miller," he said, the accusation stinging, because it was true.

"You weren't acting like you."

Holden shrugged, noticing only afterward that it was another imitation of Miller. Naomi looked down at the captain's patches on the shoulder of her *Somnambulist* jumpsuit. "Maybe I should keep these…"

A small, unkempt-looking man with salt-and-pepper hair, Chinese features, and a week's growth of beard walked up to them and nodded nervously. He was literally wringing his hands, a gesture Holden had been pretty sure only little old ladies in ancient cinema made.

He gave them another small nod and said, "You are James Holden? Captain James Holden? From the OPA?"

Holden and Naomi glanced at each other. Holden tugged at his patchy beard. "Is this actually helping at all? Be honest."

"Captain Holden, my name is Prax, Praxidike Meng. I'm a botanist."

Holden shook the man's hand.

"Nice to meet you, Prax. I'm afraid we have to—"

"You have to help me," Prax said. Holden could see that the man had been through a rough couple of months. His clothes hung off him like a starving man's, and his face was covered with yellowing bruises from a fairly recent beating.

"Sure, if you'll see the Supitayaporns at the aid station, tell them I said—"

"No!" Prax shouted. "I don't need that. I need you to *help* me!"

Holden shot a glance at Naomi. She shrugged. *Your call.*

"Okay," Holden said. "What's the problem?"

Chapter Twelve: Avasarala

A small house is a deeper kind of luxury," her husband said. "To live in a space entirely our own, to remember the simple pleasures of baking bread and washing our own dishes. This is what your friends in high places forget. It makes them less human."

He was sitting at the kitchen table, leaning back in a chair of bamboo laminate that had been distressed until it looked like stained walnut. The scars from his cancer surgery were two pale lines in the darkness of his throat, barely visible under the powdering of white stubble. His forehead was broader than when she'd married him, his hair thinner. The Sunday morning sun spilled across the table, glowing.

"That's crap," she said. "Just because you pretend to live like a dirt farmer doesn't make Errinwright or Lus or any of the others less human. There's smaller houses than this with six families living in them, and the people in those are a hundred times closer to animals than anyone I work with."

"You really think that?"

"Of course I do. Otherwise why would I go to work in the morning? If someone doesn't get those half-feral bastards out of the slums, who are you university types going to teach?"

"An excellent point," Arjun said.

"What makes them less human is they don't fucking meditate. A small house isn't a luxury," she said, then paused. "A small house and a lot of money, maybe."

Arjun grinned at her. He had always had the most beautiful smile. She found herself smiling back at him, even though part of her wanted to be cross. Outside, Kiki and Suri shrieked, their small half-naked bodies bolting across the grass. Their nurse trotted along a half second behind them, her hand to her side like she was easing a stitch.

"A big yard is a luxury," Avasarala said.

"It is."

Suri burst in the back door, her hand covered in loose black soil and a wide grin on her face. Her footsteps left crumbling dark marks on the carpet.

"Nani! Nani! Look what I found!"

Avasarala shifted in her chair. In her granddaughter's palm, an earthworm was shifting the pink and brown rings of its body, wet as the soil that dripped from Suri's fingers. Avasarala made her face into a mask of wonder and delight.

"That's wonderful, Suri. Come back outside and show your nani where you found that."

The yard smelled like cut grass and fresh soil. The gardener—a thin man hardly older than her own son would have been—knelt in the back, pulling weeds by hand. Suri pelted out toward him, and Avasarala moved along after her at a stroll. When she came near, the gardener nodded, but there was no space for conversation. Suri was pointing and gesturing and retelling the grand adventure of finding a common worm in the mud as if it were a thing of epics. Kiki appeared at Avasarala's side, quietly taking her hand. She loved her little Suri, but privately—or if not that, then only to Arjun—she thought Kiki was the smarter of her grandchildren. Quiet, but the girl's black eyes were bright, and she could mimic anyone she heard. Kiki didn't miss much.

"Darling wife," Arjun called from the back door. "There's someone to talk with you."

"Where?"

"The house system," Arjun said. "She says your terminal's not answering."

"There's a reason for that," Avasarala said.

"It's Gloria Tannenbaum."

Avasarala reluctantly handed Kiki's hand over to the nurse, kissed Suri's head, and went back toward the house. Arjun held the door open for her. His expression was apologetic.

"These cunts are digging into my grandma time," she said.

"The price of power," Arjun replied with a solemnity that was amused and serious at the same time.

Avasarala opened the connection on the system in her private office. There was a click and a moment's dislocation while the privacy screens came up, and then Gloria Tannenbaum's thin, eyebrowless face appeared on her screen.

"Gloria! I'm sorry. I had my terminal down with the children over."

"Not a problem," the woman said with a clean, brittle smile that was as close as she came to a genuine emotion. "Probably for the best anyway. Always assume those are being monitored more closely than civilian lines."

Avasarala lowered herself into her chair. The leather breathed out gently under her weight.

"I hope things are all right with you and Etsepan?"

"Fine," Gloria said.

"Good, good. Now why the fuck are you calling me?"

"I was talking to a friend of mine whose wife is stationed on the *Mikhaylov*. From what he says, it's being pulled off patrol. Going deep."

Avasarala frowned. The *Mikhaylov* was part of a small convoy monitoring the traffic between the deep stations orbiting at the far edge of the Belt.

"Going deep where?"

"I asked around," Gloria said. "Ganymede."

"Nguyen?"

"Yes."

"Your friend has loose lips," Avasarala said.

"I never tell him anything true," Gloria said. "I thought you should know."

"I owe you," Avasarala said. Gloria nodded once, the movement sharp as a crow's, and dropped the connection. Avasarala sat in silence for a long moment, fingers pressed to her lips, mind following the chains of implication like a brook flowing over stones. Nguyen was sending more ships to Ganymede, and he was doing it quietly.

The *why quietly* part was simple. If he'd done it openly, she would have stopped him. Nguyen was young and he was ambitious, but he wasn't stupid. He was drawing conclusions of his own, and somehow he'd gotten to the idea that sending more forces into the open sore that was Ganymede Station would make things better.

"Oh, Nani!" Kiki called. From the lilt of her voice, Avasarala knew there was mischief afoot. She hefted herself up from the desk and headed for the door.

"In here, Kiki," she said, stepping out into the kitchen.

The water balloon hit her in the shoulder without bursting, bobbled down to the floor, and popped at her feet, turning the stone tiles around her dark. Avasarala looked up, rage-faced. Kiki stood in the doorway leading to the yard, caught between fear and delight.

"Did you just make a mess in my house?" Avasarala asked.

Pale-faced, the girl nodded.

"Do you know what happens to bad children who make a mess in their nani's house?"

"Do they get tickled?"

"They get *tickled*!" Avasarala said, and bolted for her. Of course Kiki got away. She was a child of eight. The only time the girl's joints ached, it was from growing too fast. And of course, eventually she let her nani catch her and tickle her until she screamed. By the time Ashanti and her husband came to gather up their children for the flight back to Novgorod, Avasarala had grass stains on her sari and her hair was standing off her scalp in all directions, like the cartoon image of her lightning-struck self.

She hugged the children twice before they left, sneaking bits of chocolate to them each time, then kissed her daughter, nodded to her son-in-law, and waved to them all from her doorway. The security team followed their car. No one so closely related to her was safe from kidnapping. It was just another fact of life.

Her shower was long, using a lavish volume of water almost too hot for comfort. She'd always liked her baths to approach scalding, ever since she was a girl. If her skin didn't tingle and throb a little when she toweled off, she'd done it wrong.

Arjun was on the bed, reading seriously from his hand terminal. She walked to her closet, threw the wet towel into the hamper, and shrugged into a cotton-weave robe.

"He thinks they did it," she said.

"Who did what?" Arjun asked.

"Nguyen. He's thinking that the Martians are behind the thing. That there's going to be a second attack on Ganymede. He knows the Martians aren't moving their fleet there, and he's still reinforcing. He doesn't care if it fucks the peace talks, because he thinks they're crap anyway. Nothing to lose. Are you listening to me?"

"Yes, I am. Nguyen thinks it was Mars. He's building a fleet to respond. You see?"

"Do you know what I'm talking about?"

"As a rule? No. But Maxwell Asinnian-Koh just posted a paper about post-lyricism that's going to get him no end of hate mail."

Avasarala chuckled.

"You live in your own world, dear one."

"I do," Arjun agreed, running his thumb across the hand terminal's screen. He looked up. "You don't mind, do you?"

"I love you for it. Stay here. Read about post-lyricism."

"What are you going to do?"

"The same thing as always. Try to keep civilization from blowing up while the children are in it."

When she'd been young, her mother had tried to teach her knitting. The skill hadn't taken, but there were other lessons that had. Once, the skein of yarn had gotten knotted badly, and Avasarala's frustrated yanking had only made things progressively worse. Her mother had taken the tight-bound clump from her, but instead of fixing it herself and handing it back, her mother sat cross-legged on the floor beside her and spoke aloud about how to solve the knot. She'd been gentle, deliberate, and patient, looking for places where she could work more slack into the system until, seemingly all at once, the yarn spilled free.

There were ten ships in the list, ranging from an ancient transport past due for the scrap heap to a pair of frigates captained by people whose names she'd heard. It wasn't a huge force, but it was enough to be provocative. Gently, deliberately, patiently, Avasarala started plucking it apart.

The transport was first, because it was easiest. She'd been cultivating the boys in maintenance and safety for years. It took four hours for someone with the schematics and logs to find a bolt that hadn't been replaced on schedule, and less than half an hour after that to issue the mandatory recall. The *Wu Tsao*—better armed of the frigates—was captained by Golla Ishigawa-Marx. His service record was solid, workmanlike reading. He was competent, unimaginative, and loyal. Three conversations had him promoted to the head of the construction oversight committee, where he probably wouldn't do any harm. The full command crew of the *Wu Tsao* was requested to come back to Earth to be present when they pinned a ribbon on him. The second frigate was harder, but she found a way. And by then the convoy was small enough that the medical and support ship was a higher rating than the remaining convoy justified.

The knot unspooled in her fingers. The three ships she couldn't pry loose were old and underpowered. If it came to a fight, they wouldn't be significant. And because of that, the Martians would only take offense if they were looking for an excuse.

She didn't think they would. And if she was wrong, that would be interesting too.

"Won't Admiral Nguyen see through all this?" Errinwright asked. He was in a hotel room somewhere on the other side of the planet. It was night behind him, and his dress shirt was unbuttoned at the top.

"Let him," Avasarala said. "What's he going to do? Go crying to his mama that I took his toys away? If he can't play with the big kids, he shouldn't be a fucking admiral."

Errinwright smiled and cracked his knuckles. He looked tired.

"The ships that will get there?"

"The *Bernadette Koe*, the *Aristophanes*, and the *Feodorovna*, sir."

"Those, yes. What are you going to tell the Martians about them?"

"Nothing if they don't bring it up," Avasarala said. "If they do, I can dismiss them. A minor medical support ship, a transport, and an itty-bitty gunship to keep off pirates. I mean, it's not like we're sending a couple of cruisers. So fuck them."

"You'll say it more gently, I hope?"

"Of course I will, sir. I'm not stupid."

"And Venus?"

She took a long breath, letting the air hiss out between her teeth.

"It's the damn bogeyman," she said. "I'm getting daily reports, but we don't know what we're looking at. The network it built across the planetary surface is finished, and now it's breaking down, but there are structures coming up in a complex radial symmetry. Only it's not along the axis of rotation. It's on the plane of ecliptic. So whatever's down there, it's orienting itself with the whole solar system in mind. And the spectrographic analysis is showing an uptick in lanthanum oxide and gold."

"I don't know what that means."

"Neither does anyone else, but the brains are thinking it may be a set of very high-temperature superconductors. They're trying to replicate the crystal structures in the labs, and they've found some things they don't understand. Turns out, the thing down there's a better physical chemist than we are. No fucking surprise there."

"Any link to Ganymede?"

"Just the one," Avasarala said. "Otherwise nothing. Or at least not directly."

"What do you mean, not directly?"

Avasarala frowned and looked away. The Buddha looked back.

"Did you know that the number of religious suicide cults has doubled since Eros?" she said. "I didn't until I got the report. The bond initiative to rebuild the water reclamation center at Cairo almost failed last year because a millennialist group said we wouldn't need it."

Errinwright sat forward. His eyes were narrow.

"You think there's a connection?"

"I don't think there's a bunch of pod people sneaking up from Venus," she said, "but…I've been thinking about what it's done to us. The whole solar system. Them and us and the Belters. It's not healthy having God sleeping right there where we can all watch him dream. It scares the shit out of us. It scares the shit out of *me*. And so we all look away and go about things as if the universe were the same as when we were young, but we know better. We're all acting like we're sane, but…"

She shook her head.

"Humanity's always lived with the inexplicable," Errinwright said. His voice was hard. She was making him uncomfortable. Well, she was making herself uncomfortable too.

"The inexplicable didn't used to eat planets," she said. "Even if the thing on Ganymede didn't come up off Venus on its own, it's pretty damn clear that it's related. And if *we* did it—"

"If we built that, it's because we found a new technology, and we're using it," Errinwright said. "Flint spear to gunpowder to nuclear warheads, it's what we do, Chrisjen. Let me worry about that. You keep your eye on Venus and don't let the Martian situation get out of control."

"Yes, sir," she said.

"Everything's going to be fine."

And, looking at the dead screen where her superior had been, Avasarala decided that maybe he even thought it was true. Avasarala wasn't sure any longer. Something was bothering her, and she didn't yet know what it was. It only lurked there, just underneath her conscious mind, like a splinter in a fingertip. She opened the captured video from the UN outpost on Ganymede, went through the mandatory security check, and watched the Marines die again.

Kiki and Suri were going to grow up in a world where this had happened, where Venus had always been the colony of something utterly foreign, uncommunicative, and implacable. The fear that carried would be normal to them, something they didn't think about any more than they did their own breath. On her screen, a man no older than Soren emptied an assault rifle clip into the attacker. The enhanced images showed the dozens of impacts cutting through the thing, the trails of filament coming out its back like streamers. The soldier died again. At least it had been quick for him. She paused the image. Her fingertip traced the outline of the attacker.

"Who are you?" she asked the screen. "What do you *want*?"

She was missing something. It happened often enough that she knew the feeling, but that didn't help. It would come when it came. All she could do until it did was keep scratching where it itched. She shut down the files, waiting for the security protocols to make sure she hadn't copied anything, then signed out and turned to the window.

She found that she was thinking about the next time. What information they'd be able to get the next time. What kind of patterns she'd be able to glean from the next time. The next attack, the next slaughter. It was already perfectly clear in her mind that what had happened on Ganymede was going to happen again, sooner or later. Genies didn't get put back into bottles, and from the moment the protomolecule had been set loose on the civilian population of Eros just to see what it would do, civilization had changed. Changed so fast and so powerfully that they were still playing catch-up.

Playing catch-up.

There was something there. Something in the words, like a lyric from a song she almost remembered. She ground her teeth and stood up, pacing the length of her window. She hated this part. Hated it.

Her office door opened. When she turned to look at Soren, he flinched back. Avasarala took her scowl down a couple of notches. It wasn't fair to scare the poor bunny. He was probably just the intern who'd pulled the short straw and gotten stuck with the cranky old woman. And in a way, she liked him.

"Yes?" she said.

"I thought you'd want to know that Admiral Nguyen sent a note of protest to Mr. Errinwright. Interference in his field of command. He didn't copy the secretary-general."

Avasarala smiled. If she couldn't unlock all the mysteries of the universe, she could at least keep the boys in line. And if he wasn't appealing to the bobble-head, then it was just pouting. Nothing was going to come of it.

"Good to know. And the Martians?"

"They're here, ma'am."

She sighed, plucked at her sari, and lifted her chin.

"Let's go stop the war, then," she said.

Chapter Thirteen: Holden

Amos, who'd finally turned up a few hours after the food riot carrying a case of beer and saying he'd done some "recon," was now carrying a small case of canned food. The label claimed it was "chicken food products." Holden hoped that the hacker Prax was leading them to would see the offering as at least being in the spirit of his requested payment.

Prax led the way with the manic speed of someone who had one last thing to do before he died, and could feel the end close on his heels. Holden suspected this wasn't far from the truth. The small botanist certainly looked like he'd been burning himself up.

They'd taken him aboard the *Somnambulist* while they'd gathered the supplies they'd need, and Holden had forced the man to eat a meal and take a shower. Prax had begun stripping while Holden was still showing him how to use the ship's head, as if waiting for privacy would waste precious time. The sight of the man's ravaged body had shocked him. All the while, the botanist spoke only of Mei, of his need to find her. Holden realized that he'd never in his life needed anything as badly as this man needed to see his daughter again.

To his surprise, it made him sad.

Prax had been robbed of everything, had all his fat boiled away; he'd been rendered down to the bare minimum of humanity. All he had left was his need to find his little girl, and Holden envied him for it.

When Holden had been dying and trapped in the hell of Eros Station, he had discovered that he needed to see Naomi one last time. Or barring that, to see that she was safe. It was why he hadn't died there. That and having Miller at his side with a second gun. And that connection, even now that he and Naomi were lovers, was a pale shadow compared to the thing driving Prax. It left Holden feeling like he'd lost something important without realizing it.

While Prax had showered, Holden had gone up the ladder to ops, where Naomi had been working to hack her way into Ganymede's crippled security system, pulled her out of her chair, and held her for a few moments. She stiffened with surprise for a second, then relaxed into his embrace. "Hi," she whispered in his ear. It might be a pale shadow, but it was what he had right now, and it was pretty damn good.

Prax paused at an intersection, his hands tapping at his thighs as if he were hurrying himself along. Naomi was back on the ship, monitoring their progress through locators they all carried and with the remnants of the station's security cameras.

At Holden's back, Amos cleared his throat and said in a voice low enough that Prax wouldn't hear, "If we lose this guy, I don't like our chances of finding our way back too quick."

Holden nodded. Amos was right.

Even at the best of times, Ganymede was a maze of identical gray corridors and occasional parklike caverns. And the station certainly wasn't at her best now. Most of the public information kiosks were dark, malfunctioning, or outright destroyed. The pubnet was unreliable at best. And the local citizens moved like scavengers over the corpse of their once-great moon, alternately terrified and threatening. He and Amos were both openly wearing firearms, and Amos had mastered a sort of constant glower that made people automatically put him onto their "not to be fucked with" list. Not for the first time, Holden wondered what sort of life Amos had been leading prior to his signing up for a tour on the *Canterbury*, the old water hauler they'd served together on.

Prax came to a sudden halt in front of a door that looked like a hundred other doors they'd already passed, set into the wall of a gray corridor that looked like every other gray corridor.

"This is it. He's in here."

Before Holden could respond, Prax was hammering on the door. Holden took a step back and to the side, giving himself a clear view of the doorway past Prax. Amos stepped to the other side, tucking the case of chicken under his left arm and hooking his right thumb into his waistband just in front of the holster. A year of patrolling the Belt, cleaning up the worst jackals that the governmental vacuum had left behind, had instilled some automatic habits in his crew. Holden appreciated them, but he wasn't sure he liked them. Working security certainly hadn't made Miller's life any better.

The door was yanked open by a scrawny and shirtless teenager with a big knife in his other hand.

"The fuck—" he started, then stopped when he saw Holden and Amos flanking Prax. He glanced at their guns and said, "Oh."

"I've brought you chicken," Prax replied, pointing back at the case Amos carried. "I need to see the rest of the camera footage."

"Coulda got that for you," Naomi said in Holden's ear, "given enough time."

"It's the 'enough time' part that's a problem," Holden subvocalized back at her. "But that's definitely plan B."

The skinny teen shrugged and opened the door the rest of the way, gesturing for Prax to enter. Holden followed, with Amos bringing up the rear.

"So," the kid said. "Show it, sabé?"

Amos put down the case on a filthy table and removed a single can from the box. He held it up where the kid could see it.

"Sauce?" the kid said.

"How about a second can instead?" Holden replied, moving over to the kid and smiling up at him agreeably. "So go get the rest of the footage, and we'll get out of your hair. Sound good?"

The kid lifted his chin and pushed Holden an arm's length back.

"Don't push up on me, macho."

"My apologies," Holden said, his smile never wavering. "Now go get the damned video footage you promised my friend here."

"Maybe no," the kid said. He flapped one hand at Holden. "Adinerado, si no? Quizas you got more than chicken to pay. Maybe a lot."

"Let me get this straight," Holden replied. "Are you shaking us down? Because that would be—"

A meaty hand came down on his shoulder, cutting him off.

"I got this one, Cap," Amos said, stepping between Holden and the kid. He held one of the chicken cans in his hand, and he was tossing it lightly and catching it.

"That guy," Amos said, pointing at Prax with his left hand while continuing to toss the chicken with his right, "got his baby girl snatched. He just wants to know where she is. He's willing to pay the agreed-upon price for that information."

The kid shrugged and started to speak, but Amos held up a finger to his lips and shushed him.

"And now, when that price is ready to be paid," Amos said, his tone friendly and conversational, "you want to shake him down because you know he's desperate. He'll give anything to get his girl back. This is a fat payday, right?"

The kid shrugged again. "Que no—"

Amos smashed the can of chicken food product into the kid's face so fast that for a moment Holden couldn't figure out why the hacker was suddenly lying on the ground, blood gushing from his nose. Amos settled one knee onto his chest, pinning him to the floor. The can of chicken went up and then pistoned down into the kid's face again with a sharp crack. He started to howl, but Amos clamped his left hand over the boy's mouth.

"You piece of shit," Amos yelled, all the friendliness gone from his voice, leaving just a ragged animal rage that Holden had never heard there before. "You gonna hold a baby girl hostage for more fucking *chicken*?"

Amos smashed the can into the hacker's ear, which immediately bloomed red. His hand came away from the kid's mouth, and the boy started yelling for help. Amos raised the can of chicken one more time, but Holden grabbed his arm and pulled him up off the gibbering kid.

"Enough," he said, holding on to Amos and hoping the big man didn't decide to clobber him with the can instead. Amos had always been the kind of guy who got into bar fights because he enjoyed them.

This was something different.

"Enough," Holden said again, and then held on until Amos stopped struggling. "He can't help us if you bash his brains out."

The kid scooted backward across the floor and had his shoulders up against the wall. He nodded as Holden spoke, and held his bleeding nose between his finger and thumb.

"That right?" Amos said. "You going to help?"

The kid nodded again and scrambled to his feet, still pressed against the wall.

"I'll go with him," Holden said, patting Amos on the shoulder. "Why don't you stay here and take a breather."

Before Amos could answer, Holden pointed at the terrified hacker.

"Better get to work."

"There," Prax said when the video of Mei's abduction came up again. "That's Mei. That man is her doctor, Dr. Strickland. That woman, I don't know her. But Mei's teacher said that she came up in their records as Mei's mother. With a picture and authorization to pick her up. Security is very good at the school. They'd never let a child go without that."

"Find where they went," Holden said to the hacker. To Prax he said, "Why her doctor?"

"Mei is..." Prax started, then stopped and started over. "Mei has a rare genetic disease that disables her immune system without regular treatments. Dr. Strickland knows this. Sixteen other kids with her disorder are missing too. He could keep them...he could keep Mei alive."

"You getting this, Naomi?"

"Yep, riding the hacker's trail through security. We won't need him again."

"Good," Holden said. "Because I'm pretty sure this bridge is thoroughly burned once we walk out the door."

"We always have more chicken," Naomi said with a chuckle.

"Amos made sure the kid's next request will be for plastic surgery."

"Ouch," she replied. "He okay?"

Holden knew she meant Amos. "Yeah. But...is there something I don't know about him that would make this problematic? Because he's really—"

"Aqui," the hacker said, pointing at his screen.

Holden watched as Dr. Strickland carried Mei down an older-looking corridor, the dark-haired woman in tow. They came to a door that looked like an ancient pressure hatch. Strickland did something at the panel next to it, and the three of them went inside.

"No eyes past this," the hacker said, almost flinching as if in expectation of being punished for the failings of the Ganymede security system.

"Naomi, where does that go?" Holden said, patting the air to let the hacker know he wasn't to blame.

"Looks like an old part of the original dig," she said, her words punctuated by pauses as she worked her console. "Zoned for utility storage. Shouldn't be anything beyond that door but dust and ice."

"Can you get us there?" Holden asked.

Naomi and Prax both said, "Yes," at the same time.

"Then that's where we're going."

He gestured for Prax and the hacker to lead the way back out to the front room, then followed them. Amos was sitting at the table, spinning one of the chicken cans on its edge like a thick coin. In the light gravity of the moon, it seemed like it would keep spinning forever. His expression was distant and unreadable.

"You did the job," Holden said to the hacker, who was staring at Amos, his face twitching from fear to rage and back again. "So you'll get paid. We aren't going to stiff you."

Before the kid could reply, Amos stood up and picked up the case of canned chicken. He turned it over and dumped all the remaining cans on the floor, where a few rolled away to various corners of the small room.

"Keep the change, asshole," he said, then threw the empty box into the tiny kitchen nook.

"And with that," Holden said, "we'll take our leave."

After Amos and Prax had gone out the door, Holden backed out, keeping a watchful eye on the hacker to make sure there were no misguided attempts at revenge. He shouldn't have worried. The minute Amos was out the door, the kid just started picking up the chicken cans and stacking them on the table.

As he backed out and closed the door behind him, Naomi said, "You know what it means, don't you?"

"Which thing?" he replied, then said to Amos, "Back to the ship."

"Prax said all the kids with Mei's particular disorder were missing," Naomi continued. "And her doctor is the one who took her out of school."

"So we can probably assume he, or people working with him, took the others," Holden agreed.

Amos and Prax were walking together up the corridor, the big man still wearing his distant look. Prax put a hand on his arm, and Holden heard him whisper, "Thank you." Amos just shrugged.

"Why would he want those kids?" Naomi asked.

"The better question to me is, how did he know to take them just hours before the shooting started?"

"Yeah," Naomi said, her voice quiet. "Yeah, how did he know that?"

"Because he's the reason why things went pear-shaped," Holden replied, saying out loud what they were both thinking.

"If he's got all of those kids, and he or the people he's with were able to start a shooting war between Mars and Earth to cover up the snatch…"

"Starts to feel like a strategy we've seen before, doesn't it? We need to know what's on the other side of that door."

"One of two things," Naomi said. "Nothing, because after the snatch they got the hell off this moon…"

"Or," Holden continued, "a whole lot of guys with guns."

"Yeah."

The galley of the *Somnambulist* was quiet as Prax and Holden's crew watched the video again. Naomi had pieced together all the security footage of Mei's abduction into a single long loop. They watched as her doctor carried her through various corridors, up a lift, and finally to the door of the abandoned parts of the station. After the third viewing, Holden gestured for Naomi to turn it off.

"What do we know?" he said, his fingers drumming on the table.

"The kid's not scared. She's not fighting to get away," Amos said.

"She's known Dr. Strickland all her life," Prax replied. "He would be almost like family to her."

"Which means they bought him," Naomi said. "Or this plan has been going on for…"

"Four years," Prax said.

"Four years," Naomi repeated. "Which is a hell of a long con to run unless the stakes are huge."

"Is it kidnapping? If they want a ransom payment…"

"Doesn't wash. A couple hours after Mei disappears into that hatch," Holden said, pointing at the image frozen on Naomi's screen, "Earth and Mars are shooting each other. Somebody's going to a lot of trouble to grab sixteen sick kids and hide the fact they did it."

"If Protogen wasn't toast," Amos said, "I'd say this is exactly the kind of shit they'd pull."

"And whoever it is has significant tech resources too," Naomi said. "They were able to hack the school's system even before the Ganymede netsec was collapsing from the battle, and insert that woman's records into Mei's file without any trace of tampering."

"Some of the kids in her school had very rich or powerful parents," Prax said. "Their security would have to be top notch."

Holden drummed out a last rhythm on the tabletop with both hands, then said, "Which all leads us back to the big question. What's waiting for us on the other side of that door?"

"Corporate goons," Amos said.

"Nothing," Naomi said.

"Mei," Prax said quietly. "It might be Mei."

"We need to be prepared for all three possibilities: violence, gathering clues, or rescuing a kid. So let's put together a plan.

Naomi, I want a terminal with a radio link that I can plug into whatever network we find on the other side, and give you a doorway in."

"Yep," Naomi said, already getting up from the table and heading toward the keel ladder.

"Prax, you need to come up with a way for Mei to trust us if we find her, and give us details on any complications her illness might cause during a rescue. How quickly do we need to get her back here for her meds? Things like that."

"Okay," Prax said, pulling out his terminal and making notes.

"Amos?"

"Yeah, Cap?"

"That leaves violence to us. Let's tool up."

The smile began and ended at the corners of Amos' eyes.

"Fuck yeah."

Chapter Fourteen: Prax

Prax didn't understand how near he was to collapse until he ate. Canned chicken with some kind of spicy chutney, soft no-crumb crackers of the type usually used in zero-g environments, a tall glass of beer. He wolfed it down, his body suddenly ravenous and unstoppable.

After he finished vomiting, the woman who seemed to take care of all the small practical matters on the ship—he knew her name was Naomi, but he kept wanting to call her Cassandra, because she looked like an intern by that name he'd worked with three years earlier—switched him to a thin protein broth that his atrophied gut could actually handle. Over the course of hours, his mind started coming back. It felt like waking up over and over without falling asleep in between; sitting in the hold of Holden's ship, he'd find himself noticing the shift in his cognition, how much more clearly he could think and how good it felt to come back to himself. And then a few minutes later, some set of sugar-deprived ganglia would struggle back to function, and it would all happen again.

And with every step back toward real consciousness, he felt the drive growing, pushing him toward the door that Strickland and Mei had gone through.

"Doctor, huh?" the big one—Amos—said.

"I got my degree here. The university's really good. Lots of grant money. Or...now I suppose there used to be."

"I was never much for formal education myself."

The relief ship's mess hall was tiny and scarred by age. The woven carbon filament walls had cracks in the enameling, and the tabletop was pitted from years, maybe decades, of use. The lighting was a thin spectrum shifted toward pink that would have killed any plants living under it in about three days. Amos had a canvas sack filled with formed plastic boxes of different sizes, each of which seemed to have a firearm of some kind inside. He had unrolled a square of red felt and disassembled a huge matte-black pistol on it. The delicate metal parts looked like sculpture. Amos dipped a cotton swab into a bright blue cleaning solution and rubbed it gently on a silver mechanism attached to a black metal tube, polishing metal plates that were already bright as a mirror.

Prax found his hands moving toward the disassembled pieces, willing them to come together. To be already cleaned and polished and remade. Amos pretended not to notice in a way that meant he was very much aware.

"I don't know why they would have taken her," Prax said. "Dr. Strickland has always been great with her. He never...I mean, he'd never hurt her. I don't think he'd hurt her."

"Yeah, probably not," Amos said. He dipped the swab into the cleaning fluid again and started on a metal rod with a spring wrapped around it.

"I really need to get there," Prax said. He didn't say, *Every minute here is a minute that they could be hurting Mei. That she could be dying or getting shipped offworld.* He tried to keep his words from sounding like a whine or a demand, but they seemed to come out as both.

"Getting ready's the shitty part," Amos said, as if agreeing to something. "You want to get right out into it right the fuck now. Get it over with."

"Well, yes," Prax said.

"I get that," Amos said. "It's no fun, but you've got to get through it. Going in without your gear ready, you might as well not go. Plus which the girl's been gone for how long now?"

"Since the fighting. Since the mirror came down."

"Chances of another hour making much difference are pretty small, right?"

"But—"

"Yeah," Amos said with a sigh. "I know. This is the tough part. Not as bad as waiting for us to get back, though. That's gonna suck even worse."

Amos put down the swab and started fitting the long black spring back over the spindle of bright metal. The alcohol fumes of the cleaning solution stung Prax's eyes.

"I'm waiting for *you*," Prax said.

"Yeah, I know," Amos said. "And I'll make sure we're real quick about it. The captain's a real good guy, but he can get kind of distracted sometimes. I'll keep him on point. No trouble."

"No," Prax said, "I don't mean I'm waiting for you when you go to that door. I mean I'm waiting for you *right now*. I'm waiting to go there with you."

Amos slid the spring and spindle into the shell of the gun, twisting it gently with his fingertips. Prax didn't know when he'd risen to his feet.

"How many gunfights have you been in?" Amos asked. His voice was low and wide and gentle. "Because I've been in... shit. This'll be eleven for me. Maybe twelve, if you count the one time when the guy got up again as a different fight. Point is, if you want your little girl safe, you don't want her in a tunnel with a guy firing a gun who doesn't know what he's doing."

As if in punctuation, Amos slid the gun together. The metal clacked.

"I'll be fine," Prax said, but his legs were trembling, just standing up. Amos held up the gun.

"This ready to fire?" Amos asked.

"Sorry?"

"If you pick this gun up right now, point it at a bad guy, pull the trigger, does it go bang? You just watched me put it together. Dangerous or safe?"

Prax opened his mouth, then closed it. An ache just behind his sternum grew a notch worse. Amos started to put the gun down.

"Safe," Prax said.

"You sure about that, Doc?"

"You didn't put any bullets in it. It's safe."

"You're *sure*?"

"Yes."

Amos frowned at the gun.

"Well, yeah, that's right," he said. "But you're still not going."

Voices came from the narrow hallway from the airlock. Jim Holden's voice wasn't what Prax had thought it would be. He'd expected him to be serious, grave. Instead, even during the times like now, when the distress clipped his vowels short and tightened his voice, there was a lightness to him. The woman's voice—*Naomi*, not Cassandra—wasn't deeper, but it was darker.

"Those are the numbers," she said.

"They're wrong," Holden said, ducking into the mess. "They've got to be wrong. It doesn't make sense."

"What's the word, Cap'n?" Amos asked.

"Security's not going to be any use," Holden said. "The locals are stretched too thin trying to keep the place from straight-out catastrophe."

"Which is why maybe we shouldn't be going in with guns drawn," Naomi said.

"Please, can we not have that conversation again right now?"

Her mouth hardened and Amos pointedly looked at the gun,

polishing the parts that already shone. Prax had the sense of walking in on a much longer conversation.

"This guy who grabs a gun first and talks later..." Naomi said. "You didn't used to be him. You *aren't* him."

"Well, I need to be him today," Holden said in a voice that closed the subject. The silence was uncomfortable.

"What's wrong with the numbers?" Prax asked. Holden looked at him, confused. "You said there was something wrong with the numbers."

"They're saying that the death rate's going up. But that's got to be wrong. The fighting was...what? One day? Day and a half? Why would things be getting worse now?"

"No," Prax said. "That's right. It's the cascade. It'll get worse."

"What's the cascade?" Naomi asked. Amos slid the pistol into its box and hauled out a longer case. A shotgun maybe. His gaze was on Prax, waiting.

"It's the basic obstacle of artificial ecosystems. In a normal evolutionary environment, there's enough diversity to cushion the system when something catastrophic happens. That's nature. Catastrophic things happen all the time. But nothing we can build has the depth. One thing goes wrong, and there's only a few compensatory pathways that can step in. They get overstressed. Fall out of balance. When the next one fails, there are even fewer paths, and then they're more stressed. It's a simple complex system. That's the technical name for it. Because it's simple, it's prone to cascades, and because it's complex, you can't predict what's going to fail. Or how. It's computationally impossible."

Holden leaned against the wall, his arms folded. It was still odd, seeing him in person. He looked the same as he had on the screens, and he also didn't.

"Ganymede Station," Holden said, "is the most important food supply and agricultural center outside Earth and Mars. It can't just collapse. They wouldn't let it. People come here to have their babies, for God's sake."

Prax tilted his head. A day before, he wouldn't have been able to explain this. For one thing, he wouldn't have had the blood sugar to fuel thought. For another, he wouldn't have had anyone to say it to. It was good to be able to think again, even if it was only so he could explain how bad things had become.

"Ganymede's dead," Prax said. "The tunnels will probably survive, but the environmental and social structures are already broken. Even if we could somehow get the environmental systems back in place—and really, we can't without a lot of work—how many people are going to stay here now? How many would be going to jail? Something's going to fill the niche, but it won't be what was here before."

"Because of the cascade," Holden said.

"Yes," Prax said. "That's what I was trying to say before. To Amos. It's all going to fall apart. The relief effort's going to make the fall a little more graceful, maybe. But it's too late. It's too late, and since Mei's out there, and we don't know what's going to break, I have to go with you."

"Prax," Cassandra said. *No. Naomi.* Maybe his brain wasn't really up to full power even now.

"Strickland and that woman, even if they think they can keep her safe, they can't. You see? Even if they're not hurting her, even if they're not, everything around them is going to fall apart. What if they run out of air? What if they don't understand what's happening?"

"I know this is hard," Holden said. "But shouting about it won't help."

"I'm not shouting. I'm not shouting. I'm just telling you that they took my little girl away, and I need to go and get her. I need to be there when you open that door. Even if she's not there. Even if she's dead, I need to be the one who finds her."

The sound was crisp and professional and oddly beautiful: a magazine slipping into a pistol. Prax hadn't seen Amos take it back out of its box, but the dark metal was in the man's huge hand. Dwarfed by his fingers. While he watched, Amos chambered a round. Then he took the gun by its barrel, careful to keep it pointing at the wall, and held it out.

"But I thought…" Prax said. "You said I wasn't…"

Amos stretched his arms out another half inch. The gesture was unmistakable. *Take it.* Prax took it. It was heavier than it looked.

"Um. Amos?" Holden said. "Did you just give him a loaded gun?"

"Doc needs to go, Cap'n," Amos said with a shrug. "So I'm thinking he should probably go."

Prax saw the look that passed between Holden and Naomi.

"We might want to talk about that decision-making process, Amos," Naomi said, shaping the words carefully.

"You betcha," Amos said. "Soon as we get back."

Prax had been walking through the station for weeks as a native, a local. A refugee with nowhere to flee. He'd gotten used to how the hallways looked, how people's eyes slid over him in case he'd try to lay his burdens on them. Now that Prax was fed and armed and part of a group, the station had become a different place. People's eyes still slid across them, but the fear was different, and hunger fought against it. Holden and Amos didn't have the gray of malnutrition or the haunted look around their eyes of seeing everything they thought was immutable collapse. Naomi was back at the ship, hacked into the local security network and ready to coordinate the three of them in case they got split up.

For the first time perhaps in his life, Prax felt like an outsider. He looked at his hometown and saw what Holden would see: a huge hallway with paints and dyes worked into the ice up high on the wall; the lower half, where people might accidentally touch it, covered in thick insulation. Ganymede's raw ice would strip the flesh from bone with even the briefest contact. The hallway was too dark now, the floodlights beginning to fail. A wide corridor Prax had walked through every day he was at school was a dim chamber filled with the sounds of dripping water as the climate regulation failed. The plants that weren't dead were dying, and the air was getting the stale taste at the back of his throat that meant the emergency recyclers would be coming on soon. Should be coming on soon. Had better.

Holden was right, though. The thin-faced, desperate people they passed had been food scientists and soil technicians, gas exchange experts and agricultural support staff. If Ganymede Station died, the cascade wouldn't stop here. Once the last load of food lifted off, the Belt, the Jovian system, and the myriad long-term bases in their own orbits around the sun would have to find a different way to get vitamins and micronutrients for their kids. Prax started wondering whether the bases on the far planets would be able to sustain themselves. If they had full hydroponics rigs and yeast farms and nothing went wrong...

It was a distraction. It was grasping anything other than the fear of what would be waiting behind that door. He embraced it.

"Hold up! All y'all."

The voice was low and rough and wet, like the man's vocal cords had been taken out and dragged through mud. He stood in the center of the ice tunnels intersecting before them, military-police body armor two sizes too small straining to keep his bulk in. His accent and build said he was Martian.

Amos and Holden paused, turned, looking everywhere but at the man before them. Prax followed their gazes. Other men lurked, half hidden, around them. The sudden panic tasted like copper.

"I make six," Holden said.

"What about the guy with the gray pants?" Amos asked.

"Okay, maybe seven. He's been with us since we left the ship, though. He might be something else."

"Six is still more than three," Naomi said in their ears. "You want me to send backup?"

"Hot damn. We've got backup?" Amos asked. "Gonna have Supitayaporn come down and talk 'em all to death?"

"We can take them," Prax said, reaching for the pistol in his pocket. "We can't let anyone—"

Amos' wide hand closed over his own, keeping the gun in his pocket and out of sight.

"These aren't the ones you shoot," Amos said. "These are the ones you talk to."

Holden stepped toward the Martian. The ease with which he held himself made the assault rifle on his shoulder seem almost innocuous. Even the expensive body armor he wore didn't seem at odds with his casual smile.

"Hey," Holden said. "There a problem, sir?"

"Might be," the Martian drawled. "Might not. That's your call."

"I'll take *not*," Holden said. "Now, if you'll excuse us, we'll be on—"

"Slow down," the Martian said, sidling forward. His face was vaguely like someone Prax had seen before on the tube and never particularly remarked. "You're not from around here."

"I am," Prax said. "I'm Dr. Praxidike Meng. Chief botanist on the RMD-Southern soy farm project. Who are you?"

"Let the cap'n do this," Amos said.

"But—"

"He's pretty good at it."

"I'm thinking you're part of the relief work," the Martian said. "Long way from the docks. Looks like you lost your way. Maybe you need an escort back to where it's safe."

Holden shifted his weight. The assault rifle just happened to slide forward a few inches, not at all provocatively.

"I don't know," Holden said. "We're pretty well protected. I think we can probably take care of ourselves. What kind of fee are you...um, escorts asking?"

"Well now. I count three of you. Call it a hundred in Martian scrip. Five, local."

"How about you follow us down, and I arrange passage for all of you off this ice ball?"

The Martian's jaw dropped.

"That's not funny," he said, but the mask of power and confidence had slipped. Prax had seen the hunger and desperation behind it.

"I'm going to an old tunnel system," Holden said. "Someone

abducted a bunch of kids right before everything went to hell. They took them there. Doc's kid was one of the ones that got snatched. We're going to get her back and politely ask how they knew all this was coming down. Might be resistance. I could use a few people who know what end of the gun points forward."

"You're fucking with me," the Martian said. From the corner of his eye, Prax saw one of the others step forward. A thin woman in cheap protective weave.

"We're OPA," Amos said, then nodded at Holden. "He's James Holden of the *Rocinante*."

"Holy shit," the Martian said. "You are. You're Holden."

"It's the beard," Holden said.

"My name's Wendell. Used to work for Pinkwater Security before the bastards took off, left us here. Way I figure, that voids the contract. You want to pick up some professional firepower, you ain't gonna find better than us."

"How many you got?"

"Six, counting me."

Holden looked over at Amos. Prax felt Amos shrug as much as saw it. The other man they'd been talking about was unrelated after all.

"All right," Holden said. "We tried to talk to local security, but they didn't give us the time of day. Follow me, back us up, and I give you my word you'll get off Ganymede."

Wendell grinned. He'd had one of his incisors dyed red with a small black-and-white design on it.

"Anything you say, boss," he said. Then, lifting his gun: "Form up! We got us a new contract, people. Let's get it done!"

The whoops came from all around them. Prax found the thin woman beside him, grinning and shaking his hand like she was running for office. Prax blinked and smiled back, and Amos put his hand on Prax's shoulder.

"See? Told you. Now let's get moving."

The hallway was darker than it had seemed in the video. The ice had thin melt channels, like pale veins, but the frost covering them was fresh. The door looked like any other of a hundred they'd passed on the way in. Prax swallowed. His stomach ached. He wanted to scream for Mei, to call her name and hear her call back.

"Okay," Naomi said in his ear. "I've got the lock disabled. Whenever you guys are ready."

"No time like the present," Holden said. "Open it up."

The seal around the door hissed.

The door opened.

Chapter Fifteen: Bobbie

Three hours into the first big meeting between the Martian and UN diplomats and they'd only just got past introducing everyone and on to reading the agenda. A squat Earther in a charcoal-gray suit that probably cost more than Bobbie's recon armor droned on about Section 14, Subsection D, Items 1-11, in which they would discuss the effect of past hostilities on commodity pricing pursuant to existing trade agreements. Bobbie looked around, noticed that everyone else at the long oak table was staring with rapt attention at the agenda reader, and stifled the truly epic yawn that was struggling to get out.

She distracted herself by trying to figure out who people were. They'd all been introduced by name and title at some point, but that didn't mean much. Everyone here was an assistant secretary, or undersecretary, or director of something. There were even a few generals, but Bobbie knew enough about how politics worked to know that the military people in the room would be the least important. The people with real power would be the quiet ones with unassuming titles. There were several of those, including a moonfaced man with a skinny tie who'd been introduced as the secretary of something or other. Sitting next to him was someone's grandmother in a bright sari, a splash of yellow in the middle of all the dark brown and dark blue and charcoal gray. She sat and munched pistachios and wore an enigmatic half smile. Bobbie entertained herself for a few minutes by trying to guess if Moonface or Grandma was the boss.

She considered pouring a glass of water from one of the crystal decanters evenly distributed across the table. She wasn't thirsty, but turning her glass over, pouring water into it, and drinking it would burn a minute, maybe two. She glanced down the table and noticed that no one else was drinking the water. Maybe everyone was waiting for someone else to be first.

"Let's take a short break," charcoal-suit man said. "Ten minutes, then we can move on to Section fifteen of the agenda."

People got up and began dispersing toward restrooms and smoking areas. Grandma carried her handbag to a recycling chute and dumped pistachio shells into it. Moonface pulled out his terminal and called someone.

"Jesus," Bobbie said, rubbing her eyes with her palms until she saw stars.

"Problem, Sergeant?" Thorsson said, leaning back in his chair and grinning. "The gravity wearing on you?"

"No," Bobbie said. Then, "Well, yes, but mostly I'm ready to jab a stylus into my eye, just for a change of pace."

Thorsson nodded and patted her hand, a move he was using more often now. It hadn't gotten any less irritating and paternalistic, but now Bobbie was worried that it might mean Thorsson was working up to hitting on her. That would be an uncomfortable moment.

She pulled her hand away and leaned toward Thorsson until he turned and looked her in the eye.

"Why," she whispered, "is no one talking about the goddamned monster? Isn't that why I'm—why *we're* here?"

"You have to understand how these things work," Thorsson said, turning away from her and fiddling with his terminal. "Politics moves slow because the stakes are very high, and no one wants to be the person that screwed it up."

He put his terminal down and gave her a wink. "Careers are at stake here."

"Careers…"

Thorsson just nodded and tapped on his terminal some more.

Careers?

For a moment, she was on her back, staring up into the star-filled void above Ganymede. Her men were dead or dying. Her suit radio dead, her armor a frozen coffin. She saw the thing's face. Without a suit in the radiation and hard vacuum, the red snowfall of flash-frozen blood around its claws. And no one at this table wanted to talk about it because it might affect their careers?

To hell with that.

When the meeting's attendees had shuffled back into the room and taken their places around the table, Bobbie raised her hand. She felt faintly ridiculous, like a fifth-grade student in a room full of adults, but she had no idea what the actual protocol for asking a question was. The agenda reader shot her one annoyed glance, then ignored her. Thorsson reached under the table and sharply squeezed her leg.

She kept her hand up.

"Excuse me?" she said.

People around the table took turns giving her increasingly unfriendly looks and then pointedly turning away. Thorsson upped the pressure on her leg until she'd had enough of him and grabbed his wrist with her other hand. She squeezed until the bones creaked and he snatched his hand away with a surprised gasp. He turned his chair to look at her, his eyes wide and his mouth a flat, lipless line.

Yellow-sari placed a hand on the agenda reader's arm, and he instantly stopped talking. *Okay, that one is the boss*, Bobbie decided.

"I, for one," Grandma said, smiling a mild apology at the room, "would like to hear what Sergeant Draper has to say."

She remembers my name, Bobbie thought. *That's interesting.*

"Sergeant?" Grandma said.

Bobbie, unsure of what to do, stood up.

"I'm just wondering why no one is talking about the monster."

Grandma's enigmatic smile returned. No one spoke. The silence slid adrenaline into Bobbie's blood. She felt her legs starting to tremble. More than anything in the world, she wanted to sit down, to make them all forget her and look away.

She scowled and locked her knees.

"You know," Bobbie said, her voice rising, but she was unable to stop it. "The monster that killed fifty soldiers on Ganymede? The reason we're all here?"

The room was silent. Thorsson stared at her like she had lost her mind. Maybe she had. Grandma tugged once at her yellow sari and smiled encouragement.

"I mean," Bobbie said, holding up the agenda, "I'm sure trade agreements and water rights and who gets to screw who on the second Thursday after the winter solstice is all *very* important!"

She stopped to suck in a long breath, the gravity and her tirade seeming to have robbed her of air. She could see it in their eyes. She could see that if she just stopped now, she'd be an odd thing that happened and everyone could go back to work and quickly forget her. She could see her career not crashing off a cliff in flames.

She discovered that she didn't care.

"But," she said, throwing the agenda across the table, where a surprised man in a brown suit dodged it as though its touch might infect him with whatever Bobbie had, "*what about the fucking monster?*"

Before she could continue, Thorsson popped up from his seat.

"Excuse me for a moment, ladies and gentlemen. Sergeant

Draper is suffering from some post-combat-related stress and needs attention."

He grabbed her elbow and drove her from the room, a rising wave of murmurs pushing at their backs. Thorsson stopped in the conference room's lobby and waited for the door to shut behind him.

"You," Thorsson said, shoving her toward a chair. Normally the skinny intelligence officer couldn't have pushed her anywhere, but all the strength seemed to have run out of her legs, and she collapsed into the seat.

"You," he repeated. Then, to someone on his terminal, he said, "Get down here, now."

"You," he said a third time, pointing at Bobbie, then paced back and forth in front of her chair.

A few minutes later, Captain Martens came trotting into the conference room lobby. He pulled up short when he saw Bobbie slouched in her chair and Thorsson's angry face.

"What—" he started, but Thorsson cut him off.

"This is *your* fault," he said to Martens, then spun to face Bobbie. "And you, Sergeant, have just proven that it was a monumental mistake to bring you along. Any benefit that might have been gained from having the only eyewitness has now been squandered by your...your *idiotic* tirade."

"She—" Martens tried again, but Thorsson poked a finger into his chest and said, "You said you could control her."

Martens gave Thorsson a sad smile.

"No, I never said that. I said I could help her given enough time."

"Doesn't matter," Thorsson said, waving a hand at them. "You're both on the next ship to Mars, where you can explain yourselves to a disciplinary board. Now get out of my sight."

He spun on his heel and slipped back into the conference room, opening the door only wide enough for his narrow body to squeeze through.

Martens sat down in the chair next to Bobbie and let out a long breath.

"So," he said. "What's up?"

"Did I just destroy my career?" she asked.

"Maybe. How do you feel?"

"I feel..." she said, realizing how badly she did want to talk with Martens, and becoming angered by the impulse. "I feel like I need some air."

Before Martens could protest, Bobbie stood up and headed for the elevators.

The UN complex was a city in its own right. Just finding a way out took her the better part of an hour. Along the way, she moved through the chaos and energy of government like a ghost. People hurried past her in the long corridors, talking energetically in clumps or on their hand terminals. Bobbie had never been to Olympia, where the Martian congressional building was located. She'd caught a few minutes of congressional sessions on the government broadcast when an issue she cared about was being discussed, but compared to the activity here at the UN, it was pretty low-key. The people in this building complex governed thirty billion citizens and hundreds of millions of colonists. By comparison, Mars' four billion suddenly seemed like a backwater.

On Mars, it was a generally accepted fact that Earth was a civilization in decay. Lazy, coddled citizens who lived on the government dole. Fat, corrupt politicians who enriched themselves at the expense of the colonies. A degrading infrastructure that spent close to 30 percent of its total output on recycling systems to keep the population from drowning in its own filth. On Mars, there was virtually no unemployment. The entire population was engaged either directly or indirectly in the greatest engineering feat in human history: the terraforming of a planet. It gave everyone a sense of purpose, a shared vision of the future. Nothing like the Earthers, who lived only for their next government payout and their next visit to the drugstore or entertainment malls.

Or at least, that was the story. Suddenly Bobbie wasn't so sure.

Repeated visits to the various information kiosks scattered through the complex eventually got her to an exit door. A bored guard nodded to her as she passed by, and then she was outside.

Outside. Without a suit.

Five seconds later she was clawing at the door, which she now realized was an exit only, trying to get back in. The guard took pity on her and pushed the door open. She ran back inside and collapsed on a nearby settee, gasping and hyperventilating.

"First time?" the guard asked with a smile.

Bobbie found herself unable to speak, but nodded.

"Mars or Luna?"

"Mars," she said once her breathing had slowed.

"Yeah, I knew it. Domes, you know. People who've been in domes just panic a bit. Belters lose their shit. And I mean completely. We wind up shipping them home drugged up to keep them from screaming."

"Yeah," Bobbie said, happy to let the guard ramble while she collected herself. "No kidding."

"They bring you in when it was dark outside?"

"Yeah."

"They do that for offworlders. Helps with the agoraphobia."

"Yeah."

"I'll hold the door open a bit for you. In case you need to come back in again."

The assumption that she'd give it a second try instantly won Bobbie over, and she actually looked at the guard for the first time. Earther short, but with beautiful skin so dark it was almost blue. He had a compact, athletic frame and lovely gray eyes. He was smiling at her without a trace of mockery.

"Thank you," she said. "Bobbie. Bobbie Draper."

"Chuck," he replied. "Look at the ground, then slowly look to the horizon. Whatever you do, don't look straight up."

"I think I got it this time, Chuck, but thanks."

Chuck gave her uniform a quick glance and said, "Semper fi, Gunny."

"Oohrah," Bobbie replied with a grin.

On her second trip outside, she did as Chuck had recommended and looked down at the ground for a few moments. This helped reduce the feeling of massive sensory overload. But only a little. A thousand scents hit her nose, competing for dominance. The rich aroma of plants and soil she would expect in a garden dome. The oil and hot metal from a fabrication lab. The ozone of electric motors. All of them hit her at once, layered on top of each other and mixed with scents too exotic to name. And the sounds were a constant cacophony. People talking, construction machinery, electric cars, a transorbital shuttle lifting off, all at once and all the time. It was no wonder it had caused a panic. Just two senses' worth of data threatened to overwhelm her. Add that impossibly blue sky that stretched on forever...

Bobbie stood outside, eyes closed, breathing until she heard Chuck let the door close behind her. Now she was committed. Turning around and asking Chuck to let her back in would be admitting defeat. He'd clearly done some time in the UNMC, and she wasn't going to look weak in front of the competition. Hell no.

When her ears and nose had gotten more accustomed to the barrage of inputs, she opened her eyes again, looking down at the concrete of the walkway. Slowly, she lifted them till the horizon was in view. Ahead of her lay long sidewalks passing through meticulously tended green space. Beyond it in the distance was a gray wall that must have stood ten meters high, with guard towers regularly spaced on it. The UN complex had a surprising amount of security. She wondered if she'd be able to get out.

She needn't have worried. As she approached the guarded gate to the outside world, the security system queried her terminal, which assured it of her VIP status. A camera above the guard post scanned her face, compared it to the picture on file, and verified her identity while she was still twenty meters from the gate. When she reached the exit, the guard snapped her a sharp salute and asked if she'd need a ride.

"No, just going for a walk," she said.

The guard smiled and wished her a good day. She began walking down the street leading away from the UN complex, then turned around to see two armed security personnel following her at a discreet distance. She shrugged and walked on. Somebody would probably lose their job if a VIP like her got lost or hurt.

Once Bobbie was outside the UN compound, her agoraphobia lessened. Buildings rose around her like walls of steel and glass, moving the dizzying skyline far enough up that she no longer saw it. Small electric cars whizzed down the streets, trailing a high-pitched whine and the scent of ozone.

And people were *everywhere*.

Bobbie had gone to a couple of games at Armstrong Stadium on Mars, to watch the Red Devils play. The stadium had seats for twenty thousand fans. Because the Devils were usually at the bottom of the standings, it generally held less than half that. That relatively modest number was the greatest number of humans Bobbie had ever seen in one place at one time. There were billions of people on Mars, but there weren't a lot of open spaces for them to gather. Standing at an intersection, looking down two streets that seemed to stretch into infinity, Bobbie was sure she saw more than the average attendance of a Red Devils game just walking on the sidewalks. She tried to imagine how many people were in the buildings that rose to vertigo-inducing heights in every direction around her, and couldn't. Millions of people, probably in just the buildings and streets she could see.

And if Martian propaganda was right, most of the people she could see right now didn't have jobs. She tried to imagine that, not having any particular place you had to be on any given day.

What the Earthers had discovered is that when people have nothing else to do, they have babies. For a brief period in the twentieth and twenty-first centuries, the population had looked like it might shrink rather than continue to grow. As more and more women went into higher education, and from there to jobs, the average family size grew smaller.

A few decades of massive employment shrinkage ended that.

Or, again, that was what she'd been taught in school. Only here on Earth, where food grew on its own, where air was just a by-product of random untended plants, where resources lay thick on the ground, could a person actually choose not to do anything at all. There was enough extra created by those who felt the need to work that the surplus could feed the rest. A world no longer of the haves and the have-nots, but of the engaged and the apathetic.

Bobbie found herself standing next to a street-level coffee shop and took a seat.

"Can I get you anything?" a smiling young woman with brightly dyed blue hair asked.

"What's good?"

"We make the best soy-milk tea, if you like that."

"Sure," Bobbie said, not sure what soy-milk tea was, but liking those two things separately enough to take a chance.

The blue-haired girl bustled away and chatted with an equally young man behind the bar while he made the tea. Bobbie looked around her, noticing that everyone she saw working was about the same age.

When the tea arrived, she said, "Hey, do you mind if I ask you something?"

The girl shrugged, her smile an invitation.

"Is everyone who works here the same age?"

"Well," she said. "Pretty close. Gotta collect your pre-university credits, right?"

"I'm not from here," Bobbie said. "Explain that."

Blue seemed actually to see her for the first time, looking over her uniform and its various insignias.

"Oh, wow, Mars, right? I want to go there."

"Yeah, it's great. So tell me about the credits thing."

"They don't have that on Mars?" she asked, puzzled. "Okay, so, if you apply to a university, you have to have at least a year of work credits. To make sure you like working. You know, so they don't waste classroom space on people who will just go on basic afterward."

"Basic?"

"You know, basic support."

"I think I understand," Bobbie said. "Basic support is the money you live on if you don't work?"

"Not money, you know, just basic. Gotta work to have money."

"Thanks," Bobbie said, then sipped her milk tea as Blue trotted to another table. The tea was delicious. She had to admit, it made a sad kind of sense to do some early winnowing before spending the resources to educate people. Bobbie told her terminal to pay the bill, and it flashed a total at her after calculating the exchange rate. She added a nice tip for the blue-haired girl who wanted more from life than basic support.

Bobbie wondered if Mars would become like this after the terraforming. If Martians didn't have to fight every day to make enough resources to survive, would they turn into this? A culture where you could actually *choose* if you wanted to contribute? The work hours and collective intelligence of fifteen billion humans just tossed away as acceptable losses for the system. It made Bobbie sad to think of. All that effort to get to a point where they could live like this. Sending their kids to work at a coffee shop to see if they were up to contributing. Letting them live the rest of their lives on *basic* if they weren't.

But one thing was for sure: All that running and exercising the Martian Marines did at one full gravity was bullshit. There was no way Mars could ever beat Earth on the ground. You could drop every Martian soldier, fully armed, into just one Earth city and the citizens would overwhelm them using rocks and sticks.

Deep in the grip of pathos, she suddenly felt a massive weight lift that she hadn't even realized she'd been carrying. Thorsson and his bullshit didn't matter. The pissing contest with Earth didn't matter. Making Mars into another Earth didn't matter, not if this was where it was headed.

All that mattered was finding out who'd put that thing on Ganymede.

She tossed off the last of her tea and thought, *I'll need a ride.*

Chapter Sixteen: Holden

Beyond the door lay a long hallway that looked, to Holden, exactly the same as every other hallway on Ganymede: ice walls with moisture-resistant and insulated structural plates and inset conduit, rubberized walking surface, full-spectrum LEDs to mimic sunlight slanting down from the blue skies of Earth. They could have been anywhere.

"We're sure this is right, Naomi?"

"That's the one we saw Mei go through in the hacker's footage," she replied.

"Okay," he said, then dropped to one knee and motioned for his ad hoc army to do the same. When everyone was in a rough circle around him, he said, "Our overwatch, Naomi, has intel on the layout of these tunnels, but not much else. We have no idea where the bad guys are, or even if they're still here."

Prax started to object, but Amos quieted him with a heavy hand on his back.

"So we could conceivably leave a lot of intersections at our back. I don't like that."

"Yeah," said Wendell, the Pinkwater leader. "I don't like that much either."

"So we're going to leave a lookout at each intersection until we know where we're going," Holden replied, then said, "Naomi, put all their hand terminals on our channel. Guys, put in your earbuds. Comm discipline is don't speak unless I ask a direct question, or someone is about to die."

"Roger," said Wendell, echoed by the rest of his team.

"Once we know what we're looking at, I'll call all the lookouts up to our position if needed. If not, they're our way out of here if we're in over our heads."

Nods all around.

"Outstanding. Amos is point. Wendell, you cover our asses. Everyone else, string out at one-meter intervals," Holden said, then tapped on Wendell's breastplate. "We do this thing clean, and I'll talk to my OPA people about putting a few credits in your accounts in addition to getting you offworld."

"Righteous," the thin woman with the cheap armor said, and then racked a round in her machine pistol.

"Okay, let's go. Amos, Naomi's map says fifty meters to another pressure door, then some warehouse space."

Amos nodded, then shouldered his weapon, a heavy automatic shotgun with a thick magazine. He had several more magazines and a number of grenades dangling from his Martian armor's harness. The metal clicked a little as he walked. Amos headed off down the hallway at a fast walk. Holden gave a quick glance behind, gratified to see the Pinkwater people keeping up the pace and the spacing. They might look half starved, but they knew what they were doing.

"Cap, there's a tunnel coming off to the right just before the pressure door," Amos said, stopping and dropping to one knee to cover the unexpected corridor.

It didn't appear on the map. That meant that new tunnels had been dug *after* the station specs had last been updated. Modifications like that meant he had even less information than he'd thought. It wasn't a good thing.

"Okay," Holden said, pointing at the thin woman with the machine pistol. "You are?"

"Paula," she said.

"Paula, this is your intersection. Try not to shoot anyone that doesn't shoot at you first, but do *not* let anyone past you for any reason."

"Solid copy on that," Paula said, and took up a position looking down the side corridor with her weapon at the ready.

Amos pulled a grenade off his harness and handed it to her.

"Just in case shit goes down," he said. Paula nodded, settled her back against the wall. Amos, taking point, moved toward the pressure door.

"Naomi," Holden said, looking over the door and locking mechanism. "Pressure door, uh, 223-B6. Pop it."

"Got it," she said. A few seconds later, Holden heard the bolts retract.

"Ten meters to the next mapped intersection," he said, then looked at the Pinkwater people and picked one gruff-looking older man at random. "That's your intersection when we get there."

The man nodded, and Holden gestured at Amos. The mechanic took hold of the hatch with his right hand and began counting down from five with his left. Holden took up a position facing the door, his assault rifle at the ready.

When Amos hit one, Holden took a deep breath, and he burst through the door as Amos yanked it open a split second later.

Nothing.

Just another ten meters of corridor, dimly lit by the few LEDs that hadn't failed in the decades since its last use. Years of micro-frost melt had built a texture over the surface of the walls like dripping spiderwebs. It looked delicate, but it was mineralized as hard as stone. It reminded Holden of a graveyard.

Amos began advancing to the intersection and the next hatch, his gun aimed down the hallway. Holden followed him, his rifle tracking right as he kept it aimed at the side passage, the reflex to cover every possible ingress point to their position having become automatic over the last year.

His year as a cop.

Naomi had said this wasn't him. He'd left the Navy without see-ing live combat outside pirate hunting from the comfort of a war-ship's operations deck. He'd worked for years on the *Canterbury*, hauling ice from Saturn to the Belt without ever having to worry about something more violent than drunken ice buckers fighting out their boredom. He'd been the peacemaker, the one who always found the way to keep things cool. When tempers flared, he'd keep it calm or keep it funny or just sit for a shift and listen to someone rave and rant whatever it was out of their system.

This new person he'd become reached for his gun first and talked second. Maybe she was right. How many ships had he slagged in the year since Eros? A dozen? More? He comforted himself with the thought that they were all very bad people. The worst kind of carrion eaters, using the chaos of war and the retreat of the Coalition Navy as an opportunity to pillage. The kind of people who'd strip all the expensive parts off your engine, steal your spare air, and leave you adrift to suffocate. Every one of their ships he'd shot down had probably saved dozens of innocent ships, hundreds of lives. But doing it had taken something from him that he occasionally felt the lack of.

Occasions like when Naomi had said, *This isn't you.*

If they tracked down the secret base where Mei had been taken, there was a good chance they'd have to fight to get her back. Holden found himself hoping it would bother him, if for no other reason than to prove that it still could.

"Cap? You okay?"

Amos was staring at him.

"Yeah," Holden said, "I just need a different job."

"Might not be the best moment for a career change, Cap."

"Fair point," Holden said, and pointed to the older Pinkwater man he'd singled out before. "This is your intersection. Same instructions. Hold it unless I call you."

The older guy shrugged and nodded, then turned to Amos. "Don't I get a grenade too?"

"Nah," Amos said, "Paula's cuter than you." He counted down from five, and Holden went through the door, same as last time.

He'd been ready for another featureless gray corridor, but on the other side there was a wide-open space, with a few tables and dusty equipment scattered haphazardly around the room. A massive 3-D copier emptied of resin and partially disassembled, a few light industrial waldoes, the kind of complex automated supply cabinet that usually lurked under desks in scientific labs or medical bays. The mineralized webwork was on the walls but not the boxes or equipment. A glass-walled cube two meters to a side sat off in one corner. One of the tables had a small bundle of sheets or tarps piled on it. Across the room another hatch stood closed.

Holden pointed to the abandoned equipment and said to Wendell, "See if you can find a network access point. If you can, plug this into it." He handed Naomi's hastily rigged network bridge to him.

Amos sent two of the remaining Pinkwater people up to the next hatch to cover it, then came back to Holden and gestured with his gun toward the glass box.

"Big enough for a couple kids," he said. "Think that's where they kept 'em?"

"Maybe," Holden said, moving over to examine it. "Prax, can you—" Holden stopped when he realized the botanist had gone over to the tables and was standing next to the bundle of rags. With Prax standing next to the bundle, Holden's perspective shifted and suddenly it didn't look like a pile of rags at all. It looked very much like a small body under a sheet.

Prax was staring at it, his hand darting toward it and then pulling back. He was shaking all over.

"This...this is..." he said to no one in particular, his hand moving out and back again.

Holden looked at Amos, then gestured at Prax with his eyes. The big mechanic moved over to him and put a hand on his arm.

"How's about you let us take a look at that, okay?"

Holden let Amos guide Prax a few steps away from the table before he moved over to it. When he lifted the sheet to look under, Prax made a sharp noise like the intake of breath before a scream. Holden shifted his body to block Prax's view.

A small boy lay on the table. He was skinny, with a mop of unruly black hair and dark skin. His clothes were bright: yellow pants and a green shirt with a cartoon crocodile and daisies. It wasn't immediately clear what had killed him.

Holden heard a commotion and turned around to see Prax, red-faced and struggling to get past Amos to the table. The mechanic was restraining him with one arm in a grip that was halfway between a wrestling hold and an embrace.

"It's not her," Holden said. "It's a kid, but it's not her. A boy. Four, maybe five years old."

When Amos heard that, he let the struggling Prax go. The botanist rushed to the table, flipping the sheet over and giving one quick cry.

"That's Katoa," Prax said. "I know him. His father..."

"It's not Mei," Holden repeated, putting a hand on Prax's shoulder. "We need to keep looking."

Prax shrugged his hand off.

"It's not Mei," Holden said again.

"But Strickland was here," Prax said. "He was their doctor. I thought if he was with them, they'd be..."

Holden said nothing. He was thinking the same thing. If one of the kids was dead, they could all be.

"I thought that meant they'd keep them alive," Prax said. "But they let Katoa die. They just let him die and they put him under this sheet. Basia, I'm so sorry..."

Holden grabbed Prax and spun him around. The way he imagined a cop would.

"That," he said, pointing at the small body on the table, "is not Mei. Do you want to find her? Then we need to keep moving."

Prax's eyes were filled with tears and his shoulders shook in silent sobs, but he nodded and walked away from the table. Amos watched him carefully. The mechanic's expression was unreadable. The thought came unbidden: *I hope bringing Prax was a good idea.*

Across the room, Wendell whistled and waved a hand. He pointed at Naomi's network access rig plugged into a port in the wall and gave the thumbs-up.

"Naomi, you in?" Holden said while he pulled the sheet back up to cover the dead boy.

"Yep, I'm in," she said, her tone distracted as she worked with the incoming data. "Traffic in this node is encrypted. Got the *Somnambulist* started on it, but she's not nearly as smart as the *Roci*. This could take a while."

"Keep trying," Holden replied, and signaled to Amos. "But if there's traffic on the network, someone's still here."

"If you wait a minute," Naomi said, "I might be able to give you the security cameras and a more up-to-date floor plan."

"Feed us what you can, when you can, but we're not waiting."

Amos ambled over to Holden and tapped the visor of his helmet. Prax was standing alone by the glass cube, staring into it like there was something to see. Holden expected Amos to say something about the man, but Amos surprised him.

"Been paying attention to the temperature, Cap?"

"Yeah," Holden replied. "Every time I check it says 'cold as hell.' "

"I was just over by the door," Amos continued. "It went up about half a degree."

Holden thought about that for a moment, double-checking it on his own HUD and tapping his fingers on his thigh.

"There's climate in the next room. They're heating it."

"Seems likely," Amos said, shifting the big auto-shotgun into both hands and thumbing off the safety.

Holden motioned the remaining Pinkwater people over to them.

"It looks like we've come to the inhabited portion of this base. Amos and I go in first. You three"—Holden pointed at the three Pinkwater people who weren't Wendell—"follow and cover our flanks. Wendell, you cover our asses and make sure we can get back out in a hurry if things go bad. Prax—"

Holden stopped, looking around for the botanist. He had quietly slipped over to the door into the next room. He'd taken the handgun Amos had given him out of his pocket. As Holden watched, he reached out and opened the door, then walked deliberately through.

"Fuck me," Amos said conversationally.

"Shit," Holden said. Then, "Go, go, go," as he rushed toward the now open door.

Just before he got to the hatch, he heard Prax say, "Nobody move," in a loud but quavering voice.

Holden burst through into the room on the other side, going right while Amos came through just behind him and went left. Prax stood a few feet past the door, the large black handgun looking improbable in his pale, shaking hand. The area itself looked a lot like the one they'd just left, except that this one had a small crowd of people in it. Armed people. Holden tried to take in everything that could be used as cover. A half dozen large gray packing crates with scientific equipment in various states of disassembly in them squatted around the room. Someone's hand terminal was propped up on a bench and blaring dance music. On one of the crates sat several open boxes of pizza with most of the slices missing, several of which were still clutched in people's hands. He tried to count them. Four. Eight. An even dozen, all of them wide about the eye and glancing around, thinking about what to do.

It looked to Holden very much like a room full of people packing up to move, taking a short lunch break. Except that the people in this room all had holsters at their sides, and they had left the corpse of a small child to rot in the next room over.

"Nobody! Move!" Prax repeated, this time with more force.

"You should listen to him," Holden added, moving the barrel of his assault rifle in a slow scan across the room. To drive the point home, Amos sidled up to the nearest worker and casually slammed the butt of his auto-shotgun into the man's ribs, dropping him to the floor like a bag of wet sand. Holden heard the tramping of his Pinkwater people rushing into the room behind him and taking up cover positions.

"Wendell," Holden said, not lowering his rifle. "Please disarm these people for me."

"No," said a stern-faced woman with a slice of pizza in her hand. "No, I don't think so."

"Excuse me?" Holden said.

"No," the woman repeated, taking another bite of her pizza. Around a mouthful of food, she said, "There are only seven of you. There are twelve of us just in this room alone. And there are a lot more behind us that will come running at the first gunshot. So, no, you don't get to disarm us."

She smiled a greasy smile at Holden, then took another bite. Holden could smell the cheese-and-pepperoni smell of good pizza over the top of Ganymede's ever-present odor of ice and the scent of his own sweat. It made his stomach give an ill-timed rumble. Prax pointed his handgun at the woman, though his hand was now shaking so badly that she probably didn't feel particularly threatened.

Amos gave him a sidelong glance as if to ask, *What now, chief?*

In Holden's mind, the room shifted into a tactical problem with an almost physical click. The eleven potential combatants who were still standing were in three clusters. None of them were wearing visible armor. Amos would almost certainly drop the group of four to the far left of the room in a single burst from his auto-shotgun. Holden was pretty sure he could take down the three directly in front of him. That left four for the Pinkwater people to handle. Best not to count on Prax for any of it.

He finished the split-second tally of potential casualties, and almost of its own volition, his thumb clicked the assault rifle to full auto.

This is not you.

Shit.

"We don't have to do this," he said, instead of opening fire. "No one has to die here today. We're looking for a little girl. Help us find her, and everyone walks away from this."

Holden could see the arrogance and bravado in the woman's face for the mask it was. Behind that, there was worry as she weighed the casualties her team would suffer against the risks of talking it out and seeing where that went. Holden gave her a smile and a nod to help her decide. *Talk to me. We're all rational people here.*

Except that not all of them were.

"Where's Mei?" Prax yelled, poking the gun at her as if his gesture would be somehow translated through the air. "Tell me where Mei is!"

"I—" she started to reply, but Prax screamed out, "Where's my little girl!" and cocked his gun.

As if in slow motion, Holden saw eleven hands dart down to the holsters at their belts.

Shit.

Chapter Seventeen: Prax

In the cinema and games that formed the basis of Prax's understanding of how people of violence interacted, the cocking of a gun was less a threat than a kind of punctuation mark. A security agent questioning someone might begin with threats and slaps, but when he cocked his gun, that meant it was time to take him seriously. It wasn't something Prax had considered any more carefully than which urinal to use when he wasn't the only one in the men's room or how to step on and off a transport tube. It was the untaught etiquette of received wisdom. You yelled, you threatened, you cocked your gun, and then people talked.

"Where's my little girl!" he yelled.

He cocked his pistol.

The reaction was almost immediate: a sharp, stuttering report like a high-pressure valve failing, but much louder. He danced back, almost dropping the pistol. Had he fired it by mistake? But no, his finger hadn't touched the trigger. The air smelled sharp, acidic. The woman with the pizza was gone. No, not gone. She was on the ground. Something terrible had happened to her jaw. As he watched, her ruined mouth moved, as though she was trying to speak. Prax could hear only a high-pitched squeal. He wondered if his eardrums had ruptured. The woman with the destroyed jaw took a long, shuddering breath and then didn't take another. With a sense of detachment, he noticed that she'd drawn her pistol. It was still clutched in her hand. He wasn't sure when she'd done that. The handset playing dance music transitioned to a different song that only faintly made it past the ringing in his ears.

"I didn't shoot her," he said. His voice sounded like he was in partial vacuum, the air too thin to support the energy of sound waves. But he could breathe. He wondered again if the gunfire had ruptured his eardrums. He looked around. Everyone was gone. He was alone in the room. Or no, they were behind cover. It occurred to him that he should probably be behind cover too. Only nobody was firing and he wasn't sure where to go.

Holden's voice seemed to come from far away.

"Amos?"

"Yeah, Cap?"

"Would you please take his gun away now?"

"I'm on it."

Amos rose from behind one of the boxes nearest the wall. His Martian armor had a long pale streak across the chest and two white circles just below the ribs. Amos limped toward him.

"Sorry, Doc," he said. "Givin' it to you was my bad call. Maybe next time, right?"

Prax looked at the big man's open hand, then carefully put the gun in it.

"Wendell?" Holden said. Prax still wasn't sure where he was, but he sounded closer. That was probably just Prax's hearing coming back. The acrid smell in the air changed to something more coppery. It made him think of compost heaps gone sour: warm and organic and unsettling.

"One down," Wendell said.

"We'll get a medic," Holden said.

"Nice thought, but no point," Wendell said. "Finish the mission. We got most of them, but two or three made it through the door. They'll raise an alarm."

One of the Pinkwater soldiers stood up. Blood was running down his left arm. Another lay on the floor, half of his head simply gone. Holden appeared. He was massaging his right elbow, and the armor showed a new scar at his left temple.

"What happened?" Prax asked.

"You started a gunfight," Holden said. "Okay, let's move ahead before they can set up defenses."

Prax started noticing other bodies. Men and women who had been eating pizza and listening to music. They'd had pistols, but Holden's people carried automatic shotguns and assault rifles and some had military-looking armor. The difference in outcome hadn't been subtle.

"Amos, take point," Holden said, and the big man moved through the doorway and into the unknown. Prax moved to follow, and the head of the Pinkwater people took his elbow.

"Why don't you stay with me, professor," he said.

"Yes. I'll...all right."

On the other side of the door, the nature of the rooms changed. They were still clearly in the old tunnels of Ganymede. The walls still had their webwork of mineralized frost, the lighting was still old-fashioned LED housings, and the gray walls showed where ice had melted and refrozen during some climate system glitch years or decades before. But walking through that doorway was walking from the land of the dead into something living. The air was warmer, and it smelled of bodies and fresh soil and the subtle, sharp scent of phenol disinfectant. The wide hall they entered could have been the common room in any of a dozen labs where Prax had worked. Three metal office doors were closed along the far wall and a rolling metal freight gateway hung open ahead of them. Amos and Holden went to the three closed doors, Amos kicking each in turn. When the third flew open, Holden shouted something, but the words were lost in the bark of a pistol and Amos' return shotgun fire.

The two remaining Pinkwater soldiers who weren't Wendell scuttled forward, pressing their backs to the wall on either side of the freight gateway. Prax started toward them, but Wendell put a restraining hand on his shoulder. The man on the left side of the door ducked his head into the doorway and then out again. A bullet gouged a streak in the wall where it missed him.

"What can you give me?" Holden asked, and for a moment Prax thought he was talking to them. Holden's eyes were hard, and the scowl seemed etched into his skin. Then Naomi said something to make him smile, and he only looked tired and sad. "All right. We've got a partial floor plan. Through there, we've got an open room. It drops down about two meters, with exits to our ten o'clock and one o'clock. It's built like a pit, so if they're setting up defense here, we've got the high ground."

"Makes it a damned stupid place to set up a defense, then," Wendell said.

Gunfire chattered, three small holes appearing in the metal of the freight gateway. The people on the other side were nervous.

"And yet the evidence suggests..." Holden said.

"You want to talk to 'em, Cap?" Amos said. "Or do we head straight for the obvious thing?"

The question meant something more than Prax understood; he could tell that much. Holden started to say something, hesitated, and then nodded toward the doorway.

"Let's get this done," he said.

Holden and Amos jogged toward the gateway, Prax and Wendell close behind. Someone was shouting orders in the room beyond. Prax made out the words *payload* and *evac*, his heart going tight. *Evac.* They couldn't let anyone leave until they found Mei.

"I counted seven," one of the Pinkwater soldiers said. "Could be more."

"Any kids?" Amos asked.

"Didn't see any."

"We should probably look again," Amos said, and leaned out the door. Prax caught his breath, expecting to see the man's head dissolve in a rain of bullets, but Amos was already pulling back when the first shots started.

"What are we working with?" Holden asked.

"More'n seven," Amos said. "They're using this as a choke point, but the fella's right. Either they don't know what they're doing, or there's something in there they can't pull back from."

"So either panicking amateurs or something critical to defend," Holden said.

A metal canister the size of a fist rolled through the gateway, clanking. Amos picked the grenade up casually and tossed it back through the doorway. The detonation lit the room, the report louder than anything Prax had ever heard before. The ringing in his ears redoubled.

"Could be both," Amos shouted conversationally from very far away.

In the next room, something shattered. People were screaming. Prax imagined technicians like the ones from the previous room shredded by shrapnel from their own grenade. One of the Pinkwater soldiers leaned out, peering into the haze of smoke. An assault rifle blatted, and he pulled back, clutching his belly. Blood poured between his fingers. Wendell pushed past Prax, kneeling by his fallen soldier.

"Sorry, sir," the Pinkwater man said. "Got careless. Leave me here and I'll guard the rear as long as I can."

"Captain Holden," Wendell said. "If we're going to do something, we're better off doing it soon."

The screaming in the other room got louder. Someone was roaring inhumanly. Prax wondered if they'd had livestock in there. The bellowing sounded almost like an injured bull. He had to fight the urge to put his hands over his ears. Something loud happened. Holden nodded.

"Amos. Soften them up, then let's head in."

"Aye, aye, Cap," Amos said, putting down his shotgun. He took two grenades of his own, pulled the pink plastic strip-pins, rolled the live grenades through the gateway, and scooped his gun back up. The doubled detonation was deeper than the first one had been, but not as loud. Even before the echo faded, Amos, Holden, Wendell, and the one remaining soldier ducked through the gateway, weapons blazing.

Prax hesitated. He was unarmed. The enemy was just beyond the threshold. He could stay here and tend to the gut-shot man. But the image that wouldn't leave him was Katoa's still body. The dead boy wasn't more than a hundred meters away. And Mei...

Keeping his head down, Prax scuttled through the doorway. Holden and Wendell were to his right, Amos and the other soldier to his left. All four were crouched, weapons at the ready. Smoke stung Prax's eyes and nostrils, and the air recyclers groaned in protest, fighting to clear the air.

"Well now," Amos said, "that's fucking queer."

The room was built on two levels: an upper catwalk a meter and a half wide, and a lower floor two meters below it. A wide passage led away at ten o'clock on the lower level, and a door on the upper level stood open at one o'clock. The pit below them was chaos. Blood soaked the walls and had sprayed up to stipple the ceiling. Bodies lay on the ground below them. A thin steam rose from the gore.

They had been using equipment for cover. Prax recognized a microcentrifuge smashed almost out of its casing. Inch-thick slivers of ice or glass glittered among the carnage. A nitrogen bath was tipped on its side, the alarm indicator showing it had locked down. A massive blot array—easily two hundred kilos—lay at an improbable angle, a child's toy thrown aside in the ecstasy of play.

"What the hell kind of ordnance are you packing?" Wendell asked, his voice awed. From the wide passage at ten o'clock came shrieks and the sound of gunfire.

"I don't think this was us," Holden said. "Come on. Double-time it."

They dropped down to the killing floor. A glass cube like the one they'd seen before stood in shattered glory. Blood made the floor slick underfoot. A hand still wrapping a pistol lay in the corner. Prax looked away. Mei was here. He couldn't lose focus. Couldn't be sick.

He kept going on.

Holden and Amos led the way toward the sound of fighting. Prax trotted along behind them. When he tried to hold back, let Wendell and his compatriot go first, the Pinkwater men gently pushed him forward. They were guarding the rear, Prax realized. In case someone came up from behind. He should have thought of that.

The passageway opened out, broad but low. Industrial loading mechs, amber indicators showing idle, stood beside pallets of foam-coated supply boxes. Amos and Holden moved down the hall with a practiced efficiency that left Prax winded. But with every turn they reached, every door they opened, he found himself willing them to go faster. She was here, and they had to find her. Before she got hurt. Before something happened. And with every body they found, the sick feeling that something had already happened sank deeper in his gut.

They moved forward quickly. Too quickly. When they reached the end of the line—an airlock four meters high and at least seven across—Prax couldn't imagine that there was anyone behind it. Amos let his automatic shotgun hang at his side as he tapped at the airlock controls. Holden squinted up at the ceiling as if something might be written there. The ground trembled and set the hidden base creaking.

"Was that a launch?" Holden said. "That was a launch!"

"Yeah," Amos said. "Looks like they've got a landing pad out there. Monitors aren't showing anything else on it, though. Whatever that was, it was the last train outta here."

Prax heard someone shouting. It took him only a second to

realize it was him. Like he was watching his body move without him, he dashed to the sealed metal doors, pounding them with his clenched fists. She was there. She was just out there, on the ship lifting away from Ganymede. He could feel her like she had a rope tied to his heart and every moment pulled it out of him a little more.

He blacked out for a second. Or maybe longer. When he came back to himself, he was slung over Amos' wide shoulder, the armor biting into his belly. He pushed up to see the airlock receding slowly behind them.

"Put me down," Prax said.

"Can't do it," Amos replied. "Cap says—"

The stuttering of assault rifle fire came, and Amos dropped Prax to the ground and squatted over him, shotgun at the ready.

"What the fuck, Cap?" Amos said.

Prax glanced up in time to see the Pinkwater soldier cut down, blood spraying out of his back. Wendell was on the ground, returning fire around a sharp corner.

"Missed someone," Holden said. "Or else they called in their friends."

"Don't shoot them," Prax said. "What if it's Mei! What if they have her with them?"

"They don't, Doc," Amos said. "Stay down."

Holden was shouting, words rolling out of him too fast to follow. Prax didn't know if he was talking to Amos or Wendell or Naomi back on the ship or him. It could have been any of them. All of them. Four men came around the corner, weapons in hand. They wore the same coveralls that all the others had worn. One had long black hair and a goatee. Another was a woman with skin the color of buttercream. The two in the middle could have been brothers—the same close-cut brown hair, the same long noses.

From somewhere to Prax's right, the shotgun spoke twice. All four fell back. It was like something out of a prank comedy. Eight legs, swept at once. Four people Prax didn't know, had never met, just fell down. They just fell down. He knew they were never getting back up.

"Wendell?" Holden said. "Report?"

"Caudel's dead," Wendell said. He didn't sound sad about it. He didn't sound like anything. "I think I broke my wrist. Anyone know where they came from?"

"Nope," Holden said. "Let's not assume they were alone, though."

They retraced their steps, back through the long, wide passages. Past bodies of men and women they hadn't killed, but who were dead now anyway. Prax didn't try to keep from weeping. There was no point. If he could keep his legs moving, one foot in front of the other, it was enough.

They reached the bloodied pit after a few minutes or an hour or a week. Prax couldn't tell, and all options seemed equally plausible. The ruptured bodies stank, the spilled blood thickening to a black currant jelly, the opened viscera freeing colonies of bacteria usually held in check by the gut. On the catwalk, a woman stood. What was her name? Paula. That was it.

"Why aren't you at your post?" Wendell snapped when he saw her.

"Guthrie called for backup. Said he was gut-shot and about to pass out. I brought him some adrenaline and speed."

"Good call," Wendell said.

"Uchi and Caudel?"

"Didn't make it," Wendell said.

The woman nodded, but Prax saw something pass over her. Everyone here was losing someone. His tragedy was just one among dozens. Hundreds. Thousands. By the time the cascade had run all the way out, maybe millions. When death grew that large, it stopped meaning anything. He leaned against the nitrogen bath, his head in his hands. He'd been so close. So close...

"We have to find that ship," he said.

"We have to drop back ten and punt," Holden said. "We came here looking for a missing kid. Now we've got a covert scientific station halfway to being packed up and shipped out. And a secret landing pad. And whatever third player was fighting with these people while we were."

"Third player?" Paula asked.

Wendell gestured to the carnage.

"Not us," he said.

"We don't know what we're looking at," Holden said. "And until we do, we need to back off."

"We can't stop," Prax said. "I can't stop. Mei is—"

"Probably dead," Wendell said. "The girl's probably dead. And if she's not, she's alive someplace besides Ganymede."

"I'm sorry," Holden said.

"The dead boy," Prax said. "Katoa. His father took the family off Ganymede as soon as he could. Got them someplace safe. Someplace else."

"Wise move," Holden said.

Prax looked to Amos for support, but the big man was poking through the wreckage, pointedly not taking either side.

"The boy was alive," Prax said. "Basia said he knew the boy was dead and he packed up and he left, and when he got on that transport? His boy was here. In this lab. And he was alive. So don't tell me Mei's probably dead."

They were all silent for a moment.

"Just don't," Prax said.

"Cap?" Amos said.

"Just a minute," Holden said. "Prax, I'm not going to say that I know what you're going through, but I have people I love too. I can't tell you what to do, but let me ask you—*ask* you—to look at what kind of strategy is going to be best for you. And for Mei."

"Cap," Amos said. "Seriously, you should look at this."

Amos stood by the shattered glass cube. His shotgun hung forgotten in his hand. Holden walked up to the man's side, following his gaze to the ruined container. Prax pushed away from the nitrogen bath and joined them. There, clinging to the walls of glass that still stood, was a network of fine black filament. Prax couldn't tell if it was an artificial polymer or a natural substance. Some kind of web. It had a fascinating structure, though. He reached out to touch it and Holden grabbed his wrist, pulling him back so hard it hurt.

When Holden spoke, his words were measured and calm, which only made the panic behind them more terrifying.

"Naomi, prep the ship. We have to get off this moon. We have to do it right now."

Chapter Eighteen: Avasarala

What do you think?" the secretary-general asked from the upper left pane of the display. On the upper right, Errinwright leaned forward a centimeter, ready to jump in if she lost her temper.

"You've read the briefing, sir," Avasarala said sweetly.

The secretary-general waved his hand in a lazy circle. He was in his early sixties and wore the decades with the elfin charm of a man untroubled by weighty thoughts. The years Avasarala had spent building herself from the treasurer of the Workers Provident Fund to the district governor of the Maharshta-Karnataka-Goa Communal Interest Zone, he'd spent as a political prisoner at a minimum-security facility in the recently reconstructed Andean cloud forest. The slow, grinding wheels of power had lifted him to celebrity, and his ability to appear to be listening lent him an air of gravity without the inconvenience of an opinion of his own.

Had a man been engineered from birth to be the ideal governmental figurehead, he still wouldn't have achieved the perfection that was Secretary-General Esteban Sorrento-Gillis.

"Political briefs never capture the really important things," the bobble-head said. "Tell me what you think."

I think you haven't read the fucking briefs, Avasarala thought. *Not that I can really complain.* She cleared her throat.

"It's all sparring and no fight, sir," Avasarala said. "The players are top level. Michel Undawe, Carson Santiseverin, Ko Shu. They brought enough military to show that it's not just the elected monkeys. But so far, the only one who's said anything interesting is a marine they brought in to be a flower arrangement. Otherwise, we're all waiting for someone else to say something telling."

"And what about"—the secretary-general paused and lowered his voice—"the *alternative hypothesis*?"

"There's activity on Venus," Avasarala said. "We still don't know what any of it means. There was a massive upwelling of elemental iron in the northern hemisphere that lasted fourteen hours. There has also been a series of volcanic eruptions. Since the planet doesn't have any tectonic motion, we're assuming the protomolecule is doing something in the mantle, but we can't tell what. The brains put together a statistical model that shows the approximate energy output expected for the changes we've seen. It suggests that the overall level of activity is rising about three hundred percent per year over that last eighteen months."

The secretary-general nodded, his expression grave. It was almost as if he'd understood any part of what she'd said. Errinwright coughed.

"Do we have any evidence that ties the activity on Venus to the events on Ganymede?" he asked.

"We do," Avasarala said. "An anomalous energy spike at the same time as the Ganymede attack. But it's only one datapoint. It might have been coincidence."

A woman's voice came from the secretary-general's feed, and he nodded.

"I'm afraid I'm called to duty," he said. "You're doing fine work, Avasarala. Damn fine work."

"I can't tell you what that means coming from you, sir," she said with a smile. "You'd fire me."

Half a beat later, the secretary-general barked out a laugh and wagged his finger at the screen before the green connection-ended message took his place. Errinwright sat back, his palms pressed to his temples. Avasarala picked up her cup of tea and sipped it with her eyebrows lifted and her gaze on the camera, inviting him to say something. The tea wasn't quite down to tepid.

"All right," Errinwright said. "You win."

"We're impeaching him?"

He actually chuckled. Wherever he was, it was dark outside his windows, so he was on the same side of the planet that she was. That they were both in night gave the meeting a sense of closeness and intimacy that had more to do with her own exhaustion than anything else.

"What do you need to resolve the Venus situation?" he asked.

"Resolve?"

"Poor choice of words," he said. "From the beginning of this, you've had your eye on Venus. Keeping things calm with the Martians. Reining in Nguyen."

"Noticed that, did you?"

"These talks are stalled, and I'm not going to waste you on baby-sitting a deadlock. We need clarity, and we need it a month ago. Ask for the resources you need, Chrisjen, and either rule Venus out or get us proof. I'm giving you a blank check."

"Retirement at last," she said, laughing. To her surprise, Errinwright took it seriously.

"If you want, but Venus first. This is the most important question either of us has ever asked. I'm trusting you."

"I'll see to it," she said. Errinwright nodded and dropped the connection.

She leaned forward on her desk, fingertips pressed to her lips. Something had happened. Something had *changed*. Either

Errinwright had read enough about Venus to get his own set of the heebie-jeebies, or someone wanted her off the Martian negotiation. Someone with enough pull to get Errinwright to kick her upstairs. Did Nguyen have patrons that powerful?

Yes, it gave her what she wanted. After all she'd said—and meant when she'd said it—she couldn't refuse the project, but the success had a bitter aftertaste. Perhaps she was reading too much into it. God knew she hadn't been getting enough sleep, and fatigue left her paranoid. She checked the time. Ten o'clock p.m. She wouldn't make it back to Arjun that night. Another morning in the depressing VIP quarters, drinking the weak coffee and pretending to care what the latest ambassador from the Pashwiri Autonomous Zone thought about dance music.

Screw it, she thought, *I need a drink.*

The Dasihari Lounge catered to the full range in the complex organism that was the United Nations. At the bar, young pages and clerks leaned into the light, laughing too loud and pretending to be more important than they were. It was a mating dance only slightly more dignified than presenting like a mandrill, but endearing in its own fashion. Roberta Draper, the Martian Marine who'd shat on the table that morning, was among them, a pint glass dwarfed by her hand and an amused expression on her face. Soren would probably be there, if not that night, another time. Avasarala's son would probably have been among them if things had gone differently.

In the center of the room, there were tables with built-in terminals to pipe in encrypted information from a thousand different sources. Privacy baffles kept even the waitstaff from glimpsing over the shoulders of the middle-range administrators drinking their dinners while they worked. And in the back were dark wooden tables in booths that recognized her before she sat down. If anyone below a certain status walked too close, a discreet young man with perfect hair would sweep up and see them to a different table, elsewhere, with less important people.

Avasarala sipped her gin and tonic while the threads of implication wove and rewove themselves. Nguyen couldn't have enough influence to put Errinwright against her. Could the Martians have asked that she be removed? She tried to remember who she'd been rude to and how, but no good suspect came to mind. And if they had, what was she going to do about it?

Well, if she couldn't be party to the Martian negotiations in an official capacity, she could still have contacts on an informal basis. Avasarala started chuckling even before she knew quite why. She picked up her glass, tapped the table to let it know it was permitted to let someone else sit there, and made her way across the bar. The music was soft arpeggios in a hypermodern tonal scale, which managed to sound soothing despite itself. The air smelled of perfume too expensive to be applied tastelessly. As she neared the bar, she saw conversations pause, glances pass between one young fount of ambition and another. *The old lady*, she imagined them saying. *What's she doing here?*

She sat down next to Draper. The big woman looked over at her. There was a light of recognition in her eyes that boded well. She might not know who Avasarala was, but she'd guessed what she was. Smart, then. Perceptive. And fucking hell, the woman was enormous. Not fat either, just…*big*.

"Buy you a drink, Sergeant?" Avasarala asked.

"I've had a few too many already," she said. And a moment later: "All right."

Avasarala lifted an eyebrow, and the bartender quietly gave the marine another glass of whatever she'd been having before.

"You made quite an impression today," Avasarala said.

"I did," Draper said. She seemed serenely unconcerned about it. "Thorsson's going to ship me out. I'm done here. May just be *done*."

"That's fair. You've accomplished what they wanted from you anyway."

Draper looked down at her. Polynesian blood, Avasarala guessed. Maybe Samoan. Someplace that evolution had made humans like mountain ranges. Her eyes were narrowed, and there was a heat to them. An anger.

"I haven't done shit."

"You were here. That's all they needed from you."

"What's the point?"

"They want to convince me that the monster wasn't theirs. One argument they've made is that their own soldiers—meaning you—didn't know about it. By bringing you, they're showing that they aren't afraid to bring you. That's all they need. You could sit around with your thumb up your ass and argue about the offside rule all day. It would be just as good for them. You're a showpiece."

The marine took it in, then raised an eyebrow.

"I don't think I like that," she said.

"Yes, well," Avasarala said, "Thorsson's a cunt, but if you stop working with politicians just for that, you won't have any friends."

The marine chuckled. Then she laughed. Then, seeing Avasarala's gaze on her own, she sobered.

"That thing that killed your friends?" Avasarala said while the marine was looking her in the eye. "It wasn't one of mine."

Draper's inhalation was sharp. It was like Avasarala had touched a wound. Which made sense, because she had. Draper's jaw worked for a second.

"It wasn't one of ours either."

"Well. At least we've got that settled."

"It won't do any good, though. They won't do anything. They won't talk about anything. They don't care. You know that? They don't care what happened as long as they all protect their careers and make sure the balance of power isn't tilted the wrong way. None of them fucking *care* what that thing was or where it came from."

The bar around them wasn't silent, but it was quieter. The mating dance was now only the second most interesting thing happening at the bar.

"I care," Avasarala said. "As a matter of fact, I've just been given a very great deal of latitude in finding out what that thing was."

It wasn't entirely true. She'd been given a huge budget to impli-
cate or rule out Venus. But it was close, and it was the right frame
for what she wanted.

"Really?" Draper said. "So what are you going to do?"

"First thing, I'm going to hire you. I need a liaison with the
Martian military. That should be you. Can you handle it?"

No one at the bar was talking to anybody now. The room might
have been empty. The only sounds were the soft music and Draper's laughter. An older man wearing clove-and-cinnamon cologne
walked by, drawn by the quiet spectacle without knowing what
it was.

"I'm a Martian Marine," Draper said. "Martian. You're UN.
Earth. We aren't even citizens of the same planet. You can't
hire me."

"My name's Chrisjen Avasarala. Ask around."

They were silent for a moment.

"I'm Bobbie," Draper said.

"Nice to meet you, Bobbie. Come work for me."

"Can I think about it?"

"Of course," Avasarala said, and had her terminal send Bobbie
her private number. "So long as when you're done thinking, you
come work for me."

At the VIP apartments, Avasarala tuned the system to the kind of
music Arjun might be listening to just then. If he wasn't already
asleep. She fought back the urge to call him. It was late already,
and she was just drunk enough to get maudlin. Sobbing into her
hand terminal about how much she loved her husband wasn't
something she longed to make a habit of. She pulled off her sari
and took a long, hot shower. She didn't drink alcohol often. Usually she didn't like how it dulled her mind. That night it seemed to
loosen her up, give her brain the little extra jazz it needed to see
connections.

Draper kept her connected to Mars, even if not to the day-by-day slog of the negotiations. That was a good start. There would be other connections too. Foster, in data services, could be brought in. She'd need to start routing more work through him. Build a relationship. It wouldn't do to march in and insist on being his new best friend just because he happened to be managing the encryption requests for Nguyen. A few no-strings-attached cupcakes first. Then the hook. Who else could she—

Her hand terminal chimed a priority alert. She turned off the water and grabbed a bathrobe, wrapping herself tightly and double-knotting the stay before she accepted the connection. She was years past flashing someone over a hand terminal, no matter how much she'd drunk. The connection came from someone in priority surveillance. The image that flashed up was a middle-aged man with ill-advised mutton-chop whiskers.

"Ameer! You mad dog. What have you done that they make you work so late?"

"Moved to Atlanta, miss," the analyst said with a toothy grin. He was the only one who ever called her miss. She hadn't spoken to him in three years. "I've just come back from lunch. I had an unscheduled report flagged for you. Contact immediately. I tried your assistant, but he didn't answer."

"He's young. He still sleeps sometimes. It's a weakness. Stand by while I set privacy."

The moment of friendly banter was over. Avasarala leaned forward, tapping her hand terminal twice to add a layer of encryption. The red icon went green.

"Go ahead," she said.

"It's from Ganymede, miss. You have a standing order on James Holden."

"Yes?"

"He's on the move. He made an apparent rendezvous with a local scientist. Praxidike Meng."

"What's Meng?"

In Atlanta, Ameer transitioned smoothly to a different file. "Botanist, miss. Emigrated to Ganymede with his family when he was a child. Schooled there. Specializes in partial-pressure low-light soybean strains. Divorced, one child. No known connections to the OPA or any established political party."

"Go ahead."

"Holden, Meng, and Burton have left their ship. They're armed, and they've made contact with a small group of private-security types. Pinkwater."

"How many?"

"The on-site analyst doesn't say, miss. A small force. Should I query?"

"What lag are we at?"

Ameer's brown-black eyes flickered.

"Forty-one minutes, eight seconds, miss."

"Hold the query. If I have anything else, I can send them together."

"The on-site analyst reports that Holden negotiated with the private security, either a last-minute renegotiation or else the whole meeting was extemporaneous. It appears they reached some agreement. The full group proceeded to an unused corridor complex and forced entry."

"A what?"

"Disused access door, miss."

"What the fuck is that supposed to mean? How big is it? Where is it?"

"Should I query?"

"You should go to Ganymede and kick this sorry excuse for an on-site analyst in the balls. Add a clarification request."

"Yes, miss," Ameer said with the ghost of a smile. Then, suddenly, he frowned. "An update. One moment."

So the OPA had something on Ganymede. Maybe something they'd put there, maybe something they'd found. Either way, this mysterious door made things a degree more interesting. While Ameer read through and digested the new update, Avasarala scratched the back of her hand and reevaluated her position. She'd thought Holden was there as an observer. Forward intelligence.

That might be wrong. If he'd gone to meet with this Praxidike Meng, this utterly under-the-radar botanist, the OPA might already know quite a bit about Bobbie Draper's monster. Add the fact that Holden's boss had the only known sample of the proto-molecule, and a narrative about the Ganymede collapse began to take shape.

There were holes in it, though. If the OPA had been playing with the protomolecule, there had been no sign of it. And Fred Johnson's psychological profile didn't match with terrorist attacks. Johnson was old-school, and the monster attack was decidedly new.

"There's been a firefight, miss. Holden and his people have met armed resistance. They've set a perimeter. The on-site analyst can't approach."

"Resistance? I thought this was supposed to be unused. Who the fuck are they shooting at?"

"Shall I query?"

"God *damn* it!"

Forty light-minutes away, something important was going on, and she was here, in a bedroom that wasn't hers, trying to make sense of it by pressing her ear to the wall. The frustration was a physical sensation. It felt like being crushed.

Forty minutes out. Forty minutes back. Whatever she said, whatever order she gave, it would get there almost an hour and a half behind what was clearly a rapidly changing situation.

"Pull him in," she said. "Holden, Burton. Their Pinkwater friends. And this mysterious botanist. Bring them all in. Now."

Ameer in Atlanta paused.

"If they're in a firefight, miss…"

"Then send in the dogs, break up the fight, and take them in. We're past surveillance. Get it done."

"Yes, miss."

"Contact me as soon as it's done."

"Yes, miss."

She watched Ameer's face as he framed the order, confirmed it, sent it out. She could practically imagine the screen, the strokes of his fingers. She willed him to go faster, to press her intent out past the speed of light and get the damn thing done.

"Order's out. As soon as I hear from the on-site analyst, I'll reach you."

"I'll be here. If I don't take the connection, try again until I wake up."

She dropped the link and sat back. Her brain felt like a swarm of bees. James Holden had changed the game again. The boy had a talent for that, but that in itself made him a known quantity. This other one, this Meng, had come from her blind side. The man might be a mole or a volunteer or a stalking goat sent to lead the OPA into a trap. She considered turning off the light, trying to sleep, then abandoned it as a bad bet.

Instead, she set up a connection with the UN's intelligence research database. It was an hour and a half at earliest before she'd hear anything more. In the meantime, she wanted to know who Praxidike Meng was and why he mattered.

Chapter Nineteen: Holden

Naomi, prep the ship. We have to get off this moon. We have to do it *right now*."

All around Holden, the black filaments spread, a dark spider's web with him at the center. He was on Eros again. He was seeing thousands of bodies turning into something else. He thought he'd made it off, but Eros just kept coming. He and Miller had gotten out, but it got Miller anyway.

Now it was back for him.

"What's the matter, Jim?" Naomi said from the distance of the suit radio. "Jim?"

"Prep the ship!"

"It's the stuff," Amos said. He was talking to Naomi. "Like from Eros."

"Jesus, they..." Holden managed to gasp out before the fear welled up in his mind, robbing him of speech. His heart banged against his ribs like it wanted out, and he had to check the oxygen levels on his HUD. It felt like there wasn't enough air in the room.

Out of the corner of his eye, something appeared to scuttle up the wall like a disembodied hand, leaving a trail of brown slime in its wake. When Holden spun and pointed his assault rifle at it, it resolved into a bloodstain below a discolored patch of ice.

Amos moved toward him, a worried look on his broad face. Holden waved him off, then set the butt of his rifle on the ground and leaned on a nearby crate to catch his breath.

"We should probably move out," Wendell said. He and Paula were helping hold up the man who'd been gut-shot. The injured man was having trouble breathing. A small red bubble of blood had formed in his left nostril, and it inflated and deflated with each ragged gasp the man took.

"Jim?" Naomi said in his ear, her voice soft. "Jim, I saw it through Amos' suitcam, and I know what it means. I'm getting the ship ready. That encrypted local traffic? It's dropped way off. I think everyone's gone."

"Everyone's gone," Holden echoed.

The diminished remains of his Pinkwater team were staring at him, the concern on their faces shifting to fear, his own terror infecting them even though they had no idea what the filament meant. They wanted him to do something, and he knew he had to, but he couldn't quite think what it was. The black web filled his head with flashing images, running too quickly to make sense, like video played at high speed: Julie Mao in her shower, the black threads surrounding her, her body twisted into a nightmare; bodies scattered across the floor of a radiation chamber; the zombie-like infected staggering off the trams in Eros, vomiting brown bile on everyone around them, even a drop of the goo a death sentence; video captures of the horror show Eros had become; a torso stripped to a rib cage and one arm dragging itself through the protomolecule landscape on some unknowable mission.

"Cap," Amos said, then moved over to touch Holden's arm. Holden yanked away, almost falling over in the process.

He swallowed the thick lemony-flavored saliva building up in his throat and said, "Okay. I'm here. Let's go. Naomi. Call Alex. We need the *Roci*."

Naomi didn't answer for a moment, then said, "What about the block—"

"Right fucking now, Naomi!" Holden yelled. "Right fucking now! Call Alex right now!"

She didn't reply, but the gut-shot man took one final ragged breath and then collapsed, nearly dragging the wounded Wendell to the floor with him.

"We have to go," Holden said to Wendell, meaning *We can't help him. If we stay, we all die*. Wendell nodded but went to one knee and began taking the man's light armor off, not understanding. Amos pulled the emergency medkit off his harness and dropped down next to Wendell to begin working on the wounded man while Paula watched, her face pale.

"Have to go," Holden said again, wanting to grab Amos and shake him until he understood. "Amos, stop, we have to go right now. Eros—"

"Cap," Amos interrupted, "all due respect, but this ain't Eros." He took a syringe from the medkit and gave the downed man an injection. "No radiation rooms, no zombies puking goo. Just that broken box, a whole lotta dead guys, and these black threads. We don't know *what* the fuck it is, but it ain't Eros. And we ain't leaving this guy behind."

The small rational part of Holden's mind knew Amos was right. And more than that, the person Holden wanted to believe he still was would never consider leaving even a complete stranger behind, much less a guy who'd taken a wound for him. He forced himself to take three deep, slow breaths. Prax knelt by Amos' side, holding the medkit.

"Naomi," Holden said, meaning to apologize for yelling at her.

"Alex is on his way," she replied, her voice tight but not accusing. "He's a few hours out. Running the blockade won't be easy, but he thinks he's got an angle. Where is he putting down?"

Holden found himself answering before he realized he'd made the decision. "Tell him to land in the *Somnambulist's* berth. I'm giving her to someone. Meet us outside the airlock when we get there."

He pulled the mag-key for the *Somnambulist* out of a pocket on his harness and tossed it to Wendell. "This will get you on the ship you're taking. Consider it a down payment for services rendered."

Wendell nodded and tucked the key away, then went back to his injured man. The man appeared to be breathing.

"Can he be carried?" Holden asked Amos, proud of how steady his voice sounded again, trying not to think about the fact that he would have left the man to die a minute before.

"No choice, Cap."

"Then somebody pick him up," Holden said. "No, not you, Amos. I need you back on point."

"I got him," Wendell said. "I can't shoot for shit with this hand busted."

"Prax. Help him," Holden said. "We're getting the hell out of here."

They moved as quickly as injured people could back through the base. Back past the men and women they'd killed getting in and, more frighteningly, the ones they hadn't. Back past Katoa's small, still corpse. Prax's gaze drifted toward the body, but Holden grabbed his jacket and shoved him toward the hatch.

"It's still not Mei," he said. "Slow us down and I leave you."

The threat made him feel like an ass the moment it left his lips, but it wasn't idle. Finding the scientist's lost little girl had stopped being the priority the instant they found the black filaments. And as long as he was being honest with himself, leaving the scientist behind would mean not being there when they found his daughter twisted into a monster by the protomolecule, brown goo leaking from orifices she hadn't been born with, the black threads crawling from her mouth and eyes.

The older Pinkwater man who'd been covering their exit

rushed over to help carry the injured man without being asked. Prax handed the wounded man off to him without a word and then slid in place behind Paula as she scanned the hallways ahead with her machine pistol.

Corridors that had seemed boring on the trip in took on a sinister feel on the way back out. The frosted texture that had reminded Holden of spiderwebs when he'd come in now looked like the veins of some living thing. Their pulsing had to be caused by adrenaline making his eyes twitch.

Eight rems burning off Jupiter onto the surface of Ganymede. Even with the magnetosphere, eight rems a day. How quickly would the protomolecule grow here, with Jupiter endlessly supplying the energy? Eros had become something frighteningly powerful once the protomolecule had taken hold. Something that could accelerate at incredible speeds without inertia. Something that could, if the reports were right, change the very atmosphere and chemical composition of Venus. And that was with just over a million human hosts and a thousand trillion tons of rocky mass to work with at the beginning.

Ganymede had ten times as many humans and many orders of magnitude more mass than Eros. What could the ancient alien weapon do with such bounty?

Amos threw open the last hatch to the shadow base, and the crew was back in the higher-traffic tunnels of Ganymede. Holden didn't see anyone acting infected. No mindless zombies staggering through the corridors. No brown vomit coating the walls and floor, filled with the alien virus looking for a host. No Protogen hired thugs shepherding people into the kill zone.

Protogen is gone.

An itch at the back of his mind that Holden hadn't even been aware of pushed its way to the front. Protogen was gone. Holden had helped bring them down. He'd been in the room when the architect of the Eros experiment died. The Martian fleet had nuked Phoebe into a thin gas that was sucked into Saturn's massive gravity. Eros had crashed into the acidic and autoclave-hot atmosphere of Venus, where no human ships could go. Holden himself had taken Protogen's only sample of the protomolecule away from them.

So who had brought the protomolecule to Ganymede?

He'd given the sample to Fred Johnson as leverage to be used in the peace talks. The Outer Planets Alliance had gotten a lot of concessions in the chaos that followed the brief inner planets war. But not everything they'd wanted. The inner planets fleets in orbit around Ganymede were proof of that.

Fred had the only sample of the protomolecule left in the solar system. Because Holden had given it to him.

"It was Fred," he said out loud without realizing it.

"What was Fred?" Naomi asked.

"This. What's happening here. He did this."

"No," Naomi said.

"To drive the inner planets out, to test some kind of super-weapon, something. But he did this."

"No," Naomi said again. "We don't know that."

The air in the corridor grew smoky, the nauseating scent of burning hair and flesh choking off Holden's reply. Amos held up a hand to halt the group, and the Pinkwater people stopped and took up defensive positions. Amos moved up the corridor to the junction and looked off to his left for several moments.

"Something bad happened here," he finally said. "I've got half a dozen dead, more than that celebrating."

"Are they armed?" Holden asked.

"Oh yeah."

The Holden who would have tried to talk his way by them, the Holden who Naomi liked and wanted back, barely put up a struggle when he said, "Get us past them."

Amos leaned out around the corner and fired off a long burst from his auto-shotgun.

"Go," he said when the echoes of the gunshots had faded away.

The Pinkwater people picked up their wounded and hurried up the corridor and beyond the battle; Prax jogged along close behind, head down and thin arms pumping. Holden followed, a glance showing him dead bodies on fire at the center of a wide hallway. Burning them had to be a message. It wasn't quite bad enough yet for them to be eating each other. Was it?

There were a few bodies lying outside the fire, bleeding out on the corrugated metal floors. Holden couldn't tell if they were Amos' handiwork. The old Holden would have asked. The new one didn't.

"Naomi," he said, wanting to hear her voice.

"I'm here."

"We're seeing trouble out here."

"Is it…" He heard the dread in her voice.

"No. Not the protomolecule. But the locals may be bad enough. Seal up the 'locks," Holden told her, the words coming to him without thought. "Warm up the reactor. If something happens to us, leave and rendezvous with Alex. Don't go to Tycho."

"Jim," she said, "I—"

"Don't go to Tycho. Fred did this. Don't go back to him."

"No," she said. Her new mantra.

"If we aren't there in half an hour, go. That's an order, XO."

At least she would get away, Holden told himself. No matter what happened on Ganymede, at least Naomi would make it out alive. A vision of the nightmare Julie, dead in her shower, but with Naomi's face flashed in his mind. He didn't expect the little yelp of grief that escaped him. Amos turned and looked back at him, but Holden waved him on without a word.

Fred had done this.

And if Fred had, then Holden had too.

Holden had spent a year playing enforcer to Fred's politician. He'd hunted ships and killed them for Fred's grand OPA government experiment. He'd changed the man he'd been into the man he was now, because some part of him believed in Fred's dream of the liberated and self-governed outer planets.

And Fred had secretly been planning…this.

Holden thought of all the things he'd put off so that he could help Fred build his new solar system order. He'd never taken Naomi to meet his family back on Earth. Not that Naomi herself could have ever gone to Earth. But he could have flown his family up to Luna to meet her. Father Tom would have resisted. He hated travel. But Holden had no doubt that in the end he would have gotten them all to come meet her once he explained how important she'd become to him.

And meeting Prax, seeing his need to find his daughter, made Holden realize how badly he wanted to know what that was like. To experience that sort of hunger for the presence of another human being. To present another generation to his parents. To show them that all the effort and energy they had put into him had paid off. That he was passing it along. He wanted, almost more than he'd wanted anything before, to see the looks on their faces when he showed them a child. His child. Naomi's child.

Fred had taken that from him, first by wasting his time as the OPA's leg breaker, and now by this betrayal. Holden swore to himself that if he made it off Ganymede, Fred would pay for all of it.

Amos halted the group again, and Holden noticed that they were back at the port. He shook himself out of his reverie. He didn't remember how they'd gotten there.

"Looks clear," Amos said.

"Naomi," Holden said, "what does it look like around the ship?"

"Looks clear here," she said. "But Alex is worried that—"

Her voice was cut off by an electronic squeal.

"Naomi? Naomi!" Holden yelled, but there was no response. To Amos he said, "Go, double-time it to the ship!"

Amos and the Pinkwater people ran toward the docks as quickly as their injured bodies and the unconscious teammate would let them. Holden brought up the rear, shouldering his assault rifle and flicking off the safety as he ran.

They ran through the twisting corridors of the port sector, Amos scattering pedestrians with loud shouts and the unspoken threat of his shotgun. An old woman in a hijab scurried away before them like a leaf driven before a storm. She was dead already. If the protomolecule was loose, everyone Holden passed was dead already. Santichai and Melissa Supitayaporn and all the people they'd come to Ganymede to save. The rioters and killers who'd been normal citizens of the station before their social ecosystem collapsed. If the protomolecule was loose, all of them were as good as dead.

So why hadn't it happened?

Holden pushed the thought aside. Later—if there was a later—he could worry about it. Someone shouted at Amos, and Amos fired his shotgun into the ceiling once. If port security still existed outside of the vultures trying to take a cut of every incoming shipment, they didn't try to stop them.

The outer airlock door of the *Somnambulist* was closed when they reached it.

"Naomi, you there?" Holden asked, fumbling in his pockets for the swipe card. She didn't reply, and it took him a moment to remember he'd given the card to Wendell. "Wendell, open the door for us."

The Pinkwater leader didn't reply.

"Wendell—" Holden started, then stopped when he saw that Wendell was staring, wide-eyed, at something behind him. Holden turned to look and saw five men—Earthers, all of them—in plain gray armor without insignias. All were armed with large bore weapons.

No, Holden thought, and brought his gun up and across them in a full auto sweep. Three of the five men dropped, their armor blooming red. The new Holden rejoiced; the old was quiet. It didn't matter who these men were. Station security or inner planet military or just leftover mercenaries from the now destroyed shadow base, he'd kill them all before he let them stop him from getting his crew off this infected moon.

He never saw who fired the shot that took his leg out from under him. One second he was standing, emptying the magazine of his assault rifle into the gray-armored fire-team, and the next a sledgehammer blow hit the armor on his right thigh, knocking him off his feet. As he fell, he saw the two remaining gray-armored soldiers go down as Amos' auto-shotgun unloaded in a single long roar.

Holden rolled to his side, looking to see if anyone else was hurt, and saw that the five on his side had been only half of the enemy team. The Pinkwater people were raising their hands and dropping their weapons as five more gray-armored soldiers came down the corridor from behind.

Amos never saw them. He dropped the expended magazine from his auto-shotgun and was pulling a new one off his harness when one of the mercenaries aimed a large weapon at the back of his head and pulled the trigger. Amos' helmet flew off and he was slapped forward onto the corrugated-metal decking with a wet crunch. Blood splashed across the floor where he hit it.

Holden tried to get a new magazine into his assault rifle, but his hands wouldn't cooperate and before he could reload his gun, one of the soldiers had crossed the distance and kicked the rifle away from him.

Holden had time to see the still standing members of his Pinkwater team disappear into black bags before one came down over his own head and plunged him into darkness.

Chapter Twenty: Bobbie

The Martian delegation had been given a suite of offices in the UN building for their own use. The furniture was all real wood; the paintings on the walls were originals and not prints. The carpet smelled new. Bobbie thought that either everyone in the UN campus lived like a king, or they were just going out of their way to impress the Martians.

Thorsson had called her a few hours after she'd left her run-in with Avasarala at the bar, and had demanded that she meet with him the next day. Now she waited in the lobby of their temporary office suite, sitting in a bergère-style chair with green velvet cushions and a cherry wood frame that would have cost her two years' salary on Mars. A screen set into the wall across from her played a news channel with the sound muted. It turned the program into a confusing and occasionally macabre slide show of images: two talking heads sitting at a desk in a blue room, a large building on fire, a woman walking down a long white hallway while gesturing animatedly to both sides, a UN battleship parked at an orbital station with severe damage scarring its flank, a red-faced man talking directly into the camera against the backdrop of a flag Bobbie didn't recognize.

It all meant something and nothing at the same time. A few hours before, this would have frustrated Bobbie. She would have felt compelled to go find the remote and turn the sound up, to add context to the information being thrown at her.

Now she just let the images flow around her like canal water past a rock.

A young man she'd seen a few times on the *Dae-Jung* but had never actually met hurried through the lobby, tapping furiously on his terminal. When he was halfway across the room, he said, "He's ready for you."

It took Bobbie a moment to realize the young man had been talking to her. Apparently her stock had fallen far enough that she no longer warranted face-to-face delivery of information. More meaningless data. More water flowing past her. She pushed herself to her feet with a grunt. Her hours-long walk at one g the previous day had taken more out of her than she'd realized.

She was vaguely surprised to find that Thorsson's office was one of the smallest in the suite. That meant that either he didn't care about the unspoken status conferred through office size, or he was actually the least important member of the delegation to still rate a private workspace. She felt no compulsion to figure out which. Thorsson did not react to her arrival, his head bent over his desk terminal. Bobbie didn't care about being ignored, or about the lesson he was trying to teach her with it. The size of the office meant that Thorsson had no chair for guests, and the ache in her legs was sufficiently distracting.

"I may have overreacted earlier," he finally said.

"Oh?" Bobbie replied, thinking about where she might find more of that soy-milk tea.

Thorsson looked up at her. His face was trying its mummified-remains version of a warm smile. "Let me be clear. There's no doubt that you damaged our credibility with your outburst. But, as Martens points out, that is largely my fault for not fully understanding the extent of your trauma."

"Ah," Bobbie said. There was a framed photograph on the wall behind Thorsson of a city with a tall metal structure in the foreground. It looked like an archaic rocket gantry. The caption read PARIS.

"So instead of sending you home, I will be keeping you on staff here. You'll be given an opportunity to repair the damage you've done."

"Why," Bobbie said, looking Thorsson in the eye for the first time since coming in, "am I here?"

Thorsson's hint of a smile disappeared and was replaced by an equally understated frown. "Excuse me?"

"Why am I here?" she repeated, thinking past the disciplinary board. Thinking of how hard it would be to get reassigned to Ganymede if Thorsson didn't send her back to Mars. If he didn't, would she be allowed to resign? Just leave the corps and buy her own ticket? The thought of no longer being a marine made her sad. The first really strong feeling she'd had in a while.

"Why are you—" Thorsson started, but Bobbie cut him off.

"Not to talk about the monster, apparently. Honestly, if I'm just here as a showpiece, I think I'd rather be sent home. I have some things I could be doing…"

"You," Thorsson said, his voice getting tighter, "are here to do exactly what I say for you to do, and exactly when I say it. Is that understood, soldier?"

"Yeah," Bobbie said, feeling the water slide past her. She was a stone. It moved her not at all. "I have to go now."

She turned and walked away, Thorsson not managing to get a last word out before she left. As she moved through the suite toward the exit, she saw Martens pouring powdered creamer into a cup of coffee in the small kitchen area. He spotted her at the same time.

"Bobbie," he said. He'd gotten a lot more familiar with her over the last few days. Normally, she'd have assumed it was a buildup to romantic or sexual overtures. With Martens, she was pretty sure it was just another tool in his "how to fix broken marines" tool kit.

"Captain," she said. She stopped. She felt the front door tugging at her with a sort of psychic gravity, but Martens had never been anything but good to her. And she had a strange premonition that she was never going to see any of these people again. She held out her hand to him, and when he took it, she said, "I'm leaving. You won't have to waste your time with me anymore."

He smiled his sad smile at her. "In spite of the fact that I don't actually feel like I've accomplished anything, I don't feel like I wasted my time. Do we part friends?"

"I—" she started, then had to stop and swallow a lump in her throat. "I hope this didn't wreck your career or anything."

"I'm not worried about it," he said to her back. She was already walking out the door. She didn't turn around.

In the hallway Bobbie pulled out her terminal and called the number Avasarala had given her. It immediately went to voice mail.

"Okay," she said, "I'll take that job."

There was something liberating and terrifying about the first day on a new job. In any new assignment, Bobbie had always had the unsettling feeling that she was in over her head, that she wouldn't know how to do any of the things they would ask her to do, that she would dress wrong or say the wrong thing, or that everyone would hate her. But no matter how strong that feeling was, it was overshadowed by the sense that with a new job came the chance to totally recreate herself in whatever image she chose, that—at least for a little while—her options were infinite.

Even waiting for Avasarala finally to notice her couldn't fully dampen that feeling.

Standing in Avasarala's office reinforced Bobbie's impression that the Martian suite was intended to impress. The deputy secretary was important enough to get Bobbie transferred out of Thorsson's command and into a liaison role for the UN with a single phone call. And yet her office had cheap carpet that smelled unpleasantly of stale tobacco smoke. Her desk was old and scuffed. No cherrywood chairs here. The only things that looked lovingly tended in the room were the fresh flowers and the Buddha shrine.

Avasarala radiated weariness. There were dark circles under her eyes that hadn't been there during their official meetings and hadn't been visible in the dim lights of the bar where she'd made her offer. Sitting behind her giant desk in a bright blue sari, she looked very small, like a child pretending to be a grown-up. Only the gray hair and crow's-feet ruined the illusion. Bobbie suddenly pictured her instead as a cranky doll, complaining as children moved her arms and legs and forced her to go to tea parties with stuffed animals. The thought made her cheeks ache from restraining the grin.

Avasarala tapped at a terminal on her desk and grunted with irritation. *No more tea for you, gramma dolly, you've had enough,* Bobbie thought, then stifled a laugh. "Soren, you've moved my fucking files again. I can't find a goddamned thing anymore."

The stiff young man who'd brought Bobbie into the office and then sort of melted into the background cleared his throat. It made Bobbie jump. He was closer behind her than she'd realized.

"Ma'am, you asked me to move a few of the—"

"Yes, yes," Avasarala interrupted, tapping harder on the terminal's screen, as if that would make the device understand what she wanted. Something about that made Bobbie think of people who started talking louder when trying to communicate with someone who spoke a different language.

"Okay, there they are," Avasarala said with irritation. "Why you'd put them..."

She tapped a few more times and Bobbie's terminal chimed.

"That," she said, "is the report and all of my notes on the Ganymede situation. Read them. Today. I may have an update later, once I've had a little polite questioning done."

Bobbie pulled out her terminal and scrolled quickly through the documents she'd just been sent. It went on and on for hundreds of pages. Her first thought was *Did she really mean read all of this today?* This was quickly followed by *Did she really just hand me everything she knows?* It made her own government's recent treatment of her look even worse.

"It won't take you long," her new boss continued. "There's almost nothing there. Lots of bullshit by overpaid consultants who think they can hide the fact that they don't actually know anything by talking twice as long."

Bobbie nodded, but the feeling of being in over her head had started to outcompete her excitement at a new opportunity.

"Ma'am, is Sergeant Draper cleared to access—" Soren said.

"Yes. I just cleared her. Bobbie? You're cleared," Avasarala said right over the top of him. "Stop busting my balls, Soren. I'm out of tea."

Bobbie made a conscious effort not to turn around and look at Soren. The situation was uncomfortable enough without driving home the fact that he'd just been humiliated in front of a foreigner with exactly seventeen minutes on the job.

"Yes, ma'am," Soren said. "But I was wondering whether you should alert the security service about your decision to clear the sergeant. They do like to be in the loop on that kind of thing."

"Meow meow cry meow meow," Avasarala said. "That's all I heard you say."

"Yes, ma'am," Soren said.

Bobbie finally looked back and forth between them. Soren was being dressed down in front of a new team member who was also technically the enemy. His expression hadn't changed. He looked like he was humoring a demented grandmother. Avasarala made an impatient clicking sound with her teeth.

"Was I not clear? Have I lost the ability to speak?"

"No, ma'am," Soren said.

"Bobbie? Can you understand me?"

"Y-yes, sir."

"Good. Then get out of my office and do your jobs. Bobbie, read. Soren, tea."

Bobbie turned to leave and found Soren staring at her, his face expressionless. Which was, in its way, more disconcerting than a little well-justified anger would have been.

As she walked past him, Avasarala said, "Soren, wait. Take this to Foster in data services." She handed Soren what looked like a memory stick. "Make sure you get it to him before he leaves for the day."

Soren nodded, smiled, and took the small black wafer from her. "Of course."

When he and Bobbie had left Avasarala's office, and Soren had closed the door behind them, Bobbie let out a long whistling exhale and smiled at him.

"Wow, that was awkward. Sorry about—" she started, but stopped when Soren held up his hand, casually dismissing her concern.

"It's nothing," he said. "She's actually having a pretty good day."

While she stood gaping and looking at him, Soren turned away from her and tossed the memory stick onto his desk, where it slid under the wrapper of a half-eaten package of cookies. He sat down and put on a headset, then began scrolling through a list of phone numbers on his desktop terminal. If he noticed her continued presence, he gave no sign.

"You know," Bobbie said finally, "I just have some stuff to read, so if you're busy, I could take that thing to the data services guy. I mean, if you're busy with other stuff."

Soren finally looked at her quizzically.

"Why would I need you to do that?"

"Well," Bobbie said, glancing at the time on her terminal, "it's pretty close to eighteen hundred local, and I don't know what time you guys usually close up shop, so I just thought—"

"Don't worry about it. The thing is, my whole job is making her"—he jerked his head toward the closed door—"calm and happy. With her, everything's top priority. And so nothing is, you know? I'll do it when it needs doing. Until then, the bitch can bark a little if it makes her feel happy."

Bobbie felt a cool rush of surprise. No, not surprise. Shock.

"You just called her a bitch?"

"What would you call her, right?" Soren said with a disarming grin. Or was it mocking? Was this all a joke to him, Avasarala and Bobbie and the monster on Ganymede too? An image popped into her head of snatching the smug little assistant out of his chair and snapping him into a zigzag shape. Her hands flexed involuntarily.

Instead, she said, "Madam Secretary seemed to think it was pretty important."

Soren turned to look at her again. "Don't worry about it, Bobbie. Seriously. I know how to do my job."

She stood for a long moment.

"Solid copy on that," she said.

Bobbie was yanked from a dead sleep by sudden blaring music. She lurched upright in an unfamiliar bed in a nearly pitch-black room. The only light she could see was a faint pulsing pearly glow from her hand terminal, all the way across the room. The music suddenly stopped sounding like an atonal cacophony and became the song she'd selected as the audio alarm for incoming phone calls when she went to bed. Someone was calling. She cursed them in three languages and tried to crawl across the bed toward the terminal.

The edge of the bed came unexpectedly and plunged her face-first toward the floor, her half-asleep body not compensating for Earth's heavier gravity. She managed to avoid breaking her head open at the cost of a pair of jammed fingers on her right hand.

Cursing even louder, she continued her trek across the floor to the still glowing terminal. When she finally reached it, she opened the connection and said, "If someone isn't dead, someone *will* be."

"Bobbie," the person on the other end said. It took Bobbie's fuzzy head a moment to place the voice. *Soren.* She glanced at the time on her terminal and saw that it was 0411. She wondered if he was calling to drunkenly upbraid her or apologize. It certainly wouldn't be the strangest thing that'd happened over the last twenty-four hours.

Bobbie realized he was still talking, and put the speaker back up to her ear. "—is expecting you soonest, so get down here," Soren said.

"Can you repeat that?"

He started speaking slowly, as though to a dim child. "The boss wants you to come to the office, okay?"

Bobbie looked at the time again. "Right now?"

"No," Soren said. "Tomorrow at the normal time. She just wanted me to call at four a.m. to make sure you were coming."

The flash of anger helped wake her up. Bobbie stopped gritting her teeth long enough to say, "Tell her I'll be right there."

She fumbled her way to a wall, and then along it to a panel, which lit up at her touch. A second touch brought up the room's lights. Avasarala had gotten her a small furnished apartment within walking distance of the office. It wasn't much bigger than a cheap rent hole on Ceres. One large room that doubled as living space and bedroom, a smaller room with a shower and toilet, and an even smaller room that pretended to be a kitchen. Bobbie's duffel lay slumped in the corner, a few items pulled out of it, but mostly still packed. She'd stayed up till one in the morning reading and hadn't bothered to do anything after that but brush her teeth and then collapse into the bed that pulled down from the ceiling.

As she stood surveying the room and trying to wake up, Bobbie had a sudden moment of total clarity. It was as though a pair of dark glasses she hadn't even known she was wearing were snatched away, leaving her blinking in the light. Here she was, climbing out of bed after three hours of sleep to meet with one of the most powerful women in the solar system, and all she cared about was that she hadn't gotten her quarters shipshape and that she really wanted to beat one of her coworkers to death with his brass pen set. Oh, and she was a career marine who'd taken a job working with her government's current worst enemy because someone in naval intelligence had been mean to her. And not least of all, she wanted to get back to Ganymede and kill someone without having the foggiest idea who that someone might be.

The abrupt and crystal-clear vision of how far off the tracks her life seemed to have fallen lasted for a few seconds, and then the fog and sleep deprivation returned, leaving her with only the disquieting feeling that she'd forgotten to do something important.

She dressed in the prior day's uniform and rinsed her mouth out, then headed out the door.

Avasarala's modest office was packed with people. Bobbie recognized at least three civilians from her first meeting there on Earth. One of them was the moonfaced man who she'd later learned was Sadavir Errinwright, Avasarala's boss and possibly the second most powerful man on Earth. The pair were in an intense conversation when she came in, and Avasarala didn't see her.

Bobbie spotted a small clump of people in military uniforms and drifted in their direction until she saw that they were generals and admirals, and changed course. She wound up next to Soren, the only other person in the room standing alone. He didn't even give her a glance, but something about the way he held himself seemed to radiate that disquieting charm, powerful and insincere. It struck Bobbie that Soren was the kind of man she might take to bed if she was drunk enough, but she'd never trust him to watch her back in a fight. On second thought, no, she'd never be drunk enough.

"Draper!" Avasarala called out in a loud voice, having finally noticed her arrival.

"Yes, ma'am," Bobbie said, taking a step forward as everyone in the room stopped talking to look at her.

"You're my liaison," Avasarala said, the bags under her eyes so pronounced they looked less like fatigue and more like an undiagnosed medical condition. "So fucking *liaise*. Call your people."

"What happened?"

"The situation around Ganymede has just turned into the shit-storm to end all shit-storms," she said. "We're in a shooting war."

Chapter Twenty-One: Prax

Prax knelt, his arms zip-tied securely behind him. His shoulders ached. It hurt to hold his head up and it hurt to let it sink down. Amos lay facedown on the floor. Prax thought he was dead until he saw the zip-ties holding his arms behind his back. The nonlethal round their kidnappers had fired into the back of the mechanic's head had left an enormous blue-and-black lump there. Most of the others—Holden, some of the Pinkwater mercenaries, even Naomi—were in positions much like his own, but not all.

Four years before, they'd had a moth infestation. A containment study had failed, and inch-long gray-brown miller moths had run riot in his dome. They'd built a heat trap: a few dabs of generated pheromones on a heat-resistant fiber swatch under the big long-wave full-spectrum lighting units. The moths came too close, and the heat killed them. The smell of small bodies burning had fouled the air for days, and the scent was exactly like that of the cauterizing drill their abductors were using on the injured Pinkwater man. A swirl of white smoke rose from the formed-plastic office table on which he was laid out.

"I'm just…" the Pinkwater man said through his sedation haze. "You just go ahead, finish that without me. I'll be over…"

"Another bleeder," one of their abductors said. She was a thick-featured woman with a mole under her left eye and blood-slicked rubber gloves. "Right there."

"Check. Got it," said the man with the drill, pressing the metal tip back down into the patient's open belly wound. The sharp tapping sound of electrical discharge, and another small plume of white smoke rising from the wound.

Amos rolled over suddenly, his nose a bloody ruin, his face covered in gore. "I bight be wrong about dis, Cab'n," he said, the words fighting out past the bulbous mess of his nose, "'ut I don'd dink dese fellas are station security."

The room Prax had found himself in when the hood had been lifted had nothing to do with the usual atmosphere of law enforcement. It looked like an old office. The kind a safety inspector or a shipping clerk might have used in the ancient days before the cascade had started: a long desk with a built-in surface terminal, a few recessed lights shining up on the ceiling, a dead plant—*Sanseviera trifasciata*—with long green-brown leaves turning to dark slime. The gray-armored guards or soldiers or whatever they were had been very methodical and efficient. Prisoners were all along one wall, bound at the ankles and wrists; their hand terminals, weapons, and personal effects were stowed along the opposite wall with two guards set to do nothing but make sure no one touched them. The armor they'd stripped off Holden and Amos was in a pile on the floor next to their guns. Then the pair that Prax thought of as the medical team had started working, caring for the most desperately wounded first. They hadn't had time yet to go on to anybody else.

"Any idea who we're dealing with here?" Wendell asked under his breath.

"Not OPA," Holden said.

"That leaves a pretty large number of suspects," the Pinkwater captain said. "Is there somebody you've pissed off I should know about?"

Holden's eyes took on a pained expression and he made a motion as close to a shrug as he could manage, given the circumstances.

"There's kind of a list," he said.

"Another bleeder here," the woman said.

"Check," the drill man said. Tap, smoke, the smell of burning flesh.

"No offense meant, Captain Holden," Wendell said, "but I'm starting to wish I'd just shot you when I had the chance."

"None taken," Holden replied with a nod.

Four of the soldiers came back into the room. They were all squat Earther types. One—a dark-skinned man with a fringe of gray hair and an air of command—was subvocalizing madly. His gaze passed over the prisoners, seeing them without seeing them. Like they were boxes. When his eyes were on Prax, the man nodded but not to him.

"Are they stable?" the dark-skinned man asked the medical team.

"If I had the choice," the woman said, "I wouldn't move this one."

"If you didn't?"

"He'll probably make it. Keep the high g to a minimum until I can get him to a real medical bay."

"Excuse me," Holden said. "Can someone please tell me what the hell's going on?"

He might as well have been asking the walls.

"We've got ten minutes," the dark-skinned man said.

"Transport ship?"

"Not yet. The secure facility."

"Splendid," the woman said sourly.

"Because if you want to ask us any questions," Holden said,

"we should start by getting everybody off Ganymede. If you want your people to still be people, we have to go. That lab we were in had the protomolecule."

"I want them moved two at a time," the dark-skinned man said.

"Yes, sir," the woman replied.

"Are you listening to me?" Holden shouted. "The protomolecule is loose on this station."

"They're not listening to us, Jim," Naomi said.

"Ferguson. Mott," the dark-skinned man said. "Report."

The room was silent as someone somewhere reported in.

"My daughter's missing," Prax said. "That ship took my daughter."

They weren't listening to him either. He hadn't expected them to. With the exception of Holden and his crew, no one had. The dark-skinned man hunched forward, his expression profoundly focused. Prax felt the hair on the back of his neck rise. A premonition.

"Repeat that," the dark-skinned man said. And then a moment later: "*We're* firing? Who's *we*?"

Someone answered. The medical team and the weapons guards had their eyes on the commander too. Their faces were poker-blank.

"Understood. Alpha team, new orders. Get to the port and secure a transport ship. Use of force is authorized. Repeat that: Use of force is authorized. Sergeant Chernev, I need you to cut the prisoners' leg restraints."

One of the gun guards did a double take.

"All of them, sir?"

"All of them. And we're going to need a gurney for this gentleman."

"What's going on, sir?" the sergeant asked, his voice strained by confusion and fear.

"What's going on is I'm giving you an order," the dark-skinned man said, striding fast out the door. "Now *go*."

Prax felt the knife slash as a rough vibration against his ankles.

He hadn't realized his feet were numb until the burning pins-and-needles sensation brought tears to his eyes. Standing hurt. In the distance, something boomed like an empty freight container dropped from a great height. The sergeant cut Amos' legs free from their bonds and moved on to Naomi. One guard still stood by the supplies. The medical team was sealing the gut-shot man's belly closed with a sweet-smelling gel. The sergeant bent over.

The glance between Holden and Amos was the only warning Prax had. As casually as a man heading for the restroom, Holden started walking toward the door.

"Hey!" the weapons guard said, lifting a rifle the size of his arm. Holden looked up innocently, all eyes upon him, while behind him Amos brought his knee up into the sergeant's head. Prax yelped with surprise and the gun swung toward him. He tried to raise his hands, but they were still tied behind him. Wendell stepped forward, put a foot against the medical woman's hip, and pushed her into the guard's line of fire.

Naomi was kneeling on the sergeant's neck; his face was purple. Holden kicked the drill-wielding man in the back of the knee at the same moment that Amos tackled the man with the rifle. The cauterizing drill sparked against the floor with a sound like a finger tapping against glass. Paula had the sergeant's knife in her hands, backing up against one of her compatriots, sawing at the zip line around his wrists. The rifleman swung his elbow, and Amos' breath went out in a whoosh. Holden dropped onto the male half of the medical team, pinning the man's arms with his knees. Amos did something Prax couldn't see, and the rifleman grunted and folded over.

Paula got through the Pinkwater man's zip-tie just as the medical woman scooped up the rifle. The freed man pulled the pistol from the fallen sergeant's holster and leaned forward, pressing the barrel to the medical woman's temple as she swung the rifle up a quarter second too late.

Everyone froze. The medical woman smiled.

"Checkmate," she said, and lowered the rifle to the floor.

It had all taken no more than ten seconds.

Naomi took the knife, quickly, methodically slicing through the wrist bindings while Holden followed along behind, disabling the communication webs in the gray unmarked armor and zip-tying their hands and feet. A perfect inversion of the previous situation. Prax, rubbing the feeling back into his fingers, had the absurd image of the dark-skinned man coming back in and barking orders to him. Another boom came, another huge, resonating container being dropped and sounding out like a drum.

"I just want you to know how much I appreciate the way you looked after my people," Wendell told the pair who made up the medical team.

The woman suggested something obscene and unpleasant, but she smiled while she did it.

"Wendell," Holden said, rummaging in the box of their belongings and then tossing a card-key to the Pinkwater leader. "The *Somnambulist* is still yours, but you need to get to her now and get the hell out of here."

"Preaching to the choir," Wendell said. "Get that gurney. We're not leaving him behind now, and we've got to get out of here before reinforcements come."

"Yessir," Paula said.

Wendell turned to Holden.

"It was interesting meeting you, Captain. Let's not do this again."

Holden nodded but didn't stop putting his armor back on to shake hands. Amos did the same, then distributed their confiscated weapons and items back to them. Holden checked the magazine on his gun and then left through the same door the dark-skinned man had used, Amos and Naomi on his heels. Prax had to trot to catch up. Another detonation came, this one not so distant. Prax thought he felt the ice shake under him, but it might have been his imagination.

"What's...what's going on?"

"The protomolecule's breaking out," Holden said, tossing a hand terminal to Naomi. "The infection's taking hold."

"I don'd dink dat' whas habn'ing, Cab'n," Amos said. With a grimace he grabbed his nose with his right hand and yanked it away from his face. When he let go, it looked mostly straight. He blew a bloody-colored plug of snot out of each nostril, then took a deep breath. "That's better."

"Alex?" Naomi said into her handset. "Alex, tell me this link is still up. Talk to me."

Her voice was shaking.

Another boom, this one louder than anything Prax had ever heard. The shaking wasn't imagined now; it threw Prax to the ground. The air had a strange smell, like overheated iron. The station lights flickered and went dark; the pale blue emergency evacuation LEDs came on. A low-pressure Klaxon was sounding, its tritone blat designed to carry through thin and thinning air. When Holden spoke, he sounded almost contemplative.

"Or they might be bombarding the station."

Ganymede Station was one of the first permanent human toeholds in the outer planets. It had been built with the long term in mind, not only in its own architecture, but also in how it would fit with the grand human expansion out into the darkness at the edge of the solar system. The possibility of catastrophe was in its DNA and had been from the beginning. It had been the safest station in the Jovian system. Just the name had once brought to mind images of newborn babies and domes filled with food crops. But the months since the mirrors fell had corroded it.

Pressure doors meant to isolate atmosphere loss had been wedged open when local hydraulics had failed. Emergency supplies had been used up and not replaced. Anything of value that could be turned into food or passage on the black market had been stolen and sold. The social infrastructure of Ganymede was already in its slow, inevitable collapse. The worst of the worst-case plans hadn't envisioned this.

Prax stood in the arching common space where Nicola and he

had gone on their first date. They'd eaten together at a little *dulcería*, drinking coffee and flirting. He could still remember the shape of her face and the heart-stopping thrill he'd felt when she took his hand. The ice where the *dulcería* had been was a fractured chaos. A dozen passages intersected here, and people were streaming through them, trying to get to the port or else deep enough into the moon that the ice would shield them, or someplace they could tell themselves was safe.

The only home he'd really known was falling apart around him. Thousands of people were going to die in the next few hours. Prax knew that, and part of him was horrified by it. But Mei had been on that ship, so she wasn't one of them. He still had to rescue her, just not from this. It made it bearable.

"Alex says it's hot out there," Naomi said as the four of them trotted through the ruins. "Really hot. He's not going to be able to make it to the port."

"There's the other landing pad," Prax said. "We could go there."

"That's the plan," Holden said. "Give Alex the coordinates for the science base."

"Yes, sir," Naomi said at the same moment Amos, raising a hand like a kid in a schoolroom, said, "The one with the protomolecule?"

"It's the only secret landing pad I've got," Holden said.

"Yeah, all right."

When Holden turned to Prax, his face was gray with strain and fear.

"Okay, Prax. You're the local. Our armor is vacuum rated, but we'll need environment suits for you and Naomi. We're about to run through hell, and not all of it's going to be pressurized. I don't have time to take a wrong turn or look for something twice. You're point. Can you handle it?"

"Yes," Prax said.

Finding the emergency environment suits was easy. They were common enough to have essentially no resale value and stowed at brightly colored emergency stations. All the supplies in the main halls and corridors were already stripped, but ducking down a narrow side corridor that linked to the less popular complex where Prax used to take Mei to the skating rink was easy. The suits there were safety orange and green, made to be visible to rescuers. Camouflage would have been more appropriate. The masks smelled of volatile plastic, and the joints were just rings sewn into the material. The suit heaters looked ill cared for and likely to catch on fire if used too long. Another blast came, followed by two others, each sounding closer than the one before.

"Nukes," Naomi said.

"Maybe gauss rounds," Holden replied. They might have been talking about the weather.

Prax shrugged.

"Either way, a hit that gets into a corridor means superheated steam," he said, pressing the last seal along his side closed and checking the cheap green LED that promised the oxygen was flowing. The heating system flickered to yellow, then back to green. "You and Amos might make it if your armor's good. I don't think Naomi and I stand a chance."

"Great," Holden said.

"I've lost the *Roci*," Naomi said. "No. I've lost the whole link. I was routing through the *Somnambulist*. She must have taken off."

Or been slagged. The thought was on all their faces. No one said it.

"Over this way," Prax said. "There's a service tunnel we used to use when I was in college. We can get around the Marble Arch complex and head up from there."

"Whatever you say, buddy," Amos said. His nose was bleeding again. The blood looked black in the faint blue light inside his helmet.

It was his last walk. Whatever happened, Prax was never coming back here, because *here* wouldn't exist. The fast lope along the service corridor where Jaimie Loomis and Tanna Ibtrahmin-Sook had taken him to get high was the last time he'd see that place. The broad, low-ceilinged amphitheater under the old water treatment center where he'd had his first internship was cracked, the reservoir compromised. It wouldn't flood the corridors quickly, but in a couple of days, the passageways would be filled in. In a couple of days, it wouldn't matter.

Everything glowed in the emergency LEDs or else fell into shadow. There was slush on the ground as the heating system struggled to compensate for the madness and failed. Twice, the way was blocked, once by a pressure door that was actually still functional, once by an icefall. They met almost no one. The others were all running for the port. Prax was leading them almost directly away from it now.

Another long, curved hall, then up a construction ramp, through an empty tunnel, and…

The blue steel door that blocked their way wasn't locked, but it was in safety mode. The indicator said there was vacuum on the other side. One of the God-like fists pummeling Ganymede had broken through here. Prax stopped, his mind clicking through the three-dimensional architecture of his home station. If the secret base was *there*, and he was *here*, then…

"We can't get there," he said.

The others were silent for a moment.

"That's not a good answer," Holden said. "Find a different one."

Prax took a long breath. If they doubled back, they could go down a level, head to the west, and try getting to the corridor from below, except that a blast strong enough to break through here would almost certainly have compromised the level below too. If they kept going to the old tube station, they might be able to find a service corridor—not that he knew there was one, but maybe—and it might lead in the right direction. Three more detonations came, shaking the ice. With a sound like a baseball bat hitting a home run, the wall beside him cracked.

"Prax, buddy," Amos said, "sooner'd be better."

They had environment suits, so if they opened the door, the vacuum wouldn't kill them. But there would be debris choking it. Any strike hard enough to break through to the surface would…

Would…

"We can't get there…through the station tunnels," he said. "But we can go up. Get to the surface and go that way."

"And how do we do that?" Holden asked.

Finding an access way that wasn't locked down took twenty minutes, but Prax found one. No wider than three men walking abreast, it was an automated service unit for the dome exteriors. The service unit itself had long since been cannibalized for parts, but that didn't matter. The airlock was still working under battery power. Naomi and Prax fed it the instructions, closed the inner door, and cycled the outer open. The escaping pressure was like a wind for a moment, and then nothing. Prax walked out onto the surface of Ganymede.

He'd seen images of the aurora from Earth. He'd never imagined he'd see anything like it in the blackness of his own sky. But there, not just above him but in lines from horizon to horizon, were streaks of green and blue and gold—chaff and debris and the radiating gas of cooling plasma. Incandescent blooms marked torch drives. Several kilometers away, a gauss round slammed into the moon's surface, the seismic shock knocking them from their feet. Prax lay there for a moment, watching the water ejecta geyser up into the darkness and then begin to fall back down as snow. It was beautiful. The rational, scientific part of his mind tried to calculate how much energy transfer there was to the moon when a rail-gun-hurled chunk of tungsten hit it. It would be like a miniature nuke without all the messy radiation. He wondered if the round would stop before it hit Ganymede's nickel-iron core.

"Okay," Holden said over the cheap radio in Prax's emergency suit. The low end of the sound spectrum was lousy, and Holden sounded like a cartoon character. "Which way now?"

"I don't know," Prax said, rising to his knees. He pointed toward the horizon. "Over there somewhere."

"I need more than that," Holden said.

"I've never been on the surface before," Prax said. "In a dome, sure. But just *out*? I mean, I know we're close to it, but I don't know how to get there."

"All right," Holden said. In the high vacuum over his head, something huge and very far away detonated. It was like the old cartoon lightbulb of someone getting an idea. "We can do this. We can solve this. Amos, you head toward that hill over there, see what you can see. Prax and Naomi, start going that direction."

"I don't think we need to do that, sir," Naomi said.

"Why not?"

Naomi raised her hand, pointing back behind Holden and Prax both.

"Because I'm pretty sure that's the *Roci* setting down over there," she said.

Chapter Twenty-Two: Holden

The secret landing pad lay in the hollow of a small crater. When Holden crested the lip and saw the *Rocinante* below him, the sudden and dizzying release of tension told him how frightened he'd been for the last several hours. But the *Roci* was home, and no matter how hard his rational mind argued that they were still in terrible danger, home was safe. As he paused a moment to catch his breath, the scene was lit with bright white light, like someone had taken a picture. Holden looked up in time to see a fading cloud of glowing gas in high orbit.

People were still dying in space just over their heads.

"Wow," Prax said. "It's bigger than I expected."

"Corvette," Amos replied, obvious pride in his voice. "Frigate-class fleet escort ship."

"I don't know what any of that means," Prax said. "It looks like a big chisel with an upside-down coffee cup on the back."

Amos said, "That's the drive—"

"Enough," Holden cut in. "Get to the airlock."

Amos led the way, sliding down the crater's icy wall hunched down on his heels and using his hands for balance. Prax went next, for once not needing any help. Naomi went third, her reflexes and balance honed by a lifetime spent in shifting gravities. She actually managed to look graceful.

Holden went last, fully prepared to slip and go down the hill in a humiliating tumble, then pleasantly surprised when he didn't.

As they bounded across the flat floor of the crater toward the ship, the outer airlock door slid open, revealing Alex in a suit of Martian body armor and carrying an assault rifle. As soon as they were close enough to the ship that they could cut through the orbital radio clutter, Holden said, "Alex! Man, is it good to see you."

"Hey, Cap," Alex replied, even his exaggerated drawl not able to hide the relief in his voice. "Wasn't sure how hot this LZ would be. Anyone chasin' you?"

Amos ran up the ramp and grabbed Alex in a bear hug that yanked him off his feet.

"Man, it's fucking good to be home!" he said.

Prax and Naomi followed, Naomi patting Alex on the shoulder as she went by. "You did good. Thank you."

Holden stopped on the ramp to look up one last time. The sky was still filled with the flashes and light trails of ongoing battle. He had the sudden visceral memory of being a boy back in Montana, watching massive thunderheads flash with hidden lightning.

Alex watched with him, then said, "It was a bit hectic, comin' in."

Holden threw an arm around his shoulder. "Thanks for the ride."

Once the airlock had finished cycling and the crew had removed their environment suits and armor, Holden said, "Alex, this is Prax Meng. Prax, this is the solar system's best pilot, Alex Kamal."

Prax shook Alex's hand. "Thank you for helping me find Mei."

Alex frowned a question at Holden, but a quick shake of the head kept him from asking it. "Nice to meet you, Prax."

"Alex," Holden said, "get us warmed up for liftoff, but don't take off until I'm up in the copilot's chair."

"Roger," Alex said, and headed toward the bow of the ship.

"Everything's sideways," Prax said, looking around at the storage room just past the inner airlock door.

"The *Roci* doesn't spend much time on her belly like this," Naomi said, taking his hand and leading him to the crew ladder, which now appeared to run across the floor. "We're standing on a bulkhead, and that wall to our right is normally the deck."

"Grew up in low grav and don't spend much time on ships, apparently," Amos said. "Man, this next part is really gonna suck for you."

"Naomi," Holden said. "Get to ops and get belted in. Amos, take Prax to the crew deck and then head down to engineering and get the *Roci* ready for a rough ride."

Before they could leave, Holden put a hand on Prax's shoulder.

"This takeoff and flight is going to be fast and bumpy. If you haven't trained for high-g flight, it will probably be very uncomfortable."

"Don't worry about me," Prax said, making what he probably thought was a brave face.

"I know you're tough. You couldn't have survived the last couple weeks otherwise. You don't have anything to prove at this point. Amos will take you to the crew deck. Find a room without a name on the door. That will be your room now. Get in the crash couch and buckle in, then hit the bright green button on the panel to your left. The couch will pump you full of drugs that will sedate you and keep you from blowing a blood vessel if we have to burn hard."

"My room?" Prax said, an odd note in his voice.

"We'll get you some clothes and sundries once we're out of this shit. You can keep them there."

"My room," Prax repeated.

"Yeah," Holden said. "Your room." He could see Prax fighting down a lump in his throat, and he realized what the simple offer of comfort and safety probably meant to someone who'd been through what the small botanist had over the last month.

There were tears in the man's eyes.

"Come on, let's get you settled in," Amos said, leading Prax aft toward the crew deck.

Holden headed the other way, past the ops deck, where Naomi was already strapped down into a chair at one of the workstations, then forward into the cockpit. He climbed into the copilot's seat and belted in.

"Five minutes," he said over the shipwide channel.

"So," Alex said, dragging the word out to two syllables while he flicked switches to finish the preflight check, "we're lookin' for someone named Mei?"

"Prax's daughter."

"We do that now? Seems like the scope of our mission is creepin' a bit."

Holden nodded. Finding lost daughters was not part of their mandate. That had been Miller's job. And he'd never be able to adequately explain the certainty he felt that this lost little girl was at the center of everything that had happened on Ganymede.

"I think this lost little girl is at the center of everything that's happened on Ganymede," he said with a shrug.

"Okay," Alex replied, then hit something on a panel twice and frowned. "Huh, we have a red on the board. Gettin' a 'no seal' on the cargo airlock. Might've caught some flak on the way down, I guess. It was pretty hot up there."

"Well, we're not going to stop and fix it now," Holden said. "We keep the bay in vacuum most of the time anyway. If the inner hatch into the cargo area is showing a good seal, just override the alarm and let's go."

"Roger," Alex said, and tapped the override.

"One minute," Holden said over the shipwide, then turned to Alex. "So I'm curious."

"'Bout?"

"How'd you manage to slip through that shit-storm up above us, and can you do it again on the way out?"

Alex laughed.

"Simple matter of never bein' higher than the second-highest threat on anyone's board. And, of course, not bein' there anymore when they decide to get around to you."

"I'm giving you a raise," Holden said, then began the ten-second countdown. At one, the *Roci* blasted off of Ganymede on four pillars of superheated steam.

"Rotate us for a full burn as soon as you can," Holden said, the rumble of the ship's takeoff giving him an artificial vibrato.

"This close?"

"There's nothing below us that matters," Holden said, thinking of the remnants of black filament they'd seen in the hidden base. "Melt it."

"Okay," Alex said. Then, once the ship had finished orienting straight up, he said, "Givin' her the spurs."

Even with the juice coursing through his blood, Holden blacked out for a moment. When he came to, the *Roci* was veering wildly from side to side. The cockpit was alive with the sounds of warning buzzers.

"Whoa, honey," Alex was saying under his breath. "Whoa, big girl."

"Naomi," Holden said, looking at a confusing mass of red on the threat board and trying to decipher it with his blood-starved brain. "Who's firing at us?"

"Everyone." She sounded as groggy as he felt.

"Yeah," Alex said, his tension draining some of the good-old-boy drawl out of his voice. "She's not kidding."

The swarm of threats on his display began to make sense, and Holden saw they were right. It looked like half of the inner planets ships on their side of Ganymede had lobbed at least one missile at them. He entered the command code to set all the weapons to free fire and sent control of the aft PDCs to Amos. "Amos, cover our asses."

Alex was doing his best to keep any of the incoming missiles from catching them, but ultimately that was a lost cause. Nothing with meat inside it could outrun metal and silicon.

"Where are we—" Holden said, stopping to target a missile that wandered into the front starboard PDC's firing arc. The point defense cannon fired off a long burst at it. The missile was smart enough to turn sharply and evade, but its sudden course change bought them a few more seconds.

"Callisto's on our side of Jupiter," Alex said, referring to the next sizable moon out from Ganymede. "Gonna get in its shadow."

Holden checked the vectors of the ships that had fired at them. If any of them were pursuing, Alex's gambit would only buy them a few minutes. But it didn't appear they were. Of the dozen or so that had attacked them, over half were moderately to severely damaged, and the ones that weren't were still busy shooting at each other.

"Seems like we were everyone's number one threat there for a second," Holden said. "But not so much anymore."

"Yeah, sorry about that, Cap. Not sure why that happened."

"I don't blame you," Holden said.

The *Roci* shuddered, and Amos gave a whoop over the ship-wide comm. "Don't be trying to touch my girl's ass!"

Two of the closer missiles had vanished off the threat board.

"Nice work, Amos," Holden said, checking the updated times to impact and seeing that they'd bought another half minute.

"Shit, Cap, the *Roci* does all the work," Amos said. "I just encourage her to express herself."

"Going to duck and cover around Callisto. I'd appreciate a distraction," Alex said to Holden.

"Okay, Naomi, another ten seconds or so," Holden said. "Then hit them with everything you've got. We'll need them blind for a few seconds."

"Roger," Naomi said. Holden could see her prepping a massive assault package of laser clutter and radio jamming.

The *Rocinante* lurched again, and the moon Callisto suddenly filled Holden's forward screen. Alex hurtled toward it at a suicidal rate, flipping the ship and hard burning at the last second to throw them into a low slingshot orbit.

"Three...two...one...now," he said, the *Roci* diving tail first toward Callisto, whipping past it so low that Holden felt like he could have reached out the airlock and scooped up some snow. At the same time, Naomi's jamming package hammered the sensors of the pursuing missiles, blinding them while their processors worked to cut through the noise.

By the time they'd reacquired the *Rocinante*, she'd been thrown around Callisto by gravity and her own drive in a new vector and at high speed. Two of the missiles gamely tried to come about and pursue, but the rest either limped off in random directions or slammed into the moon. When their two pursuers had gotten back on course, the *Roci* had opened up an enormous lead and could take her time shooting them down.

"We made it," Alex said. Holden found the disbelief in his pilot's voice fairly disconcerting. Had it been that close?

"Never doubted it," Holden said. "Take us to Tycho. Half a g. I'll be in my cabin."

When they were finished, Naomi flopped onto her side in their shared bunk, sweat plastering her curly black hair to her forehead. She was still panting. He was too.

"That was...vigorous," she said.

Holden nodded but didn't have enough air to actually speak yet. When he'd climbed down the ladder from the cockpit, Naomi had been waiting, already out of her restraints. She'd grabbed him and kissed him so hard his lip had split. He hadn't even noticed. They'd barely reached the cabin with their clothes on. What had happened afterward was sort of a blur now to Holden, though his legs were tired and his lip hurt.

Naomi rolled across him and climbed out of the bunk.

"I've got to pee," she said, pulling on a robe and heading out the door. Holden just nodded to her, still not quite capable of speech.

He shifted over to the middle of the bed, stretching out his arms and legs for a moment. The truth was the *Roci*'s cabins were not built for two occupants, least of all the crash couches that doubled as beds. But over the course of the last year, he'd spent more and more time sleeping in Naomi's cabin, until it sort of became *their* cabin and he just didn't sleep anywhere else anymore. They couldn't share the bunk during high-g maneuvers, but so far they'd never been asleep anytime the ship had needed to do high-g maneuvering. A trend that was likely to continue.

Holden was starting to doze off when the hatch opened and Naomi came back in. She tossed a cold, wet washcloth onto his belly.

"Wow, that's bracing," Holden said, sitting up with a start.

"It was hot when I left the head with it."

"That," Holden said while he cleaned up, "sounded very dirty."

Naomi grinned, then sat on the edge of the bunk and poked him in the ribs. "You can still think of sex? I would've thought we got that out of your system."

"A close brush with death does wonderful things for my refractory period."

Naomi climbed into the bunk next to him, still wrapped in her robe.

"You know," she said, "this was my idea. And I'm all in favor of reaffirming life through sex."

"Why do I get the feeling that there is a 'but' missing at the end of that sentence?"

"But—"

"Ah, there it is."

"There's something we need to talk about. And this seems a good time."

Holden rolled over onto his side, facing her, and pushed up onto one elbow. A thick strand of hair was hanging in her face, and he brushed it back with his other hand.

"What did I do?" he said.

"It's not exactly anything you've done," Naomi said. "It's more what we're heading off to do right now."

Holden put his hand on her arm but waited for her to continue. The soft cloth of her robe clung to the wet skin beneath it.

"I'm worried," she said, "that we're flying off to Tycho to do something really rash."

"Naomi, you weren't there, you didn't see—"

"I saw it, Jim, through Amos' suitcam. I know what it is. I know how much it scares you. It scares the hell out of me too."

"No," Holden said, his voice surprising him with its anger. "No you don't. You weren't on Eros when it got out, you never—"

"Hey, I was there. Maybe not for the worst of it. Not like you," Naomi said, her voice still calm. "But I did help carry what was left of you and Miller to the med bay. And I watched you try to die there. We can't just accuse Fred of—"

"Right now—and I mean *right now*—Ganymede could be changing."

"No—"

"*Yes*. Yes it could. We could be leaving a couple million dead people behind right now who don't know it yet. Melissa and Santichai? Remember them? Now think of them stripped down to whatever pieces the protomolecule finds most useful at the moment. Think of them as *parts*. Because if that bug is loose on Ganymede, then that's what they are."

"Jim," Naomi said, a warning in her voice now. "This is what I'm talking about. The intensity of your feelings isn't *evidence*. You are about to accuse a man who's been your friend and patron for the last year of maybe killing an entire moon full of people. That isn't the Fred we know. And you owe him better than that."

Holden pushed up to a sitting position, part of him wanting to physically distance himself from Naomi, the part of him that was angry with her for not sympathizing enough.

"*I* gave Fred the last of it. *I gave it to him*, and he swore right to my face he'd never use it. But that's not what I saw down there.

You call him my friend, but Fred has only ever done what would advance his own cause. Even helping us was just another move in his political game."

"Experiments on kidnapped children?" Naomi said. "A whole moon—one of the most important in the outer planets—put at risk and maybe killed outright? Does that make any sense to you? Does that sound like Fred Johnson?"

"The OPA wants Ganymede even more than either inner planet does," Holden said, finally admitting the thing he'd feared since they'd found the black filament. "And they wouldn't give it to him."

"Stop," Naomi said.

"Maybe he's trying to drive them off, or he sold it to them in exchange for the moon. That would at least explain the heavy inner planets traffic we've been seeing—"

"No. Stop," she said. "I don't want to sit here and listen to you talk yourself into this."

Holden started to speak, but Naomi sat up facing him and gently put her hand over his mouth.

"I didn't like this new Jim Holden you've been turning into. The guy who'd rather reach for his gun than talk? I know being the OPA's bagman has been a shitty job, and I know we've had to do a lot of pretty rotten things in the name of protecting the Belt. But that was still you. I could still see you lurking there under the surface, waiting to come back."

"Naomi," he said, pulling her hand away from his face.

"This guy who can't wait to go all *High Noon* in the streets of Tycho? That's not Jim Holden at all. I don't recognize that man," she said, then frowned. "No. That's not right. I do recognize him. But his name was Miller."

For Holden, the most awful part was how calm she was. She never raised her voice, never sounded angry. Instead, infinitely worse, there was only a resigned sadness.

"If that's who you are now, you need to drop me off somewhere. I can't go with you anymore," she said. "I'm out."

Chapter Twenty-Three: Avasarala

Avasarala stood at her window, looking out at the morning haze. In the distance, a transport lifted off. It rode an exhaust plume that looked like a pillar of bright white cloud, and then it was gone. Her hands ached. She knew that some of the photons striking her eyes right now had come from explosions light-minutes away. Ganymede Station, once the safest place without an atmosphere, then a war zone, and now a wasteland. She could no more pick out the light of its death than pluck a particular molecule of salt from the ocean, but she knew it was there, and the fact was like a stone in her belly.

"I can ask for confirmation," Soren said. "Nguyen should be filing his command report in the next eighteen hours. Once we have that—"

"We'll know what he said," Avasarala snapped. "I can tell you that right now. The Martian forces took a threatening position, and he was forced to respond aggressively. La la fucking la. *Where did he get the ships?*"

"He's an admiral," Soren said. "I thought he came with them."

She turned. The boy looked tired. He'd been up since the small hours of the morning. They all had. His eyes were bloodshot, and his skin pallid and clammy.

"I took apart that command group myself," she said. "I pared it down until you could have drowned it in a bathtub. And he's out there now with enough firepower to take on the Martian fleet?"

"Apparently," Soren said.

She fought the urge to spit. The rumble of the transport engines finally reached her, the sound muffled by distance and the glazing. The light was already gone. To her sleep-deprived mind, it was exactly like playing politics in the Jovian system or the Belt. Something happened—she could see it happen—but she heard it only after the fact. When it was too late.

She'd made a mistake. Nguyen was a war hawk. The kind of adolescent boy who still thought any problem could be solved by shooting it enough. Everything he'd done was as subtle as a lead pipe to the kneecap, until this. Now he'd reassembled his command without her knowing it. And he'd had her pulled from the Martian negotiations.

Which meant that he hadn't done any of it. Nguyen had either a patron or a cabal. She hadn't seen that he was a bit player, so whoever called his tune had surprised her. She was playing against shadows, and she hated it.

"More light," she said.

"Excuse me?"

"Find out how he got those ships," she said. "Do it before you go to sleep. I want a full accounting. Where the replacement ships came from, who ordered them, how they were justified. Everything."

"Would you also like a pony, ma'am?"

"You're fucking right I would," she said, and sagged against her desk. "You do good work. Someday you might get a real job."

"I'm looking forward to it, ma'am."

"Is she still around?"

"At her desk," Soren said. "Should I send her in?"

"You better had."

When Bobbie came into the room, a film of cheap paper in her fist, it struck Avasarala again how poorly the Martian fit in. It wasn't only her accent or the difference in build that spoke of a childhood in the lower Martian gravity. In the halls of politics, the woman's air of physical competence stood out. She looked like she'd been rousted out of bed in the middle of the night, just like all of them; it was only that it looked good on her. Might be useful, might not, but certainly it was worth remembering.

"What have you got?" Avasarala asked.

The marine's frown was all in her forehead.

"I've gotten through to a couple of people in the command. Most of them don't know who the hell I am, though. I probably spent as much time telling them I was working for you as I did talking about Ganymede."

"It's a lesson. Martian bureaucrats are stupid, venal people. What did they say?"

"Long story?"

"Short."

"You shot at us."

Avasarala leaned back in her chair. Her back hurt, her knees hurt, and the knot of sorrow and outrage that was always just under her heart felt brighter than usual.

"Of course we did," she said. "The peace delegation?"

"Already gone," Bobbie said. "They'll be releasing a statement sometime tomorrow about how the UN was negotiating in bad faith. They're still fighting out the exact wording."

"What's the hold?"

Bobbie shook her head. She didn't understand.

"What words are they fighting over, and which side wants which words?" Avasarala demanded.

"I don't know. Does it matter?"

Of course it mattered. The difference between *The UN has been negotiating in bad faith* and *The UN was negotiating in bad faith* could be measured in hundreds of lives. Thousands. Avasarala tried to swallow her impatience. It didn't come naturally.

"All right," she said. "See if there's anything else you can get me."

Bobbie held out the paper. Avasarala took it.

"The hell is this?" she asked.

"My resignation," Bobbie said. "I thought you'd want all the paperwork in place. We're at war now, so I'll be shipping back. Getting my new assignment."

"Who recalled you?"

"No one, yet," Bobbie said. "But—"

"Will you please sit down? I feel like I'm at the bottom of a fucking well, talking to you."

The marine sat. Avasarala took a deep breath.

"Do you want to kill me?" Avasarala asked. Bobbie blinked, and before she could answer, Avasarala lifted her hand, commanding silence. "I am one of the most powerful people in the UN. We're at war. So do you want to kill me?"

"I…guess so?"

"You don't. You want to find out who killed your men and you want the politicians to stop greasing the wheels with Marine blood. And holy shit! What do you know? I want that too."

"But I'm active-duty Martian military," Bobbie said. "If I stay working for you, I'm committing treason." The way she said it wasn't complaint or accusation.

"They haven't recalled you," Avasarala said. "And they're not going to. The wartime diplomatic code of contact is almost exactly the same for you as it is for us, and it's ten thousand pages of nine-point type. If you get orders right now, I can put up enough queries and requests for clarifications that you'll die of old age in that chair. If you just want to kill someone for Mars, you're not going to get a better target than me. If you want to stop this idiotic fucking war and find out who's actually behind it, get back to your desk and find out who wants what wording."

Bobbie was silent for a long moment.

"You mean that as a rhetorical device," she said at last, "but it would make a certain amount of sense to kill you. And I can do it."

A tiny chill hit Avasarala's spine, but she didn't let it reach her face.

"I'll try not to oversell the point in the future. Now get back to work."

"Yes, sir," Bobbie said, then stood and walked out of the room. Avasarala blew out a breath, her cheeks ballooning. She was inviting Martian Marines to slaughter her in her own office. She needed a fucking nap. Her hand terminal chimed. An unscheduled high-status report had just come through, the deep red banner overriding her usual display settings. She tapped it, ready for more bad news from Ganymede.

It was about Venus.

Until seven hours earlier, the *Arboghast* had been a third-generation destroyer, built at the Bush Shipyards thirteen years before and later refitted as a military science vessel. For the last eight months, she'd been orbiting Venus. Most of the active scanning data that Avasarala had relied on had come from her.

The event she was watching had been captured by two lunar telescopic stations with broad-spectrum intelligence feeds that happened to be at the correct angles, and about a dozen shipborne optical observers. The dataset they collected agreed perfectly.

"Play it again," Avasarala said.

Michael-Jon de Uturbé had been a field technician when she'd first met him, thirty years before. Now he was the de facto head of the special sciences committee and married to Avasarala's roommate from university. In that time, his hair had fallen out or grown white, his dark brown skin had taken to draping a bit off of his bones, and he hadn't changed the brand of cheap floral cologne he wore.

He had always been an intensely shy, almost antisocial, man. In order to maintain the connection, she knew not to ask too much of him. His small, cluttered office was less than a quarter of a mile from hers, and she had seen him five times in the last decade, each of them moments when she needed to understand something obscure and complex quickly.

He tapped his hand terminal twice, and the images on the display reset. The *Arboghast* was whole once more, floating in false color detail above the haze of Venusian cloud. The time stamp started moving forward, one second per second.

"Walk me through," she said.

"Um. Well. We start from the spike. It's just like the one we saw that last time Ganymede started going to hell."

"Splendid. That's two datapoints."

"This came before the fighting," he said. "Maybe an hour. A little less."

It had come during Holden's firefight. Before she could bring him in. But how could Venus be responding to Holden's raid on Ganymede? Had Bobbie's monsters been part of that fight?

"Then the radio ping. Right"—he froze the display—"here. Massive sweep in three-second-by-seven-second grid. It was looking, but it knew where to look. All those active scans, I'd assume. Called attention."

"All right."

He started the playback again. The resolution went a few degrees grainier, and he made a pleased sound.

"This was interesting," he said, as if the rest were not. "Radiative pulse of some kind. Interfered with all the telescopy except a strictly visible spectrum kit on Luna. Only lasted a tenth of a second, though. The microwave burst after it was pretty normal active sensor scanning."

You sound disappointed perched at the back of Avasarala's tongue, but the dread and anticipation of what would come next stopped it. The *Arboghast*, with 572 souls aboard her, came apart like a cloud. Hull plates peeled away in neat, orderly rows. Superstructural girders and decks shifted apart. The engineering bays detached, slipping away. In the image before her, the full crew had been exposed to hard vacuum. In the moment she was looking at now, they were all dying and not yet dead. That it was like watching a construction plan animation—crew quarters here, the engineering section here, the plates cupping the drive thus and so—only made it more monstrous.

"Now this is especially interesting," Michael-Jon said, stopping the playback. "Watch what happens when we increase magnification."

Don't show them to me, Avasarala wanted to say. *I don't want to watch them die.*

But the image he moved in on wasn't a human being, but a knot of complicated ducting. He advanced it slowly, frame by frame, and the image grew misty.

"It's ablating?" she asked.

"What? No, no. Here, I'll bring you closer."

The image jumped in again. The cloudiness was an illusion created by a host of small bits of metal: bolts, nuts, Edison clamps, O-rings. She squinted. It wasn't a loose cloud either. Like iron filings under the influence of a magnet, each tiny piece was held in line with the ones before and behind it.

"The *Arboghast* wasn't torn apart," he said. "It was disassembled. It looks as though there were about fifteen separate waves, each one undoing another level of the mechanism. Stripped the whole thing down to the screws."

Avasarala took a deep breath, then another, then another, until the sound lost its ragged edge and the awe and fear grew small enough that she could push it to the back of her mind.

"What does this?" she said at last. She'd meant it as a rhetorical question. Of course there was no answer. No force known to humanity could do what had just been done. That wasn't the meaning he took.

"Graduate students," he said brightly. "My Industrial Design final was just the same. They gave us all machines and we had to take them apart and figure out what they did. Extra credit was to deliver an improved design." And a moment later, his voice melancholy: "Of course we also had to put them back together, yes?"

On the display, the rigidity and order of the floating bits of metal stopped, and the bolts and girders, vast ceramic plates and minute clamps began to drift, set in chaotic motion by the departure of whatever had been holding them. Seventy seconds from first burst to the end. A little over a minute, and not a shot fired in response. Not even something clearly to be shot.

"The crew?"

"Took their suits apart. Didn't bother disassembling the bodies. Might have interpreted them as a logical unit or might already know all it needs to about human anatomy."

"Who's seen this?"

Michael-Jon blinked, then shrugged, then blinked again.

"*This* this, or a version of this? We're the only one with both high-def feeds, but it's Venus. Everyone who was looking saw it. Not like it's in a sealed lab."

She closed her eyes, pressing her fingers against the bridge of her nose as if she were fighting a headache while she struggled to keep the mask in place. Better to seem in pain. Better to seem impatient. The fear shook her like a seizure, like something happening to somebody else. Tears welled up in her eyes, and she bit her lip until they went away. She pulled up the personnel locator on her hand terminal. Nguyen was out of the question even if he'd been in conversational range. Nettleford was with a dozen ships burning toward Ceres Station, and she wasn't entirely certain of him. Souther.

"Can you send this version to Admiral Souther?"

"Oh, no. It's not cleared for release."

Avasarala looked at him, her expression empty.

"Are you clearing it for release?"

"I am clearing it for release to Admiral Souther. Please send it immediately."

Michael-Jon bobbed a quick nod, tapping with the tips of both pinkies. Avasarala took out her own hand terminal and sent a simple message to Souther. WATCH AND CALL ME. When she stood, her legs ached.

"It was good seeing you again," Michael-Jon said, not looking at her. "We should all have dinner sometime."

"Let's," Avasarala said, and left.

The women's restroom was cold. Avasarala stood at the sink, her palms flat against the granite. She wasn't used to fear or awe. Her life had been about control, talking and bullying and teasing whoever needed it until the world turned the direction she wanted it to. The few times the implacable universe had overwhelmed her haunted her: an earthquake in Bengal when she'd been a girl, a storm in Egypt that had trapped her and Arjun in their hotel room for four days as the food supplies failed, the death of her son. Each one had turned her constant pretense of certainty and pride against her, left her curled in her bed at night for weeks afterward, her fingers bent in claws, her dreams nightmares.

This was worse. Before, she could comfort herself with the idea that the universe was empty of intent. That all the terrible things were just the accidental convergences of chance and mindless forces. The death of the *Arboghast* was something else. It was intentional and inhuman. It was like seeing the face of God and finding no compassion there.

Shaking, she pulled up her hand terminal. Arjun answered almost immediately. From the set of his jaw and the softness of his eyes, she knew he had seen some version of the event. And his thought hadn't been for the fate of mankind, but for her. She tried to smile, but it was too much. Tears ran down her cheeks. Arjun sighed gently and looked down.

"I love you very much," Avasarala said. "Knowing you has let me bear the unbearable."

Arjun grinned. He looked good with wrinkles. He was a more handsome man now that he was older. As if the round-faced, comically earnest boy who'd snuck to her window to read poems in the night had only been waiting to become this.

"I love you, I have always loved you, if we are born into new lives, I will love you there."

Avasarala sobbed once, wiped her eyes with the back of her hand, and nodded.

"All right, then," she said.

"Back to work?"

"Back to work. I may be home late."

"I'll be here. You can wake me."

They were silent for a moment; then she released the connection. Admiral Souther hadn't called. Errinwright hadn't called. Avasarala's mind was leaping around like a terrier attacking a troop transport. She rose to her feet, forced herself to put one foot in front of the other. The simple physical act of walking seemed to clear her head. Little electric carts stood ready to whisk her back to her office, but she ignored them, and by the time she reached it, she was almost calm again.

Bobbie sat hunched at her desk, the sheer physical bulk of the woman making the furniture seem like something from grade school. Soren was elsewhere, which was fine. His training wasn't military.

"So you're in an entrenched position with a huge threat coming down onto you, right?" Avasarala said, sitting down on the edge of Soren's desk. "Say you're on a moon and some third party has thrown a comet at you. Massive threat, you understand?"

Bobbie looked at her, confused for a moment, and then, with a shrug, played along.

"All right," the marine said.

"So why do you choose that moment to pick a fight with your neighbors? Are you just frightened and lashing out? Are you thinking that the other bastards are responsible for the rock? Are you just that stupid?"

"We're talking about Venus and the fighting in the Jovian system," Bobbie said.

"It's a pretty fucking thin metaphor, yes," Avasarala said. "So why are you doing it?"

Bobbie leaned back in her chair, plastic creaking under her. The big woman's eyes narrowed. She opened her mouth once, closed it, frowned, and began again.

"I'm consolidating power," Bobbie said. "If I use my resources stopping the comet, then as soon as that threat's gone, I lose. The other guy catches me with my pants down. Bang. If I kick his ass first, then when it's over, I win."

"But if you cooperate—"

"Then you have to trust the other guy," Bobbie said, shaking her head.

"There's a million tons of ice coming that's going to kill you both. Why the hell wouldn't you trust the other guy?"

"Depends. Is he an Earther?" Bobbie said. "We've got two major military forces in the system, plus whatever the Belters can gin up. That's three sides with a lot of history. When whatever's going to happen on Venus actually happens, someone wants to already have all the cards."

"And if both sides—Earth and Mars—are making that same calculation, we're going to spend all our energy getting ready for the war after next."

"Yep," Bobbie said. "And yes, that's how we all lose together."

Chapter Twenty-Four: Prax

Prax sat in his cabin. For sleeping space on a ship, he knew it was large. Spacious, even. Altogether, it was smaller than his bedroom on Ganymede had been. He sat on the gel-filled mattress, the acceleration gravity pressing him down, making his arms and legs feel heavier than they were. He wondered whether the sense of suddenly weighing more—specifically the discontinuous change of space travel—triggered some evolutionary cue for fatigue. The feeling of being pulled to the floor or the bed was so powerfully like the sensation of bone-melting tiredness it was easy to think that sleeping a little more would fix it, would make things better.

"Your daughter is probably dead," he said aloud. Waited to see how his body would react. "Mei is probably dead."

He didn't start sobbing this time, so that was progress.

Ganymede was a day and a half behind him and already too

small to pick out with the naked eye. Jupiter was a dim disk the size of a pinky nail, kicking back the light of a sun that was little more than an extremely bright star. Intellectually, he knew that he was falling sunward, heading in from the Jovian system toward the Belt. In a week, the sun would be close to twice the size it was now, and it would still be insignificant. In a context of such immensity, of distances and speeds so far above any meaningful human experience, it seemed like nothing should matter. He should be agreeing that he hadn't been there when God made the mountains, whether it meant the ones on Earth or on Ganymede or somewhere farther out in the darkness. He was in a tiny metal-and-ceramic box that was exchanging matter for energy to throw a half dozen primates across a vacuum larger than millions of oceans. Compared to that, how could anything matter?

"Your daughter is probably dead," he said again, and this time the words caught in his throat and started to choke him.

It was, he thought, something about the sense of being suddenly safe. On Ganymede, he'd had fear to numb him. Fear and malnutrition and routine and the ability at any moment to move, to do something even if it was utterly useless. Go check the boards again, go wait in line at security, trot along the hallways and see how many new bullet holes pocked them.

On the *Rocinante*, he had to slow down. He had to stop. There was nothing for him to do here but wait out the long sunward fall to Tycho Station. He couldn't distract himself. There was no station—not even a wounded and dying one—to hunt through. There were only the cabin he'd been given, his hand terminal, a few jumpsuits a half size too big for him. A small box of generic toiletries. That was everything he had left. And there was enough food and clean water that his brain could start working again.

Each passing hour felt like waking up a little more. He knew how badly his body and mind had been abused only when he got better. Every time, he felt like this had to be back to normal, and then not long after, he'd find that, no, there had been more.

So he explored himself, probing at the wound at the center of his personal world like pressing the tip of his tongue into a dry socket.

"Your daughter," he said through the tears, "is probably dead. But if she isn't, you have to find her."

That felt better—or, if not better, at least right. He leaned forward, his hands clasped, and rested his chin. Carefully, he imagined Katoa's body, laid out on its table. When his mind rebelled, trying to think about something—anything—else, he brought it back and put Mei in the boy's place. Quiet, empty, dead. The grief welled up from a place just above his stomach, and he watched it like it was something outside himself.

During his time as a graduate student, he had done data collection for a study of *Pinus contorata*. Of all the varieties of pine to rise off Earth, lodgepole pine had been the most robust in low-g environments. His job had been to collect the fallen cones and burn them for the seeds. In the wild, lodgepole pine wouldn't geminate without fire; the resin in the cones encouraged a hotter fire, even when it meant the death of the parental tree. To get better, it had to get worse. To survive, the plant had to embrace the unsurvivable.

He understood that.

"Mei is dead," he said. "You lost her."

He didn't have to wait for the idea to stop hurting. It would never stop hurting. But he couldn't let it grow so strong it overwhelmed him. He had the sense of doing himself permanent spiritual damage, but it was the strategy he had. And from what he could tell, it seemed to be working.

His hand terminal chimed. The two-hour block was up. Prax wiped the tears away with the back of his hand, took a deep breath, blew it back out, and stood. Two hours, twice a day, he'd decided, would be enough time in the fire to keep him hard and strong in this new environment of less freedom and more calories. Enough to keep him functional. He washed his face in the communal bathroom—the crew called it the head—and made his way to the galley.

The pilot—Alex, his name was—stood at the coffee machine, talking to a comm unit on the wall. His skin was darker than Prax's, his thinning hair black, with the first few stray threads of white. His voice had the odd drawl some Martians affected.

"I'm seein' eight percent and falling."

The wall unit said something cheerful and obscene. Amos.

"I'm tellin' you, the seal's cracked," Alex said.

"I been over it twice," Amos said from the comm. The pilot took a mug with the word *Tachi* printed on it from the coffee machine.

"Third time's the charm."

"Arright. Stand by."

The pilot took one long, lip-smacking sip from the mug, then, noticing Prax, nodded. Prax smiled uncomfortably.

"Feelin' better?" Alex asked.

"Yes. I think so," Prax said. "I don't know."

Alex sat at one of the tables. The design of the room was military—all soft edges and curves to minimize damage if someone was caught out of place by an impact or a sudden maneuver. The food inventory control had a biometric interface that had been disabled. Built for high security, but not used that way. The name ROCINANTE was on the wall in letters as broad as his hand, and someone had added a stencil of a spray of yellow narcissus. It looked desperately out of place and very appropriate at the same time. When he thought about it that way, it seemed to fit most things about the ship. Her crew, for instance.

"You settlin' in all right? You need anything?"

"I'm fine," Prax said with a nod. "Thank you."

"They beat us up pretty good gettin' out of there. I've been through some ugly patches of sky, but that was right up there."

Prax nodded and took a food packet from the dispenser. It was textured paste, sweet and rich with wheat and honey and the subterranean tang of baked raisins. Prax sat down before he thought about it, and the pilot seemed to take it as an invitation to continue the conversation.

"How long have you been on Ganymede?"

"Most of my life," Prax said. "My family went out when my mother was pregnant. They'd been working on Earth and Luna, saving up to get to the outer planets. They had a short posting on Callisto first."

"Belters?"

"Not exactly. They heard that the contracts were better out past the Belt. It was the whole 'make a better future for the family' idea. My father's dream, really."

Alex sipped at his coffee.

"And so, Praxidike. They named you after the moon?"

"They did," Prax said. "They were a little embarrassed to find out it was a woman's name. I never minded it, though. My wife—my ex-wife—thought it was endearing. It's probably why she noticed me in the first place, really. It takes something to stand out a little, and you can't swing a dead cat on Ganymede without hitting five botany PhDs. Or, well, you couldn't."

The pause was just long enough that Prax knew what was coming and could steel himself for it.

"I heard your daughter went missing," Alex said. "I'm sorry about that."

"She's probably dead," Prax said, just the way he'd practiced.

"It had to do with that lab y'all found down there, did it?"

"I think so. It must have. They took her just before the first incident. Her and several of the others in her group."

"Her group?"

"She has an immune disorder. Myers-Skelton Premature Immunosenescence. Always has had."

"My sister had a brittle bone disorder. Hard," Alex said. "Is that why they took her?"

"I assume so," Prax said. "Why else would you steal a child like that?"

"Slave labor or sex trade," Alex said softly. "But can't see why you'd pick out kids with a medical condition. It true you saw protomolecule down there?"

"Apparently," Prax said. The food bulb was cooling in his hand. He knew he should eat more—he wanted to, as good as it tasted—but something was turning at the back of his mind. He'd thought this all through before, when he'd been distracted and starving. Now, in this civilized coffin hurtling through the void, all the old familiar thoughts started to touch up against each other. They'd specifically targeted the children from Mei's group. Immunocompromised children. And they'd been working with the protomolecule.

"The captain was on Eros," Alex said.

"It must have been a loss for him when it happened," Prax said to have something to say.

"No, I don't mean he lived there. He was on the station when it happened. We all were, but he was on it the longest. He actually saw it starting. The initial infected. That."

"Really?"

"Changed him, some. I've been flyin' with him since we were just fartin' around on this old ice bucket running from Saturn to the Belt. He didn't used to like me, I suspect. Now we're family. It's been a hell of a trip."

Prax took a long pull from his food bulb. Cool, the paste tasted less of wheat and more of honey and raisin. It wasn't as good. He remembered the look of fear on Holden's face when they'd found the dark filaments, the sound of controlled panic in his voice. It made sense now.

And as if summoned by the thought, Holden appeared in the doorway, a formed aluminum case under his arm with electromagnetic plates along the base. A personal footlocker designed to stay put even under high g. Prax had seen them before, but he'd never needed one. Gravity had been a constant for him until now.

"Cap'n," Alex said with a vestigial salute. "Everything all right?"

"Just moving some things to my bunk," Holden said. The tightness in his voice was unmistakable. Prax had the sudden feeling that he was intruding on something private, but Alex and Holden didn't give any further sign. Holden only moved off down the hall. When he was out of earshot, Alex sighed.

"Trouble?" Prax asked.

"Yeah. Don't worry. It's not about you. This has been brewin' for a while now."

"I'm sorry," Prax said.

"Had to happen. Best to get it over with one way or the other," Alex said, but there was an unmistakable dread in his voice. Prax felt himself liking the man. The wall terminal chirped and then spoke in Amos' voice.

"What've you got now?"

Alex pulled the terminal close, the articulated arm bending and twisting on complicated joints, then tapped on it with the fingers of one hand while keeping hold of the coffee with the other. The terminal flickered, datasets converting to graphs and tables in real time.

"Ten percent," Alex said. "No. Twelve. We're moving up. What'd you find?"

"Cracked seal," Amos said. "And yeah, you're very fucking clever. What else we got?"

Alex tapped on the terminal and Holden reappeared from the hallway, now without his case.

"Port sensor array took a hit. Looks like we burned out a few of the leads," Alex said.

"All right," Amos said. "Let's get those bad boys swapped out."

"Or maybe we can do something that doesn't involve crawling on the outside of a ship under thrust," Holden said.

"I can get it done, Cap," Amos said. Even through the tinny wall speaker, he sounded affronted. Holden shook his head.

"One slip, and the exhaust cooks you down to component atoms. Let's leave that for the techs on Tycho. Alex, what else have we got?"

"Memory leak in the navigation system. Probably a fried network that grew back wrong," the pilot said. "The cargo bay's still in vacuum. The radio array's as dead as a hammer for no apparent reason. Hand terminals aren't talking. And one of the medical pods is throwing error codes, so don't get sick."

Holden went to the coffee machine, talking over his shoulder as he keyed in his preferences. His cup said *Tachi* too. Prax realized with a start that they all did. He wondered who or what a Tachi was.

"Does the cargo bay need EVA?"

"Don't know," Alex said. "Lemme take a look."

Holden took his coffee mug out of the machine with a little sigh and stroked the brushed metal plates like he was petting a cat. On impulse, Prax cleared his throat.

"Excuse me," he said. "Captain Holden? I was wondering, if the radio gets fixed or there's a tightbeam available, if maybe there was a way I could use some time on the communications array?"

"We're kind of trying to be quiet right now," Holden said. "What are you wanting to send?"

"I need to do some research," Prax said. "The data we got on Ganymede from when they took Mei. There are images of the woman who was with them. And if I can find what happened to Dr. Strickland...I've been on a security-locked system since the day she went missing. Even if it was just the public access databases and networks, it would be a place to start."

"And it's that or sit around and stew until we get to Tycho," Holden said. "All right. I'll ask Naomi to get you an access account for the *Roci*'s network. I don't know if there'll be anything in the OPA files, but you might as well check them too."

"Really?"

"Sure," Holden said. "They've got a pretty decent face-recognition database. It's inside their secure perimeter, so you might need to have one of us make the request."

"And that would be all right? I don't want to get you in trouble with the OPA."

Holden's smile was warm and cheerful.

"Really, don't worry about that," he said. "Alex, what've we got?"

"Looks like cargo door's not sealin', which we knew. We may

have taken a hit, blown a hole in her. We've got the video feed back up...hold on..."

Holden shifted to peer over Alex's shoulder. Prax took another swallow of his food and gave in to curiosity. An image of a cargo bay no wider than Prax's palm took up one corner of the display. Most of the cargo was on electromagnetic pallets, stuck to the plates nearest the wide bay door, but some had broken loose, pressed by thrust gravity to the floor. It gave the room an unreal, Escher-like appearance. Alex resized the image, zooming in on the cargo door. In one corner, a thick section of metal was bent inward, bright metal showing where the bend had cracked the external layers. A spray of stars showed through the hole.

"Well, at least it ain't subtle," Alex said.

"What hit it?" Holden said.

"Don't know, Cap," Alex said. "No scorching as far as I can see. But a gauss round wouldn't have bent the metal in like that. Just would have made a hole. And the bay isn't breached, so whatever did it didn't make a hole on the other side."

The pilot increased the magnification again, looking closely at the edges of the wound. It was true there were no scorch marks, but thin black smudges showed against the metal of the door and the deck. Prax frowned. He opened his mouth to speak, then closed it again.

Holden said what Prax had been thinking.

"Alex? Is that a handprint?"

"Looks like one, Cap, but..."

"Pull out. Look at the decking."

They were small. Subtle. Easy to overlook on the small image. But they were there. A handprint, smeared in something dark that Prax had the strong suspicion had once been red. The unmistakable print of five naked toes. A long smear of darkness.

The pilot followed the trail.

"That bay's in hard vacuum, right?" Holden asked.

"Has been for a day and a half, sir," Alex said. The casual air was gone. They were all business now.

"Track right," Holden said.

"Yes, sir."

"Okay, stop. What's that?"

The body was curled into a fetal ball, except where its palms were pressed against the bulkhead. It lay perfectly still, as if they were under high g and it was held against the deck, crushed by its own weight. The flesh was the black of anthracite and the red of blood. Prax couldn't tell if it had been a man or a woman.

"Alex, do we have a stowaway?"

"Pretty sure that ain't on the cargo manifest, sir."

"And did that fellow there bend his way through my ship with his bare hands?"

"Looks like maybe, sir."

"Amos? Naomi?"

"I'm looking at it too." Naomi's voice came from the terminal a moment before Amos' low whistle. Prax thought back to the mysterious sounds of violence in the lab, the bodies of guards they hadn't fought, the shattered glass and its black filament. Here was the experiment that had slipped its leash back at that lab. It had fled to the cold, dead surface of Ganymede and waited there until a chance came to escape. Prax felt the gooseflesh crawling up his arms.

"Okay," Holden said. "But it's dead, right?"

"I don't think so," Naomi said.

Chapter Twenty-Five: Bobbie

Bobbie's hand terminal began playing reveille at four thirty a.m. local time: what she and her mates might have grumbled and called "oh dark thirty" back when she'd been a marine and had mates to grumble with. She'd left her terminal in the living room, lying next to the pull-down cot she used as a bed, the volume set high enough to have left her ears ringing if she'd been in there with it. But Bobbie had already been up for an hour. In her cramped bathroom, the sound was only annoying, bouncing around her tiny apartment like radio in a deep well. The echoes were a sonic reminder that she still didn't have much furniture or any wall hangings.

It didn't matter. She'd never had a guest.

The reveille was a mean-spirited little joke Bobbie was playing on herself. The Martian military had formed hundreds of years after trumpets and drums had been a useful means of transmitting information to troops. Martians lacked the nostalgia the UN military had for such things. The first time Bobbie had heard a morning reveille, she'd been watching a video on military history. She'd been happy to realize that no matter how annoying the Martian equivalent—a series of atonal electronic blats—was, it would never be as annoying as what the Earth boys woke up to.

But now Bobbie wasn't a Martian Marine anymore.

"I am not a traitor," Bobbie said to her reflection in the mirror. Mirror Bobbie looked unconvinced.

After the blaring trumpet call's third repetition, her hand terminal beeped once and fell into a sullen silence. She'd been holding her toothbrush for the last half hour. The toothpaste had started to grow a hard skin. She ran it under warm water to soften it back up and started brushing her teeth.

"I'm not a traitor," she said to herself, the toothbrush making the words unintelligible. "Not."

Not even standing here in the bathroom of her UN-provided apartment, brushing her teeth with UN toothpaste and rinsing the sink with UN-provided water. Not while she clutched her good Martian toothbrush and scrubbed until her gums bled.

"Not," she said again, daring mirror Bobbie to disagree.

She put the toothbrush back into her small toiletry case, carried it into the living room, and placed it in her duffel. Everything she owned stayed in the duffel. She'd need to move fast when her people called her home. And they would. She'd get a priority dispatch on her terminal, the red-and-gray border of the MCRN CINC-COM flashing around it. They'd tell her that she needed to return to her unit immediately. That she was still one of them.

That she wasn't a traitor for staying.

She straightened her uniform, slid her now quiet terminal into her pocket, and checked her hair in the mirror next to the door. It was pulled into a bun so tight it almost gave her a face-lift, not one single hair out of place.

"I'm not a traitor," she said to the mirror. Front hallway mirror Bobbie seemed more open to this idea than bathroom mirror

Bobbie had. "Damn straight," she said, then slammed the door behind her when she left.

She hopped on one of the little electric bikes the UN campus made available everywhere, and was in the office three minutes before five a.m. Soren was already there. No matter what time she came in, Soren always beat her. Either he slept at his desk or he was spying on her to see what time she set her alarm for each morning.

"Bobbie," he said, his smile not even pretending to be genuine.

Bobbie couldn't bring herself to respond, so she just nodded and collapsed into her chair. One glance at the darkened windows in Avasarala's office told her the old lady wasn't in yet. Bobbie pulled up her to-do list on the desktop screen.

"She had me add a lot of people," Soren said, referring to the list of people Bobbie was supposed to call in her role as Martian military liaison. "She really wants to get a hold of an early draft of the Martian statement on Ganymede. That's your top priority for the day. Okay?"

"Why?" Bobbie said. "The actual statement came out yesterday. We both read it."

"Bobbie," Soren said with a sigh that said he was tired of explaining simple things to her, but a grin that said he really wasn't. "This is how the game is played. Mars releases a statement condemning our actions. We go back channel and find an early draft. If it was harsher than the actual statement that was released, then someone in the dip corps argued to tone it down. That means they're trying to avoid escalating. If it was milder in the early draft, then they're deliberately escalating to provoke a response."

"But since they know you'll get those early drafts, then that's meaningless. They'll just make sure you get leaks that give you the impression they want you to have."

"See? Now you're getting it," Soren said. "What your opponent wants *you* to think is useful data in figuring out what *they* think. So get the early draft, okay? Do it before the end of the day."

But no one talks to me anymore because now I'm the UN's pet Martian, and even though I'm not a traitor, it is entirely possible that everyone else thinks I am.

"Okay."

Bobbie pulled up the newly revised list and made the first connection request of the day.

"Bobbie!" Avasarala yelled from her desk. There was any number of electronic means for getting Bobbie's attention, but she almost never saw Avasarala use them. She yanked her earbud free and stood up. Soren's smirk was of the psychic variety; his face didn't change at all.

"Ma'am?" Bobbie said, taking a short step into Avasarala's office. "You bellowed?"

"No one likes a smart-ass," Avasarala said, not looking up from her desk terminal. "Where's my first draft of that report? It's almost lunchtime."

Bobbie stood a little straighter and clasped her arms behind her back.

"Sir, I regret to inform you that I have been unable to find anyone willing to release the early draft of the report to me."

"Are you standing at attention?" Avasarala said, looking up at her for the first time. "Jesus. I'm not about to march you out to the firing squad. Did you try everyone on the list?"

"Yes, I—" Bobbie stopped for a moment and took a deep breath, then took a few more steps into the office. Quietly she said, "No one talks to me."

The old woman lifted a snow-white eyebrow.

"That's interesting."

"It is?" Bobbie said.

Avasarala smiled at her, a warm, genuine smile, then poured tea out of a black iron pot into two small teacups.

"Sit down," she said, waving at a chair next to her desk. When Bobbie remained standing, Avasarala said, "Seriously, sit the fuck down. Five minutes talking to you and I can't tilt my head forward again for an hour."

Bobbie sat, hesitated, and took one of the small teacups. It wasn't much larger than a shot glass, and the tea inside it was very dark and smelled unpleasant. She took a small sip and burned her tongue.

"It's a Lapsang souchong," Avasarala said. "My husband buys it for me. What do you think?"

"I think it smells like hobo feet," Bobbie replied.

"No shit, but Arjun loves it and it's not bad once you get used to drinking it."

Bobbie nodded and took another sip but didn't reply.

"Okay, so," Avasarala said, "you're the Martian who was unhappy and got tempted over to the other side by a powerful old lady with lots of shiny prizes to offer. You're the worst kind of traitor, because ultimately everything that's happened to you since you came to Earth was because you were pouting."

"I—"

"Shut the fuck up now, dear, the grown-up is talking."

Bobbie shut up and drank her awful tea.

"But," Avasarala continued, the same sweet smile on her wrinkled face, "if I were on the other team, you know who I'd send misinformation leaks to?"

"Me," Bobbie said.

"You. Because you're desperate to prove your value to your new boss, and they can send you blatantly false information and not really care if they fuck your shit up in the long run. If I were the Martian counterespionage wonks, I'd have already recruited one of your closest friends back home and be using them to funnel a mountain's worth of false data your direction."

My closest friends are all dead, Bobbie thought.

"But no one—"

"Is talking to you from back home. Which means two things. They are still trying to figure out my game in keeping you here, and they don't have a misinformation campaign in place because they're as confused as we are. You'll be contacted by someone in the next week or so. They'll ask you to leak information from my office, but they'll ask it in such a way that winds up giving you a whole lot of false information. If you're loyal and spy for them, great. If not and you tell me what they asked for, also great. Maybe they'll get lucky and you'll do both."

Bobbie put the teacup back on the desk. Her hands were in fists.

"This," Bobbie said, "is why everyone hates politicians."

"No. They hate us because we have power. Bobbie, this isn't how your mind likes to work, and I respect that. I don't have time to explain things to you," Avasarala said, the smile disappearing like it had never been. "So just assume I know what I'm doing, and that when I ask you to do the impossible, it's because even your failure helps our cause somehow."

"*Our* cause?"

"We're on the same team here. Team Let's-Not-Lose-Together. That is us, isn't it?"

"Yes," Bobbie said, glancing at the Buddha in his shrine. He smiled at her serenely. *Just one of the team*, his round face seemed to say. "Yes it is."

"Then get the fuck back out there and start calling everyone all over again. This time take detailed notes on who refuses to help you and the exact words they use in their refusal. Okay?"

"Solid copy on that, ma'am."

"Good," Avasarala said, smiling gently again. "Get out of my office."

Familiarity might breed contempt, but Bobbie hadn't much liked Soren right from the start. Sitting next to him for several days had ratcheted up her dislike to a whole new level. When he wasn't ignoring her, he was condescending. He talked too loud on his phone, even when she was trying to carry on a conversation of her own. Sometimes he sat on her desk, talking to visitors. He wore too much cologne.

The worst thing was he ate cookies all day.

It was impressive, given his rail-thin build, and Bobbie was not generally the kind of person who cared at all about other people's dietary habits. But his preferred brand of cookie came out of the break room vending machine in a foil packet that crinkled every time he reached into it. At first, this had only been annoying. But after a couple of days of the Crinkle, Crunch, Chomp, and Smack Radio Theater, she'd had enough. She dropped her latest pointless connection and turned to stare at him. He ignored her and tapped on his desk terminal.

"Soren," she said, meaning to ask him to dump the damn cookies out on a plate or a napkin so she didn't have to hear that infuriating crinkle sound anymore. Before she could get more than his name out, he held up a finger to shush her and pointed at his earbud.

"No," he said, "not really a good—"

Bobbie wasn't sure if he was talking to her or someone on the phone, so she got up and moved over to his desk, sitting on the edge of it. He gave her a withering glare, but she just smiled and mouthed, "I'll wait." The edge of his desk creaked a little under her weight.

He turned his back to her.

"I understand," he said. "But this is not a good time to discuss— I see. I can probably— I see, yes. Foster won't— Yes. Yes, I understand. I'll be there."

He turned back around and tapped his desk, killing the connection.

"What?"

"I hate your cookies. The constant crinkle of the package is driving me insane."

"Cookies?" Soren said, a baffled expression on his face. Bobbie thought that it might be the first honest emotion she'd ever seen there.

"Yeah, can you put them on a—" Bobbie started, but before she could finish, Soren grabbed up the package and tossed them into the recycling bin next to his desk.

"Happy?"

"Well—"

"I don't have time for you right now, Sergeant."

"Okay," Bobbie said, and went back to her desk.

Soren kept fidgeting like he had more to say, so Bobbie didn't call the next person on her list. She waited for him to speak. Probably the cookie thing had been a mistake on her part. Really, it wasn't a big deal. If she weren't under so much pressure, it wasn't the sort of thing she'd probably even notice. When Soren finally spoke up, she'd apologize for being so pushy about it and then offer to buy him a new package. Instead of speaking, he stood up.

"Soren, I—" Bobbie started, but Soren ignored her and unlocked a drawer on his desk. He pulled out a small bit of black plastic. Probably because she'd just heard him say the name Foster, Bobbie recognized it as the memory stick Avasarala had given him a few days earlier. Foster was the data services guy, so she assumed he was finally getting around to taking care of that little task, which would at least get him away from the office for a few minutes.

Until he turned and headed for the elevators.

Bobbie had done a little gofer work running things back and forth to data services and knew that their office was on the same floor and in the opposite direction of the elevators.

"Huh."

She was tired. She was half sick with guilt and she wasn't even all that sure what she felt guilty about. She disliked the man anyway. The hunch that popped into her head was almost certainly a result of her own paranoia and addled image of the world.

She got up, following him.

"This is really stupid," she said to herself, smiling and nodding at a page who hurried by. She was over two meters tall on a planet of short people. She wasn't going to blend.

Soren climbed into an elevator. Bobbie stopped outside the doors and waited. Through the aluminum-and-ceramic doors, she heard him ask someone to press one. Going all the way to the street level, then. She hit the down button and took the next elevator to the bottom floor.

Of course, he wasn't in sight when she got there.

A giant Martian woman running around the lobby of the UN building would draw a little attention, so she scrapped that as a plan. A wave of uncertainty, failure, and despair lapped at the shoreline of her mind.

Forget that it was an office building. Forget that there were no armed enemy, no squad behind her. *Forget that, and look at the logic of the situation on the ground. Think tactically. Be smart.*

"I need to be smart," she said. A short woman in a red suit who had just come up and pressed the elevator call button overheard her and said, "What?"

"I need to be smart," Bobbie told her. "Can't go running off half-cocked." *Not even when doing something insane and stupid.*

"I...see," the woman said, then pushed the elevator call button again several times. Next to the elevator control panel was a courtesy terminal. *If you can't find the target, restrict the target's degrees of freedom. Make them come to you. Right.* Bobbie hit the button for the lobby reception desk. An automated system with an extremely realistic and sexually ambiguous voice asked how it could assist her.

"Please page Soren Cottwald to the lobby reception desk," Bobbie said. The computer on the other end of the line thanked her for using the UN automated courtesy system and dropped the connection.

Soren might not have his terminal on, or it could be set to ignore incoming pages. Or he might ignore this one all on his own. She found a couch with a sight line to the desk and shifted a ficus to provide her cover.

Two minutes later, Soren trotted up to the reception desk, his hair more windblown than usual. He must have already been all the way outside when he got the page. He began talking to one of the human receptionists. Bobbie moved across the lobby to a little coffee and snack kiosk and hid as best she could. After typing on her desk for a moment, the receptionist pointed at the terminal next to the elevators. Soren frowned and took a few steps toward it, then looked around nervously and headed toward the building entrance.

Bobbie followed.

Once Bobbie was outside, her height was both an advantage and a disadvantage. Being a head and a half taller than most everyone around her meant that she could afford to stay pretty far behind Soren as he hurried along the sidewalk. She could spot the top of his head from half a city block away. At the same time, if he looked behind him, he couldn't miss her face sticking up a good third of a meter out of the crowd.

But he didn't turn around. In fact, he appeared to be in something of a hurry, pushing his way through the knots of people on the busy sidewalks around the UN campus with obvious impatience. He didn't look around or pause by a good reflective surface or backtrack. He'd been nervous answering the page, and he was being pointedly, angrily not nervous now.

Whistling past the graveyard. Bobbie felt her muscles soften, her joints grow loose and easy, her hunch slip a centimeter closer to certainty.

After three blocks he turned and went into a bar.

Bobbie stopped a half block away and considered. The front of the bar, a place creatively named Pete's, was darkened glass. If you wanted to duck in somewhere and see if people were following you, it was the perfect place to go. Maybe he'd gotten smart.

Maybe he hadn't.

Bobbie walked over to the front door. Getting caught following him had no consequences. Soren already hated her. The most ethically suspect thing she was doing was cutting out early to pop into a neighborhood bar. Who was going to rat on her? Soren? The guy who cut out just as early and went to the same damn bar?

If he was in there and doing nothing more than grabbing an early beer, she'd just walk up to him, apologize for the cookie thing, and buy him his second round.

She pushed the door open and went inside.

It took her eyes a moment to adjust from the early-afternoon sunlight outside to the dimly lit bar. Once the glare had faded, she saw a long bamboo bar top manned by a human bartender, half a dozen booths with about as many patrons, and no Soren. The air smelled of beer and burnt popcorn. The patrons gave her one look and then carefully went back to their drinks and mumbled conversations.

Had Soren ducked out the back to ditch her? She didn't think he'd seen her, but she wasn't exactly trained for tailing people. She was about to ask the bartender if he'd seen a guy run through, and where that guy might have gone, when she noticed a sign at the back of the bar that said POOL TABLES with an arrow pointing left.

She walked to the back of the bar, turned left, and found a smaller, second room with four pool tables and two men. One of them was Soren.

They both looked up as she turned the corner.

"Hi," she said. Soren was smiling at her, but he was always smiling. Smiling, for him, was protective coloration. Camouflage. The other man was large, fit, and wearing an excessively casual outfit that tried too hard to look like it belonged in a seedy pool hall. It clashed with the man's military haircut and ramrod-straight posture. Bobbie had a feeling she'd seen his face before, but in a different setting. She tried to picture him with a uniform on.

"Bobbie," Soren said, giving his companion one quick glance and then looking away. "You play?" He picked up a pool cue that had been lying on one of the tables, and began chalking the tip. Bobbie didn't point out that there were no balls on any of the tables, and that a sign just behind Soren said RENTAL BALLS AVAILABLE ON REQUEST.

His companion said nothing but slid something into his pocket. Between his fingers Bobbie caught a glimpse of black plastic.

She smiled. She knew where she'd seen the second man before.

"No," she said to Soren. "It's not popular where I come from."

"Slate, I guess," he replied. His smile became a bit more genuine and a lot colder. He blew the chalk dust off the pool cue's tip and moved a step to the side, shifting toward her left. "Too heavy for the early colony ships."

"Makes sense," Bobbie said, moving back until the doorway protected her flanks.

"Is this a problem?" Soren's companion said, looking at Bobbie.

Before Soren could reply, Bobbie said, "You tell me. You were at that late-night meeting in Avasarala's office when Ganymede went to shit. Nguyen's staff, right? Lieutenant something or other."

"You're digging a hole, Bobbie," Soren said, the pool cue held lightly in his right hand.

"And," she continued, "I know Soren handed you something his boss had asked him to take to data services a couple days ago. I bet you don't work in data services, do you?"

Nguyen's flunky took a menacing step toward her, and Soren shifted to her left again.

Bobbie burst out laughing.

"Seriously," she said, looking at Soren. "Either stop jerking that pool cue off or take it somewhere private."

Soren looked down at the cue in his hand as though surprised to see it there, then dropped it.

"And you," Bobbie said to the flunky. "You trying to come through this door would literally be the high point of my month." Without moving her feet she shifted her weight forward and flexed her elbows slightly.

The flunky looked her in the eye for one long moment. She grinned back.

"Come on," she said. "I'm gonna get blue balls you keep teasing me like this."

The flunky put up his hands. Something halfway between a fighting stance and a gesture of surrender. Never taking his eyes off Bobbie, he turned his face slightly toward Soren and said, "This is your problem. Handle it." He backed up two slow steps, then turned and walked across the room and into a hallway Bobbie couldn't see from where she was standing. A second later, she heard a door slam.

"Shit," Bobbie said. "I bet I'd have scored more points with the old lady if I'd gotten that memory stick back."

Soren began to shuffle toward the back door. Bobbie crossed the space between them like a cat, grabbing the front of his shirt and pulling him up until their noses were almost touching. Her body felt alive and free for the first time in a long time.

"What are you going to do," he said through a forced smirk, "beat me up?"

"Naw," Bobbie replied, shifting to an exaggerated Mariner Valley drawl. "I'm gonna tell on you, boy."

Chapter Twenty-Six: Holden

Holden watched the monster quiver as it huddled against the cargo bay bulkhead. On the video monitor, it looked small and washed out and grainy. He concentrated on his breathing. *Long slow breath in, fill up the lungs all the way to the bottom. Long slow breath out. Pause. Repeat. Do not lose your shit in front of the crew.*

"Well," Alex said after a minute. "There's your problem."

He was trying to make a joke. *Had* made a joke. Normally, Holden would have laughed at his exaggerated drawl and comic obviousness. Alex could be very funny, in a dry, understated sort of way.

Right now, Holden had to clench his hands to stop from strangling the man.

Amos said, "I'm coming up," at the same moment Naomi said, "I'm coming down."

"Alex," Holden said, pretending a calm he didn't feel. "What's the status of the cargo bay airlock?"

Alex tapped twice on the terminal and said, "Airtight, Cap. Zero loss."

Which was good, because as frightened of the protomolecule as he was, Holden also knew that it wasn't magic. It had mass and it occupied space. If not even a molecule of oxygen could sneak out through the airlock seal, then he was pretty sure none of the virus could get in. But…

"Alex, crank up the O2," Holden said. "As rich as we can get it without blowing the ship up."

The protomolecule was anaerobic. If any of it did somehow get in, he wanted the environment as hostile as possible.

"And get up to the cockpit," he continued. "Seal yourself in. If the goo somehow gets loose on the ship, I need your finger on the reactor overrides."

Alex frowned and scratched his thin hair. "That seems a little extreme—"

Holden grabbed him by the upper arms, hard. Alex's eyes went wide and his hands came up in an automatic gesture of surrender. Beside him, the botanist blinked in confusion and alarm. This was not the best way to instill confidence. In other circumstances, Holden might have cared.

"Alex," Holden said, not able to stop himself from shaking even while clutching the pilot's arms. "Can I count on you to blow this ship into gas if that shit gets in here? Because if I can't, consider yourself relieved of duty and confined to quarters immediately."

Alex surprised him, not by reacting in anger, but by reaching up and putting his hands on Holden's forearms. Alex's face was serious, but his eyes were kind.

"Seal myself into the cockpit and prepare to scuttle the ship. Aye, aye, sir," he said. "What's the stand-down order?"

"Direct order from myself or Naomi," Holden replied with a hidden sigh of relief. He didn't have to say, *If that thing gets in here and kills us, you're better off going up with the ship*. He let go of Alex's arms and the pilot took one step back, his broad dark face wrinkled with concern. The panic that threatened to overwhelm Holden might get out of his control if he allowed anyone to feel sympathy for him, so he said, "Now, Alex. Do it now."

Alex nodded once, looked like he wanted to say something else, then spun on his heel and went to the crew ladder and up toward the cockpit. Naomi descended the same ladder a few moments later, and Amos came up from below a short time after that.

Naomi spoke first. "What's the plan?" They'd been intimate long enough for Holden to recognize the barely concealed fear in her voice.

Holden paused to take two more long breaths. "Amos and I will go see if we can't drive it out the cargo bay doors. Get them open for us."

"Done," she said, and headed up the ladder to ops.

Amos was watching him, a speculative look in his eyes.

"So, Cap, how do we 'drive it' out those doors?"

"Well," Holden replied. "I was thinking we shoot the shit out of it and then take a flamethrower to any pieces that fall off. So we better gear up."

Amos nodded. "Damn. I feel like I just took that shit off."

Holden was not claustrophobic.

No one who chose long-flight space travel as a career was. Even if a person could somehow con their way past the psychological profiles and simulation runs, one trip was usually enough to separate those who could handle long periods in confined spaces from those who went bugfuck and had to be sedated for the trip home.

As a junior lieutenant Holden had spent days in scout ships so small that you literally could not bend over to scratch your feet. He'd climbed around between the inner and outer hulls of warships. He'd once been confined to his crash couch for twenty-one days during a fast-burn trip from Luna to Saturn. He never had nightmares of being crushed or being buried alive.

For the first time in his decade and a half of nearly constant space travel, the ship he was on felt too small. Not just cramped, but terrifyingly constricted. He felt trapped, like an animal in a snare.

Less than twelve meters away from where he stood, someone infected with the protomolecule was sitting in his cargo bay. And there was nowhere he could go to get away from it.

Putting on his body armor didn't help this feeling of confinement.

The first thing that went on was what the grunts called the full-body condom. It was a thick black bodysuit, made of multiple layers of Kevlar, rubber, impact-reactive gel, and the sensor network that kept track of his injury and vitals status. Over that went the slightly looser environment suit, with its own layers of self-sealing gel to instantly repair tears or bullet holes. And finally, the various pieces of strap-on armor plating that could deflect a high-velocity rifle shot or ablate the outer layers to shed the energy of a laser.

To Holden, it felt like wrapping himself in his own death shroud.

But even with all its layers and weight, it still wasn't as frightening as the powered armor that recon Marines wore would have been. What the Navy boys called walking coffins. The idea behind the name being that anything powerful enough to break the armor would liquefy the marine inside, so you didn't bother to open it. You just tossed the whole thing into the grave. This was hyperbole, of course, but the idea of going into that cargo bay wearing something that he wouldn't even be able to move without the power-enhanced strength would have scared the shit out of him. What if the batteries died?

Of course, a nice suit of strength-augmenting armor might be handy when trying to throw monsters off the ship.

"That's on backward," Amos said, pointing at Holden's thigh.

"Shit," Holden said. Amos was right. He'd been so far up his own ass that he'd screwed up the buckles on his thigh armor. "Sorry, I'm having a hard time staying focused here."

"Scared shitless," Amos said with a nod.

"Well, I wouldn't say—"

"Wasn't talking about you," Amos said. "Me. I'm scared shit-less of walking into the cargo bay with that thing in there. And I didn't watch Eros turn into goo at close range. So I get it. Right there with you, Jim."

It was the first time in Holden's memory that Amos had called him by his first name. Holden nodded back at him, then went about straightening out his thigh armor.

"Yeah," he said. "I just yelled at Alex for not being scared enough."

Amos had finished with his armor and was pulling his favorite auto-shotgun out of his locker.

"No shit?"

"Yeah. He made a joke and I'm scared out of my skull, so I yelled at him and threatened to relieve him."

"Can you do that?" Amos asked. "He's kind of our only pilot."

"No, Amos. No, I can't kick Alex off the ship any more than I can kick you or Naomi off the ship. We're not even a skeleton crew. We're whatever you have when you don't have a skeleton."

"Worried about Naomi leaving?" Amos said. He kept his voice light, but his words hit like hammer blows. Holden felt the air go out of him, and had to focus on breathing again for a minute.

"No," he said. "I mean, yes, of course I am. But that's not what has me freaked out right now."

Holden picked up his assault rifle and looked at it, then put it back in his locker and took out a heavy recoilless pistol instead. The self-contained rockets that were its ammunition wouldn't impart thrust and send him flying all over the place if he fired it in zero g.

"I watched you die," he said, not looking at Amos.

"Huh?"

"I watched you die. When that kidnap team, whoever the hell *they* were, took us. I saw one of them shoot you in the back of the head, and I saw you drop face-first on the floor. There was blood everywhere."

"Yeah, but I—"

"I know it was a nonlethal round. I know they wanted us alive. I know the blood was your broken nose when your head slammed into the floor. I know all of that *now*. At the time, what I knew was that you'd just been shot in the head and killed."

Amos slid a magazine into his shotgun and racked a round but, other than that, didn't make a sound.

"All of this is really fragile," Holden said, waving around at Amos and the ship. "This little family we have. One fuckup, and something irreplaceable gets lost."

Amos was frowning at him now. "This is still about Naomi, right?"

"No! I mean, yes. But no. When I thought you were dead, it knocked all the wind out of me. And right now, I need to focus on getting that thing off the ship, and all I can think about is losing one of the crew."

Amos nodded, slung the shotgun over his shoulder, and sat down on the bench next to his locker.

"I get it. So what do you want to do?"

"I want," Holden said, sliding a magazine into his pistol, "to get that fucking monster off my ship. But please promise me you won't die doing it. That would help a lot."

"Cap," Amos said with a grin. "Anything that kills me has already killed everyone else. I was born to be the last man standing. You can count on it."

The panic and fear didn't leave Holden. They squatted on his chest now just the way they had before. But at least he didn't feel so alone with them.

"Then let's go get rid of this stowaway."

The wait inside the cargo bay airlock was endless as the inner door sealed, the pumps sucked all the air out of the room, and then the outer door cycled open. Holden fidgeted and rechecked his gun half a dozen times while he waited. Amos stood in a relaxed slump, his huge shotgun cradled loosely in his arms. The upside, if there was an upside to the wait, was that with the cargo bay in vacuum, the airlock could make as much noise as it wanted without alerting the creature to their presence.

The last of the external noise disappeared, and Holden could hear only himself breathing. A yellow light came on near the outer airlock door, warning them of the null atmosphere on the other side.

"Alex," Holden said, plugging a hardline into the airlock terminal. Radio was still dead all over the ship. "We're about to go in. Kill the engines."

"Roger that," Alex replied, and the gravity dropped away. Holden kicked the slide controls on his heels to turn up his magnetic boots.

The cargo bay on the *Rocinante* was cramped. Tall and narrow, it occupied the starboard side of the ship, crammed into the unused space between the outer hull and the engineering bay. On the port side, the same space was filled with the ship's water tank. The *Roci* was a warship. Any cargo it carried would be an afterthought.

The downside to this was that while under thrust, the cargo bay turned into a well with the cargo doors at the bottom. The various crates that occupied the space latched on to mounts on the bulkheads or in some cases were attached with electromagnetic feet. With thrust gravity threatening to send a person tumbling seven meters straight down to the cargo doors, it would be an impossible place to fight effectively.

In microgravity, it became a long hallway with lots of cover.

Holden entered the room first, walking along the bulkhead on magnetic boots, and took cover behind a large metal crate filled with extra rounds for the ship's point defense cannons. Alex followed, taking up a position behind another crate two meters away.

Below them, the monster seemed to be asleep.

It huddled motionless against the bulkhead that separated the cargo bay from engineering.

"Okay, Naomi, go ahead and open it up," Holden said. He jiggled the trailing line of cable to get it unhooked from a corner of the crate and gave it a little slack.

"Doors opening now," she replied, her voice thin and fuzzy in his helmet. The cargo doors at the bottom of the room silently swung open, exposing several square meters of star-filled blackness. The monster either didn't notice the doors opening or didn't care.

"They hibernate sometimes, right?" Amos said, the cable running from his suit to the airlock looking like a high-tech umbilical cord. "Like Julie did when she got the bug. Hibernated in that hotel room on Eros for a couple weeks."

"Maybe," Holden replied. "How do you want to approach this? I'm almost thinking we should just go down there, grab the thing, and toss it out the door. But I have strong reservations about touching it."

"Yeah, wouldn't want to take our suits back inside with us," Amos agreed.

Holden had a sudden memory of coming in after playing outside, and taking all his clothes off in the mudroom before Mother Tamara would let him into the rest of the house. This would be pretty much the same, only a lot colder.

"I find myself wishing we had a really long stick," Holden said, looking around at the various objects stored in the cargo bay, hoping to find one that suited his need.

"Uh, Cap'n?" Amos said. "It's looking at us."

Holden turned back around and saw Amos was right. The creature hadn't moved anything but its head, but it was definitely staring up at them now, its eyes a creepy illuminated-from-within blue.

"Well, okay," Holden said. "It's not hibernating."

"You know, if I can knock it off that bulkhead with a shot or two, and Alex kicks on the engine, it might just tumble right out the back door and into the exhaust plume. That oughta take care of it."

"Let's think about—" Holden said, but before he could finish his thought, the room strobed several times with the muzzle flash of Amos' shotgun. The monster was hit multiple times and knocked into a spinning lump floating toward the door.

"Alex, just—" Amos said.

The monster blurred into action. It flung one arm toward the bulkhead, the limb actually seeming to get longer to reach it, and yanked down hard enough to bend the steel plates. The creature hurtled up to the top of the cargo bay so fast that when it hit the crate Holden was hiding behind, the magnetic feet lost their seal. The cargo bay seemed to spin as the impact threw Holden back. The crate, just behind him, matched his velocity. Holden slammed against the bulkhead a split second before the crate did, and the magnetic pallet snapped onto the new wall, trapping Holden's leg beneath it.

Something in his knee bent badly, and the pain turned the world red for a moment.

Amos began firing his gun into the monster at close range, but it casually backhanded him and threw him into the cargo airlock hard enough to bend the inner door. The outer door slammed shut the second the inner door was compromised. Holden tried to move but his leg was pinned by the crate, and with electromagnets rated to hold a quarter ton of weight under a ten-g burn, he wouldn't be moving it anytime soon. The crate controls that would shut the magnets off showed the orange glow of a full seal ten centimeters beyond his reach.

The monster turned back to look at him. Its blue eyes were far too large for its head, giving the creature a curious, childlike look. It reached out one oversized hand.

Holden fired into it until his gun was empty.

The miniature, self-contained rockets the recoilless gun used as ammunition exploded in tiny puffs of light and smoke as they hit the creature, each one pushing it farther back and tearing large chunks of its torso away. Black filaments sprayed out and across the room like a line drawing representation of blood splatter.

When the last rocket hit, the monster was blown off the bulkhead and thrown down the cargo bay toward the open doors.

The black-and-red body tumbled toward the vast swatch of stars and darkness, and Holden let himself hope. Less than a meter from the doors, it reached out one long arm and caught the edge of a crate. Holden had seen what kind of strength was in those hands, and knew it wouldn't lose its grip.

"Captain," Amos was yelling in his ear. "Holden, are you still with us?"

"Here, Amos. In a little trouble."

As he spoke, the monster pulled itself up onto the crate it had caught and sat motionless. A hideous gargoyle turned suddenly to stone.

"Gonna hit the override and get you," Amos said. "The inner door is fucked, so we'll lose some atmo, but not too much—"

"Okay, but do it soon," Holden said. "I'm pinned. I need you to cut the mags on this crate."

A moment later, the airlock door opened in a puff of atmosphere. Amos started to step out into the bay when the monster jumped off the crate it was sitting on, grabbed the heavy plastic container with one hand and the bulkhead with the other, and threw the container at him. It slammed into the bulkhead hard enough that Holden felt the vibration through his suit. It missed taking Amos' head off by centimeters. The big mechanic fell back with a curse and the airlock doors shot closed again.

"Sorry," Amos said. "Panicked. Let me get this open—"

"No!" Holden yelled. "Stop opening the damn door. I'm trapped behind two goddamn crates now. And one of these times, the door is going to cut my cable. I really don't want to be stuck in here without a radio."

With the airlock closed, the monster moved back over to the bulkhead next to the engine room and curled up into a ball again. The tissue in the gaping wounds caused by Holden's gun pulsed wetly.

"I can see it, Cap," Alex said. "If I stomp on the gas, I think I can knock it right out those doors."

"No," Naomi and Amos said at almost the same time.

"No," Naomi repeated. "Look where Holden is under those crates. If we go high g, it'll break every bone in his body, even if he somehow isn't thrown out the door too."

"Yeah, she's right," Amos said. "That plan'll kill the captain. It's off the table."

Holden listened for a few moments to his crew argue about how to keep him alive, and watched the creature snuggle itself up the bulkhead and seem to go back to sleep.

"Well," Holden said, breaking into their discussion. "A high-g burn would almost certainly break me into tiny pieces right now. But that doesn't necessarily take it off the table."

The new words that came over the channel seemed like a thing from another world. Holden didn't even recognize the botanist's voice at first.

"Well," Prax said. "That's interesting."

Chapter Twenty-Seven: Prax

When Eros died, everyone watched. The station had been designed as a scientific data extraction engine, and every change, death, and metamorphosis had been captured, recorded, and streamed out to the system. What the governments of Mars and Earth had tried to suppress had leaked out in the weeks and months that followed. How people viewed it had more to do with who they were than the actual footage. To some people, it had been news. For others, evidence. For more than Prax liked to think, it had been an entertainment of terrible decadence—a Busby Berkeley snuff flick.

Prax had watched it too, as had everyone on his team. For him, it had been a puzzle. The drive to apply the logic of conventional biology to the effects of the protomolecule had been overwhelming and, for the most part, fruitless. Individual pieces were tantalizing—the spiral curves so similar to nautilus shell, the heat signature of the infected bodies shifting in patterns that almost matched certain hemorrhagic fevers. But nothing had come together.

Certainly someone, somewhere, was getting the grant money to study what had happened, but Prax's work wouldn't wait for him. He'd turned back to his soybeans. Life had gone on. It hadn't been an obsession, just a well-known conundrum that someone else was going to have to solve.

Prax hung weightless at an unused station in ops and watched the security camera feed. The creature reached out for Captain Holden, and Holden shot it and shot it and shot it. Prax watched the filamentous discharge from the creature's back. That was familiar, certainly. It had been one of the hallmarks of the Eros footage.

The monster began to tumble. Morphologically, it wasn't very far off from human. One head, two arms, two legs. No autonomous structures, no hands or rib cages repurposed to some other function.

Naomi, at the controls, gasped. It was odd, hearing it only through the actual air they shared and not through the comm channel. It seemed intimate in a way that left him a little uncomfortable, but there was something more important. His mind had a fuzzy feeling, like his head was full of cotton ticking. He recognized the sensation. He was thinking something that he wasn't yet aware of.

"I'm pinned," Holden said. "I need you to cut the mags on this crate."

The creature was at the far end of the cargo bay. As Amos went in, it braced itself with one hand, throwing a large crate with the other. Even in the poor-quality feed, Prax could see its massive trapezius and deltoids, the muscles enlarged to a freakish degree. And yet not particularly relocated. So the protomolecule was working under constraints. Whatever the creature was, it wasn't doing what the Eros samples had done. The thing in the cargo bay was unquestionably the same technology, but harnessed for some different application. The cotton ticking shifted.

"No! Stop opening the damn door. I'm trapped behind two goddamn crates now."

The creature moved back to the bulkhead, near where it had first been at rest. It huddled there, the wounds in its body pulsing visibly. But it hadn't *settled* there. With the engines off-line, there wasn't even a trace of gravity to pull it back in place. If it was comfortable there, there had to be a reason.

"No!" Naomi said. Her hands were on the support rings by the controls. Her face had an ashy color. "No. Look where Holden is under those crates. If we go high g, it'll break every bone in his body, even if he somehow isn't thrown out the door too."

"Yeah, she's right," Amos said. He sounded tired. Maybe that was how he expressed sorrow. "That plan'll kill the captain. It's off the table."

"Well. A high-g burn would almost certainly break me into tiny pieces right now. But that doesn't necessarily take it off the table."

On the bulkhead, the creature moved. It wasn't much, but it was there. Prax zoomed in on it as best he could. One massive clawed hand—clawed but still with four fingers and a thumb—braced it, and the other tore at the bulkhead. The first layer was fabric and insulation and it came off in rubbery strips. Once it was gone, the creature attacked the armored steel underneath. Tiny curls of metal floated in the vacuum beside it, catching the light like little stars. Now why was it doing that? If it was trying to do structural damage, there was any number of better ways. Or maybe it was trying to tunnel through the bulkhead, trying to reach something, following some signal...

The cotton ticking disappeared, resolving into the image of a pale, new root springing from a seed. He felt himself smile. *Well, that's interesting.*

"What is, Doc?" Amos asked. Prax realized he must have spoken aloud.

"Um," Prax said, trying to gather the words that would explain what he'd seen. "It's trying to move up a radiation gradient. I mean...the version of the protomolecule that was loose on Eros fed off radiation energy, and so I guess it makes sense that this one would too—"

"This one?" Alex asked. "What one?"

"This version. I mean, this one's obviously been engineered to repress most of the changes. It's hardly changed the host body at all. There have to be novel constraints on it, but it still seems to need a source of radiation."

"Why, Doc?" Amos asked. He was trying to be patient. "Why do we think it needs radiation?"

"Oh," Prax said. "Because we shut down the drive, and so the reactor is running at maintenance level, and now it's trying to dig through to the core."

There was a pause, and then Alex said something obscene.

"Okay," Holden said. "There's no choice. Alex, you need to get that thing out of here before it gets through the bulkhead. We don't have time to build a new plan."

"Captain," Alex said. "Jim—"

"I'll be in one second after it's gone," Amos said. "If you aren't there, it's been an honor serving with you, Cap."

Prax waved his hands, as if the gesture could get their attention. The movement sent him looping slowly through the operations deck.

"Wait. No. That *is* the new plan," he said. "It's moving up a radiation gradient. It's like a root heading toward water."

Naomi had turned to look at him as he spun. She seemed to spin, and Prax's brain reset to feeling that she was below him, spiraling away. He closed his eyes.

"You're going to have to walk us through this," Holden said. "Quickly. How can we control it?"

"Change the gradient," Prax said. "How long would it take to put together a container with some unshielded radioisotopes?"

"Depends, Doc," Amos said. "How much do we need?"

"Just more than is leaking through from the reactor right now," Prax said.

"Bait," Naomi said, catching hold of him and pulling him to a handhold. "You want to make something that looks like better food and lure that thing out the door with it."

"I just said that. Didn't I just say that?" Prax asked.

"Not exactly, no," Naomi said.

On the screen, the creature was slowly building a cloud of metal shavings. Prax wasn't sure, because the resolution of the image wasn't actually all that good, but it seemed like its hand might be changing shape as it dug. He wondered how much the constraints placed on the protomolecule's expression took damage and healing into account. Regenerative processes were a great opportunity for constraining systems to fail. Cancer was just cell replication gone mad. If it was starting to change, it might not stop.

"Regardless," Prax said, "I think we should probably hurry."

The plan was simple enough. Amos would reenter the cargo bay and free the captain as soon as the bay doors had shut behind the intruder. Naomi, in ops, would trigger the doors to close the moment the creature had gone after the radioactive bait. Alex would fire the engines as soon as doing so wouldn't kill the captain. And the bait—a half-kilo cylinder with a thin case of lead foil to keep it from attracting the beast too early—would be walked out through the main airlock and tossed into the vacuum by the only remaining crewman.

Prax floated in the airlock, bait trap in the thick glove of the environment suit. Regrets and uncertainty flooded through his mind.

"Maybe it would be better if Amos did this part," Prax said. "I've never actually done any extravehicular anything before."

"Sorry, Doc. I've got a ninety-kilo captain to haul," Amos said.

"Couldn't we automate this? A lab waldo could—"

"Prax," Naomi said, and the gentleness of the syllable carried the weight of a thousand *get-your-ass-out-there*s. Prax checked the seals on his suit one more time. Everything reported good. The suit was much better than the one he'd worn leaving Ganymede. It was twenty-five meters from the personnel airlock near the front of the ship to the cargo bay doors at the extreme aft. He wouldn't even have to go all the way there. He tested the radio tether to make sure it was clipped tightly into the airlock's plug.

That was another interesting question. Was the radio-jamming effect a natural output of the monster? Prax tried to imagine how such a thing could be generated biologically. Would the effect end when the monster left the ship? When it was burned up by the exhaust?

"Prax," Naomi said. "Now is good."

"All right," he said. "I'm going out."

The outer airlock door cycled open. His first impulse was to push out into the darkness the way he would into a large room. His second was to crawl on his hands and knees, keeping as much of his body against the skin of the ship as humanly possible. Prax took the bait in one hand and used the toe rings to lift himself up and out.

The darkness around him was overwhelming. The *Rocinante* was a raft of metal and paint on an ocean. More than an ocean. The stars wrapped around him in all directions, the nearest ones hundreds of lifetimes away, and then more past those and more past those. The sense of being on a tiny little asteroid or moon looking up at a too-wide sky flipped and he was at the top of the universe, looking down into an abyss without end. It was like a visual illusion flipping between a vase and then two faces, then back again at the speed of perception. Prax grinned up, spreading his arms into the nothingness even as the first taste of nausea crawled up the back of his tongue. He'd read accounts of extravehicular euphoria, but the experience was unlike anything he'd imagined. He was the eye of God, drinking in the light of infinite stars, and he was a speck of dust on a speck of dust, clipped by his mag boots to the body of a ship unthinkably more powerful than himself, and unimportant before the face of the abyss. His suit's speakers crackled with background radiation from the birth of the universe, and eerie voices whispered in the static.

"Uh, Doc?" Amos said. "There a problem out there?"

Prax looked around, expecting to see the mechanic beside him. The milk-white universe of stars was all that met him. With so many, it seemed like they should sum to brightness. Instead, the *Rocinante* was dark except for the EVA lights and, toward the rear of the ship, a barely visible white nebula where atmosphere had blown out from the cargo bay.

"No," Prax said. "No problems."

He tried to take a step forward, but his suit didn't budge. He pulled, straining to lift his foot from the plating. His toe moved forward a centimeter and stopped. Panic flared in his chest. Something was wrong with the mag boots. At this rate, he'd never make it to the cargo bay door before the creature dug through and into engineering and the reactor itself.

"Um. I have a problem," he said. "I can't move my feet."

"What are the slide controls set to?" Naomi asked.

"Oh, right," Prax said, moving the boot settings down to match his strength. "I'm fine. Never mind."

He'd never actually walked with mag boots before, and it was a strange sensation. For most of the stride, his leg felt free and almost uncontrolled, and then, as he brought his foot toward the hull, there would be a moment, a critical point, when the force took hold and slammed him to the metal. He made his way floating and being snatched down, step by step. He couldn't see the cargo bay doors, but he knew where they were. From his position looking aft, they were to the left of the drive cone. But on the right side of the ship. *No, starboard side. They call it starboard on ships.*

He knew that just past the dark metal lip that marked the edge of the ship, the creature was digging at the walls, clawing through the flesh of the ship toward its heart. If it figured out what was going on—if it had the cognitive capacity for even basic reasoning—it could come boiling up out of the bay at him.

Vacuum didn't kill it. Prax imagined himself trying to clomp away on his awkward magnetic boots while the creature cut him apart; then he took a long, shuddering breath and lifted the bait.

"Okay," he said. "I'm in position."

"No time like the present," Holden said, his voice strained with pain but attempting to be light.

"Right," Prax said.

He pressed the small timer, hunched close to the hull of the ship, and then, with every muscle in his body, uncurled and flung the little cylinder into nothing. It flew out, catching the light from the cargo bay interior and then vanishing. Prax had the nauseating certainty that he'd forgotten a step, and that the lead foil wouldn't come off the way it was supposed to.

"It's moving," Holden said. "It smelled it. It's going out."

And there it was, long black fingers folding up from the ship, the dark body pulling itself up to the ship's exterior like it had been born to the abyss. Its eyes glowed blue. Prax heard nothing but his own panicked breathing. Like an animal in the ancient grasslands of Earth, he had the primal urge to be still and silent, though through the vacuum, the creature wouldn't have heard him if he'd shrieked.

The creature shifted; the eerie eyes closed, opened again, closed; and then it leapt. The un-twinkling stars were eclipsed by its passage.

"Clear," Prax said, shocked by the firmness of his voice. "It's clear of the ship. Close the cargo doors now."

"Check," Naomi said. "Closing doors."

"I'm coming in, Cap'n," Amos said.

"I'm passing out, Amos," Holden said, but there was enough laughter in the words that Prax was pretty sure he was joking.

In the darkness, a star blinked out and then came back. Then another. Prax mentally traced the path. Another star eclipsed.

"I'm heating her back up," Alex said. "Let me know when you're all secure, right?"

Prax watched, waited. The star stayed solid. Shouldn't it have gone dark like the others? Had he misjudged? Or was the creature looping around? If it could maneuver in raw vacuum, could it have noticed Alex bringing the reactor back online?

Prax turned back toward the main airlock.

The *Rocinante* had seemed like nothing—a toothpick floating on an ocean of stars. Now the distance back to the airlock was immense. Prax moved one foot, then the other, trying to run without ever having both feet off the deck. The mag boots wouldn't let him release them both at the same time, the trailing foot trapped until the lead one signaled it was solid. His back itched, and he fought the urge to look behind. Nothing was there, and if something was, looking wouldn't help. The cable of his radio link turned from a line into a loop that trailed behind him as he moved. He pulled on it to take up the slack.

The tiny green-and-yellow glow of the open airlock called to him like something from a dream. He heard himself whimpering a little, but the sound was lost in a string of profanity from Holden.

"What's going on down there?" Naomi snapped.

"Captain's feeling a little under the weather," Amos said. "Think he maybe wrenched something."

"My knee feels like someone gave birth in it," Holden said. "I'll be fine."

"Are we clear for burn?" Alex asked.

"We are not," Naomi said. "Cargo doors are as closed as they're going to get until we hit the docks, but the forward airlock isn't sealed."

"I'm almost in," Prax said, thinking, *Don't leave me here. Don't leave me in the pit with that thing.*

"Right, then," Alex said. "Let me know when I can get us the hell out of here."

In the depth of the ship, Amos made a small sound. Prax reached the airlock, pulling himself in with a violence that made the joints of his suit creak. He yanked on his umbilical to pull it the rest of the way in after him. He flung himself against the far wall, slapping at the controls until the cycle started and the outer door slid closed. In the dim light of the airlock proper, Prax spun slowly on all three axes. The outer door remained closed. Nothing ripped it open; no glowing blue eyes appeared to crawl in after him. He bumped gently against the wall as the distant sound of an air pump announced the presence of atmosphere.

"I'm in," he said. "I'm in the airlock."

"Is the captain stable?" Naomi asked.

"Was he ever?" Amos replied.

"I'm fine. My knee hurts. Get us out of here."

"Amos?" Naomi said. "I'm seeing you're still in the cargo bay. Is there a problem?"

"Might be," Amos said. "Our guy left something behind."

"Don't touch it!" Holden's voice was harsh as a bark. "We'll get a torch and burn it down to its component atoms."

"Don't think that'd be a good idea," Amos said. "I've seen these before, and they don't take well to cutting torches."

Prax levered himself up to standing, adjusting the slides on his boots to keep him lightly attached to the airlock floor. The inner airlock door chimed that it was safe to remove his suit and reenter the ship. He ignored it and activated one of the wall panels. He switched to a view of the cargo bay. Holden was floating near the cargo airlock. Amos was hanging on to a wall-mounted ladder and examining something small and shiny stuck to the bulkhead.

"What is it, Amos?" Naomi asked.

"Well, I'd have to clean some of this yuck off it," Amos said. "But it looks like a pretty standard incendiary charge. Not a big one, but enough to vaporize about two square meters."

There was a moment of silence. Prax released the seal on his helmet, lifted it off, and took a deep breath of the ship's air. He switched to an outside camera. The monster was drifting behind the ship, suddenly visible again in the faint light coming out of the cargo bay, and slowly receding from view. It was wrapped around his radioactive bait.

"A bomb," Holden said. "You're telling me that thing left a *bomb*?"

"And pretty damn peculiar too. If you ask me," Amos replied.

"Amos, come with me into the cargo airlock," Holden said. "Alex, what's left to do before we burn that monster up? Is Prax back inside?"

"You guys in the 'lock?" Alex said.

"We are now. Do it."

"Don't need to say it twice," Alex said. "Brace for acceleration."

The biochemical cascade that came from euphoria and panic and the reassurance of safety slowed Prax's response time so that when the burn began, he didn't quite have his legs under him. He stumbled against the wall, knocking his head against the inner door of the airlock. He didn't care. He felt wonderful. He'd gotten the monster off the ship. It was burning up in the *Rocinante*'s fiery tail even as he watched.

Then an angry god kicked the side of the ship and sent it spinning across the void. Prax was ripped from his feet, the gentle magnetic tug of his boots not enough to stop it. The outer airlock door rushed at him, and the world went black.

Chapter Twenty-Eight: Avasarala

There was another spike. A third one. Only this time, there didn't seem to be any chance of Bobbie's monsters being involved. So maybe...maybe it was coincidence. Which opened the question. If the thing hadn't come from Venus, then where?

The world, however, had conspired to distract her.

"She's not what we thought she was, ma'am," Soren said. "I fell for the little lost Martian thing too. She's good."

Avasarala leaned back in her chair. The intelligence report on her screen showed the woman she'd called Roberta Draper in civilian clothes. If anything, they made her look bigger. The name listed was Amanda Telelé. Free operative of the Martian Intelligence Service.

"I'm still looking into it," Soren said. "It looks like there really was a Roberta Draper, but she died on Ganymede with the other marines."

Avasarala waved the words away and scrolled through the report. Records of back-channel steganographic messages between the alleged Bobbie and a known Martian operative on Luna beginning the day that Avasarala had recruited her. Avasarala waited for the fear to squeeze her chest, the sense of betrayal. They didn't come. She kept turning to new parts of the report, taking in new information and waiting for her body to react. It kept not happening.

"We looked into this why?" she asked.

"It was a hunch," Soren said. "It was just the way she carried herself when she wasn't around you. She was a little too...slick, I guess. She just didn't seem right. So I took the initiative. I said it was from you."

"So that I wouldn't look like such a fucking idiot for inviting a mole into my office?"

"Seemed like the polite thing to do," Soren said. "If you're looking for ways to reward my good service, I do accept bonuses and promotion."

"I fucking bet you do," Avasarala said.

He waited, leaning a little forward on his toes. Waiting for her to give the order to have Bobbie arrested and submitted for a full intelligence debriefing. As euphemisms went, "full intelligence debriefing" was among the most obscene, but they were at war with Mars, and a high-value intelligence agent planted in the heart of the UN would know things that were invaluable.

So, Avasarala thought, *why am I not reacting to this?*

She reached out to the screen, paused, pulled back her hand, frowning.

"Ma'am?" Soren said.

It was the smallest thing, and the least expected. Soren bit at the inside of his bottom lip. It was a tiny movement, almost invisible. Like a tell at a poker table. And as she saw it, Avasarala knew.

There was no thinking it out, no reasoning, no struggle or second-guessing. It was all simply there, clear in her mind as if she had always known it, complete and perfect. Soren was nervous because the report she was looking at wouldn't hold up to rigorous scrutiny.

It wouldn't hold up because it was a fake.

It was a fake because Soren was working for someone else, someone who wanted to control the information getting to Avasarala's desk. Nguyen had re-created his little fleet without her knowing it because Soren was the one watching the data traffic. Someone had known that she would need controlling. Handling. This was something that had been prepared for since well before Ganymede had gone pear-shaped. The monster on Ganymede had been anticipated.

And so it was Errinwright.

He had let her demand her peace negotiations, let her think she'd undermined Nguyen, let her take Bobbie onto her staff. All of it, so that she wouldn't get suspicious.

This wasn't a shard of Venus that had escaped; it was a military project. A weapon that Earth wanted in order to break its rivals before the alien project on Venus finished whatever it was doing. Someone—probably Mao-Kwikowski—had retained a sample of the protomolecule in some separate and firewalled lab, weaponized it, and opened bidding.

The attack on Ganymede had been on one hand a proof of concept assault, on the other a crippling blow to the outer planets' food supply. The OPA had never been on the list of bidders. And then Nguyen had gone to the Jovian system to collect the goods, James Holden and his pet botanist had walked in on some part of it, and Mars had figured out they were about to lose the trade.

Avasarala wondered how much Errinwright had given Jules-Pierre Mao to outbid Mars. It would have had to be more than just money.

Earth was about to get its first protomolecule weapon, and Errinwright had kept her out of the loop because whatever he was going to do with it, she wasn't going to like it. And she was one of the only people in the solar system who might have been able to stop him.

She wondered whether she still was.

"Thank you, Soren," she said. "I appreciate this. Do we know where she is?"

"She's looking for you," Soren said, and a sly smile tugged at his lips. "She may be under the impression that you're asleep. It is pretty late."

"Sleep? Yes, I remember that vaguely," Avasarala said. "All right. I'm going to need to talk to Errinwright."

"Do you want me to have her arrested?"

"No, I don't."

The disappointment barely showed.

"How *should* we move forward?" Soren asked.

"I'll talk to Errinwright," she said. "Can you get me some tea?"

"Yes, ma'am," he said, and practically bowed his way out of the room.

Avasarala leaned back in her chair. Her mind felt calm. Her body was centered and still, like she'd ended a particularly long and effective meditation. She pulled up the connection request and waited to see how long Errinwright or his assistant would take to respond. As soon as she made the request, it was flagged PRIORITY PENDING. Three minutes later, Errinwright was there. He spoke from his hand terminal, the picture jumping as the car he was in bumped and turned. It was full night wherever he was.

"Chrisjen!" he said. "Is anything wrong?"

"Nothing in particular," Avasarala said, silently cursing the connection. She wanted to see his face. She wanted to watch him lie to her. "Soren's brought me something interesting. Intelligence thinks my Martian liaison's a spy."

"Really?" Errinwright said. "That's unfortunate. Are you arresting her?"

"I don't think so," Avasarala said. "I think I'll put my own flag on her traffic. Better the devil we know. Don't you agree?"

The pause was hardly noticeable.

"That's a good idea. Do that."

"Thank you, sir."

"Since I've got you here, I needed to ask you something. Do you have anything that requires you in the office, or can you work on a ship?"

She smiled. Here was the next move, then.

"What are you thinking about?"

Errinwright's car reached a stretch of smoother pavement and his face came into clearer focus. He was wearing a dark suit with a high-collared shirt and no tie. He looked like a priest.

"Ganymede. We need to show that we're taking the situation out there seriously. The secretary-general wants someone senior to go there physically. Report back on the humanitarian angle. Since you're the one who's taken point on this, he thought you'd be the right face to put on it. And I thought it would give you the chance to follow up on the initial attack too."

"We're in a shooting war," Avasarala said. "I don't think the Navy would want to spare a ship to haul my old bones out there. Besides which, I'm coordinating the investigation into Venus, aren't I? Blank check and all."

Errinwright grinned exactly as if he'd meant it.

"I've got you taken care of. Jules-Pierre Mao is taking a yacht from Luna to Ganymede to oversee his company's humanitarian aid efforts. He's offered a berth. It's better accommodations than you get at the office. Probably better bandwidth too. You can monitor Venus from there."

"Mao-Kwik is part of the government now? I hadn't known," she said.

"We're all on the same side. Mao-Kwik is as interested as anyone in seeing those people cared for."

Avasarala's door opened and Roberta Draper loomed into the office. She looked like crap. Her skin had the ashy look of that of someone who hadn't slept in too long. Her jaw was set. Avasarala nodded toward the chair.

"I take up a lot of bandwidth," she said.

"Won't be a problem. You'll get first priority on all communications channels."

The Martian sat down across the desk, well out of the camera's cone. Bobbie braced her hands on her thighs, elbows to the sides, like a wrestler getting ready to step into the cage. Avasarala made herself not glance at the woman.

"Can I think about it?"

"Chrisjen," Errinwright said, bringing his hand terminal closer in, his wide, round face filling the screen. "I told the secretary-general that this might not fly. Even in the best yacht, traveling out to the Jovian system is a hard journey. If you've got too much to do or if you're at all uncomfortable with the trip, you just say so and I'll find someone else. They just won't be as good as you."

"Who is?" Avasarala said with a toss of her hand. Rage was boiling in her gut. "Fine. You've talked me into it. When do I leave?"

"The yacht's scheduled for departure in four days. I'm sorry for the tight turnaround, but I didn't have confirmation until about an hour ago."

"Serendipity."

"If I were a religious man, I'd say it meant something. I'll have the details sent to Soren."

"Better send it to me directly," Avasarala said. "Soren's going to have a lot on his plate already."

"Whatever you like," he said.

Her boss had secretly started a war. He was working with the same corporations that had let the genie out of the bottle on Phoebe, sacrificed Eros, and threatened everything human. He was a frightened little boy in a good suit picking a fight he thought he could win because he was pissing himself over the real threat. She smiled at him. Good men and women had already died because of him and Nguyen. Children had died on Ganymede. Belters would be scrambling for calories. Some would starve.

Errinwright's round cheeks fell a millimeter. His brows knotted just a bit. He knew that she knew. Because of course he did. Players at their level didn't deceive each other. They won even though their opponents knew exactly what was happening. Just like he was winning against her right now.

"Are you feeling all right?" he asked. "I think this is the first conversation we've had in ten years where you haven't said something vulgar."

Avasarala grinned at the screen, reaching out her fingertips as if she could caress him.

"Cunt," she said carefully.

When the connection dropped, she put her head in her hands for a moment, blowing out her breath and sucking it back in hard, focusing. When she sat up, Bobbie was watching her.

"Evening," Avasarala said.

"I've been trying to find you," Bobbie said. "My connections were blocked."

Avasarala grunted.

"We need to talk about something. Someone. I mean, Soren," Bobbie said. "You remember that data you wanted him to take care of a couple days ago? He handed it off to someone else. I don't know who, but they were military. I'll swear to that."

So that's what spooked him, Avasarala thought. Caught with his hands in the cookie jar. Poor idiot had underestimated her pet Marine.

"All right," she said.

"I understand that you don't have any reason to trust me," Bobbie said, "but...Okay. Why are you laughing?"

Avasarala stood up, stretching until the joints in her shoulders ached pleasantly.

"At this moment, you are literally the only one on my staff who I trust as far as I can piss. You remember when I said that the thing on Ganymede wasn't us? It wasn't then but it is now. We've bought it, and I assume we're planning to use it against you."

Bobbie stood up. Her face, once just ashen, was bloodless.

"I have to tell my superiors," she said, her voice thick and strangled.

"No, you don't. They know. And you can't prove it yet any more than I can. Tell them now and they'll broadcast it, and we'll deny it and blah blah blah. The bigger problem is that you're coming back to Ganymede with me. I'm being sent."

She explained everything. Soren's false intelligence report, what it implied, Errinwright's betrayal, and the mission to Ganymede on the Mao-Kwik yacht.

"You can't do that," Bobbie said.

"It's a pain in the ass," Avasarala agreed. "They'll be monitoring my connections, but they're probably doing the same here. And if they're shipping me to Ganymede, you can be dead sure that nothing is going to happen there. They're putting me in a box until it's too late to change anything. Or that's what they're trying, anyway. I'm not giving away the fucking game yet."

"You can't get on that ship," Bobbie said. "It's a trap."

"Of course it's a trap," Avasarala said, waving a hand. "But it's a trap I have to step into. Refuse a request from the secretary-general? That comes out, and everyone starts thinking I'm about to retire. No one backs a player who's going to be powerless next year. We play for the long term, and that means looking strong for the duration. Errinwright knows that. It's why he played it this way."

Outside, another shuttle was lifting off. Avasarala could already hear the roar of the burn, feel the press of thrust and false gravity pushing her back. It had been thirty years since she'd been out of Earth's gravity well. This wasn't going to be pleasant.

"If you get on that ship, they'll kill you," Bobbie said, making each word its own sentence.

"That's not how this game gets played," Avasarala said. "What they—"

The door opened again. Soren had a tray in his hands. The teapot on it was cast iron, with a single handleless enamel cup. He opened his mouth to speak, then saw Bobbie. It was easy to forget how much larger she was until a man Soren's height visibly cowered before her.

"My tea! That's excellent. Do you want any, Bobbie?"

"No."

"All right. Well, put it down, Soren. I'm not drinking it with you standing there. Good. And pour me a cup."

Avasarala watched him turn his back on the marine. His hands didn't shake; she'd give the boy that much. Avasarala stood silent, waiting for him to bring it to her as if he were a puppy learning to retrieve a toy. When he did, she blew across the surface of the tea, scattering the thin veil of steam. He carefully didn't turn to look at Bobbie.

"Will there be anything else, ma'am?"

Avasarala smiled. How many people had this boy killed just by lying to her? She would never know for certain, and neither would he. The best she could do was *not another*.

"Soren," she said. "They're going to know it was you."

It was too much. He looked over his shoulder. Then he looked back, greenish with anxiety.

"Who do you mean?" he said, trying for charm.

"Them. If you're counting on them to help your career, I just want you to understand that they won't. The kind of men you're working for? Once they know you've slipped, you're nothing to them. They have no tolerance for failure."

"I—"

"Neither do I. Don't leave anything personal at your desk."

She watched it in his eyes. The future he'd planned and worked for, defined himself by, fell away. A life on basic support rose in its place. It wasn't enough. It wasn't nearly enough. But it was all the justice she could manage on short notice.

When the door was closed, Bobbie cleared her throat.

"What's going to happen to him?" she asked.

Avasarala sipped her tea. It was good, fresh green tea, brewed perfectly—rich and sweet and not even slightly bitter.

"Who gives a shit?" she said. "The Mao-Kwik yacht leaves in four days. That's not much time. And neither of us is going to be able to take a dump without the bad guys knowing. I'm going to get you a list of people I need to have drinks or lunch or coffee with before we leave. Your job is to arrange it so I do."

"I'm your social secretary now?" Bobbie said, bristling.

"You and my husband are the only two people alive who I know aren't trying to stop me," Avasarala said. "That's how far down I am right now. This has to happen, and there is no one else I can rely on. So yes. You're my social secretary. You're my bodyguard. You're my psychiatrist. All of it. You."

Bobbie lowered her head, breathing out through flared nostrils. Her lips pursed and she shook her massive head once quickly—left, then right, then back to center.

"You're fucked," she said.

Avasarala took another sip of her tea. She should have been ruined. She should have been in tears. She'd been cut off from her own power, tricked. Jules-Pierre Mao had sat there, not a meter from where she was now, and laughed down his sleeve at her. Errinwright and Nguyen and whoever else was in his little cabal. They'd tricked her. She'd sat there, pulling strings and trading favors and thinking that she was doing something real. For months—maybe years—she hadn't noticed that she was being closed out.

They'd made a fool of her. She should have been humiliated. Instead, she felt alive. This was her game, and if she was behind at halftime, it only meant they expected her to lose. There was nothing better than being underestimated.

"Do you have a gun?"

Bobbie almost laughed.

"They don't like having Martian soldiers walking around the United Nations with guns. I have to eat lunch with a dull spork. We're at war."

"All right, fine. When we get on the yacht, you're in charge of security. You're going to need a gun. I'll arrange that for you."

"You can? Honestly, though, I'd rather have my suit."

"Your suit? What suit?"

"I had custom-fit powered armor with me when I came here.

The video feed of the monster was copied from it. They said they were turning it over to your guys to confirm the original footage hadn't been faked."

Avasarala looked at Bobbie and sipped her tea. Michael-Jon would know where it was. She'd call him the next morning, arrange to have it brought on board the Mao-Kwik yacht with an innocuous label like WARDROBE stamped on the side.

Probably thinking she needed to be convinced, Bobbie kept talking. "Seriously. Get me a gun, I'm a soldier. Get that suit for me, I'm a superhero."

"If we've still got it, you'll have it."

"All right, then," Bobbie said. She smiled. For the first time since they'd met, Avasarala was afraid of her.

God help whoever makes you put it on.

Chapter Twenty-Nine: Holden

Gravity returned as Alex brought the engine up, and Holden floated down to the deck of the cargo bay airlock at a gentle half g. They didn't need to go fast now that the monster was outside the ship. They just needed to put some distance between the ship and it, and get it into the drive's star-hot exhaust plume, where it would be broken down into its various subatomic particles. Even the protomolecule couldn't survive being reduced to ions.

He hoped, anyway.

When he touched down on the deck, he intended to turn on the wall monitor and check the aft cameras. He wanted to watch the thing be torched, but the moment his weight came down, a white-hot spike of pain took his knee. He yelped and collapsed.

Amos drifted down next to him, then kicked off his boot mags and started to kneel. "You okay, Cap?" he said.

"Fine. I mean, for I-think-I-blew-out-my-knee levels of fine."

"Yeah. Joint injury's a lot less painful in microgravity, ain't it?"

Holden was about to reply when a massive hammer hit the side of the ship. The hull rang like a gong. The *Roci*'s engine cut off almost instantly, and the ship snapped into a flat spin. Amos was lifted away from Holden and thrown across the airlock to slam against the outer door. Holden slid along the deck to land standing upright against the bulkhead next to him, his knee collapsing under him so painfully he nearly blacked out.

He chinned a button in his helmet, and his body armor shot him full of amphetamines and painkillers. Within seconds, his knee still hurt, but the pain was very far away and easy to ignore. The threatening tunnel vision vanished and the airlock became very bright. His heart started to race.

"Alex," he said, knowing the answer before he asked, "what was that?"

"When we torched our passenger there, the bomb in the cargo bay went off," the pilot replied. "We've got serious damage to that bay, to the outer hull, and to engineering. Reactor went into emergency shutdown. The cargo bay turned into a second drive during the blast and put us into a spin. I have no control over the ship."

Amos groaned and began moving his limbs. "That sucks."

"We need to kill this spin," Holden said. "What do you need to get the attitude thrusters back up?"

"Holden," Naomi cut in, "I think Prax may be injured in the airlock. He's not moving in there."

"Is he dying?"

The hesitation lasted for one very long second.

"His suit doesn't think so."

"Then ship first," Holden said. "First aid after. Alex, we've got radios again. And the lights are on. So the jamming is gone, and the batteries must still be working. Why can't you fire the thrusters?"

"Looks like…primary and secondary pumps are out. No water pressure."

"Confirmed," Naomi said a second later. "Primary wasn't in the blast area. If it's toast, engineering must be a mess. Secondary's on the deck above. It shouldn't have been physically damaged, but there was a big power spike just before the reactor went off-line. Might have fried it or blown a breaker."

"Okay, we're on it. Amos," Holden said, pulling himself over to where the mechanic lay on the cargo airlock's outer door. "You with me?"

Amos gave a one-handed Belter nod, then groaned. "Just knocked the wind out of me, is all."

"Gotta get up, big man," Holden said, pushing himself to his feet. In the partial gravity of their spin, his leg felt heavy, hot, and stiff as a board. Without the drugs pouring through him, standing on it would have probably made him scream. Instead, he pulled Amos up, putting even more pressure on it.

I will pay for this later, he thought. But the amphetamines made later seem very far away.

"What?" Amos said, slurring the word. He probably had a concussion, but Holden would get him some medical attention later when the ship was back under their control.

"We need to get to the secondary water pump," Holden said, forcing himself to speak slowly in spite of the drugs. "What's the fastest access point?"

"Machine shop," Amos replied, then closed his eyes and seemed to fall asleep on his feet.

"Naomi," Holden said. "Can you control Amos' suit from there?"

"Yes."

"Shoot him full of speed. I can't drag his ass around with me, and I need him."

"Okay," she said. A couple of seconds later, Amos' eyes popped open.

"Shit," he said. "Was I asleep?" His words were still slurred but now had a sort of manic energy to them.

"We need to get to the bulkhead access point in the machine

shop. Grab whatever you think we'll need to get the pump running. It might have blown a breaker or fried some wiring. I'll meet you there."

"Okay," Amos said, then pulled himself along the toe rings set into the floor to get to the inner airlock door. A moment later it was open and he crawled out of view.

With the ship spinning, gravity was pulling Holden to a point halfway between the deck and the starboard bulkhead. None of the ladders and rings set into the ship for use in low g or under thrust would be oriented in the right direction. Not really a problem with four working limbs, but it would make maneuvering with one useless leg difficult.

And of course, once he moved past wherever the ship's center of spin was, everything would reverse.

For a moment, his perspective shifted. The vicious Coriolis rattled the fine bones inside his ears, and he was riding a spinning hunk of metal lost in permanent free fall. Then he was under it, about to be crushed. He flushed with the sweat that came a moment before nausea as his brain ran through scenarios to explain the sensations of the spin. He chinned the suit controls, pumping a massive dose of emergency antinausea drugs into his bloodstream.

Without giving himself more time to think about it, Holden grabbed the toe rings and pulled himself up to the inner airlock door. He could see Amos filling a plastic bucket with tools and supplies he was yanking out of drawers and lockers.

"Naomi," Holden said. "Going to take a peek in engineering. Do we have any cameras left in there?"

She made a sort of disgusted grunt he interpreted as a negative, then said, "I've got systems shorted out all over the ship. Either they're destroyed, or the power is out on that circuit."

Holden pulled himself over to the deck-mounted pressure hatch that separated the machine shop from engineering. A status light on the hatch blinked an angry red.

"Shit, I was afraid of that."

"What?" Naomi asked.

"You don't have environmental readings either, do you?"

"Not from engineering. That's all down."

"Well," Holden said with a long sigh. "The hatch thinks there's no atmosphere on the other side. That incendiary charge actually blew a hole through the bulkhead, and engineering is in vacuum."

"Uh-oh," Alex said. "Cargo bay's in vacuum too."

"And the cargo bay door is broken," Naomi added. "And the cargo airlock."

"And a partridge in a fucking pear tree," Amos said with a disgusted snort. "Let's get the damn ship to stop spinning and I'll go outside and take a look at it."

"Amos is right," Holden said, giving up on the hatch and pushing himself to his feet. He staggered down a steeply angled bulkhead to the access panel where Amos was now waiting, bucket in hand. "First things first."

While Amos used a torque wrench to unbolt the access panel, Holden said, "Actually, Naomi, pump all the air out of the machine shop too. No atmo below deck four. Override the safeties so we can open the engineering hatch if we need to."

Amos ran out the last bolt and pulled the panel off the bulkhead. Beyond it lay a dark, cramped space filled with a confusing tangle of pipes and cabling.

"Oh," Holden added. "Might want to prep an SOS if we can't get this fixed."

"Yeah, because we got a lot of people out there who we really want coming to help us right now," Amos said.

Amos pulled himself into the narrow passage between the two hulls and then out of sight. Holden followed him in. Two meters beyond the hatch loomed the blocky and complex-looking pump mechanism that kept water pressure to the maneuvering thrusters. Amos stopped next to it and began pulling parts off. Holden waited behind him, the narrow space not allowing him to see what the big mechanic was doing.

"How's it look?" Holden asked after a few minutes of listening to Amos curse under his breath while he worked.

"It looks fine here," Amos said. "Gonna swap this breaker any-way, just to be sure. But I don't think the pump's our problem."

Shit.

Holden backed out of the maintenance hatch and half crawled up the steep slope of bulkhead back to the engineering hatch. The angry red light had been replaced with a morose yellow one now that there was no atmosphere on either side of the hatch.

"Naomi," Holden said. "I've got to get into engineering. I need to see what happened in there. Have you killed the safeties?"

"Yes. But I've got no sensors in there. The room could be flooded with radiation—"

"But you have sensors here in the machine shop, right? If I open the hatch and you get radiation warnings, just let me know. I'll shut it immediately."

"Jim," Naomi said, the stiffness that had been in her voice every time she'd spoken to him for the last day slipping a bit. "How many times can you get yourself massively irradiated before it catches up with you?"

"At least once more?"

"I'll tell the *Roci* to prep a bed in sick bay," she said, not quite laughing.

"Get one of the ones that's not throwing errors."

Without giving himself time to rethink it, Holden slapped the release on the deck hatch. He held his breath while it opened, expecting to see chaos and destruction on the other side, followed by his suit's radiation alarm.

Instead, other than one small hole in the bulkhead closest to the explosion, it looked fine.

Holden pulled himself through the opening and hung by his arms for a few moments, examining the space. The massive fusion reactor that dominated the center of the compartment looked untouched. The bulkhead on the starboard side bowed in precari-ously, with a charred hole in its center, like a miniature volcano had formed there. Holden shuddered at the thought of how much energy had to have been released to bend the heavily armored and radiation-shielded bulkhead in like that, and how close it had come to punching a hole in their reactor. How many more joules to go from a badly dented wall to full containment breach?

"God, this one was close," he said out loud to no one in particular.

"Swapped out all the parts I can think to," Amos said. "The problem is somewhere else."

Holden let go of the rim of the hatch and dropped a half meter to the bulkhead, which angled below him, then slid to the deck. The only other visible damage was a hunk of bulkhead plating stuck in the wall exactly on the other side of the reactor. Holden couldn't see any way that the shrapnel could have gotten there without passing directly through the reactor, or else bouncing off two bulkheads and around it. There was no sign of the first, so the second, incredibly unlikely though it was, had to be what had happened.

"I mean, really close," he said, touching the jagged metal fragment. It was sunk a good fifteen centimeters into the wall. Plenty far enough to have at least breached the shielding on the reactor. Maybe worse.

"Grabbing your camera," Naomi said. A moment later she whistled. "No kidding. The walls in there are mostly cabling. Can't make a hole like that without breaking something."

Holden tried to pull the shrapnel out of the wall by hand and failed. "Amos, bring some pliers and a lot of patch cabling."

"So no on the distress call, then," Naomi said.

"No. But if someone could point a camera aft and reassure me that for all this trouble we actually killed that damned thing, that would be just swell."

"Watched it go myself, Cap," Alex said. "Nothin' but gas now."

Holden lay on one of the sick bay beds, letting the ship look his leg over. Periodically a manipulator prodded his knee, which was swelled up to the size of a cantaloupe, the skin stretched tight as a drum's head. But the bed was also making sure to keep him perfectly medicated, so the occasional pokes and prods registered only as pressure without any pain.

The panel next to his head warned him to remain still; then two arms grabbed his leg while a third injected a needle-thin flexible tube into his knee and started doing something arthroscopic. He felt a vague tugging sensation.

At the next bed over lay Prax. His head was bandaged where a three-centimeter flap of skin had been glued back down. His eyes were closed. Amos, who had turned out not to have a concussion, just another nasty bump on his head, was belowdecks doing makeshift repairs on everything the monster's bomb had broken, including putting a temporary patch on the hole in their engineering bulkhead. They wouldn't be able to fix the cargo bay door until they docked at Tycho. Alex was flying them there at a gentle quarter g to make it easier to work.

Holden didn't mind the delay. The truth was he was in no hurry to get back to Tycho and confront Fred about what he'd seen. The longer he thought about it, the further he got from his earlier blind panic, and the more he thought Naomi was right. It made no sense for Fred to be behind any of this.

But he wasn't sure. And he had to be sure.

Prax mumbled something and touched his head. He started pulling on the bandages.

"I wouldn't mess with those," Holden said.

Prax nodded and closed his eyes again. Sleeping, or trying to. The auto-doc pulled the tube out of Holden's leg, sprayed it with antiseptic, and began wrapping it with a tight bandage. Holden waited until the medical pod was done doing whatever it was doing to his knee, then turned sideways on the bed and tried to stand up. Even at a quarter g, his leg wouldn't support him. He hopped on one foot over to a supply locker and got himself a crutch.

As he moved past the botanist's bed, Prax grabbed his arm. His grip was surprisingly strong.

"It's dead?"

"Yeah," Holden said, patting his hand. "We got it. Thanks."

Prax didn't reply; he just rolled onto his side and shook. It took Holden a moment to realize Prax was weeping. He left without saying anything else. What else was there to say?

Holden took the ladder-lift up, planning to go to ops and read the detailed damage reports Naomi and the *Roci* were compiling. He stopped when he got to the personnel deck and heard two people speaking. He couldn't hear what they were saying, but he recognized Naomi's voice, and he recognized the tone she used when she was having an intimate conversation.

The voices were coming from the galley. Feeling a little like a Peeping Tom, Holden moved closer to the galley hatch until he could make out the words.

"It's more than that," Naomi was saying. Holden almost walked into the galley, but something in her tone stopped him. He had the terrible feeling she was talking about him. About them. About why she was leaving.

"Why does it have to be more?" the other person said. Amos.

"You almost beat a man to death with a can of chicken on Ganymede," Naomi replied.

"Gonna hold a little girl hostage for some food? Fuck him. If he was here, I'd smash him again right now."

"Do you trust me, Amos?" Naomi said. Her voice was sad. More than that. Frightened.

"More than anyone else," Amos replied.

"I'm scared out of my wits. Jim is rushing off to do something really dumb on Tycho. This guy we're taking with us seems like he's one twitch from a nervous breakdown."

"Well, he's—"

"And you," she continued. "I depend on you. I know you've always got my back, no matter what. Except maybe not now, because the Amos I know doesn't beat a skinny kid half to death, no matter how much chicken he asks for. I feel like everyone's losing themselves. I need to understand, because I'm really, really frightened."

Holden felt the urge to go in, take her hand, hold her. The need in her voice demanded it, but he held himself back. There was a long pause. Holden heard a scraping sound, followed by the sound of metal hitting glass. Someone was stirring sugar into coffee. The sounds were so clear he could almost see it.

"So, Baltimore," Amos said, his voice as relaxed as if he were going to talk about the weather. "Not a nice town. You ever heard of squeezing? Squeeze trade? Hooker squeeze?"

"No. Is it a drug?"

"No," Amos said with a laugh. "No, when you squeeze a hooker, you put her on the street until she gets knocked up, then peddle her to johns who get off on pregnant girls, then send her back to the streets after she pops the kid. With procreation restrictions, banging pregnant girls is quite the kink."

"Squeeze?"

"Yeah, you know, 'squeezing out puppies'? You never heard it called that?"

"Okay," Naomi said, trying to hide her disgust.

"Those kids? They're illegal, but they don't just vanish, not right away," Amos continued. "They got uses too."

Holden felt his chest tighten a little. It wasn't something he'd ever thought about. When, a second later, Naomi spoke, her horror echoed his.

"Jesus."

"Jesus got nothing to do with it," Amos said. "No Jesus in the squeeze trade. But some kids wind up in the pimp gangs. Some wind up on the streets…"

"Some wind up finding a way to ship offworld, and they never go back?" Naomi asked, her voice quiet.

"Maybe," Amos said, his voice as flat and conversational as ever. "Maybe some do. But most of them just…disappear, eventually. Used up. Most of them."

For a time, no one spoke. Holden heard the sounds of coffee being drunk.

"Amos," she said, her voice thick. "I never—"

"So I'd like to find this little girl before someone uses her up, and she disappears. I'd like to do that for her," Amos said. His voice caught for a moment, and he cleared it with a loud cough. "For her dad."

Holden thought they were done, and started to slip away when he heard Amos, his voice calm again, say, "Then I'm going to kill whoever snatched her."

Chapter Thirty: Bobbie

Prior to working for Avasarala at the UN, Bobbie had never even heard of Mao-Kwikowski Mercantile, or if she had, she hadn't noticed. She'd spent her whole life wearing, eating, or sitting on products carted through the solar system by Mao-Kwik freighters without ever realizing it. After she'd gone through the files Avasarala had given her, she'd been astonished at the size and reach of the company. Hundreds of ships, dozens of stations, millions of employees. Jules-Pierre Mao owned significant properties on every habitable planet and moon in the solar system.

His eighteen-year-old daughter had owned her own racing ship. And that was the daughter he *didn't* like.

When Bobbie tried to imagine being so wealthy you could own a spaceship just to compete in races, she failed. That the same girl had run away to be an OPA rebel probably said a lot about the relationship of wealth and contentment, but Bobbie had a hard time being that philosophical.

She'd grown up solidly Martian middle class. Her father had done twenty as a Marine noncom and had gone into private security consulting after he'd left the corps. Bobbie's family had always had a nice home. She and her two older brothers had attended a private primary school, and her brothers had both gone on to university without having to take out student loans. Growing up, she'd never once thought of herself as poor.

She did now.

Owning your own racing ship wasn't even wealth. It was like speciation. It was conspicuous consumption befitting ancient Earth royalty, a pharaoh's pyramid with a reaction drive. Bobbie had thought it was the most ridiculous excess she'd ever heard of.

And then she climbed off the short flight shuttle onto Jules-Pierre Mao's private L5 station.

Jules didn't park his ships in orbit at a public station. He didn't even use a Mao-Kwik corporate station. This was an entire fully functioning space station in orbit around Earth solely for his private spaceships, and the whole thing done up like peacock feathers. It was a level of extravagance that had never even occurred to her.

She also thought it made Mao himself very dangerous. Everything he did was an announcement of his freedom from constraint. He was a man without boundaries. Killing a senior politician of the UN government might be bad business. It might wind up being expensive. But it would never actually be risky to a man with this much wealth and power.

Avasarala didn't see it.

"I hate spin gravity," Avasarala said, sipping at a cup of steaming tea. They'd be on the station for only three hours, while cargo was transferred from the shuttle to Mao's yacht, but they'd been assigned a suite of four full-sized bedrooms, each with its own shower, and a massive lounge area. A huge screen pretended to be a window, the crescent Earth with her continent-veiling clouds hung on the black. They had a private kitchen staffed by three people, whose biggest task so far had been making the assistant undersecretary's tea. Bobbie considered ordering a large meal just to give them something to do.

"I can't believe we're about to climb on a ship owned by this man. Have you ever known anyone this wealthy to go to jail? Or even be prosecuted? This guy could probably walk in here and shoot you in the face on a live newsfeed and get away with it."

Avasarala laughed at her. Bobbie suppressed a surge of anger. It was just fear looking for an outlet.

"That's not the game," Avasarala said. "No one gets shot. They get marginalized. It's worse."

"No, it's not. I've seen people shot. I've seen my friends shot. When you say, 'That's not the game,' you mean for people like you. Not like me."

Avasarala's expression cooled.

"Yes, that's what I mean," the old woman said. "The level we're playing at has different rules. It's like playing go. It's all about exerting influence. Controlling the board without occupying it."

"Poker is a game too," Bobbie said. "But sometimes the stakes get so high that one player decides it's easier to kill the other guy and walk away with the money. It happens all the time."

Avasarala nodded at her, not replying right away, visibly thinking over what Bobbie had said. Bobbie felt her anger replaced with a sudden rush of affection for the grumpy and arrogant old lady.

"Okay," Avasarala said, putting her teacup down and placing her hands in her lap. "I hear what you're saying, Sergeant. I think it's unlikely, but I'm glad you're here to say it."

But you aren't taking it seriously, Bobbie wanted to shout at her. Instead, she asked the servant who hovered nearby for a mushroom and onion sandwich. While she ate it, Avasarala sipped tea, nibbled on a cookie, and made small talk about the war and her grandchildren. Bobbie tried to be sure to make concerned noises during the war parts and *awww, cute* noises when the kids were the topic. But all she could think about was the tactical nightmare defending Avasarala on an enemy-controlled space-craft would be.

Her recon suit was in a large crate marked FORMAL WEAR and being loaded onto the Mao yacht even as they waited. Bobbie wanted to sneak off and put it on. She didn't notice when Ava-sarala stopped speaking for several minutes.

"Bobbie," Avasarala said, her face not quite a frown. "Are my stories about my beloved grandchildren boring you?"

"Yeah," Bobbie replied. "They really are."

Bobbie had thought that Mao Station was the most ludicrous dis-play of conspicuous wealth she'd ever seen right up until they boarded the yacht.

While the station was extravagant, it at least served a function. It was Jules Mao's personal orbital garage, where he could store and service his fleet of private spacecraft. Underneath the glitz there was a working station, with mechanics and support staff doing actual jobs.

The yacht, the *Guanshiyin*, was the size of a standard cheapjack people-mover that would have transported two hundred custom-ers, but it only had a dozen staterooms. Its cargo area was just large enough to contain the supplies they'd need for a lengthy voyage. It wasn't particularly fast. It was, by any reasonable mea-surement, a miserable failure as a useful spacecraft.

But its job was not to be useful.

The *Guanshiyin*'s job was to be comfortable. Extravagantly comfortable.

It was like a hotel lobby. The carpet was plush and soft under-foot, and actual crystal chandeliers caught the light. Everyplace that should have had a sharp corner was rounded. Softened. The walls were papered with raw bamboo and natural fiber. The first thing Bobbie thought was how hard it would be to clean, and the second thing was that the difficulty was intentional.

Each suite of rooms took up nearly an entire deck of the ship. Each room had its own private bath, media center, game room, and lounge with a full bar. The lounge had a gigantic screen showing the view outside, which would not have been higher definition had it been an actual glass window. Near the bar was a dumbwaiter next to an intercom, which could deliver food prepared by Cordon Bleu chefs any hour of the day or night.

The carpet was so thick Bobbie was pretty sure mag boots wouldn't work. It wouldn't matter. A ship like this would never break down, never have to stop the engines during flight. The kind of people who flew on the *Guanshiyin* had probably never actually worn an environment suit in their lives.

All the fixtures in her bathroom were gold plated.

Bobbie and Avasarala were sitting in the lounge with the head of her UN security team, a pleasant-looking gray-haired man of Kurdish descent named Cotyar. Bobbie had been worried when she first met him. He looked like a friendly high school teacher, not a soldier. But then she'd watched him go through Avasarala's rooms with practiced efficiency, laying out their security plan and directing his team, and her worries eased.

"Well, impressions?" Avasarala asked, leaning back in a plush armchair with her eyes closed.

"This room is not secure," Cotyar said, his accent exotic to Bobbie's ears. "We should not discuss sensitive matters here. Your private room has been secured for such discussions."

"This is a trap," Bobbie said.

"Aren't we finished with that shit yet?" Avasarala said, then leaned forward to give Bobbie a glare.

"She is right," Cotyar said quietly, clearly unhappy to be discussing such matters in an unsecured room. "I've counted fourteen crew on this ship already, and I would estimate that is less than one-third of the total crew of this vessel. I have a team of six for your protection—"

"Seven," Bobbie interrupted, raising her hand.

"As you say," Cotyar continued with a nod. "Seven. We do not control any of the ship's systems. Assassination would be as simple as sealing the deck we are on and pumping out the air."

Bobbie pointed at Cotyar and said, "See?"

Avasarala waved a hand as if she were shooing flies. "What's communications look like?"

"Robust," Cotyar said. "We've set up a private network and have been given the backup tightbeam and radio array for your personal use. Bandwidth is significant, though light delay will be an increasing factor as we move away from Earth."

"Good," Avasarala said, smiling for the first time since they'd come on the ship. She'd stopped looking tired a while ago and had moved on to whatever tired turns into when it became a lifestyle.

"None of this is secure," Cotyar said. "We can secure our private internal network, but if they are monitoring outbound and inbound traffic through the array we're using, there will be no way to detect that. We have no access to ship operations."

"And," Avasarala said, "that is exactly why I'm here. Bottle me up, send me on a long trip, and read all my fucking mail."

"We're lucky if that's all they do," Bobbie said. Thinking about how tired Avasarala looked had reminded her how tired she was too. She felt herself drift away for a moment.

Avasarala finished saying something, and Cotyar nodded and said yes to her. She turned to Bobbie and said, "Do you agree?"

"Uh," Bobbie said, trying to rewind the conversation in her head and failing. "I'm—"

"You're practically falling out of your fucking chair. When's the last time you got a full night's sleep?"

"Probably about the last time you did," Bobbie said. *The last time all my squaddies were alive, and you weren't trying to keep the solar system from catching on fire.* She waited for the next scathing comment, the next observation that she couldn't do her job if she was that compromised. That weak.

"Fair enough," Avasarala said. Bobbie felt another little surge of affection for her. "Mao's throwing a big dinner tonight to welcome us aboard. I want you and Cotyar to come with. Cotyar will be security, so he'll stand at the back of the room and look menacing."

Bobbie laughed before she could stop herself. Cotyar smiled and winked at her.

"And," Avasarala continued, "you'll be there as my social secretary, so you can chat people up. Try to get a feel for the crew and the mood of the ship. Okay?"

"Roger that."

"I noticed," Avasarala said, her tone shifting to the one she used when she was going to ask for an unpleasant favor, "the executive officer staring at you when we did the airlock meet and greet."

Bobbie nodded. She'd noticed it too. Some men had a large-woman fetish, and Bobbie had gotten the hair-raising sense that he might be a member of that tribe. They tended to have unresolved mommy issues, so she generally steered clear.

"Any chance you could talk him up at dinner?" Avasarala finished.

Bobbie laughed, expecting everyone else to laugh too. Even Cotyar was looking at her as though Avasarala had made a perfectly reasonable request.

"Uh, no," Bobbie said.

"Did you say no?"

"Yeah, no. Hell no. Fuck no. *Nein und abermals nein. Nyet. La. Siei,*" Bobbie said, stopping when she ran out of languages. "And I'm actually a little pissed now."

"I'm not asking you to sleep with him."

"Good, because I don't use sex as a weapon," Bobbie said. "I use weapons as weapons."

"Chrisjen!" Jules Mao said, enveloping Avasarala's hand in his and shaking it.

The lord of the Mao-Kwik empire towered over Avasarala. He had the kind of handsome face that made Bobbie instinctively want to like him, and medically untreated male-pattern hair loss that said he didn't care whether she did. Choosing not to use his wealth to fix a problem as treatable as thinning hair actually made him seem even more in control. He wore a loose sweater and cotton pants that hung on him like a tailored suit. When Avasarala introduced Bobbie to him, he smiled and nodded while barely glancing in her direction.

"Is your staff settled in?" he asked, letting Avasarala know that Bobbie's presence reminded him of underlings. Bobbie gritted her teeth but kept her face blank.

"Yes," Avasarala replied with what Bobbie would have sworn was genuine warmth. "The accommodations are lovely, and your crew has been wonderful."

"Excellent," Jules said, placing Avasarala's hand on his arm and leading her to an enormous table. They were surrounded on all sides by men in white jackets with black bow ties. One of them darted forward and pulled a chair out. Jules placed Avasarala in it. "Chef Marco has promised something special tonight."

"How about straight answers? Are those on the menu?" Bobbie asked as a waiter pulled out a chair for her.

Jules settled into his chair at the head of the table. "Answers?"

"You guys won," Bobbie said, ignoring the steaming soup one of the servers placed in front of her. Mao tapped salt onto his and began eating it as though they were just having casual dinner conversation. "The assistant undersecretary is on the ship. No reason to bullshit us now. What's going on?"

"Humanitarian aid," he replied.

"*Bullshit*," Bobbie said. She glanced at Avasarala, but the old woman was just smiling. "You can't tell me that you have time to spend a couple months doing the transit to Jupiter just to oversee handing out rice and juice boxes. And you couldn't get enough relief supplies onto this ship to feed Ganymede lunch, much less make a long-term difference."

Mao settled back in his chair, and the white jackets bustled around the room, clearing the soup away. Bobbie's was whisked away as well, even though she hadn't eaten any of it.

"Roberta," Mao began.

"Don't call me Roberta."

"*Sergeant*, you should be questioning your superiors at the UN foreign office, not me."

"I'd love to, but apparently asking questions is against the rules in this *game*."

His smile was warm, condescending, and empty. "I made my ship available to provide Madam Undersecretary the most comfortable ride to her new assignment. And while you have not yet met them, there are personnel currently on this vessel whose expertise will be invaluable to the citizens of Ganymede once you arrive."

Bobbie had been around Avasarala long enough to see the game being played right in front of her. Mao was laughing at her. He knew this was all bullshit, and he knew she knew it as well. But as long as he remained calm and gave reasonable answers, no one could call him on it. He was too powerful to be called a liar to his face.

"You're a liar, and—" she started; then something he'd said made her stop. "Wait, 'once *you* arrive'? You aren't coming?"

"I'm afraid not," Mao said, smiling up at the white jacket who placed another plate in front of him. This one had what appeared to be a whole fish, complete with head and staring eyes.

Bobbie gaped at Avasarala, who was frowning at Mao now.

"I was told you were personally leading this relief effort," Avasarala said.

"That was my intention. But I'm afraid other business has removed that option. Once we finish with this excellent dinner, I'll be taking the shuttle back to the station. This ship, and its crew, are at your disposal until your vital work on Ganymede is complete."

Avasarala just stared at Mao. For the first time in Bobbie's experience, the old lady was struck speechless.

A white jacket brought Bobbie a fish while her lush prison flew at a leisurely quarter g toward Jupiter.

Avasarala hadn't said a word on the ride down the lift to their suite. In the lounge, she stopped long enough to grab a bottle of gin off the bar, and waggled a finger at Bobbie. Bobbie followed her into the master bedroom, Cotyar close behind.

Once the door was closed and Cotyar had used his handheld security terminal to scan the room for bugs, Avasarala said, "Bobbie, start thinking of a way to either get control of this ship or get us off of it."

"Forget that," Bobbie said. "Let's go grab that shuttle Mao's leaving on right now. It's within range of his station or he wouldn't be taking it."

To her surprise, Cotyar nodded. "I agree with the sergeant. If we plan to leave, the shuttle will be easier to commandeer and control against a hostile crew."

Avasarala sat down on her bed with a long exhale that turned into a heavy sigh. "I can't leave yet. It doesn't work that way."

"The fucking game!" Bobbie yelled.

"Yes," Avasarala snapped. "*Yes*, the fucking game. I've been ordered by my superiors to make this trip. If I leave now, I'm out. They'll be polite and call it a sudden illness or exhaustion, but the excuse they give me will also be the reason I'm not allowed to keep doing my job. I'll be safe, and I'll be powerless. As long as I pretend I'm doing what they asked me to, I can keep working. I'm still the assistant undersecretary of executive administration. I still have connections. Influence. If I run now, I lose them. If I lose them, these fuckers might as well shoot me."

"But," Bobbie said.

"But," Avasarala repeated. "If I continue to be effective, they'll find a way to cut me off. Unexplained comm failure, something. Something to keep me off the network. When that happens, I will demand that the captain reroute to the closest station for repairs. If I'm right, he won't do it."

"Ah," Bobbie said.

"Oh," Cotyar said a moment later.

"Yes," Avasarala said. "When that happens, I will declare this an illegal seizure of my person, and you will get me this ship."

Chapter Thirty-One: Prax

With every day that passed, the question came closer: What was the next step? It didn't feel all that different from those first, terrible days on Ganymede, making lists as a way of telling himself what to do. Only now he wasn't only looking for Mei. He was looking for Strickland. Or the mysterious woman in the video. Or whoever had built the secret lab. In that sense, he was much better off than he had been before.

On the other hand, he had been searching Ganymede. Now the field had expanded to include everywhere.

The lag time to Earth—or Luna, actually, since Persis-Strokes Security Consultants was based in orbit rather than down the planet's gravity well—was a little over twenty minutes. It made actual conversation essentially impossible, so in practice, the hatchet-faced woman on his screen was making a series of promotional videos more and more specifically targeted to what Prax wanted to hear.

"We have an intelligence-sharing relationship with Pinkwater, which is presently the security company with the largest physical and operational presence in the outer planets," she said. "We also have joint-action contracts with Al Abbiq and Star Helix. With those, we can take immediate action either directly or through our partners, on literally any station or planet in the system."

Prax nodded to himself. That was exactly what he needed. Someone with eyes everywhere, with contacts everywhere. Someone who could help.

"I'm attaching a release," the woman said. "We will need payment for the processing fee, but we won't be charging your accounts for anything more than that until we've agreed on the scope of the investigation you're willing to be liable for. Once we have that in hand, I will send you a detailed proposal with an itemized spreadsheet and we can decide the scope of work that works best for you."

"Thank you," Prax said. He pulled up the document, signed off, and returned it. It would be twenty minutes at the speed of light before it reached Luna. Twenty minutes back. Who knew how long in between?

It was a start. He could feel good about that, at least.

The ship was quiet in a way that felt like anticipation, but Prax didn't know exactly what of. The arrival at Tycho Station, but beyond that, he wasn't sure. Leaving his bunk behind, he went through the empty galley and up the ladder toward the ops center and then the pilot's station. The small room was dim, most of the light coming from the control panels and the sweep of high-definition screens that filled 270 degrees of vision with starlight, the distant sun, and the approaching mass of Tycho Station, the oasis in the vast emptiness.

"Hey there, Doc," Alex said from the pilot's couch. "Come up to see the view?"

"If…I mean, if that's all right."

"Not a problem. I haven't been running with a copilot since we got the *Roci*. Strap in right there. Just if somethin' happens, don't touch anything."

"I won't," Prax promised as he scrambled into the acceleration couch. At first, the station seemed to grow slowly. The two counter-rotating rings were hardly larger than Prax's thumb, the sphere they surrounded little more than a gum ball. Then, as they drew nearer, the fuzzy texture at the edge of the construction sphere began to resolve into massive waldoes and gantries reaching toward a strangely aerodynamic form. The ship under construction was still half undressed, ceramic and steel support beams open to the vacuum like bones. Tiny fireflies flickered inside and out: welders and sealant packs firing off too far away to see apart from the light.

"Is that built for atmosphere?"

"Nope. Kinda looks that way, though. That's the *Chesapeake*. Or it will be, anyway. She's designed for sustained high g. I think they're talkin' about running the poor bastard at something like eight g for a couple of months."

"All the way where?" Prax asked, doing a little napkin-back math in his head. "It would have to be outside the orbit of… anything."

"Yep, she'll be going deep. They're going after that *Nauvoo*."

"The generation ship that was supposed to knock Eros into the sun?"

"That's the one. They cut her engines when the plan went south, but she's been cruisin' on ever since. Wasn't finished, so they can't bring her around on remote. Instead, they're buildin' a retriever. Hope they manage too. The *Nauvoo* was an amazin' piece of work. Of course, even if they get her back, it won't keep the Mormons from suing Tycho into nonexistence if they can figure out how."

"Why would that be hard?"

"OPA doesn't recognize the courts on Earth and Mars, and they run the ones in the Belt. So it's pretty much win in a court that doesn't matter or lose in one that does."

"Oh," Prax said.

On the screens, Tycho Station grew larger and more detailed. Prax couldn't tell what detail of it brought it into perspective, but between one heartbeat and the next, he understood the scope and size of the station before him and let out a little gasp. The construction sphere had to be half a kilometer across, like two complete farm domes stuck bottom to bottom. Slowly, the great industrial sphere grew until it filled the screens, starlight replaced by the glow from equipment guides and a glass-domed observation bubble. Steel-and-ceramic plates and scaffolds took the place of the blackness. There were the massive drives that could push the entire station, like a city in the sky, anywhere in the solar system. There were the complex swivel points, like the gimbals of a crash couch made by giants, that would reconfigure the station as a whole when thrust gravity took rotation's place.

It took his breath away. The elegance and functionality of the structure lay out before him, as beautiful and simple and effective as a leaf or a root cluster. To have something so much like the fruits of evolution, but designed by human minds, was awe-inspiring. It was the pinnacle of what creativity meant, the impossible made real.

"That's good work," Prax said.

"Yup," Alex said. And then on the shipwide channel: "We've arrived. Everyone strap in for docking. I'm going to manual."

Prax half rose in his couch.

"Should I go to my quarters?"

"Where you are's as good as anyplace. Just put the web on in case we bump against somethin'," Alex said. And then, his voice changing to a stronger, more clipped cadence: "Tycho control, this is the *Rocinante*. Are we cleared for docking?"

Prax heard a distant voice speaking to Alex alone.

"Roger that," Alex said. "We're comin' in."

In the dramas and action films that Prax had watched back on Ganymede, piloting a ship had always looked like a fairly athletic thing. Sweating men dragging hard against the control bars.

Watching Alex was nothing like it. He still had the two joysticks, but his motions were small, calm. A tap, and the gravity under Prax changed, his couch shifting under him by a few centimeters. Then another tap and another shift. The heads-up display showed a tunnel through the vacuum outlined in a blue and gold that swept up and to the right, ending against the side of the turning ring.

Prax looked at the mass of data being sent to Alex and said, "Why fly at all? Couldn't the ship just use this data to do the docking itself?"

"Why fly?" Alex repeated with a laugh. "'Cuz it's fun, Doc. Because it's fun."

The long bluish lights of the windows in Tycho's observation dome were so clear Prax could see the people looking out at him. He could almost forget that the screens in the cockpit weren't windows: The urge to look out and wave, to watch someone wave back, was profound.

Holden's voice came over Alex's line, the words unidentifiable and the tone perfectly clear.

"We're looking fine, Cap," Alex said. "Ten more minutes."

The crash couch shifted to the side, the wide plane of the station curving down as Alex matched the rotation. To generate even a third of a g on a ring that wide would demand punishing inertial forces, but under Alex's hand, ship and station drifted together slowly and gently. Before Prax had gotten married, he'd seen a dance performance based on neo-Taoist traditions. For the first hour, it had been utterly boring, and then after that, the small movements of arms and legs and torso, shifting together, bending, and falling away, had been entrancing. The *Rocinante* slid into place beside an extending airlock port with the same beauty Prax had seen in that dance, but made more powerful by the knowledge that instead of skin and muscles, this was tons of high-tensile steel and live fusion reactors.

The *Rocinante* eased into her berth with one last correction, one last shifting of the gimbaled couches. The final matching spin had been no more than any of the small corrections Alex had made on the way in. There was a disconcerting bang as the station's docking hooks latched on to the ship.

"Tycho control," Alex said. "This is the *Rocinante* confirming dock. We have seal on the airlock. We are reading the clamps in place. Can you confirm?"

A moment passed, and a mutter.

"Thank you too, Tycho," Alex said. "It's good to be back."

Gravity in the ship had shifted subtly. Instead of thrust from the drive creating the illusion of weight, it now came from the spin of the ring they were clamped to. Prax felt like he was tilting slightly to the side whenever he stood up straight, and had to fight the urge to overcompensate by leaning the other way.

Holden was in the galley when Prax reached it, the coffee machine pouring black and hot, with just the slightest bend to the stream. Coriolis effect, a dimly remembered high school class reminded Prax. Amos and Naomi came in together. They were all together now, and Prax felt the time was right to thank them all for what they'd done for him. For Mei, who was probably dead. The naked pain on Holden's face stopped him.

Naomi stood in front of him, a duffel bag over her shoulder.

"You're heading out," Holden said.

"I am." Her voice was light, but it had meaning radiating from it like harmonic overtones. Prax blinked.

"All right, then," Holden said.

For a few seconds, no one moved; then Naomi darted in, kissing Holden lightly on the cheek. The captain's arms moved out to embrace her, but she'd already stepped away, marching out through the narrow hallway with the air of a woman on her way someplace. Holden took his coffee. Amos and Alex exchanged glances.

"Ah, Cap'n?" Alex asked. Compared to the voice of the man who'd just put a nuclear warship against a spinning metal wheel in the middle of interplanetary space, this voice was hesitant and concerned. "Are we lookin' for a new XO?"

"We're not looking for anything until I say so," Holden said. Then, his voice quieter: "But, God, I hope not."

"Yessir," Alex said. "Me too."

The four men stood for a long, awkward moment. Amos was the first to speak.

"You know, Cap," he said, "the place I've got booked has room for two. If you want the spare bunk, it's yours."

"No," Holden said. He didn't look at them as he spoke, but reached out his hand and pressed his palm to the wall. "I'm staying on the *Roci*. I'll be right here."

"You sure?" Amos asked, and again it seemed to mean something more than Prax could understand.

"*I'm* not going anywhere," Holden said.

"All right, then."

Prax cleared his throat, and Amos took his elbow.

"What about you?" Amos said. "You got a place to bunk down?"

Prax's prepared speech—*I wanted to tell you all how much I appreciate...*—ran into the question, derailing both thoughts.

"I...ah...I don't, but—"

"Right, then. Get your stuff, and you can come with me."

"Well, yes. Thank you. But first I wanted to tell you all—"

Amos put a solid hand on his shoulder.

"Maybe later," the big man said. "Right now, how about you just come with me?"

Holden leaned against the wall now. His jaw was set hard, like that of a man about to scream or vomit or weep. His eyes were looking at the ship but seeing past it. Sorrow welled up in Prax as if he were looking into a mirror.

"Yeah," he said. "Okay."

Amos' rooms were, if anything, smaller than the bunks on the *Rocinante*: two small privacy areas, a common space less than half the size of the galley, and a bathroom with a fold-out sink and toilet in the shower stall. It would have induced claustrophobia if Amos had actually been there.

Instead, he'd seen Prax settled in, taken a quick shower, and headed out into the wide, luxurious passageways of the station. There were plants everywhere, but for the most part they seemed decorative. The curve of the decks was so slight Prax could almost imagine he was back on some unfamiliar part of Ganymede, that his hole was no more than a tube ride away. That Mei would be there, waiting for him. Prax let the outer door close, pulled out his hand terminal, and connected to the local network.

There was still no reply from Persis-Strokes, but it was probably too early to expect one. In the meantime, the problem was money. If he was going to fund this, he couldn't do it alone.

Which meant Nicola.

Prax set up his terminal, turning the camera on himself. The image on the screen looked thin, wasted. The weeks had dried him out, and his time on the *Rocinante* hadn't completely rebuilt him. He might never be rebuilt. The sunken cheeks on the screen might be who he was now. That was fine. He started recording.

"Hi, Nici," he said. "I wanted you to know I'm safe. I got to Tycho Station, but I still don't have Mei. I'm hiring a security consultant. I'm giving them everything I know. They seem like they'll really be able to help. But it's expensive. It may be very expensive. And she may already be dead."

Prax took a moment to catch his breath.

"She may already be dead," he said again. "But I have to try. I know you aren't in a great financial position right now. I know you've got your new husband to think of. But if you have anything you can spare—not for me. I don't want anything from you. Just Mei. For her. If you can give her anything, this is the last chance."

He paused again, his mind warring between *Thank you* and *It's the least you can fucking do*. In the end, he just shut off the recording and sent it.

The lag between Ceres and Tycho Station was fifteen minutes, given their relative positions. And even then, he didn't know what the local schedule there was. He might be sending his message in the middle of the night or during dinnertime. She might not have anything to say to him.

It didn't matter. He had to try. He could sleep if he knew he'd done everything he could to try.

He recorded and sent messages to his mother, to his old roommate from college who'd taken a position on Neptune Station, to his postdoctorate advisor. Each time, the story got a little easier to tell. The details started coming together, one leading into another. With them, he didn't talk about the protomolecule. At best, it would have scared them. At worst, they'd have thought the loss had broken his mind.

When the last message was gone, he sat quietly. There was one other thing he thought he had to do now that he had full communication access. It wasn't what he wanted.

He started the recording.

"Basia," he said. "This is Praxidike. I wanted you to know that I know Katoa is dead. I saw the body. It didn't…it didn't look like he suffered. And I thought, if I was in your place, that wondering…wondering would be worse. I'm sorry. I'm just…"

He turned off the recording, sent it, and crawled onto the small bed. He'd expected it to be hard and uncomfortable, but the mattress was as cradling as crash couch gel, and he fell asleep easily and woke four hours later like someone had flipped a switch on the back of his head. Amos was still gone, even though it was station midnight. There was still no message from Persis-Strokes, so Prax recorded a polite inquiry—just to be sure the information hadn't gotten lost in transit—then watched it and erased it. He took a long shower, washing his hair twice, shaved, and recorded a new inquiry, looking less like a raving lunatic.

Ten minutes after he sent it, a new-message alert chimed. Intellectually, he knew it couldn't be a response. With lag, his message wouldn't even be at Luna yet. When he pulled it up, it was Nicola. The heart-shaped face looked older than he remembered it. There was the first dusting of gray at her temples. But when she made that soft, sad smile, he was twenty again, sitting across from her in the grand park while bhangra throbbed and lasers traced living art on the domed ice above them. He remembered what it had been like to love her.

"I have your message," she said. "I'm...I'm so sorry, Praxidike. I wish there was more I could do. Things aren't so good here on Ceres. I will talk with Taban. He makes more than I do, and if he understands what's happened, he might want to help too. For my sake.

"Take care of yourself, old man. You look tired."

On the screen, Mei's mother leaned forward and stopped the recording. An icon showed an authorized transfer code for eighty FusionTek Reál. Prax checked the exchange rates, converting the company scrip to UN dollars. It was almost a week's salary. Not enough. Not near enough. But still, it had been a sacrifice for her.

He pulled the message back up, pausing it in the gap between two words. Nicola looked out at him from the terminal, her lips parted barely enough for him to see her pale teeth. Her eyes were sad and playful. He'd thought for so long that it was her soul and not just an accident of physiology that gave her that look of fettered joy. He'd been wrong.

As he sat, lost in history and imagination, a new message appeared. It was from Luna. Persis-Strokes. With a feeling somewhere between anxiety and hope, he went to the attached spreadsheet. At the first set of numbers, his heart sank.

Mei might be out there. She might be alive. Certainly Strickland and his people were there. They could be found. They could be caught. There was justice to be had.

He just couldn't afford it.

Chapter Thirty-Two: Holden

Holden sat in a pull-down chair in the *Rocinante*'s engineering bay reviewing the damage and making notes for Tycho's repair crew. Everyone else was gone. *Some more than others*, he thought.

REPLACE STARBOARD ENGINEERING BULKHEAD.

SIGNIFICANT DAMAGE TO PORT-SIDE POWER CABLE JUNCTION, POSSIBLY REPLACE ENTIRE JUNCTION BOX.

Two lines of text representing hundreds of work hours, hundreds of thousands of dollars in parts. It also represented the aftermath of coming within a hand's breadth of fiery annihilation for the ship and crew. Describing it in two quick sentences felt almost sacrilegious. He made a footnote of the types of civilian parts that Tycho was likely to have available that would work with his Martian warship.

Behind him, a wall monitor streamed a Ceres-based news show.

Holden had turned it on to keep his mind occupied while he tinkered with the ship and made notes.

Which was all bullshit, of course. Sam, the Tycho engineer who usually took the lead on their repair jobs, didn't need his help. She didn't need him making lists of parts for her. She was, in every sense, better qualified to be doing what he was doing right now. But as soon as he turned the job over to her, he wouldn't have any reason to stay on the ship. He would have to confront Fred about the protomolecule on Ganymede.

And maybe lose Naomi in the process.

If his early suspicion was correct and Fred actually had bartered using the protomolecule as currency or, worse, as a weapon, Holden would kill him. He knew that like he knew his own name, and he feared it. That it would be a capital offense and would almost certainly get him burned down on the spot was actually less important than the fact that it would be the final proof that Naomi was right to leave. That he'd turned into the man she feared he was becoming. Just another Detective Miller, dispensing frontier justice from the barrel of his gun. But whenever he pictured the scene, Fred's admission of guilt and heartfelt appeal for mercy, Holden couldn't picture not killing him for what he'd done. He remembered being the sort of man who would make a different choice, but he couldn't actually remember what being that man was *like*.

If he was wrong, and Fred had nothing to do with the tragedy on Ganymede, then she'd have been right all along, and he had just been too stubborn to see it. He might be able to apologize for that with sufficient humility to win her back. Stupidity was usually a lesser crime than vigilantism.

But if Fred *wasn't* the one playing God with the alien supervirus, that was much, much worse for humanity in general. It was an unpleasant thought that the truth that would be worst for humanity was the one that would be best for him. Intellectually, he knew he wouldn't hesitate to sacrifice himself or his happiness to save everyone else. But that didn't stop the tiny voice at the back of his head that said, *Fuck everyone else, I want my girl-friend back.*

Something half remembered pushed up from his subconscious and he wrote MORE COFFEE FILTERS on his list of needed supplies.

The wall panel behind him chimed an alert half a second before his hand terminal buzzed to let him know someone was at the airlock, requesting permission to board. He tapped the screen to switch to the airlock's outer door camera and saw Alex and Sam waiting in the corridor. Sam was still the adorable red-haired pixie in the oversized gray coveralls he remembered. She was carrying a large toolbox and laughing. Alex said something else and she laughed harder, almost dropping her tools. With the intercom off, it was a silent movie.

Holden tapped the intercom button and said, "Come on in, guys." Another tap cycled the outer airlock doors open. Sam waved at the camera and stepped inside.

A few minutes later, the pressure hatch to engineering banged open, and the ladder-lift whined its way down. Sam and Alex stepped off, Sam dropping her tools onto the metal deck with a loud crash.

"What's up?" she said, giving Holden a quick hug. "You getting my girl all shot up again?"

"*Your* girl?" Alex said.

"Not this time," Holden replied, pointing out the damaged bulkheads in the engineering bay to her. "Bomb went off in the cargo bay, burned a hole there and threw some shrapnel into the power junction there."

Sam whistled. "Either that shrapnel took the long way around, or your reactor knows how to duck."

"How long, you think?"

"Bulkhead's simple," she said, punching something into her terminal, then tapping her front teeth with its corner. "We can bring a patch in through the cargo bay in a single piece. Makes the job a lot easier. Power junction takes longer, but not a lot. Say four days if I get my crew on it right now."

"Well," Holden said, wincing like a man who had to keep admitting to new wrongdoings. "We also have a damaged cargo bay door that will either have to be fixed or replaced. And our cargo bay airlock is kind of messed up."

"Couple more days, then," Sam said, then knelt down and began pulling things out of her toolbox. "Mind if I start taking some measurements?"

Holden waved at the wall. "Be my guest."

"Been watching the news a lot?" Sam said, pointing at the talking heads on the wall monitor. "Ganymede is fucked, right?"

"Yeah," Alex said. "Pretty much."

"But it's only Ganymede so far," Holden said. "So that means something I haven't quite figured out yet."

"Naomi's staying with me right now," Sam said as if they'd been talking about that all along. Holden felt his face go still and tried to fight against it, forcing himself to smile.

"Oh. Cool."

"She won't talk about it, but if I find out you did something shitty to her, I'm using this on your dick," she said, holding up a torque wrench. Alex laughed nervously for a second, then trailed off and just looked uncomfortable.

"I consider myself fairly warned," Holden said. "How is she?"

"Quiet," Sam said. "Okay, got what I need. Gonna scoot now and get fabrication to work on cutting this bulkhead patch. See you boys around."

"Bye, Sam," Alex said, watching her ride the ladder-lift until the pressure door closed behind her. "I'm twenty years too old, and I'm pretty sure I've got the wrong plumbin', but I like that gal."

"You and Amos just trade this crush back and forth?" Holden said. "Or should I be worried about you two doing pistols at dawn over her?"

"My love is a pure love," Alex said with a grin. "I wouldn't sully it by actually, you know, doin' anything about it."

"The kind poets write about, then."

"So," Alex said, leaning against a wall and looking at his nails. "Let's talk about the XO situation."

"Let's not."

"Oh, let's do," Alex said, then took a step forward and crossed his arms like a man who was not going to give any ground. "I've been flyin' this boat solo for over a year now. That only works because Naomi is a brilliant ops officer and takes up a whole lotta slack. If we lose her, we don't fly. And that's a fact."

Holden dropped the hand terminal he'd been using into his pocket and slumped back against the reactor shielding.

"I know. I *know*. I never thought she'd actually do this."

"Leave," Alex said.

"Yeah."

"We've never talked about pay," Alex said. "We don't get salaries."

"Pay?" Holden frowned at Alex and banged out a quick drumbeat on the reactor behind him. It echoed like a metal tomb. "Every dime that Fred's given us that hasn't gone to pay for operating the ship is in the account I set up. If you need some of it, twenty-five percent of that money belongs to you."

Alex shook his head and waved his hands. "No, don't get me wrong. I don't need money, and I don't think you're stealin' from us. Just pointing out that we never talked about pay."

"So?"

"So that means we aren't a normal crew. We aren't workin' the ship for money, or because a government drafted us. We're here because we want to be. That's all you've got over us. We believe in the cause, and we want to be part of what you're doing. The minute we lose that, we might as well take a real payin' job."

"But Naomi—" Holden started.

"Was your *girlfriend*," Alex said with a laugh. "Damn, Jim, have you *seen* her? She can get another boyfriend. In fact, you mind if I—"

"I take your point. I hear you. I fucked it up, it's my fault. I know that. All of it. I need to go see Fred and start thinking about how to put it all back together again."

"Unless Fred actually *did* do it."

"Yeah. Unless that."

"I've been wondering when you'd finally drop by," Fred Johnson said as Holden walked through his office door. Fred was looking both better and worse than when Holden had first met him a year earlier. Better because the Outer Planets Alliance, the quasi government that Fred was the titular head of, was no longer a terrorist organization, but a de facto government that could sit at the diplomatic table with the inner planets. And Fred had taken to the role of administrator with a relish he must not have felt for being a freedom fighter. It was visible in the relaxed set of his shoulders, and the half smile that had become his default expression.

And worse because the last year and all the pressures of governance had aged him. His hair was both thinner and whiter, his neck a confusion of loose flesh and old, ropy muscle. His eyes had permanent bags under them now. His coffee-colored skin didn't show many wrinkles, but it had a tinge of gray to it.

But the smile he gave Holden was genuine, and he came around the desk to shake his hand and guide him to a chair.

"I read your report on Ganymede," Fred said. "Talk to me about it. Impressions on the ground."

"Fred," Holden said. "There's something else."

Fred nodded to him as he moved back around his desk and sat down. "Go on."

Holden started to speak, then stopped. Fred was staring at him. His expression hadn't changed, but his eyes were sharper, more focused. Holden felt a sudden and irrational fear that Fred already knew everything he was about to say.

The truth was Holden had always been afraid of Fred. There was a duality to the man that left him on edge. Fred had reached out to the crew of the *Rocinante* at the exact moment they'd needed help the most. He'd become their patron, their safe harbor against the myriad enemies they'd gathered over the last year. And yet Holden couldn't forget that this was still Colonel Frederick Lucius Johnson, the Butcher of Anderson Station. A man who had spent the last decade helping to organize and run the Outer Planets Alliance, an organization that was capable of murder and terrorism to further its goals. Fred had almost certainly ordered some of those murders personally. It was entirely possible that the OPA leader version of Fred had killed more people than even the United Nations Marine colonel version of Fred had.

Would he really balk at using the protomolecule to further his agenda?

Maybe. Maybe that would be going too far. And he'd been a friend, and he deserved the chance to defend himself.

"Fred, I—" Holden started, then stopped.

Fred nodded again, the smile slipping off his face and being replaced by a slight frown. "I'm not going to like this." It was a statement of fact.

Holden grabbed the arms of the office chair and pushed himself to his feet. He shoved more violently than he wanted to and, in the low .3 g of station spin, flew off his feet for a second. Fred chuckled and the frown shifted back into a grin.

And that was it. The grin and the laugh broke the fear and turned it into anger. When Holden settled back to his feet, he leaned forward and slammed both palms onto Fred's desk.

"You," he said, "don't get to laugh. Not until I know for sure it wasn't all your fault. If you can do what I think you might have done and still laugh, I will shoot you right here and now."

Fred's smile didn't change, but something in his eyes did. He wasn't used to being threatened, but it wasn't new territory either.

"What I might have done," Fred said, not turning it into a question, just repeating it back.

"It's the protomolecule, Fred. That's what's happening on Ganymede. A lab with kids as experiments and that black webbing shit and a monster that almost killed my ship. That's my fucking *impression on the ground*. Someone has been playing with the bug, and it might be loose, and the inner planets are shooting each other to shit in orbit around it."

"You think I did this," Fred said. Again, just a flat statement of fact.

"*We threw this shit into Venus*," Holden yelled. "*I gave* you *the only sample*. And suddenly Ganymede, breadbasket of your future empire, the one place the inner navies won't cede control of, gets a fucking outbreak?"

Fred let the silence answer for a beat.

"Are you asking me if I'm using the protomolecule to drive the inner planets troops off Ganymede, and strengthen my control of the outer planets?"

Fred's quiet tone made Holden realize how loud he'd gotten, and he took a moment to take several deep breaths. When his pulse had slowed a bit, he said, "Yes. Pretty much exactly that."

"You," Fred said with a broad smile that did not extend to his eyes, "do not get to ask me that."

"What?"

"In case you've forgotten, you are an employee of this organization." Fred stood up, stretching to his full height, a dozen centimeters taller than Holden. His smile didn't change, but his body shifted and sort of spread out. Suddenly he looked very large. Holden took a step back before he could stop himself.

"I," Fred continued, "owe you nothing but the terms of our latest contract. Have you completely lost your mind, boy? Charging in here? Shouting at me? *Demanding* answers?"

"No one else could have—" Holden started, but Fred ignored him.

"You gave me the only sample we knew of. But you assume that if you don't know about it, it doesn't exist. I've been putting up with your bullshit for over a year now," Fred said. "This idea you have that the universe owes you answers. This righteous indignation you wield like a club at everyone around you. But I don't *have* to put up with your shit.

"Do you know why that is?"

Holden shook his head, afraid if he spoke, it might come out as a squeak.

"It's because," Fred said, "I'm the *fucking boss*. I run this outfit. You've been pretty useful, and you might be again in the future. But I have enough shit to deal with right now without you starting another one of your crusades at my expense."

"So," Holden said, letting the word drag to two syllables.

"So you're fired. This was your last contract with me. I'll finish fixing the *Roci* and I'll pay you, because I don't break a deal. But I think we've finally built enough ships to start policing our own sky without your help, and even if we haven't, I'm just about done with you."

"Fired," Holden said.

"Now get the hell out of my office before I decide to take the *Roci* too. She's got more Tycho parts on her now than originals. I think I might be able to make a good argument I own that ship."

Holden backed up toward the door, wondering how serious that threat might actually be. Fred watched him go but didn't move. When he reached the door, Fred said, "It wasn't me."

Their gazes met for a long, breathless moment.

"It wasn't me," Fred repeated.

Holden said, "Okay," and backed out the door.

When the door slid shut and blocked Fred from view, Holden let out a long sigh and collapsed against the corridor wall. Fred was right about one thing: He'd been excusing himself with his fear for far too long. *This righteous indignation you wield like a club at everyone around you.* He'd seen humanity almost end due to its own stupidity. It had left him shaken to the core. He'd been running on fear and adrenaline ever since Eros.

But it wasn't an excuse. Not anymore.

He started to pull out his terminal to call Naomi when it hit him like a light turning on. *I'm fired.*

He'd been on an exclusive contract with Fred for over a year. Tycho Station was their home base. Sam had spent almost as much time tuning and patching the *Roci* as Amos had. That was all gone. They'd have to find their own jobs, find their own ports, buy their own repairs. No more patron to hold his hand. For the first time in a very long time, Holden was a real independent captain. He'd need to earn his way by keeping the ship in the air and the crew fed. He paused for a moment, letting that sink in.

It felt great.

Chapter Thirty-Three: Prax

Amos sat forward in his chair. The sheer physical mass of the man made the room seem smaller, and the smell of alcohol and old smoke came off him like heat from a fire. His expression couldn't have been more gentle.

"I don't know what to do," Prax said. "I just don't know what to do. This is all my fault. Nicola was just…she was so lost and so angry. Every day, I woke up and I looked over at her, and all I saw was how trapped she was. And I knew Mei was going to grow up with that. With trying to get her mommy to love her when all Nici wanted to do was be somewhere else. And I thought it would be better. When she started talking about going, I was ready for her to do it, you know? And when Mei…when I had to tell Mei that…"

Prax dropped his head into his hands, rocking slowly back and forth.

"You gonna sick up again, Doc?"

"No. I'm fine. If I'd been a better father to her, she'd still be here."

"We talking about the ex-wife or the kid?"

"I don't care about Nicola. If I'd been there for Mei. If I'd gone to her as soon as we got the warning. If I hadn't waited there in the dome. And for what? Plants? They're dead now anyway. I had one, but I lost it, too. I couldn't even save one. But I could have gotten there. Found her. If I'd—"

"You know she was gone before the shit hit the fan, right?"

Prax shook his head. He wasn't about to let reality forgive him.

"And this. I had a chance. I got out. I got some money. And I was stupid. It was her last chance, and I was stupid about it."

"Yeah, well. You're new at this, Doc."

"She should have had a better dad. She deserved a better dad. Was such a good…she was such a good girl."

For the first time, Amos touched him. The wide hand took his shoulder, gripping him from collarbone to scapula and bending Prax's spine until it was straight. Amos' eyes were more than bloodshot, white sclera marbled with red. His breath was hot and astringent, the platonic ideal of a sailor on a shore leave bender. But his voice was sober and steady.

"She's got a fine daddy, Doc. You give a shit, and that's more than a lot of people ever do."

Prax swallowed. He was tired. He was tired of being strong, of being hopeful and determined and preparing for the worst. He didn't want to be himself anymore. He didn't want to be anyone at all. Amos' hand felt like a ship clamp, keeping Prax from spinning away into darkness. All he wanted was to be let go.

"She's gone," Prax said. It felt like a good excuse. An explanation. "They took her away from me, and I don't know who they are, and I can't get her back, and I don't understand."

"It ain't over yet."

Prax nodded, not because he was actually comforted, but

because this was the moment when he knew he should act like he was.

"I'm never going to find her."

"You're wrong."

The door chimed and slid open. Holden stepped in. Prax couldn't see at first what was different about him, but that something had happened...had changed...was unmistakable. The face was the same; the clothes hadn't changed. Prax had the uncanny memory of sitting through a lecture on metamorphosis.

"Hey," Holden said. "Everything all right?"

"Little bumpy," Amos said. Prax saw his own confusion mirrored in Amos' face. They were both aware of the transformation, and neither of them knew what it was. "You get laid or something, Cap?"

"No," Holden said.

"I mean, good on you if you did," Amos said. "It just wasn't how I pictured—"

"I didn't get laid," Holden said hesitantly. The smile that came after was almost radiant. "I got fired."

"Just you got fired, or all of us?"

"All of us."

"Huh," Amos said. He went still for a moment, then shrugged. "All right."

"I need to talk to Naomi, but she's not accepting connections from me. Do you think you could track her down?"

Discomfort pursed Amos' lips like he'd sucked on an old lemon.

"I'm not going to pick a fight," Holden said. "We just didn't leave it in the right place. And it's my fault, so I need to fix it."

"I know she was hanging out down in that one bar Sam told us about last time. The Blauwe Blome. But you make a dick of yourself and I'm not the one that told you."

"Not a problem," Holden said. "Thanks."

The captain turned to leave and then stopped in the doorway. He looked like someone still half in a dream.

"What's bumpy?" he asked. "You said it was bumpy."

"The doc was looking to hire on some Luna private security squad to track the kid down. Didn't work out and he kind of took it bad."

Holden frowned. Prax felt the heat of a blush pushing up his neck.

"I thought *we* were finding the kid," Holden said. He sounded genuinely confused.

"Doc wasn't clear on that."

"Oh," Holden said. He turned to Prax. "We're finding your kid. You don't need to get someone else."

"I can't pay you," Prax said. "All my accounts were on the Ganymede system, and even if they're still there, I can't access them. I just have what people are giving me. I can probably get something like a thousand dollars UN. Is that enough?"

"No," Holden said. "That won't buy a week's air, much less water. We'll have to take care of that."

Holden tilted his head like he was listening to something only he could hear.

"I've already talked to my ex-wife," Prax said. "And my parents. I can't think of anyone else."

"How about everyone?" Holden said.

"I'm James Holden," the captain said from the huge screen of the *Rocinante*'s pilot capsule, "and I'm here to ask for your help. Four months ago, hours before the first attack on Ganymede, a little girl with a life-threatening genetic illness was abducted from her day care. In the chaos that—"

Alex stopped the playback. Prax tried to sit up, but the gimbaled copilot's chair only shifted under him, and he lay back.

"I don't know," Alex said from the pilot's couch. "The green background kinda makes him look pasty, don't you think?"

Prax narrowed his eyes a degree, considered, then nodded.

"It's not really his color," Prax said. "Maybe if it was darker."

"I'll try that," the pilot said, tapping at his screen. "Normally it's Naomi who does this stuff. Communications packages ain't exactly my first love. But we'll get it done. How about this?"

"Better," Prax said.

"I'm James Holden, and I'm here to ask for your help. Four months ago..."

Holden's part of the little presentation was less than a minute, speaking into the camera from Amos' hand terminal. After that, Amos and Prax had spent an hour trying to create the rest. Alex had been the one to suggest using the better equipment on the *Rocinante*. Once they'd done that, putting together the information had been easy. He'd taken the start he'd made for Nicola and his parents as the template. Alex helped him record the rest—an explanation of Mei's condition; the security footage of Strickland and the mysterious woman taking her from the day care; the data from the secret lab, complete with images of the protomolecule filament; pictures of Mei playing in the parks; and a short video from her second birthday party, when she smeared cake frosting on her forehead.

Prax felt odd watching himself speak. He had seen plenty of recordings of himself, but the man on the screen was thinner than he'd expected. Older. His voice was higher than the one he heard in his own ears, and less hesitant. The Praxidike Meng who was about to be broadcast out to the whole of humanity was a different man than he was, but it was close enough. And if it helped to find Mei, it would do. If it brought her back, he'd be anyone.

Alex slid his fingers across his controls, rearranging the presentation, connecting the images of Mei to the timeline to Holden. They had set up an account with a Belt-based credit union that had a suite of options for short-term unincorporated nonprofit concerns so that any contributions could be accepted automatically. Prax watched, wanting badly to offer comment or take control. But there was nothing more to do.

"All right," Alex said. "That's about as pretty as I can make it."

"Okay, then," Prax said. "What do we do with it now?"

Alex looked over. He seemed tired, but there was also an excitement.

"Hit send."

"But the review process…"

"There is no review process, Doc. This isn't a government thing. Hell, it's not even a business. It's just us monkeys flying fast and tryin' to keep our butts out of the engine plume."

"Oh," Prax said. "Really?"

"You hang around the captain long enough, you get used to it. You might want to take a day, though. Think it through."

Prax lifted himself on one elbow.

"Think what through?"

"Sending this out. If it works the way we're thinking, you're about to get a lot of attention. Maybe it'll be what we're hoping for; maybe it'll be something else. All I'm saying is you can't unscramble that egg."

Prax considered for a few seconds. The screens glowed.

"It's Mei," Prax said.

"All right, then," Alex said, and shifted communication control to the copilot's station. "You want to do the honors?"

"Where is it going? I mean, where are we sending it?"

"Simple broadcast," Alex said. "Probably get picked up by some local feeds in the Belt. But it's the captain, so folks will watch it, pass it around on the net. And…"

"And?"

"We didn't put our hitchhiker in, but the filament out of that glass case? We're kind of announcing that the protomolecule's still out there. That's gonna boost the signal."

"And we think that's going to help?"

"First time we did something like this, it started a war," Alex said. " 'Help' might be a strong word for it. Stir things up, though."

Prax shrugged and hit send.

"Torpedoes away," Alex said, chuckling.

Prax slept on the station, serenaded by the hum of the air recyclers. Amos was gone again, leaving only a note that Prax shouldn't wait up. It was probably his imagination that made the spin gravity seem to feel different. With a diameter as wide as Tycho's, the Coriolis effect shouldn't have been uncomfortably noticeable, and certainly not when he lay there, motionless, in the darkness of his room. And still, he couldn't get comfortable. He couldn't forget that he was being turned, inertia pressing him against the thin mattress as his body tried to fly out into the void. Most of the time he'd been on the *Rocinante*, he'd been able to trick his mind into thinking that he had the reassuring mass of a moon under him. It wasn't, he decided, an artifact of how the acceleration was generated so much as what it meant.

As his mind slowly spiraled down, bits of his self breaking apart like a meteor hitting atmosphere, he felt a massive welling-up of gratitude. Part of it was to Holden and part to Amos. The whole crew of the *Rocinante*. Half-dreaming, he was on Ganymede again. He was starving, walking down ice corridors with the certainty that somewhere nearby, one of his soybeans had been infected with the protomolecule and was tracking him, bent on revenge. With the broken logic of dreams, he was also on Tycho, looking for work, but all the people he gave his CV to shook their heads and told him he was missing some sort of degree or credential he didn't recognize or understand. The only thing that made it bearable was a deeper knowledge—certain as bone—that none of it was true. That he was sleeping, and that when he woke, he would be somewhere safe.

What did wake him at last was the rich smell of beef. His eyes were crusted like he'd been crying in his sleep, the tears leaving salt residues where they'd evaporated. The shower was hissing and splashing. Prax pulled on his jumpsuit, wondering again why it had TACHI printed across the back.

Breakfast waited on the table: steak and eggs, flour tortillas, and black coffee. Real food that had cost someone a small fortune. There were two plates, so Prax chose one and started eating. It had probably cost a tenth of the money he had from Nicola, but it tasted wonderful. Amos ducked out of the shower, a towel wrapped around his hips. A massive white scar puckered the right side of his abdomen, pulling his navel off center, and a nearly photographic tattoo of a young woman with wavy hair and almond-shaped eyes covered his heart. Prax thought there was a word under the tattooed face, but he didn't want to stare.

"Hey, Doc," Amos said. "You're looking better."

"I got some rest," Prax said as Amos walked into his own room and closed the door behind him. When Prax spoke again, he raised his voice. "I want to thank you. I was feeling low last night. And whether you and the others can actually help find Mei or not—"

"Why wouldn't we be able to find her?" Amos asked, his voice muffled by the door. "You ain't losing respect for me, are you, Doc?"

"No," Prax said. "No, not at all. I only meant that what you and the captain are offering is...it's a huge..."

Amos came back out grinning. His jumpsuit covered scars and tattoos as if they'd never been.

"I knew what you meant. I was just joshing you. You like that steak? Keep wondering where they put the cows on this thing, don't you?"

"Oh no, this is vat-grown. You can tell from the way the muscle fibers grow. You see how these parts right here are layered? Actually makes it easier to get a good marbled cut than when you carve it out of a steer."

"No shit?" Amos said, sitting across from him. "I didn't know that."

"Microgravity also makes fish more nutritious," Prax said around a mouthful of egg. "Increases the oil production. No one knows why, but there are a couple very interesting studies about it. They think it may not be the low g itself so much as the constant flow you have to have so that the animals don't stop swimming, make a bubble of oxygen-depleted water, and suffocate."

Amos ripped a bit of tortilla and dipped it into the yolk.

"This is what dinner conversation's like in your family, ain't it?"

Prax blinked.

"Mostly, yes. Why? What do you talk about?"

Amos chuckled. He seemed to be in a very good mood. There was a relaxed look about his shoulders, and something in the set of his jaw had changed. Prax remembered the previous night's conversation with the captain.

"You got laid, didn't you?"

"Oh hell yes," Amos said. "But that's not the best part."

"It's not?"

"Oh, it's a fucking good part, but there's nothing better in the world than getting a job the day after your ass gets canned."

A pang of confusion touched Prax. Amos pulled his hand terminal out of his pocket, tapped it twice, and slid it across the table. The screen showed a red security border and the name of the credit union Alex had been working with the night before. When he saw the balance, his eyes went wide.

"Is...is that...?"

"That's enough to keep the *Roci* flying for a month, and we got it in seven hours," Amos said. "You just hired yourself a team, Doc."

"I don't know...really?"

"Not just that. Take a look at the messages you've got coming in. Captain made a pretty big splash back in the day, but your kiddo? All that shit that came down on Ganymede just got itself a face, and it's her."

Prax pulled up his own terminal. The mailbox associated with the presentation had over five hundred video messages and thousands of texts. He began going through them. Men and women he didn't know—some of them in tears—offered up their prayers and anger and support. A Belter with a wild mane of gray-black hair gibbered in patois so thick Prax could barely make it out. As near as he could tell, the man was offering to kill someone for him.

Half an hour later, Prax's eggs had congealed. A woman from Ceres told him that she'd lost her daughter in a divorce, and that she was sending him her month's chewing tobacco money. A group of food engineers on Luna had passed the hat and sent along what would have been a month's salary if Prax had still been a botanist. An old Martian man with skin the color of chocolate and powdered-sugar hair gazed seriously into a camera halfway across the solar system and said he was with Prax.

When the next message began, it looked just like the others before it. The man in the image was older—eighty, maybe ninety—with a fringe of white hair clinging to the back of his skull and a craggy face. There was something about his expression that caught Prax's attention. A hesitance.

"Dr. Meng," the man said. He had a slushy accent that reminded Prax of recordings of his own grandfather. "I'm very sorry to hear of all you and your family have suffered. Are suffering." The man licked his lips. "The security video on your presentation. I believe I know the man in it. But his name isn't Strickland..."

Chapter Thirty-Four: Holden

According to the station directory, the Blauwe Blome was famous for two things: a drink called the Blue Meanie and its large number of Golgo tables. The guidebook warned potential patrons that the station allowed the bar to serve only two Blue Meanies to each customer due to the drink's fairly suicidal mixture of ethanol, caffeine, and methylphenidate. And, Holden guessed, some kind of blue food coloring.

As he walked through the corridors of Tycho's leisure section, the guidebook began explaining the rules of Golgo to him. After a few moments of utter confusion—*goals are said to be "borrowed" when the defense deflects the drive*—he shut it off. There was very little chance he was going to be playing games. And a drink that removed your inhibitions and left you wired and full of energy would be redundant right now.

The truth was Holden had never felt better in his life.

He'd messed a lot of things up over the last year. He'd driven his crew away from him. He'd aligned himself with a side he wasn't sure he agreed with in exchange for safety. He might have ruined the one healthy relationship he'd had in his life. He'd been driven by his fear to become someone else. Someone who handled fear by turning it into violence. Someone who Naomi didn't love, who his crew didn't respect, who he himself didn't like much.

The fear wasn't gone. It was still there, making his scalp crawl every time he thought about Ganymede, and about what might be loose and growing there right now. But for the first time in a long time, he was aware of it and wasn't hiding from it. He had given himself permission to be afraid. It made all the difference.

Holden heard the Blauwe Blome several seconds before he saw it. It began as a barely audible rhythmic thumping, which gradually increased in volume and picked up an electronic wail and a woman's voice singing in mixed Hindi and Russian. By the time he reached the club's front door, the song had changed to two men in an alternating chant that sounded like an argument set to music. The electronic wail was replaced by angry guitars. The bass line changed not at all.

Inside, the club was an all-out assault on the senses. A massive dance floor dominated the center space, and the dozens of bodies writhing on it were bathed in a constantly changing light show that shifted and flashed in time to the music. The music had been loud out in the corridor, but inside, it became deafening. A long chrome bar was set against one wall, and half a dozen bartenders were frantically filling drink orders.

A sign on the back wall read GOLGO and had an arrow pointing down a long hallway. Holden followed it, the music fading with each step so that by the time he reached the back room with the game tables, it was back to being muted bass lines.

Naomi was at one of the tables with her friend Sam the engineer and a cluster of other Belters. Her hair was pulled back with a red elastic band wide enough to be decorative. She'd switched out her jumpsuit for a pair of gray tailored slacks he hadn't known she owned and a yellow blouse that made her caramel-colored skin seem darker. Holden had to stop for a moment. She smiled at someone who wasn't him, and his chest went tight.

As he approached, Sam threw a small metal ball at the table. The group at the other end reacted with sudden violent movements. He couldn't see exactly what was happening from where he stood, but the slumped shoulders and halfhearted curses coming from the second group led Holden to believe that Sam had done something good for her team.

Sam spun around and threw up her hand. The group at her end of the table, which included Naomi, took turns slapping her palm. Sam saw him first and said something he couldn't hear. Naomi turned around and gave him a speculative look that stopped him in his tracks. She didn't smile and she didn't frown. He raised his palms in what he hoped was an *I didn't come to fight* gesture. For a moment, they stood facing each other across the noisy room.

Jesus, he thought, *how did I let it come to this?*

Naomi nodded at him and pointed at a table in one corner of the room. He sat down and ordered himself a drink. Not one of the blue liver-killers the bar was famous for, just a cheap Belt-produced scotch. He'd grown to, if not appreciate, at least tolerate the faint mold aftertaste it always had. Naomi said goodbye to the rest of her team for a few minutes and then walked over. It wasn't a casual stroll, but it wasn't the gait of someone going to a dreaded meeting either.

"Can I order you something?" Holden asked as she sat.

"Sure, I'll take a grapefruit martini," she said. While Holden entered the order on the table, she looked him over with a mysterious half smile that turned his belly to liquid.

"Okay," he said, authorizing his terminal to open a bar tab and pay for the drinks. "One hideous martini on its way."

Naomi laughed. "Hideous?"

"A near-fatal case of scurvy being the only reason I can imagine drinking something with grapefruit juice in it."

She laughed again, untying at least one of the knots in Holden's gut, and they sat together in companionable silence until the drinks arrived. She took a small sip and smacked her lips in appreciation, then said, "Okay. Spill."

Holden took a much longer drink, nearly finishing off the small glass of scotch in a single gulp, trying to convince himself that the spreading warmth in his belly could stand in for courage. *I didn't feel comfortable with where we left things, and I thought that we should talk. Kind of process this together.* He cleared his throat.

"I fucked everything up," he said. "I've treated my friends badly. Worse than badly. You were absolutely right to do what you did. I couldn't hear what you were saying at the time, but you were right to say it."

Naomi took another drink of her martini, then casually reached up and pulled out the elastic band holding her masses of black curls behind her head. Her hair fell down around her face in a tangle, making Holden think of ivy-covered stone walls. He realized that for as long as he'd known her, Naomi had always let her hair down in emotional situations. She hid behind it, not literally, but because it was her best feature. The eye was just naturally drawn to its glossy black curls. A distraction technique. It made her suddenly seem very human, as vulnerable and lost as he was. Holden felt a rush of affection for her that must have showed on his face, because she looked at him and then blushed.

"What is this, Jim?"

"An apology?" he said. "An admission that you were right, and that I was turning into my own screwed-up version of Miller? Those at the very least. Hopefully opening the dialogue to reconciliation, if I'm lucky."

"I'm glad," Naomi said. "I'm glad you're figuring that out. But I've been saying this for months now, and you—"

"Wait," Holden said. He could feel her pulling back from him, not letting herself believe. All he had left to offer her was absolute truth, so he did. "I couldn't hear you. Because I've been terrified, and I've been a coward."

"Fear doesn't make you a coward."

"No," he said. "Of course it doesn't. But refusing to face up to it. To not admit to you how I felt. To not let you and Alex and Amos help me. That was cowardice. And it may have cost me you, the crew's loyalty, everything I really care about. It made me keep a bad job a lot longer than I should have because the job was safe."

A small knot of the Golgo players began drifting toward their table, and Holden was gratified when he saw Naomi wave them off. It meant she wanted to keep talking. That was a start.

"Tell me," she said. "Where are you going from here?"

"I have no idea," Holden replied with a grin. "And that's the best feeling I've had in ages. But no matter what happens next, I need you there."

When she started to protest, Holden quickly put up a hand to stop her and said, "No, I don't mean like that. I'd love to win you back, but I'm perfectly okay with the idea that it might take some time, or never happen at all. I mean the *Roci* needs you back. The crew needs you there."

"I don't want to leave her," Naomi said with a shy smile.

"She's your home," Holden said. "Always will be as long as you want it. And that's true no matter what happens between us."

Naomi began wrapping one thick strand of hair around her finger and drank off the last of her drink. Holden pointed at the table menu, but she shook her hand at him.

"This is because you confronted Fred, right?"

"Yeah, partly," Holden said. "I was standing in his office feeling terrified and realizing I'd been afraid for a long, long time. I've screwed things up with him too. Some of that's probably his fault. He's a true believer, and those are bad people to climb into bed with. But it's mostly still mine."

"Did you quit?"

"He fired me, but I was probably going to quit."

"So," Naomi said. "You've lost us our paying gig and our patron. I guess I feel a little flattered that the part you're trying to patch up is me."

"You," Holden said, "are the only part I really care about fixing."

"You know what happens now, right?"

"You move back onto the ship?"

Naomi just smiled the comment away. "Now we pay for our own repairs. If we fire a torpedo, we have to find someone to sell us a new one. We pay for water, air, docking fees, food, and medical supplies for our very expensive automated sick bay. Have a plan for that?"

"Nope!" Holden said. "But I have to say, for some reason, it feels great."

"And when the euphoria passes?"

"I'll make a plan."

Her smile grew reflective and she tugged on her lock of hair.

"I'm not ready to move back to the ship right now," Naomi said, reaching across the table to take his hand in hers. "But by the time the *Roci* is patched up, I'll need my cabin back."

"I'll move the rest of my stuff out immediately."

"Jim," she said, squeezing his fingers once before letting go. "I love you, and we're not okay yet. But this is a good start."

And yes, Holden thought, it really was.

Holden woke up in his old cabin on the *Rocinante* feeling better than he had in months. He climbed out of his bunk and wandered naked through the empty ship to the head. He took an hour-long shower in water he actually had to pay for now, heated by electricity the dock would be charging him for by the kilowatt-hour. He walked back to his bunk, drying skin made pink by the almost scalding water as he went.

He made and ate a large breakfast and drank five cups of coffee while catching up on the technical reports on the *Roci*'s repairs until he was sure he understood everything about what had been done. Holden had switched to reading a column about the state of Mars-Earth relations by a political humorist when his terminal buzzed at him, and a call came through from Amos.

"Hey, Cap," he said, his big face filling the small screen. "You coming over to the station today? Or should we come meet you on the *Roci*?"

"Let's meet here," Holden replied. "Sam and her team will be working today and I want to keep an eye on things."

"See you in a few, then," Amos said, and killed the connection.

Holden tried to finish the humor column but kept getting distracted and having to read the same passage over again. He finally gave up and cleaned the galley for a while, then set the coffeemaker to brew a fresh pot for Amos and the work crew when they arrived.

The machine was gurgling happily to itself like a content infant when the deck hatch clanged open and Amos and Prax climbed down the crew ladder and into the galley.

"Cap," Amos said, dropping into a chair with a thump. Prax followed him into the room but didn't sit. Holden grabbed mugs and pulled two more cups of coffee, then set them on the table.

"What's the news?" he said.

Amos answered with a shit-eating grin and spun his terminal across the table to Holden. When Holden looked at it, it was displaying the account information for Prax's "save Mei" fund. It had just over half a million UN dollars in it.

Holden whistled and slumped into a chair. "Jesus grinned, Amos. I'd hoped we might...but never this."

"Yeah, it was a little under 300k this morning. It's gone up another 200k just over the last three hours. Seems like everyone following the Ganymede shit on the news has made little Mei the poster child for the tragedy."

"Is this enough?" Prax cut in, anxiety in his voice.

"Oh, hell yes," Holden said with a laugh. "Way more than enough. This will fund our rescue mission just fine."

"Also, we got a clue," Amos said, pausing dramatically to sip his coffee.

"About Mei?"

"Yep," Amos said, adding a little more sugar to his cup. "Prax, send him that message you got."

Holden watched the message three times, grinning wider with each viewing. "The security video on your presentation. I believe I know the man in it," the elderly gentleman on the screen was saying. "But his name isn't Strickland. When I worked with him at Ceres Mining and Tech University, his name was Merrian. Carlos Merrian."

"That," Holden said after his final viewing, "is what my old buddy Detective Miller might have called a *lead*."

"What now, chief?" Amos asked.

"I think I need to make a phone call."

"Okay. The doc and I will get out of your hair and watch his money roll in."

They left together, Holden waiting until the deck hatch slammed behind them to send a connection request to the switchboard at Ceres M&T. The lag was running about fifteen minutes with Tycho's current location, so he settled back and played a simple puzzle game on his terminal that left his mind free to think and plan. If they knew who Strickland had been before he was Strickland, they might be able to trace his career history. And somewhere along the way, he'd stopped being a guy named Carlos who worked at a tech school, and became a guy named Strickland who stole little kids. Knowing *why* would be a good start to learning where he might be now.

Almost forty minutes after sending out the request, he received a reply. He was a little surprised to see the elderly man from the video message. He hadn't expected to connect on his first try.

"Hello," the man said. "I'm Dr. Moynahan. I've been expecting your message. I assume you want to know the details about Dr. Merrian. To make a long story short, he and I worked together at the CMTU biosciences lab. He was working on biological development constraint systems. He was never good at playing the university game. Didn't make many allies while he was here. So when he crossed some ethical gray areas, they were only too happy to run him out of town. I don't know the details on that. I wasn't his department head. Let me know if you need anything else."

Holden watched the message twice, taking notes and cursing the fifteen-minute lag. When he was ready, he sent a reply back.

"Thank you so much for the help, Dr. Moynahan. We really appreciate it. I don't suppose you know what happened after he was kicked out of the university, do you? Did he go to another institution? Take a corporate job? Anything?"

He hit send and sat back to wait again. He tried the puzzle game but got annoyed and turned it off. Instead, he pulled up the Tycho public entertainment feed and watched a children's cartoon that was frantic and loud enough to distract him.

When his terminal buzzed with the incoming message, he almost knocked it off the table in his haste to start the video.

"Actually," Dr. Moynahan said, scratching at the gray stubble on his chin while he spoke, "he never even made it in front of the ethics review. Quit the day before. Made a lot of fuss, walking through the lab and yelling that we weren't going to be able to push him around anymore. That he had a bigwig corporate job with all the funding and resources he wanted. Called us small-minded pencil pushers stagnating in a quagmire of petty ethical constraints. Can't remember the name of the company he was going to work for, though."

Holden hit pause and felt a chill go down his spine. *Stagnating in a quagmire of petty ethical constraints.* He didn't need Moynahan to tell him which company would snatch a man like that up. He'd heard almost those exact words spoken by Antony Dresden, the architect of the Eros project that had killed a million and a half people as part of a grand biology experiment.

Carlos Merrian had gone to work for Protogen and disappeared. He'd come back as Strickland, abductor of small children.

And, Holden thought, the murderer too.

Chapter Thirty-Five: Avasarala

On the screen, the young man laughed as he had laughed twenty-five seconds earlier on Earth. It was the level of lag Avasarala hated the most. Too much for the conversation to feel anything like normal, but not quite enough to make it impossible. Everything she did took too long, every reading of reaction and nuance crippled by the effort to guess what exactly in her words and expression ten seconds before had elicited it.

"Only you," he said, "could take another Earth-Mars war, turn it into a private cruise, and then seem pissed off about it. Anyone in my office would give their left testicle to go with you."

"Next time I'll take up a collection, but—"

"As far as an accurate military inventory," he said twenty-five seconds ago, "there are reports in place, but they're not as good as I'd like. Because it's you, I've got a couple of my interns building search parameters. My impression is that the research budget is about a tenth of the money going to actual research. With your clearances, I have rights to look at it, but these Navy guys are pretty good at obscuring things. I think you'll find…" His expression clouded. "A collection?"

"Forget it. You were saying?"

She waited fifty seconds, resenting each individually.

"I don't know that we'll be able to get a definitive answer," the young man said. "We might get lucky, but if it's something they want to hide, they can probably hide it."

Especially since they'll know you're looking for it, and what I asked you to look for, Avasarala thought. Even if the income stream between Mao-Kwikowski, Nguyen, and Errinwright was in all the budgets right now, by the time Avasarala's allies looked, it would be hidden. All she could do was keep pushing on as many fronts as she could devise and hope that they fucked up. Three more days of information requests and queries, and she could ask for traffic analysis. She couldn't know exactly what information they were hiding, but if she could find out what kinds and categories of data they were keeping away from her, that would tell her something.

Something, but not much.

"Do what you can," she said. "I'll luxuriate out here in the middle of nowhere. Get back to me."

She didn't wait fifty seconds for a round of etiquette and farewell. Life was too short for that shit.

Her private quarters on the *Guanshiyin* were gorgeous. The bed and couch matched the deep carpet in tones of gold and green that should have clashed but didn't. The light was the best approximation of mid-morning sunlight that she'd ever seen, and the air recyclers were scented to give everything just a note of turned earth and fresh-cut grass. Only the low thrust gravity spoiled the illusion of being in a private country club somewhere in the green belt of south Asia. The low gravity and the goddamned lag.

She hated low gravity. Even if the acceleration was perfectly smooth and the yacht never had to shift or move to avoid debris, her guts were used to a full g pulling things down. She hadn't digested anything well since she'd come on board, and she always felt short of breath.

Her system chimed. A new report from Venus. She popped it open. The preliminary analysis of the wreckage from the *Arboghast* was under way. There was some ionizing in the metal that was apparently consistent with someone's theory of how the proto-molecule functioned. It was the first time a prediction had been confirmed, the first tiny toehold toward a genuine understanding of what was happening on Venus. There was an exact timing of the three energy spikes. There was a spectral analysis of the upper atmosphere of Venus that showed more elemental nitrogen than expected. Avasarala felt her eyes glazing over. The truth was she didn't care.

She should. It was important. Possibly more important than anything else that was happening. But just like Errinwright and Nguyen and all the others, she was caught up in this smaller, human struggle of war and influence and the tribal division between Earth and Mars. The outer planets too, if you took them seriously.

Hell, at this point she was more worried about Bobbie and Cotyar than she was about Venus. Cotyar was a good man, and his disapproval left her feeling defensive and pissed off. And Bobbie looked like she was about to crack. And why not? The woman had watched her friends die around her, had been stripped of her context, and was now working for her traditional enemy. The marine was tough, in more ways than one, and having someone on the team with no allegiance or ties to anyone on Earth was a real benefit. Especially after fucking Soren.

She leaned back in her chair, unnerved by how different it felt when she weighed so little. Soren still smarted. Not the betrayal itself; betrayal was an occupational hazard. If she started getting her feelings hurt by that, she really should retire. No, it was that she hadn't seen it. She'd let herself have a blind spot, and Errin-wright had known how to use it. How to disenfranchise her. She hated being outplayed. And more than that, she hated that her failure was going to mean more war, more violence, more children dying.

That was the price for screwing up. More dead children.

So she wouldn't screw up anymore.

She could practically see Arjun, the gentle sorrow in his eyes. *It isn't all your responsibility*, he would say.

"It's everyone's fucking responsibility," she said out loud. "But I'm the one who's taking it seriously."

She smiled. Let Mao's monitors and spies make sense of that. She let herself imagine them searching her room for some other transmission device, trying to find who she'd been speaking to. Or they'd just think the old lady was losing her beans.

Let 'em wonder.

She closed out the Venus report. Another message had arrived while she was in her reverie, flagged as an issue she'd requested follow-up on. When she read the intelligence summary, her eyebrows rose.

"I'm James Holden, and I'm here to ask for your help."

Avasarala watched Bobbie watching the screen. She looked exhausted and restless both. Her eyes weren't bloodshot so much as dry-looking. Like bearings without enough grease. If she'd needed an example to demonstrate the difference between sleepy and tired, it would have been the marine.

"So he got out, then," Bobbie said.

"Him and his pet botanist and the whole damned crew," Avasarala said. "So now we have one story about what they were doing on Ganymede that got your boys and ours so excited they started shooting each other."

Bobbie looked up at her.

"Do you think it's true?"

"What is truth?" Avasarala said. "I think Holden has a long

history of blabbing whatever he knows or thinks he knows all over creation. True or not, he believes it."

"And the part about the protomolecule? I mean, he just told everyone that the protomolecule is loose on Ganymede."

"He did."

"People have got to be reacting to that, right?"

Avasarala flipped to the intelligence summary, then to feeds of the riots on Ganymede. Thin, frightened people, exhausted by tragedy and war and fueled by panic. She could tell that the security forces arrayed against them were trying to be gentle. These weren't thugs enjoying the use of force. These were orderlies trying to keep the frail and dying from hurting themselves and each other, walking the line between necessary violence and ineffectiveness.

"Fifty dead so far," Avasarala said. "That's the estimate, anyway. That place is so ass-fucked right now, they might have been going to die of sickness and malnutrition anyway. But they died of this instead."

"I went to that restaurant," Bobbie said.

Avasarala frowned, trying to make it into a metaphor for something. Bobbie pointed at the screen.

"The one they're dying in front of? I ate there just after I arrived at the deployment. They had good sausage."

"Sorry," Avasarala said, but the marine only shook her head.

"So that cat's out of the bag," she said.

"Maybe," Avasarala said. "Maybe not."

"James Holden just told the whole system that the protomolecule's on Ganymede. In what universe is that *maybe not*?"

Avasarala pulled up a mainstream newsfeed, checked the flags, and pulled the one with the listed experts she wanted. The data buffered for a few seconds while she lifted her finger for patience.

"—totally irresponsible," a grave-cheeked man in a lab coat and kufi cap said. The contempt in his voice could have peeled paint.

The interviewer appeared beside him. She was maybe twenty years old, with hair cut short and straight and a dark suit that said she was a serious journalist.

"So you're saying the protomolecule *isn't* involved?"

"It isn't. The images James Holden and his little group are sending have nothing to do with the protomolecule. That webbing is what happens when you have a binding agent leak. It happens all the time."

"So there isn't any reason to panic."

"Alice," the expert said, turning his condescension to the interviewer. "Within a few days of exposure, Eros was a living horror show. In the time since hostilities opened, Ganymede hasn't shown one sign of a live infection. Not one."

"But he has a scientist with him. The botanist Dr. Praxidike Meng, whose daughter—"

"I don't know this Meng fellow, but playing with a few soybeans makes him as much an expert on the protomolecule as it makes him a brain surgeon. I'm very sorry, of course, about his missing daughter, but no. If the protomolecule were on Ganymede, we'd have known long ago. This panic is over *literally* nothing."

"He can go on like that for hours," Avasarala said, shutting down the screen. "And we have dozens like him. Mars is going to be doing the same thing. Saturating the newsfeeds with the counter-story."

"Impressive," Bobbie said, pushing herself back from the desk.

"It keeps people calm. That's the important thing. Holden thinks he's a hero, power to the people, information wants to be free blah blah blah, but he's a fucking moron."

"He's on his own ship."

Avasarala crossed her arms. "What's your point?"

"He's on his own ship and we're not."

"So we're all fucking morons," Avasarala said. "Fine."

Bobbie stood up and started pacing the room. She turned well before she reached the wall. The woman was used to pacing in smaller quarters.

"What do you want me to do about it?" Bobbie asked.

"Nothing," Avasarala said. "What the hell could you do about it? You're stuck out here with me. I can hardly do anything, and I've got friends in high places. You've got *nothing*. I only wanted to talk to someone I didn't have to wait two minutes to let interrupt me."

She'd taken it too far. Bobbie's expression eased, went calm and closed and distant. She was shutting down. Avasarala lowered herself to the edge of the bed.

"That wasn't fair," Avasarala said.

"If you say so."

"I fucking say so."

The marine tilted her head. "Was that an apology?"

"As close to one as I'm giving right now."

Something shifted in Avasarala's mind. Not about Venus, or James Holden and his *poor lost girl* appeal, or even Errinwright. It had to do with Bobbie and her pacing and her sleeplessness. Then she got it and laughed once mirthlessly. Bobbie crossed her arms, her steady silence a question.

"It isn't funny," Avasarala said.

"Try me."

"You remind me of my daughter."

"Yeah?"

She'd pissed Bobbie off, and now she was going to have to explain herself. The air recyclers hummed to themselves. Something far off in the bowels of the yacht groaned like they were on an ancient sailing ship made from timber and tar.

"My son died when he was fifteen," Avasarala said. "Skiing. Did I tell you this? He was on a slope that he'd run twenty, thirty times before. He knew it, but something happened and he ran into a tree. They guessed he was going something like sixty kilometers an hour when he hit. Some people survive an impact like that, but not him."

For a moment, she was there again, in the house with the medic on the screen giving her the news. She could still smell the incense

Arjun had been burning at the time. She could still hear the rain-drops against the window, tapping like fingertips. It was the worst memory she had, and it was perfect and clear. She took a long, deep shuddering breath.

"I almost got divorced three times in the next six months. Arjun was a saint, but saints have their limits. We fought about anything. About nothing. Each of us blamed ourselves for not saving Charanpal, and we resented it when the other one tried to take some responsibility. And so, of course, my daughter suffered the worst.

"There was a night when we were out at something, Arjun and I. We got home late, and we'd been fighting. Ashanti was in the kitchen, washing dishes. Washing clean dishes by hand. Scrubbing them with a cloth and this terrible abrasive cleanser. Her fingers were bleeding, but she didn't seem to notice, you know? I tried to stop her, pull her away, but she started screaming and she wouldn't be quiet again until I let her resume her washing. I was so angry I couldn't see. I hated my daughter. For that moment, I hated her."

"And I remind you of her how exactly?"

Avasarala gestured to the room. Its bed with real linen sheets. The textured paper on the walls, the scented air.

"You can't compromise. You can't see things the way I tell you that they are, and when I try and make you, you go away."

"Is that what you want?" Bobbie said. Her voice was crawling up to a higher energy level. It was anger, but it brought her back to being present. "You want me to agree with whatever you say, and if I don't, you're going to hate me for it?"

"Of course I want you to call me on my bullshit. That's what I pay you for. I'm only going to hate you for the moment," Avasarala said. "I love my daughter very much."

"I'm sure you do, ma'am. I'm not her."

Avasarala sighed.

"I didn't call you in here and show you all of this because I was tired of the lag. I'm worried. Fuck it, I'm *scared*."

"About what?"

"You want a list?"

Bobbie actually smiled. Avasarala felt herself smiling back.

"I'm scared that I've been outplayed already," she said. "I'm afraid that I won't be able to stop the hawks and their cabal from using their pretty new toys. And…and I'm afraid that I might be wrong. What happens, Bobbie? What happens if whatever the hell that is on Venus rises up and finds us as divided and screwed up and ineffective as we are right now?"

"I don't know."

Avasarala's terminal chimed. She glanced at the new message. A note from Admiral Souther. Avasarala had sent him an utterly innocuous note about having lunch when they both got back to Earth, then coded it for high-security clearance with a private encryption schema. It would take her handlers a couple of hours at least to crack it. She tabbed it open. The reply was plain text.

LOVE TO.
THE EAGLE LANDS AT MIDNIGHT. PETTING ZOOS
ARE ILLEGAL IN ROME.

Avasarala laughed. It was real pleasure this time. Bobbie loomed up over her shoulder, and Avasarala turned the screen so that the big marine could peer down at it.

"What's that mean?"

Avasarala motioned her down close enough that her lips were almost against Bobbie's ear. At that intimate distance, the big woman smelled of clean sweat and the cucumber-scented emollient that was in all Mao's guest quarters.

"Nothing," Avasarala whispered. "He's just following my lead, but they'll chew their livers out guessing at it."

Bobbie stood up. Her expression of incredulity was eloquent.

"This really is how government works, isn't it?"

"Welcome to the monkey house," Avasarala said.

"I think I might go get drunk."

"And I'll get back to work."

At the doorway, Bobbie paused. She looked small in the wide frame. A doorframe on a spaceship that left Roberta Draper looking small. There was nothing about the yacht that wasn't tastefully obscene.

"What happened with her?"

"Who?"

"Your daughter."

Avasarala closed her terminal.

"Arjun sang to her until she stopped. It took about three hours. He sat on the counter and went through all the songs we'd sung to them when they were little. Eventually, Ashanti let him lead her to her room and tuck her into bed."

"You hated him too, didn't you? For being able to help her when you couldn't."

"You're catching on, Sergeant."

Bobbie licked her lips.

"I want to hurt someone," she said. "I'm afraid if it's not them, it's going to wind up being me."

"We all grieve in our own ways," Avasarala said. "For what it's worth, you'll never kill enough people to keep your platoon from dying. No more than I can save enough people that one of them will be Charanpal."

For a long moment, Bobbie weighed the words. Avasarala could almost hear the woman's mind turning the ideas one way and then another. Soren had been an idiot to underestimate this woman. But Soren had been an idiot in a lot of ways. When at length she spoke, her voice was light and conversational, as if her words weren't profound.

"No harm trying, though."

"It's what we do," Avasarala said.

The marine nodded curtly. For a moment, Avasarala thought she might be going to salute, but instead, she lumbered out toward the complimentary bar in the wide common area. There was a fountain out there with sprays of water drifting down fake bronze sculptures of horses and underdressed women. If that didn't make someone want a stiff drink of something, then nothing would.

Avasarala thumbed on the video feed again.

"This is James Holden—"

She turned it off again.

"At least you lost that fucking beard," she said to no one.

Chapter Thirty-Six: Prax

Prax remembered his first epiphany. Or possibly, he thought, the one he remembered as his first. In the absence of further evidence, he went with it. He'd been in second form, just seventeen, and in the middle of a genetic engineering lab. Sitting there among the steel tables and microcentrifuges, he'd struggled with why exactly his results were so badly off. He'd rechecked his calculations, read through his lab notes. The error was more than sloppy technique could explain, and his technique wasn't even sloppy.

And then he'd noticed that one of the reagents was chiral, and he knew what had happened. He hadn't figured anything wrong but he had assumed that the reagent was taken from a natural source rather than generated de novo. Instead of being uniformly left-handed, it had been a mix of chiralities, half of them inactive. The insight had left him grinning from ear to ear.

It had been a failure, but it was a failure he understood, and that made it a victory. The only thing he regretted was that seeing what should have been clear had taken him so long.

The four days since he had sent the broadcast, he'd hardly slept. Instead, he'd read through the comments and messages pouring in with the donations, responding to a few, asking questions of people all over the system whom he didn't know. The goodwill and generosity pouring out to him was intoxicating. For two days, he hadn't slept, borne up on the euphoria of feeling effective. When he had slept, he'd dreamed of finding Mei.

When the answer came, he only wished he'd found it before.

"The time they had, they could have taken her anywhere, Doc," Amos said. "I mean, not to bust your balls or nothing."

"They could," Prax said. "They could take her anywhere as long as they had a supply of her medications. But she's not the limiting factor. The question is where they were coming from."

Prax had called the meeting without a clear idea of where to have it. The crew of the *Roci* was small, but Amos' rooms were smaller. He'd considered the galley of the ship, but there were still technicians finishing the repairs, and Prax wanted privacy. In the end, he'd checked the incoming stream of contributions from Holden's broadcast and taken enough to rent a room from a station club.

Now they were in a private lounge. Outside the wall-screen window, the great construction waldoes shifted by tiny degrees, attitude rockets flaring and going still in patterns as complex as language. Another thing Prax had never thought about before coming here: The station waldoes had to fire attitude rockets to keep their movements from shifting the station they were attached to. Everything, everywhere, a dance of tiny movements and the ripples they made.

Inside the room, the music that floated between the wide tables and crash-gel chairs was soft and lyrical, the singer's voice deep and soothing.

"From?" Alex said. "I thought they were from Ganymede."

"The lab on Ganymede wasn't equipped to deal with serious research," Prax said. "And they arranged things so that Ganymede would turn into a war zone. That'd be a bad idea if they were doing their primary work in the middle of it. That was a field lab."

"I try not to shit where I eat," Amos said, agreeing.

"You live on a spaceship," Holden said.

"I don't shit in the galley, though."

"Fair point."

"Anyway," Prax said, "we can safely assume they were working from a better-protected base. And that base has to be somewhere in the Jovian system. Somewhere nearby."

"You lost me again," Holden said. "Why does it need to be close?"

"Transport time. Mei can go anywhere if there's a good supply of medications, but she's more robust than the...the things."

Holden raised his hand like a schoolboy asking a question.

"Okay, I could be hearing you wrong, but did you just say that the thing that ripped its way into my ship, threw a five-hundred-kilo storage pallet at me, and almost chewed a path straight to the reactor core is more delicate than a four-year-old girl with no immune system?"

Prax nodded. A stab of horror and grief went through him. She wasn't four anymore. Mei's birthday had been the month before, and he'd missed it. She was five. But grief and horror were old companions by now. He pushed the thought aside.

"I'll be clearer," he said. "Mei's body isn't fighting its situation. That's her disease, if you think about it. There's a whole array of things that happen in normal bodies that don't happen in hers. Now you take one of the things, one of the creatures. Like the one from the ship?"

"That bastard was pretty active," Amos said.

"No," Prax said. "I mean, yes, but no. I mean active on a biochemical level. If Strickland or Merrian or whoever is using the protomolecule to reengineer a human body, they're taking one complex system and overlaying another one. We know it's unstable."

"Okay," Naomi said. She was sitting beside Amos and across the table from Holden. "*How* do we know that?"

Prax frowned. When he'd practiced making the presentation, he hadn't expected so many questions. The things he'd thought were obvious from the start hadn't even occurred to the others. This was why he hadn't gone in for teaching. Looking at their faces now, he saw blank confusion.

"All right," he said. "Let me take it from the top. There was something on Ganymede that started the war. There was also a secret lab staffed with people who at the very least knew about the attack before it happened."

"Check," Alex said.

"Okay," Prax said. "In the lab, we had signs of the protomolecule, a dead boy, and a bunch of people getting ready to leave. And when we got there, we only had to fight halfway in. After that, something else was going ahead of us and killing everyone."

"Hey!" Amos said. "You think that was the same fucker that got into the *Roci*?"

Prax stopped the word *obviously* just before it fell from his lips.

"Probably," he said instead. "And it seems likely that the original attack involved more like that one."

"So two got loose?" Naomi asked, but he could see that she already sensed the problem with that.

"No, because they knew it was going to happen. One got loose when Amos threw that grenade back at them. One was released intentionally. But that doesn't matter. What matters is that they're using the protomolecule to remake human bodies, and they aren't able to control it with perfect fidelity. The programming they're putting in fails."

Prax nodded, as if by doing it he could will them to follow his chain of reasoning. Holden shook his head, paused, and then nodded.

"The bomb," he said.

"The bomb," Prax agreed. "Even when they didn't know that the second thing was going to get loose, they'd outfitted it with a powerful incendiary explosive device."

"Ah!" Alex said. "I get it! You figure they knew it was going to go off the rails eventually, so they wired it to blow if it got out of hand."

In the depths of space, a construction welder streaked across the hull of the half-built ship, the light of its flare casting a sudden, sharp light across the pilot's eager face.

"Yes," Prax said. "But it could be also be an ancillary weapon, or a payload that the thing was supposed to deliver. I think it's a fail-safe. It probably is, but it could be any number of other things."

"Okay, but it left it behind," Alex said.

"Given time, it *ejected* the bomb," Prax said. "You see? It chose to reconfigure itself to remove the payload. It didn't place it to destroy the *Roci*, even though it could have. It didn't deliver it to a preset target. It just decided to pop it loose."

"And it knew to do that—"

"It's smart enough to recognize threat," Prax said. "I don't know the mechanism yet. It could be cognitive or networked or some kind of modified immune response."

"Okay, Prax. So if the protomolecule can eventually get out of whatever constraints they're putting on it and go rogue, where does that get us?" Naomi asked.

Square one, Prax thought, and launched in on the information he'd intended to give them in the first place.

"It means that wherever the main lab is—the place they didn't release one of those things on—it has to be close enough to Ganymede to get it there before it slipped its leash. I don't know how long that is, and I'm betting they don't either. So closer is better."

"A Jovian moon or a secret station," Holden said.

"You can't have a secret station in the Jovian system," Alex said. "There's too much traffic. Someone'd see something. Shit, it's where most of the extrasolar astronomy was going on until we got out to Uranus. Put something close, the observatories are gonna get pissed because it's stinking up their pictures, right?"

Naomi tapped her fingers against the tabletop, the sound like the ticking of condensate falling inside sheet metal vents.

"Well, the obvious choice is Europa," she said.

"It's Io," Prax said, impatience slipping into his voice. "I used some of the money to get a tariff search on the kinds of arylamines and nitroarenes that you use for mutagentic research." He paused. "It's all right that I did that, isn't it? Spent the money?"

"That's what it's there for," Holden said.

"Okay, so mutagens that only start functioning after you activate them are very tightly controlled, since you can use them for bioweapons research, but if you're trying to work with that kind of biological cascade and constraint systems, you'd need them. Most of the supplies went to Ganymede, but there was a steady stream to Europa too. And when I looked at that, I couldn't find a final receiver listed. Because they shipped back out of Europa about two hours after they landed."

"Bound for Io," Holden said.

"It didn't list a location, but the shipping containers for them have to follow Earth and Mars safety specifications. Very expensive. And the shipping containers for the Europa shipment were returned to the manufacturer for credit on a transport bound from Io."

Prax took a breath. It had been like pulling teeth, but he was pretty sure he'd made all the points he needed to for the evidence to be, if not conclusive, at least powerfully suggestive.

"So," Amos said, drawing the word out to almost three syllables. "The bad guys are probably on Io?"

"Yes," Prax said.

"Well shit, Doc. Coulda just said so."

The thrust gravity was a full g but without the subtle Coriolis of Tycho Station. Prax sat in his bunk, bent over his hand terminal. There had been times on the journey to Tycho Station when being half starved and sick at heart were the only things that distracted him. Nothing physical had changed. The walls were still narrow and close. The air recycler still clicked and hummed. Only now, rather than feeling isolated, Prax felt he was in the center of a vast network of people, all bent toward the same end that he was.

MR. MENG, I SAW THE REPORT ON YOU AND MY HEART AND PRAYERS ARE WITH YOU. I'M SORRY I CAN'T SEND MONEY BECAUSE I'M ON BASIC, BUT I HAVE INCLUDED THE REPORT IN MY CHURCH NEWS-LETTER. I HOPE YOU CAN FIND YOUR DAUGHTER SAFE AND HEALTHY.

Prax had composed a form letter for responding to all the general well-wishers, and he'd considered trying to find a filter that could identify those messages and reply automatically with the canned response. He held off because he wasn't sure how well he could define the conditions set, and he didn't want anyone to feel that their sentiments were being taken for granted. And after all, he had no duties on the *Rocinante*.

I'M WRITING YOU BECAUSE I MAY HAVE INFORMA-TION THAT WILL HELP WITH THE QUEST TO RECLAIM YOUR DAUGHTER. SINCE I WAS VERY YOUNG, I HAVE HAD POWERFUL PREMONITIONS IN MY DREAMS, AND THREE DAYS BEFORE I SAW JAMES HOLDEN'S ARTICLE ABOUT YOU AND YOUR DAUGHTER, I SAW HER IN A DREAM. SHE WAS ON LUNA IN A VERY SMALL PLACE WITHOUT LIGHT, AND SHE WAS SCARED. I TRIED TO COMFORT HER, BUT I FEEL SURE NOW THAT YOU ARE MEANT TO FIND HER ON LUNA OR IN A NEARBY ORBIT.

Prax didn't respond to *everything*, of course.

The journey to Io wouldn't take much more time than the one to Tycho had. Probably less, since they were unlikely to have the chaos of a stowaway protomolecule construct blowing out the cargo bay this time. If Prax thought about it too long, it made his palm itch. He knew where she was—or where she had been. Every hour was bringing him closer, and every message flowing into his charitable account gave him a little more power. Someone else who might know where Carlos Merrian was and what he was doing.

There were a few he'd set up conversations with, mostly video conversations sent back and forth. He'd spoken with a security broker based out of Ceres Station, who'd run some of his tariff searches and seemed like a genuinely nice man. He'd exchanged a few video recordings with a grief counselor on Mars before he started to get an uncomfortable feeling that she was hitting on him. An entire school of children—at least a hundred of them—had sent him a recording of them singing a song in mixed Spanish and French in honor of Mei and her return.

Intellectually, he knew that nothing had changed. The chances were still very good that Mei was dead, or at least that he would never see her again. But to have so many people—and in such a steady stream—telling him that it would be all right, that they hoped it would be all right, that they were pulling for him made despair less possible. It was probably something like group reinforcement effect. It was something common to some species of crop plant: An ill or suffering plant could be moved into a community of well members of the species and, through proximity, improve, even if soil and water were supplied separately. Yes, it was chemically mediated, but humans were social animals, and a woman smiling up from the screen, her eyes seeming to look deeply into your own, and saying what you wanted to believe was almost impossible to wholly disbelieve.

It was selfish, and he knew that, but it was also addictive. He'd stopped paying attention to the donations that were coming in once he knew there was enough to fund the ship as far as Io. Holden had given him an expense report and a detailed spreadsheet of costs, but Prax didn't think Holden would cheat him, so he'd barely glanced at anything other than the total at the bottom. Once there was enough money, he'd stopped caring about money.

It was the commentary that took his time and attention.

He heard Alex and Amos in the galley, their voices calm and conversational. It reminded him of living in the group housing at university. The awareness of other voices, other presences, and the comfort that came from those familiar sounds. It wasn't that different from reading the comment threads.

I LOST MY SON FOUR YEARS AGO, AND I STILL CAN'T IMAGINE WHAT YOU ARE GOING THROUGH RIGHT NOW. I WISH THERE WAS MORE I COULD DO.

He had the list down to only a few dozen. It was mid-afternoon in the arbitrary world of ship time, but he was powerfully sleepy. He debated leaving the remaining messages until after a nap, and decided to read through them without requiring himself to respond to each one. Alex laughed. Amos joined him.

Prax opened the fifth message.

YOU ARE A SICK, SICK, SICK MOTHERFUCKER, AND IF I EVER SEE YOU, I SWEAR TO GOD I WILL KILL YOU MYSELF. PEOPLE LIKE YOU SHOULD BE RAPED TO DEATH JUST SO YOU KNOW WHAT IT FEELS LIKE.

Prax tried to catch his breath. The sudden ache in his body was just like the aftermath of being punched in the solar plexus. He deleted the message. Another came in, and then three more. And then a dozen. With a sense of dread, Prax opened one of the new ones.

I HOPE YOU DIE.

"I don't understand," Prax said to the terminal. The vitriol was sudden and constant and utterly inexplicable. At least, it was until he opened one of the messages that had the link to a public news-feed. Prax put in a request, and five minutes later, his screen went blank, the logo of one of the big Earth-based news aggregators glowed briefly in blue, and the title of the feed series—The Raw Feed—appeared.

When the logo faded out, Nicola was looking out at him. Prax reached for the controls, part of his mind insisting that he'd somehow slipped into his private messages, even as the rest of him knew better. Nicola licked her lips, looked away, then back at the camera. She looked tired. Exhausted.

"My name's Nicola Mulko. I used to be married to Praxidike Meng, the man who put out a call for help finding our daughter... my daughter, Mei."

A tear dripped down her cheek, and she didn't wipe it away.

"What you don't know—what no one knows—is that Praxidike Meng is a monster of a human being. Ever since I got away from him, I've been trying to get Mei back. I thought his abuse of me was between us. I didn't think he'd hurt her. But information has come back to me from friends who stayed on Ganymede after I left that..."

"Nicola," Prax said. "Don't. Don't do this."

"Praxidike Meng is a violent and dangerous man," Nicola said. "As Mei's mother, I believe that she has been emotionally, physically, and sexually abused by him since I left. And that her alleged disappearance during the troubles on Ganymede are to hide the fact that he's finally killed her."

The tears were flowing freely down Nicola's cheeks now, but her voice and eyes were dead as last week's fish.

"I don't blame anyone but myself," she said. "I should never have left when I couldn't get my little girl away too..."

Chapter Thirty-Seven: Avasarala

I don't blame anyone but myself," the teary-eyed woman said, and Avasarala stopped the feed, sitting back in her chair. Her heart was beating faster than usual and she could feel thoughts swimming just under the ice of her conscious mind. She felt like someone could press an ear to her skull and listen to her brain humming.

Bobbie was sitting on the four-poster. She made the thing look small, which was impressive in itself. She had one leg tucked up under her and a pack of real playing cards laid out in formation on the crisp gold-and-green bedspread. The game of solitaire was forgotten, though. The Martian's gaze was on her, and Avasarala felt a slow grin pulling at her lips.

"Well, I'll be fucked," she said. "They're scared of him."

"Who's scared of who?"

"Errinwright is moving against Holden and this Meng bastard, whoever he is. They actually forced him to take action. *I* couldn't get that out of him."

"You don't think the botanist was diddling his kid?"

"Might have been, but that"—she tapped on the still, tearful face of the botanist's ex-wife—"is a smear campaign. I'll bet you a week's pay that I've had lunch with the woman coordinating it."

Bobbie's skeptical look only made Avasarala smile more broadly.

"This," Avasarala said, "is the first genuinely good thing that's happened since we got on this floating whorehouse. I've got to get to work. Goddamn, but I wish I was back at the office."

"You want some tea?"

"Gin," she said, engaging the camera on her terminal. "We're celebrating."

In the focus window, she looked smaller than she felt. The rooms had been designed to command attention whatever angle she put herself in, like being trapped in a postcard. Anyone who rode in the yacht would be able to brag without saying a word, but in the weak gravity her hair stood out from her head like she'd just gotten out of bed. More than that, she looked emotionally exhausted and physically diminished.

Put it away, she told herself. *Find the mask.*

She took a deep breath, made a rude gesture into the camera, and then started recording.

"Admiral Souther," she said. "Thank you so much for your last message. Something's come to my attention that I thought you might find interesting. It looks like someone's taken a fresh dislike to James Holden. If I were with the fleet instead of floating around the fucking solar system, I'd take you out for a cup of coffee and talk this over, but since that's not happening, I'm going to open some of my private files for you. I've been following Holden. Take a look at what I've got and tell me if you're seeing the same things I am."

She sent the message. The next thing that would have made sense would be contacting Errinwright. If the situation had been what they were both pretending it was, she'd have kept him involved and engaged. For a long moment, she considered following the form, pretending. Bobbie loomed up on her right, putting the glass of gin on the desk with a soft click. Avasarala picked it up and sipped a small taste of it. Mao's private-label gin was excellent, even without the lime twist.

Nah. Fuck Errinwright. She pulled up her address book and started leafing through entries until she found what she wanted and pressed record.

"Ms. Corlinowski, I've just seen the leaked video accusing Praxidike Meng of screwing his cute little five-year-old daughter. When exactly did UN media relations turn into a fucking divorce court? If it gets out that we were behind that, I would like to know whose resignation I'm going to hand to the newsfeeds, and right now I'm thinking it's yours. Give my love to Richard, and get back to me before I fire your incompetent ass out of spite."

She ended the recording and sent it.

"She was the one that arranged it?" Bobbie asked.

"Might have been," Avasarala said, taking another bite of gin. It was too good. If she wasn't careful, she'd drink a lot of it. "If it wasn't, she'll find who it was and serve them up on a plate. Emma Corlinowski's a coward. It's why I love her."

Over the next hour, she sent a dozen more messages out, performance after performance after performance. She started a liability investigation into Meng's ex-wife and whether the UN could be held responsible for slander. She put the Ganymede relief coordinator on high alert, demanding everything she could get about Mei Meng and the search for her. She put in high-priority requests to have the doctor and the woman from Holden's broadcast identified, and then sent a twenty-minute rambling message to an old colleague in data storage, with a small, tacit request for the same information made in the middle of it all.

Errinwright had changed the game. If she'd had freedom, she'd have been unstoppable. As it was, she had to assume that every move she made would be cataloged and acted against almost as soon as she made it. But Errinwright and his allies were only human, and if she kept a solid flow of demands and requests, screeds and wheedling, they might overlook something. Or someone on a newsfeed might notice the uptick in activity and look into it. Or, if nothing else, her efforts might give Errinwright a bad night's sleep.

It was what she had. It wasn't enough. Long years of practice with the fine dance of politics and power had left her with expectations and reflexes that couldn't find their right form there. The lag was killing her with frustration, and she took it out on whomever she was recording for at the moment. She felt like a world-class musician standing before a full auditorium and handed a kazoo.

She didn't notice when she finished her gin. She only put the glass to her mouth, found it empty, and realized it wasn't the first time she'd done it. Five hours had passed. She'd had only three responses so far out of almost fifty messages she'd sent out. That was more than lag. That was someone else's damage control.

She didn't realize that she was hungry until Cotyar came with a plate, the smell of curried lamb and watermelon wafting in with him. Avasarala's belly woke with a roar, and she turned off her terminal.

"You've just saved my life," she told him, gesturing at the desk.

"It was Sergeant Draper's idea," he said. "After the third time you ignored her asking."

"I don't remember that," she said as he put the dish in front of her. "Don't they have servants on this thing? Why are you bringing the food?"

"They do, ma'am. I'm not letting them in here."

"That seems extreme. Feeling jumpy, are you?"

"As you say."

She ate too quickly. Her back was aching, and her left leg was tingling with the pins and needles she got now from sitting too long in one position. As a young woman, she'd never suffered that. On the other hand, she hadn't had the ability to pepper every major player in the United Nations and be taken seriously. Time took her strength but it gave her power in exchange. It was a fair trade.

She couldn't wait to finish her meal, turning on the terminal while she gulped the last of it down. Four waiting messages. Souther, God bless his shriveled little heart. One from someone at the legal council whose name she didn't recognize, and another from someone she did. One from Michael-Jon, which was probably about Venus. She opened the one from Souther.

The admiral appeared on her screen and she had to stop herself from saying hello. It was only a video recording, not a real conversation. She hated it.

"Chrisjen," the admiral said. "You're going to have to be careful with all this information you're sending me. Arjun's going to get jealous. I wasn't aware of our friend Jimmy's part in instigating this latest brouhaha."

Our friend Jimmy. He wasn't saying the name Holden out loud. That was interesting. He was expecting some kind of filtering to be sniffing out Holden's name. She tried to guess whether he thought the filter would be on his outgoing messages or her incoming. If Errinwright had half a brain—which he did—he'd be watching the traffic both ways for both of them. Was he worried about someone else? How many players were there at the table? She didn't have enough information to work with, but it was interesting, at least.

"I can see where your concerns might lead you," Souther said. "I'm making some inquiries, but you know how these things are. Might find something in a minute, might find something in a year. You don't be a stranger, though. There's more than enough going on out here that I can wish I could take you up on that lunch. We're all looking forward to seeing you again."

There was a barefaced lie, Avasarala thought. Still, nice of him to say it. She scraped her fork along the bottom of the plate, a thin residue of curry clinging to the silver.

The first message was some young man with a Brazilian accent explaining to her that the UN had nothing to do with the video footage released of Nicola Mulko, and therefore could not be held responsible for it. The second was the boy's supervisor, apologizing for him and promising a fully formed brief by the end of the day, which was considerably more like it. The smart people were still afraid of her. That thought was more nourishing than the lamb.

As she reached for the screen, the ship shifted under her, gravity pulling her slightly to the side. She put her hand on the desk; the curry and the remnants of gin churned her gut.

"Were we expecting that?" she shouted.

"Yes, ma'am," Cotyar called from the next room. "Scheduled course correction."

"Never happens at the fucking office," she said, and Michael-Jon appeared on her screen. He looked mildly confused, but that could have been just the angle of his face. She felt a sick dread.

For a moment, the *Arboghast* floated before her again, coming apart. Without intending it, she paused the feed. Something in the back of her mind wanted to turn away. Not to know.

It wasn't hard to understand how Errinwright and Nguyen and their cabal would turn their backs on Venus, on the alien chaos that was becoming order and more than order. She felt it too, the atavistic fear lurking at the back of her mind. How much easier to turn to the old games, the old patterns, the history of warfare and conflict, deception and death. For all its horror, it was familiar. It was known.

As a girl, she'd seen a film about a man who saw the face of God. For the first hour of the film, he had gone through the drab life of someone living on basic on the coast of southern Africa. When he saw God, the film switched to ten minutes of the man wailing and then another hour of slowly building himself back up to do the same idiot life he'd had at the beginning. Avasarala had hated it. Now, though, she almost understood. Turning away was natural. Even if it was moronic and self-destructive and empty, it was natural.

War. Slaughter. Death. All the violence that Errinwright and his men—and she felt certain they were almost all of them men—were embracing, they were drawn to because it was comforting. And they were scared.

Well, so was she.

"Pussies," she said, and restarted the playback.

"Venus can think," Michael-Jon said instead of *hello* or any other social pleasantry. "I've had the signal analysis team running the data we saw from the network of water and electrical currents, and we've found a model. It's only about a sixty percent correlation, but I'm comfortable putting that above chance. It's got different anatomy, of course, but its functional structure is most like a cetacean doing spatial reasoning problems. I mean, there's still the problem of the explanatory gap, and I can't help with that part, but with what we've seen, I'm fairly sure that the patterns we saw were it thinking. They were the actual thoughts, like neurons firing off."

He looked into the camera as if expecting her to answer and then looked mildly disappointed when she didn't.

"I thought you'd want to know," he said, and ended the recording.

Before she could formulate a response, a new message from Souther appeared. She opened it with a sense of gratitude and relief that she was slightly ashamed of.

"Chrisjen," he said. "We have a problem. You should check the force assignments on Ganymede and let me know if we're seeing the same things."

Avasarala frowned. The lag now was over twenty-eight minutes. She put in a standard request, expedited it, and stood up. Her back was a solid knot. She walked to the common area of the suite. Bobbie, Cotyar, and three other men were sitting in a circle, the deck of cards distributed among them. Poker. Avasarala walked toward them, rolling through the hips where movement hurt. Something about lower gravity made her joints ache. She lowered herself to Bobbie's side.

"Next hand, you can deal me in," she said.

The order had come from Nguyen, and at first glance it made no sense at all. Six UN destroyers had been ordered off the Ganymede patrol, sent out at high burn on a course that seemed to lead essentially to nowhere. Initial reports showed that after a decent period of wondering what the fuck, a similar detachment of Martian ships matched course.

Nguyen was up to something, and she didn't have the first clue what it could be. But Souther had sent it and thought she would see something.

It took another hour to find it. Holden's *Rocinante* had departed Tycho Station on a gentle burn for the Jovian system. He might have filed a flight plan with the OPA, but he hadn't informed Earth or Mars of anything, which meant Nguyen was watching him too.

They weren't just scared. They were going to kill him.

Avasarala sat quietly for a long moment before she stood up and went back toward the game. Cotyar and Bobbie were at the end of a high-stakes round, which meant the pile of little bits of chocolate candy they were using for chips was almost five centimeters deep.

"Mr. Cotyar," Avasarala said. "Sergeant Draper. With me, please."

The cards all vanished. The men looked at each other nervously as she walked back into her bedroom. She closed the door behind them carefully. It didn't even click.

"I am about to do something that may pull a trigger," she said. "If I do this, the complexion of our situation may change."

Cotyar and Bobbie exchanged looks.

"I have some things I'd like to get out of storage," Bobbie said.

"I'll brief the men," Cotyar said.

"Ten minutes."

The lag between the *Guanshiyin* and the *Rocinante* was still too long for conversation, but it was less than it took to get a message back to Earth. The sense of being so far from home left her a little light-headed. Cotyar stepped into the room and nodded once. Avasarala opened her terminal and requested a tightbeam connection. She gave the transponder code for the *Rocinante*. Less than a minute later, the connection came back refused. She smiled to herself and opened a channel to ops.

"This is Assistant Undersecretary Avasarala," she said, as if there were anyone else on board who it might be. "What the fuck is wrong with your tightbeam?"

"I apologize, Madam Secretary," a young man with bright blue eyes and close-cut blond hair said. "That communication channel isn't available right now."

"Why the fuck isn't it available?"

"It's not available, ma'am."

"Fine. I didn't want to do this on the radio, but I can broadcast if I have to."

"I'm afraid that won't be possible," the boy said. Avasarala took a long breath and let it out through her teeth.

"Put the captain on," she said.

A moment later, the image jumped. The captain was a thin-faced man with the brown eyes of an Irish setter. The set of his mouth and his bloodless lips told her that he knew what was coming, at least in outline. For a moment, she just looked into the camera. It was a trick she'd learned when she'd just started off. Looking at the screen image let the other person feel they were being seen. Looking into the tiny black pinpoint of the lens itself left them feeling stared down.

"Captain. I have a high-priority message I need to send."

"I am very sorry. We're having technical difficulties with the communication array."

"Do you have a backup system? A shuttle we can power up? Anything?"

"Not at this time."

"You're lying to me," she said. Then, when he didn't answer: "I am making an official request that this yacht engage its emergency beacon and change course to the nearest aid."

"I'm not going to be able to do that, ma'am. If you will just be patient, we'll get you to Ganymede safe and in one piece. I'm sure any repairs we need can be done there."

Avasarala leaned close to the terminal.

"I can come up there and we can have this conversation personally," she said. "Captain. You know the laws as well as I do. Turn on the beacon or give me communications access."

"Ma'am, you are the guest of Jules-Pierre Mao, and I respect that. But Mr. Mao is the owner of this vessel, and I answer to him."

"No, then."

"I'm very sorry."

"You're making a mistake, shithead," Avasarala said, and dropped the connection.

Bobbie came into the room. Her face was bright, and there was a hunger about her, like a running dog straining at the leash. Gravity shifted a degree. A course correction, but not a change.

"How'd it go?" Bobbie asked.

"I am declaring this vessel in violation of laws and standards," Avasarala said. "Cotyar, you're witness to that."

"As you say, ma'am."

"All right, then. Bobbie. Get me control of this fucking ship."

Chapter Thirty-Eight: Bobbie

What else do you need from us?" Cotyar asked. Two of his people were moving the big crate marked FORMAL WEAR into Avasarala's room. They were using a large furniture dolly and grunting with effort. Even in the gentle quarter g of the *Guanshiyin*'s thrust, Bobbie's armor weighed over a hundred kilos.

"We're sure this room isn't under surveillance?" Bobbie said. "This is going to work a lot better if they have no idea what's about to happen."

Cotyar shrugged. "It has no functioning eavesdropping devices I've been able to detect."

"Okay, then," Bobbie said, rapping on the fiberglass crate with her knuckle. "Open it up."

Cotyar tapped something on his hand terminal and the crate's locks opened with a sharp click. Bobbie yanked the opened panel off and leaned it against the wall. Inside the crate, suspended in a web of elastic bands, was her suit.

Cotyar whistled. "A Goliath III. I can't believe they let you keep it."

Bobbie removed the helmet and put it on the bed, then began pulling the various other pieces out of the webbing and setting them on the floor. "They gave it to your tech guys to verify some video stored in the suit. When Avasarala tracked it down, it was in a closet, collecting dust. No one seemed to care when she took it."

She pulled out the suit's right arm. She hadn't expected them to get her any of the 2mm ammo the suit's integrated gun used, but was surprised to find that they'd completely removed the gun from the housing. It made sense to remove all the weapons before handing the suit off to a bunch of civilians, but it still annoyed her.

"Shit," she said. "Won't be shooting anyone, I guess."

"If you did," Cotyar said with a smile, "would the bullets even slow down as they went through both of the ship's hulls and let all the air out?"

"Nope," Bobbie said, laying the last piece of the suit on the floor, then pulling out the tools necessary to put it all back together again. "But that might be a point in my favor. The gun on this rig is designed to shoot through other people wearing comparable armor. Anything that will shoot through my suit here will probably also hole the ship. Which means—"

"None of the security personnel on this vessel will have weapons capable of penetrating your armor," Cotyar finished. "As you say. How many of my people will you want with you?"

"None," Bobbie said, attaching the fresh battery pack Avasarala's techs had provided to the back of the armor and getting a lovely green "fully charged" light from the panel. "Once I get started, the obvious counterplay will be to grab the undersecretary and hold her hostage. Preventing that is your job."

Cotyar smiled again. There was no humor in it.

"As you say."

It took Bobbie just under three hours to assemble and field prep her suit. It should have taken only two, but she forgave herself the extra hour by remembering that she was out of practice. The closer the suit got to completion, the tighter the knot in her stomach grew. Some of it was the natural tension that came before combat. And her time in the Marines had taught her to use it. To let the stress force her to recheck everything three times. Once she was in the thick of it, it would be too late.

But deep down, Bobbie knew that the possibility of violence wasn't the only thing twisting up her insides. It was impossible to forget what had happened the last time she'd worn this suit. The red enamel of her Martian camouflage was pitted and scraped from the exploding monster and her high-speed skid across Ganymede's ice. A tiny bit of fluid leakage on the knee reminded her of Private Hillman. Hilly, her friend. Wiping off the helmet's faceplate made her think of the last time she'd spoken to Lieutenant Givens, her CO, just before the monster had ripped him in two.

When the suit was finished and lying on the floor, opened up and waiting for her to climb inside, she felt a shudder run up her spine. For the first time ever, the inside looked small. Sepulchral.

"No," she said to no one but herself.

"No?" Cotyar asked, sitting on the floor next to her, holding the tools he thought she might need next. He'd been so quiet during the assembly procedure she'd sort of forgotten he was there.

"I'm not afraid of putting this back on," she said.

"Ah," Cotyar replied with a nod, then put the tools into the toolbox. "As you say."

Bobbie pushed herself to her feet and yanked the black unitard she wore under the armor out of the crate. Without thinking about it, she stripped down to her panties and pulled the skintight garment on. She was pulling the wire leads out of her armor and connecting them to the various sensors on the bodysuit when she noticed that Cotyar had turned his back to her, and that his usually light brown neck was turning beet red.

"Oh," she said. "Sorry. I've stripped down and put this on in front of my squaddies so many times I don't even think about it anymore."

"No reason to apologize," Cotyar said without turning around. "I was only taken by surprise."

He risked a peek over his left shoulder, and when he saw that she was fully covered by the bodysuit, he turned back to help her wire it up to the armor.

"You are," he said, then paused for a beat. "Lovely."

It was her turn to blush.

"Aren't you married?" Bobbie asked with a grin, happy for the distraction. The simple humanity in discomfort with mating signals made the monster in her head seem very far away.

"Yes," Cotyar replied, attaching the final lead to a sensor at the small of her back. "Very. But I'm not blind."

"Thank you," Bobbie said, and gave him a friendly pat on the shoulder. After a few moments' struggle with the tight spaces, she sat down into the suit's open chest and slid down until her legs and arms were fully inside. "Button me up."

Cotyar sealed up the chest as she'd shown him, then put the helmet on her and locked it in place. Inside the suit, her HUD flashed through the boot routine. A gentle, almost subliminal hum surrounded her. She activated the array of micro-motors and pumps that powered the exo-musculature, and then sat up.

Cotyar was looking at her, his face a question. Bobbie turned on the external speaker and said, "Yeah, it all looks good in here. Green across the board."

She pushed herself to her feet effortlessly and felt the old sensation of barely restrained power running through her limbs. She knew if she pushed off hard with her legs, she'd hit the ceiling with enough force to severely damage it. A sudden motion of her arm could hurl the heavy four-poster bed across the room or shatter Cotyar's spine. It made her move with the deliberate gentleness of long training.

Cotyar reached under his jacket and pulled out a sleek black pistol of the slug-throwing variety. Bobbie knew the security team had loaded them with high-impact plastic rounds, guaranteed not to knock holes in the ship. It was the same kind of round Mao's security team would be using. He started to hold it out to her, but then looked at the thickness of her armored fingers, and at the much smaller opening of the trigger guard, and shrugged apologetically.

"I won't need it," she said. Her voice sounded harsh, metallic, inhuman.

Cotyar smiled again.

"As you say."

Bobbie punched the button to call the keel elevator, then walked back and forth in the lounge, letting her reflexes get used to her armor. There was a nanosecond delay between attempting to move a limb and having the armor react. It made walking around feel vaguely dreamlike, as if the act of wanting to move your limbs and the moving of the limbs themselves were separate events. Hours of training and use had mostly overcome the sensation when Bobbie wore her armor, but it always took a few minutes of moving around to get past the oddness of it.

Avasarala walked into the lounge from the room they were using as the communications center and sat down at the bar. She poured herself a stiff shot of gin, then squeezed a piece of lime into it almost as an afterthought. The old lady had been drinking a lot more lately, but it wasn't Bobbie's place to point it out. Maybe it was helping her sleep.

When the elevator didn't arrive after several minutes, she thumped over to the panel and hit the button a few more times. A small display said OUT OF SERVICE.

"Damn," Bobbie said to herself. "They really are kidnapping us."

She'd left the external speakers on, and the harsh voice coming out of her suit echoed around the room. Avasarala didn't look up from her drink but said, "Remember what I said."

"Huh?" Bobbie said, not paying attention. She climbed awkwardly up the crew ladder to the deck hatch above her head and hit the button. The hatch slid open. That meant that everyone was still pretending that this wasn't a kidnapping. They could explain away the elevator. Explaining why the undersecretary was locked out of the rest of the ship would be harder. Maybe they figured a woman in her seventies would be reluctant to climb around the ship on ladders, so killing the lift was good enough. They might have been right. Avasarala certainly didn't look like she was up to a two-hundred-foot climb, even in the low gravity.

"None of these people were on Ganymede," Avasarala said.

"Okay," Bobbie replied to the seeming non sequitur.

"You won't be able to kill enough of them to bring your platoon back," Avasarala finished, tossing off the last of her gin, then pushing away from the bar and heading off to her room.

Bobbie didn't reply. She pulled herself up to the next deck and let the hatch slide shut behind her.

Her armor had been designed for exactly this sort of mission. The original Goliath-class scout suits had been built for Marine boarding parties in ship-to-ship engagements. That meant they were designed for maximum maneuverability in tight spaces. No matter how good the armor was, it was useless if the soldier wearing it couldn't climb ladders, slip through human-sized hatches, and maneuver gracefully in microgravity.

Bobbie climbed the ladder to the next deck hatch and hit the button. The console responded with a red warning light. A few moments of looking at the menus revealed why: They'd parked the crew elevator just above the hatch and then disabled it, creating a barricade. And that meant they knew something was up.

Bobbie looked around the room she was in, another relaxation lounge, nearly identical to the one she'd just left, until she found the likeliest place for them to have hidden their cameras. She waved. *This won't stop me, guys.*

She climbed back down and went into the luxurious bathroom space. On a ship this nice, it couldn't properly be called the head.

A few moments' probing found the fairly well-hidden bulkhead service hatch. It was locked. Bobbie tore it off the wall.

On the other side were a tangle of piping and a narrow corridor barely large enough to stuff her armor into. She climbed in and pulled herself along the pipes for two decks, then kicked the service hatch into the room and climbed in.

The compartment turned out to be a secondary galley, with a bank of stoves and ovens along one wall, several refrigeration units, and lots of counter space, all in gleaming stainless steel.

Her suit warned her that she was being targeted, and changed the HUD so that the normally invisible infrared beams aimed at her became faint red lines. Half a dozen were painting her chest, all coming from compact black weapons held by Mao-Kwik security personnel at the other end of the room.

Bobbie stood up. To their credit, the security goons didn't back up. Her HUD ran through the weapons database and informed her that the men were armed with 5mm submachine guns with a standard ammo capacity of three hundred rounds and a cyclic rate of ten rounds per second. Unless they were using high-explosive armor-piercing rounds, unlikely with the ship's hull right behind her, the suit rated their danger level as low.

Bobbie made sure her external speakers were still on and said, "Okay, fellas, let's—"

They opened fire.

For one long second, the entire galley was in chaos. High-impact plastic rounds bounced off her armor, deflected off the bulkheads, and skipped around the room. They blew apart containers of dried goods, hurled pots and pans off their magnetic hooks, and flung smaller utensils into the air in a cloud of stainless steel and plastic shards. One round took a particularly unlucky bounce and hit one of the security guards in the center of his nose, punching a hole into his head and dropping him to the floor with an almost comic look of surprise on his face.

Before two seconds could tick by, Bobbie was in motion, launching herself across the steel island in the center of the room and plowing into all five remaining guards with her arms out-stretched, like a football player going in for a tackle. They were hurled against the far bulkhead with a meaty thud, then slumped to the ground motionless. Her suit started to put up life-sign indicators on her HUD for them, but she shut it off without looking. She didn't want to know. One of the men stirred, then started to raise his gun. Bobbie gently shoved him, and he flew across the room to crumple against the far bulkhead. He didn't move again.

She glanced around the room, looking for cameras. She couldn't find one but hoped it was there anyway. If they'd seen this, maybe they wouldn't throw any more of their people at her.

At the keel ladder, she discovered that they'd blocked the elevator by jamming the floor hatch open with a crowbar. Basic ship safety protocols wouldn't allow the elevator to move to another deck unless the deck above was sealed. Bobbie yanked out the crowbar and threw it across the room, then hit the call button. The lift climbed up the ladder shaft to her level and stopped. She jumped on and hit the button that would take her to the bridge, eight decks up. Eight more pressure hatches.

Eight more possible ambushes.

She tightened her hands into fists until the knuckles stretched painfully inside her gauntlets. *Bring it.*

Three decks up the elevator stopped, the panel informing her that all the pressure hatches between her and the bridge had been overridden and forced open. They were willing to risk a hole in the ship emptying out half the ship's air rather than let her up to the bridge. It was sort of gratifying to be scarier than sudden decompression.

She climbed off the lift onto a deck that appeared to be mostly crew quarters, though it must have been evacuated. There wasn't a soul in sight. A quick tour revealed twelve small crew cabins and two bathrooms that could reasonably be called heads. No gold plating on the fixtures for the crew. No open bar. No twenty-four-hour-a-day food service. Looking at the fairly Spartan living conditions of the average crew member on the *Guanshiyin* brought home Avasarala's last words to her. These were just sailors. None of them deserved to die for what had happened on Ganymede.

Bobbie found herself glad she didn't have a gun.

She found another access hatch in the head and tore it open. But to her surprise, the service corridor ended just a few feet above her head. Something in the structure of the ship was cutting her off. Having never seen the *Guanshiyin* from the outside, she had no idea what it might be. But she needed to get another five decks up, and she wasn't about to let this stop her.

A ten-minute search turned up a service hatch through the outer hull. She'd torn off two inner hull hatches on two different decks, so if she got it open, those two decks would lose their air. But the central ladder corridor was sealed at Avasarala's deck, so her people would be fine. And the whole reason she was doing this was the sealed hatch to the upper decks, which seemed to be where most of the crew was.

She thought about the six men down in the galley and felt a pang. Sure, they'd shot first, but if any of them were still alive, she had no desire to asphyxiate them in their sleep.

It turned out not to be a problem. The hatch led into a small airlock chamber, about the size of a closet. A minute later it had cycled through and she climbed out onto the outer hull of the ship.

Triple-hulled. Of course. The lord of the Mao-Kwik empire wasn't going to trust his expensive skin to anything that wasn't the safest humans could build. And the ostentatious design of the ship extended to her outer hull as well. While most military ships were painted a flat black that made them hard to spot visually in space, most civilian ships either were left an unpainted gray or were painted in basic corporate colors.

The *Guanshiyin* had a mural painted on it in vivid colors. Bobbie was too close to see what it was, but under her feet were what appeared to be grass and the hoof of a giant horse. Mao had the hull of his ship painted with a mural that included horses and grass. When almost no one would ever see it.

Bobbie made sure her boot and glove mags were set strong enough to handle the quarter-g thrust the ship was still under, and started climbing up the side. She quickly reached the spot where the dead end between the hulls began, and saw that it was an empty shuttle bay. If only Avasarala had let her do this *before* Mao had run off with the shuttle.

Triple hulls, Bobbie thought. Maximum redundancy.

On a hunch, she crawled across the ship to the other side. Sure enough, there was a second shuttle bay. But the ship in it wasn't a standard short-flight shuttle. It was long and sleek, with an engine housing twice as large as that of a normal ship its size. Written in proud red letters across the bow of the ship was the name *Razorback*.

A racing pinnace.

Bobbie crawled back around to the empty cargo bay and used the airlock there to enter the ship. The military override codes her suit sent to the locked door worked, to her surprise. The airlock led to the deck just below the bridge, the one used for shuttle supply storage and maintenance. The center of the deck was taken up by a large machine shop. Standing in it were the captain of the *Guanshiyin* and his senior staff. There were no security personnel or weapons in sight.

The captain tapped his ear in an ancient *can you hear me?* gesture. Bobbie nodded one fist at him, then turned the external speakers back on and said, "Yes."

"We are not military personnel," the captain said. "We can't defend ourselves from military hardware. But I'm not going to turn this vessel over to you without knowing your intentions. My XO is on the deck above us, prepared to scuttle the ship if we can't come to terms."

Bobbie smiled at him, though she didn't know if he could see it through her helmet. "You've illegally detained a high-level member of the UN government. Acting in my role as a member of her security team, I have come to demand that you deliver her immediately to the port of her choosing, at best possible speed."

She shrugged with her hands in the Belter way. "Or, you can blow yourselves up. Seems like a drastic overreaction to having to give the undersecretary her radio privileges back."

The captain nodded and relaxed visibly. Whatever happened next, it wasn't like he had any choice. And since he didn't have any choice, he didn't have any responsibility. "We were following orders. You'll note that in the log when you take command."

"I'll see that she knows."

The captain nodded again. "Then the ship is yours."

Bobbie opened her radio link to Cotyar. "We win. Put Her Majesty on, will you?"

While she waited for Avasarala, Bobbie said to the captain, "There are six injured security people down below. Get a medical team down there."

"Bobbie?" Avasarala said over the radio.

"The ship is yours, madam."

"Great. Tell the captain we need to make best possible speed to intercept Holden. We're getting to him before Nguyen does."

"Uh, this is a pleasure yacht. It's built to run at low g for comfort. I'd bet it can do a full g if it needs to, but I doubt it does much more than that."

"Admiral Nguyen is about to kill everyone that actually might know what the fuck is going on." Avasarala didn't quite yell. "We don't have time to cruise around like we're trying to pick up fucking rent boys!"

"Huh," Bobbie said. Then, a moment later: "If this is a race, I know where there's a racing ship…"

Chapter Thirty-Nine: Holden

Holden pulled himself a cup of coffee from the galley coffeepot, and the strong smell filled the room. He could feel the eyes of the crew on his back with an almost physical force. He'd called them all there, and once they'd assembled and taken their seats, he'd turned his back on them and started making coffee. *I'm stalling for time, because I forgot how I wanted to say this.* He put some sugar in his coffee even though he always drank it black, just because stirring took a few more seconds.

"So. Who are we?" he said as he stirred.

His question was met with silence, so he turned around and leaned back against the countertop, holding his unwanted cup of coffee and continuing to stir.

"Seriously," he said. "Who are we? It's the question I keep coming back to."

"Uh," Amos said, and shifted in his seat. "My name's Amos, Cap. You feeling okay?"

No one else spoke. Alex was staring at the table in front of him, his dark scalp shining through his thinning hair under the harsh white of the galley lights. Prax was sitting on the counter next to the sink and looking at his hands. He flexed them periodically as though trying to figure out what they were for.

Only Naomi was looking at him. Her hair was pulled up into a thick tail, and her dark, almond-shaped eyes were staring right into his. It was fairly disconcerting.

"I've recently figured out something about myself," Holden continued, not letting Naomi's unblinking stare throw him off. "I've been treating you all like you owe me something. And none of you do. And that means I've been treating you like shit."

"No," Alex started without looking up.

"Yes," Holden said, and stopped until Alex looked up at him. "Yes. You maybe more than anyone else. Because I've been scared to death and cowards always look for an easy target. And you're about the nicest person I know, Alex. So I treated you badly because I could get away with it. And I hope you forgive me for that, because I really hate that I did it."

"Sure, I forgive you, Cap," Alex said with a smile and his heavy drawl.

"I'll try to earn it," Holden answered, bothered by the easy reply. "But Alex said something else to me recently that I've been thinking about a lot. He reminded me that none of you are employees. We're not on the *Canterbury*. We don't work for Pur'n'Kleen anymore. And I don't own this ship any more than any of you do. We took contracts from the OPA in exchange for pocket money and ship expenses, but we never talked about how to handle the excess."

"You opened that account," Alex said.

"Yeah, there's a bank account with all of the extra money in it. Last I checked, there was just under eighty grand in there. I said we'd keep it for ship expenses, but who am I to make that decision for the rest of you? That's not *my* money. It's *our* money. *We* earned it."

"But you're the captain," Amos said, then pointed at the coffeepot.

While Holden fixed him a cup, he said, "Am I? I was the XO on the *Canterbury*. It made sense for me to be the captain after the *Cant* got nuked."

He handed the cup to Amos and sat down at the table with the rest of the crew. "But we haven't been those guys for a long time now. Who we are now is four people who don't actually work for anyone—"

Prax cleared his throat at this, and Holden nodded an apology at him. "Anyone long term, let's say. There is no corporation or government granting me authority over this crew. We're just four people who sort of own a ship that Mars will probably try to take back the first chance they get."

"This is legitimate salvage," Alex said.

"And I hope the Martians find that compelling when you explain it to them," Holden replied. "But it doesn't change my point: Who are we?"

Naomi nodded a fist at him. "I see where you're going. We've left a lot of this kind of stuff just up in the air because we've been running full tilt since the *Canterbury*."

"And this," Holden said, "is the perfect time to figure that stuff out. We've got a contract to help Prax find his little girl, and he's paying us so we can afford to run the ship. Once we find Mei, how do we find the next job? Do we go looking for a *next* job? Do we sell the *Roci* to the OPA and retire on Titan? I think we need to know those things."

No one spoke. Prax pushed himself off the counter and started rummaging through the cabinets. After a minute or two, he pulled out a package that read CHOCOLATE PUDDING on the side and said, "Can I make this?"

Naomi laughed. Alex said, "Knock yourself out, Doc."

Prax pulled a bowl out and began mixing ingredients into it.

Oddly enough, because the botanist was paying attention to something else, it created a sense of intimacy for the crew. The outsider was doing outside things, leaving them to talk among themselves. Holden wondered if Prax knew that and was doing it on purpose.

Amos slurped down the last of his coffee and said, "So, you called this meeting, Cap. You have something in mind?"

"Yeah," Holden said, taking a moment to think. "Yeah, kind of."

Naomi put a hand on his arm and smiled at him. "We're listening."

"I think we get married," he said with a wink at Naomi. "Make it all nice and legal."

"Wait," she said. The look on her face was more horrified than Holden would have hoped.

"No, no, that's sort of a joke," Holden said. "But only sort of. See, I was thinking about my parents. They formed their initial collective partnership because of the farm. They were all friends, they wanted to buy the property in Montana, and so they made a group large enough to afford it. It wasn't sexual. Father Tom and Father Caesar were already sexual partners and monogamous. Mother Tamara was single. Fathers Joseph and Anton and Mothers Elise and Sophie were already a polyamorous civil unit. Father Dimitri joined a month later when he started dating Tamara. They formed a civil union to own the property jointly. They wouldn't have been able to afford it if they were all paying taxes for separate kids, so they had me as a group."

"Earth," Alex said, "is a weird freakin' place."

"Eight parents to a baby ain't exactly common," Amos said.

"But it makes a lot of economic sense with the baby tax," Holden said. "So it's not unheard of, either."

"What about people making babies without paying the tax?" Alex asked.

"It's tougher to get away with than you think," Holden said. "Unless you never go to a doctor or only use black markets."

Amos and Naomi shared a quick look that Holden pretended not to see.

"Okay," Holden continued. "Forget babies for a minute. What I'm talking about is incorporating. If we plan to stick together, let's make it legal. We can draft up incorporation papers with one of the independent outer planets stations, like Ceres or Europa, and become joint owners of this enterprise."

"What," Naomi said, "does our little company do?"

"Exactly," Holden said in triumph.

"Uh," Amos said again.

"No, I mean, that's exactly what I've been asking," Holden continued. "Who are we? What do we want to do? Because when this contract with Prax is over, the bank account will be well padded, we'll own a high-tech warship, and we'll be free to do whatever we damn well want to do."

"Jesus, Cap," Amos said. "I just got half a hard-on."

"I know, right?" Holden replied with a grin.

Prax stopped mixing things in his bowl and stuck it in the refrigerator. He turned and looked at them with the careful movements of someone who feared he'd be asked to leave if anyone noticed him. Holden moved over to him and put an arm around his shoulder. "Our friend Prax here can't be the only guy who needs to hire a ship like this, right?"

"We're faster and meaner than just about anything a civvy can dig up," Alex said with a nod.

"And when we find Mei, it will be as high profile as you could hope for," Holden said. "What better advertising could we get than that?"

"Admit it, Cap," Amos said. "You just kind of like being famous."

"If it gets us jobs, sure."

"We're much more likely to wind up broke, out of air, and drifting through space dead," Naomi said.

"That's always a possibility," Holden admitted. "But, man, aren't you ready to be your own boss for a change? If we find we can't make it on our own, we can always sell the ship for a giant sack of money and go our separate ways. We have an escape plan."

"Yeah," Amos said. "Fuck yeah. Let's do this. How do we start?"

"Well," Holden said. "That's another new thing. I think we have to vote. No one of us owns the ship, so I think we vote on important stuff like this from now on."

Amos said, "All in favor of making ourselves into a company to own the ship, raise your hand."

To Holden's delight, they all raised their hands. Even Prax started to, realized he was doing it, and then put it back down.

"I'll get us an attorney on Ceres and start the paperwork," Holden said. "But that leads to something else. A company can own a ship, but a company can't be the registered captain. We'll need to vote for whoever holds that title."

Amos started laughing. "Gimme a fucking break. Raise your hand if Holden isn't the captain."

No hands went up.

"See?" Amos said.

Holden started to speak but stopped when something uncomfortable happened in his throat and behind his sternum.

"Look," Amos said, his face kind. "You're just that guy."

Naomi nodded and smiled at Holden, which only made the ache in his chest pleasantly worse. "I'm an engineer," she said. "There isn't a program on this ship I haven't tweaked or rewritten, and I could probably take her apart and put her back together by myself at this point. But I can't bluff at cards. And I'm never going to be the one that stares down the joint navies of the inner planets and says, 'Back the hell off.' "

"Roger that," Alex said. "And I just want to fly my baby. That's all and that's it. If I get to do that, I'm happy."

Holden started to speak, but to his surprise and embarrassment, the minute his mouth opened, his eyes teared up. Amos saved him.

"I'm just a grease monkey," he said. "I push tools. And I mostly wait for Naomi to tell me when and where to push 'em. I got no desire to run anything bigger than that machine shop. You're the talker. I've seen you face down Fred Johnson, UN naval captains, OPA cowboys, and drugged-up space pirates. You talk out your ass better than most people do using their mouth and sober."

"Thank you," Holden finally said. "I love you guys. You know that, right?"

"Plus which," Amos continued, "no one on this ship will try harder to jump in front of a bullet for me than you will. I find that appealing in a captain."

"Thanks," Holden said again.

"Sounds settled to me," Alex said, getting up and heading toward the ladder. "Gonna go make sure we're not aimed at a rock or somethin'."

Holden watched him go and was gratified to see him wiping his eyes as soon as he got out of the room. It was okay to be a weepy little kid as long as everyone else was being a weepy little kid.

Prax gave him an awkward pat on the shoulder and said, "Come back to the galley in an hour. Pudding will be ready." Then he wandered out and into his cabin. He was already reading messages on his hand terminal as he closed the door.

"Okay," Amos said. "What now?"

"Amos," Naomi said, getting up and walking over to stand in front of Holden. "Please take ops for me for a while."

"Roger that," Amos said, the grin existing only in his voice. He climbed the ladder up and out of sight, the pressure hatch opening for him, then slamming behind him when he went.

"Hi," Holden said. "Was that right?"

She nodded. "I feel like I got you back. I was worried I'd never see you again."

"If you hadn't yanked me out of that hole I was digging for myself, neither of us would have."

Naomi leaned forward to kiss him, and he wrapped his arms around her and pulled her tight. When they stopped to breathe, he said, "Is this too soon?"

She said, "Shut up," and kissed him again. Without breaking the kiss, she pulled her body away from his and began fumbling with the zipper of his jumpsuit. Those ridiculous Martian military jumpsuits that had come with the ship, TACHI stenciled across the back. Now that they were going to have their own company, they'd need to get something better. Jumpsuits made a lot of sense for shipboard life, with changing gravities and oily mechanical parts. But something actually tailored to fit them all, and in their own colors. ROCINANTE on the back.

Naomi's hand got inside the jumpsuit and under his T-shirt, and he lost all thought of fashion choices.

"My bunk or yours?" he said.

"You have your own bunk?"

Not anymore.

Making love to Naomi had always been different than with anyone else. Some of it was physical. She was the only Belter he'd ever been with, and that meant she was physiologically different in some ways. But that wasn't the most notable part for him. What made Naomi different was that they'd been friends for five years before they'd slept together.

It wasn't a flattering testament to his character, and it made him cringe when he thought about it now, but he'd always been pretty shallow when it came to sex. He'd picked out potential sexual partners within minutes of meeting a new woman, and because he was pretty and charming, he usually got the ones he was interested in. He'd always been quick to allow himself to mistake infatuation for genuine affection. One of his most painful memories was the day Naomi had called him on it. Exposed for him the little game he played in which he convinced himself he genuinely cared for the women he was sleeping with so that he wouldn't feel like a user.

But he had been. The fact that the women were using him in turn didn't make him feel better about it.

Because Naomi was so physically different from the ideal that growing up on Earth had created, he had just not seen her as a potential sexual partner when they'd first met. And that meant he'd grown to know her as a person without any of the sexual baggage he usually carried. When his feelings for her grew beyond friendship, he was surprised.

And somehow, that changed everything about sex. The movements might all be the same, but the desire to communicate affection rather than demonstrate prowess changed what everything meant. After their first time together, he'd lain in bed for hours feeling like he'd been doing it wrong for years and only just realized it.

He was doing that again now.

Naomi slept on her side next to him, her arm thrown across his chest and her thigh across his, her belly against his hip and her breast against his ribs. It had never been like this with anyone before her, and this was what it was supposed to be like. This sense of complete ease and contentment. He could imagine a future in which he hadn't been able to prove he'd changed, and in which she never came back to him. He could see years and decades of sexual partners, always trying to recapture this feeling and never being able to because, of course, it wasn't really about the sex.

Thinking about it made his stomach hurt.

Naomi talked in her sleep. Her mouth whispered something mysterious into his neck, and the sudden tickle woke him up enough to realize he'd been drifting off to sleep. He hugged her head to his chest and kissed the top of it, then rolled over onto his side and let himself fade.

The wall monitor over the bed buzzed.

"Who is it?" he said, suddenly as tired as he could remember ever having been. He'd just closed his eyes a second earlier, and he knew he'd never be able to open them now.

"Me, Cap," Alex said. Holden wanted to shout at him but couldn't find the energy.

"Okay."

"You need to see this," was all Alex said, but something in his voice woke Holden up. He sat up, moving Naomi's arm out of the way. She said something in sleep-talk but didn't wake.

"Okay," he said again, turning on the monitor.

A white-haired older woman with very strange facial features looked out at him. It took his addled mind a second to recognize that she wasn't deformed, just being crushed by a heavy burn. With a voice distorted by g-forces mashing down on her throat, she said, "My name is Chrisjen Avasarala. I'm the UN assistant undersecretary of executive administration. A UN admiral has dispatched six Munroe-class destroyers from the Jupiter system to destroy your ship. Track this transponder code and come meet me or you and everyone on your ship will die. This is not a fucking joke."

Chapter Forty: Prax

Thrust pressed him into the crash couch. It was only four g, but even a single full g called for very nearly the full medical cocktail. He had lived in a place that kept him weak. He'd known that, of course, but mostly in terms of xylem and phloem. He had taken the normal low-g medical supplements to encourage bone growth. He had exercised as much as the guidelines asked. Usually. But always in the back of his mind, he'd thought it was idiocy. He was a botanist. He'd live and die in the familiar tunnels, with their comfortable low gravity—less than a fifth of Earth's. An Earth he would never have reason to go to. There was even less reason he would ever need to suffer through a high-g burn. And yet here he lay in the gel like he was at the bottom of an ocean. His vision was blurred, and he fought for every inhalation. When his knee hyperextended, he tried to scream but couldn't catch his breath.

The others would be better. They'd be used to things like this.

They knew that they'd survive. His hindbrain wasn't at all sure. Needles dug into the flesh of his thigh, injecting him with another cocktail of hormones and paralytics. Cold like the touch of ice spread from the injection points, and a paradoxical sense of ease and dread filled his mind. At this point, it was a balancing act between keeping his blood vessels elastic enough that they wouldn't burst and robust enough that they wouldn't collapse. His mind slid out from under him, leaving something calculating and detached in its place. It was like pure executive function without a sense of self. What had been his mind knew what he had known, remembered the things he remembered, but wasn't him.

In this altered state of consciousness, he found himself taking inventory. Would it be okay to die now? Did he want to live, and if he did, on what terms? He considered the loss of his daughter as if it were a physical object. Loss was the soft pink of crushed seashell, where once it had been the red of old, scabby blood. The red of an umbilical cord waiting to drop free. He remembered Mei, what she had looked like. The delight in her laugh. She wasn't like that anymore. If she was alive. But she was probably dead.

In his gravity-bent mind, he smiled. Of course, his lips couldn't react. He'd been wrong. All along, he'd been wrong. The hours of sitting by himself, telling himself that Mei was dead. He'd thought he was toughening himself. Preparing himself for the worst. That wasn't right at all. He'd said it, he'd tried to believe it, because the thought was comforting.

If she was dead, she wasn't being tortured. If she was dead, she wasn't scared. If she was dead, then the pain would be all his, entirely his, and she would be safe. He noticed without pleasure or pain that it was a pathological mental frame. But he'd had his life and his daughter taken from him, had survived in near starvation while the cascade effect ate what was left of Ganymede, had been shot at, had faced a half-alien killing machine, and was now known throughout the solar system as a wife beater and pedophile. He had no reason to be sane. It wouldn't help him.

And on top of that, his knee *really* hurt.

Somewhere far, far away, in a place with light and air, something buzzed three times, and the mountain rolled off his sternum. Coming back to himself was like rising from the bottom of a pool.

"Okay, y'all," Alex said across the ship's system. "We're callin' this dinner. Take a couple minutes for your livers to crawl up off your spinal cords, and we'll meet up in the galley. We've only got fifty minutes, so enjoy it while you can."

Prax took a deep breath, blowing it out between his teeth, and then sat up. His whole body felt bruised. His hand terminal claimed the thrust was at one-third g, but it felt like more and less than that. He swung his legs over the edge, and his knee made a wet, grinding pop. He tapped at his terminal.

"Um, I'm not sure I can walk," he said. "My knee."

"Hang tight, Doc." Amos' voice came from the speaker. "I'll come take a look at it. I'm pretty much the closest thing we've got to a medic unless you wanna hand it over to the med bay."

"Just don't try to weld him back together," Holden said. "It doesn't work."

The link went silent. While he waited, Prax checked his incoming messages. The list was too long for the screen, but that had been true since the initial message had gone out. The message titles had changed.

> BABY RAPERS SHOULD BE TORTURED TO DEATH
> DON'T LISTEN TO THE HATERS
> I BELIEVE YOU
> MY FATHER DID THE SAME THING TO ME
> TURN TO JESUS BEFORE IT'S TOO LATE

He didn't open them. He checked the newsfeeds under his own name and Mei's and had seven thousand active feeds with those keywords. Nicola's only had fifty.

There had been a time that he'd loved Nicola, or thought that he had. He'd wanted to have sex with her as badly as he'd wanted anything before in his life. He told himself there had been good times. Nights they'd spent together. Mei had come from Nicola's body. It was hard to believe that something so precious and central to his life had also been part of a woman who, by the evidence, he'd never really known. Even as the father of her child, he hadn't known the woman who could have made that recording.

He opened the hand terminal's recording fields, centered the camera on himself, and licked his lips.

"Nicola..."

Twenty seconds later, he closed the field and erased the recording. He had nothing to say. *Who are you, and who do you think I am?* came closest, and he didn't care about the answer to either one.

He went back to the messages, filtering on the names of the people who'd been helping him investigate. There was nothing new since the last time.

"Hey, Doc," Amos said, lumbering into the small room.

"I'm sorry," Prax said, putting his terminal back into its holder beside the crash couch. "It was just that during that last burn..."

He gestured to his knee. It was swollen, but not as badly as he'd expected. He'd thought it would be twice its normal size, but the anti-inflammatories that had been injected into his veins were doing their job. Amos nodded, put a hand on Prax's sternum, and pushed him back into the gel.

"I got a toe that pops out sometimes," Amos said. "Little tiny joint, but get it at the wrong angle on a fast burn, hurts like a bitch. Try not to tense up, Doc."

Amos bent the knee twice, feeling the joint grind. "This ain't that bad. Here, straighten it out. Okay."

Amos wrapped one hand around Prax's ankle, braced the other on the frame of the couch, and pulled slowly and irresistibly. Prax's knee bloomed with pain, and then a deep, wet pop and a nauseating sensation of tendons shifting against bone.

"There you go," Amos said. "We go back into burn, make sure you got that leg in the right place. Hyperextend that again right now, we'll pop your kneecap off, okay?"

"Right," Prax said, starting to sit up.

"I'm sorry as hell to do this, Doc," Amos said, putting a hand on his chest, pushing him back down. "I mean, you're having a lousy day and all. But you know how it is."

Prax frowned. Every muscle in his face felt bruised.

"What is it?"

"All this bullshit they're saying about you and the kid? That's all just bullshit, right?"

"Of course," Prax said.

"Because you know, sometimes things happen, you didn't even mean them to. Have a hard day, lose your temper, maybe? Or shit, you get drunk. Some of the things I've done when I really tied one on? I don't even know about until later." Amos smiled. "I'm just saying if there's a grain of truth, something that's getting all exaggerated, it'd be better if we knew it now, right?"

"I never did anything that she said."

"It's okay to tell me the truth, Doc. I understand. Sometimes guys do stuff. Doesn't make 'em bad."

Prax pushed Amos' hand aside and brought himself up to sitting. His knee felt much better.

"Actually," he said, "it does. That makes them bad."

Amos' expression relaxed, his smile changed in a way Prax couldn't quite understand.

"All right, Doc. Like I said, I'm sorry as hell. But I did have to ask."

"It's okay," Prax said, standing up. For a moment, the knee seemed like it might give, but it didn't. Prax took a tentative step, then another. It would work. He turned toward the galley, but the conversation wasn't finished. "If I had. If I had done those things, that would have been okay with you?"

"Oh, fuck no. I'd have broken your neck and thrown you out the airlock," Amos said, clapping him on the shoulder.

"Ah," Prax said, a gentle relief loosening in his chest. "Thank you."

"Anytime."

The other three were in the galley when Prax and Amos got

there, but it still felt half full. Less. Naomi and Alex were sitting across the table from each other. Neither of them looked as ruined as Prax felt. Holden turned from the wall with a formed-foam bowl in either hand. The brown slurry in them smelled of heat and earth and cooked leaves. As soon as it caught his nose, Prax was ravenous.

"Lentil soup?" Holden asked as Prax and Amos sat on either side of Alex.

"That would be wonderful," Prax said.

"I'll just take a tube of goo," Amos said. "Lentils give me gas, and I can't see popping an intestine next time we accelerate being fun for anyone."

Holden put a fresh bowl in front of Prax and handed a white tube with a black plastic nipple to Amos, then sat beside Naomi. They didn't touch, but the connection between them was unmistakable. He wondered whether Mei had ever wanted him to reconcile with Nicola. Impossible now.

"Okay, Alex," Holden said. "What've we got?"

"Same thing we had before," Alex said. "Six destroyers burning like hell toward us. A matching force burning after them, and a racing pinnace heading away from us on the other side."

"Wait," Prax said. "Away from us?"

"They're matching our course. Already did the turnaround, and they're getting up to speed to join us."

Prax closed his eyes, picturing the vectors.

"We're almost there, then?" he said.

"Very nearly," Alex said. "Eighteen, twenty hours."

"How's it going to play out? Are the Earth ships going to catch us?"

"They're gonna catch the hell out of us," Alex said, "but not before we get that pinnace. Call it four days after, maybe."

Prax took a spoonful of the soup. It tasted just as good as it smelled. Green, dark leaves were mixed in with the lentils, and he spread one open with his spoon, trying to identify it. Spinach, maybe. The stem margin didn't look quite right, but it had been cooked, after all...

"How sure are we this isn't a trap?" Amos asked.

"We aren't," Holden said. "But I don't see how it would work."

"If they want us in custody instead of dead," Naomi suggested. "We are talking about opening our airlock for someone way high up in the Earth government."

"So she is who she says she is?" Prax asked.

"Looks like it," Holden said.

Alex raised a hand.

"Well, if it's talk to some little gramma from the UN or get my ass shot off by six destroyers, I'm thinkin' we can break out the cookies and tea, right?"

"It would be late in the game to go for another plan," Naomi said. "It makes me damn uncomfortable having Earth saving me from Earth, though."

"Structures are never monolithic," Prax said. "There's more genetic variation within Belters or Martians or Earthers than there is between them. Evolution would predict some divisions within the group structures and alliances with out-members. You see the same thing in ferns."

"Ferns?" Naomi asked.

"Ferns can be very aggressive," Prax said.

A soft chime interrupted them: three rising notes, like bells gently struck.

"Okay, suck it down," Alex said. "That's the fifteen-minute warning."

Amos made a prodigious sucking sound, the white tube withering at his lips. Prax put down his spoon and lifted the soup bowl to his lips, not wanting to leave a drop of it. Holden did the same, then started gathering up the used bowls.

"Anyone needs to hit the head, this is the time," he said. "We'll talk again in..."

"Eight hours," Alex said.

"Eight hours," Holden repeated.

Prax felt his chest go tight. Another round of crushing acceleration. Hours of the couch's needles propping up his failing metab-
olism. It sounded like hell. He rose from the table, nodded to
everyone, and went back to his bunk. His knee was much better.
He hoped it would still be when he next got up. The ten-minute
chime sounded. He lay down on the couch, trying to align his
body perfectly, then waited. Waited.

He rolled over and grabbed his hand terminal. Seven new
incoming messages. Two of them supportive, three hateful, one
addressed to the wrong person, and one a financial statement from
the charity fund. He didn't bother reading them.

He turned on the camera.

"Nicola," he said. "I don't know what they told you. I don't
know if you really think all those things that you said. But I know
I never touched you in anger, even at the end. And if you really
felt afraid of me, I don't know why it was. Mei is the one thing
that I love more than anything in life. I'd die before I let anyone
hurt her. And now half the solar system thinks I hurt her…"

He stopped the recording and began again.

"Nicola. Honestly, I didn't think we had anything left between
us to betray."

He stopped. The five-minute warning chimed as he ran his fingers through his hair. Each individual follicle ached. He wondered
if this was why Amos kept his head shaved. There were so many
things about being on a ship that didn't occur to you until you
were actually there.

"Nicola…"

He erased all the recordings and logged into the charity bank
account interface. There was a secure request format that could
encrypt and send an authorized transfer as soon as light-speed
delivered it to the bank's computers. He filled it all out quickly.
The two-minute warning sounded, louder and more insistent.
With thirty seconds left, he sent her money back. There was nothing else for them to say.

He put the hand terminal in place and lay back. The computer counted backward from twenty, and the mountain rolled back over him.

"How's the knee?" Amos asked.

"Pretty good," Prax said. "I was surprised. I thought there'd be more damage."

"Didn't hyperextend this time," Amos said. "Did okay with my toe too."

A deep tone rang through the ship, and the deck shifted under Prax. Holden, standing just to Prax's right, moved the rifle to his left hand and touched a control panel.

"Alex?"

"Yeah, it was little rough. Sorry about that, but... Hold on. Yeah, Cap. We've got seal. And they're knocking."

Holden shifted the rifle back to his other hand. Amos also had a weapon at the ready. Naomi stood beside him, nothing in her hands but a terminal linked to ship operations. If something went wrong, being able to control ship functions might be more useful than a gun. They all wore the articulated armor of the Martian military that had come with the ship. The paired ships were accelerating at a third of a g. The Earth destroyers still barreled down toward them.

"So I'm guessing the firearms mean you're thinking trap, Cap'n?" Amos asked.

"Nothing wrong with an honor guard," Holden said.

Prax held up his hand.

"You don't ever get one again," Holden said. "No offense."

"No, I was just... I thought honor guards were usually on the same side as the people they're guarding?"

"We may be stretching the definitions a little here," Naomi said. Her voice had just a trace of tension in it.

"She's just a little old politician," Holden said. "And that pinnace can't hold more than two people. We've got her outnumbered. And if things get ugly, Alex is watching from the pilot's seat. You are watching, right?"

"Oh yeah," Alex said.

"So if there are any surprises, Naomi can pop us loose and Alex can get us out of here."

"That won't help with the destroyers, though," Prax said.

Naomi put a hand on his arm, squeezing him gently.

"I'm not sure you're helping, Prax."

The outer airlock cycled open with a distant hum. The lights clicked from red to green.

"Whoa," Alex said.

"Problem?" Holden snapped.

"No, it's just—"

The inner door opened, and the biggest person Prax had seen in his entire life stepped into the room wearing a suit of some sort of strength-augmenting armor. If it weren't for the transparent faceplate, he would have thought it was a two-meter-tall bipedal robot. Through the faceplate, Prax saw a woman's features: large dark eyes and coffee-with-cream skin. Her gaze raked them with the palpable threat of violence. Beside him, Amos took an unconscious step back.

"You're the captain," the woman said, the suit's speakers making her voice sound artificial and amplified. It didn't sound like a question.

"I am," Holden said. "I've got to say, you looked a little different on-screen."

The joke fell flat and the giant stepped into the room.

"Planning to shoot me with that?" she asked, pointing toward Holden's gun with a massive gauntleted fist.

"Would it work?"

"Probably not," the giant said. She took another small step forward, her armor whining when she moved. Holden and Amos took a matching step back.

"Call it an honor guard, then," Holden said.

"I'm honored. Will you put them away now?"

"Sure."

Two minutes later, the guns were stowed, and the huge woman, who still hadn't given her name, tapped something inside the helmet with her chin and said, "Okay. You're clear."

The airlock cycled again, red to green, with the hum of the opening doors. The woman who came in this time was smaller than any of them. Her gray hair was spiking out in all directions, and the orange sari she wore hung strangely in the low thrust gravity.

"Undersecretary Avasarala," Holden said. "Welcome aboard. If there's anything I can—"

"You're Naomi Nagata," the wizened little woman said.

Holden and Naomi exchanged glances, and Naomi shrugged.

"I am."

"How the fuck do you keep your hair like that? I look like a hedgehog's been humping my skull."

"Um—"

"Looking the part is half of what's going to keep you all alive. We don't have time to screw around. Nagata, you get me looking pretty and girlish. Holden—"

"I'm an engineer, not a damned hairstylist," Naomi said, anger creeping into her voice.

"Ma'am," Holden said, "this is my ship and my crew. Half of us aren't even Earth citizens, and we don't just take your commands."

"All right. Ms. Nagata, if we're going to keep this ship from turning into an expanding ball of hot gas, we need to make a press statement, and I'm not prepared to do that. Would you please assist me?"

"Okay," Naomi said.

"Thank you. And, Captain? You need a fucking shave."

Chapter Forty-One: Avasarala

After the *Guanshiyin*, the *Rocinante* seemed dour, mean, and utilitarian. There was no plush carpeting, only fabric-covered foam to soften corners and angles where soldiers might be thrown when the ship maneuvered violently. Instead of cinnamon and honey, the air had the plastic-and-heat smell of military air recyclers. And there were no expansive desk, no wide solitaire-ready bed, and no private space apart from a captain's lounge the size of a public toilet stall.

Most of the footage they'd taken had been in the cargo bays, angled so that no ammunition or weaponry was in the image. Someone who knew Martian military vessels could tell where they were. To everyone else, it would be an open space with cargo crates in the background. Naomi Nagata had helped put the release together—she was a surprisingly good visual editor—and when it became clear that none of the men could manage a professional-sounding voice-over, she'd done that too.

The crew assembled in the medical bay, where the mechanic Amos Burton had changed the feed to display from her hand terminal. Now he was sitting on one of the patient beds, his legs crossed, smiling amiably. If Avasarala hadn't seen the intelligence files on Holden's crew, she'd never have guessed what the man was capable of.

The others were spread out in a rough semicircle. Bobbie was sitting beside Alex Kamal, the Martians unconsciously grouping together. Praxidike Meng stood at the back of the room. Avasarala couldn't tell if her presence made him uncomfortable or if he was always like that.

"Okay," she said. "Last chance for feedback."

"Wish I had some popcorn," Amos said, and the medical scanner flashed once, showed a broadcast code and then white block letters: FOR IMMEDIATE RELEASE.

Avasarala and Holden appeared on the screen. She was speaking, her hands out before her as if illustrating a point. Holden, looking sober, leaned toward her. Naomi Nagata's voice was calm, strong, and professional.

"In a surprising development, the deputy to Undersecretary of Executive Administration Sadavir Errinwright met with OPA representative James Holden and a representative of the Martian military today to address concerns over the potentially earth-shattering revelations surrounding the devastating attack on Ganymede."

The image cut to Avasarala. She was leaning forward to make her neck longer and hide the loose skin under her chin. Long practice made her look natural, but she could almost hear Arjun laughing. A runner at the bottom of the screen identified her by name and title.

"I expect to be traveling with Captain Holden to the Jovian system," Avasarala said. "The United Nations of Earth feel very strongly that a multilateral investigation into this is the best way to restore balance and peace to the system."

The image shifted to Holden and Avasarala sitting in the galley with the botanist. This time the little scientist was talking and she and Holden pretended to listen. The voice-over came again.

"When asked about the accusations leveled against Praxidike Meng, whose search for his daughter has become the human face of the tragedy on Ganymede, the Earth delegation was unequivocal."

Then back to Avasarala, her expression now sorrowful. Her head shaking in an almost subliminal negation.

"Nicola Mulko is a tragic figure in this, and I personally condemn the irresponsibility of these raw newsfeeds that allow statements from mentally ill people to be presented as if they were verified fact. Her abandonment of her husband and child is beyond dispute, and her struggles with her psychological issues deserve a more dignified and private venue."

From off camera, Nagata asked, "So you blame the media?"

"Absolutely," Avasarala said as the image shifted to a picture of a toddler with smiling black eyes and dark pigtails. "We have absolute faith in Dr. Meng's love and dedication to Mei, and we are pleased to be part of the effort to bring her safely home."

The recording ended.

"All right," Avasarala said. "Any comments?"

"I don't actually work for the OPA anymore," Holden said.

"I'm not authorized to represent the Martian military," Bobbie said. "I'm not even sure I'm still supposed to be working with you."

"Thank you for that. Are there any comments that matter?" Avasarala asked. There was a moment's silence.

"Worked for me," Praxidike Meng said.

There was one way that the *Rocinante* was infinitely more expansive than the *Guanshiyin*, and it was the only one that she cared about. The tightbeam was hers. Lag was worse and every hour took her farther from Earth, but knowing that the messages she sent were getting off the ship without being reported to Nguyen and Errinwright gave her the feeling of breathing free. What happened once they reached Earth, she couldn't control, but that was always true. That was the game.

Admiral Souther looked tired, but on the small screen it was hard to tell much more than that.

"You've kicked the beehive, Chrisjen," he said. "It's looking an awful lot like you just made yourself a human shield for a bunch of folks that don't work for us. And I'm guessing that was the plan.

"I did what you asked, and yes, Nguyen took meetings with Jules-Pierre Mao. First one was just after his testimony on Protogen. And yes, Errinwright knew about them. But that doesn't mean very much. I've met with Mao. He's a snake, but if you stopped dealing with men like him, you wouldn't have much left to do.

"The smear campaign against your scientist friend came out of the executive office, which, I've got to say, makes a damn lot of us over here in the armed forces a bit twitchy. Starts looking like there's divisions inside the leadership, and it gets a little murky whose orders we're supposed to be following. If it gets there, our friend Errinwright still outranks you. Him or the secretary-general comes to me with a direct order, I'm going to have to have a hell of a good reason to think it's illegal. This whole thing smells like skunk, but I don't have that reason yet. You know what I'm saying."

The recording stopped. Avasarala pressed her fingers to her lips. She understood. She didn't like it, but she understood. She levered herself up from her couch. Her joints still ached from the race to the *Rocinante*, and the way the ship would sometimes shift beneath her, course corrections moving gravity a degree or two, left her vaguely nauseated. She'd made it this far.

The corridor that led to the galley was short, but it had a bend just before it entered. The voices carried well enough that Avasarala walked softly. The low Martian drawl was the pilot, and Bobbie's vowels and timbre were unmistakable.

"—that tellin' the captain where to stand and how to look. I thought Amos was going to toss her in the airlock a couple of times."

"He could try," Bobbie said.

"And you work for her?"

"I don't know who the hell I work for anymore. I think I'm still pulling a salary from Mars, but all my dailies are out of her office budget. I've pretty much been playing it all as it comes."

"Sounds rough."

"I'm a marine," Bobbie said, and Avasarala paused. The tone was wrong. It was calm, almost relaxed. Almost at peace. That was interesting.

"Does anyone actually like her?" the pilot asked.

"No," Bobbie said almost before the question was done being asked. "Oh hell no. And she keeps it like that. That shit she pulled with Holden, marching on his ship and ordering him around like she owned it? She's always like that. The secretary-general? She calls him a bobble-head to his face."

"And what's with the potty mouth?"

"Part of her charm," Bobbie said.

The pilot chuckled, and there was a little slurp as he drank something.

"I may have misunderstood politics," he said. And a moment later: "You like her?"

"I do."

"Mind if I ask why?"

"We care about the same things," Bobbie said, and the thoughtful note in her voice made Avasarala feel uncomfortable eavesdropping. She cleared her throat and walked into the galley.

"Where's Holden?" she asked.

"Probably sleeping," the pilot said. "The way we've been keepin' the ship's cycle, it's about two in the morning."

"Ah," Avasarala said. For her, it was mid-afternoon. That was going to be a little awkward. Everything in her life seemed to be about lag right now, waiting for the messages to get through the vast blackness of the vacuum. But at least she could prepare.

"I'm going to want a meeting with everyone on board as soon as they're up," she said. "Bobbie, you'll need your formal wear again."

It took Bobbie only a few seconds to understand.

"You'll show them the monster," she said.

"And then we're going to sit here and talk until we figure out what exactly it is they know on this ship. It has the bad guys worried enough they were willing to send their boys to kill them," she said.

"Yeah, about that," the pilot said. "Those destroyers cut back to a cruising acceleration, but they aren't turning back yet."

"Doesn't matter," Avasarala said. "Everybody knows I'm on this ship. No one's going to shoot at it."

In the local morning and Avasarala's subjective early evening, the crew gathered again. Rather than bring the whole powered suit into the galley, she'd copied the stored video and given it to Naomi. The crew members were bright and well rested apart from the pilot, who had stayed up entirely too late talking to Bobbie, and the botanist, who looked like he might just be permanently exhausted.

"I'm not supposed to show this to anyone," Avasarala said, looking pointedly at Holden. "But on this ship, right now, I think we all need to put our cards on the table. And I'm willing to go first. This is the attack on Ganymede. The thing that started it all off. Naomi?"

Naomi started the playback, and Bobbie turned away and stared at the bulkhead. Avasarala didn't watch it either, her attention on the faces of the others. As the blood and carnage played out behind her, she studied them and learned a little more about the people she was dealing with. The engineer, Amos, watched with the calm reserve of a professional killer. No surprise there. At first Holden, Naomi, and Alex were horrified, and she watched as Alex and Naomi slid into a kind of shock. There were tears in the pilot's eyes. Holden, on the other hand, curled in. His shoulders bent outward from each other, and an expression of banked rage smoldered in his eyes and around the corners of his mouth. That was interesting. Bobbie wept openly with her back to the screen, and her expression was melancholy, like a woman at a funeral. A memorial service. Praxidike—everyone else called him Prax—was the only one who seemed almost happy. When at the segment's end, the monstrosity detonated, he clapped his hands and squealed in pleasure.

"That was it," he said. "You were right, Alex. Did you see how it was starting to grow more limbs? Catastrophic restraint failure. It *was* a fail-safe."

"Okay," Avasarala said. "Why don't you try that again with an antecedent. What was a fail-safe?"

"The other protomolecule form ejected the explosive device from its body before it could detonate. You see, these… things—protomolecule soldiers or whatever—are breaking their programming, and I think Merrian knows about it. He hasn't found a way to stop it, because the constraints fail."

"Who's Marion, and what does she have to do with anything?" Avasarala said.

"You wanted more nouns, Gramma," Amos said.

"Let me take this from the top," Holden said, and recounted the attack by the stowaway beast, the damage to the cargo door, Prax's scheme to lure it out of the ship and reduce it to its component atoms with the drive's exhaust.

Avasarala handed over the data she had about the energy spikes on Venus, and Prax grabbed that data, looking it over while talking about his determination of a secret base on Io where the things were being produced. It left Avasarala's head spinning.

"And they took your kid there," Avasarala said.

"They took all of them," Prax said.

"Why would they do that?"

"Because they don't have immune systems," Prax said. "And so they'd be easier to reshape with the protomolecule. There would be fewer physiological systems fighting against the new cellular constraints, and the soldiers would probably last a lot longer."

"Jesus, Doc," Amos said. "They're going to turn Mei into one of those fucking things?"

"Probably," Prax said, frowning. "I only just figured that out."

"But why do it at all?" Holden said. "It doesn't make sense."

"In order to sell them to a military force as a first-strike weapon," Avasarala said. "To consolidate power before...well, before the fucking apocalypse."

"Point of clarification," Alex said, raising his hand. "We have an apocalypse comin'? Was that a thing we knew about?"

"Venus," Avasarala said.

"Oh. That apocalypse," Alex said, lowering his hand. "Right."

"Soldiers that can travel without ships," Naomi said. "You could fire them off at high g for a little while, then cut engines and let them go ballistic. How would you find them?"

"But it won't *work*," Prax said. "Remember? They escape constraint. And since they can share information, they're going to get harder to hold to any kind of new programming."

The room went silent. Prax looked confused.

"They can *share information*?" Avasarala said.

"Sure," Prax said. "Look at your energy spikes. The first one happened while the thing was fighting Bobbie and the other marines on Ganymede. The second spike came when the other one got loose in the lab. The third spike was when we killed it with the *Rocinante*. Every time one of them has been attacked, Venus reacted. They're networked. I'd assume that any critical information could be shared. Like how to escape constraints."

"If they use them against people," Holden said, "there won't be any way to stop them. They'll ditch the fail-safe bombs and just keep going. The battles won't end."

"Um. No," Prax said. "That's not the problem. It's the cascade again. Once the protomolecule gets a little freedom, it has more tools to erode other constraints, which gets it more tools to erode more constraints and on and on like that. The original program or something like it will eventually swamp the new program. They'll revert."

Bobbie leaned forward, her head canted a few degrees to the

right. Her voice was quiet, but it had a threat of violence that was louder than shouting.

"So if they set those things loose on Mars, they stay soldiers like the first one for a while. And then they start dropping the bombs out like your guy did. And then they turn Mars into Eros?"

"Well, worse than Eros," Prax said. "Any decent-sized Martian city is going to have an order of magnitude more people than Eros did."

The room was quiet. On the monitor, Bobbie's suit camera looked up at star-filled sky while battleships killed each other in orbit.

"I've got to send some messages out," Avasarala said.

"These half-human things you've made? They aren't your servants. You can't control them," Avasarala said. "Jules-Pierre Mao sold you a bill of goods. I know why you kept me out of this, and I think you're a fucking moron for it, but put it aside. It doesn't matter now. Just do not pull that fucking trigger. Do you understand what I'm saying? Don't. You will be personally responsible for the single deadliest screwup in the history of humankind, and I'm on a ship with Jim fucking Holden, so the bar's not low."

The full recording clocked in at almost half an hour. The security footage from the *Rocinante* with its stowaway was attached. A fifteen-minute lecture by Prax had to be scrapped when he reached the part about his daughter being turned into a protomolecule soldier, and this time broke into uncontrollable weeping. Avasarala did her best to recapitulate it, but she wasn't at all certain she had the details right. She'd considered bringing Jon-Michael into it, but decided against it. Better to keep it in the family.

She sent the message. If she knew Errinwright, he wouldn't get back to her immediately. There would be an hour or two of evaluation, weighing what she'd said, and then when she'd been left to stew for a while, he'd reply.

She hoped he'd be sane about it. He had to.

She needed to sleep. She could feel the fatigue gnawing at the edges of her mind, slowing her, but when she lay down, rest felt as far away as home. As Arjun. She thought about recording a message for him, but it would only have left her feeling more powerfully isolated. After an hour, she pulled herself up and walked through the halls. Her body told her it was midnight or later, and the activity on board—music ringing out of the machine shop, a loud conversation between Holden and Alex about the maintenance of the electronics systems, even Praxidike's sitting in the galley by himself, apparently grooming a box of hydroponics cuttings—had a surreal late-night feeling.

She considered sending another message to Souther. The lag time would be much less to him, and she was hungry enough for a response that anything would do. When the answer came, it wasn't a message.

"Captain," Alex said over the ship-wide comm. "You should come up to ops and look at this."

Something in his voice told Avasarala that this wasn't a maintenance question. She found the lift to ops just as Holden went up, and pulled herself up the ladder rather than wait. She wasn't the only one who'd followed the call. Bobbie was in a spare seat, her eyes on the same screen as Holden's. The blinking tactical data scrolled down the screen, and a dozen bright red dots displayed changes. She didn't understand most of what she saw, but the gist was obvious. The destroyers were on the move.

"Okay," Holden said. "What're we seeing?"

"All the Earth destroyers hit high burn. Six g," Alex said.

"Are they going to Io?"

"Oh, hell no."

This was Errinwright's answer. No messages. No negotiations. Not even an acknowledgment that she'd asked him to restrain himself. Warships. The despair only lasted for a moment. Then came the anger.

"Bobbie?"

"Yeah."

"That part where you told me I didn't understand the danger I was in?"

"And you told me that I didn't how the game was played."

"That part."

"I remember. What about it?"

"If you wanted to say 'I told you so,' this looks like the right time."

Chapter Forty-Two: Holden

Holden had spent a month at the Diamond Head Electronic Warfare Lab on Oahu as his first posting after officer candidate school. During that time, he'd learned he had no desire to be a naval intelligence wonk, really disliked poi, and really liked Polynesian women. He'd been far too busy at the time to actively chase one, but he'd thoroughly enjoyed spending his few spare moments down at the beach looking at them. He'd had a thing for curvy women with long black hair ever since.

The Martian Marine was like one of those cute little beach bunnies that someone had used editing software on and blown up to 150 percent normal size. The proportions, the black hair, the dark eyes, everything was the same. Only, giant. It short-circuited his neural wiring. The lizard living at the back of his brain kept jumping back and forth between *Mate with it!* and *Flee from it!* What was worse, she knew it. She seemed to have sized him up and decided he was only worth a tired smirk within moments of their meeting.

"Do you need me to go over it again?" she said, the smirk mocking him. They were sitting together in the galley, where she'd been describing for him the Martian intelligence on the best way to engage the Munroe-class light destroyer.

No! he wanted to yell. *I heard you. I'm not a freak. I have a lovely girlfriend that I'm totally committed to, so stop treating me like some kind of bumbling teenage boy who's trying to look down your dress!*

But then he'd look up at her again, and his hindbrain would start bouncing back and forth between attraction and fear, and his language centers would start misfiring. Again.

"No," he said, staring at the neatly organized list of bullet points she'd forwarded to his hand terminal. "I think this information is very…informative."

He saw the smirk widen out of the corner of his eye and focused more intently on the list.

"Okay," Bobbie said. "I'm going to go catch some rack time. With your permission, of course. Captain."

"Permission granted," Holden said. "Of course. Go. Rack."

She pushed herself to her feet without touching the arms of the chair. She'd grown up in Martian gravity. She had to mass a hundred kilos at one g, easy. She was showing off. He pretended to ignore it, and she left the galley.

"She's something, isn't she?" Avasarala said, coming into the galley and collapsing into the recently vacated chair. Holden looked up at her and saw a different kind of smirk. One that said the old lady saw right through him to the warring lizards at the back of his head. But she wasn't a giant Polynesian woman, so he could vent his frustration on her.

"Yeah, she's a peach," he said. "But we're still going to die."

"What?"

"When those destroyers catch us, which they will, we are going to die. The only reason they aren't raining torpedoes down on us already is because they know our PDC network can take out anything fired at this range."

Avasarala leaned back in her chair with a heavy sigh, and the smirk shifted into a tired but genuine smile. "I don't suppose there's any chance you could find an old woman a cup of tea, could you?"

Holden shook his head. "I'm sorry. No tea drinkers on the crew. Lots of coffee, though, if you'd like a cup."

"I'm actually tired enough to do that. Lots of cream, lots of sugar."

"How about," Holden said, pulling her a cup, "lots of sugar, lots of a powder that's called 'whitener.'"

"Sounds like piss. I'll take it."

Holden sat down and pushed the sweetened and "whitened" cup of coffee across to her. She took it and grimaced through several long swallows.

"Explain," she said after another drink, "everything you just said."

"Those destroyers are going to kill us," Holden repeated. "The sergeant says you refuse to believe that UN ships will fire on you, but I agree with her. That's naive."

"Okay, but what's a 'PDC network'?"

Holden tried not to frown. He'd expected any number of things from the woman, but ignorance hadn't been one.

"Point defense cannons. If those destroyers fire torpedoes at us from this distance, the targeting computer for the PDCs won't have any trouble shooting them down. So they'll wait until they get close enough that they can overwhelm us. I give it three days before they start."

"I see," Avasarala said. "And what's your plan?"

Holden barked out a laugh with no humor in it. "Plan? My plan is to die in a ball of superheated plasma. There is literally no way that a single fast-attack corvette, which is us, can successfully fight six light destroyers. We aren't in the same weight class as even one of them, but against one, a lucky shot maybe. Against six? No chance. We die."

"I've read your file," Avasarala said. "You faced down a UN corvette during the Eros incident."

"Yeah, one corvette. We were a match for her. And I got her to back down by threatening the unarmed science ship she was escorting. This isn't even remotely the same thing."

"So what does the infamous James Holden do at his last stand?"

He was silent for a while.

"He rats," Holden said. "We know what's going on. We have all the pieces now. Mao-Kwik, the protomolecule monsters, where they're taking the kids…everything. We put all the data in a file and broadcast it to the universe. They can still kill us if they want to, but we can make it a pointless act of revenge. Keep it from actually helping them."

"No," Avasarala said.

"Uh, no? You might be forgetting whose ship you're on."

"I'm sorry, did I seem to give a fuck that this is your ship? If I did, really, I was just being polite," Avasarala said, giving him a withering glare. "You aren't going to fuck up the whole solar system just because you're a one-trick pony. We have bigger fish to fry."

Holden counted to ten in his head and said, "Your idea is?"

"Send it to these two UN admirals," she said, then tapped something on her terminal. His buzzed with the received file. "Souther and Leniki. Mostly Souther. I don't like Leniki, and he hasn't been in the loop on this, but he's a decent backup."

"You want my last act before being killed by a UN admiral to be sending all of the vital information I have to a UN admiral."

Avasarala leaned back into her chair and rubbed her temples with her fingertips. Holden waited. "I'm tired," she said after a few moments. "And I miss my husband. It's like an ache in my arms that I can't hold him right now. Do you know what that's like?"

"I know exactly what that ache feels like."

"So I want you to understand that I'm sitting here, right now, coming to terms with the idea that I won't see him again. Or my grandchildren. Or my daughter. My doctors said I probably had a good thirty years left in me. Time to watch my grandkids grow up, maybe even see a great-grandchild or two. But instead, I'm going to be killed by a limp-dick, whiny sonofabitch like Admiral Nguyen."

Holden could feel the massive weight of those six destroyers bearing down on them, murder in their hearts. It felt like having a pistol pushed into his ribs from behind. He wanted to shake the old woman and tell her to hurry up.

She smiled at him.

"My last act in this universe isn't going to be fucking up everything I did right up to now."

Holden made a conscious effort to ignore his frustration. He got up and opened the refrigerator. "Hey, there's leftover pudding. Want some?"

"I've read your psych profile. I know all about your 'everyone should know everything' naive bullshit. But how much of the last war was *your* fault, with your goddamned endless pirate broadcasts? Well?"

"None of it," Holden said. "Desperate psychotic people do desperate psychotic things when they're exposed. I refuse to grant them immunity from exposure out of fear of their reaction. When you do, the desperate psychos wind up in charge."

She laughed. It was a surprisingly warm sound.

"Anyone who understands what's going on is at least desperate and probably psychotic to boot. Dissociative at the least. Let me explain it this way," Avasarala said. "You tell everyone, and yeah, you'll get a reaction. And maybe, weeks, or months, or years from now, it will all get sorted out. But you tell the *right* people, and we can sort it out right now."

Amos and Prax walked into the galley together. Amos had his big thermos in his hand and headed straight toward the coffeepot. Prax followed him and picked up a mug. Avasarala's eyes narrowed and she said, "Maybe even save that little girl."

"Mei?" Prax said immediately, putting the mug down and turning around.

Oh, that was low, Holden thought. *Even for a politician.*

"Yes, Mei," Avasarala replied. "That's what this is about, right, Jim? Not some personal crusade, but trying to save a little girl from very bad people?"

"Explain how—" Holden started, but Avasarala kept talking right over the top of him.

"The UN isn't one person. It isn't even one corporation. It's a thousand little, petty factions fighting against each other. Their side's got the floor, but that's temporary. That's always temporary. I know people who can move against Nguyen and his group. They can cut off his support, strip him of ships, even recall and court-martial him given enough time. But they can't do any of that if we're in a shooting war with Mars. And if you toss everything you know into the wind, Mars won't have time to wait and figure out the subtleties; they'll have no choice but to preemptively strike against Nguyen's fleet, Io, what's left of Ganymede. Everything."

"Io?" Prax said. "But Mei—"

"So you want me to give all the info to your little political cabal back on Earth, when the entire reason for this problem is that there are little political cabals back on Earth."

"Yes," Avasarala said. "And I'm the only hope she's got. You have to trust me."

"I don't. Not even a little bit. I think you're part of the problem. I think you see all of this as political maneuvering and power games. I think you want to *win*. So no, I don't trust you at all."

"Hey, uh, Cap?" Amos said, slowly screwing the top onto his thermos. "Ain't you forgetting something?"

"What, Amos? What am I forgetting?"

"Don't we vote on shit like this now?"

"Don't pout," Naomi said. She was stretched out on a crash couch next to the main operations panel on the ops deck. Holden was seated across the room from her at the comm panel. He'd just sent out Avasarala's data file to her two UN admirals. His fingers itched with the desire to dump it into a general broadcast. But they'd debated the issue for the crew, and she'd won the vote. The whole voting thing had seemed like such a good idea when he'd first brought it up. After losing his first vote, not so much. They'd all be dead in two days, so at least it probably wouldn't happen again.

"If we get killed, and Avasarala's pet admirals don't actually do anything with the data we just sent, this was all for nothing."

"You think they'll bury it?" Naomi said.

"I don't know, and that's the problem. I don't know what they'll do. We met this UN politician two days ago and she's already running the ship."

"So send it to someone else too," Naomi said. "Someone who you can trust to keep it quiet, but can get the word out if the UN guys turn out to be working for the wrong team."

"That's not a bad idea."

"Fred, maybe?"

"No." Holden laughed. "Fred would see it as political capital. He'd use it to bargain with. It needs to be someone that has nothing to gain or lose by using it. I'll have to think about it."

Naomi got up, then came over to straddle his legs and sit on his lap facing him. "And we're all about to die. That's not making any of this any easier."

Not all of us.

"Naomi, gather the crew up, the marine and Avasarala too. The galley, I guess. I have some last business to announce. I'll meet you guys there in ten minutes."

She kissed him lightly on the nose. "Okay. We'll be there."

When she disappeared from sight down the crew ladder, Holden opened up the chief of the watch's locker. Inside were a set of very out-of-date codebooks, a manual of Martian naval law, and a side-arm and two magazines of ballistic gel rounds. He took out the gun, loaded it, and strapped the belt and holster around his waist.

Next he went back to the comm station and put Avasarala's data package into a tightbeam transmission that would bounce from Ceres to Mars to Luna to Earth, using public routers all the way. It would be unlikely to send up any red flags. He hit the video record button and said, "Hi, Mom. Take a look at this. Show it to the family. I have no idea how you'll know when the right time to use it is, but when that time comes, do with it whatever seems best. I trust you guys, and I love you."

Before he could say anything else or think better of the whole thing, he hit the transmit key and turned the panel off.

He called up the ladder-lift, because riding it would take longer than climbing the ladder and he needed time to think out exactly how to play the next ten minutes. When he reached the crew deck, he still didn't have it all figured out, but he squared his shoulders and walked into the galley anyway.

Amos, Alex, and Naomi were sitting on one side of the table, facing him. Prax was in his usual perch on the counter. Bobbie and Avasarala sat sideways on the other side of the table so that they could see him. That put the marine less than two meters away, with nothing between her and him. Depending on how this went, that might be a problem.

He dropped his hand to the butt of the gun at his hip to make sure everyone saw it, then said, "We have about two days before elements of the UN Navy get close enough to overwhelm our defenses with a torpedo salvo and destroy this ship."

Alex nodded, but no one spoke.

"But we have the Mao racing pinnace that brought Avasarala to us attached to the hull. It holds two. We're going to stick two people on it and get them away. Then we're going to turn around and head straight for those UN ships to buy the pinnace time. Who knows, we may even take one with us. Get ourselves a few servants in the afterlife."

"Fucking A," Amos said.

"I can support that," Avasarala said. "Who're the lucky bastards? And how do we stop the UN ships from just killing it after they kill this ship?"

"Prax and Naomi," Holden said immediately, before anyone else could speak. "Prax and Naomi go on the ship."

"Okay," Amos said, nodding.

"Why?" Naomi and Avasarala said at the same moment.

"Prax because he's the face of this whole thing. He's the guy who figured it all out. And because when someone finally rescues his little girl, it'd be nice if her daddy was there," Holden said. Then, tapping the butt of the gun with his fingers: "And Naomi because I fucking said so. Questions?"

"Nope," Alex said. "Works for me."

Holden was watching the marine closely. If someone tried to take the gun from him, it would be her. And she worked for Avasarala. If the old lady decided she wanted to be on the *Razorback* when it left, the marine would be the one who tried to make that happen. But to his surprise, she didn't move except to raise her hand.

"Sergeant?" Holden said.

"Two of those six Martian ships that are tailing the UN boys are new Raptor-class fast cruisers. They can probably catch the *Razorback* if they really want to."

"Would they?" Holden asked. "It was my impression that they were there to keep an eye on the UN ships and nothing else."

"Well, probably not, but…" She drifted off mid-sentence with a distant look in her eyes.

"So that's the plan," Holden said. "Prax, Naomi, get whatever supplies you need packed up and get on the *Razorback*. Everyone else, I'd appreciate it if you waited here while they did that."

"Hold on a minute—" Naomi protested, her voice angry.

Before Holden could respond, Bobbie spoke again.

"Hey, you know? I just had an idea."

Chapter Forty-Three: Bobbie

They were all missing something. It was like someone knocking at the back of her mind, demanding to be let in. Bobbie went over it in her head. Sure, that prick Nguyen showed every sign he was willing to kill the *Rocinante*, ranking UN politician on board or not. Avasarala had made a gamble that her presence would back the UN ships off. It seemed she was about to lose that bet. There were still six UN destroyers bearing down on them.

But there were six more ships tailing *them*.

Including, as she'd just pointed out to Holden, two *Raptor*-class fast-attack cruisers. Top-of-the-line Martian military hardware, and more than a match for any UN destroyer. Along with the two cruisers were four Martian destroyers. They might or might not be better than their UN counterparts, but with the two cruisers in their wing, they had a significant tonnage and fire-power advantage. And they were following the UN ships to see that they weren't about to do something to escalate the shooting war.

Like killing the one UN politician who wasn't straining at the leash for a war with Mars.

"Hey, you know?" Bobbie said before she realized she was going to say anything. "I just had an idea..."

The galley fell silent.

Bobbie had a sudden and uncomfortable memory of speaking up in the UN conference room and wrecking her military career in the process. Captain Holden, the cute one who was a little too full of himself, was staring at her, a not particularly flattering gape on his face. He looked like a very angry person who'd lost his train of thought mid-rant. And Avasarala was staring at her too. Though, having learned to read the old lady's expression better, she didn't see anger there. Just curiosity.

"Well," Bobbie said, clearing her throat. "There are six Martian ships following those UN ships. And the Martian ships outclass them. Both navies are at high alert."

No one moved or spoke. Avasarala's curiosity had turned to a frown. "So," Bobbie continued, "they might be willing to back us up."

Avasarala's frown had only gotten deeper. "Why," she said, "would the Martians give a fuck about protecting me from being killed by my own damn Navy?"

"Would it hurt to ask?"

"No," Holden said. "I'm thinking no. Is everyone else here thinking it wouldn't hurt?"

"Who'd make the call?" Avasarala asked. "You? The traitor?"

The words were like a gut punch. But Bobbie realized what the old lady was doing. She was hitting Bobbie with the worst possible Martian response. Gauging her reaction to it.

"Yeah, I'd open the door," Bobbie said. "But you're the one that will have to convince them."

Avasarala stared at her for one very long minute, then said, "Okay."

"Repeat that, *Rocinante*," the Martian commander said. The connection was as clear as if they were standing in the room with the man. It wasn't the sound quality that was throwing him. Avasarala spoke slowly, enunciating carefully, all the same.

"This is Assistant Undersecretary Chrisjen Avasarala of the United Nations of Earth," Avasarala said again. "I am about to be attacked by a rogue element of the UN Navy while on my way to a peacekeeping mission in the Jupiter system. Fucking save me! I will reward you by talking my government out of glassing your planet."

"I'm going to have to send this up the chain," the commander said. They weren't using a video link, but the grin was audible in his voice.

"Call whoever you need to call," Avasarala said. "Just make a decision before these cunts start raining missiles down on me. All right?"

"I'll do my best, ma'am."

The skinny one—her name was Naomi—killed the connection and swiveled to look at Bobbie. "Why would they help us, again?"

"Mars doesn't want a war," Bobbie replied, hoping she wasn't talking completely out her ass. "If they find out that the UN's voice of reason is on a ship that's about to be killed by rogue UN war hawks, it only makes sense for them to step in."

"Kind of sounds like you're talking out your ass there," Naomi said.

"Also," Avasarala said, "I just gave them permission to shoot at the UN Navy without political repercussions."

"Even if they help," Holden said, "there's no way they can completely stop the UN ships from taking some shots at us. We'll need an engagement plan."

"We just got this damn thing put back together," Amos said.

"I still say we stick Prax and Naomi on the *Razorback*," Holden said.

"I'm starting to think that's a bad idea," Avasarala said. She took a sip of coffee and grimaced. The old lady was definitely missing her five cups of tea a day.

"Explain," Holden said.

"Well, if the Martians decide they're on our side, that changes the whole landscape for those UN ships. They can't beat all seven of us, if I understand the math right."

"Okay," Holden said.

"That makes it in their interest not to be called a rogue element in the history books. If Nguyen's cabal fails, everyone on his team gets at minimum a court-martial. The best way to make sure that doesn't happen is to make sure I don't survive this fight, no matter who wins."

"Which means they'll be shooting at the *Roci*," Naomi said. "Not the pinnace."

"Of course not," Avasarala said with a laugh. "Because of course I'll be on the pinnace. You think for a second they'll believe that you're desperately trying to protect an escape craft that I'm *not* on? And I bet the *Razorback* doesn't have those PDCs you were talking about. Does it?"

To Bobbie's surprise, Holden was nodding as Avasarala spoke. She'd sort of pegged him as a know-it-all who fell in love only with his own ideas.

"Yeah," Holden said. "You're absolutely right. They'll fling everything they've got at the *Razorback* as she tries to get away, and she'll have no defense."

"Which means we all live or we all die, right here on this ship," Naomi said with a sigh. "As usual."

"So, again," Holden said. "We need an engagement plan."

"This is a pretty thin crew," Bobbie said now that the conversation had moved back to her area of expertise. "Where's everyone usually sit?"

"Operations officer," Holden said, pointing at Naomi. "She also does electronic warfare and countermeasures. And she's a savant, considering she'd never worked it before we got this ship."

"Mechanic—" Holden started, pointing at Amos.

"Grease monkey," Amos said, cutting him off. "I do my best to keep the ship from falling apart when there's holes in it."

"I usually man the combat ops board," Holden said.

"Who's the gunner?" Bobbie asked.

"Yo," said Alex, pointing at himself.

"You fly *and* do target acquisition?" Bobbie said. "I'm impressed."

Alex's already dark skin grew a shade darker. His *aw shucks* Mariner Valley drawl had started to go from annoying to charming. And the blush was sweet. "Aw, no. The cap'n does acquisition from combat ops, generally. But I have to manage fire control."

"Well, there you go," Bobbie said, turning to Holden. "Give me weps."

"No offense, Sergeant…" Holden said.

"Gunny," Bobbie replied.

"Gunny," Holden agreed with a nod. "But are you qualified to operate fire control on a naval vessel?"

Bobbie decided not to be offended and grinned at him instead. "I saw your armor and the weapons you were carrying in the airlock. You found a MAP in the cargo bay, right?"

"Map?" Avasarala asked.

"Mobile assault package. Marine assault gear. Not as good as my Force Recon armor, but full kit for half a dozen ground pounders."

"Yeah," Holden said. "That's where we got it."

"That's because this is a multi-role fast-attack ship. Torpedo bomber is just one of them. Boarding party insertion is another. And gunnery sergeant is a rank with a very specific meaning."

"Yeah," Alex said. "Equipment specialist."

"I'm required to be proficient in all of the weapons systems my platoon or company might need to operate during a typical deployment. Including the weapons systems on an assault boat like this."

"I see—" Holden started, but Bobbie cut him off with a nod.

"I'm your gunner."

Like most things in Bobbie's life, the weapons officer's chair had been made for someone smaller than her. The five-point harness was digging into her hips and her shoulders. Even at its farthest setting, the fire control console was just a bit too close for her to comfortably rest her arms on the crash couch while using it. All of which would be a problem if they had to do any really high-g maneuvering. Which, of course, they would once the fight started.

She tucked her elbows in as close as she could to keep her arms from wrenching out of their sockets at high g, and fidgeted with the harness. It would have to be good enough.

From his seat behind and above her, Alex said, "This'll be over quick one way or the other. You probably won't have time to get too uncomfortable."

"That's reassuring."

Over the 1MC Holden said, "We're inside the maximum-effective weapon range now. They could fire immediately or twenty hours from now. So stay belted in. Only leave your station in life-threatening emergency and at my direct order. I hope everyone got their catheter on right."

"Mine's too tight," Amos said.

Alex spoke behind her, and it was echoed a split second later over the comm channel. "It's a condom catheter, partner. It goes on the *out*side."

Bobbie couldn't help laughing and held one hand up behind her until Alex slapped it.

Holden said, "We have greens across the board down here in ops. Everyone check in with go/no-go status."

"All green at flight control," Alex said.

"Green at electronic warfare," Naomi said.

"We're go down here," Amos said.

"Weapons are green and hot," Bobbie said last. Even strapped into a chair two sizes too small for her, on a stolen Martian warship captained by one of the most wanted men in the inner planets, it felt really goddamned good to be there. Bobbie restrained a whoop of joy and instead pulled Holden's threat display up. He'd already marked the six pursuing UN destroyers. Bobbie tagged the lead ship and let the *Rocinante* try to come up with a target solution on it. The *Roci* calculated the odds of a hit at less than .1 percent. She jumped from target to target, getting a feel for the response times and controls. She tapped a button to pull up target info and looked over the UN destroyer specs.

When reading ship specs bored her, she pulled out to the tactical view. One tiny green dot pursued by six slightly larger red dots, which were in turn pursued by six blue dots. That was wrong. The Earth ships should be blue, and the Martians' red. She told the *Roci* to swap the color scheme. The *Rocinante* was oriented toward the pursuing ships. On the map, it looked like they were flying directly at each other. But in reality, the *Rocinante* was in the middle of a deceleration burn, slowing down to let the UN ships catch up faster. All thirteen of the ships in this particular engagement were hurtling sunward. The *Roci* was just doing it ass first.

Bobbie glanced at the time and saw that her noodling with the controls had burned less than fifteen minutes. "I hate waiting for a fight."

"You and me both, sister," Alex said.

"Got any games on this thing?" Bobbie asked, tapping on her console.

"I spy with my little eye," Alex replied, "something that begins with *D*."

"Destroyer," Bobbie said. "Six tubes, eight PDCs, and a keel-mounted rapid-fire rail gun."

"Good guess. Your turn."

"I fucking hate waiting for a fight."

When the battle began, it began all at once. Bobbie had expected some early probing shots. A few torpedoes fired from extreme range, just to see if the crew of the *Rocinante* had full control of all the weapon systems and everything was in working order.

Instead, the UN ships had closed the distance, the *Roci* slamming on the brakes to meet them.

Bobbie watched the six UN ships creep closer and closer to the red line on her threat display. The red line that represented the point at which a full salvo from all six ships would overwhelm the *Roci*'s point defense network.

Meanwhile, the six Martian ships moved closer to the green line on her display that represented their optimal firing range to engage the UN ships. It was a big game of chicken, and everyone was waiting to see who would flinch first.

Alex was juggling their deceleration thrust to try to make sure the Martians got in range before the Earthers did. When the shooting started, he would put the throttle down and try to move through the active combat zone as quickly as possible. It was why they were going to meet the UN ships in the first place. Running away would just have kept them in range a lot longer.

Then one of the red dots—a Martian fast-attack cruiser—crossed the green line, and alarms started going off all over the ship.

"Fast movers," Naomi said. "The Martian cruiser has fired eight torpedoes!"

Bobbie could see them. Tiny yellow dots shifting to orange as they took off at high g. The UN ships immediately responded. Half of them spun around to face the pursuing Martian ships and opened up with their rail guns and point defense cannons. The space on the tactical display between the two groups was suddenly filled with yellow-orange dots.

"Incoming!" Naomi yelled. "Six torpedoes on a collision course!"

Half a second later, the torpedoes' vector and speed information popped up on Bobbie's PDC control display. Holden had been right. The skinny Belter was good at this. Her reaction times were astonishing. Bobbie flagged all six torpedoes for the PDCs, and the ship began to vibrate as they fired in a rapid staccato.

"Juice coming," Alex said, and Bobbie felt her couch prick her in half a dozen places. Cold pumped into her veins, quickly becoming white-hot. She shook her head to clear the threatening tunnel vision while Alex said, "Three...two..."

He never said *one*. The *Rocinante* smashed into Bobbie from behind, crushing her into her crash couch. She remembered at the last second to keep her elbows lined up, and avoided having her arms broken as every part of her tried to fly backward at ten gravities.

On her threat display, the initial wave of six torpedoes fired at them winked out one by one as the *Roci* tracked and shot them down. More torpedoes were in the air, but now the entire Martian wing had opened up on the Earthers, and the space around the ships had become a confusion of drive tails and detonations. Bobbie told the *Roci* to target anything on an approach vector and shoot at it with the point defenses, leaving it up to Martian engineering and the universe's good graces.

She switched one of the big displays to the forward cameras, turning it into a window on the battle. Ahead of her the sky was filled with bright white flashes of light and expanding clouds of gas as torpedoes detonated. The UN ships had decided that the Martians were the real threat, and all six of them had spun to face the enemy ships head-on. Bobbie tapped a control to throw a threat overlay onto the video image, and suddenly the sky was full of impossibly fast blobs of light as the threat computer put a glowing outline on every torpedo and projectile.

The *Rocinante* was coming up fast on the UN destroyers, and the thrust dropped to two g. "Here we go," Alex said.

Bobbie pulled up the torpedo targeting system and targeted the drive cones of two of the ships. "Two away," she said, releasing her first two fish into the water. Bright drive trails lit the sky as they streaked off. The ready-to-fire indicator went red as the ship reloaded the tubes. Bobbie was already selecting the drive cones of the next two UN ships. The instant the ready indicator went green, she fired them both. She targeted the last two destroyers, then checked on the progress of her first two torpedoes. They were both gone, shot down by the destroyers' aft PDCs. A wave of fast-moving blobs of light hurtled toward them, and Alex threw the ship sideways, dancing out of the line of fire.

It wasn't enough. A yellow atmosphere warning light began rotating in the cockpit, and a ditone Klaxon sounded.

"We're hit," Holden said, his voice calm. "Dumping the atmosphere. Hope everyone has their hat on tight."

As Holden shut down the air system, the sounds of the ship faded until Bobbie could hear only her own breathing and the faint hiss of the 1MC channel on her headset.

"Wow," Amos said over the comm. "Three hits. Small projectiles, probably PDC rounds. Managed to go right through us without hitting anything that mattered."

"It went through my room," the scientist, Prax, said.

"Bet that woke you up," Amos said, his voice a grin.

"I soiled myself," Prax replied without a hint of humor.

"Quiet," Holden said, but there was no malice in it. "Stay off the channel, please."

Bobbie let the rational, thinking part of her mind listen to the back-and-forth. She had no use for that part of her brain right now. The part of her mind that had been trained to acquire targets and fire torpedoes at them worked without her interference. The lizard was driving now.

She didn't know how many torpedoes she'd fired when there was an enormous flash of light and the camera display blacked out for a second. When it came back, one of the UN destroyers was torn in two, the rapidly separating pieces of hull spinning away from each other, trailing a faint gas cloud and small bits of jetsam. Some of those things flying out of the shattered ship would be UN sailors. Bobbie ignored that. The lizard rejoiced.

The destruction of the first UN ship tipped the scales, and within minutes the other five were heavily damaged or destroyed. A UN captain sent out a distress call and immediately signaled surrender.

Bobbie looked at her display. Three UN ships destroyed. Three heavily damaged. The Martians had lost two destroyers, and one of their cruisers was badly damaged. The *Rocinante* had three bullet wounds that had let all her air out, but no other damage.

They'd won.

"Holy shit," Alex said. "Captain, we have *got* to get one of these."

It took Bobbie a minute to realize he was talking about her.

"You have the gratitude of the UN government," Avasarala was saying to the Martian commander. "Or at least the part of the UN government I run. We're going to Io to blow up some more ships and maybe stop the apocalypse. Want to come with?"

Bobbie opened a private channel to Avasarala.

"We're all traitors now."

"Ha!" the old lady said. "Only if we lose."

Chapter Forty-Four: Holden

From the outside, the damage to the *Rocinante* was barely noticeable. The three point defense cannon rounds fired by one of the UN destroyers had hit her just forward of the sick bay and, after a short diagonal trip through the ship, exited through the machine shop, two decks below. Along the way, one of them had passed through three cabins in the crew deck.

Holden had expected the little botanist to be a wreck, especially after his crack about soiling himself. But when Holden had checked on him after the battle, he'd been surprised by the nonchalant shrug the scientist had given.

"It was very startling," was all he'd said.

It would be easy to write it off as shell shock. The kidnapping of his daughter, followed by months of living on Ganymede as the social structure collapsed. Easy to see Prax's calm as the precursor to a complete mental and emotional breakdown. God knew the man had lost control of himself half a dozen times, and most of them inconvenient. But Holden suspected there was a lot more to Prax than that. There was a relentless forward motion to the man. The universe might knock him down over and over again, but unless he was dead, he'd just keep getting up and shuffling ahead toward his goal. Holden thought he had probably been a very good scientist. Thrilled by small victories, undeterred by setbacks. Plodding along until he got to where he needed to be.

Even now, just hours after nearly being cut in two by a high-speed projectile, Prax was belowdecks with Naomi and Avasarala, patching holes inside the ship. He hadn't even been asked. He'd just climbed out of his bunk and pitched in.

Holden stood above one of the bullet entry points on the ship's outer hull. The small projectile had left a perfectly round hole and almost no dimpling. It had passed through five centimeters of high-tensile alloy armor so quickly it hadn't even dented it.

"Found it," Holden said. "No light coming out, so it looks like they've already patched it on the inside."

"Coming," Amos said, then clumped across the hull on magnetic boots, a portable welding torch in his hand. Bobbie followed in her fancy powered armor, carrying big sheets of patch material.

While Bobbie and Amos worked on sealing up the outer hull breach, Holden wandered off to find the next hole. Around him, the three remaining Martian warships drifted along with the *Rocinante* like an honor guard. With their drives off, they were visible only as small black spots that moved across the star field. Even with the *Roci* telling his armor where to look, and with the HUD pointing the ships out, they were almost impossible to see.

Holden tracked the Martian cruiser on his HUD until it passed across the bright splash of the Milky Way's ecliptic. For a moment, the entire ship was a black silhouette framed in the ancient white of a few billion stars. A faint cone of translucent white sprayed out from one side of the ship, and it drifted back into the star-speckled black. Holden felt a desire to have Naomi standing next to him, looking up at the same sights, that bordered on a physical ache.

"I forget how beautiful it is out here," he said to her over their private channel instead.

"You daydreaming and letting someone else do all the work?" she replied.

"Yeah. More of these stars have planets around them than don't. Billions of worlds. Five hundred million planets in the habitable zone was the last estimate. Think our great-grandkids will get to see any of them?"

"*Our* grandkids?"

"When this is over."

"Also," Naomi said, "at least one of those planets has the proto-molecule masters on it. Maybe we should avoid that one."

"Honestly? That's one I'd like to see. Who made this thing? What's it all for? I'd love to be able to ask. And at the very least, they share the human drive to find every habitable corner and move in. We might have more in common than we think."

"They also kill whoever lived there first."

Holden snorted. "We've been doing that since the invention of the spear. They're just scary good at it."

"You found that next hole yet?" Amos said over the main channel, his voice an unwelcome intrusion. Holden pulled his gaze away from the sky and back to the metal beneath his feet. Using the damage map the *Roci* was feeding to his HUD, it took only a moment to find the next entry wound.

"Yeah, yeah, right here," he said, and Amos and Bobbie began moving his direction.

"Cap," Alex said, chiming in from the cockpit. "The captain of that MCRN cruiser is lookin' to talk to you."

"Patch him through to my suit."

"Roger," Alex said, and then the static on the radio shifted in tone. "Captain Holden?"

"I read you. Go ahead."

"This is Captain Richard Tseng of the MCRN *Cydonia*. Sorry we weren't able to speak sooner. I've been dealing with damage control and arranging for rescue and repair ships."

"I understand, Captain," Holden said, trying to spot the *Cydonia* again but failing. "I'm out on my hull patching a few holes myself. I saw you guys drive by a minute ago."

"My XO says you'd asked to speak to me."

"Yes, and thank her on my behalf for all the help so far," Holden said. "Listen, we burned through an awful lot of our stores in that skirmish. We fired fourteen torpedoes and nearly half of our point defense ammunition. Since this used to be a Martian ship, I thought maybe you'd have reloads that would fit our racks."

"Sure," Captain Tseng said without a moment's hesitation. "I'll have the destroyer *Sally Ride* pull alongside for munitions transfer."

"Uh," Holden said, shocked by the instant agreement. He'd been prepared to negotiate. "Thanks."

"I'll pass along my intel officer's breakdown of the fight. You'll find it interesting viewing. But the short version is that first kill, the one that broke open the UN defense screen and ended the fight? That was yours. Guess they shouldn't have turned their backs on you."

"You guys can take credit for it," Holden said with a laugh. "I had a Martian Marine gunnery sergeant doing the shooting."

There was a pause; then Tseng said, "When this is over, I'd like to buy you a drink and talk about how a dishonorably discharged UN naval officer winds up flying a stolen MCRN torpedo bomber crewed by Martian military personnel and a senior UN politician."

"It's a damn good story," Holden replied. "Say, speaking of Martians, I'd like to get one of mine a present. Do you carry a Marine detachment on the *Cydonia*?"

"Yes, why?"

"Got any Force Recon Marines in that group?"

"Yes. Again, why?"

"There's some equipment we'll need that you've probably got in storage."

He told Captain Tseng what he was looking for, and Tseng said, "I'll have the *Ride* give you one when we do the transfer."

The MCRN *Sally Ride* looked like she'd come through the fight without a scratch. When she pulled up next to the *Rocinante*, her dark flank looked as smooth and unmarred as a pool of black water. After Alex and the *Ride*'s pilot had perfectly matched course, a large hatch in her side opened up, dim red emergency lighting spilling out. Two magnetic grapples were fired across, connecting the ships with ten meters of cable.

"This is Lieutenant Graves," a girlish voice said. "Prepared to begin cargo transfer on your order."

Lieutenant Graves sounded like she should still be in high school, but Holden said, "Go ahead. We're ready on this end."

Switching channels to Naomi, he said, "Pop the hatches, new fish coming aboard."

A few meters from where he was standing, a large hatch that was normally flush with the hull opened up into a meter-wide and eight-meter-long gap in the skin of the ship. A complicated-looking system of rails and gears ran down the sides of the opening. At the bottom sat three of the *Rocinante*'s remaining ship-to-ship torpedoes.

"Seven in here," Holden said, pointing at the open torpedo rack. "And seven on the other side."

"Roger," said Graves. The long, narrow white shape of a plasma torpedo appeared in the *Ride*'s open hatch, with sailors wearing EVA packs flanking it. With gentle puffs of compressed nitrogen, they flew the torpedo down along the two guidelines to the *Roci*; then, with the help of Bobbie's suit-augmented strength, they maneuvered it into position at the top of the rack.

"First one in position," Bobbie said.

"Got it," Naomi replied, and a second later the motorized rails came to life and grabbed the torpedo, pulling it down into the magazine.

Holden glanced at the elapsed time on his HUD. Getting all fourteen torpedoes transferred and loaded would take hours.

"Amos," he said. "Where are you?"

"Just finishing that last patch down by the machine shop," the mechanic replied. "You need something?"

"When you're done with that, grab a couple EVA packs. You and I will go get the other supplies. Should be three crates of PDC rounds and some sundries."

"I'm done now. Naomi, pop the cargo door for me, wouldja?"

Holden watched Bobbie and the *Ride*'s sailors work, and they had two more torpedoes loaded by the time Amos arrived with two EVA packs.

"Lieutenant Graves, two crew from the *Rocinante* requesting permission to board and pick up the rest of the supplies."

"Granted, *Rocinante*."

The PDC rounds came in crates of twenty thousand and at full gravity would have weighed more than five hundred kilos. In the microgravity of the coasting ships, two people with EVA packs could move one if they were willing to take their time and recharge their compressed nitrogen after every trip. Without a salvage mech or a small work shuttle available, there wasn't any other choice.

Each crate had to be pushed slowly toward the aft of the *Rocinante* through a twenty-second-long "burn" from Amos' EVA pack. When it got to the aft of the ship next to the cargo bay door, Holden would do an equally long thrust from his pack to bring the crate to a stop. Then the two of them would maneuver it inside and lock it to a bulkhead. The process was long, and at least for Holden, each trip had one heart-racing moment when he was firing the brakes to stop the crate. Every time, he had a brief, panicky vision of his EVA pack failing and him and the crate of ammo drifting off into space while Amos watched. It was ridiculous, of course. Amos could easily grab a fresh EVA pack and come get him, or the ship could drop back, or the *Ride* could send a rescue shuttle, or any other of a huge number of ways he'd be quickly saved.

But humans hadn't been living and working in space nearly long enough for the primitive part of the brain not to say, *I'll fall. I'll fall forever.*

The people from the *Ride* finished bringing over torpedoes about the time Holden and Amos had locked the last crate of PDC ammo into the cargo bay.

"Naomi," Holden called on the open channel. "We all green?"

"Everything looks good from here. All of the new torpedoes are talking to the *Roci* and reporting operational."

"Outstanding. Amos and I are coming in through the cargo bay airlock. Go ahead and seal the bay up. Alex, as soon as Naomi gives the all clear, let the *Cydonia* know we can do a fast burn to Io at the captain's earliest pleasure."

While the crew prepped the ship for the trip to Io, Holden and Amos stripped off their gear and stowed it in the machine shop. Six gray disks, three on each bulkhead across the compartment from each other, showed where the rounds had ripped through this part of the ship.

"What's in that other box the Martians gave you?" Amos asked, pulling off one oversized magnetic boot.

"A present for Bobbie," Holden said. "I'd like to keep it quiet until I give it to her, okay?"

"Sure, no problem, Cap'n. If it turns out to be a dozen long-stemmed roses, I don't want to be there when Naomi finds out. Plus, you know, Alex..."

"No, it's a lot more practical than roses—" Holden started, then rewound the conversation in his head. "Alex? What about Alex?"

Amos shrugged with his hands, like a Belter. "I think he might have a wee bit of a thing for our ample marine."

"You're kidding." Holden couldn't picture it. It wasn't as though Bobbie were unattractive. Far from it. But she was also very big, and quite intimidating. And Alex was such a quiet and mild guy. Sure, they were both Martians, and no matter how cosmopolitan a person got, there was something comforting in reminders of home. Maybe just being the only two Martians on the ship was enough. But Alex was pushing fifty, balding without complaint, and wore his love handles with the quiet resignation of a middle-aged man. Sergeant Draper couldn't be more than thirty and looked like a comic book illustration, complete with muscles *on* her muscles. Unable to stop himself, his mind began trying to figure out how the two of them would fit together. It didn't work.

"Wow," was all he could say. "Is it mutual?"

"No idea," Amos replied with another shrug. "The sergeant ain't easy to read. But I don't think she'd do him any deliberate harm, if that's what you're asking. Not that, you know, we could stop her."

"Scares you too, does she?"

"Look," Amos said with a grin. "When it comes to scrapes, I'm what you might call a talented amateur. But I've gotten a good look at that woman in and out of that fancy mechanical shell she wears. She's a pro. We're not playing the same sport."

Gravity began to return in the *Rocinante*. Alex was bringing up the drive, which meant they were beginning their run to Io. Holden stood up and took a moment to let his joints adjust to the sensation of weight again. He clapped Amos on the back and said, "Well, you've got a full load of torpedoes and bullets, three Martian warships trailing you, one angry old lady in tea withdrawal, and a Martian Marine who could probably kill you with your own teeth. What do you do?"

"You tell me, Captain."

"You find someone else for them to fight."

Chapter Forty-Five: Avasarala

"As I see it, sir," Avasarala said, "the die is already cast. We effectively have two courses of policy already in play. The question now is how we move forward. So far I've been able to keep the information from getting out, but once it does, it will be devastating. And since it is all but certain that the artifact is able to communicate, the chances of an effective military usage of these protomolecule-human hybrids is essentially nil. If we use this weapon, we will be creating a second Venus, committing genocide, and removing any moral argument against using weapons like accelerated asteroids against the Earth itself.

"I hope you will excuse the language, sir, but this was a cock-up from the start. The damage done to human security is literally unimaginable. It seems clear at this point that the protomolecule project under way on Venus is aware of events in the Jovian system. It's plausible that the samples out here have the information gained from the destruction of the *Arboghast*. To say that makes our position problematic is to radically understate the case.

"If it had gone through the appropriate channels, we would not be in this position. As it stands, I have done all that is presently within my capabilities, given my situation. The coalition I have built between Mars, elements of the Belt, and the legitimate government of Earth are ready to take action. But the United Nations must distance itself from this plan and move immediately to isolate and defang the faction within the government that has been doing this weasel shit. Again, excuse the language.

"I have sent copies of the data included here to Admirals Souther and Leniki as well as to my team on the Venus problem. They are, of course, at your disposal to answer any questions if I am not available.

"I'm very sorry to put you in the position, sir, but you are going to have to choose sides in this. And quickly. Events out here have developed a momentum of their own. If you're going to be on the right side of history on this, you must move now."

If there's any history to be on the right side of, she thought. She tried to come up with something else that she could say, some other argument that would penetrate the layers of old-growth wood that surrounded the secretary-general's brain. There weren't any, and repeating herself in simple storybook rhyme would probably come off as condescending. She stopped the recording, cut off the last few seconds of her looking into the camera in despair, and sent it off with every high-priority flag there was and diplomatic encryption.

So this was what it came to. All of human civilization, everything it had managed, from the first cave painting to crawling up the gravity well and pressing out into the antechamber of the stars, came down to whether a man whose greatest claim to fame was that he'd been thrown in prison for writing bad poetry had the balls to back down Errinwright. The ship corrected under her, shifting like an elevator suddenly slipping its tracks. She tried to sit up, but the gimbaled couch moved. God, but she hated space travel.

"Is it going to work?"

The botanist stood in her doorway. He was stick-thin, with a slightly larger head than looked right. He wasn't built as awkwardly as a Belter, but he couldn't be mistaken for someone who'd grown to maturity living at a full gravity. Standing in her doorway, trying to find something to do with his hands, he looked awkward and lost and slightly otherworldly.

"I don't know," she said. "If I were there, it would happen the way I want it to happen. I could go squeeze a few testicles until they saw it my way. From here? Maybe. Maybe not."

"You can talk to anyone from here, though, can't you?"

"It isn't the same."

He nodded, his attention shifting inward. Despite the differences in skin color and build, the man suddenly reminded her of Michael-Jon. He had the same sense of being a half step back from everything. Only, Michael-Jon's detachment verged on autism, and Praxidike Meng was a little more visibly interested in the people around him.

"They got to Nicola," he said. "They made her say those things about me. About Mei."

"Of course they did. That's what they do. And if they wanted to, they'd have papers and police reports to back it all up, backdated and put in the databases of everywhere you ever lived."

"I hate it that people think I did that."

Avasarala nodded, then shrugged.

"Reputation never has very much to do with reality," she said. "I could name half a dozen paragons of virtue that are horrible, small-souled, evil people. And some of the best men I know, you'd walk out of the room if you heard their names. No one on the screen is who they are when you breathe their air."

"Holden," Prax said.

"Well. He's the exception," she said.

The botanist looked down and then up again. His expression was almost apologetic.

"Mei's probably dead," he said.

"You don't believe that."

"It's been a long time. Even if they had her medicine, they've probably turned her into one of these...things."

"You still don't believe that," she said. The botanist leaned forward, frowning like she'd given him a problem he couldn't immediately solve. "Tell me it's all right to bomb Io. I can have thirty nuclear warheads fired now. Turn off the engines, let them fly ballistic. They won't all get through, but some will. Say the word now, and I can have Io reduced to slag before we even get there."

"You're right," Prax said. And then, a moment later: "Why aren't you doing that?"

"Do you want the real reason, or my justification?"

"Both?"

"I justify it this way," she said. "I don't know what is in that lab. I can't assume that the monsters are only there, and if I destroy the place, I might be slagging the records that will let me find the missing ones. I don't know everyone involved in this, and I don't have proof against some of the ones I do know. It may be down there. I'll go, I'll find out, and then I will reduce the lab to radioactive glass afterward."

"Those are good reasons."

"They're good justifications. I find them very convincing."

"But the reason is that Mei might still be alive."

"I don't kill children," she said. "Not even when it's the right thing to do. You would be surprised how often it's hurt my political career. People used to think I was weak until I found the trick."

"The trick."

"If you can make them blush, they think you're a hard-ass," she said. "My husband calls it the mask."

"Oh," Prax said. "Thank you."

Waiting was worse than the fear of battle. Her body wanted to move, to get away from her chair and walk through the familiar halls. The back of her mind shouted for action, movement, confrontation. She paced the ship top to bottom and back again. Her mind went through trivia about all the people she met in the halls, the small detritus from the intelligence reports she'd read. The mechanic, Amos Burton. Implicated in several murders, indicted, never tried. Took an elective vasectomy the day he was legally old enough to do so. Naomi Nagata, the engineer. Two master's degrees. Offered full-ride scholarship for a PhD on Ceres Station and turned it down. Alex Kamal, pilot. Seven drunk and disorderlies when he was in his early twenties. Had a son on Mars he still didn't know about. James Holden, the man without secrets. The holy fool who'd dragged the solar system into war and seemed utterly blind to the damage he caused. An idealist. The most dangerous kind of man there was. And a good man too.

She wondered whether any of it mattered.

The only real player near enough to talk to without lag turning the conversation utterly epistolary was Souther, and as he was still putatively on the same side as Nguyen and preparing to face battle with the ships protecting her, the opportunities were few and far between.

"Have you heard anything?" he asked from her terminal.

"No," she said. "I don't know what's taking the fucking bobble-head so long."

"You're asking him to turn his back on the man he's trusted the most."

"And how fucking long does that take? When I did it, it was over in maybe five minutes. 'Soren,' I said. 'You're a douche bag. Get out of my sight.' It isn't harder than that."

"And if he doesn't come through?" Souther asked.

She sighed.

"Then I call you back and try talking you into going rogue."

"Ah," Souther said with a half smile. "And how do you see that going?"

"I don't like my chances, but you never know. I can be damned persuasive."

An alert popped up. A new message. From Arjun.

"I have to go," she said. "Keep an ear to the ground or whatever the hell you do out here where the ground doesn't mean anything."

"Be safe, Chrisjen," Souther said, and vanished into the green background of a dead connection.

Around her, the galley was empty. Still, someone might come in. She lifted the hem of her sari and walked to her little room, sliding her door closed before she gave her terminal permission to open the file.

Arjun was at his desk, his formal clothes on but undone at the neck and sleeves. He looked like a man just returned from a bad party. The sunlight streamed in behind him. Afternoon, then. It had been afternoon when he'd sent it. And it might still be. She touched the screen, her fingertips tracing the line of his shoulder.

"So I understand from your message that you may not come home," he said.

"I'm sorry," she said to the screen.

"As you imagine, I find the thought…distressing," he said, and then a smile split his face, dancing in eyes she now saw were red with tears. "But what can I do about it? I teach poetry to graduate students. I have no power in this world. That has always been you. And so I want to offer you this. Don't think about me. Don't take your mind from what you're doing on my account. And if you don't…"

Arjun took a deep breath.

"If life transcends death, then I will seek for you there. If not, then there too."

He looked down and then up again.

"I love you, Kiki. And I will always love you, from whatever distance."

The message ended. Avasarala closed her eyes. Around her, the ship was as close and confining as a coffin. The small noises of it pressed in against her until she wanted to scream. Until she wanted to sleep. She let herself weep for a moment. There was nothing else to be done. She had taken her best shot, and there was nothing to be done but meditate and worry.

Half an hour later, her terminal chimed again, waking her from troubled dreams. Errinwright. Anxiety knotted her throat. She lifted a finger to begin the playback, and then paused. She didn't want to. She didn't want to go back into that world, wear her heavy mask. She wanted to watch Arjun again. Listen to his voice.

Only, of course, Arjun had known what she would want. It was why he'd said the things he had. She started the message.

Errinwright looked angry. More than that, he looked tired. His pleasant demeanor was gone, and he was a man made entirely of salt water and threat.

"Chrisjen," he said. "I know you won't understand this, but I have been doing everything in my power to keep you and yours safe. You don't understand what you've waded into, and you are fucking things up. I wish you had had the moral courage to come to me with this before you ran off like a horny sixteen-year-old with James Holden. Honestly, if there was a better way to destroy any professional credibility you once had, I can't think what it would have been.

"I put you on the *Guanshiyin* to take you off the board because I knew that things were about to go hot. Well, they are, only you're in the middle of them and you don't understand the situation. Millions of people stand in real danger of dying badly because of your egotism. You're one of them. Arjun's another. And your daughter. All of them are in threat now because of *you*."

In the image, Errinwright clasped his hands together, pressing his knuckles against his lower lip, the platonic ideal of a scolding father.

"If you come back now, I might—might—be able to save you. Not your career. That's gone. Forget it. Everyone down here sees that you're working with the OPA and Mars. Everyone thinks you've betrayed us, and I can't undo that. Your life and your family. That's all I can salvage. But you have to get away from this circus you've started, and you have to do it now.

"Time's short, Chrisjen. Everything important to you hangs in the balance, and I cannot help you if you don't help yourself. Not with this.

"It's last-chance time. Ignore me now, and the next time we talk, someone will have died."

The message ended. She started it again, and then a third time. Her grin felt feral.

She found Bobbie in the ops deck with the pilot, Alex. They stopped talking as she came in, a question in Bobbie's expression. Avasarala held up a finger and switched the video feed to display on the ship monitors. Errinwright came to life. On the big screens, she could see his pores and the individual hairs in his eyebrows. As he spoke, Avasarala saw Alex and Bobbie grow sober, leaning in toward the screen as if they were all at a poker table and coming to the end of a high-stakes hand.

"All right," Bobbie said. "What do we do?"

"We break out the fucking champagne," Avasarala said. "What did he just tell us? There is nothing in that message. Nothing. He is walking around his words like they've got poisoned spikes on them. And what's he got? Threats. No one makes threats."

"Wait," Alex said. "That was a good sign?"

"That was excellent," Avasarala said, and then something else, something small, fell into place in the back of her mind and she started laughing and cursing at the same time.

"What? What is it?"

" 'If life transcends death, then I will seek for you there. If not, then there too,' " she said. "It's a fucking haiku. That man has a one-track mind and one train on it. Poetry. Save me from poetry."

They didn't understand, but they didn't need to. The real message came five hours later. It came on a public newsfeed, and it was delivered by Secretary-General Esteban Sorrento-Gillis. The old man was brilliant at looking somber and energetic at the same time. If he hadn't been the executive of the largest governing body in the history of the human race, he'd have made a killing promoting health drinks.

The whole crew had gathered by now—Amos, Naomi, Holden, Alex. Even Prax. They were sandwiched into the ops deck, their combined breaths just slightly overloading the recyclers and giving the deck a feeling of barn heat. All eyes were on the screen as the secretary-general took the podium.

"I have come here tonight to announce the immediate formation of an investigative committee. Accusations have been made that some individuals within the governing body of the United Nations and its military forces have taken unauthorized and possibly illegal steps in dealing with certain private contractors. If these accusations are true, they must be addressed in the most expedient possible manner. And if unfounded, they must be dispelled and those responsible for spreading these lies called to account.

"I need not remind you all of the years I spent as a political prisoner."

"Oh fuck me," Avasarala said, clapping her hands in glee. "He's using the outsider speech. That man's asshole must be tight enough right now to bend space."

"I have dedicated my terms as secretary-general to rooting out corruption, and as long as I have this gavel, I shall continue to do so. Our world and the solar system we all share must be assured that the United Nations honors the ethical, moral, and spiritual values that hold us all together as a species."

On the feed, Esteban Sorrento-Gillis nodded, turned, and strode away in a clamor of unacknowledged questions, and the commentators flowed into the space, talking over each other in all the political opinions of the spectrum.

"Okay," Holden said. "So did he actually say anything?"

"He said Errinwright is finished," Avasarala said. "If he had any influence left at all, that announcement would never have been made. God*damn*, I wish I was there."

Errinwright was off the board. All that left was Nguyen, Mao, Strickland or whoever he was, their half-controlled protomolecule warriors, and the building threat of Venus. She let a long breath rattle through her throat and the spaces behind her nose.

"Ladies and gentlemen," she said, "I have just solved our smallest problem."

Chapter Forty-Six: Bobbie

One of Bobbie's most vivid memories was of the day she got her orders to report to the 2nd Expeditionary Force Spec War training facility. Force Recon. The top of the heap for a Martian ground pounder. In boot camp, they'd trained with a Force Recon sergeant. He'd been wearing a suit of gleaming red power armor, and they'd watched him demonstrate its use in a variety of tactical situations. At the end, he'd told them that the top four boots from her class would be transferred to the Spec War facility on the slopes of Hecates Tholus and trained to wear the armor and join the baddest fighting unit in the solar system.

She decided that meant her.

Determined to win one of those four coveted slots, she'd thrown herself into her boot camp training with everything she had. It turned out that was quite a lot. Not only did she make it into the top four, she was number one by an embarrassing margin. And then the letter came, ordering her to report to Hecate Base for recon training, and it was all worth it. She called her father and just screamed for two minutes. When he finally got her to calm down and tell him what she was calling about, he screamed back for even longer. *You're one of the best now, baby*, he'd said at the end, and the warmth those words put in her heart had never really faded.

Even now, sitting on the gray metal deck in the dirty machine shop on a stolen Martian warship. Even with all her mates torn into pieces and scattered across the frozen surface of Ganymede. Even with her military status in limbo and her loyalty to her nation justifiably in question. Even with all that, *You're one of the best now, baby* made her smile. She felt an ache to call her father and tell him what had happened. They'd always been close, and when neither of her brothers had followed in his footsteps by choosing a military career, she had. It had just strengthened the connection. She knew he'd understand what it was costing her to turn her back on everything she held sacred to avenge her team.

And she had a powerful premonition she'd never see him again.

Even if they made it through to Jupiter with half the UN fleet hunting them, and even if when they got there, Admiral Nguyen and the dozen or more ships he controlled didn't immediately blow them out of the sky, and even if they managed to stop whatever was happening in orbit around Io with the *Rocinante* intact, Holden was still planning to land and save Prax's daughter.

The monsters would be there.

She knew it as surely as she'd ever known anything in her life. Each night she dreamed of facing it again. The thing flexing its long fingers and staring at her with its too-large glowing blue eyes, ready to finish what it had started all those months earlier on Ganymede. In her dream, she raised a gun that grew out of her hand, and started shooting it as it ran toward her, black spider-webs spilling from holes that closed like water. She always woke before it reached her, but she knew how the dream would end: with her shattered body left cooling on the ice. She also knew that when Holden led his team down to the laboratories on Io where the monsters were made, she'd go along with him. The scene from her dream would play out in real life. She knew it like she knew her father's love. She welcomed it.

On the floor around her lay the pieces of her armor. With weeks of travel on the way to Io, she had time to completely strip and refit it. The *Rocinante*'s machine shop was well stocked, and the tools were of Martian make. It was the perfect location. The suit had seen a lot of use without much maintenance, but if she was being honest with herself, the distraction was the payoff. A suit of Martian reconnaissance armor was an incredibly complex machine, finely tuned to its wearer. Stripping and reassembling it wasn't a trivial task. It required full concentration. Every moment she spent working on it was another moment when she didn't think about the monster waiting to kill her on Io.

Sadly, that distraction was over now. She'd finished with the maintenance, even finding the micro-fracture in a tiny valve that was causing the slow but persistent leak of fluid in the suit's knee actuator. It was time to just put it all back together. It had the feeling of ritual. A final cleansing before going out to meet death on the battlefield.

I've watched too many Kurosawa movies, she thought, but couldn't quite abandon the idea. The imagery was a lovely way of turning angst and suicidal ideation into honor and noble sacrifice.

She picked up the torso assembly and carefully wiped it off with a damp cloth, removing the last bits of dust and machine oil that clung to the outside. The smell of metal and lubricant filled the air. And while she bolted armor plating back onto the frame, the red enameled surface covered with a thousand dings and scratches, she stopped fighting the urge to ritualize the task and just let it happen. She was very likely assembling her death shroud. Depending on how the final battle went, this ceramic and rubber and alloy might house her corpse for the rest of eternity.

She flipped the torso assembly over and began working on the back. A long gouge in the enamel showed the violence of her passage across Ganymede's ice when the monster had self-destructed right in front of her. She picked up a wrench, then put it back down, tapping on the deck with her knuckle.

Why then?

Why had the monster blown itself up at that moment? She remembered the way it had started to shift, new limbs bursting from its body as it watched her. If Prax was right, that was the moment the constraint systems that Mao's scientists had installed failed. And they'd set the bomb up to detonate if the creature was getting out of their control. But that just pushed the question one level back. Why had their control over the creature's physiology failed at that precise moment? Prax said that regenerative processes were a good place for constraint systems to fail. And her platoon had riddled the creature with gunfire as it had charged their lines. It hadn't seemed to hurt it at the time, but each wound represented a sudden burst of activity inside the creature's cells, or whatever it had in place of cells, as the monster healed. Each was a chance for the new growth to slip the leash.

Maybe that was the answer. *Don't try to kill the monster. Just damage it enough that the program starts to break down and the self-destruct kicks in.* She wouldn't even have to survive, just last long enough to harm the monster beyond its ability to safely repair itself. All she needed was enough time to really hurt it.

She put down the armor plate she was working on and picked up the helmet. The suit's memory still had the gun camera footage of the fight on it. She hadn't watched it again after Avasarala's presentation to the crew of the *Roci*. She hadn't been able to.

She pushed herself to her feet and hit the comm panel on the wall. "Hey, Naomi? You in ops?"

"Yep," Naomi said after a few seconds. "You need something, Sergeant?"

"Do you think you can tell the *Roci* to talk to my helmet? I've got the radio on, but it won't talk to civilian stuff. This is one of our boats, so I figure the *Roci* has the keys and codes."

There was a long pause, so Bobbie put the helmet on a work-table next to the closest wall monitor and waited.

"I'm seeing a radio node that the *Roci* is calling 'MCR MR Goliath III 24397A15.' "

"That's me," Bobbie said. "Can you send control of that node down to the panel in the machine shop?"

"Done," Naomi said after a second.

"Thanks," Bobbie said, and killed the comm. It took her a moment to re-familiarize herself with the Martian military video software, and to convince the system to use out-of-date data-unpacking algorithms. After a few false starts, the raw gun camera footage from her fight on Ganymede was playing on the screen. She set it to endless loop and sat back down on the deck with her suit.

She finished bolting the back armor on and began attaching the torso's power supply and main hydraulic system during the first play-through. She tried not to feel anything about the images on screen, nor to attach any significance to them or think of them as a puzzle to be solved. She just concentrated on her work on the suit with her mind and let her subconscious chew on the data from the screen.

The distraction caused her to redo things occasionally as she worked, but that was fine. She wasn't on a deadline. She finished attaching the power supply and main motors. Green lights lit up on the hand terminal she had plugged into the suit's brain. On the wall screen by her helmet, a UN soldier was hurled across the surface of Ganymede at her. A confusion of images as she dodged away. When the image steadied, both the UN Marine and her friend Tev Hillman were gone.

Bobbie picked up an arm assembly and began reattaching it to the torso. The monster had picked up a soldier in a suit of armor comparable to her own and then thrown him with enough force to kill instantly. There was no defense against that kind of strength except not to get hit. She concentrated on putting the arm back together.

When she looked up at the screen again, the feed had restarted. The monster was running across the ice, chasing the UN soldiers. It killed one of them. The Bobbie on the video began firing, followed by her entire platoon opening up.

The creature was fast. But when the UN soldiers suddenly turned to open a firing lane for the Martians, the creature didn't react quickly. So maybe fast in a straight line, but not a lot of lateral speed. That might be useful. The video caught up again to the UN soldier being thrown into Private Hillman. The creature reacted to gunfire, to injuries, even though they didn't slow it down. She thought back to the video she'd seen of Holden and Amos engaging the creature in the *Rocinante*'s cargo hold. It had largely ignored them until Amos started shooting it, and then it had erupted into violence.

But the first creature had attacked the UN troop station. So at least to some degree, they could be directed. Given orders. Once they no longer had orders, they seemed to lapse into a default state of trying to get increased energy and break the constraints. While in that state, they ignored pretty much everything but food and violence. The next time she ran into one, unless it had specifically been ordered to attack her, she could probably pick her own battleground, draw it to her where she wanted to be. That was useful too.

She finished attaching the arm assembly and tested it. Greens across the board. Even if she wasn't sure whom she was working for, at least she hadn't forgotten how to do her job.

On the screen, the monster ran up the side of the big mech *Yojimbo* and tore the pilot's hatch off. Sa'id, the pilot, was hurled away. Again with the ripping and throwing. It made sense. With a combination like enormous strength and virtual immunity to ballistic damage as your tool set, running straight at your opponent, then ripping them in two was a pretty winning strategy. Throwing heavy objects at lethal speeds went hand in hand with the strength. And kinetic energy was a bitch. Armor might deflect bullets or lasers, and it might help cushion impacts, but no one had ever made armor that could shrug off all the kinetic energy imparted by a large mass moving at high speed. At least not in something a human could wear. If you were strong enough, a garbage Dumpster was better than a gun.

So when the monster attacked, it ran straight at its enemy, hoping to get a grip on them, which pretty much ended the fight. If it couldn't do that, it tried to hurl heavy objects at the opponent. The one in the cargo bay had nearly killed Jim Holden by throwing a massive crate. Unfortunately, her armor had a lot of the same restrictions it had. While it made her very fast when she wanted to be, it was not particularly good at lateral movement. Most things built for speed weren't. Cheetahs and horses didn't do a lot of sideways running. She was strong in her suit, but not nearly as strong as it was. She did have an advantage with firearms in that she could run away from the creature while continuing to attack from range. The creature couldn't throw a massive object at her without stopping and anchoring itself. It might be ungodly strong, but it still only weighed what it weighed, and Newton had a few things to say about a light object throwing a heavy one.

By the time she'd finished assembling her suit, she'd watched the video over a hundred times, and the tactics of the fight were starting to take shape in her head. In hand-to-hand combat training, she'd been able to overpower most of her opponents. But the small and quick fighters, the ones who knew how to stick-and-move, gave her trouble. That was who she'd be in this fight. She'd have to hit and run, never stopping for a moment. And even then she'd need a lot of luck, because she was fighting way out of her weight class, and one shot from the monster was a guaranteed knockout.

Her other advantage was that she didn't really have to *win*. She just had to do enough damage to make the monster kill itself. By the time she'd climbed into her newly refurbished suit and let it close around her for a final test, she was pretty sure she could do that.

Bobbie thought her newfound peace about the battle to come would finally let her sleep, but after three hours of tossing and turning in her rack, she gave up. Something still itched at the back of her head. She was trying to find her *Bushido*, and there were still too many things she couldn't let go of. Something wasn't giving her permission yet.

So she pulled on a large fuzzy bathrobe she'd stolen from the *Guanshiyin*, and rode the ladder-lift up toward the ops deck. It was third watch, so the ship was deserted. Holden and Naomi had a cabin together, and she found herself envying that human contact right now. Something certain to cling to amid all the other uncertainty. Avasarala was in her borrowed cabin, probably sending messages to people back on Earth. Alex would be asleep in his room, and for a brief moment she considered waking him. She liked the gregarious pilot. He was genuine in a way she hadn't seen much of since leaving active duty. But she also knew that waking a man up at three a.m. while in her bathrobe sent signals she didn't intend. Rather than try to explain that she just needed to talk to someone, she passed the crew deck by and kept going.

Amos was sitting at a station in ops with his back to her, taking the late watch. To avoid startling him, she cleared her throat. He didn't move or react, so she walked to the comm station. Looking back at him, she saw that his eyes were closed and his breathing was very deep and regular. Sleeping on a duty watch would get you captain's mast, at the least, on an MCRN ship. It seemed Holden had let discipline lapse a bit since his Navy days.

Bobbie opened up the comms and found the closest relay for tightbeam traffic. First she called her father. "Hi, Pop. Not sure you should try and answer this. The situation here is volatile and evolving rapidly. But you may hear a lot of crazy shit over the next few days. Some of it might be about me. Just know that I love you guys, and I love Mars. Everything I did was to try and protect you and my home. I might have lost my way a little bit, because things got complicated and hard to figure out. But I think I see a clear path now, and I'm going to take it. I love you and Mom. Tell the boys they suck." Before she turned off the recording, she reached out and touched the screen. "Bye, Dad."

She pressed send, but something still felt incomplete. Outside her family, anyone who'd tried to help her in the last three months was sitting on the same ship she was, so it didn't make sense.

Except, of course, that it did. Because not *everyone* was on this ship.

Bobbie punched up another number from memory and said, "Hi, Captain Martens. It's me. I think I know what you were trying to help me see. I wasn't ready for it then, but it stuck with me. So you didn't waste your time. I get it now. I know this wasn't my fault. I know I was just at the wrong place at the wrong time. I'm going back to the start now *because* I understand. Not angry, not hurt, not blaming myself. Just my duty to finish the fight."

Something loosened in her chest the moment she hit the send button. All the threads had been neatly tied up, and now she could go to Io and do what she needed to do without regret. She let out a long sigh and slid down in the crash couch until she was almost prone. She suddenly felt bone tired. Like she could sleep for a week. She wondered if anyone would get mad if she just crashed out in ops instead of going all the way back down the lift.

She didn't remember having fallen asleep, but here she was stretched out in the comm station's crash couch, a small puddle of drool next to her head. To her relief, her robe seemed to have remained mostly in place, so at least she hadn't bare-assed everyone walking through.

"Gunny?" Holden said in a tone of voice that meant he was saying it again. He was standing over her, a concerned look on his face.

"Sorry, sorry," she said, sitting up and pulling her robe more tightly around her middle. "I needed to send out some messages last night. Must have been more tired than I thought."

"Yeah," Holden said. "It's no problem. Sleep wherever you like."

"Okay," Bobbie said, backing toward the crew ladder. "With

that, I think I'll go down and take a shower and try to turn back into a human."

Holden nodded as she went, a strange smile on his face. "Sure. Meet me in the machine shop when you're dressed."

"Roger that," she said, and bolted down the ladder.

After a decadently long shower and a change into her clean red-and-gray utility uniform, she grabbed a cup of coffee from the galley and made her way back down to the machine shop. Holden was already there. He had a crate the size of a guitar case sitting on one of the workbenches, and a larger square crate next to his feet on the deck. When she entered the compartment, he patted the crate on the table. "This is for you. I saw when you came on board that you seemed to be missing yours."

Bobbie hesitated a moment, then walked over to the crate and flipped it open. Inside sat a 2mm electrically fired three-barrel Gatling gun, of the type the Marines designated a Thunderbolt Mark V. It was new and shiny and exactly the type that would fit into her suit.

"This is amazing," Bobbie said after catching her breath. "But it's just an awkward club without ammo."

Holden kicked the crate on the floor. "Five thousand rounds of two-millimeter caseless. Incendiary-tipped."

"Incendiary?"

"You forget, I've seen the monster up close too. Armor piercing doesn't help at all. If anything, it reduces soft-tissue damage. But since the lab stuck an incendiary bomb into all of them, I figure that means they aren't fireproof."

Bobbie lifted the heavy weapon out of the crate and put it on the floor next to her newly reassembled suit.

"Oh, *hell* yes."

Chapter Forty-Seven: Holden

Holden sat at the combat control console on the operations deck and watched Ragnarok gather. Admiral Souther, who Avasarala had assured everyone was one of the good guys, had joined his ships with their small but growing fleet of Martians as they sped toward Io. Waiting for them in orbit around that moon were the dozen ships in Admiral Nguyen's fleet. More Martian and UN ships sped toward that location from Saturn and the Belt. By the time everyone got there, there would be something like thirty-five capital ships in the kill zone, and dozens of smaller interceptors and corvettes, like the *Rocinante*.

Three dozen capital ships. Holden tried to remember if there had ever been a fleet action of this size, and couldn't think of one. Including Admiral Nguyen's and Admiral Souther's flagships, there would be four *Truman*-class UN dreadnoughts in the final tally, and the Martians would have three *Donnager*-class battleships of their own, any one of which could depopulate a planet. The rest would be a mix of cruisers and destroyers. Not quite the heavy hitters the battleships were, but plenty powerful enough to vaporize the *Rocinante*. Which, if he was being honest, was the part Holden was most worried about.

On paper, his team had the most ships. With Souther and the Martians joining forces, they outnumbered the Nguyen contingent two to one. But how many Earth ships would be willing to fire on their own, just because one admiral and a banished politician said so? It was entirely possible that if actual shooting started, a lot of UN ships might have unexplained comm failures and wait to see how it all came out. And that wasn't the worst case. The worst case was that a number of Souther's ships would switch sides once Martians starting killing Earthers. The fight could turn into a whole lot of people pointing guns at each other, with no one knowing whom to trust.

It could turn into a bloodbath.

"We have twice as many ships," Avasarala said from her constant perch at the comm station. Holden almost objected but changed his mind. In the end, it wouldn't matter. Avasarala would believe what she wanted to believe. She needed to think all her efforts had been worthwhile, that they were about to pay off when the fleet arrived and this Nguyen clown surrendered to her obviously superior force. The truth was her version wasn't any more or less a fantasy than his. No one would know for sure until everyone knew for sure.

"How long now?" Avasarala said, then sipped at the bulb of weak coffee she'd started making for herself in place of tea.

Holden considered pointing out the navigation information the *Roci* made available at every console, and then didn't. Avasarala didn't want him to show her how to find it herself. She wanted him to tell her. She wasn't accustomed to pressing her own buttons. In her mind, she outranked him. Holden wondered what the chain of command actually looked like in this situation. How many illegal captains of stolen ships did it take to equal one disgraced UN official? That could tie a courtroom up for a few decades.

He also wasn't being fair to Avasarala. It wasn't about making him take her orders, not really. It was about being in a situation that she was utterly untrained for, where she was the least useful person in the room and trying to assert some control. Trying to reshape the space around her to fit with her mental image of herself.

Or maybe she just needed to hear a voice.

"Eighteen hours now," Holden said. "Most of the other ships that aren't part of our fleet will beat us there. And the ones that don't won't show up until it's over, so we can ignore them."

"Eighteen hours," Avasarala said. There was something like awe in her voice. "Space is too fucking big. It's the same old story."

He'd guessed right. She just wanted to talk, so he let her. "What story?"

"Empire. Every empire grows until its reach exceeds its grasp. We started out fighting over who got the best branches in one tree. Then we climb down and fight over a few kilometers' worth of trees. Then someone starts riding horses, and you get empires of hundreds or thousands of kilometers. Ships open up empire expansion across the oceans. The Epstein drive gave us the outer planets…"

She trailed off and tapped out something on the comm panel. She didn't volunteer who she was sending messages to, and Holden didn't ask. When she was done, she said, "But the story is always the same. No matter how good your technology is, at some point you'll conquer territory that you can't hold on to."

"You're talking about the outer planets?"

"Not specifically," she said, her voice growing soft and thoughtful. "I'm talking about the entire fucking concept of empire. The Brits couldn't hold on to India or North America because why should people listen to a king who's six thousand kilometers away?"

Holden tinkered with the air-circulation nozzle on his panel, aiming it at his face. The cool air smelled faintly of ozone and oil. "Logistics is always a problem."

"No kidding. Taking a dangerous trip six thousand kilometers across the Atlantic so you can fight with colonists gives the enemy one hell of a home-court advantage."

"At least," Holden said, "we Earthers figured that out before we picked a fight with Mars. It's even further. And sometimes the sun is in the way."

"Some people have never forgiven us for not humbling Mars when we had the chance," Avasarala said. "I work for a few of them. Fucking idiots."

"I thought the point of your story was that those people always lose in the end."

"Those people," she said, pushing herself to her feet and slowly heading toward the crew ladder, "are not the real problem. Venus might be housing the advance party of the first empire whose grasp is as long as its reach. And this fucking protomolecule has exposed us for the petty, small-town bosses we are. We're getting ready to trade our solar system away because we thought we could build airports out of bamboo and summon the cargo."

"Get some sleep," Holden said to her while she called up the ladder-lift. "We'll defeat one empire at a time."

"Maybe," she said as she dropped out of sight, and the deck hatch banged shut behind her.

"Why isn't anyone shooting?" Prax said. He'd come up to the operations deck trailing after Naomi like a lost child. Now he was sitting at one of the many unused crash couches. He stared up at the main screen, his face a mix of fear and fascination.

The big tactical display showed a muddled mass of red and green dots representing the three dozen capital ships parked in orbit around Io. The *Roci* had marked all the Earth ships green and the Martian ships red. It created a confusing simplicity out of what was in actuality a far more complex situation. Holden knew that friend-or-foe identification was going to be a problem if anyone started shooting.

For now, the various ships drifted quietly above Io, their enormous threat merely implied. They made Holden think of the crocodiles he'd seen at the zoo as a child. Huge, armored, filled with teeth, but drifting on the surface of the water like statues. Not even their eyes blinking. When food had been thrown into the pen, they'd exploded out of the water with frightening speed.

We're just waiting for some blood to hit the water.

"Why isn't anyone shooting?" Prax repeated.

"Hey, Doc," Amos said. He was lounging in one of the crash couches next to Prax. He projected a calm laziness that Holden wished he himself felt. "Remember how on Ganymede we were facing down those guys with guns and no one was shooting right up until you decided to cock your gun?"

Prax blanched. Holden guessed he was remembering the bloody aftermath of that fight. "Yes," Prax said. "I remember."

"This is like that," Amos said. "Only no one's cocked their gun just yet."

Prax nodded. "Okay."

If someone finally did break the whole situation loose, Holden knew that figuring out who was shooting at whom would be their first problem. "Avasarala, any word yet on the political landscape? There's a whole lot of green on that board. How many of those dots belong to us?"

Avasarala shrugged and went on listening to the ship-to-ship cross talk.

"Naomi?" Holden said. "Any ideas?"

"So far Nguyen's fleet is targeting only Martian ships," she replied, marking ships on the main tactical board for everyone to see. "The Martian ships are targeting back. Souther's ships aren't targeting anyone, and Souther hasn't even opened his tubes. I'm guessing he's still hoping for a peaceful resolution."

"Please send the intel officer on Souther's ship my compliments," Holden said to Naomi. "And ask him to get us some new

IFF data so this doesn't turn into the solar system's biggest clusterfuck."

"Done," Naomi said, and made the call.

"Get everyone buttoned up in their suits, Amos," Holden continued. "Do a hat check here before you go below. I hope we don't start shooting, but what I hope will happen and what actually happens are almost never the same."

"Roger," Amos said, then climbed out of his couch and began clumping around the deck on magnetic boots, checking the seals on everyone's helmets.

"Test test test," Holden said over the crew radio. One by one everyone on the ship responded with the affirmative. Until someone with a higher pay grade than his decided which way things were going to go, there wasn't much else he could do.

"Wait," Avasarala said, then hit a button on her console, and an outside channel started playing on their suit radios.

"—launch immediately against targets on Mars. We have a battery of missiles carrying a lethal biological weapon ready to fire. You have one hour to leave Io orbit or we will launch immediately against targets on Mars. We have a—"

Avasarala turned the channel off again.

"It seems a third party has joined the circle jerk," Amos said.

"No," Avasarala replied. "It's Nguyen. He's outnumbered, so he's ordered his Mao cronies on the surface to make the threat to back us off. He'll— Oh, shit."

She hit her panel again and a new voice spoke over the radio. This one was a woman's voice with a cultured Martian accent.

"Io, this is Admiral Muhan of the Martian Congressional Republic Navy. You fire anything bigger than a bottle rocket and we will glass the whole fucking moon. Do you read me?"

Amos leaned over to Prax. "Now, you see, all this is them cocking their guns."

Prax nodded. "Got it."

"This," Holden said, listening to the barely restrained fury in the Martian admiral's voice, "is about to get seriously out of hand."

"This is Admiral Nguyen aboard the UNN *Agatha King*," a new voice said. "Admiral Souther is here illegally, at the behest of a civilian UN official with no military authority. I hereby order all ships under Admiral Souther's command to immediately stand down. I further order that the captain of Souther's flagship place the admiral under arrest for treason and—"

"Oh, do shut up," Souther replied over the same channel. "I'm here as part of a legal fact-finding mission regarding improper use of UN funds and material for a secret biological weapon project on Io. A project which Admiral Nguyen is directly responsible for in contravention of UN directives—"

Avasarala cut the link.

"Oh, this ain't good," Alex said.

"Well," Avasarala said, then opened the faceplate on her helmet and let out a long sigh. She opened her purse and pulled a pistachio out of it. She cracked it and thoughtfully ate the meat, then put the shell in the nearby recycling chute. A tiny bit of the skin floated away in the microgravity. "No, actually, it should be fine. This is all posturing. As long as they keep comparing dicks, no one will shoot."

"But we can't just wait here," Prax said, shaking his head. Amos was floating in front of him, checking his helmet. Prax shoved him away and tried to get to his feet. He drifted away from his crash couch but didn't think to turn on his boot mags. "If Mei is down there, we have to go. They're talking about glassing the moon. We have to get there before they do it."

There was a high violin-string whine at the back of Prax's voice. The tension was getting to him. It was getting to all of them, but Prax was the one who was going to show it worst and first. Holden shot a look at Amos, but the big man just looked surprised at having been pushed away by the much smaller scientist.

"They're talking about destroying the base. We have to go

down there!" Prax continued, the panic in his voice starting to shine through.

"We're not doing anything," Holden said. "Not until we have a better idea how this is going to shake out."

"We came all this way so that we can not do anything?" Prax demanded.

"Doc, we don't want to be the ones to move first," Amos said, and put a hand on Prax's shoulder, pulling him back down to the deck. The little botanist violently shrugged it off without turning around, then shoved off his couch toward Avasarala.

"Give me the channel. Let me talk to them," Prax said, reaching for her comm panel. "I can—"

Holden launched himself out of his crash couch, catching the scientist mid-flight and hurling them both across the deck and into the bulkhead. The thick layer of anti-spalling padding absorbed their impact, but Holden felt the air go out of Prax when his hip slammed into the smaller man's belly.

"Gah," Prax said, and curled up into a floating fetal ball.

Holden kicked on his boot mags and pushed himself down to the deck. He grabbed Prax and pushed him across the compartment to Amos. "Take him below, stuff him in his bunk, and sedate the shit out of him. Then get to engineering and get us ready for a fight."

Amos nodded and grabbed the floating Prax. "Okay." A moment later the two of them disappeared down the deck hatch.

Holden looked around the room, seeing the shocked looks from Avasarala and Naomi but ignoring them. Prax's need for his daughter to take precedence over everything else had almost put them all in danger again. And while Holden intellectually understood the man's drive, having to stop him from killing them all every time Mei's name came up was stress he didn't need right then. It left him angry and needing to snap at someone.

"Where the hell is Bobbie?" he said to no one in particular. He hadn't seen her since they had put in to orbit around Io.

"Just saw her in the machine shop," Amos replied over the

radio. "She was fieldstripping my shotgun. I think she's doing all the guns and armor."

"That's—" Holden started, ready to yell about something. "That's actually really helpful. Tell her to button up her suit and turn her radio on. Things might be going south in a hurry here."

He took a few seconds to breathe and calm himself down, then returned to the combat operations station.

"You okay?" Naomi asked over their private channel.

"No," he said, chinning the button to make sure only she heard his reply. "No, I'm actually scared to death."

"I thought we were past that."

"Past being scared?"

"No," she said, the smile audible in her voice. "Past blaming yourself for it. I'm scared too."

"I love you," Holden said, feeling that same electric thrill he always got when he told her, part fear, part boast.

"You should probably keep your eye on your station," she said, her tone teasing. She never told him she loved him when he said it first. She'd said that when people did it too often, it made the word lose all its power. He understood the argument, but he'd kind of hoped she'd break her rule this once. He needed to hear it.

Avasarala was hunched over the comm station like an ancient mystic peering into a murky crystal ball. The space suit hung on her like a scarecrow's oversized coveralls. Holden considered ordering her to button up her helmet, then shrugged. She was old enough to decide for herself the relative risks and rewards of eating during a battle.

Periodically she reached into her purse and pulled out another nut. The air around her was a growing cloud of tiny pieces of pistachio skin. It was annoying to watch her cluttering up his ship, but no warship was built so fragile that a little airborne waste would break anything. Either the tiny pieces of shell would be sucked into the air recycling system and trapped by the filters, or they'd go under thrust and all the garbage would fall to the floor, where they could sweep it up. Holden wondered if Avasarala had ever had to clean anything in her life.

While he watched her, the old lady cocked her head to one side, listening with sudden interest to something only she could hear. Her hand darted forward, bird quick, to tap at the screen. A new voice came over the ship's radios, this one with the faint hiss transmissions picked up when traveling for millions of kilometers through space.

"—eneral Esteban Sorrento-Gillis. Some time ago, I announced the formation of an exploratory committee to look into possible misuse of UN resources for illegal biological weapon research. While that investigation is ongoing, and the committee is not prepared to bring charges at this time, in the interests of public safety and to better facilitate a thorough and comprehensive investigation, certain UN personnel in key positions are to be recalled to Earth for questioning. First, Admiral Augusto Nguyen, of the United Nations Navy. Second—"

Avasarala hit the panel to shut off the feed and stared at the console with her mouth open for several seconds. "Oh, fuck me."

All over the ship, alarms started blaring.

Chapter Forty-Eight: Avasarala

I 've got fast movers," Naomi said over the blaring alarms. "The UN flagship is firing."

Avasarala closed her helmet, watching the in-suit display confirm the seal, then tapped at the communications console, her mind moving faster than her hands. Errinwright had cut a deal, and now Nguyen knew it. The admiral had just been hung out to dry, and he was taking it poorly. A flag popped up on the console: incoming high-priority broadcast. She thumbed it, and Souther appeared on her terminal and every other one in the ops deck.

"This is Admiral Souther. I am hereby taking command of—"

"Okay," Naomi said. "I need my real screen back now. Got some work to do."

"Sorry, sorry," Avasarala said, tapping at the console. "Wrong button."

"—this task force. Admiral Nguyen is relieved of duty. Any hostilities will be—"

Avasarala switched the feed to her own screen and in the process switched to a different broadcast. Nguyen was flushed almost purple. He was wearing his uniform like a boast.

"—illegal and unprecedented seizure. Admiral Souther is to be escorted to the brig until—"

Five incoming comm requests lit up, each listing a name and short-form transponder ID. She ignored them all for the broadcast controls. As soon as the live button went active, she looked into the camera.

"This is Assistant Undersecretary Chrisjen Avasarala, representing the civilian government of Earth," she said. "Legal and appropriate command of this force is given to Admiral Souther. Anyone rejecting or ignoring his orders will be subject to legal action. I repeat, Admiral Souther is in legally authorized command of—"

Naomi made a low grunting sound. Avasarala stopped the broadcast and turned.

"Okay," Holden said. "That was bad."

"What?" Avasarala said. "What was bad?"

"One of the Earth ships just took three torpedo hits."

"It that a lot?"

"The PDCs aren't stopping them," Naomi said. "Those UN torpedoes all have transponder codes that mark them as friends, so they're sailing right through. They typically don't expect to be getting shot at by other UN ships."

"Three is a lot," Holden said, strapping into the crash couch. She didn't see him touch any of the controls, but he must have, because when he spoke, it echoed through the ship as well as the speakers in her helmet. "We have just gone live. Everyone has to the count of twenty to get strapped in someplace safe."

"Solid copy on that," Bobbie replied from wherever she was on the ship.

"Just got the doc strapped in and happy," Amos said. "I'm on my way to engineering."

"Are we heading into this?" Alex asked.

"We've got something like thirty-five capital ships out there, all of them much, much bigger than us. How about we just try to keep anyone from shooting us full of holes."

"Yes, sir," Alex said from the pilot's deck. Any vestige of democracy and vote taking was gone. That was a good thing. At least Holden had control when there had to be a single voice in command.

"I have two fast movers coming in," Naomi said. "Someone still thinks we're the bad guys."

"I blame Avasarala," Bobbie said.

Before Avasarala could laugh, gravity ticked up and slewed to the side, the *Rocinante* taking action beneath her. Her couch shifted and creaked. The protective gel squeezed her and let her go.

"Alex?"

"On 'em," Alex said. "I wouldn't mind getting a real gunner, sir."

"Are we going to have enough time to get her up here safely?"

"Nope," Alex said. "I've got three more incoming."

"I can take PDC control from here, sir," Bobbie said. "It's not the real thing, but it's something the rest of you won't have to do."

"Naomi, give the PDCs to the sergeant."

"PDC control transferred. It's all yours, Bobbie."

"Taking control," Bobbie said.

Avasarala's screen was a tangle of incoming messages in a flickering array. She started going through them. The *Kennedy* was announcing that Souther's command was illegal. The *Triton*'s first officer was reporting that the captain had been relieved of duty, and requested orders from Souther. The Martian destroyer *Iani Chaos* was trying to reach Avasarala for clarification of which Earth ships it was permitted to shoot at.

She pulled up the tactical display. Circles in red and green marked the swarm of ships; tiny silver threads showed what might have been streams of PDC fire or the paths of torpedoes.

"Are we red or green?" Avasarala asked. "Who's who on this fucking thing?"

"Mars is red, Earth is green," Naomi said.

"And which Earth ones are on our side?"

"Find out," Holden said as one of the green dots suddenly vanished. "Alex?"

"The *Darius* took the safeties off its PDCs, and now it's spraying down everything in range whether it's friend or foe. And... shit."

Avasarala's chair shifted again, seeming to rise from under her, pressing her back into the gel until it was hard to lift her arms. On the tactical screen, the cloud of ships, enemy and friendly and ambiguous, shifted slightly, and two golden dots grew larger, proximity notations beside them counting quickly down.

"Madam Assistant whatever you are," Holden said, "you could respond to some of those comm requests now."

Avasarala's gut felt like someone was squeezing it from below. The taste of salt and stomach acid haunted the back of her tongue. She was beginning to sweat in a way that had less to do with temperature than nausea. She forced her hands out to the control panel just as the two golden dots vanished.

"Thank you, Bobbie," Alex said. "I'm heading up. Gonna try to get the Martians between us and the fighting."

She started making calls. In the heat of a battle, all she had to offer was this: making calls. Talking. The same things she always did. Something about it was actually reassuring. The *Greenville* was accepting Souther's command. The *Tanaka* wasn't responding. The *Dyson* opened the channel, but the only sound was men shouting at each other. It was bedlam.

A message came in from Souther, and she accepted it. It included a new IFF code, and she manually accepted the update. On the tactical, most of the green dots shifted to white.

"Thank you," Holden said. Avasarala swallowed her *You're welcome*. The antinausea drugs seemed to be working for everyone else. She really, *really* didn't want to throw up inside her helmet. One of the six remaining green dots blinked out of existence and another turned suddenly to white.

"Ooh, right in the back," Alex said. "That was cold."

Souther's ID showed up again on Avasarala's console, and she hit accept just as the *Roci* shifted again.

"—the immediate surrender of the flagship *King* and Admiral Augusto Nguyen," Souther was saying. His shock of white hair was standing up off his head as if the low thrust gravity was letting it expand like a peacock's tail. His smile was sharp as a knife. "Any vessel that still refuses to acknowledge my orders as legal and legitimate will forfeit this amnesty. You have thirty seconds from this mark."

On the tactical display, the threads of silver and gold had, for the most part, vanished. The ships shifted positions, each moving along its own complex vectors. As she watched, all the remaining green dots turned to white. All except one.

"Don't be an asshole, Nguyen," Avasarala said. "It's over."

The ops deck was silent for a long moment, the tension almost unbearable. Naomi's voice was the one to break it.

"I've got more fast movers. Oh, I've got a *lot* of them."

"Where?" Holden snapped.

"From the surface."

Avasarala didn't do anything, but her tactical display resized, pulling back until the cluster of ships, red and white and the single defiant green, were less than a quarter of their original size and the massive curve of the moon's surface impinged on the lower edge of the display. Rising like a solid mass, hundreds of fine yellow lines.

"Get me a count," Holden said. "I need a count here."

"Two hundred nineteen. No. Wait. Two hundred thirty."

"What the hell are they? Are those torpedoes?" Alex asked.

"No," Bobbie said. "They're monsters. They launched the monsters."

Avasarala opened a broadcast channel. Her hair probably looked worse than Souther's but she was well past vanity. That she could speak without fear of vomiting was blessing enough.

"This is Avasarala," she said. "The launch you are all seeing right now is a new protomolecule-based weapon that is being used as an unauthorized first strike against Mars. We need to shoot those fuckers out of the sky and do it now. Everyone."

"We've got a coordination override request coming through from Souther's flagship," Naomi said. "Surrender control?"

"The hell I will," Alex said.

"No, but track requests," Holden said. "I'm not handing control of my ship to a military fire-control computer, but we still need to be part of the solution here."

"The *King*'s starting a hard burn," Alex said. "I think he's trying to hightail it."

On the display, the attack from the surface of Io was beginning to bloom, individual threads coming apart in unexpected angles, some corkscrewing, some reaching out in bent paths like an insect's articulated legs. Any one of them was the death of a planet, and the acceleration data put them at ten, fifteen, twenty g's. Nothing human survived at a sustained twenty g. Nothing human had to.

Golden flickers of light appeared from the ships, drifting down to meet the threads of Io. The slow, stately pace of the display was undercut by the data. Plasma torpedoes burning full out, and yet it took long seconds for them to reach the main stem. Avasarala watched the first of them detonate, saw the column of protomolecule monsters split into a dozen different streams. Evasive action.

"Some of those are coming toward us, Cap," Alex said. "I don't think they're designed to hole a ship's hull, but I'm pretty damn sure they'd do it anyway."

"Let's get in there and do what we can. We can't let any of these…Okay, where'd they go?"

On the tactical display, the attacking monsters were blinking out of existence, the threads vanishing.

"They're cutting thrust," Naomi said. "And the RF transponders are going dark. Must have radar-absorbing hull materials."

"Do we have tracking data? Can we anticipate where they're going to be?"

The tactical display began to flicker. Fireflies. The monsters shifting in and out, thrusting in what looked like semi-random directions, but the bloom of them always expanding.

"This is going to be a bitch," Alex said. "Bobbie?"

"I've got some target locks. Get us in PDC range."

"Hang on, kids," Alex said. "We're going for a ride."

The *Roci* bucked hard, and Avasarala pressed back into her seat. The shuddering rhythm seemed to be her own trembling muscles and then the firing PDCs and then her body again. On the display, the combined forces of Earth and Mars spread out, running after the near-invisible foes. Thrust gravity shifted, spinning her couch one way and then another without warning. She tried closing her eyes, but that was worse.

"Hmm."

"What, Naomi?" Holden said. " 'Hmm' what?"

"The *King* was doing something strange there. Huge activity from the maneuvering thrusters and...Oh."

" 'Oh' what? Nouns. I need nouns."

"She's holed," Naomi said. "One of the monsters holed her."

"Told you they could do that," Alex said. "Hate to be on the ship right now. Still. Couldn't have happened to a nicer fella."

"His men aren't responsible for his actions," Bobbie said. "They may not even know Souther's in command. We've got to help them."

"We can't," Holden said. "They'll shoot at us."

"Would you all please shut the fuck up?" Avasarala said. "And stop moving the goddamned ship around. Just pick a direction and calm down for two minutes."

Her comm request went ignored for five minutes. Then ten. When the *King*'s distress beacon kicked in, she still hadn't answered. A broadcast signal came in just after.

"This is Admiral Nguyen of the United Nations battleship *Agatha King*. I am offering to surrender to UN ships with the condition of immediate evacuation. Repeat: I am offering surrender to any United Nations military vessel on the condition of immediate evacuation."

Souther answered on the same frequency.

"This is the *Okimbo*. What's your situation?"

"We have a possible biohazard," Nguyen said. His voice was so tight and high it sounded like someone was strangling him. On the tactical display, several white dots were already moving toward the green.

"Hold tight, *King*," Souther said. "We're on our way."

"Like hell you are," Avasarala said, then cursed quietly as she opened a broadcast channel. "Like hell you are. This is Avasarala. I am declaring a quarantine and containment order on the *Agatha King*. No vessel should dock with her or accept transfer of materiel or personnel. Any ship that does will be placed under a quarantine and containment order as well."

Two of the white dots turned aside. Three others continued on. She opened the channel again.

"Am I the only one here who remembers Eros? What the fuck do you people think is loose on the *King*? Do not approach."

The last of the white dots turned aside. When Nguyen answered her comm request, she'd forgotten she still had it open. He looked like shit. She didn't imagine she looked much better. How many wars had ended this way? she wondered. Two exhausted, nauseated people staring at each other while the world burned around them.

"What more do you want from me?" Nguyen said. "I've surrendered. I lost. My men shouldn't have to die for your spite."

"It's not spite," Avasarala said. "We can't do it. The protomolecule gets loose. Your fancy control programs don't work. It's infectious."

"That's not proven," he said, but the way he said it told her everything.

"It's happening, isn't it?" she said. "Turn on your internal cameras. Let us see."

"I'm not going to do that."

She felt the air go out of her. It had happened.

"I am so sorry," Avasarala said. "Oh. I am so sorry."

Nguyen's eyebrows rose a millimeter. His lips pressed, blood-less and thin. She thought there were tears in his eyes, but it might have been only a transmission artifact.

"You have to turn on the transponders," Avasarala said. And then, when he didn't reply: "We can't weaponize the protomole-cule. We don't understand what it is. We can't control it. You just sent a death sentence to Mars. I can't save you, I cannot. But turn those transponders back on and help me save them."

The moment hung in the air. Avasarala could feel Holden's and Naomi's attention on her like warmth radiating from the heating grate. Nguyen shook his head, his lips twitching, lost in conversa-tion with himself.

"Nguyen," she said. "What's happening? On your ship. How bad is it?"

"Get me out of here, and I'll turn the transponders on," he said. "Throw me in the brig for the rest of my life, I don't care. But get me off of this ship."

Avasarala tried to lean forward, but it only made her crash couch shift. She looked for the words that would bring him back, the ones that would tell him that he had been wrong and evil and now he was going to die badly at the hands of his own weapon and somehow make it all right. She looked at this angry, small, shortsighted, frightened little man and tried to find the way to pull him back to simple human decency.

She failed.

"I can't do that," she said.

"Then stop wasting my time," he said, and cut the connection.

She lay back, her palm over her eyes.

"I'm gettin' some mighty strange readings off that battleship," Alex said. "Naomi? You seeing this?"

"Sorry. Give me a second."

"What have you got, Alex?" Holden asked.

"Reactor activity's down. Internal radiation through the ship's spiking huge. It's like they're venting the reactor into the air recycling."

"That don't sound healthy," Amos said.

The ops deck went silent again. Avasarala reached to open a channel to Souther but stopped. She didn't know what she'd say. The voice that came over the ship channel was slushy and drugged. She didn't recognize Prax at first, and then he had to repeat himself twice before she could make out the words.

"Incubation chamber," Prax said. "It's making the ship an incubation chamber. Like on Eros."

"It knows how to do that?" Bobbie said.

"Apparently so," Naomi said.

"We're going to have to slag that thing," Bobbie said. "Do we have enough firepower for that?"

Avasarala opened her eyes again. She tried to feel something besides great, oceanic sorrow. There had to be hope in there somewhere. Even Pandora got that much.

Holden was the one who said what she was thinking.

"Even if we can, it won't save Mars."

"Maybe we got them all?" Alex said. "I mean, there were a shitload of those things, but maybe…maybe we got 'em?"

"Hard to tell when they were running ballistic," Bobbie said. "If we missed just one, and it gets to Mars…"

It was all slipping away from her. She had been so close to stopping it, and now here she was, watching it all slip past. Her gut was a solid knot. But they hadn't failed. Not yet. Somewhere in all this there had to be a way. Something that could still be done.

She forwarded her last conversation with Nguyen to Souther. Maybe he'd have an idea. A secret weapon that could come out of nowhere and force the codes out. Maybe the great brotherhood of military men would draw some vestige of humanity out of Nguyen.

Ten minutes later, a survival pod came loose from the *King*. Souther didn't bother contacting her before they shot it down. The ops deck was like a mourning chamber.

"Okay," Holden said. "First things first. We've got to get down to the base. If Mei's there, we need to get her out."

"I'm on that," Amos said. "And we got to take the doc. He ain't gonna outsource that one."

"That's what I was thinking," Holden said. "So you guys take the *Roci* down to the surface."

"*Us* guys?" Naomi asked.

"I'll take the pinnace over to the battleship," Holden said. "The transponder activation codes are going to be in the CIC."

"You?" Avasarala asked.

"Only two people got off Eros," Holden said with a shrug. "And I'm the one that's left."

Chapter Forty-Nine: Holden

Don't do this," Naomi said. She didn't beg, or cry, or make demands. All the power of her request lay in its quiet simplicity. "Don't do it."

Holden opened the suit locker just outside the main airlock and reached for his Martian-made armor. A sudden and visceral memory of radiation sickness on Eros stopped him. "They've been pumping radiation into the *King* for hours now, right?"

"Don't go over there," Naomi said again.

"Bobbie," Holden said over the comm.

"Here," she replied with a grunt. She was helping Amos prep their gear for the assault on the Mao science station. After his one encounter with the Mao protomolecule hybrid, he could only imagine they were going loaded for bear.

"What are these standard Martian armor suits rated for radiation-wise?"

"Like mine?" Bobbie asked.

"No, not a powered suit. I know they harden you guys for close-proximity blasts. I'm talking about this stuff we pulled out of the MAP crate."

"About as much as a standard vacuum suit. Good enough for short walks outside the ship. Not so much for constant exposure to high radiation levels."

"Shit," Holden said. Then: "Thanks." He killed the comm panel and closed the locker. "I'll need a full-on hazard suit. Which means I'll be better in the radiation, and not bullet resistant at all."

"How many times can you get yourself massively irradiated before it catches up with you?" Naomi said.

"Same as last time. At least one more," Holden replied with a grin. Naomi didn't smile back. He hit the comm again and said, "Amos, bring me up a hazard suit from engineering. Whatever's the hardest thing we've got on board."

"Okay," Amos replied.

Holden opened his equipment locker and took out the assault rifle he kept there. It was large, black, and designed to be intimidating. It would immediately mark anyone who carried it as a threat. He put it back and decided on a pistol instead. The hazmat suit would make him fairly anonymous. It was the sort of thing any member of the damage-control team might wear during an emergency. If he was wearing only a service pistol in a hip holster, it might keep anyone from singling him out as part of the problem.

And with the protomolecule loose on the *King*, and the ship flooded with radiation, there would be a big problem.

Because if Prax and Avasarala were right, and the protomolecule was linked even without a physical connection, then the goo on the *King* knew what the goo on Venus knew. Part of that was how human spaceships were put together, ever since it had disassembled the *Arboghast*. But it also meant it knew a lot about how to turn humans into vomit zombies. It had performed that trick a million times or so on Eros. It had practice.

It was entirely possible that every single human on the *King* was now a vomit zombie. And sadly, that was the best-case scenario. Vomit zombies were walking death to anyone with exposed skin, but to Holden, in his fully sealed and vacuum-rated hazmat suit, they would be at worst a mild annoyance.

The worst-case scenario was that the protomolecule was so good at changing humans now, the ship would be full of lethal hybrids like the one he'd fought in the cargo bay. That would be an impossible situation, so he chose to believe it wasn't true. Besides, the protomolecule hadn't made any soldiers on Eros. Miller hadn't really taken the time to describe what he'd run into there, but he'd spent a lot of time on the station looking for Julie and he'd never reported being attacked by anything. The protomolecule was incredibly aggressive and invasive. It would kill a million humans in hours and turn them into spare parts for whatever it was working on. But it invaded at the cellular level. It acted like a virus, not an army.

Just keep telling yourself that, Holden thought. It made what he was about to do seem possible.

He took a compact semiautomatic pistol and holster out of the locker. Naomi watched while he loaded the weapon's magazine and three spares, but she didn't speak. He had just pushed the last round into the final magazine when Amos floated into the compartment, dragging a large red suit behind him.

"This is our best, Cap," he said. "For when shit has gone truly wrong. Should be plenty for the levels they've got in that ship. Max exposure time is six hours, but the air supply only lasts two, so that's not an issue."

Holden examined the bulky suit. The surface was a thick, flexible rubbery substance. It might deter someone attacking with their fingernails or teeth, but it wouldn't stop a knife or a bullet. The air supply was contained under the suit's radiation-resistant skin, so it made for a big, awkward lump on the wearer's back. The difficulty he had pulling the suit to himself and then stopping it told him its mass was considerable.

"Won't be moving fast in this, will I?"

"No," Amos said with a grimace. "They're not made for a fire-fight. If the bullets start flying, you're fucked."

Naomi nodded but said nothing.

"Amos," Holden said, grabbing the mechanic's arm as he turned to leave. "The gunny's in charge once you hit the surface. She's a pro, and this is her show. But I need you to keep Prax safe, because he's kind of an idiot. The only thing I ask you to do is get that man and his little girl safely off the moon and back to this ship."

Amos looked hurt for a moment. "Of course I will, Captain. Anything that gets to him or that baby will already have killed me. And that ain't easy to do."

Holden pulled Amos to him and gave the big man a quick hug. "I feel sorry for anything that tries. No one could ask for a better crewman, Amos. Just want you to know that."

Amos pushed him away. "You act like you're not coming back."

Holden shot a look at Naomi, but her expression hadn't changed. Amos just laughed for a minute, then clapped Holden on the back hard enough to rattle his teeth. "That's bullshit," Amos said. "You're the toughest guy I know." Without waiting for Holden to reply, he headed out to the crew ladder, and then down to the deck below.

Naomi pushed lightly against the bulkhead and drifted over to Holden. Air resistance brought her to a stop half a meter from him. She was still the most agile person in microgravity he'd ever met, a ballerina of null g. He had to stop himself from hugging her to him. The expression on her face told him it wasn't what she wanted. She just floated in front of him for a moment, not saying anything, then reached out and put one long, slender hand against his cheek. It felt cool and soft.

"Don't go," she said, and something in her voice told him it would be the last time.

He backed up and began shrugging his way into the hazmat suit. "Then who? Can you see Avasarala fighting through a mob of vomit zombies? She wouldn't know the CIC from the galley. Amos has to go get that little girl. You know he does, and you know why. Prax has to be there. Bobbie keeps them both alive."

He got the bulky suit over his shoulders and sealed up the front but left the helmet lying against his back. The boot mags came on when he hit them with his heels, and he pushed down to the deck and stuck there.

"You?" he asked Naomi. "Do I send you? I'd bet on you against a thousand zombies any day of the week. But you don't know the CIC any better than Avasarala does. How does that make sense?"

"We just got right again," she said. "That's not fair."

"But," he said, "tell the Martians that me saving their planet makes us even on this whole 'you stole our warship' issue, okay?" He knew he was making light of the moment and immediately hated himself for it. But Naomi knew him, knew how afraid he was, and she didn't call him on it. He felt a rush of love for her that sent electricity up his spine and made his scalp tingle.

"Fine," she said, her face hardening. "But you're coming back. I'll be here on the radio the whole time. We'll work through this together, every step. No hero bullshit. Brains instead of bullets, and we work the problems together. You give me that. You better give me that."

Holden finally pulled her into his arms and kissed her. "I agree. Please, please help me make it back alive. I'd really like that."

Flying the *Razorback* to the crippled *Agatha King* was like taking a race car to the corner market. The *King* was only a few thousand kilometers from the *Rocinante*. It seemed close enough for an EVA pack and a really strong push. Instead, he flew what was probably the fastest ship in the Jupiter system in teakettle mode at about 5 percent thrust through the debris of the recent battle. He could sense the *Razorback* straining at the leash, responding to his tiny bursts of steam with sullen reproach. The distance to the stricken flagship was short enough, and the path treacherous enough, that programming in a course would take more time than just flying by stick. But even at his languid pace, the *Razorback* seemed to have a hard time keeping its nose pointed at the *King*.

You don't want to go there, the ship seemed to be saying. *That's an awful place.*

"No, no, I really don't," he said, patting the console in front of him. "But just get me there in one piece, okay, honey?"

A massive chunk of what must have once been a destroyer floated past, the ragged edges still glowing with heat. Holden tapped the stick and pushed the *Razorback* sideways to get a bit more distance from the floating wreckage. The nose drifted off course. "Fight all you want, we're still going to the same place."

Some part of Holden was disappointed that the transit was so dangerous. He'd never flown to Io before, and the view of the moon at the edge of his screens was spectacular. A massive volcano of molten silicate on the opposite side of the moon was throwing particles so high into space he could see the trail it left in the sky. The plume cooled into a spray of silicate crystals, which caught Jupiter's glow and glittered like diamonds scattered across the black. Some of them would drift off to become part of Jupiter's faint ring system, blown right out of Io's gravity well. In any other circumstance, it would have been beautiful.

But the hazardous flight kept his attention on his instruments and the screens in front of him. And always, the growing bulk of the *Agatha King*, floating alone at the center of the junk cloud.

When he was within range, Holden signaled the ship's automated docking system, but as he'd suspected, the *King* didn't respond. He piloted up to the nearest external airlock and told the *Razorback* to maintain a constant distance of five meters. The racing ship was not designed to dock with another ship in space. It lacked even a rudimentary docking tube. His trip to the *King* would be a short spacewalk.

Avasarala had gotten a master override code from Souther, and Holden had the *Razorback* transmit it. The airlock immediately cycled open.

Holden topped off the hazmat suit's air supply in the *Razorback*'s airlock. Once he got onto Nguyen's flagship, he couldn't trust the air, even in the suit-recharging stations. Nothing from the *King* could be allowed inside his suit. Nothing.

When his stored-air gauge read 100 percent, he turned on the radio and called Naomi. "I'm going in now."

He kicked off his boot mags, and a sharp push against the inner airlock door sent him across the short gap to the *King*.

"I'm getting a good picture," Naomi said. The video link light on his HUD was on. Naomi could see everything he could see. It was comforting and lonely at the same time, like making a call to a friend who lived very far away.

Holden cycled the airlock. The two minutes while the *King* closed the outer door and then pumped air into the chamber seemed to last forever. There was no way to know what would be on the other side of the inner airlock door when it finally opened. Holden put his hand on the butt of his pistol with a nonchalance he didn't feel.

The inner door slid open.

The sudden screech of his hazmat suit's radiation alarm nearly gave him a heart attack. He chinned the control that killed the audible alarm, though he kept the outside radiation level meter running. It wasn't data that actually did him any good, but the suit was reassuring him that it could handle the current levels, and that was nice.

Holden stepped out of the airlock into a small compartment filled with storage lockers and EVA equipment. It looked empty, but a small noise from one of the lockers alerted him, and he turned just in time to see a man in a UN naval uniform burst out of the locker and swing a heavy wrench at his head. The bulky hazmat suit kept him from moving quickly, and the wrench struck a ringing blow off the side of his helmet.

"Jim!" Naomi yelled over the radio.

"Die, you bastard!" the Navy man yelled at the same time. He took a second swing, but he wasn't wearing mag boots, and without the push off the bulkhead to give him momentum, the swing did little more than start spinning the man around in the air. Holden grabbed the wrench out of his hand and threw it away. He caught the man to stop his spinning with his left hand and drew his pistol with his right.

"If you cracked my suit, I'm going to throw you out that airlock," Holden said. He began flipping through suit status screens while keeping his pistol pointed at the wrench enthusiast.

"It looks okay," Naomi said, relief evident in her voice. "No reds or yellows. That helmet is tougher than it looks."

"What the hell were you doing in that locker?" Holden asked the man.

"I was working here when the…it…came on board," the man said. He was a compact-looking Earther, with pale skin and flaming red hair cut close to the scalp. A patch on his suit said LARSON. "All the doors sealed up during emergency lockdown. I was trapped in here, but I could watch what was happening on the internal security system. I was hoping to grab a suit and get out the airlock, but it was sealed too. Say, how'd you get in here?"

"I have admiralty-level overrides," Holden said to him. Quietly, to Naomi he said, "At current radiation levels, what's survival odds for our friend here?"

"Not bad," Naomi said. "If we get him into sick bay in the next couple of hours."

To Larson he said, "Okay, you're coming with me. We're going to CIC. Get me there fast, and you've got a ride off this tub."

"Yes, sir!" Larson said with a salute.

"He thinks you're an admiral." Naomi laughed.

"Larson, put on an environment suit. Do it fast."

"Sir, yes sir!"

The suits they had in the airlock storage lockers would at least have their own air supplies. That would cut down on damage from the radiation the young sailor was absorbing. And an airtight suit would reduce the risk of protomolecule infection as they made their way through the ship.

Holden waited until Larson had shrugged into a suit, then

transmitted the override code to the hatch and it slid open. "After you, Larson. Command information center, as fast as you can. If we run into anyone, especially if they're throwing up, stay away and let me deal with them."

"Yes, sir," Larson said, his voice fuzzy over the static-filled radio, then pushed off into the corridor. He took Holden at his word and led him on a fast trip through the crippled *Agatha King*. They stopped only when a sealed hatch blocked their way, and then only long enough for Holden's suit to convince it to open.

The areas of the ship they moved through didn't look damaged at all. The bioweapon pod had hit farther aft, and the monster had headed straight to the reactor room. According to Larson, it had killed a number of people on the way, including the ship's entire contingent of Marines when they tried to stop it. But once it had entered engineering, it mostly ignored the rest of the crew. Larson said that shortly after it got into engineering, the shipwide security camera system had gone off-line. With no way to know where the monster was, and no way out of the airlock storage room, Larson had hidden in a locker to wait it out.

"When you came in, all I could see was this big, lumpy red thing," Larson explained. "I thought maybe you were another one of those monsters."

The lack of visible damage was a good thing. It meant all the hatches and other systems they came across still worked. The lack of a monster rampaging through the ship was even better. The thing that had Holden worried was the lack of people. A ship this size had over a thousand crew persons. At least some of them should be in the areas of the ship they were passing through, but so far they hadn't run across a single one.

The occasional puddle of brown goo on the floor was not an encouraging sign.

Larson stopped at a locked hatch to let Holden catch his breath. The heavy hazmat suit was not built for long treks, and it was starting to fill up with the stink of his own sweat. While he took a minute to rest and let the suit's cooling systems try to bring his temperature down, Larson said, "We'll be going past the forward galley to one of the elevator bays. The CIC is on the deck just above. Five, ten minutes tops."

Holden checked his air supply and saw that he had burned nearly half of it. He was rapidly approaching the point of no return. But something in Larson's voice caught his ear. It was the way he said *galley*.

"Is there something I should know about the galley?"

Larson said, "I'm not sure. But after the cameras went out, I kept hoping someone was going to come get me. So I started trying to call people on the comm. When that didn't work, I started having the *King* do location checks on people I knew. After a while, no matter who I asked about, the answer was always 'the forward galley.'"

"So," Holden said. "There might be upwards of a thousand infected Navy people crammed into that galley?"

Larson gave a shrug barely visible in his environment suit. "Maybe the monster killed them and put them there."

"Oh, I think that's exactly what happened," Holden said, taking out his gun and working the slide to chamber a round. "But I seriously doubt they stayed dead."

Before Larson could ask what he meant, Holden had his suit unlock the hatch. "When I open this door, you head to the elevator as fast as you can. I'll be right behind you. Don't stop no matter what. You *have* to get me to that CIC. Are we clear?"

Larson nodded inside his helmet.

"Good. On three."

Holden began counting, one hand on the hatch, the other holding his gun. When he hit three, he shoved the hatch open. Larson put his feet against a bulkhead and pushed off down the corridor on the other side.

Tiny blue flickers floated in the air around them like fireflies. Like the lights Miller had reported when he was on Eros the second time. The time he didn't come back from. The fireflies were here now too.

At the end of the corridor, Holden could see the elevator door. He began clumping after Larson on his magnetic boots. When Larson was halfway down the corridor, he passed an open hatch.

The young sailor started screaming.

Holden ran as fast as the clumsy hazmat suit and his magnetic boots would let him go. Larson kept flying down the corridor, but he was screaming and flailing at the air like a drowning man trying to swim. Holden was almost to the open hatch when something crawled out of it and into his path. At first he thought it was the kind of vomit zombie he'd run into on Eros. It moved slowly, and the front of its Navy uniform was covered in brown vomit. But when it turned to look at Holden, its eyes glowed with a faint inner blue. And there was an intelligence in them the Eros zombies hadn't had.

The protomolecule had learned some lessons on Eros. This was the new, improved version of the vomit zombie.

Holden didn't wait to see what it was going to do. Without slowing his pace, he raised his pistol and shot it in the head. To his relief, the light went out of its eyes, and it spun away from the deck, spraying brown goo in an arc as it rotated. When he passed the open hatch, he risked a glance inside.

It was full of the new vomit zombies. Hundreds of them. All their disconcertingly blue eyes were aimed at him. Holden turned back to the corridor and ran. From behind, he heard a rising wave of sounds as the zombies moaned as one and began climbing along the bulkheads and deck after him.

"Go! Get in the elevator!" he screamed at Larson, cursing at how much the heavy hazmat suit slowed him down.

"God, what was that?" Naomi said. He'd forgotten she was watching. He didn't waste breath answering. Larson had come out of his panic-induced fugue and was busily working the elevator doors open. Holden ran up to him and then turned around to look behind. Dozens of the blue-eyed vomit zombies filled the corridor behind him, crawling on the bulkheads, ceiling, and deck like spiders. The floating blue lights swirled on air currents Holden couldn't feel.

"Go faster," he said to Larson, sighting down his pistol at the lead zombie and putting a bullet in its head. It floated off the wall, spraying goo as it went. The zombie behind it shoved it out of the way, which sent it spinning down the corridor toward them. Holden moved in front of Larson to protect him, and a spray of brown slime hit his chest and visor. If they hadn't both been wearing sealed suits, it would have been a death sentence. He repressed a shudder and shot two more zombies. The rest didn't even slow down.

Behind him, Larson cursed as the partially opened doors snapped shut again, pinning his arm. The sailor worked them back open, pushing them with his back and one leg.

"We're in!" Larson yelled. Holden began backing up toward the elevator shaft, emptying the rest of his magazine as he went. Half a dozen more zombies spun away, spraying goo; then he was in the shaft and Larson shoved the doors shut.

"Up one level," Larson said, panting with fear and exertion. He pushed off the bulkhead and floated up to the next set of doors, then levered them open. Holden followed, replacing the magazine in his gun. Directly across from the elevator was a heavily armored hatch with CIC stenciled in white on the metal. Holden moved toward it, having his suit transmit the override code. Behind him, Larson let the elevator doors slam shut. The howling of the zombies echoed up the elevator shaft.

"We should hurry," Holden said, hitting the button to open the CIC and bulling his way in before the hatch had finished cycling open. Larson floated through after him.

There was a single man still in the CIC: a squat, powerfully built Asian man with an admiral's uniform and a large-caliber pistol in one shaky hand.

"Stay where you are," the man said.

"Admiral Nguyen!" Larson blurted out. "You're alive!"

Nguyen ignored him. "You're here for the bioweapon launch vehicle remote codes. I have them here." He held up a hand terminal. "They're yours in exchange for a ride off of this ship."

"He's taking us," Larson said, pointing at Holden. "He said he'd take me too."

"No fucking way," Holden said to Nguyen. "Not a chance. Either give me those codes because there's a scrap of humanity left in you, or give them to me because you're dead. I don't give a shit either way. You decide."

Nguyen looked back and forth from Larson to Holden, clutching the hand terminal and the pistol so tightly that his knuckles were white. "No! *You* have to—"

Holden shot him in the throat. Somewhere in his brain stem, Detective Miller nodded in approval.

"Start working on an alternate route back to my ship," Holden said to Larson as he walked across the room to grab the hand terminal floating by Nguyen's corpse. It took him a moment to find the *King*'s self-destruct switch hidden behind a locked panel. Souther's override code gave him access to that too.

"Sorry," Holden said quietly to Naomi as he opened it. "I know I sort of agreed not to do that anymore. But I didn't have time to—"

"No," Naomi said, her voice sad. "That bastard deserved to die. And I know you'll feel like shit about it later. That's good enough for me."

The panel opened, and a simple button lay on the other side. It wasn't even red, just a plain industrial white. "This is what blows the ship?"

"No timer," Naomi said.

"Well, this is an anti-boarding fail-safe. If someone opens this panel and presses this button, it's because the ship is lost. They don't want it on a timer someone can just disarm."

"This is an engineering problem," Naomi said. She already knew what he was thinking, and she was trying to get an answer out before he could say it. "We can solve this."

"We can't," Holden said, waiting to feel the sorrow but instead feeling a sort of quiet peace. "There are a couple hundred very angry zombies trying to get up the elevator shaft right now. We won't come up with a solution that doesn't leave me stranded in here anyway."

A hand squeezed his shoulder. He looked up, and Larson said, "I'll press it."

"No, you don't have to—"

Larson held out his arm. The sleeve of his environment suit had a tiny tear where the elevator doors had closed on it. Around the tear was a palm-sized brown stain.

"Just rotten fucking luck, I guess. But I watched the Eros feeds like everyone else," Larson said. "You can't risk taking me. Pretty soon I might be…" He paused and pointed back toward the elevator with his head. "Might be one of those."

Holden took Larson's hand in his. The thick gloves made it impossible to feel anything. "I'm very sorry."

"Hey, you tried," Larson said with a sad smile. "At least now I won't die of thirst in a suit locker."

"Admiral Souther will know about this," Holden said. "I'll make sure everyone knows."

"Seriously," Larson said, floating next to the button that would turn the *Agatha King* into a small star for a few seconds. He pulled off his helmet and took a long breath. "There's another airlock three decks up. If they aren't in the elevator shaft yet, you can make it."

"Larson, I—"

"You should go away now."

Holden had to strip off his suit in the *King*'s airlock. It was covered in the goo, and he couldn't risk taking it onto the *Razorback*. He absorbed a few rads while he stole another UN vac suit from one of the lockers and put it on instead. It looked exactly like the one Larson was wearing. As soon as he was back on the *Razorback*, he sent the remote command codes to Souther's ship. He was nearly back to the *Rocinante* when the *King* vanished in a ball of white fire.

Chapter Fifty: Bobbie

T he captain just left," Amos said to Bobbie when he came back
into the machine shop. She floated half a meter above the deck
inside a small circle of deadly technology. Behind her sat her
cleaned and refitted recon suit, a single barrel of the newly
installed gun gleaming inside the port on its right arm. To her left
floated the recently reassembled auto-shotgun Amos favored. The
rest of the circle was formed by pistols, grenades, a combat knife,
and a variety of weapon magazines. Bobbie took one last mental
inventory and decided she'd done all she could do.

"He thinks maybe he's not coming back from this one," Amos
continued, then bent down to grab the auto-shotgun. He looked it
over with a critical eye, then gave her an appreciative nod.

"Going into a fight where you know you aren't coming back
gives you a sort of clarity," Bobbie said. She reached out and
grabbed her armor, pulling herself into it. Not an easy thing to do

in microgravity. She had to twist and shimmy to get her legs down into the suit before she could start sealing up the chest. She noticed Amos watching her. He had a dopey grin on his face.

"Seriously. Now?" she said. "We're talking about your captain going off to his death, and all that's going through your head right now is 'Ooh, boobies!'"

Amos continued to grin, not chastened at all. "That bodysuit don't leave a lot to the imagination. That's all."

Bobbie rolled her eyes. "Believe me, if I could wear a bulky sweater inside my fully articulated, power-assisted combat suit, I still wouldn't. Because that would be stupid." She hit the controls to seal the suit, and her armor folded around her like a second skin. She closed the helmet, using the suit's external speakers to talk to Amos, knowing it would make her voice robotic and inhuman.

"Better put your big-boy pants on," she said, the sound echoing around the room. Amos took an unconscious step back. "The captain isn't the only one that might not be coming back."

Bobbie climbed onto the ladder-lift and let it take her all the way up to the ops deck. Avasarala was belted into her couch at the comm station. Naomi was in Holden's usual spot at the tactical panel. Alex would be up in the cockpit already. Bobbie opened her visor to speak using her normal voice.

"We cleared?" she asked Avasarala.

The old lady nodded and held up one hand in a *wait* gesture while she spoke to someone on her headset mic. "The Martians have already dropped a full platoon," she said, pushing the mic away from her face. "But their orders are to set up a perimeter and seal the base while someone further up the food chain decides what to do."

"They're not going to—" Bobbie started, but Avasarala cut her off with a dismissive wave of her hand.

"Fuck no," she said. "*I'm* further up the food chain, and I've already decided we're going to glass this abattoir as soon as you're off the surface. I'm letting them think we're still discussing it so you have time to go get the kids."

Bobbie nodded her fist at Avasarala. Recon Marines were trained to use the Belters' physical idiom when in their combat armor. Avasarala just looked baffled at the gesture and said, "So stop playing with your hand and go get the fucking kids."

Bobbie headed back to the ladder-lift, connecting to the ship's 1MC as she went. "Amos, Prax, meet me in the airlock in five minutes, geared up and ready to go. Alex, put us on the deck in ten."

"Roger that," Alex replied. "Good hunting, soldier." She wondered if they might have become friends, given enough time. It was a pleasant thought.

Amos was waiting for her outside the airlock when she arrived. He wore his Martian-made light armor and carried his oversized gun. Prax rushed into the compartment a few minutes later, still struggling to get into his borrowed gear. He looked like a boy wearing his father's shoes. While Amos helped him get buttoned up, Alex called down to the airlock and said, "Heading down. Hang on to something."

Bobbie turned her boot mags to full, locking herself to the deck while the ship shifted under her. Amos and Prax both sat down on chairs that pulled out from the wall, and belted in.

"Let's go over the plan one more time," she said, calling up the aerial photos they'd shot of the facility. She patched into the *Roci* and threw the pictures onto a wall monitor. "This airlock is our entrance. If it's locked, Amos will blast it with explosives to open the outer door. We need to get inside fast. Your armor isn't going to protect you from the vicious radiation belt Io orbits in for long. Prax, you have the radio link Naomi rigged, so once we're inside, you start looking for a network node to plug it into. We have no information about the layout of the base, so the faster we can get Naomi hacking their system, the faster we can find those kids."

"I like the backup plan better," Amos said.

"Backup plan?" Prax asked.

"The backup plan is I grab the first guy we see, and beat him until he tells us where the kids are."

Prax nodded. "Okay. I like that one too."

Bobbie ignored the macho posturing. Everyone dealt with pre-combat jitters in their own way. Bobbie preferred obsessive list making. But flexing and threats were good too. "Once we have a location, you guys move with all haste to the kids, while I ensure a clear path of egress."

"Sounds good," Amos said.

"Make no mistake," Bobbie said. "Io is one of the worst places in the solar system. Tectonically unstable and radioactive as hell. Easy to see why they hid here, but do not underestimate the peril that just being on this shit moon carries."

"Two minutes," Alex said over the comm.

Bobbie took a deep breath. "And that isn't the worst. These assholes launched a couple hundred human-protomolecule hybrids at Mars. We can hope that they shot their entire wad, but I have a feeling they didn't. We might very well run into one of those monsters once we get inside."

She didn't say, *I've seen it in my dreams*. It seemed counterproductive.

"If we see one, *I deal with it*. Amos, you almost got your captain killed blasting away at the one you found in the cargo bay. You try that shit with me, I'll snap your arm off. Don't test me."

"Okay, chief," Amos replied. "Don't get your panties in a twist. I heard you."

"One minute," Alex said.

"There are Martian Marines controlling the perimeter, but they've been given the okay to let us in. If someone escapes past us, no need to apprehend them. The Marines will pick them up before they get far."

"Thirty seconds."

"Get ready," Bobbie said, then pulled up her HUD's suit status display. Everything was green, including the ammo indicator, which showed two thousand incendiary rounds.

The air sucked out of the airlock in a long, fading hiss, leaving only a thin wisp of atmosphere that would be the same density as Io's own faint haze of sulfur. Before the ship hit the deck, Amos jumped up out of his chair and stood on his toes to put his helmet against hers. He yelled, "Give 'em hell, marine."

The outer airlock door slid open, and Bobbie's suit blatted a radiation alarm at her. It also helpfully informed her that the outside atmosphere was not capable of supporting life. She shoved Amos toward the open lock and then pushed Prax after him. "Go, go, go!"

Amos took off across the ground in a weird, hopping run, his breath panting in her ears over the radio link. Prax stayed close behind him and seemed more comfortable in the low gravity. He had no trouble keeping up. Bobbie climbed out of the *Roci* and then jumped in a long arc that took her about seven meters above the surface at its apex. She visually scanned the area while her suit reached out with radar and EM sensors, trying to pinpoint targets. Neither she nor it found any.

She hit the ground next to the lumbering Amos and hopped again, beating them both to the airlock door. She tapped the button and the outer door cycled open. Of course. Who locks their door on Io? No one is going to hike across a wasteland of molten silicon and sulfur to steal the family silver.

Amos plowed past her into the airlock, stopping for breath only once he was inside. Bobbie followed Prax in a second later, and she was about to tell Amos to cycle the airlock when her radio died.

She spun around, looking out across the surface of the moon for movement. Amos came up behind her and put his helmet against her back armor. When he yelled, it was barely audible. "What is it?"

Instead of yelling back, she stepped outside the airlock and pointed to Amos, then pointed at the inner door. She mimed a person walking with her fingers. Amos nodded at her with one hand, then moved back into the airlock and shut the outer door.

Whatever happened inside, it was up to Amos and Prax now. She wished them well.

She spotted the movement before her suit did. Something shifting against the sulfurous yellow background. Something not quite the same color. She tracked it with her eyes and had the suit hit it with a targeting laser. She wouldn't lose track of it now. It might gobble radio waves, but the fact that she could see it meant that light bounced off it just fine.

It moved again. Not quickly, and staying close to the ground. If she hadn't been looking right at it, she'd have missed the motion entirely. Being sneaky. Which probably meant it didn't know she'd spotted it. Her suit's laser range finder marked it as just over three hundred meters away. According to her theory, once it realized it had been spotted, it would charge her, moving in a straight line to try to grab and rip. If it couldn't reach her quickly, it would try to throw things at her. And all she needed to do was hurt it until its program failed and it self-destructed. Lots of theories.

Time to test them out.

She aimed her gun at it. The suit helped her correct for deflection based on the range, but she was using ultrahigh velocity rounds on a moon with fractional gravity. Bullet drop at three hundred meters would be trivial. Even though there was no way the creature could see it through her helmet's darkened visor, she blew it a kiss. "I'm back, sweetie. Come say hi to momma."

She tapped the trigger on her gun. Fifty rounds streaked downrange, crossing the distance from her gun to the creature in less than a third of a second. All fifty slammed into it, shedding very little of their kinetic energy as they passed through. Just enough to burst the tip of each round open and ignite the self-oxidizing flammable gel they carried. Fifty trails of short-lived but very intense flame burned through the monster.

Some of the black filament bursting from the exit wounds actually caught fire, disappearing with a flash.

The monster launched itself toward Bobbie at a dead run that should have been impossible in low gravity. Each push of its limbs should have launched it high into the air. It stuck to the silicate surface of Io as though it were wearing magnetic boots on a metal deck. Its speed was breathtaking. Its blue eyes blazed like lightning. The long, improbable hands reached out for her, clenching and grasping at nothing as it ran. It was all just like in her dreams. And for a split second, Bobbie just wanted to stand perfectly still and let the scene play out to the conclusion she'd never gotten to see. Another part of her mind expected her to wake up, soaking with sweat, as she had so many times before.

Bobbie watched as it ran toward her, and noted with pleasure the burnt black injuries the incendiary bullets had cut through its body. No sprays of black filament and then the wounds closing like water. Not this time. She'd hurt it, and she wanted to go on hurting it.

She turned away and took off in a bounding run at a ninety-degree angle to its path. Her suit kept the targeting laser locked on to the monster, so she could track its location even without turning around to look. As she'd suspected, it turned to follow her, but it lost ground. "Fast on the straightaways," Bobbie said to it. "But you corner like shit."

When the creature realized she wasn't going to just stand still and let it get close to her, it stopped. Bobbie stumbled to a stop, turning to watch it. It reached down and tore up a big chunk of ancient lava bed, then reached down to grip the ground with its other hand.

"Here it comes," Bobbie said to herself.

She threw herself to the side as the creature's arm whipped forward. The rock missed her by centimeters as she hurtled sideways. She hit the moon's surface and skidded, already returning fire. This time she fired for several seconds, sending hundreds of rounds into and through the creature.

"Anything you can do I can do better," she sang under her breath. "I can do anything better than you." The bullets tore great flaming chunks out of the monster and nearly severed its left arm. The creature spun around and collapsed. Bobbie bounced back to her feet, ready to run again if the monster got back up. It didn't. Instead, it rolled over onto its back and shook. Its head began to swell, and the blue eyes flashed even brighter. Bobbie could see things moving beneath the surface of its chitinous black skin.

"Boom, motherfucker!" she yelled at it, waiting for the bomb to go off.

Instead, it bounced suddenly to its feet, tore a portion of its own abdomen off, and threw it at her. By the time Bobbie realized what had just happened, the bomb was only a few meters from her. It detonated and blew her off her feet. She went skidding across Io's surface, her armor blaring warnings at her. When she finally came to a stop, her HUD was flashing a Christmas display of red and green lights. She tried to move her limbs, but they were as heavy as stone. The suit's motion control processor, the computer that interpreted her body's movements and turned them into commands for the suit's actuators, had failed. The suit was trying to reboot it while simultaneously trying to reroute and run the program in a different location. A flashing amber message on the HUD said PLEASE STAND BY.

Bobbie couldn't turn her head yet, so when the monster leaned down over her, it took her completely by surprise. She stifled a scream. It wouldn't have mattered. The sulfur atmosphere on Io was far too thin for sound waves to travel in. The monster couldn't have heard her. But while the new Bobbie was at peace with the idea of dying in battle, enough of the old Bobbie remained that she was not going to go out screaming like a baby.

It leaned down to look at her; its overlarge and curiously child-like eyes glowed bright blue. The damage her gun had done seemed extensive, but the creature appeared not to notice. It poked at her chest armor with one long finger, then convulsed and vomited a thick spray of brown goo all over her.

"Oh, that's *disgusting*," she yelled at it. If her suit had been opened up to the outside, getting that protomolecule shit on her would have been the least of her problems. But still, how the hell was she going to wash this crap off?

It cocked its head and regarded her curiously. It poked again at her armor, one finger wriggling into gaps, trying to find a way in to her skin. She'd seen one of these things rip a nine-ton combat mech apart. If it wanted into her suit, it was coming in. But it seemed reluctant to damage her for some reason. As she watched, a long, flexible tube burst out of its midsection and began probing at her armor instead of the finger. Brown goo dribbled out of this new appendage in a constant stream.

Her gun status light flickered from red to green. She spun up the barrels to test it and it worked. Of course, her suit was still telling her to "please stand by" when it came to actually moving. Maybe if the monster got bored and wandered in front of her gun, she could get some shots off.

The tube was probing at her armor more insistently now. It pushed its way into gaps, periodically shooting brown liquid into them. It was as repulsive as it was frightening. It was like being threatened by a serial killer that was also fumbling at her clothing with a teenager's horny insistence.

"Oh, to hell with *this*," she said to it. She was about through with letting this thing grope her while she lay helpless on her back. The suit's right arm was heavy, and the actuators that made her strong when it was working also resisted movement when it was not. Pushing her arm up was like doing a one-arm bench press while wearing a lead glove. She pressed up anyway until she felt something pop. It might have been in the suit. It might have been in her arm. She couldn't tell yet, because she was too wired for pain to set in.

But when it popped, her arm came up, and she pushed her fist up against the monster's head.

"Buh-bye," she said. The monster turned to look curiously at her hand. She held down the trigger until the ammo counter read zero and the gun stopped spinning. The creature had ceased to exist from the shoulders up. She dropped her arm back to the ground, exhausted.

REROUTE SUCCESSFUL, her suit told her. REBOOTING, it said. When the subliminal hum came back, she started laughing and found she couldn't stop. She shoved the monster's corpse off her and sat up.

"Good thing. It's a really long walk back to the ship."

Chapter Fifty-One: Prax

Prax ran.

Around him, the station walls formed angles at the center to make an elongated hexagon. The gravity was barely higher than Ganymede standard, and after weeks at a full-g burn, Prax had to pay attention to keep himself from rising to the ceiling with each step. Amos loped beside him, every stride low, long, and fast. The shotgun in the man's hands remained perfectly level.

At a T intersection ahead, a woman appeared. Dark hair and skin. Not the one who'd taken Mei. Her eyes went wide and she darted off.

"They know we're coming," Prax said. He was panting a little.

"That probably wasn't their first clue, Doc," Amos said. His voice was perfectly conversational, but there was an intensity in it. Something like anger.

At the intersection, they paused, Prax leaning over and resting elbows on knees to catch his breath. It was an old, primitive reflex. In less than .2 g, the blood return wasn't significantly increased by putting his head even with his heart. Strictly speaking, he would have been better off standing and keeping his posture from narrowing any of his blood vessels. He forced himself to stand.

"Where should I plug in this radio link for Naomi?" he asked Amos.

Amos shrugged and pointed at the wall. "Maybe we can just follow the signs instead."

There was a legend on the wall with colored arrows pointing in different directions. ENV CONTROL and CAFETERIA and PRIMARY LAB. Amos tapped PRIMARY LAB with the barrel of his shotgun.

"Sounds good to me," Prax said.

"You good to go?"

"I am," Prax said, though he probably wasn't.

The floor seemed to shift under him, followed immediately by a long, ominous rumbling that he could feel in the soles of his feet.

"Naomi? You there?"

"I am. I have to keep track of the captain on the other line. I might pop in and out. Everything all right?"

"Might be stretching the point," Amos said. "We got something sounded like someone shooting at us. They ain't shooting at the base, are they?"

"They aren't," Naomi said from the ship, her voice pressed thin and tinny by the attenuated signal. "It looks like some of the locals are mounting a defense, but so far our Marines aren't returning fire."

"Tell 'em to calm that shit down," Amos said, but he was already moving down the corridor toward the primary lab. Prax jumped after him, misjudged, and cracked his arm against the ceiling.

"Soon as they ask me," Naomi said.

The corridors were a maze, but it was the kind of maze Prax had been running through his whole life. The institutional logic of a research facility was the same everywhere. The floor plans were different; budget concerns could change how richly appointed the details were; the fields being supported determined what equipment was present. But the soul of the place was the same, and it was Prax's home.

Twice more, they caught sight of people scattering through the halls with them. The first was a young Belter woman in a white lab coat. The second was a massively obese dark-skinned man with the squat build of Earth. He was wearing a crisp suit, the signature of the administrative class everywhere. Neither one tried to stop them, so Prax forgot about them almost as soon as he saw them.

The imaging suite was behind a set of negative-pressure seals. When Prax and Amos went through, the gust of air seemed to push them faster, urging them on. The rumble came again, louder this time and lasting almost fifteen seconds. It could be fighting. It could be a volcano forming nearby. No way to know. Prax knew this base would have to have been built with tectonic instability in mind. He wondered what the safeguards were for a moment, then put it out of his mind. Nothing he could do about it anyway.

The lab's imaging suite was at least the equal of the one he'd shared on Ganymede, with everything from the spidery full-resonance displays to the inferential gravity lens. In the corner, a squat orange table showed a holographic image of a colony of rapidly dividing cells. Two doors led out apart from the one they'd come through. Somewhere nearby, people were shouting at each other.

Prax pointed at one of the doors.

"This one," he said. "Look at the hinges. It's built to allow a gurney through."

The passageway on the other side was warmer and the air was more humid. It wasn't quite greenhouse level, but near to it. It opened into a long gallery with five-meter ceilings. Fitted tracks on the ceiling and floor allowed for moving high-mass equipment and containment cages. Bays lined it, each, it seemed, with a research bench not so different from the ones Prax had used as an undergraduate: smart table, wall display, inventory control box, specimen cages. The shouting voices were louder now. He was about to say as much, but Amos shook his head and pointed down the gallery toward one of the farther bays. A man's voice came from that direction, his tone high and tight and angry.

"...not an evacuation if there's no place to evacuate to," he was saying. "I'm not giving up the one bargaining chip I have left."

"You don't have that option," a woman said. "Put the gun down, and let's talk this through. I've been handling you for seven years, and I will keep you in business for seven more, but you do not—"

"Are you delusional? You think there's a tomorrow after this?"

Amos pointed forward with his shotgun, then began a slow, deliberate advance. Prax followed, trying to be silent. It had been months since he'd heard Dr. Strickland's voice, but the shouting man could be him. It was possible.

"Let me make this perfectly clear," the man said. "We have nothing. Nothing. The only hope of negotiation is if we have a card to play. That means them. Why do you think they're *alive*?"

"Carlos," the woman said as Prax came to the corner of the bay. "We can have this conversation later. There's a hostile enemy force on the base right now, and if you're still here when they come through that hatch—"

"Yeah," Amos interrupted, "what happens then?"

The bay was just like the others. Strickland—it was unmistakably Strickland—stood beside a gray metal transport crate that went from the floor to just above his hip. In the specimen cages, a half dozen children lay motionless, sleeping or drugged. Strickland also had a small gun in his hand, pointed at the woman from the video. She was in a harshly cut uniform, the sort of thing that security forces adopted to make their staff look hard and intimidating. It worked for her.

"We came in the other hatch," Prax said, pointing back over his shoulder.

"Da?"

One syllable, spoken softly. It rang out from the transport cart louder than all the weeks of explosions and gauss rounds and screams of the wounded and dying. Prax couldn't breathe; he couldn't move. He wanted to tell them all to put the guns away, to be careful. There was a child. His child.

Strickland's pistol barked, and some sort of high-explosive round destroyed the woman's neck and face in a spray of blood and cartilage. She tried to scream once, but with significant portions of her larynx already compromised, what she managed was more of a powerful, wet exhalation. Amos lifted the shotgun, but Strickland—Merrian, whatever his name was—put his pistol on the top of the crate and seemed almost to sag with relief. The woman drifted to the floor, blood and flesh fanning out and falling gently to the ground like a blanket of red lace.

"Thank God you came," the doctor said. "Oh, thank God you came. I was stalling her as long as I could. Dr. Meng, I can't imagine how hard this has been for you. I am so, *so* sorry."

Prax stepped forward. The woman took another jerking breath, her nervous system firing at random now. Strickland smiled at him, the same reassuring smile he recognized from any number of doctor's visits over the previous years. Prax found the transport's control pad and knelt to open it. The side panel clicked as the magnetic locks gave up their grip. The panel rolled up, disappearing into the cart's frame.

For a terrible, breathless moment, it was the wrong girl. She had the black, lustrous hair, the egg-brown skin. She could have been Mei's older sister. And then the child moved. It wasn't much more than shifting her head, but it was all that his brain needed to see his baby in this older girl's body. All the months on Ganymede, all the weeks to Tycho and back, she'd been growing up without him.

"She's so big," he said. "She's grown so much."

Mei frowned, tiny ridges popping into being just above her brow. It made her look like Nicola. And then her eyes opened. They were blank and empty. Prax yanked at the release on his helmet and lifted it off. The station air smelled vaguely of sulfur and copper.

Mei's gaze fastened on him and she smiled.

"Da," she said again, and put out one hand. When he reached for her, she took his finger in her fist and pulled herself into his arms. He held her to his chest; the warmth and mass of her small body—no longer tiny, only small—was overwhelming. The void between the stars was smaller than Mei was at that moment.

"She's sedated," Strickland said. "But her health is perfect. Her immune system has been performing at peak."

"My baby," Prax said. "My perfect girl."

Mei's eyes were closed, but she smiled and made a small, animal grunt of satisfaction.

"I can't tell you how sorry I am for all this," Strickland said. "If I had any way of reaching you, of telling you what was happening, I swear to you I would have. This has been beyond a nightmare."

"So you're saying they kept you prisoner here?" Amos asked.

"Almost all the technical staff was here against their will," Strickland said. "When we signed on, we were promised resources and freedom of a kind most of us had only dreamed about. When I started, I thought I could make a real difference. I was terribly, terribly wrong, and I will never be able to apologize enough."

Prax's blood was singing. A warmth spread from the center of his body, radiating out to his hands and feet. It was like being dosed with the most perfect euphoric in the history of pharmacy. Her hair smelled like the cheap lab shampoo he'd used to wash dogs in the laboratories of his youth. He stood too quickly, and her mass and momentum pulled him a few centimeters off the floor. His knees and feet were slick, and it took him a moment to realize he'd been kneeling in blood.

"What happened to these kids? Are there others somewhere else?" Amos asked.

"These are the only ones I was able to save. They've all been sedated for evacuation," Strickland said. "But right now, we need to leave. Get off the station. I have to get to the authorities."

"And why do you need to do that?" Amos asked.

"I have to tell them what's been going on here," Strickland said. "I have to tell everyone about the crimes that were committed here."

"Yeah, okay," Amos said. "Hey, Prax? You think you could get that?" He pointed his shotgun at something on a nearby crate.

Prax turned to look at Amos. It was almost a struggle to remember where he was and what they were doing.

"Oh," he said. "Sure."

Holding Mei against him with one arm, he took Strickland's gun and trained it on the man.

"No," Strickland said. "You don't...you don't understand. I'm the victim here. I had to do all this. They forced me. She forced me."

"You know," Amos said, "maybe I'm coming across as what a guy like you might call working class. Doesn't mean I'm stupid. You're one of Protogen's pet sociopaths, and I ain't buying any damn thing you're trying to sell."

Strickland's face turned to cold rage like a mask had fallen away.

"Protogen's dead," he said. "There is no Protogen."

"Yeah," Amos said. "I got the brand name wrong. That's the problem here."

Mei murmured something, her hand reaching up behind Prax's ear to grip his hair. Strickland stepped back, his hands in fists.

"I saved her," he said. "That girl's alive because of me. She was slated for the second-generation units, and I pulled her off the project. I pulled all of them. If it wasn't for me, every child here would be worse than dead right now. Worse than dead."

"It was the broadcast, wasn't it?" Prax said. "You saw that we might find out, so you wanted to make sure that you had the girl from the screen. The one everyone was looking for."

"You'd rather I hadn't?" Strickland said. "It was still me that saved her."

"Actually, I think that makes it Captain Holden," Prax said. "But I take your point."

Strickland's pistol had a simple thumb switch on the back. He pressed it to turn the safety on.

"My home is gone," Prax said, speaking slowly. "My job is gone. Most of the people I've ever known are either dead or scattered through the system. A major government is saying I abuse women and children. I've had more than eighty explicit death threats from absolute strangers in the last month. And you know what? I don't care."

Strickland licked his lips, his eyes shifting from Prax to Amos and back again.

"I don't need to kill you," Prax said. "I have my daughter back. Revenge isn't important to me."

Strickland took a deep breath and let it out slowly. Prax could see the man's body relax, and something on the dividing line of relief and pleasure appeared at the corners of his mouth. Mei twitched once when Amos' auto-shotgun fired, but she lay back down against Prax's shoulder without crying or looking around. Strickland's body drifted slowly to the ground, the arms falling to the sides. The space where the head had been gouted bright arterial blood against the walls, each pulse smaller than the one before.

Amos shrugged.

"Or that," Prax said.

"So you got any ideas how we—"

The hatch behind them opened and a man ran in.

"What happened? I heard—"

Amos raised the auto-shotgun. The new man backpedaled, a thin whine of fear escaping from him as he retreated. Amos cleared his throat.

"Any idea how we get these kids out of here?"

Putting Mei back in the transport cart was one of the hardest things Prax had ever done. He wanted to carry her against him, to press his face against hers. It was a primate reaction, the deepest centers of his brain longing for the reassurance of physical contact. But his suit wouldn't protect her from the radiation or near vacuum of Io's sulfuric atmosphere, and the transport would. He nestled her gently against two other children while Amos put the other four in a second cart. The smallest of them was still in newborn diapers. Prax wondered if she had come from Ganymede too. The carts glided against the station flooring, only rattling when they crossed the built-in tracks.

"You remember how to get back to the surface?" Amos asked.

"I think so," Prax said.

"Uh, Doc? You really want to put your helmet back on."

"Oh! Right. Thank you."

At the T intersection, half a dozen men in security uniforms had built a barricade, preparing to defend the lab against attack. Because Amos tossed in his grenades from the rear, the cover was less effective than the locals had anticipated, but it still took a few minutes to clear the bodies and the remains of the barricade to let the carts roll through.

There was a time, Prax knew, that the violence would have bothered him. Not the blood or bodies. He'd spent more than enough time doing dissections and even autonomous-limb vivisection to be able to wall off what he was seeing from any particular sense of visceral horror. But that it was something done in anger, that the men and women he'd just seen blown apart hadn't donated their bodies or tissues, would have affected him once. The universe had taken that from him, and he couldn't say now exactly when it had happened. Part of him was numb, and maybe it always would be. There was a feeling of loss in that, but it was intellectual. The only emotions he felt were a glowing, transforming relief that Mei was here and alive and a vicious animal protectiveness that meant he would never let her leave his sight, possibly until she left for university.

On the surface, the transports were rougher, the wheels less suited to the uneven surface of the land. Prax followed Amos' example, turning the boxes around to pull them rather than push. Looking at the vectors, it made sense, but it wouldn't have occurred to him if he hadn't seen Amos doing it.

Bobbie was walking slowly toward the *Rocinante*. Her suit was charred and stained and moving poorly. A clear fluid was leaking down the back.

"Don't get close to me," she said. "I've got protomolecule goo all over this thing."

"That's bad," Amos said. "You got a way to clean that off?"

"Not really," she replied. "How'd the extraction go?"

"Got enough kids to start a singing group, but a little shy of a baseball team," Amos said.

"Mei's here," Prax said. "She's all right."

"I'm glad to hear that," Bobbie said, and even though she was clearly exhausted, she sounded like she meant it.

At the airlock, Amos and Prax got in and nestled the transports against the back wall while Bobbie stood on the rough ground outside. Prax checked the transport indicators. There was enough onboard air to last another forty minutes.

"All right," Amos said. "We're ready."

"Going for emergency blow," Bobbie said, and her armored suit came apart around her. It was a strange sight, the hard curves and layers of combat plate peeling themselves back, blooming out like a flower and then falling apart, and the woman, eyes closed and mouth open, being revealed. When she put her hand out for Amos to pull her in, the gesture reminded Prax of Mei seeing him again.

"Now, Doc," Amos said.

"Cycling," Prax said. He closed the outer door and started fresh air coming into the lock. Ten seconds later, Bobbie's chest started to pump like a bellows. Thirty seconds, and they were at seven-eighths of an atmosphere.

"Where do we stand, guys?" Naomi asked as Prax opened the

transport. The children were all asleep. Mei was sucking on her first two fingers, the way she had when she was a baby. He couldn't get past how much older she looked.

"We're solid," Amos said. "I say we get the fuck out of here and glass the place."

"A-fucking-men," Avasarala's voice said in the background.

"Copy that," Naomi said. "We're prepping for launch. Let me know when you've got all our new passengers safely in."

Prax pulled off his helmet and sat beside Bobbie. In the black sheath of her base garments, she looked like someone just coming back from the gym. She could have been anybody.

"Glad you got your kid back," she said.

"Thank you. I'm sorry you lost the suit," he said.

She shrugged.

"At this point, it was mostly a metaphor anyway," she said, and the inner airlock opened.

"Cycle's done, Naomi," Amos said. "We're home."

Chapter Fifty-Two: Avasarala

It was over, except that it wasn't. It never was.

"We're all friends now," Souther said. Talking to him without lag was a luxury she was going to miss. "But if we all limp back to our corners, we're more likely to stay that way. I'm thinking it's going to be a question of years before either of our fleets are back up to what we were. There was a lot of damage."

"The children?"

"Processing them. My medical officer's in communication with a list of doctors who deal with pediatric immune problems. It's just about finding their parents and getting them all home now."

"Good," she said. "That's what I like to hear. And the other thing?"

Souther nodded. He looked younger in low gravity. They both did. Skin didn't sag when there was nothing to tug it down, and she could see what he'd looked like as a boy.

"We've got transponder locks on a hundred and seventy-one packages. They're all moving sunward pretty fast, but they're not accelerating or evading. Pretty much we're standing back and letting them get close enough to Mars that disposal is trivial."

"You sure that's a good idea?"

"By 'close,' I mean still weeks away at current speed. Space is big."

There was a pause that meant something other than distance.

"I wish you'd ride back on one of ours," Souther said.

"And be stuck out here for another few weeks with the paperwork? Not going to happen. And besides, heading back with James Holden and Sergeant Roberta Draper and Mei Meng? It has all the right symbolism. Press will eat it up. Earth, Mars, the Outer Planets, and whatever the hell Holden is now."

"Celebrity," Souther said. "A nation of its own."

"He's not that bad once you get past the self-righteousness. And anyway, this is the ship I'm on, and there's nothing it's waiting to repair before it starts its burn. And I've already hired him. No one's giving me any shit about discretionary spending right now."

"All right," Souther said. "Then I'll see you back down the well."

"See you there," she said, and cut the connection.

She pulled herself up and launched gently across the ops deck. It would have been easy to push down the crew ladder shaft, flying the way she'd dreamed of as a child. It tempted. In practice, she figured she'd either push too hard and slam into something or else too gently and have air resistance stop her with nothing solid close enough to reach. She used the handholds and pulled herself slowly down toward the galley. Pressure doors opened at her approach and closed behind her with soft hydraulic hisses and metallic bangs. When she reached the crew deck, she heard the voices before she could make out the words, and the words before she saw the people.

"...have to shut it down," Prax was saying. "I mean, it's false pretenses now. You don't think I could be sued, do you?"

"You can always be sued," Holden said. "Chances are they wouldn't win."

"But I don't want to be sued in the first place. We have to shut it down."

"I put a notice on the site so it gives a status update and asks for confirmation before any more money gets moved."

She pulled herself into the galley. Prax and Holden were floating near the coffee machine. Prax wore a stunned expression, whereas Holden looked slightly smug. They both had bulbs of coffee, but Prax seemed to have forgotten his. The botanist's eyes were wide and his mouth hung open, even in the microgravity.

"Who's getting sued?" Avasarala asked.

"Now that we have Mei," Holden said, "Prax wants people to stop giving him money."

"It's too much," the botanist said, looking at her as if he expected her to do something about it. "I mean..."

"Surplus funds?" Avasarala asked.

"He can't *quite* retire on what he's got," Holden said. "Not in luxury, anyway."

"But it's yours," Prax said, turning to Holden with something like hope. "You set up the account."

"I took the *Rocinante*'s fees already. Trust me, you paid us generously," Holden said, hand out in a gesture of refusal. "What's still in there's all yours. Well, yours and Mei's."

Avasarala scowled. That changed her personal calculus a little. She'd thought this would be the right time to lock Prax into a contract, but Jim Holden had once again ridden in at the last moment and screwed everything up.

"Congratulations," Avasarala said. "Has either of you seen Bobbie? I need to talk to her."

"Last I saw, she was heading for the machine shop."

"Thanks," Avasarala said, and kept pulling herself along. If Praxidike Meng was independently wealthy, that made him less likely to take on the job of rebuilding Ganymede for purely financial reasons. She could probably work the civic pride angle. He and his daughter were the face of the tragedy there, and having him running the show would mean more to people than all the facts and figures of how screwed they'd all be without the food supplies back online. He might be the kind of man who'd be swayed by that. She needed to think about it.

Once again, she was moving slowly and carefully enough that she heard the voices before she reached the machine shop. Bobbie and Amos, both of them laughing. She couldn't believe that she was walking in on an intimate moment, but it had that tickle-fight sound to it. Then Mei shrieked with delight, and Avasarala understood.

The machine shop was the last place in the ship, with the possible exception of engineering, that Avasarala would have thought about playing with a little girl, but there she was, arms and legs flailing through the air. Her shoulder-length black hair flowed around her in a whirl, following the gentle end-over-end spin of her body. Her face was bright with pleasure. Bobbie and Amos stood at opposite ends of the shop. As Avasarala watched, Bobbie caught the little girl out of the air and launched her back toward Amos. Soon, Avasarala thought, the girl would start losing her milk teeth. She wondered how much of all this Mei would remember when she was an adult.

"Are you people crazy?" Avasarala said as Amos caught the girl. "This isn't a playground."

"Hey there," Amos said, "we weren't planning on staying long. The captain and the doc needed a minute, so I figured I'd haul the kiddo down here. Give her the tour."

"When they send you to play catch with a child, they don't mean that she's the f— that she's the ball," Avasarala said, moving across to him. "Give that child to me. None of you people has any idea how to take care of a little girl. It's amazing you all lived to adulthood."

"Ain't wrong about that," Amos said amiably, holding out the kid.

"Come to your nana," Avasarala said.

"What's a nana?" Mei asked.

"I'm a nana," Avasarala said, gathering the child to her. Her body wanted to put the girl against her hip, to feel the weight bearing down on her. In microgravity holding a child felt odd. Good, but odd. Mei smelled of wax and vanilla. "How much longer before we can get some thrust? I feel like a f— like a balloon floating around in here."

"Soon as Alex and Naomi finish maintenance on the drive computers, we're out of here," Amos said.

"Where's my daddy?" Mei asked.

"Good," Avasarala said. "We've got a schedule to keep, and I'm not paying you people for floating lessons. Your daddy's talking to the captain, Mei-Mei."

"Where?" the girl demanded. "Where is he? I want my da!"

"I'll get you back to him, kiddo," Amos said, holding out a massive hand. He shifted his attention to Avasarala. "She's good for about five minutes, then it's 'Where's Daddy?'"

"Good," Avasarala said. "They deserve each other."

"Yeah," the big mechanic said. He pulled the child close to his center of gravity and launched up toward the galley. No handhold for him. Avasarala watched him go, then turned to Bobbie.

Bobbie floated, her hair sprayed softly out around her. Her face and body were more relaxed than Avasarala remembered ever having seen them. It should have made her seem at peace, but all she could think was that the girl looked drowned.

"Hey," Bobbie said. "Did you hear back from your tech guys on Earth?"

"I did," Avasarala said. "There was another energy spike. Bigger than the last ones. Prax was right. They are networked, and worse than that, they don't suffer lag. Venus reacted before the information about the battle could have reached it."

"Okay," Bobbie said. "That's bad, right?"

"It's weird as tits on a bishop, but who knows if it means anything? They're talking about spin-entanglement webs, whatever the hell those are. The best theory we've got is that it's like a little adrenaline rush for the protomolecule. Some part of it is involved with violence, and the rest goes on alert until it's clear the danger's passed."

"Well, then it's scared of something. Nice to know it might have a vulnerability somewhere."

They were silent for a moment. Somewhere far off in the ship, something clanged and Mei shrieked. Bobbie tensed, but Avasarala didn't. It was interesting to see people who hadn't been around a child react to Mei. They couldn't tell the difference between pleasure and alarm. Avasarala found that on this ship, she and Prax were the only experts in children's screaming.

"I was looking for you," Avasarala said.

"I'm here," Bobbie said, shrugging.

"Is that a problem?"

"I don't follow. Is what a problem?"

"That you're here?"

She looked away, her expression closing down. It was what Avasarala had expected.

"You were going down there to die, only the universe fucked you over again. You won. You're alive. None of the problems go away."

"Some of them do," Bobbie said. "Just not all. And at least we won your game."

Avasarala's cough of a laugh was enough to set her spinning slightly. She reached out to the wall and steadied her drift.

"That's the game I play. You never win. You just don't lose yet. Errinwright? He lost. Soren. Nguyen. I took them out of the game and I stayed in, but now? Errinwright's going to retire with extreme prejudice, and I'm going to be given his job."

"Do you want it?"

"It doesn't matter if I want it. I'll be offered it because if the bobble-head doesn't offer it, people will think he's slighting me. And I'll take it because if I don't, people will think I'm not hungry enough to be afraid of any longer. I'll be answering directly to the secretary-general. I'll have more power, more responsibility. More friends and more enemies. It's the price of playing."

"Seems like there should be an alternative."

"There is. I could retire."

"Why don't you?"

"Oh, I will," Avasarala said. "The day my son comes home. What about you? Are you looking to quit?"

"You mean am I still planning to get myself killed?"

"Yes, that."

There was a pause. That was good. It meant Bobbie was actually thinking about her answer.

"No," she said. "I don't think so. Going down in a fight's one thing. I can be proud of that. But just getting out to get out. I can't do that."

"You're in an interesting position," Avasarala said. "You think about what to do with it."

"And what position is that? Ronin?"

"A traitor to your government and a patriotic hero. A martyr who didn't die. A Martian whose best and only friend is about to run the government of Earth."

"You're not my only friend," Bobbie said.

"Bullshit. Alex and Amos don't count. They only want to get into your pants."

"And you don't?"

Avasarala laughed again. Bobbie was at least smiling. It was more than she'd done since she'd come back. Her sigh was deep and melancholy.

"I still feel haunted," she said. "I thought it would go away. I thought if I faced it, it would all go away."

"It doesn't go away. Ever. But you get better at it."

"At what?"

"At being haunted," Avasarala said. "Think about what you want to do. Think about who you want to become. And then see me, and I will make it happen for you if I can."

"Why?" Bobbie asked. "Seriously, why? I'm a soldier. I did the mission. And yes, it was harder and stranger than anything I've ever done, but I *got* it done. I did it because it needed doing. You don't owe me anything."

Avasarala hoisted an eyebrow.

"Political favors are how I express affection," she said.

"Okay, people," Alex's voice said across the ship's PA. "We're back up and commencing burn in thirty seconds unless someone says otherwise. Everybody get ready to weigh something."

"I appreciate the offer," Bobbie said. "But it may be a while before I know if I want to take it."

"What will you do, then? Next, I mean."

"I'm going home," she said. "I want to see my family. My dad. I think I'll stay there for a while. Figure out who I am. How to start over. Like that."

"The door's open, Bobbie. Whenever you want it, the door is open."

The flight back to Luna was a pain in the ass. Avasarala spent seven hours a day in her crash couch, sending messages back and forth against different levels of lag. On Earth, Sadavir Errinwright was quietly celebrated, his career with the UN honored with a small and private ceremony, and then he went off to spend more time with his family or farm chickens or whatever he was going to do with the remaining decades until death. Whatever it was, it wouldn't involve wielding political power.

The investigation into the Io base was ongoing, and heads were quietly rolling on Earth. But not on Mars. Whoever in the Martian government had been bidding against Errinwright, they were going to get away with it. By losing the most powerful biological weapon in human history, they'd saved their own careers. Politics was full of little ironies like that.

Avasarala put together her own new office in absentia. By the time she stepped into it, it would already have been running for a month. It felt like driving a car while sitting in the backseat. She hated it.

In addition, Mei Meng had decided she was funny, and spent part of each day monopolizing her attention. She didn't have time to play with a little girl, except that of course she did. So she did. And she had to exercise so that they wouldn't have to put her in a nursing home when she got back to a full g. The steroid cocktail gave her hot flashes and made it hard to sleep. Both her granddaughters had birthdays she could attend only on a screen. One had twenty minutes' lag; one had four.

When they passed the cloud of protomolecule monsters speeding in toward the sun, she had nightmares for two nights running, but they gradually stopped. Every one of them was being tracked by two governments, and Errinwright's little packets of death were all quiescent and speeding quietly and happily toward their own destruction.

She couldn't wait to be home.

When they docked on Luna, it was like a starving woman with a slice of apple touched to her lips, but not allowed to bite. The soft blue and white of the daylight planet, the black and gold of night. It was a beautiful world. Unmatched in the solar system. Her garden was down there. Her office. Her own bed.

But Arjun was not.

He was waiting for her on the landing pad in his best suit with a spray of fresh lilacs in his hand. The low gravity made him look younger too, if a little bloodshot about the eyes. She could feel the curiosity of Holden and his crew as she walked toward him. Who was this man that he could stand to be married to someone as abrasive and hard as Chrisjen Avasarala? Was this her master or her victim? How would that even work?

"Welcome home," Arjun said softly as she leaned into his arms.

He smelled like himself. She put her head against his shoulder, and she didn't need Earth so badly any longer.

This was home enough.

Chapter Fifty-Three: Holden

"Hi, Mom. We're on Luna!"

The light delay from Luna was less than six seconds for a round trip, but it was enough to add an awkward pause before each response. Mother Elise stared out at him from his hotel room's video screen for five long heartbeats; then her face lit up. "Jimmy! Are you coming down?"

She meant down the well. Coming home. Holden felt an ache to do exactly that. It had been years since he'd been to the farm in Montana that his parents owned. But this time he had Naomi with him, and Belters didn't go to Earth. "No, Mom, not this time. But I want all of you to come meet me up here. The shuttle ride is my treat. And UN Undersecretary Avasarala is hosting, so the accommodations are pretty posh."

When there was comm lag, it was difficult not to ramble on. The other person never sent the subtle physical cues that signaled it was their turn to talk. Holden forced himself to stop babbling and wait for a reply. Elise stared at the screen, waiting out the lag. Holden could see how much she'd aged in the years since his last trip home. Her dark brown, almost black, hair was streaked with gray, and the laugh lines around her eyes and mouth had deepened. After five seconds, she waved a hand at the screen in a dismissive gesture. "Oh, Tom will never ride a shuttle to Luna. You know that. He hates microgravity. Just come down and see us here. We'll throw a party. You can bring your friends here."

Holden smiled at her. "Mom, I need you guys to come up here because I have someone I want you to meet. Remember the woman? Naomi Nagata, the one I told you about? I told you I've been seeing her. I think it might be more than that. In fact, I'm kind of sure about it now. And now we'll be on Luna while a whole lot of political bullshit gets straightened out. I really want you guys to come up. See me, meet Naomi."

It was almost too subtle to catch, the way his mother flinched five seconds later. She covered it with a big smile. "More than that? What does that mean? Like, getting married? I always thought you'd want kids of your own someday..." She trailed off, maintaining an uncomfortably stiff smile.

"Mom," Holden said. "Earthers and Belters can have kids just fine. We're not a different species."

"Sure," she said a few seconds later, nodding too quickly. "But if you have children out there—" She stopped, her smile fading a bit.

"Then they'll be Belters," Holden said. "Yeah, you guys are just going to have to be okay with that."

After five seconds, she nodded. Again, too quickly. "Then I guess we better come up and meet this woman you're willing to leave Earth behind for. She must be very special."

"Yeah," Holden said. "She is."

Elise shifted uncomfortably for a second; then her smile came back, far less forced. "I'll get Tom on that shuttle if I have to drag him by the hair."

"I love you, Mom," Holden said. His parents had spent their whole lives on Earth. The only outer planets types they knew were the caricature villains that showed up on bad entertainment feeds. He didn't hold their ingrained prejudices against them, because he knew that meeting Naomi would be the cure for it. A few days spent in her company and they wouldn't be able to help falling in love with her. "Oh, one last thing. That data I sent you a while back? Hang on to that for me. Keep it quiet, but keep it. Depending on how things fall out over the next couple of months, I may need it."

"My parents are racists," Holden said to Naomi later that night. She lay curled against his side, her face against his ear. One long brown leg thrown across his hips.

"Okay," she whispered.

The hotel suite Avasarala had provided for them was luxurious to the point of opulence. The mattress was so soft that in the lunar gravity it was like floating on a cloud. The air recycling system pumped in subtle scents handcrafted by the hotel's in-house perfumer. That night's selection was called Windblown Grass. It didn't exactly smell like grass to Holden, but it was nice. Just a hint of earthiness to it. Holden had a suspicion that all perfumes were named randomly, anyway. He also suspected that the hotel ran the oxygen just a little higher than normal. He felt a little *too* good.

"They're worried our babies will be Belters," he said.

"No babies," Naomi whispered. Before Holden could ask what she meant, she was snoring in his ear.

The next day, he woke before Naomi, dressed in the best suit he owned, and headed out into the station. There was one last thing he had to do before he could call this whole bloody affair truly over.

He had to see Jules Mao.

Avasarala had told him that Mao was one of several dozen high-ranking politicians, generals, and corporate leaders rounded up in the mass of arrests following Io. He was the only one Avasarala was going to see personally. And, since they'd caught him on his L5 station frantically trying to get on a fast ship to the outer planets, she'd just had him brought to her on Luna.

That day was the day of their meeting. He'd asked Avasarala if he could be there, expecting a no. Instead, she laughed a good, long time and said, "Holden, there is literally nothing I can think of that will be more humiliating to that man than having you watch me dismantle him. Fuck yes, you can come."

So Holden hurried out of the hotel and onto the streets of Lovell City. A quick pedicab ride got him to the tube station, and a twenty-minute tube ride took him to the New Hague United Nations complex. A perky young page was waiting for him when he arrived, and he was escorted efficiently through the complex's twisty maze of corridors to a door marked CONFERENCE ROOM 34.

"You can wait inside, sir," the perky page chirped at him.

"No, you know?" Holden said, clapping the boy on the shoulder. "I think I'll wait out here."

The page dipped his head slightly and bustled off down the corridor, already looking at his hand terminal for whatever his next task was. Holden leaned against the corridor wall and waited. In the low gravity, standing was hardly any more effort than sitting, and he really wanted to see Mao perp-walked down the hallway to his meeting.

His terminal buzzed, and he got a short text message from Avasarala. It said ON OUR WAY.

Less than five minutes later, Jules-Pierre Mao climbed off an elevator into the corridor, flanked by two of the largest military police officers Holden had ever seen. Mao had his hands cuffed in front of him. Even wearing a prisoner's jumpsuit, hands in restraints, and with armed guards escorting him, he managed to look arrogant and in control. As they approached, Holden stood up straight and stepped in their way. One of the MPs yanked on Mao's arm to stop him and gave Holden a subtle nod. It seemed to say, *I'm down for whatever with this guy.* Holden had a sense that if he yanked a pistol out of his pants and shot Mao right there in the corridor, the two MPs would discover they had both been struck with blindness at the same moment and failed to see anything.

But he didn't want to shoot Mao. He wanted what he always seemed to want in these situations. He wanted to know *why.*

"Was it worth it?"

Even though they were the same height, Mao managed to frown down at him. "You are?"

"Awww, come on," Holden said with a grin. "You know me. I'm James Holden. I helped bring down your pals at Protogen, and now I'm about to finish that job with you. I'm also the one that found your daughter after the protomolecule had killed her. So I'll ask again: Was it worth it?"

Mao didn't answer.

"A dead daughter, a company in ruins, millions of people slaughtered, a solar system that will probably never have peaceful stability again. *Was it worth it?*"

"Why are you here?" Mao finally asked. He looked smaller when he said it. He wouldn't make eye contact.

"I was there, in the room, when Dresden got his and I'm the man who killed your pet admiral. I just feel like there's this wonderful symmetry in being there when you get yours."

"Antony Dresden," Mao said, "was shot in the head three times execution style. Is that what passes for justice with you?"

Holden laughed. "Oh, I doubt Chrisjen Avasarala is going to shoot you in the face. Do you think what's coming will be better?"

Mao didn't reply, and Holden looked at the MP and gestured toward the conference room door. They almost looked disappointed as they pushed Mao into the room and attached his restraints to a chair.

"We'll be waiting out here, sir, if you need us," the larger of the two MPs said. They took up flanking positions next to the door.

Holden went into the conference room and took a chair, but he didn't say anything else to Mao. A few moments later, Avasarala shuffled into the room, talking on her hand terminal.

"I don't give a fuck whose birthday it is, you make this happen before my meeting is over or I'll have your nuts as paperweights." She paused as the person on the other end said something. She grinned at Mao and said, "Well, go fast, because I have a feeling my meeting will be short. Good talking to you."

She sank into a chair directly across the table from Mao. She didn't look at Holden or acknowledge him at all. He suspected that the record would never reflect his presence in the room. Avasarala put her terminal on the tabletop and leaned back in her chair. She didn't speak for several tense seconds. When she did, it was to Holden. She still didn't look at him.

"You've gotten paid for hauling me back here?"

"Payment's cleared," Holden said.

"That's good. I wanted to ask you about a longer-term contract. It would be civilian, of course, but—"

Mao cleared his throat. Avasarala smiled at him.

"I know you're there. I'll be right with you."

"I've already got a contract," Holden said. "We're escorting the first reconstruction flotilla to Ganymede. And after that, I'm thinking we'll probably be able to get another escort gig from there. Still a lot of people relocating who'd rather not get stopped by pirates along the way."

"You're sure?"

Mao's face was white with humiliation. Holden let himself enjoy it.

"I've just gotten done working for a government," Holden said. "I didn't wear it well."

"Oh please. You worked for the OPA. That's not a government, it's a rugby scrum with a currency. Yes, Jules, what is it? You need to go to the potty?"

"This is beneath you," Mao said. "I didn't come here to be insulted."

Avasarala's smile was incandescent.

"You're sure about that? Let me ask, do you remember what I said the first time we met?"

"You asked me to tell you about any involvement I might have had with the protomolecule project run by Protogen."

"No," Avasarala replied. "I mean, yes, I did ask that. But that's not the part that you should be caring about right now. You lied to me. Your involvement with weaponizing the Protogen project is fully exposed, and that question is like asking what color Tuesday was. It's meaningless."

"Let's get down to brass tacks," Mao said. "I can—"

"No," Avasarala interrupted. "The part you should be caring about is what I said just before you left. Do you remember that?"

He looked blankly up at her.

"I didn't think so. I told you that if I found out later you'd hidden something from me, I wouldn't take it well."

"Your exact words," Mao said with a mocking grin, "were 'I am not someone you want to fuck with.'"

"So you do remember," she said, not a hint of humor in her tone. "Good. This is where you get to find out what that means."

"I have additional information that could be of benefit—"

"Shut the fuck up," Avasarala said, real anger creeping into her voice for the first time. "Next time I hear your voice, I have those two big MPs in the hallway hold you down and beat you with a fucking chair. Do you understand me?"

Mao didn't reply, which showed that he did.

"You don't have any idea what you've cost me," she said. "I'm being promoted. The economic planning council? I run it now. The public health service? I never had to worry about it because that was Errinwright's pain in the ass. It's mine now. The committee on financial regulation? Mine. You've fucked up my calendar for the next two decades.

"This is not a negotiation," Avasarala continued. "This is me gloating. I'm going to drop you into a hole so deep even your wife will forget you ever existed. I'm going to use Errinwright's old position to dismantle everything you ever built, piece by piece, and scatter it to the winds. I'll make sure you get to watch it happening. The one thing your hole will have is twenty-four-hour news. And since you and I will never meet again, I want to make sure my name is on your mind every time I destroy something else you left behind. I am going to *erase* you."

Mao stared back defiantly, but Holden could see it was just a shell. Avasarala had known exactly where to hit him. Because men like him lived for their legacy. They saw themselves as the architects of the future. What Avasarala was promising was worse than death.

Mao shot a quick look at Holden, and it seemed to say, *I'll take those three shots to the head now, please.*

Holden smiled at him.

Chapter Fifty-Four: Prax

Mei sat on Prax's lap, but her attention was focused with a laser intensity to her left. She put her hand up to her mouth and gently, deliberately deposited a wad of half-chewed spaghetti into her palm, then held it out toward Amos.

"It's yucky," she said.

The big man chuckled.

"Well, if it wasn't before, it sure is now, pumpkin," he said, unfolding his napkin. "Why don't you put that right here?"

"I'm sorry," Prax said. "She's just—"

"She's just a kid, Doc," Amos said. "This is what she's supposed to do."

They didn't call the dinner a dinner. It was a reception sponsored by the United Nations at the New Hague facilities on Luna. Prax couldn't tell if the wall was a window or an ultrahigh-definition screen. On it, Earth glowed blue and white on the horizon. The tables were spread around the room in a semi-organic array that Avasarala had explained was the current fashion. *Makes it look like some asshole just put them up anywhere.*

The room was almost equally people he knew and people he didn't, and watching them segregate was fascinating in its way. To his right, several small tables were filled with short, stocky men and women in professional suits and military uniforms orbiting around Avasarala and her amused-looking husband, Arjun. They gossiped about funding-system analysis and media-relations control. Every outer planets hand they shook was an inclusion that their subjects of conversation denied. To his left, the scientific group was dressed in the best clothes they had, dress jackets that had fit ten years before, and suits representing at least half a dozen different design seasons. Earthers and Martians and Belters all mixed in that group, but the talk was just as exclusionary: nutrient grades, adjustable permeability membrane technologies, phenotypic force expressions. Those were both his people from the past and his future. The shattered and reassembled society of Ganymede. If it hadn't been for the middle table with Bobbie and the crew of the *Rocinante*, he would have been there, talking about cascade arrays and non-visible-feeding chloroplasts.

But in the center, isolated and alone, Holden and his crew were as happy and at peace as if they'd been in their own galley, burning through the vacuum. And Mei, who had taken a fancy to Amos, still wouldn't be physically parted from Prax without starting to yell and cry. Prax understood exactly how the girl felt, and didn't see it as a problem.

"So living on Ganymede, you know a lot about low-gravity childbearing, right?" Holden said. "It's not really that much riskier for Belters, is it?"

Prax swallowed a mouthful of salad and shook his head.

"Oh, no. It's tremendously difficult. Especially if it's just a shipboard situation without extensive medical controls. If you look at naturally occurring pregnancies, there's a developmental or morphological abnormality five times out of six."

"Five..." Holden said.

"Most of them are germ line issues, though," Prax said. "Nearly all of the children born on Ganymede were implanted after a full genetic analysis. If there's a lethal equivalent, they just drop the zygote and start over. Non–germ line abnormalities are only twice as common as on Earth, though, so that's not so bad."

"Ah," Holden said, looking crestfallen.

"Why do you ask?"

"No reason," Naomi said. "He's just making conversation."

"Daddy, I want tofu," Mei said, grabbing his earlobe and yanking it. "Where's tofu?"

"Let's see if we can't find you some tofu," Prax said, pushing his chair back from the table. "Come on."

As he walked across the room, scanning the crowd for a dark, formal suit belonging to a waiter as opposed to a dark, formal suit belonging to a diplomat, a young woman came up to him with a drink in one hand and a flush on her cheeks.

"You're Praxidike Meng," she said. "You probably don't remember me."

"Um. No," he said.

"I'm Carol Kiesowski," she said, touching her collarbone as if to clarify what she meant by *I*. "We wrote to each other a couple of times right after you put out the video about Mei."

"Oh, right," Prax said, trying desperately to remember anything about the woman or the comments she might have left.

"I just want to say I think both of you are just so, so brave," the woman said, nodding. It occurred to Prax that she might be drunk.

"Son of a fucking *whore*," Avasarala said, loud enough to cut through the background buzz of conversations.

The crowd turned to her. She was looking at her hand terminal.

"What's a whore, Daddy?"

"It's a kind of frost, honey," Prax said. "What's going on?"

"Holden's old boss beat us to the punch," Avasarala said. "I guess we know what happened to all those fucking missiles he stole."

Arjun touched his wife's shoulder and pointed at Prax. She actually looked abashed.

"Sorry for the language," she said. "I forgot about her."

Holden appeared at Prax's shoulder.

"My boss?"

"Fred Johnson just put on a display," Avasarala said. "Nguyen's monsters? We've been waiting for them to come closer to Mars before we took them down. Transponders are all chirping away, and we've got them all tracked tighter than a fly's... Well, they crossed into the Belt, and he nuked them. All of them."

"That's good, though," Prax said. "I mean, isn't that good?"

"Not if he's doing it," Avasarala said. "He's flexing muscles. Showing that the Belt's got an offensive arsenal now."

A man in uniform to Avasarala's left started talking at the same time as a woman just behind her, and in a moment, the need to declaim had spread through the whole group. Prax pulled away. The drunk woman was pointing at a man and talking rapidly, Prax and Mei forgotten. He found a waiter at the edge of the room, extracted a promise of tofu, and went back to his seat. Amos and Mei immediately started playing at who could blow their nose the hardest, and Prax turned to Bobbie.

"Are you going to go back to Mars, then?" he asked. It seemed like a polite, innocuous question until Bobbie pressed her lips tight and nodded.

"I am," she said. "Turns out my brother's getting married. I'm going to try to get there in time to screw up his bachelor party. What about you? Taking the old lady's position?"

"Well, I think so," Prax said, a little surprised that Bobbie had heard about Avasarala's offer. It hadn't been made public yet. "I mean, all of the basic advantages of Ganymede are still there. The magnetosphere, the ice. If even some of the mirror arrays can be salvaged, it would still be better than starting again from nothing. I mean, the thing you have to understand about Ganymede..."

Once he started on the subject, it was hard for him to stop. In many ways, Ganymede had been the center of civilization in the outer planets. All the cutting-edge plant work had been there. All the life sciences issues. But it was more than that. There was something exciting about the prospect of rebuilding that was, in its fashion, even more interesting than the initial growth. To do something the first time was an exploration. To do it again was to take all the things they had learned, and refine, improve, perfect. It left Prax a little bit giddy. Bobbie listened with a melancholy smile on her face.

And it wasn't only Ganymede. All of human civilization had been built out of the ruins of what had come before. Life itself was a grand chemical improvisation that began with the simplest replicators and grew and collapsed and grew again. Catastrophe was just one part of what always happened. It was a prelude to what came next.

"You make it sound romantic," Bobbie said, and the way she said it was almost an accusation.

"I don't mean to—" Prax began, and something cold and wet wriggled its way into his ear. He pulled back with a yelp, turning to face Mei's bright eyes and brilliant smile. Her index finger dripped with saliva, and beyond her Amos was laughing himself crimson, one hand grasping at his belly and the other slapping the table hard enough to make the plates rattle.

"What was *that*?"

"Hi, Daddy. I love you."

"Here," Alex said, passing Prax a clean napkin. "You're gonna want that."

The startling thing was the silence. He didn't know how long it had been going on, but the awareness of it washed over him like a wave. The political half of the room was still and quiet. Through the forest of their bodies, he saw Avasarala bending forward, her elbows on her knees, her hand terminal inches in front of her face. When she stood up, they parted before her. She was such a small woman, but she commanded the room just by walking out of it.

"That's not good," Holden said, rising to his feet. Without another word, Prax and Naomi, Amos and Alex and Bobbie all followed after her. The politicians and the scientists came too, all of them mixing at last.

The meeting room was across a wide hall and set up in the model of an ancient Greek amphitheater. The podium at the front stood before a massive high-definition screen. Avasarala marched down to a seat, talking fast and low into her hand terminal. The others trailed in after her. The sense of dread was physical. The screen went black and someone dimmed the lights.

In the darkness of the screen, Venus stood in near silhouette against the sun. It was an image Prax had seen hundreds of times before. The feed could have come from any of a dozen monitoring stations. The time stamp on the lower left said they were looking back in time forty-seven minutes. A ship name, the *Celestine*, floated beneath the numbers.

Every time the protomolecule soldiers had been involved in violence, Venus had reacted. The OPA had just destroyed a hundred of its half-human soldiers. Prax felt himself caught between excitement and dread.

The image scattered and re-formed, some kind of interference confusing the sensors. Avasarala said something sharp that could have been *show me*. A few seconds later, the image stopped and reframed. A detail screen showing a gray-green ship. A heads-up display marked it the *Merman*. The image scattered again, and when it re-formed, the *Merman* had moved half an inch to the left and was spinning end over end, tumbling. Avasarala spoke again. A few seconds' lag, and the screen went back to its original image. Now that Prax knew to look, he could see the tiny dot of the *Merman* moving near the penumbra. There were other tiny specks like it.

The dark side of Venus pulsed like a sudden, planetary flash of lightning under the obscuring clouds. And then it glowed.

Vast filaments thousands of kilometers long like spokes on a wheel lit white and vanished. The clouds of Venus shifted, disturbed from below. Prax had the powerful memory of seeing a wake on the surface of a water tank when a fish passed close underneath. Vast and glowing, it rose through the cloud cover. Spoke-like strands of iridescence arced with vast lightning storms, coming together like the arms of an octopus but connected to a rigid central node. Once it had climbed out of Venus' thick cloud cover, it launched itself away from the sun, toward the viewing ship, but passing it. The other ships in its path were scattered and hurled away. A long plume of displaced Venusian atmosphere caught the sun and glowed like snowflakes and slivers of ice. Prax tried to make sense of the scale. As large as Ceres Station. As large as Ganymede. Larger. It folded its arms—its tentacles—together, accelerating without any visible drive plume. It swam in the void. His heart was racing, but his body was still as stone.

Mei patted his cheek with her open palm and pointed to the screen.

"What's that?" she asked.

Epilogue: Holden

Holden started the replay again. The wall screen in the *Rocinante*'s galley was too small to really catch all the details of the high-resolution imagery the *Celestine* had taken. But Holden couldn't stop watching it no matter what room he was in. An ignored cup of coffee cooled on the table in front of him next to the sandwich he hadn't eaten.

Venus flashed with light in an intricate pattern. The heavy cloud cover swirled as though caught in a planetwide storm. And then it rose from the surface, pulling a thick contrail of Venus' atmosphere in its wake.

"Come to bed," Naomi said, then leaned forward in her chair and took his hand. "Get some sleep."

"It's so big. And the way it swatted all those ships out of the way. Effortless, like a whale swimming through a school of guppies."

"Can you do anything about it?"

"This is the end, Naomi," Holden said, pulling his eyes away from the screen to look at her. "What if this is the end? This isn't some alien virus anymore. This thing is what the protomolecule came here to make. This is what it was going to hijack all life on the Earth to make. It could be *anything*."

"Can you do anything about it?" she repeated. Her words were harsh, but her voice was kind and she squeezed his fingers affectionately.

Holden turned back to the screen, restarting the image. A dozen ships blew away from Venus as though a massive wind had caught them and sent them spinning like leaves. The surface of the atmosphere began to roil and twist.

"Okay," Naomi said, standing up. "I'm going to bed. Don't wake me when you come in. I'm exhausted."

Holden nodded to her without looking away from the video feed. The massive shape folded itself into a streamlined dart, like a piece of wet cloth plucked up from the center, then flew away. The Venus it left behind looked diminished, somehow. As though something vital had been stolen from it to construct the alien artifact.

And here it was. After all the fighting, with human civilization left in chaos just from its presence, the protomolecule had finished the job it came billions of years before to do. Would humanity survive it? Would the protomolecule even notice them, now that it had finished its grand work?

It wasn't the ending of one thing that left Holden terrified. It was the prospect of something beginning that was utterly outside the human experience. Whatever happened next, no one could be prepared for it.

It scared the hell out of him.

Behind him, a man cleared his throat.

Holden turned reluctantly away from the image on the screen. The man stood next to the galley refrigerator as if he'd always been there, rumpled gray suit and dented porkpie hat. A bright blue firefly flew off his cheek, then hung in the air beside him. He waved it away like it was a gnat. His expression was one of discomfort and apology.

"Hey," Detective Miller said. "We gotta talk."

Acknowledgments

The process of making a book is never as solitary as it seems. This book and this series wouldn't exist without the hard work of Shawna McCarthy and Danny Baror and the support and dedication of DongWon Song, Anne Clarke, Alex Lencicki, the inimitable Jack Womack, and the brilliant crew at Orbit. Also gratitude goes to Carrie, Kat, and Jayné for feedback and support, and also to the whole Sakeriver gang. Much of the cool in the book belongs to them. The errors and infelicities and egregious fudging was all us.

extras

www.orbitbooks.net

about the author

James S. A. Cory is the pen name of fantasy author Daniel Abraham and Ty Franck, George R. R. Martin's assistant. They both live in Albuquerque, New Mexico. Find out more about this series at www.the-expanse.com

Find out more about James S. A. Corey and other Orbit authors by registering for the free monthly newsletter at www.orbit.net

if you enjoyed

CALIBAN'S WAR

look out for

EXISTENCE

by

David Brin

1.

I, AMPHORUM

The universe had two great halves.

A hemisphere of glittering stars surrounded Gerald on the right.

Blue-brown Earth took up the other side. *Home,* after this job was done. Cleaning the mess left by another generation.

Like a fetus in its sac, Gerald floated in a crystal shell, perched at the end of a long boom, some distance from the space station

Endurance. Buffered from its throbbing pulse, this bubble was more space than station.

Here, he could focus on signals coming from a satellite hundreds of kilometers away. A long, narrow ribbon of whirling fiber, far overhead.

> *The bola. His lariat. His tool in an ongoing chore.*
> *The bola is my arm.*
> *The grabber is my hand.*
> *Magnetic is the lever that I turn.*
> *A planet is my fulcrum.*

Most days, the little chant helped Gerald to focus on his job – that of a glorified garbageman. *There are still people who envy me. Millions, down in that film of sea and cloud and shore.*

Some would be looking up right now, as nightfall rushed faster than sound across teeming Sumatra. Twilight was the best time to glimpse this big old station. It made him feel connected with humanity every time *Endurance* crossed the terminator – whether dawn or dusk – knowing a few people still looked up.

Focus, Gerald. On the job.

Reaching out, extending his right arm fully along the line of his body, he tried again to adjust tension in that far-off, whirling cable, two thousand kilometers overhead, as if it were a languid extension of his own self.

And the cable replied. Feedback signals pulsed along Gerald's neuro-sens suit ... but they felt wrong.

My fault, Gerald realized. The orders he sent to the slender satellite were too rapid, too impatient. Nearby, little Hachi complained with a screech. The other occupant of this inflated chamber wasn't happy.

'All right.' Gerald grimaced at the little figure, wearing its own neuro-sens outfit. 'Don't get your tail in a knot. I'll fix it.'

Sometimes a monkey has more sense than a man.

Especially a man who looks so raggedy, Gerald thought. A chance glimpse of his reflection revealed how stained his elastic garment had become – from spilled drinks and maintenance fluids. His grizzled cheeks looked gaunt. Infested, even haunted, by bushy, unkempt eyebrows.

If I go home to Houston like this, the family won't even let me in our house. Though, with all my accumulated flight pay . . .

Come on, focus!

Grimly, Gerald clicked down twice on his lower left premolar and three times on the right. His suit responded with another jolt of Slow Juice through a vein in his thigh. Coolness, a lassitude that should help clear thinking, spread through his body—

– and time seemed to crawl.

Feedback signals from the distant bola now had time to catch up. He felt more a *part* of the thirty kilometer strand, as it whirled ponderously in a higher orbit. Pulsing electric currents that throbbed *up there* were translated as a faint tingle *down here,* running from Gerald's wrist, along his arm and shoulder, slanting across his back and then down to his left big toe, where they seemed to *dig* for leverage. When he pushed, the faraway cable-satellite responded, applying force against the planet's magnetic field.

Tele-operation. In an era of ever more sophisticated artificial intelligence, some tasks still needed an old-fashioned human pilot. Even one who floated in a bubble, far below the real action.

Let's increase the current a bit. To notch down our rate of turn. A tingle in his toe represented several hundred amps of electricity, spewing from one end of the whirling tether, increasing magnetic drag. The great cable rotated across the stars a bit slower.

Hachi – linked-in nearby – hooted querulously from his own web of support fibers. This was better, though the capuchin still needed convincing.

'Cut me some slack,' Gerald grumbled. 'I know what I'm doing.'

The computer's dynamical model agreed with Hachi, though. It still forecast no easy grab when the tether's tip reached its brief rendezvous with . . . whatever piece of space junk lay in Gerald's sights.

Another tooth-tap command, and night closed in around him more completely, simulating what he would see if he were *up there*, hundreds of klicks higher, at the tether's speeding tip, where stars glittered more clearly. From that greater altitude, Earth seemed a much smaller disc, filling just a quarter of the sky.

Now, everything he heard, felt or saw came from the robotic cable. His lasso. A vine to swing upon, suspended from some distant constellation.

Once an ape . . . always an ape.

The tether *became* Gerald's body. An electric tingle along his spine – a sleeting breeze – was the Van Allen radiation wind, caught in magnetic belts that made a lethal sizzle of the middle-orbit heights, from nine hundred kilometers all the way out to thirty thousand or so.

The Bermuda Triangle of outer space. No mere human could survive in that realm for more than an hour. The Apollo astronauts accumulated half of all their allotted radiation dosage during a few minutes sprinting across the belt, toward the relative calm and safety of the Moon. Expensive communications satellites suffered more damage just passing through those middle altitudes than they would in a decade, higher up in placid geosynchronous orbit.

Ever since that brief time of bold lunar missions – and the even-briefer *Zheng He* era – no astronaut had ventured beyond the radiation belt. Instead, they hunkered in safety, just above the atmosphere, while robots explored the solar system. This made Gerald the Far-Out Guy! With his bola for an arm, and the grabber for a hand, he reached beyond. Just a bit, into the maelstrom. No one else got as high.

Trawling for garbage.

'All right . . .,' he murmured. 'Where are you . . . ?'

Radar had the target pinpointed, about as well as machines could manage amid a crackling fog of charged particles. Position and trajectory kept jittering, evading a fix with slipperiness that seemed almost alive. Worse – though no one believed him – Gerald swore that orbits tended to *shift* in this creepy zone, by up to a few thousandths of a percent, translating into tens of meters. That could make a bola-snatch more artistic guesswork than physics. Computers still had lots to learn, before they took over *this* job from a couple of primates.

Hachi chirped excitedly.

'Yeah, I see it.' Gerald squinted, and optics at the tether-tip automatically magnified a glitter, just ahead. The *target* – probably some piece of space junk, left here by an earlier, wastrel generation. Part of an exploding Russian second stage, perhaps. Or a connector ring from an Apollo flight. Maybe one of those capsules filled with human ashes that used to get fired out here, willy-nilly, during the burial-in-space fad. Or else the remnants of some foolish weapon experiment. Space Command claimed to have all the garbage radar charted and imaged down to a dozen centimeters.

Gerald knew better.

Whatever this thing was, the time had come to bring it home before collision with other debris caused a cascade of secondary impacts – a runaway process that already forced weather and research satellites to be replaced or expensively armored.

Garbage collecting wasn't exactly romantic. Then again, neither was Gerald. Far from the square-jawed, heroic image of a spaceman, he saw only a middle-aged disappointment, on the rare occasions that he looked in a mirror at all, a face lined from squinting in the sharp light of orbit, where sunrise came at you like a wall, every ninety minutes.

At least he was good at achieving a feat of imagination – that he *really* existed far above. That his true body spun out there, thousands of kilometers away.

The illusion felt perfect, at last. Gerald *was* the bola. Thirty kilometers of slender, conducting filament, whirling a slow turn every thirty minutes, or five times during each elongated orbit. At both ends of the pivoting tether were compact clusters of sensors (*my eyes*), cathode emitters (*my muscles*), and grabbers (*my clutching hands*), that felt more part of him, right now, than anything made of flesh. More real than the meaty parts he had been born with, now drifting in a cocoon far below, near the bulky, pitted space station. That distant human body seemed almost imaginary.

Like a hunter with his faithful dog, man and monkey grew silent during final approach, as if sound might spook the prey, glittering in their sights.

It's got an odd shine, he thought, as telemetry showed the distance rapidly narrowing. Only a few kilometers now, till the complex dance of two orbits and the tether's own, gyrating spin converged, like a fielder leaping to snatch a hurtling line drive. Like an acrobat, catching his partner in midair. After which . . .

. . . the bola's natural spin would take over, clasping the seized piece of debris into its whirl, absorbing its old momentum and giving that property new values, new direction. Half a spin later, with this tether-tip at *closest approach* to Earth, the grabber would let go, hurling the debris backward, westward, and *down* to burn in the atmosphere.

The easy part. By then, Gerald would be sipping coffee in the station's shielded crew lounge. Only now—

That's no discarded second stage rocket, he pondered, studying the glimmer. *It's not a cargo faring, or shredded fuel tank, or urine-icicle, dumped by a manned mission.* By now, Gerald knew how all kinds of normal junk reflected sunlight – from archaic launch vehicles and satellites to lost gloves and tools – each playing peek-aboo tricks of shadow. But this thing . . .

Even the colors weren't right. Too blue. Too many *kinds* of blue. And light levels remained so steady! As if the thing had no facets or flat surfaces. Hachi's questioning hoot was low and worried. How can you make a firm grab, without knowing where the edges are?

As relative velocity ebbed toward zero, Gerald made adjustments by spewing electrons from cathode emitters at either cable end, creating torque against the planetary field, a trick for maneuvering without rockets or fuel. Ideal for a slow, patient job that had to be done on the cheap.

Now Hachi earned his keep. The little monkey stretched himself like a strand of spaghetti, smoothly taking over final corrections – his instincts honed by a million generations of swinging from jungle branches – while Gerald focused on the grab itself. There would be no second chance.

Slow and patient . . . except at the last, frenetic moment . . . when you wish you had something quicker to work with than magnetism. When you wish—

There it was, ahead. The Whatever.

Rushing toward rendezvous, the bola's camera spied something glittery, vaguely oval in shape, gleaming with a pale blueness that pulsed like something eager.

Gerald's hand *was* the grabber, turning a fielder's mitt of splayed fingers, reaching as the object loomed suddenly.

Don't flinch, he chided ancient intuitions while preparing to snatch whatever this hurtling thing might be.

Relax. It never hurts.

Only this time – in a strange and puzzling way – it did.

A MYRIAD PATHS OF ENTROPY

Does the universe hate us? How many pitfalls lie ahead, waiting to shred our conceited molecule-clusters back into unthinking dust? Shall we count them?

Men and women always felt besieged. By monsters prowling the darkness. By their oppressive rulers, or violent neighbors, or capricious gods. Yet, didn't they most often blame themselves? Bad times were viewed as punishment, brought on by wrong behavior. By unwise belief.

Today, our means of self-destruction seem myriad. (Though *Pandora's Cornucopia* will try to list them all!) We modern folk snort at the superstitions of our ancestors. We know *they* could never really wreck the world, but we can! Zeus or Moloch could not match the destructive power of a nuclear missile exchange, or a dusting of plague bacilli, or some ecological travesty, or ruinous mismanagement of the intricate aiconomy.

Oh, we're mighty. But are we *so* different from our forebears?

Won't our calamity (when it comes) also be blamed on some arrogant mistake? A flaw in judgment? Some obstinate belief? *Culpa nostra.* Won't it be the same old plaint, echoing across the ruin of our hopes?

'We never deserved it all! Our shining towers and golden fields. Our overflowing libraries and full bellies. Our long lives and overindulged children. Our happiness. Whether by God's will or our own hand, we always expected it would come to this.

'To dust.'

—Pandora's Cornucopia

2.

AFICIONADO

Meanwhile, far below, cameras stared across forbidden desert, monitoring disputed territory in a conflict so bitter, antagonists couldn't agree what to call it.

One side named the struggle *righteous war*, with countless innocent lives in peril.

Their opponents claimed there were no victims, at all.

And so, suspicious cameras panned, alert for encroachment. Camouflaged atop hills or under highway culverts or innocuous stones, they probed for a hated adversary. And for some months the guardians succeeded, staving off incursions. Protecting sandy desolation.

Then, technology shifted advantages again.

The enemy's first move? Take out those guarding eyes.

Infiltrators came at dawn, out of the rising sun – several hundred little machines, skimming low on whispering gusts. Each one, resembling a native hummingbird, followed a carefully scouted path toward its target, landing *behind* some camera or sensor, in its blind spot. It then unfolded wings that transformed into holo-displays, depicting perfect false images of the same desert scene to the guardian lens, without even a suspicious flicker. Other spy-machines sniffed out camouflaged seismic sensors and embraced them gently – cushioning to mask approaching tremors.

The robotic attack covered a hundred square kilometers. In eight minutes, the desert lay unwatched, undefended.

Now, from over the horizon, large vehicles converged along multiple roadways toward the same open area – seventeen hybrid-electric rigs, disguised as commercial cargo transports, complete with company hologos. But when their paths intersected, crews in dun-colored jumpsuits leaped to unlash cargoes. Generators roared and the air swirled with exotic stench as pungent volatiles gushed from storage tanks to fill pressurized vessels. Consoles sprang to life. Hinged panels fell away, revealing long, tapered cylinders on slanted ramps.

Ponderously, each cigar shape raised its nose skyward while fins popped open at the tail. Shouts grew tense as tightly coordinated countdowns commenced. Soon the enemy – sophisticated and wary – would pick up enough clues. They would realize ... and act.

When every missile was aimed, targets acquired, all they lacked were payloads.

A dozen figures emerged from an air-conditioned van, wearing snug suits of shimmering material and garishly painted helmets. Each carried a satchel that hummed and whirred to keep them cool. Several moved with a gait that seemed rubbery with anxious excitement. One skipped a little caper, about every fourth step.

A dour-looking woman awaited them, with badge and uniform. Holding up a databoard, she confronted the first vacuum-suited figure.

'Name and scan,' she demanded. 'Then affirm your intent.'

The helmet visor, decorated with gilt swirls, swiveled back, revealing heavily tanned features, about thirty years old, with eyes the color of a cold sea – till the official's instrument cast a questioning ray. Then, briefly, one pupil flared retinal red.

'Hacker Sander,' the tall man said, in a voice both taut and restrained. 'I affirm that I'm doing this of my own free will, according to documents on record.'

His clarity of purpose must have satisfied the ai-clipboard, which uttered an approving beep. The inspector nodded. 'Thank you, Mr Sander. Have a safe trip. Next?'

She indicated another would-be rocketeer, who carried his helmet in the crook of one arm, bearing a motif of flames surrounding a screaming mouth.

'What rubbish,' the blond youth snarled, elbowing Hacker as he tried to loom over the bureaucrat. 'Do you have any idea who we are? Who I am?'

'Yes, Lord Smit. Though whether I *care* or not doesn't matter.' She held up the scanner. '*This* matters. It can prevent you from being lasered into tiny fragments by the USSF, while you're passing through controlled airspace.'

'Is that a threat? Why you little ... *government* ... pissant. You had better not be trying to—'

'Government *and* guild,' Hacker Sander interrupted, suppressing his own hot anger over that elbow in the ribs. 'Come on, Smitty. We're on a tight schedule.'

The baron whirled on him, tension cracking the normally smooth aristocratic accent. 'I warned you about nicknames, Sander, you third-generation poser. I had to put up with your seniority during pilot training. But just wait until we get back. I'll take you apart!'

'Why wait?' Hacker kept eye contact while reaching up to unlatch his air hose. A quick punch ought to lay this blue-blood out, letting the rest of them get on with it. There were good reasons to hurry. Other forces, more formidable than mere government, were converging right now, eager to prevent what was planned here.

Besides, nobody called a Sander a 'poser.'

The other rocket jockeys intervened before he could use his fist – probably a good thing, at that – grabbing the two men and separating them. Pushed to the end of the queue, Smit stewed and cast deadly looks toward Hacker. But when his turn came again, the nobleman went through ID check with composure, as cold and brittle as some glacier.

'Your permits are in order,' the functionary concluded, unhurriedly addressing Hacker, because he was most experienced. 'Your liability bonds and Rocket Racing League waivers have been accepted. The government won't stand in your way.'

Hacker shrugged, as if the statement was both expected and irrelevant. He flung his visor back down and gave a sign to the other suited figures, who rushed to the ladders that launch personnel braced against each rocket, clambering awkwardly, then squirming into cramped couches and strapping in. Even the novices had practiced countless times.

Hatches slammed, hissing as they sealed. Muffled shouts told of final preparations. Then came a distant chant, familiar, yet always thrilling, counting backward at a steady cadence. A rhythm more than a century old.

Is it really that long, since Robert Goddard came to this same desert? Hacker pondered. *To experiment with the first controllable rockets? Would he be surprised at what we've done with the thing he started? Turning them into weapons of war ... then giant exploration vessels ... and finally playthings of the superrich?*

Oh, there were alternatives, like commercial space tourism. One Japanese orbital hotel and another under construction. Hacker owned stock. There were even multipassenger suborbital jaunts, available to the merely well-off. For the price of maybe twenty college educations.

Hacker felt no shame or regret. *If it weren't for us, there'd be almost nothing left of the dream.*

Countdown approached zero for the first missile.

His.

'Yeeeee-haw!' Hacker Sander shouted ...

... before a violent kick flattened him against the airbed. A mammoth hand seemed to plant itself on his chest and *shoved*, expelling half the contents of his lungs in a moan of sweet agony. Like every other time, the sudden shock brought physical surprise and visceral dread – followed by a sheer ecstatic rush, like nothing else on Earth.

Hell ... he wasn't even *part* of the Earth! For a little while, at least.

Seconds passed amid brutal shaking as the rocket clawed its way skyward. Friction heat and ionization licked the transparent nose cone only centimeters from his face. Shooting toward heaven at Mach ten, he felt pinned, helplessly immobile ...

... and completely omnipotent.

I'm a freaking god!

At Mach fifteen somehow he drew enough breath for another cry – this time a shout of elated greeting as black space spread before the missile's bubble nose, flecked by a million glittering stars.

Back on the ground, cleanup efforts were even more frenetic than setup. With all rockets away, men and women sprinted across the scorched desert, packing to depart before the enemy arrived. Warning posts had already spotted flying machines, racing this way at high speed.

But the government official moved languidly, tallying damage to vegetation, erodible soils, and tiny animals – all of it localized, without appreciable effect on endangered species. A commercial reconditioning service had already been summoned. Atmospheric pollution was easier to calculate, of course. Harder to ameliorate.

She knew these people had plenty to spend. And nowadays, soaking up excess accumulated wealth was as important as any other process of recycling. Her ai-board printed a bill, which she handed over as the last team member revved his engine, impatient to be off.

'Aw, man!' he complained, reading the total. 'Our club will barely break even on this launch!'

'Then pick a less expensive hobby,' she replied, and stepped back as the driver gunned his truck, roaring away in clouds of dust, incidentally crushing one more barrel cactus en route to the highway. Her vigilant clipboard noted this, adjusting the final tally.

Sitting on the hood of her jeep, she waited for another 'club' whose members were as passionate as the rocketeers. Equally skilled and dedicated, though both groups despised each other. Sensors showed them coming fast, from the west – *radical environmentalists*. The official knew what to expect when they arrived. Frustrated to find their opponents gone and two acres of desert singed, they'd give her a tongue-lashing for being 'evenhanded' in a situation where – obviously – you could only choose sides.

Well, she thought. *It takes a thick skin to work in government nowadays. No one thinks you matter much.*

Overhead the contrails were starting to shear, ripped by stratospheric winds, a sight that always tugged the heart. And while her intellectual sympathies lay closer to the eco-activists, not the spoiled rocket jockeys . . .

. . . a part of her still thrilled, whenever she witnessed a launch. So ecstatic – almost orgiastic.

'Go!' she whispered with a touch of secret envy toward those distant glitters, already arcing toward the pinnacle of their brief climb, before starting their long plummet to the Gulf of Mexico.

WAIST

Wow, ain't it strange that ...

... doomcasters keep shouting the end of the world? From Ragnarok to Armageddon, was there ever a time without Jeremiahs, Jonahs, and Johns, clamoring some imminent last day? The long list makes you say *Wow*—

– *ain't it strange that* millenarians kept expecting the second coming every year of the first century C.E.? Or that twenty thousand 'Old Believers' in Russia burned themselves alive, to escape the Antichrist? Or that the most popular book of the 1790s ingeniously tied every line of Revelation to Napoleon and other current figures, a feat of pattern-seeking that's been repeated every generation since? Like when both sides of the U.S. Civil War saw their rivals as *the Beast*. Later mystics ascribed that role to the Soviet Union, then blithely reassigned it to militant Islam, then to the rising empire of the Han ... and now to *artificial reality* and the so-called Tenth Estate.

Can anyone doubt the agility of human imagination?

Nor is it always religion. Comets and planet alignments sent people scooting to caves or hilltops in 1186, 1524, 1736, 1794, 1919, 1960, 1982, 2011, 2012, 2014, 2020, and so on. Meanwhile, obsessive scribblers seek happy closure in Bible codes and permutations of 666, 1260, or 1,000. And temporal hypochondriacs keep seeing themselves in the vague, Rorschach mirror of Nostradamus.

And wow, ain't it strange that ... computers didn't stop in 2000, nor jets tumble from the sky? Remember 2012's Mayan calendar fizzle? Or when Comet Bui-Buri convinced millions to *buy* gas masks and *bury* time capsules? Or when that amalgam of true believers built their *Third Temple* in Jerusalem, sacrificed some goats, then walked naked to Meggido? Or when the New Egyptian Reconstructionists foresaw completion of a full, 1,460-year Sophic Cycle after the birth of Muhammad? Or the *monthly* panics from 2027 to 2036, depending on your calculation for the two-thousandth Easter?

... or other false alarms, from the green epiphany of Gaia to the Yellowstone Scare, to Awfulday's horror. Will we ever exhaust the rich supply of dooms?

And *wow, ain't it strange that* ... people who know nothing of Isaac Newton the physicist now cite his *biblical forecast* that the end might come in 2060? (Except Newton himself didn't believe it.)

And *WAIST* ... humanity survived at all, with so many rubbing their hands, hoping we'll fail?

Or that some of us keep offering *wagers*? Asking doomlovers to back up their next forecast with confidence, courage, and honest *cash*? Oh, but they-of-little-faith never accept. Refusing to bet, they hold on, like iron, to their money.

Enter the monthly
Orbit sweepstakes at
www.orbitloot.com

With a different prize every month,
from advance copies of books by
your favourite authors to exclusive
merchandise packs,
**we think you'll find something
you love.**